IRON
GOLD

BY PIERCE BROWN

Red Rising

Golden Son

Morning Star

Iron Gold

IRON GOLD

PIERCE BROWN

HODDER &
STOUGHTON

First published in Great Britain in 2018 by Hodder & Stoughton
An Hachette UK company

1

Copyright © Pierce Brown 2018

The right of Pierce Brown to be identified as the Author of the Work has been asserted by him in accordance with the Copyright, Designs and Patents Act 1988.

All characters in this publication are fictitious and any resemblance to real persons, living or dead, is purely coincidental.

A CIP catalogue record for this title is available from the British Library

Hardback ISBN 978 1 473 64655 1
Trade Paperback ISBN 978 1 473 64656 8
eBook ISBN 978 1 473 64658 2

Printed and bound in Great Britain by Clays Ltd, St Ives plc

Hodder & Stoughton policy is to use papers that are natural, renewable and recyclable products and made from wood grown in sustainable forests. The logging and manufacturing processes are expected to conform to the environmental regulations of the country of origin.

Hodder & Stoughton Ltd
Carmelite House
50 Victoria Embankment
London EC4Y 0DZ

www.hodder.co.uk

For the Howlers.

THE SOLAR SYSTEM

In the tenth year of the Solar War

Commissioned by Sovereign Virginia au
Augustus, 753 PCE

WHITE
FLEET

MERCURY

EARTH

VENUS
DOCKYARDS

ASH LORD'S
FLEET

VENUS

LUNA

HOME
GUARD

SOCIETY
REMNANT

Planets controlled
by the Ash Lord

SOLAR
REPUBLIC

Spheres liberated
by the Republic

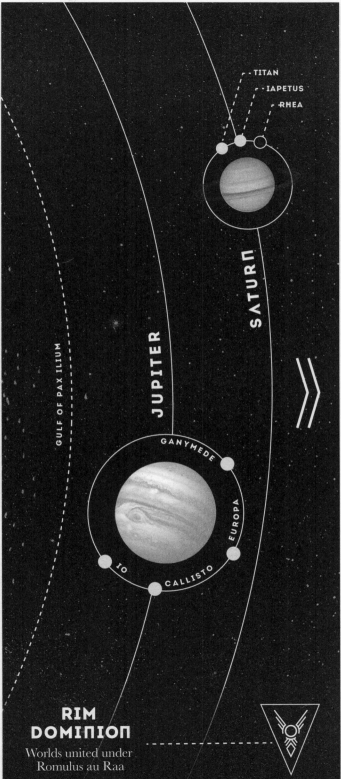

ECLIPTIC
GUARD

PHOBOS
DOCKYARDS

PHOBOS

DEIMOS

MARS

TITAN
IAPETUS
RHEA

SATURN

JUPITER

GULF OF PAX ILIUM

GANYMEDE

EUROPA

IO

CALLISTO

RIM
DOMINION

Worlds united under
Romulus au Raa

DRAMATIS PERSONAE

REDS

DARROW OF LYKOS/THE REAPER   ArchImperator of the Republic, husband to Virginia

RHONNA   Niece of Darrow

LYRIA OF LAGALOS   A Gamma Red

DANCER, SENATOR O'FARAN   Senator of the Republic, Ares lieutenant

DANO   Colleague of Ephraim

GOLDS

VIRGINIA AU AUGUSTUS/MUSTANG   Reigning Sovereign of the Republic, wife to Darrow, mother to Pax

PAX   Son of Darrow and Virginia

MAGNUS AU GRIMMUS/THE ASH LORD   Former ArchImperator to Octavia

ATALANTIA AU GRIMMUS   Daughter of the Ash Lord

CASSIUS AU BELLONA   Former Morning Knight, guardian to Lysander

LYSANDER AU LUNE   Grandson of former Sovereign Octavia, heir to House Lune

SEVRO AU BARCA/THE GOBLIN   Howler, husband to Victra

VICTRA AU BARCA   Wife to Sevro, née Victra au Julii

ELECTRA AU BARCA   Daughter of Sevro and Victra

KAVAX AU TELEMANUS   Head of House Telemanus, father to Daxo

NIOBE AU TELEMANUS   Wife to Kavax

DAXO AU TELEMANUS   Heir and son of Kavax

THRAXA AU TELEMANUS   Daughter of Kavax and Niobe

ROMULUS AU RAA   Head of House Raa, Lord of the Dust, Sovereign of the Rim Dominion

DIDO AU RAA   Wife to Romulus, née Dido au Saud

SERAPHINA AU RAA   Daughter of Romulus and Dido

DIOMEDES AU RAA/THE STORM KNIGHT   Son of Romulus and Dido

MARIUS AU RAA   Quaestor, son of Romulus and Dido

APOLLONIUS AU VALII-RATH/THE MINOTAUR   Heir to House Valii-Rath

THARSUS AU VALII-RATH   Brother to Apollonius

ALEXANDAR AU ARCOS   Eldest grandson of Lorn, a Howler

VANDROS   a Howler

CLOWN   a Howler

PEBBLE   a Howler

OTHER COLORS

HOLIDAY TI NAKAMURA   Legionnaire, sister to Trigg, a Gray

EPHRAIM TI HORN   Freelancer, former Son of Ares

SEFI   Queen of the Valkyrie, sister to Ragnar, an Obsidian

WULFGAR THE WHITETOOTH   ArchWarden of the Republic, an Obsidian

VOLGA FJORGAN   Colleague of Ephraim, an Obsidian

QUICKSILVER/REGULUS AG SUN   Richest man in the Republic, a Silver

PYTHA   Blue pilot, companion to Cassius and Lysander

CYRA SI LAMENSIS   Locksmith, colleague of Ephraim, a Green

PUBLIUS CU CARAVAL   The Copper Tribune, leader of the Copper bloc, a
    Copper

MICKEY   Carver, a Violet

THE FALL OF MERCURY

THE FURY

SILENT, SHE WAITS FOR the sky to fall, standing upon an island of volcanic rock amidst a black sea. The long moonless night yawns before her. The only sounds, a flapping banner of war held in her lover's hand and the warm waves that kiss her steel boots. Her heart is heavy. Her spirit wild. Peerless knights tower behind her. Salt spray beads on their family crests—emerald centaurs, screaming eagles, gold sphinxes, and the crowned skull of her father's grim house. Her Golden eyes look to the heavens. Waiting. The water heaves in. Out. The heartbeat of her silence.

THE CITY

Tyche, the jewel of Mercury, hunches in fear between the mountains and the sun. Her famed glass and limestone spires are dark. The Ancestor Bridge is empty. Here, Lorn au Arcos wept as a young man when he saw the messenger planet at sunset for the first time. Now, trash rolls through her streets, pushed by salty summer wind. Gone are the calls of the fishmongers at the wharf. Gone are the patter of pedestrian feet on the cobbles and the rumble of aircars and the laughter of the lowColor children who jump from the bridges into the waves on scorching summer days when the Trasmian sea winds are still. The city is quiet, its wealthy already gone to desert mountain retreats or government bunkers, its soldiers on its rooftops watching the sky, its poor having left for the desert or upon cramped boats destined for the Ismere Islands.

But the city is not empty.

Huddled masses fill the public transit systems that wend beneath the waves. And in the upstairs window of a tenement complex on the ugly fringes of the city, far from the water, where the working poor are kept, a little girl with Orange eyes fogs the window with her breath. The night sky sparks. Flashing and flaring with spurts of light like the fireworks her brother sometimes buys at the corner shop. She's been told there is a battle between big fleets high up there. She has never seen a starship. Her mother lies sick in the bedroom, unable to travel. Her father, who builds parts for engines, sits at the little plastic dinner table with his sons, knowing he cannot protect them. The holoCan washes them in pale light. Government news programs tell them to seek shelter. In her pocket the girl carries a folded piece of paper that she found in the gutter. On it is a little curved sword. She's seen it before on the cube. Her teachers at the government school say it brings chaos. War. It has set the spheres on fire. But now she secretly draws the blade in the fog her breath has made on the window, and she feels brave.

Then the bombs begin to fall.

THE BOMBS

They come from high-orbit Thor-class bombers piloted by farmboys from Earth and miners from Mars of the Twelfth Sunshine Squadron. Curses and prayers and tribal dragons and curved scythes have been sprayed upon them in aerosol paint. They dip through the clouds and fall over the sea, outracing their own sound. Their guidance chips are made by freeColors on Phobos. Their steel is mined and smelted by entrepreneurs in the Belt. Their ion propulsion engines are stamped with the winged heel of a company that makes consumer electronics and toiletries and weapons. Down and down they go to race shadowless over the desert, then the sea, carrying the weight of the newest empire under the sun.

The first bomb destroys the Hall of Justice on Tyche's Vespasian Island. Then it burrows a hundred meters into the earth before detonating against the bunker buried there, killing all inside. The second lands in the sea, fifteen kilometers from a fleet of refugees, where it sinks a Society warship, hiding under the chop. The third races over a spine of mountains north of Tyche when it is struck with a railgun round fired from a defense installation by a Gray teenager with acne scars and the charm of a sweetheart around his neck. It careens off its course and sputters across the sky before falling to the earth.

It detonates on the fringes of the city, far from the water, where it turns four blocks of tenement housing to dust.

THE REAPER

Silent, he lies encased in mankilling metal in the belly of a starship called the *Morning Star*. The fear swallows him now as it has done time and time before. The only sound is the whir of his armor's air filtration unit and the radio chatter of distant men and women. Around him lie his friends, they too cocooned in metal. Waiting. Eyes Red and Gold and Gray and Obsidian. Wolfheads mark their pauldrons. Tattoos their necks and arms. Wild empire breakers from Mars and Luna and Earth. Beyond them fly ships with names like *Spirit of Lykos, Hope of Tinos,* and *Echo of Ragnar.* They are painted white and led by a woman with onyx-dark skin. The Lion Sovereign said the white was for spring. For a new beginning. But the ships are stained. Smeared with char and patched wounds and mismatched panels. They broke the Sword Armada and the martyr Fabii. They conquered the heart of the Gold empire. They battled back the Ash Lord to the Core and have kept the dragons of the Rim at bay.

How could they ever stay clean?

Alone in his armor, waiting to fall from the sky, he remembers the girl who began it all. He remembers how her Red hair fell over her eyes. How her mouth danced with laughter. How she breathed as she lay atop him, so warm and fragile in a world far too cold. She has been dead longer than she was ever alive. And now that her dream has spread, he wonders if she would recognize it. And he wonders too if he were to die today, would he recognize the echo of his own life? What sort of man would his son become in this world he has made? He thinks of his son's face and how soon he will become a man. And he thinks of his Golden wife. How she stood on the landing pad, looking up at him, wondering if he'd ever return home again.

More than anything, he wants this to end.

Then the machine takes hold.

He feels the tug on his body. The pounding of his heart. The mad cackling of the Goblin and the howls of his friends as they try to forget their children, their loves, and be brave. Nausea in his gut rises as the magnetic rails charge behind him. With a shudder of metal, they fire him forward through the launch tube out into silent space at six times the speed of sound.

Men call him father, liberator, warlord, Slave King, Reaper. But he feels a boy as he falls toward the war-torn planet, his armor red, his army vast, his heart heavy.

It is the tenth year of war and the thirty-third of his life.

PART I

WIND

There is a poor, blind Samson in this land,

Shorn of his strength and bound in bonds of steel,

Who may, in some grim revel, raise his hand,

And shake the pillars of this Commonweal,

Till the vast Temple of our liberties

A shapeless mass of wreck and rubbish lies.

—HENRY WADSWORTH LONGFELLOW

1

DARROW

Hero of the Republic

WEARY, I WALK UPON FLOWERS at the head of an army. Petals carpet the last of the stone road before me. Thrown by children from windows, they twirl lazily down from the steel towers that grow to either side of the Luna boulevard. In the sky, the sun dies its slow, weeklong death, staining the tattered clouds and gathered crowd in bloody hues. Waves of humanity lap against security barricades, pressing inward on our parade as Hyperion City Watchmen in gray uniforms and cyan berets guard the route, shoving drunken revelers back into the crowd. Behind them, antiterrorism units prowl up and down the pavement, their fly-eyed goggles scanning irises, hands resting on energy weapons.

My own eyes rove the crowd.

After ten years of war, I no longer believe in moments of peace.

It's a sea of Colors that line the twelve-kilometer Via Triumphia. Built by my people, the Red slaves of the Golds, hundreds of years ago, the Triumphia is the avenue by which the Conquerors who tamed Earth held their own processions as they claimed continent after continent. Iron-spined murderers with eyes of gold and haughty menace once consecrated these same stones. Now, nearly a millennium later, we sully the Triumphia's sacred white marble by honoring Liberators with eyes of jet and ash and rust and soil.

Once, this would have filled me with pride. Jubilant crowds celebrating the Free Legions returned from vanquishing yet another threat to our fledgling Republic. But today I see holosigns of my head with a bloody crown atop it, hear the jeers from the Vox Populi as they wave banners emblazoned with their upside-down pyramid, and feel nothing but the weight of an endless war and a desperate longing to be once again in the embrace of my family. It has been a year since I've seen my wife and son. After the long voyage back from Mercury, all I want is to be with them, to fall into a bed, and to sleep for a dreamless month.

The last of my journey home lies before me. As the Triumphia widens and abuts the stairs that lead up to the New Forum, I face one final summit.

Faces drunk on jubilation and new commercial spirits gape up at me as I reach the stairs. Hands sticky with sweets wave in the air. And tongues, loose from those same commercial spirits and delights, cry out, shouting my name, or cursing it. Not the name my mother gave me, but the name my deeds have built. The name the fallen Peerless Scarred now whisper as a curse.

"Reaper, Reaper, Reaper," they cry, not in unison, but in frenzy. The clamor suffocates, squeezing with a billion-fingered hand: all the hopes, all the dreams, all the pain constricting around me. But so close to the end, I can put one foot after the other. I begin to climb the stairs.

Clunk.

My metal boots grind on stone with the weight of loss: Eo, Ragnar, Fitchner, and all the others who've fought and fallen at my side while somehow I have remained alive.

I am tall and broad. Thicker at my age of thirty-three than I was in my youth. Stronger and more brutal in my build and movement. Born Red, made Gold, I have kept what Mickey the Carver gave me. These Gold eyes and hair feel more my own than those of that boy who lived in the mines of Lykos. That boy grew, loved, and dug the earth, but he lost so much it often feels like it happened to another soul.

Clunk. Another step.

Sometimes I fear that this war is killing that boy inside. I ache to remember him, his raw, pure heart. To forget this city moon, this Solar War, and return to the bosom of the planet that gave birth to me before the boy inside is dead forever. Before my son loses the chance to ever know him. But the worlds, it seems, have plans of their own.

Clunk.

I feel the weight of the chaos I've unleashed: famines and genocide on Mars, Obsidian piracy in the Belt, terrorism, radiation sickness and disease spreading through the lower reaches of Luna, and the two hundred million lives lost in my war.

I force a smile. Today is our fourth Liberation Day. After two years of siege, Mercury has joined the free worlds of Luna, Earth, and Mars. Bars stand open. War-weary citizens rove the streets, looking for reason to celebrate. Fireworks crackle and blaze across the sky, shot from the roofs of skyscraper and tenement complex alike.

With our victory on the first planet from the sun, the Ash Lord has been pushed back to his last bastion, the fortress planet Venus, where his battered fleet guards precious docks and the remaining loyalists. I have come home to convince the Senate to requisition ships and men of the war-impoverished Republic for one final campaign. One last push on Venus to put this bloodydamn war to rest. So I can set down the sword and go home to my family for good.

Clunk.

I take a moment to glance behind me. Waiting at the foot of the stairs is my Seventh Legion, or the remnants of it. Twenty-eight thousand men and women where once there were fifty. They stand in casual order around a fourteen-pointed ivory star with a pegasus galloping at its center—held aloft by the famous Thraxa au Telemanus. The Hammer. After losing her left arm to Atalantia au Grimmus's razor, she had it replaced by a metal prototype appendage from Sun

Industries. Wild gold hair flutters behind her head, garlanded with white feathers given to her by Obsidian admirers.

In her mid-thirties, a stout woman with thighs thick as water drums and a freckled, bluff face. She grins past the shoulders of the Obsidians and Golds around her. Blue and Red and Orange pilots wave to the crowd. Red, Gray, and Brown infantry smile and laugh as pretty young Pinks and Reds duck under barriers and rush to drape necklaces of flowers around their necks, push bottles of liquor into their hands and kisses onto their mouths. They are the only full legion in today's parade. The rest remain on Mercury with Orion and Harnassus, battling with the Ash Lord's legions stranded there when his fleet retreated.

Clunk.

"Remember, you are but mortal," Sevro's bored voice drawls in my ear as white-haired Wulfgar and the Republic Wardens descend to greet us midway up the Forum stairs. Sevro sniffs my neck and makes a noise of distaste. "By Jove. You wretch. Did you dip yourself in piss before the occasion?"

"It's cologne," I say. "Mustang bought it for me last Solstice."

He's quiet for a moment. "Is it made out of piss?"

I scowl back at him, wrinkling my nose at the heaviness of liquor on his breath, and eye the ragged wolfcloak he wears over his ceremonial armor. He claims he hasn't washed it since the Institute. "You're really lecturing me about stenches? Just shut up and behave like an Imperator," I say with a grin.

Snorting, Sevro drops back to where the legendary Obsidian, Sefi Volarus, stands in her customary silence. He feigns an air of domesticity, but next to the giant woman, he looks a little like some sort of gutter dog an alcoholic father might ill-advisedly bring home to play with the children—washed and rid of fleas, but still possessing that weird mania behind the eyes. Pinched, thin lipped, with a nose crooked as an old knifefighter's fingers. He eyes the crowd with resigned distaste.

Behind him lope the pack of mangy Howlers he brought with us to Mercury. My bodyguards, now drunk as gallants at a Lykos Laureltide. Stalwart Holiday walks at their center, the snub-nosed woman doing her best to keep them in line.

There used to be more of them. So many more.

I smile as Wulfgar descends the stairs to meet me. A favorite son of the Rising, the Obsidian is a tree root of a man, gnarled and narrow, armored all in pale blue. He's in his early forties. His face angular as a raptor's, his beard braided like that of his hero, Ragnar.

One of the Obsidians to fight alongside Ragnar at the walls of Agea, Wulfgar was with the Sons of Ares that freed me from the Jackal in Attica. Now ArchWarden of the Republic, he smiles down at me from the step above, his black eyes crinkling at the corners.

"Hail libertas," I say with a smile.

"Hail libertas," he echoes.

"Wulfgar. Fancy meeting you here. You missed the Rain," I say.

"You did not wait for me to return, did you?" Wulfgar clucks his tongue. "My children will ask where I was when the Rain fell upon Mercury, and you know what I will have to tell them?" He leans forward with a conspiratorial smile. "I was making night soil, wiping my ass when I heard Barca had taken Mount Caloris." He rumbles out a laugh.

"I told you not to leave," Sevro says. "You'd miss out on all the fun, I said. You should have seen the Ashies route. Trails of piss all the way to Venus. You'd have loved it." Sevro grins at the Obsidian. It was Sevro who put a razor in his hand in the river mud of Agea. Wulfgar has his own razor now. Its hilt made from the fang of an ice dragon from Earth's South Pole.

"My blade would have sung that day were I not summoned by the Senate," he says.

Sevro sneers. "That's right. You ran home like a good little dog."

"A dog? I am a servant of the People, my friend. As are we all." His eyes find me with mild accusation and I understand the true meaning to his words. Wulfgar is a believer, like all Wardens. Not in me, but in the Republic, in the principles for which it stands, and the orders that the Senate gives. Two days before the Iron Rain over Mercury, the Senate, led by my old friend Dancer, voted against my proposal. They told me to maintain the siege. To not waste men, resources, on an assault.

I disobeyed and let the Rain fall.

Now a million of my men lie in the sands of Mercury and we have our Liberation Day.

Were Wulfgar with me on Mercury, he would not have joined our Rain against the Senate's permission. In fact, he might have tried to stop me. He's one of the few men alive who might manage. For a spell at least.

He spares a nod for Sefi. *"Njar ga hae, svester."* A rough translation is "Respect to you, sister" in *nagal.*

"Njar ga hir, bruder," she replies. No love lost between them. They have different priorities.

"Your weapons." Wulfgar gestures to my razor.

Sefi and I hand his Wardens our weapons. Muttering under his breath, Sevro hands over his as well. "Did you forget your toothpick?" Wulfgar asks, looking at Sevro's left boot.

"Treasonous yeti," Sevro mutters, and pulls a wicked blade long as a baby's body from his boot. The Warden who takes it looks terrified.

"Odin's fortune with the togas, Darrow," Wulfgar says to me as he motions for us to continue upward. "You will need it."

Arrayed at the top of the steps of the New Forum are the 140 Senators of the Republic. Ten per Color, all draped in white togas that flutter in the breeze. They peer down at me like a row of haughty pigeons on a wire. Red and Gold, mortal enemies in the Senate, bookend the row to either side. Dancer is missing. But I have eyes only for the lonely bird of prey that stands at the center of all the silly, vain, power-hungry little pigeons.

Her golden hair is bound tight behind her head. Her tunic is pure white, without the ribbons of their Color the others wear. And in her hand, she carries the Dawn Scepter—now a multi-hued gold baton half a meter long, with the pyramid of the Society recast into the fourteen-pointed star of the Republic at its tip. Her face is elegant and distant. A small nose, piercing eyes behind thick eyelashes, and a mischievous cat's smile growing on her face. The Sovereign of our Republic. Here at the summit of the stairs, her eyes shed the weight from my shoulders, the fear from my heart that I would never see her again. Through war and space and this damnable parade, I have traveled to find her again, my life, my love, my home.

I bend to my knee and look up into the eyes of the mother of my child.

" 'Lo, wife," I say with a smile.

" 'Lo, husband. Welcome home."

2

DARROW

Father

Silene Manor, the Sovereign's traditional Luna country retreat, is nestled five hundred kilometers north of Hyperion at the base of the Atlas Mountains on a small lake. The northern hemisphere of the moon, comprised of mountains and seas, is less populous than the belt of cities that girdle the equator. Though Mustang governs from the Palace of Light in the Citadel, Silene is the true home of my family, at least until we return to Mars. Built to resemble one of the papal villas on Earth's Lake Como, the stone house sits along the edge of a rocky cove, and spills down to the lake by means of switchbacked stairs cut into the rock.

Here the thin conifers whisper to heights four times those possible on Earth. They sway nearly two hundred meters in the air around the raised concrete landing pad where the steward of House Augustus, Cedric cu Platuu, waits with my wife's Lionguards as our shuttle lands. The small Copper greets Sevro and me with great alacrity, bowing deeply and flourishing his hand. Thraxa runs past him without even a greeting, eager to find her mother.

"ArchImperator," he gushes, plump cheeks flushing with delight. He's a short but ample man, built a bit like a plum with knobby arms and legs added as an afterthought. A whisper of a mustache, nearly as thin as the graying copper hair upon his head, wavers in the wind. "What gladness to see you again!"

"Cedric," I say, greeting the short man warmly. "I hear you've just had a birthday."

"Yes, my lord! My seventy-first. Though I do maintain one should stop counting after sixty."

"Prime work," Sevro says. "You look positively prepubescent."

"Thank you, my lord!"

Few know the secrets of the Citadel as well as Cedric; he was one of the gems of the Sovereign's court. Mustang, having thought highly of him during her time with Octavia, saw no need to dismiss a man so knowledgeable and dedicated to his duty.

"Where's the welcoming party?" Sevro asks, looking for his wife, Victra. Mustang and Daxo remained behind in Hyperion to deal with their unruly Senate, but promised to rejoin by dinnertime.

"Oh, the children are recently returned from a three-day adventure," Cedric says. "The Lady Telemanus took them to the ruins of the USS *Davy Crockett* in the Atlas Mountains. Merrywater's own! I hear they had quite a time around that old wreck. Quite. A. Time, yes. Learned many lessons and expanded their individual initiative. As your curriculum requested, *dominu—*" Cedric's eyes nearly pop out of his head before he corrects himself. "As your curriculum requested, *sir.*"

"Is my wife here yet?" Sevro asks gruffly.

"Not yet, sir. Her valet said she would be late to dinner. I believe there were labor strikes in her warehouses in Endymion and Echo City. It's all over the holoNews."

"She didn't even show to the Triumph," Sevro mutters. "I looked fabulous."

"She has missed you at your most prime, sir."

"Right. See, Darrow? Cedric agrees." What he hasn't noticed is Cedric shuffling away from the odious stench of his wolfcloak.

"Cedric, where is my son?" I ask the man.

He smiles. "I think you can guess, sir."

———

The sounds of neoPlast swords knocking together and boots on stone greet Sevro and me as we enter the dueling grotto. There, vines crawl over granite fountains and along the damp stone floor. Evergreen needles drift in cumulous shapes from the top of the trees. And in the center of the grotto, under the watching eyes of the gargoyles adorning the fountains, a young boy and girl circle each other at the center of a chalk circle. The seven other children of their pack watch on, along with two Gold women. Sevro pulls me to the side so we remain unseen and sit out of sight on the edge of a granite fountain to watch.

The boy at the center of the circle is ten, lean and proud. He laughs like his mother and broods like his father. His hair is the color of straw, his face round and flushed with youth. Rose-gold eyes burn from under long lashes. He's larger than I remember, older, and it feels so impossible that he could have come from me. That he could have thoughts of his own. That he'll love, smile, die like the rest of us.

His brow is furrowed now in concentration. Sweat pours down his face, matting his hair as his opponent strikes his knee a glancing blow.

The girl is nine and narrow-faced like a sleek hunting dog. Electra, the eldest of Sevro's three daughters, is taller than my son and twice as thin. But while Pax radiates an inner joy that makes adults' eyes twinkle, there's a deep grimness to the girl. Her eyes are dusky gold and hidden behind heavy lids. Sometimes when they look at me, I feel them judging with an aloofness that reminds me of her mother.

Sevro leans forward eagerly. "I'll wager Aja's razor against Apollonius's helm that my wee monster beats the piss out of your boy."

"I'm not going to bet on our children," I whisper in indignation.

"I'll throw Aja's Institute ring in as well."

"Have some decency, Sevro. They're our children."

"And Octavia's cape."

"I want the Falthe Ivory Tree."

Sevro gasps. "I love the Ivory Tree. Where else will I hang my trophies?"

I shrug. "No Ivory Tree, no bet."

"Bloodydamn savage," he says, sticking out a hand to shake. "You have a deal." Sevro's become quite the collector—acquiring a hoard of trophies from Gold Imperators, knights, and would-be kings. He hangs their rings and weapons and crests from the boughs of the ivory tree he uprooted from the House Falthe compound on Earth and moved to his home on Luna.

We watch as Electra redoubles her onslaught against Pax. My son continues to back away, to sidestep, allowing her to overextend. Once she does, he twirls his plastic razor toward her rib cage. It connects lightly. "Point!" he shouts.

"I'm counting, Pax. Not you," Niobe au Telemanus says. Kavax's wife is a serene woman with a bird's nest of untamable graying hair and skin the color of cherrywood. The tribal tattoos of her Pacific Islander ancestors cover her arms. "Three to two, for Pax."

"Mind your balance, and stop overextending, Electra," says Thraxa. "You'll lose your footing if you're on an unstable surface, like a ship deck or ice." She sits on the edge of a fountain, miraculously already having found a bottle of beer.

Brow furrowed in anger, Electra rushes Pax again. They move fast for children, but since they're still shy of puberty, their movements are not yet graceful. Electra feints high, then twists her wrist to slash savagely down, hitting Pax's shoulder. "Point for Electra," Niobe says. Sevro has to stop himself from clapping. Pax tries to recover, but Electra is on him. Three more quick blows knock his razor from his hand. He falls down and Electra lifts her razor to smash him hard on the head.

Thraxa slips forward and catches the blade mid-swing with her metal hand. "Temper, temper, little lady." She pours a little beer on her head.

Electra glares up at her.

Sevro can't contain himself any longer. "My little harpy!" He lunges up off the bench and I follow through to the grotto. "Daddy's home!" A smile slashes across Electra's dour face as she turns to see her father. She runs to him and lets him scoop her up off the ground. Looks rather like he's hugging a limp fish. Some of the children flinch back when they see Sevro. And when they see me emerge from behind the vines, they stiffen and bow with perfect manners. Not one born since the fall of House Lune has the sigils implanted on their hands.

We raise them in packs of nine now, setting children of disparate

Colors together early in their schooling with hopes of creating the bonds that I found at the Institute, but without the murder and starvation. Pax's best friend, Baldur, a quiet gap-toothed Obsidian boy who is already nearly as tall as Sevro, helps Pax up. He tries to dust Pax off before Pax shoos him away and looks over at us.

I expected him to rush to me like Electra, but he doesn't. And in that moment, a very sharp spasm of pain goes through the deeper part of me. When I left him, he was a boy, brimming with reckless life, but the hesitation, the coldness in him now, is from the world of men. Minding his pack, he walks forward very calmly and bows at the waist, no deeper than manners require. "Hello, Father."

"My boy," I say with a smile. "You've grown like a weed."

"That's what happens when you age," he says, an edge to his words. I always thought when I became a man, I'd feel more confident, but towering over this boy, I feel so very small. I lost my own father to a cause; have I doomed Pax to the same fate?

"He's not generally such a snot," Niobe says later as we stand to the side after the children are dismissed from the day's practice. Pax leaves quickly and in a mood. Baldur rushes to keep up.

"Take the angst as a compliment, Darrow," Thraxa mumbles. "He just misses his father. I felt the same way anytime the old man was away on one of Augustus's errands." She pulls a slim burner from her pocket and lights it in the coals of one of the copper braziers that line the crumbling walls of the grotto. Niobe plucks it from her fingers and puts it out on her daughter's metal arm.

"Was Daxo ever like that?" I ask.

"Daxo?" Niobe laughs. "Daxo was born stoic as a stone."

"Plotting in the womb from conception," Thraxa mutters, and sips her beer. "We used to make owl hoots at him. Always watching the rest of us out the window. Big brother never wanted to play our games. Only his own."

"And you were such a paragon?" Niobe asks. "You used to eat cow pies."

Thraxa shrugs. "Better than your cooking." She steps out of range of her mother's reach and lights a replacement burner. "Thank Jove we had Browns."

Niobe rolls her eyes and touches my arm. "The miscreant is right, Darrow. Pax just missed you. You've time to make up."

I smile at her but watch Sevro walking away toward the water with Electra. "You know you're Daddy's favorite, don't you?" he's saying to her. I fight back my jealousy. He always seems able to pick right back up where he left off with his family. I wish I had that same gift.

I seek my mother out in the garden that runs along the side of one of the stone storage sheds. She's hunched in the black dirt with two other Red servant women and a Red man, her bare feet sticking out behind her as she plants bulbs in the ground in tidy rows. I pause a moment at the edge of the garden to watch her, just as I used to watch from the stairwell in our little home in Lykos as she made her night tea. I was afraid of her after Father died. She was always quick with a swat or a barbed word. I thought I deserved the treatment. How much easier the love between us would have been if I'd known as a child that her anger and my fear came from a pain neither one of us deserved. The love in me wells up for her as I remember what she's endured, and for a brief flicker, I ache to see my father again. For him to see my mother free.

"Are you just going to watch like a wastrel or are you going to help us plant?" she asks without looking up.

"I'm not sure I'd be a good farmer," I say.

She stands with the help of one of her companions, dusts the dirt from her pants, and takes her time setting her tools away before coming to say hello. She's only eighteen years older than I am, but she wears the years hard. Still, she is stronger by leagues than when she lived below. Her joints are worn from years in the mines. But her cheeks are ruddy with life now. Our physicians have helped relieve most of the symptoms of the stroke and heart condition that ravaged her. I know she feels guilty for this life. This luxury, when my father and so many others wait for us in the Vale. Her work in the garden and on the grounds is a penance for surviving.

My mother gives me a hard hug. "My son." She breathes me in before pulling back to look all the way up to my face. "You put the death in me when I heard of that damn Iron Rain. You put the death in all of us."

"I'm sorry. They shouldn't have told you before that I was unaccounted for."

She nods and says nothing, and I realize how deep her worry went. How they must have huddled in the living room here or in the Citadel and listened to the holoNews just like everyone else. The Red man shuffles to join us, his bad leg dragging behind.

"'Lo, Dancer," I say past my mother. My old mentor wears laborer's garments instead of his senatorial robes. His hair is gray, his face fatherly and creased from hard years. But there's still mischief in his rebel eyes. "Given up the Senate for gardening, have you?"

"I'm a man of the people," he says with a shrug. "Good to have dirt under the nails again. The gardeners in that museum the Senate gave me won't let me touch a damn weed. 'Lo, Sevro."

"Politician," Sevro says, joining me from behind. Heedless of the mood, he pretends like he's going to scoop my mother up into the air, but she scowls at him and he turns the scoop into a gentle hug.

"Better," she says. "You nearly broke my hip the last time."

"Oh, don't be such a Pixie," he mutters.

"Say that again?"

He steps back. "Nothing, ma'am."

"What word from Leanna?" I ask.

"They're well. Was hoping to visit them soon. Maybe take Pax along to Icaria in the winter. This place gets too cold for these old bones."

"All the way to Mars?" I ask.

"It's his home," she says sharply. "You want him to forget where he came from? Red's as deep in his blood as Gold. Not that he's ever reminded it, 'cept by me."

Dancer looks away, as if to give us privacy.

"He'll go to Mars," I say. "We all will when it's safe."

We might control Mars, but that's a far cry from it being a world of harmony. The Sirenian continent is still infested by a Gold army of iron-skinned veterans, just like the battleground of South Pacifica on Earth. The Ash Lord hasn't risked putting a major fleet in orbit in years, but ground wars are decidedly more stubborn than their astral counterparts.

"And when will it be safe, according to you?" my mother asks.

"Soon."

Neither Dancer nor my mother is impressed by that answer. "And how long are you staying here?" she asks.

"A month, at least. Rhonna and Kieran will be coming, like you asked."

"About bloody time. Thought Mercury had stolen them."

"Victra and the girls will come up for a spell too. Though I do have business in Hyperion at the end of the week."

"With the Senate. Asking for more men." Her tone's as sour as her eyes.

I sigh and look at Dancer. "Infecting my mother with your politics now?"

He laughs. "Deanna most certainly has a mind of her own."

"With both of you in my ears I'll go deaf," she says.

"Plug your ears," Sevro replies. "It's what I do when they jabber about politics."

Dancer snorts. "If only your wife did the same."

"Careful, boyo. She's got ears everywhere. She could be listening now."

"Why weren't you at the Triumph?" I ask Dancer.

He grimaces. "Please. We both know I've got no stomach for pomp. Especially on this damn moon. Give me dirt and air and friends." He looks fondly at the trees around. A shadow passes over his face at the thought of returning to Hyperion. "But I must be heading back to the mechanized Babylon. Deanna, thank you for letting me garden with you. It's just what I needed."

"You're not staying for supper?" my mother asks.

"Unfortunately, there are other gardens that need tending. Speaking of which . . . Darrow, could I have a moment?"

———

Dancer and I leave my mother and Sevro bickering about the smell of his wolfcloak to walk along a dirt footpath leading into the trees toward the lake. A patrol skiff skims the water on the far shore. "How are you?" he asks me. "None of that patriotic hero shit. Remember, I know all your tells."

"Tired," I admit. "You'd think a month's journey back would let me catch up on sleep. But there's always something."

"*Can* you sleep?" he asks.

"Sometimes."

"Lucky bastard. I piss the bed," he admits. "Probably twice a month. I don't ever remember the bloodydamn dreams, but my body sure as hell does." He was in the thick of the fighting to free Mars. The tunnel wars there were even nastier than the block fighting on Luna. Even the Obsidians don't sing songs of their victories in the tunnels. The Rat War, they call it. Over the course of three years, Dancer personally liberated over a hundred mines with the Sons of Ares. If Fitchner is the father of the Rising, it'd be fair to call Dancer the favorite uncle, despite the dissolution of the Sons of Ares.

"You can take meds," I say. "Most of the vets do."

"*Psych meds?* I don't need Yellow synthetics. I'm a Red of Faran. My wits are damn sure more important than a dry bed." On that we agree. Even though he's my wife's main opposition in the Senate, and thereby mine, he's still as dear to me as my own family. Only when Mars and her moons were declared free did Dancer give up the gun and take up the senatorial toga to found the Vox Populi, the "Voice of the People," a socialist lowColor party to counter what he saw as undue Gold influence over the Republic. It's a bloodydamn thorn in my boots every time he gives a speech on proportional representation. If he had his way, there'd be five hundred lowColor senators to every Gold senator. Good math. Bad reality.

"Still, must be good to feel grass under your boots instead of sand and metal," he says softly. "Must be good to be home."

"It is." I hestitate and look out at the rocky shore below. "Gets harder every time. To come back. You'd think I look forward to it, but . . . I don't know. I dread it in a way. Every time Pax grows a centimeter, it feels like an indictment against me for not being there to see it." I pick a loose thread impatiently. "Not to mention the longer I spend here, the more time the Ash Lord has to prepare Venus, and the longer this all stretches out."

His face hardens at the mention of the war. "And how long do you think this will . . . stretch out?"

"That depends, doesn't it?" I ask. "You're the only thing standing in my way of getting the men I need to end this."

"That's always your answer. Isn't it? More men." He sighs. "I'm the mouth of the Vox Populi, not the brain."

"You know, Dancer, humility isn't always a virtue."

"You disobeyed the Senate," he says flatly. "We did not give you permission to launch an Iron Rain. We preached caution and—"

"I won, didn't I?"

"This isn't the Sons of Ares any longer, much as you and I both wish it were. Virginia and her Optimates were content to let you run roughshod over the Senate, but the people are learning just how strong their voice is." He steps close to me. "Still, they revere you."

"Not all of them."

"Please. You've got cults that say prayers in your name. Who else has that?"

"Ragnar." I hesitate. "And Lysander au Lune."

"The line of Silenius died with Octavia. You were a fool to let that boy go, but if he was alive we'd know it. He got swallowed up by the war just like the rest of them. That leaves only you. The people love you, Darrow. You can't abuse that love. Whatever you do, you set an example. So if you don't follow the law, why should our Imperators, our Governors? Why should anyone else? How are we supposed to govern if you go off and do whatever you damn well please, like you're a—" He catches himself.

"A Gold."

"You know what I mean. The Senate was elected. You were not."

"I do what's necessary. You and I always have. But the rest of them, they do what gets them reelected. Why should I listen to them?" I smile at him. "Maybe you want an apology. Will that get me the men I need?"

"It may be too late for apologies."

I raise an eyebrow. I wish I could say his coldness is alien to me, but that bond between us has never been the same since he learned how I bought my peace with Romulus. I gave Romulus the Sons of Ares. Those were Dancer's men I left to die on the Rim. The guilt I felt for that defined our relationship for years, made me desperate for his approval. I thought if I could destroy the Ash Lord, I could amend the horror I consigned those men and women to. Nothing has been amended. Nothing will be. And it breaks my heart to know Dancer will never love me again the way I love him.

"Are we threatening each other now, Dancer? Thought you and I were beyond that. We started this together."

"Aye. We did. I care for you as if you were my own blood. Have ever since you came to me covered in dirt, no taller than my nose. But even you have to follow the laws of the Republic you helped build. Because when the law is not obeyed, the ground is fertile for tyrants."

I sigh. "You've been reading again."

"Damn right. The Golds hoarded our history so they could pretend they owned it. It's my duty as a free man to read so I'm not blind, being led around by my nose."

"No one is leading you around by your nose."

He snorts his disagreement. "When I was a soldier, I watched as your wife gave pardons to murderers, to slavers, and I bore it because I was told it was necessary to win the war. I watch now as our people live fifteen to a room with scraps for food, rags for healthcare, while the highColor aristocracy live in towers, and I bear it because I'm told it is necessary to win the war. I'll be damned if I sit back and watch another tyrant replace the one we left behind because it is necessary to win the fucking war."

"Spare me the speeches, man. My wife's no tyrant. It was her idea to diminish the strength of the Sovereign in the New Compact. Her choice to give that strength to the Senate. She helped give our people a voice. You think that was convenient for her? You think that's what a tyrant would do?"

He fixes me with hard eyes. "I wasn't talking about her."

I see.

"I remember when you told me I was a good man who'd have to do bad things," I say. "Your stomach go soft? Or have you spent so much time with politicians that you've forgotten what the enemy looks like? Usually they're about seven foot tall, wear a big Pyramid badge, oh, and they've got Red blood all over their hands."

"And so do you," he says. "One million was the total loss, wasn't it? One million for Mercury. You might be willing to bear that. But the rest of us tire of the weight. I know the Obsidians do. I know I do."

"So that leaves us at an impasse."

"It does. You're my friend," he says, voice heavy with emotion. "You will always be my friend. I won't put a dagger in your back. But I will stand up to you. I will do what is right."

"And so will I." I put out my hand. He takes it and lingers for a moment before walking down the path. He turns before it bends into the trees. "Is there something you're not telling me, Darrow? If there is, now is the time. When it's between just us friends."

"I've no secrets from you," I say, wishing it were true, wishing he believed me. Wishing he were still the leader of the Sons of Ares, so we could bear our secrets together like we once did. Sadly, not all adversaries are enemies.

He turns and limps back to the garden to say farewell to my mother. They embrace and he makes his way to the southern landing pads where his Warden escorts wait. He takes a white wool toga from one and puts it on over his shirt before he goes up the ramp.

"What did he want?" Sevro asks.

"What do all politicians want?"

"Prostitutes."

"Control."

"He knows about the emissaries?"

"He couldn't."

Sevro watches Dancer's wool toga billow in the wind as he boards his shuttle. "I liked the bastard better in armor."

"So did I."

3

DARROW

The Fantasy

DINNER IS SERVED SHORTLY AFTER Daxo and Mustang arrive from Hyperion with my brother Kieran and niece, Rhonna. We eat at a long wooden table covered with candles and hearty provincial Martian dishes spiced with curry and cardamom. Sevro, swarmed by his daughters, makes faces at them as they eat. But when the air cracks with a sonic boom, he bolts upright, looks at the sky, and runs off into the house, urging his children to stay put. He returns a whole half an hour later arm in arm with his wife, hair a mess, two jacket buttons missing, touching a white napkin to a bloodied, split lip. My old friend Victra, immaculate in a high-collared green jacket threaded with gemstones, beams devilishly across the patio at me. She's seven months pregnant with their fourth daughter. "Well, if it isn't the Reaper in the leathery flesh. Apologies, my goodman. I'm dreadfully late."

Her long legs cover the distance in three strides.

I greet her with a hug. She squeezes my butt hard enough to make me jump. She kisses Mustang on the head and slides into a chair, dominating the table. "Hello, gloomy one," she says to Electra. She looks at young Pax and Baldur, who've been huddled conspiratorially at the far end of the table. Both boys blush furiously. "Will one of you handsome lads pour Aunty Victra some juice? She's had a hellish day." They scramble over one another to be the first to grab the pitcher. Baldur wins, and, pleased as a peacock, the quiet Obsidian lad solemnly pours Victra a towering glass. "Damnable mechanics union is on strike again. I've got docks full of freight that's ready to move, but the little bastards got all spiced up by a Vox Populi mouthpiece and took the power couplings out of more than half the ships in my Luna food haulers and hid them."

"What do they want?" Mustang asks.

"Aside from the moon to starve? Higher wages, better living conditions . . . the usual tripe. They say it's too expensive to live on Luna with their wages. Well, there's plenty of room on Earth!"

"How ungrateful of the unwashed peasants," my mother says.

"I detect your sarcasm, Deanna, and I'm choosing to ignore it in honor of our recently returned heroes. There will be enough debate later in the week. Anyway, I'm practically a saint. Mother would have sent Grays in to crack their ungrateful skulls. Thank Jove the tinmen still bloody any Vox they see."

"It's their right to bargain collectively," Mustang says, reaching down to wipe a bit of hummus off the face of Sevro's youngest, Diana. "Written in ink in the New Compact."

"Yes, of course it is. Unions are the heart of fair labor," Victra mutters. "It's the only thing Quicksilver and I agree upon."

Mustang smiles. "Better. You're a paragon of the Republic once again."

"You only just missed Dancer," Sevro says.

"I thought it reeked of self-righteousness." Victra goes to sip her juice and jumps in surprise. Baldur still stands at her side, smiling a bit too earnestly. "Oh, you're still here. Begone, creature." She kisses her fingers and then presses them to Baldur's cheek, pushing him away. He goes, drifting on air back to my envious son.

Afterwards, as the children go off into the vineyard to play, we retire to the back grotto. My family, those by blood and by choice, surround me. For the first time in over a year, I feel peace settling into me. My wife puts her feet in my lap and instructs me to rub them.

"I think Pax is in love with you, Victra," Mustang laughs as Daxo pours her a glass of wine. His hands dwarf the bottle. A taller man than I am, he has difficulty sitting in his chair and keeps accidentally kicking my shins under the table. Kieran and his wife, Dio, hold hands on a bench by the fire. When I was younger, I remember thinking how much she looked like Eo. But now, as time passes, the shadow of my wife's face fades and I see only the woman who is the center of my brother's being. She lurches forward suddenly, away from a shower of embers as Niobe dumps another log on the flames. Thraxa sits off in the corner, furtively lighting a burner.

"Well, Pax could have worse an idol than his godmother," Victra says, eyeing her husband, who is picking his teeth with a splinter of wood he's pried from the outdoor table. She pushes him with her foot. "That's grotesque. Stop."

"Sorry."

"Yet you're not stopping."

"Bit of gristle, my love." He turns like he's throwing the splinter away, but keeps picking. "Got it," he says gloomily. Instead of throwing the salvaged gristle to the side, he chews on it and swallows. "Beef."

"Beef?" Mustang looks back at the table. "We had chicken and lamb."

Sevro frowns. "Odd. Kieran, when did we last have beef?"

"At the Howler dinner, three days ago." Noses wrinkle around the table.

Sevro chuckles to himself. "Then it was well aged."

Daxo shakes his head and continues sketching angels for Diana, who sits on his lap admiring the man's work. He's no fool with a razor, but his true art is made with a stylus. Victra looks helplessly at Mustang over her juice, despairing of her husband. "Proof, my dear, that love is blind."

"Mickey can fix that face if you're tired of looking at it," I say.

"Good luck. You'd have to pry the decadent sprite away from his laboratory," Daxo says. The bald man considers Diana's addition of a cruelly barbed trident to the angel he's drawn. "Not to mention his admirers. He brought quite the menagerie to the Opera last September. It was a bit like a Hieronymus Bosch painting come alive. One of them was even an actress. Can you imagine?" he asks Mustang. "Your father would have chewed through his cheek to see lowColors sitting in the Elorian."

"He's not the only one," Victra says. "Too much new money these days. Quicksilver's friends." She shivers.

"Well, money doesn't buy culture, does it?" Daxo replies.

"Not at all, my goodman. Not at all."

As the night deepens, the orange fingers of the slow sunset thread their way through the trees. I let go of the strain in my shoulders and sink deeper into my cup, listening to my friends chatter and joke while little blue bugs flicker and stab violent light into the late summer twilight. The trees rustle beyond the terrace; the shouts of children come from the grounds as they play night games. The blistering sand seas of Mercury seem so far away now. The stench of war so remote in my mind they are little more than shards of half-forgotten dreams.

This is how life should be.

This peace. This laughter.

But even now I feel it slipping through my fingers like that faraway sand. I sense the House Augustus Lionguards out in the darkness of the forest, watching the sky, the shadows, helping us stay inside the fantasy a moment longer. Mustang catches my eye and nods toward the door.

Forcing myself to part ways from my friends as the Telemanuses give a rousing, drunken rendition of their family's song, "The Fox of Summerfall," I follow several minutes after Mustang disappears into the main house. The manor halls here are older even than those of the Citadel of Light. History is the mortar of the place. Relics from older ages adorn walls, festoon shelves. Octavia called this place home as a child. Her essence lingers in the rafters and the attic and the gardens, as do those of her ancestors and child. It is where Lysander would have played long before his path crossed mine. I feel the imprint the Lunes have left on the home. At first I thought it strange living in the house of my greatest enemy, but in all humanity, who knew the burdens Mustang and I face as well as Octavia? In life, I loathed her. In death, I understand her.

The scent of my wife reaches me before the sight of her. Our room is warm and the door shudders shut behind me on a rusted metal latch. A bottle of wine is open on the table beside the fireplace, where eagles and crescent moons of House Lune are carved into the stone corbels. Mustang's slippers lie discarded on the floor. The ring of her father and my House Mars ring rest on the table beside her datapad, which flashes away with new messages.

She's spooled herself into a chair on our veranda like a bit of golden yarn, reading the dog-eared book of Shelley's poetry Roque gave her years ago during their summer of opera and art in Agea, after the Institute. She doesn't look up as I approach. I stand behind her, considering better of speaking, and slide a hand through her hair. I knead my thumbs into the muscles of her neck and back. Her proud shoulders relent against my fingers and she turns her book over in her lap. Sharing a life threads more than flesh and blood together. It weaves her memories in and around and through mine.

The more I know of her, the more I share of her, the more I love her in a way the boy I used to be never knew how to love. Eo was a flame, dancing against the wind. I tried to catch her. Tried to hold her. But she was never meant to be held.

My wife is not as fickle as a flame. She is an ocean. I knew from the first that I cannot own her, cannot tame her, but I am the only storm that moves her depths and stirs her tides. And that is more than enough.

I lower my lips to her neck and taste the alcohol and sandalwood of her perfume. I breathe slow and easy, feeling the lightness of love and the wordless unspooling of the sea of space that kept us apart. Impossible, it seems, that we were ever so distant. That there was ever a time where she existed and I was not with her. Everything that she is, every scent, taste, touch, makes me know I am home. She reaches up, dragging her slender fingers through my hair. "I missed you," I say.

"What's not to miss?" she asks, giving me a sly smile. I move to sit with her on the chaise, but she clucks her tongue. "You're not done yet. Keep rubbing, Imperator. Your Sovereign commands it."

"I think power's gone to your head." She glances up at me. "Yes, ma'am." I continue massaging her neck.

"I'm drunk," she mutters. "I can already feel the hangover."

"Thraxa's good at making it feel like a moral obligation to keep pace."

"Ten credits says we have to scrape Sevro off the patio tomorrow."

"Poor Goblin. All spirit, no body mass."

She laughs. "I put him and Victra in the west wing so we can actually get some sleep. Last time, I woke up in the middle of the night thinking a coyote was caught in the air recycler. I swear, at the pace they're going they'll be able to single-handedly populate Pluto in a few years."

She pats the cushion beside her. I join her on the chaise and wrap my arms around her. The lake breeze sighs through the trees. In the silence we share, I feel her heartbeat and wonder what her eyes see as they look out over the tops of the trees to the orange sky.

"Dancer was here," I say.

She makes a small noise of acknowledgment, to let me know she resents my reminder of the world beyond our balcony. "He's not happy with you."

"Half the Senate looked like they wanted to poison my wine."

"I warned you. Luna's changed since you were gone. The Vox Populi can't be ignored any longer."

"I noticed."

"Yet when they passed a resolution, you spat in their eye."

"And now they'll spit in mine."

"Seems that's the bed you made."

"Do they have the votes to block my request?"

"They might."

"Even if you apply pressure?"

"You mean even if I clean up your mess." It wasn't a question.

"I made the right decision," I say. "I know I did. You know I did.

They don't know war. They were afraid of being held responsible for failure. What was I supposed to do? Comb my hair while they protected their reputations?"

"Maybe you should learn from them."

"I'm not going to hold a poll in the middle of a war. You could have vetoed them."

"I could have. But then they'd cry that I was protecting my husband, and the Vox would gain more even supporters."

"Copper and Obsidian are still in play?"

"No. Caraval says the Coppers will back you. As goes Sefi, so goes Obsidian. What will she choose? You'd know better than I."

"I don't know," I admit. "She was against the Rain, but she came with me."

She's silent at that.

"You think I've shot us in the foot, don't you?"

"Does Dancer have anything else he can use against you?"

"No," I say. I know she doesn't believe me. And she knows I know, but she can't ask any more. Though I want to tell her about the emissaries, it would incriminate her as well. Sevro and I agreed it was a secret that must stay within the Howlers. She would be bound by oath to tell the Senate. And she tried so hard to honor her new oaths.

"Dancer's not the only one angry with me," I say. "Pax would hardly look at me at dinner."

"I saw."

"I don't know what to do."

"I think you do." She goes quiet. "We're missing this," she says eventually. "Life. The dinner tonight, I'll remember forever. The lightning bugs. The children in the yard. The smell of rain on its way." She looks over at me. "Just seeing you laughing. I shouldn't remember it. It should be one of thousands."

"What are you saying?"

"I'm saying that when my term of office ends in two years, maybe I won't run again. Maybe I let the torch pass to someone else. You hand the reins to Orion or Harnassus. Maybe the rest of this isn't our responsibility." A tiny, hopeful smile crosses her lips. "We will go back to Mars and live in my estate. We'll raise our children with your brother and sister's and put our lives into helping our family, our planet. And each night we'd have a dinner like this one. Friends could come and go in our house whenever they passed through. The door would always be open. . . ."

And an army would always have to guard it.

Her words carry away into the night, into the arms of the swaying trees, along with the current of the wind, up and up into the sky, where it seems all fantasies go. But I sit cold as a stone beside her, because I know she doesn't believe any of this. We've played the game far too long to walk away. I take her hand. And as my wife is quiet and the fantasy drifts away, our familiar friend, dread, creeps onto the balcony with us, because deep inside, in the shadowy chasms of ourselves, we know Lorn was right. For those who dine with war and empire, the bill always comes at the end.

And almost as if the world was listening to my thoughts, a knock comes at the door. Mustang answers it, and when she returns her face belongs to the Sovereign, not my wife. "It was Daxo. Dancer's called an emergency session of the Senate. They've moved your hearing up to tomorrow night."

"What does that mean?"

"Nothing good."

4

LYRIA

Welcome to the Worlds

S KY.
     That's what my da would call the roof of stone and metal that stretched over our home in the mine of Lagalos. It's what we all used to call it, going back generations of our clan to the first Pioneers. *The sky be crumbling. The sky needs reinforcing.*

It stretched over us like a great shield, keeping us safe from the fabled Martian storms raging outside. There were dances for the sky, songs wishing it luck and blessings. I even knew two lasses named for it.

But the sky wasn't a shield. It was a lid. A cage.

I was sixteen years of knobby knees and freckles when I first saw the true sky. Took six years from the death of the Sovereign on Luna for the Rising to push the last of the Golds off our continent of Cimmeria. Two more years for them to finally free our mine from the Gray warlord who set up his own little kingdom in their absence.

Then the Rising came to Lagalos.

Our saviors looked more like manic Laureltide jesters than soldiers draped with trophies of gray and blond hair and iron pyramid badges. SlingBlades and spiked red helmets were painted on their chests. And standing at their front was a weary, bearded Red man old enough to be a grandfather. He had a large gun in one hand and in the other a tattered white flag with the fourteen-pointed morning star. He wept when he saw the bloated bellies and skeletal evidence of our starvation under the Gray warlord. His gun dropped to the floor, and though he was a stranger to us, he came forward and hugged me. "Sister," he said. Then he hugged the man beside me. "Brother."

Four weeks later, kind-faced men and women wearing white helmets and fourteen-pointed stars on their chests took us to the surface. I'll never forget their eyes. They were Yellow and Brown and Pink. They had bottles of water, sparkling sweet drinks and candy for the children. And they gave us clunky goggles marked with winged feet to cover our cave eyes from the sun. I didn't want to wear the goggles. Rather look at the true sky and its sun with my own eyes. But a kind Yellow nurse told me I might lose my sight. So on they went.

When the doors of the lift opened, we walked from a basin littered with ships, up metal stairs and out onto an endless plain of tall grass vibrating with the sound of insects, and I saw it: blue and vast, so large I felt I was falling up into it. The true sky. And there, hanging like a sullen coal on the impossible horizon, was the sun. Giving us warmth. Filling my eyes with tears. So small I could block it with a thumb. Our sun. *My* sun.

The Republic's relief ships arrived the next morning to bawdy choruses hurled out from the throats of young gallants and lasses. The ships were cleaner than anything I'd ever seen. White as my nephew's baby teeth as they coasted down. On their bellies blazed the star of the Republic. To us, then, the star meant hope.

"Reaper's compliments," a young soldier said as he handed me a chocolate bar. "Welcome to the worlds, lass."

Welcome to the worlds.

On the shuttle away from our mine, a video appeared before each of us, the hologram so lifelike I thought my fingers would touch the Gold face that sprung into the air. I'd seen her before, but here above ground on one of her ships, she seemed like a goddess from one of our songs. Virginia the Lionheart. Her eyes a terrifying gold. Her hair like spun silk held back from her poreless face. She shone brighter than that little coal of a sun. Making me feel little more than a shadow of a girl.

"Child of Mars, welcome to the worlds . . ." the young Sovereign began gently. "You are about to embark upon a great journey to your rightful place upon the surface of the planet your ancestors built. Your sweat, your blood, and that of your kin, gave this planet life. Now it is your turn to share in the bounty of mankind, to live and prosper in this new Solar Republic and pave a way for the next generation. My heart is with you. The hopes and dreams of people everywhere rise with you. Good luck and may you and yours find joy under the stars."

That was two years and a thousand broken promises ago.

Now, under a boiling sun, I hunch over the scant, piddling river beyond Assimilation Camp 121. My back bent and fingers crooked as I rub an abrasive brush into a pair of pants soiled by Ava's work in the slaughter yards where she kills cattle to fill our pot.

My arms, once ashen brown like most from Lagalos, are wiry and now baked dark by the sun and bitten ragged by the bugs that rise up out of the riverbed mud. The summers of the Cimmerian Plains are humid and thick with mosquitoes. I swat three away that've found a gap in the lyder flower paste.

I'm eighteen now with stubborn baby fat in my cheeks. My hair leaps from my head at a thick tangle. Like a rabid animal trying to escape my skull. I don't blame it. Eyes never rest long on me. The boys on Da's drillteam used to call me Mudbug for the color of my eyes. Da always said Ava's got the looks in our family. I've just got the temper.

Along the riverbank are hardpacked men and women—two score Gammas of my clan humming "The Ballad of Bloody Mary the Fool." My mother used to hum it as she worked. Rust-red hair bursts from under broad-brimmed hats and headwraps of bright cloth. Off the bank, fishermen laze on boats smoking tobacco as they drag their nets farther into the river.

Lambda doesn't let us use the Solar Republic washers in the center of the camp anymore. Bastards think they have the right, since they are the same clan as the Reaper. Never mind that they're as related to him as I am to bats that come out of the jungle at night to hunt for the camp's mosquitoes.

The Solar Republic ships don't come much anymore without a full military escort, what with the Red Hand marauders running mad in the South. Those that do come drop the supplies in little parachute crates from the sky. And the soldiers who actually land in the camp now cradle weapons instead of candy.

We see it on the HC news every day. Red Hand raids on helpless camps. Sons kidnapped, fathers killed, and the rest savaged. They claim they're bringing justice to my clan, the Gammas, for being the pets of our former oppressors. In every camp they raid, they purge us like a strain of diseased rats.

Ava believes the Republic will stop the Hand. That the Reaper will come with his howling legions and smite the bastards right and good. Or somesuch. She's always been a pretty fool. The Sovereign brought us out of the dirt and forgot us in the mud. The Reaper hasn't even been to Mars in years. Got more to worry about than his own Color, it seems.

Bitten ragged by the mosquitoes, I haul the basket up onto my head and make my way back to the camp. The pawing electricity of a coming storm fills the air. In the distance, across the green-stained savannah, huge thunderheads begin to bruise the sky purple and black. They're forming fast.

Heaps of trash hump the violent green landscape closer to the camp. Here and there range slim burner boys blackened dark with soot. They wear rags tied over their faces as they douse heaps of clothing and trash infected by the malaria outbreak with engine oil. The blazes choke the sky with cancerous black veins.

My brother, Tiran, is out there amidst the stacks, face wrapped like the rest, squinting into a blaze for one token an hour. In the mine, all he wanted to be was a Helldiver. It's all any of us wanted to be. I used to sneak downstairs late at night and don my father's workboots and his helmet and sit at the dinner table with forks and spoons pinched between my fingers, acting as if I were running a clawDrill.

But then my da fell into a pitviper nest and lost his legs. Soon after,

Mum died and the rest of Da went with her. I used to think my world permanent. That clansmen and women would always tip their heads to my father, that my mother would always be there to wake me and give me a spot of syrup before school. But that life is gone. More miners are lured up every day by the promise of freedom. And in their wake, the mines are bought by big companies from big cities and manned by robots stamped with a silver heel. Just like ours was. They say we're to receive a share soon as it makes a profit. We've yet to see so much as a half-credit chit.

A throaty din rises from Assimilation Camp 121 as I enter its open gates. It's a muck-soaked town of plastic, tin, and dog shit. Fifty thousand of us now in a place meant for twenty, with more coming every day. Gloomy squadrons of mosquitoes buzz low over the soup of the streets, searching for meat to suck. All the lads old enough for the Free Legions have gone to war. And those boys and girls who stay behind work shit jobs for food tokens so the old don't starve. No child dreams of being a Helldiver anymore, because in this new world there are no Helldivers left.

5

LYRIA

Camp 121

I MAKE IT TO MY FAMILY's hut using the sheeting and wood planks that serve as roads through the mud. I slip under the mosquito netting just as thunder cracks open the sky overhead. Rain pours down, hammering the thin plastic roofs all down the narrow lane. Inside the dry hut, I'm greeted with the thick smell of stew. I set the basket down inside the door. Our home is five meters by seven, made of neoPlast stamped with the star of the Republic and a tiny little winged heel where the plastic meets the ground. It's separated into two small rooms by opaque plastic dividers that fall from the ceiling. The kitchen and living room in the front. The bunks in the back. My sister Ava is hunched over a little solar stove stirring a pot. She glances back at me as I stand panting.

"Either you're getting faster or the clouds are getting slower."

"Bit of both, I'd say." I rub the stitch in my side and sit down at the little plastic dinner table. "Tiran still burnin'?"

"That he is."

"Poor lad's gonna get drenched. Bloodydamn, it smells kind in here." I inhale the scent of stew.

Ava glows. "A bit of garlic found its way into the pot."

"Garlic? How'd that sneak through Lambda? They stop hoarding the new freight?"

"No." She goes back to stirring the pot. "One of the soldiers gave it to me."

"Gave? Out of the goodness of his high heart?"

"And that's not all." She hikes up her skirt to show off two brilliant blue shoes. Not government-issue clogs. Real shoes of leather and quality rubber.

"Bloodydamn. What you give him in return?" I ask in shock.

"Nothing!" Ava scrunches her nose at the accusation.

"Men don't give gifts for *nothing*."

"I'm married." She crosses her arms.

"Sorry. Forgot," I say with bite. Her husband, Varon, is as good a man as I've ever met, and as absent a one. He, along with our two eldest brothers, Aengus and Dagan, volunteered for the Free Legions right after we entered the camp. Last we heard from them was from a Legion com bank on Phobos. Three of them crowded together to fit into the frame. Said they were sailing with the White Fleet toward Mercury. Seems just yesterday I was following Aengus through the vents of Lagalos to look for fungus to fill his still.

"Where're the boys?" I ask.

"Liam's at the infirmary."

"Again?" A pang of pity goes through me.

"Another ear infection," she says. "Could you go visit him in the morning? You know how much—"

"Course," I interrupt. Liam, her second youngest, is just past six and has been blind from birth. He's always been my favorite. Sweet little thing. "I'll bring him some leftover candy if the other rats don't gobble it up."

"You spoil him."

"Some lads oughta be spoiled."

I find my niece, Ella, bundled up in her carriage by the table. She's playing with a little mobile of one of her brother's broken toys suspended above her. "How's my little haemanthus blossom on this *dreadful* stormy eve?" I say, poking her nose. She giggles and grabs my finger, then tries to eat it. "She got a mouth on her."

"I'll feed her after dinner. You mind checkin' Da's diaper?"

My father sits in his chair watching the HC box I stole from a Lambda too drunk to mind his tent. His eyes are pearly and distant, reflecting the static of the dead channel that writhes on the screen.

"Lemme help you with that, Da," I say. I change the channel till an image of a gravBike shooting over a Mercurian desert appears. Bad men pursue the roguish Blue hero, who looks not just a bit like Colloway xe Char.

"Is this all right?" I ask. Thunder rolls outside.

He doesn't answer. Doesn't even look at me, so I bite back the resentment and try to remember him as the man who used to take us to the deep mines. His rough hands would light the gas fire, and he'd whisper ghost stories of Golback the Dark Creeper or Old Shuffle-foot in his hoarse voice. The flames from the fire would saw the air and he would boom out a hilarious laugh at our terrified faces.

I don't recognize this man . . . this creature wearing my father's skin. It just eats and shits and sits there watching the HC. Still, I shove the anger away, feeling guilty for it, and kiss him on the forehead. I tuck his blanket a little bit under his bearded chin and thank the Vale there's no soil in his diaper.

There's a clatter from the door as my sister's young sons bowl into the house, drenched in mud and rain. Next comes our remaining brother, Tiran, smelling of smoke from the burning stacks. He's the tallest in the family, but frighteningly thin. Most nights, he looks like a curled weed, hunched over the little books he writes for the children. Fills them with stories of castles and vales and flying knights. He whips his wet hair at us and tries to give Ava a hug. My sister shows off her shoes to her jealous boys with false modesty. They debate what one of the brighter blue colors on the tongues ought to be called while I set the dishes.

"Cerulean!" they decide. "Like Colloway xe Char's tattoos."

"Colloway xe Char. Colloway xe Char," Tiran mocks.

"Warlock's the best pilot in the worlds," Conn says in indignation.

Tiran scoffs. "I'd take the Reaper in a starShell against Char in a ripWing any day."

Conn puts his arms on his hips. "You're stupid. Warlock would blast him to bloody bits."

"Well, they're friends, so they won't be blasting each other to anything," my sister says. "They're too busy protecting your father and uncles, aren't they?"

"Do you think Da has met them?" Conn asks. "Char and the Reaper?"

"And Ares?" Barlow adds. "Or Wulfgar the Whitetooth?" He slams his hands like he's a menacing Obsidian. "Or Dancer of Faran! Or Thraxa au—"

"Aye, they're probably the best of friends. Now eat."

We eat dinner huddled around the plastic table as the rain drums the roof. There's barely enough room for bowls and elbows, but we layer around the thin soup and chatter on about the merits of rip-Wings against starShells in atmosphere. My sister smiles when the boys say the soup tastes better today.

After dinner, we gather around with Da to watch one of his programs. I break half of a Cosmos chocolate bar into seven pieces to share. I pocket my piece for Liam and smile when I see Tiran give his piece to Ava. No wonder he's so skinny. The program is a news show. The host a Violet who reminds me a bit of the helions—a tropical bird that lives off our trash. He has an incredible shock of white hair and a jaw you could carve granite with, but pathetically delicate hands for a man.

The very important man is reporting on the Reaper's Triumph in Hyperion City. My nephews all nudge each other as he theorizes that the next push will be toward Venus to finish off the Ash Lord and his daughter, the Last Fury, once and for all. My sister watches in silence, stroking her new shoes. So far our brothers and her husband have not been named in the casualty report that scrolls along the bottom of the holo.

Tiran leans toward the far-off world. He's always been the softest of our family, and the most eager to prove himself. Soon it'll be his turn. He becomes sixteen in just a few months. Then he'll leave all this mud behind for the stars. I can't help but resent him already. None of them should have left their family.

The boys don't see my sister's quiet desperation. The images of the HC dance in their Red eyes. The color. The spectacle of the Triumph on Luna. The glory of the greatest son of Red standing with his Gold wife—the Sovereign who promised us so much—lifting his clenched fist into the air as they howl. They think they could rise like the Reaper. They're too young to see our life is the lie behind the lights.

"Reaper! Reaper!" the crowd shouts.

My little nephews join in the chant. And I reach for my sister's hand, glaring at the HC, remembering the promises undelivered, and wonder if I'm the only one who misses the mines.

I wake in the night to a distant roar. The room is still. Sweat slicks my legs. I sit up in bed, listening. There's a clamor in the distance. The snoring of far-off engines. Mosquitoes buzz outside the netting that's wrapped around our bunks. "Aunt Lyria," Conn whispers from beside me. "What's that noise?"

"Quiet, love." I strain to hear. The engines fade. I push my legs off the edge of my bunk. Father's soft breathing comes from below. He's still asleep. My sister's bunk is empty. So is Tiran's sleeping pallet on the ground.

I slip past the mosquito netting and out of my bed in shorts and a cotton shirt soggy from the humidity. "Where are you going?" Conn asks. "Aunt Lyria . . ." I seal the netting behind me with the adhesive strip.

"Just going to take a peek, love," I say. "Go back to sleep." I slip on my sandals and leave the room. My sister is already awake, standing near the door and watching nervously as Tiran puts on his boots. "What's what?" I ask quietly. "Thought I heard a ship."

"Probably just some idiot SR airhead buzzing the camp," Tiran says.

"Not bloody likely," I snap. "We ain't had a supply ship land in a month."

"Lower your voice," he hisses. "The little ones'll hear."

"Well, if you weren't being thick, I wouldn't have to shout."

"Stop it, you two." Ava looks nervous. "What if it's the Red Hand?"

Tiran brushes his tangled hair from his eyes. "Don't get your fry-suit in a twist. The Hand's hundreds of klicks south. Republic wouldn't let anyone in our airspace."

"Like that means pissall," I mutter.

"They own the skies," he replies like he's a Praetor.

"They don't even own their own cities," I say, remembering the bombings in Agea.

He sighs. "I'll go take a look. You both mind the house."

"Mind the house?" I laugh. "Stop acting the maggot. I'm coming with."

"No, you're not," Tiran replies.

"I'm just as fast as you."

"Not the bloody point. I'm the man of the house," he says, and I snort. "Remember what happened to Vanna, Torron's daughter? Girls shouldn't wander the township at night. Especially not us." He means Gamma, and he's right. I knew Vanna since I was a child. She was tattered flesh when they found her, hands cut off. We buried her by the treeline of the jungle south of the camp. "Besides, if I'm wrong, you gotta to be here to help Ava and the little ones. I'll go take a look and I'll be back fastlike. I promise." He leaves without another word. Ava closes the door behind him. She wrings her hands and sits at the kitchen table. I sit down with her, picking at the scratches on the plastic top in irritation. *Man of the house.*

"Slag this." I stand up. "I'm gonna go have a look."

"Tiran's already gone!"

"Please. His balls have barely dropped. I'll be back in a tick." I head to the door.

"Lyria . . ."

"What?"

She grabs our lone frying pan from the kitchen. "At least take this."

"In case I find eggs? Fine. Fine." I take the pan. "Might want to get water and food ready just in case." She nods and I leave her behind.

The night is grim and humid as air in a smoker's mouth. By the time I've made it out of Gamma township and into the main camp, a tongue of sweat licks down the small of my back. It's quiet but for the hissing insects. A withered gaboon lizard watches me from the roof of a refugee domicile as it chews on a night moth. Lights glow from the far end of the camp where the landing pads lie. Eyes glint out from plastic doorways as I pass, peering out from behind mosquito netting. The streets are empty. I'm afraid in a way I never was in the mines. Feeling smaller now than I did in our hut.

There's men's voices arguing ahead. I creep carefully forward till I'm crouched behind a stack of discarded cargo containers. Two rusty pelican transport vessels have landed on the concrete pads. One is painted with the face of a lithe Pink model drinking a bottle of Ambrosia, a sweet pepper cola beverage that's given half the camp cavities. She smiles and winks at me, her mouth full of white, gleaming teeth. The lights of the ships blaze in the predawn, silhouetting the group of men from our camp who've woken and gone out to inspect the landed ships. My brother is amongst them, loitering in the back self-consciously. I suddenly feel guilt for snorting when he said "man of the house." He's just a boy. My boy, my little brother trying to be big. The clansmen are exchanging words with another group of men who've come down the ships' ramps. These ones are Reds too, but they carry weapons and long bandoliers stocked with ammunition across their bare chests.

The new men are asking where to find the Gammas. There's an argument amongst the men from our camp, then one of them is pointing toward our township. Another shoves him, but soon several other men begin to point not just at our homes, but toward Tiran and several others amongst their group. The other men drift away from my brother and the three other Gammas. The smallest of the men from the ship says something, but I don't catch it. One of the Gammas rushes him just as the man lifts a long dark object from his side. Acid-green light churns in the ammunition globe of his plasma rifle, then lunges from the muzzle in a rippling ball that gashes the darkness. It cleaves clean through the center of the man. He teeters to the ground like a township drunk. I'm frozen to the spot. My brother flees with the other pair of Gammas. One of the outsiders raises his rifle.

Metal chatters like a broken silk-threading machine.

My brother's chest erupts. The other gunmen shatter the quiet night, flashing and bleeding fire from their weapons. Tiran spasms, jerks. Not falling quickly. But stumbling one step, two steps, then another gunshot cracks the air and he is tumbling. Half his head is gone. A wailing cry rises from my belly. The whole world rushes past and goes silent as I stare at that shadowy mound in the mud.

Tiran . . .

The first man to fire walks over to my brother's body and rakes the corpse with the plasma weapon. Then he looks up at me, the acid-green fire illuminating a face like a demon's. It's not a man. It's a Red woman with terrible scars covering half of her face.

"Justice to Gamma!" Synced to the speakers on both of the ships behind her, her voice bellows out into the night. "Death to the collaborators! Justice to Gamma!"

6

EPHRAIM

Eternal City

I YAWN IN THE HUMID DARK, craving a burner because the vapor inhaler I'm sucking on is about as satisfying as fucking through a tarpaulin sheet. My left foot is numb and sweating through the sock in its rubber shoe, and my right arm is bent so awkwardly into the stone that my knock-off Valenti chronometer is drilling into the bone of my wrist with every. Arterial. Pulse.

The only thing that has kept me sane over the past nine hours has been the holocontacts I bought off the rack from that lemur-looking bastard, Kobachi, on 198th, 56th, and 17th in Old Town. But the contacts shorted out, and now I've got a corneal abrasion and worse, plenty of time to kill. Perfect.

I try in vain to stretch. The stone box doesn't give me much room to wriggle my 1.75-meter frame. My main grudge against ancient Egyptians isn't that they pioneered the institution of mass slavery for public works, it's that they were all so damn tiny. Still smells like the old raisin we dragged out of it late last night before the delivery.

I check my watch. It was a gift from my late fiancé. One of the cheap silvery types cobbled together by half-blind immigrant low-Colors in sweatshops deep in the armpits of Luna. Probably Tycho

City. Maybe Endymion or the Mass. Somewhere half a world away from the beating heart of Hyperion—where I am currently entombed. He didn't know it was a knockoff, so he paid nearly sixty percent market value, half his quarterly pay. His face glowed when he gave it to me. I didn't have the heart to tell him he could have bought it for the price of a decent bottle of vodka. Poor kid.

Check the watch again. Almost time.

Two minutes to midnight, only several hours left of dusk before Hyperion is plunged into the last dark month of summer. Dark or light, a day in Hyperion never truly ends. The caretakers of the day just lock their doors and hand the reins of the town over to the nocturnal creatures. Under Gold it wasn't exactly a Pink's paradise. But now, it's the law of the jungle when the lights go out. Outside the museum, the hot city will be stretching and crooning in the sweaty dusk, readying to make some trouble. On the lamplit Promenade, decent citizens will skitter to their private housing complexes, fleeing the yapping of young music and the roar of hoverbike gangs echoing up from Lost City.

Hyperion. Jewel of Luna. The Eternal City. She's a beautiful wartime mess. So much to look at, you can only afford to see what you want to see. If you plan on staying sane, that is.

But here, in the Hyperion Museum of Antiquities, behind thick walls of marble is a world with a different set of rules. During day hours, packs of drooling lowColor schoolchildren and Martian and Terran immigrants waddle their way through the marble corridors, rubbing snotty noses against glass containment boxes. At night, though, the museum is a fortress crypt. Impenetrable from the outside, occupied only by a contingent of pale night guards and the dead residents of crypts, statues, and paintings. The only way in was to become a resident. So we bribed a docker and snuck aboard a freighter from Earth as it landed at Atlas Interplanetary. A freighter that happened to hold numerous relics liberated from the private stash of some exiled Gold overlord dead or fled to Venus. Probably old Scorpio. Whole slew of goodies. Fourteen paintings from neoclassical Europe, a crate of Phoenician urns, twenty-five crates of Roman scrolls, and four sarcophagi.

What was yesterday filled with mummified Egyptians is tonight filled with freelancers.

By now the janitorial technicians will be herding up their robot charges and moving to the east wing. A team of security guards occupies a headquarters in the basement.

Tick. Tock. Tick. Tock.

I'm sick of waiting. Sick of the carousel of thoughts in my brain. I stare at the watch, willing the hands forward on their cheap gears that lose seconds every day. Can't think of anything but a ghost and how each tick, each tock, takes me farther from him. Farther from the ridiculous slicked-back hair he wore because he thought it made him look like a holostar I liked, or the knockoff Duverchi jackets he'd wear thinking it hid the farmboy underneath. That was his problem—always trying to be something he wasn't. Always trying to be *more*. Ate him up in the end and spat him out.

I pull my zoladone dispenser from my pack. I thumb the silver cylinder and it dispenses a black pill the size of a rat's pupil into my hand. Particularly wicked new designer drug. Absurdly illegal. Jacks up your dopamine and suppresses activity in the bit of gray matter responsible for empathy. Spec ops teams ate Zs like candy during the Battle of Luna. If you have to melt a city block, it's better to save the tears till you're back in your bunk.

I keep the dose low. One milligram worth of emotion-numbing molecules lances through my blood. The thoughts of my fiancé lose their dimensionality, becoming nothing but flat, monochrome pictures in a faded memory.

Tick. Tock. Tick. Tock.

Beep.

Shine time. I click my com once. Three more clicks echo.

Then there's a grating sound from the stone. It begins to move on its own. Blue light from the warehouse overheads seeps through the cracks as the lid of the sarcophagus levitates. A dark mass stands above me, holding the stone lid in the air as if it were made of neo-Plast.

"Evening, Volga," I mouth in gratitude to the giant woman. I sit up and feel a series of satisfying pops as my spinal cord stretches. Half my age, my Obsidian accomplice smiles with a mouth mangled by second-rate dental work. Unlike ice Obsidians, her face is absent the dense wind calluses that usually hide the sloping of cheekbones. Volga's small for an Obsidian, lean and a stunted six and a half feet. It makes her look less threatening than the average crow. It's not what her makers intended. She was born in a lab, courtesy of a Society breeding program. Poor kid didn't measure up with the rest of the crop and was tossed down to Earth for slave labor.

Met her five years back at a loading dock outside Echo City. I had delivered an item to a collector and had to celebrate with a few cocktails. Volga found me ten drinks and two centimeters deep in a pool of my own blood in an alley, mugged, cut, and left for dead by two local blackteeth. She carried me to a hospital and I paid her back with a ride to Luna, the one place she really wanted to go. Been following me around ever since. Teaching her the trade is my own little pet project.

Like me, she wears a black neoPlast suit to hide her thermal signature. She's still holding the lid of the sarcophagus above my head in the gloom of the museum's warehouse.

"You can stop showing off now," I mutter.

"Do not be jealous, tiny man, that I can lift what you cannot lift."

"Shhh. Don't bark so damn loud."

She winces. "Sorry. I thought Cyra turned off the security system."

"Just shut up," I say irritably. "Don't skip in a minefield." The old legion adage makes me feel even older than does the old ache in my right knee.

"Yes, boss." She makes an embarrassed face and sets the stone down gently before extending a hand to lift me out. I groan. Even with the Z, I feel every drink and snort and puff of my forty-six years. I blame the legion for stealing a good quarter of them. The Rising for stealing three more before I wised up and split. And then myself for spending all the rest like there'd be more coming at the end of the rainbow.

I don't need a mirror to tell me I'm the secondhand model of myself. I've got the telltale swollen face of a man who's gone one too many rounds with the bottle, and a slight body even a decade in legion gravity gymnasiums couldn't broaden.

I gather the green wrappers from my dinner of sirloin cubes and Venusian ginger seaweed and spray an aerosol can of blackmarket DNA into the sarcophagus before stuffing the can and the garbage into my backpack. Up goes my bodysuit's facial hood and I motion to Volga to don hers. We find the other two members of my team past a stack of crates four meters high, crouched in front of the security door leading out of the warehouse.

"Top of the evening," my team's cat, Dano, a young, pimply Red, says without looking back. "Could hear your knees creaking from a hundred meters, Tinman. Need some street grease in them. I know a louse at a chop shop who'll do you good."

I ignore him and his Terran overfamiliarity.

I need more Lunese associates. Hell, I'd even take a grumpy Martian. Terrans are all such talkers.

My Green locksmith, Cyra, another Terran, is on a knee working the interior of the biometric lock. Her gear is set out on the floor near the door, where she'll run support. Bit twitchy, that one. She doesn't usually like coming to the dancefloor. I've hired Cyra sporadically over the past few years, but we're not close. She's like most Limies—petulant and selfish, with a processor in place of a heart. Especially nasty to Volga. Doesn't bother me. I came to the conclusion at the age of nine that most people are liars, bastards, or just plain stupid. She's a good hacker, and that's all I care about. There's few enough of them freelancing these days. Corporations, criminal and reputable alike, are gobbling up all the talent.

Both Cyra and Dano are short, and the only way to tell them apart in their hooded black bodysuits is the sizable paunch around Cyra's midsection, that and the fact that Dano is doing the splits stretching for his part in the play, and humming an asinine Red ditty to himself.

I mind Dano less than Cyra. I've known him since he was a street rat fresh off the boat from Earth, pickpocketing on the Promenade with more acne on his face than hair in his head.

Cyra's hands work the innards of the door, her left holding an output jack that transmits a wireless signal from the door to the hardware in her head. Two metal crescents packed with hardware and two hardline uplinks embedded in her skull run from her temples, over her ears, and back toward the base of her cranium. I see their bulge from underneath her thermal hood.

"Door alarm?" I ask, when she leans back from the door.

"Off, obviously," she snaps, voice muffled through the hood. "The magnetic seal is dead." She glances over at Volga, who has kneeled to unfold her compact assault rifle from its black case. "Planning to break your rule tonight, crow?"

"Wait, are we murder positive?" Dano asks eagerly.

"No. We're not breaking any rules," I reply. "But if chance strikes, the pale lady is my walking, talking insurance policy. You know what they say. Hell hath no fury like a woman packing a railgun." Volga's gloved hands assemble the black weapon. She pulls free three curved clips of ammunition and attaches them to the outside of her suit with bonding tape. Each clip is marked with a colored band coordinating with the type of projectile—venom paralytic, electrical disrupter, hallucinogenic round. Never killing rounds. Damn inconvenient having a killing-machine bodyguard who refuses to kill.

I've no such reservations. I touch the pistol on my own hip, making sure the leg holster is tight. Muscle reflex by this point. I look back at Cyra. "You going to make me ask about the rest of the alarms?"

"Limey couldn't get all of 'em," Dano says from the ground where he contorts his leg behind his head in a bizarre hamstring stretch.

"That right?"

"Yeah," Cyra mutters.

Dano looks over at me, his face hidden behind the tight black plastic of his thermal. "Told you we shoulda hired Geratrix."

"Geratrix is Syndicate now," I mutter.

Dano bows his head in mock sorrow. "Another one for the bloody black."

"It's not my fault," Cyra says in a low voice. "They updated their system. New protocols are government. Would take me near thirty minutes to punch in. Shit, it'd take a team of Republic astral hackers at least twelve—"

I hold up a hand. "Hear that?" I whisper. They listen. "That's the sound of your take getting cut in half."

"Half?"

"Half a job, half pay."

Cyra's got a temper on her as short as a tick's tooth. Her hand drops to the multigun on her hip. Still, Volga takes one step toward her and Cyra looks like a kitten hearing thunder. I bend on a knee in front of the Green. "It's not my fault . . ." she says. I take her chin through the mask and guide it so she's looking at me.

"Calm down, and tell me the problem." I snap my fingers. "Today, pissant."

"I can't access the Conquerors Exhibit systems," she admits.

"At all?"

"It's on an isolated server. Real relics in there, real security."

I feel a spasm of annoyance in my left eyelid. Damn. Dano's gonna have to do some acrobatics. "You know how I hate surprises, Cyra. . . ."

"Told you we shoulda bought the gravBelts," Dano says.

"Say 'I told you we shoulda' one more time. See what happens." He meets my eyes, then glances down at the floor. Thought so. "Spider gloves are good enough," I say. "Recyclers on." Dano, Volga, and I pull our recyclers from our bags and strap them over our thermals' mouth holes. "I trust you still have the doors figured. . . ."

She nods.

"Thirty seconds in each room," I remind them as Volga slings her gun on her back and approaches the door. Dano rolls up from his stretch and Volga pushes a large flat magnet against the door. It makes a dull thump as it locks onto the metal. We stare at the magnet as its sound reverberates. Through the door our voices won't be heard, but that might have been. I look to Cyra. She shakes her head. Decibel levels were too low. Clear, Volga wraps her massive mitts around the handle.

My body welcomes the adrenaline, sucking it down like water on cracked asphalt. I look at the watch and feel nothing. My focus narrows to the here and now. I grin.

"No one better sprain their fucking ankle," I say, warming up my legs. "Go on, V. Shine time." Volga heaves on the door, rolling it back into the wall.

"And grid one is down," Cyra says quietly into our coms. Dano goes first into the hall on sound-dampening shoes. I go next and look to see if Volga's following. She's right behind me, freakishly silent despite her size. Cyra stays behind, monitoring the security systems and the guard level.

Down a narrow staff corridor lies another heavy security door. *"Hold,"* Cyra says. *"Grid two is down. Twenty-nine, twenty-eight . . ."* Volga puts a mechanical lever under the door and activates it. The heavy door slides upward, jolting along with the lever. We shimmy under the door. A painting of a furious warhorse strapped to a chariot is suspended mid-stride from the ceiling. In the chariot is an archer firing at men in bronze armor and horsehair helms. I stand quickly to look around the vast room. Weeping stone children peer down from the floral columns. Great frescoes explode with color along marble walls. Soon the floor pressure sensors, cameras, and lasers will come back on.

"Twenty."

A sense of nostalgia sweeps over me as we run across the floor. Seems just yesterday I was here as a legion pledge. I remember boarding the tram to come to the city center wearing the winged pyramid pin they give us, puffing my chest out when highColors would nod to me or lowColors would step out of my path. Stupid kid. He thought that pin made him a man. It just made him a pet. And nowadays it'll get you scalped.

"Eight. Seven . . ."

After three more halls and a stitch in my side later as I try to keep up with my younger crew, we reach the Conquerors Exhibit, where we prop open the door with the lever and shimmy under. Carefully, we stand on a narrow slip of metal, just shy of the marble floor that has the inbuilt pressure sensors.

The room is as domineering as its subjects. Built by enraptured

Golds to honor their psychotic ancestors who conquered Earth, it is grand and brutal, and unchanged by the Republic except for a few modifications. They've included a list of the conquered amongst the conquerors. Representations of pre-Color humans stand beside casualty statistics. One hundred and ten million died for Gold to rule. Then their bombers dropped solocene into the troposphere and neutered an entire race. Didn't even have to convert them to the Color hierarchy. Just had to wait a century for them to die out. Bloodless genocide. Give one thing to the Conquerors. They were efficient.

Pricks.

At the center of the exhibit, under a stone archway with the legend CONQUERORS EXHIBIT, twenty ancient Ionic columns line an ascending stairway. At the top, a Delphic temple sits, and inside that, past priceless relics encased in duroglass, lies the object of my collector's desire. It is a sword of the first overlord, a razor belonging to the great bastard, hero of the Conquerors, Silenius au Lune. The Lightbringer.

"That don't look so scary," Dano said when we first got the contract.

I smiled and nodded to Volga. "What if she were holding it?"

"She'd look scary waving a bloodydamn muffin."

"If I had a muffin, I would eat it," Volga said.

The blade sits behind two fingers of duroglass and is on loan to the museum from a private collector for only one week longer. Liberation Day is a perfect time for it to go missing. Volga and I scan the ceiling of the exhibit, looking for the telltale sign of a drone garage. We see it in the top left corner of the room, a small titanium flap built into the marble. I nod to Volga, and she slips on her spider gloves and jumps onto the wall. They stick to the marble and she crawls along the wall till she's hanging beneath the garage door. She pulls four laser nodes from her pack and puts them on either side of the door and activates them. Two green lasers crisscross over the door. She gives me an eager thumbs-up and looks for more garages.

I nudge Dano. He's up.

The boy does an ironic two-step dance on the narrow slip of the doorframe, jumps up onto the wall with his spider gloves, then pushes off with his legs, backflipping onto a glass case holding a Gold war helmet. He catches himself, turns, then leapfrogs case to case till he can jump onto one of the Ionic columns. He hits it midway up, hugs it and shimmies up. As he moves, I summon the autoflier from its garage five klicks away via my datapad. It drives autonomously through traffic toward the museum. Dano moves along the columns like some sort of human flea till he's picked his way directly above the glass case. He lets himself fall, turning in the air so he lands on all fours in a way that makes my knees ache just to watch.

Dano stands and delivers an obnoxious bow before pulling his laser cutter from his pack. The glass glows as he cuts a circular hole into it. Then, with a triumphant smile, he plucks up the blade and holds it aloft.

The alarm goes off on schedule.

A high-pitched frequency screams out of speakers. It would shred our eardrums if we didn't have sonic plugs. As it is, it's little more than the annoying whine of a hungry dog. A second security door closes behind us, sealing us in. Two nodes on the ceiling lower and begin to pump disabling gas into the room. Does nothing with our recyclers running. Up high on the wall, the drone garage opens and a metal drone rips out of its hiding place, right into Volga's laser grid. It smokes down to the floor in four pieces. A second follows and meets the same fate as she shoots out the cameras. At the windows, metal security doors fall to block us in. I stand still like a conductor at the center of his orchestra. All these variables falling into place just as I planned. And a deep, formless depression falls on me as the adrenaline fades.

"Locksmith, find your exit," I mutter into my com.

Volga drops from her place on the wall to join me. She moves excitably, still young enough to be impressed by this. Dano hops along the columns back to the arch, where he graffities profanity with his laser drill. "The razor?" I ask.

He twirls it in his hand. It's meant for a man twice his size. "A nasty little dick tickler."

"The razor," I say again.

"Course, boss." He flips it to me casually. I snag it out of the air. Its handle is too big for my hand. Real ivory exterior and inlaid with gold filigree. The rest is brutally economical. In whip form it coils like a thin, sleeping snake. Eager to be rid of it, I shove it in a foam carry case and tuck it into my pack.

"All right, kids." I open the canister of custom acid and tip it onto the marble floor. "Time to go."

7

EPHRAIM

The Arbiter

Tʜᴇ ᴍᴏʀɴɪɴɢ ᴀꜰᴛᴇʀ ᴛʜᴇ ʜᴇɪꜱᴛ, on my least favorite day of the year, I drain the vodka from my glass, waiting for the arbiter to finish his inspection. "So, is there a verdict yet?" I ask without bothering to hide my impatience. The slender man makes a show of remaining silent at the desk over which he has been hunched for the better part of an hour. It's overdramatic White slush. Anemic assholes think it profound to feign an air of aloofness, hiding behind contracts and commerce the way spiders hide and wait behind their webs. Two hundred were sentenced to life in Deepgrave during the Hyperion Trials for their part in the Gold judicial system. Should have been ten thousand. Rest were saved by the Amnesty declared by the Sovereign.

Bored, I survey the rest of the penthouse. It is painfully tasteful, done up in the restrained ostentation popular in Luna's upper circles—minimalist decor with rose-quartz floors and large windows that look out over the glowing nightscape. On a moon where three billion souls clamor atop each other to breathe, only the offensively rich can afford to waste space.

It reminds me of so many of the decadent flats I encountered as a high-end claims investigator for Piraeus Insurance, before the Rising. Back when I was the help.

HighColors looked down on Grays because we took out the trash. LowColors hated us because they were the trash. Everyone else feared us, because for seven hundred years we have been the all-purpose knife of the state. Obsidians? Circus freaks, the lot of 'em. Grays do work. We are adaptable, efficient, and bred for systematic loyalty. Little has changed for most of them: new masters, same collar.

I yawn. I'm thinking too much again, so I pop a zoladone, stand and pace as the drug leads my wandering thoughts back to my employer with a cold, distant hand.

Oslo, if that is in fact his name, is an inoffensive, impossibly meticulous creature with a dreadful sense of calm that borderlines on the robotic. Slender, and professional in his white business tunic with a starched high collar and sleeves to his knuckles. His skin is squid ink black. His head bald and the irises of his eyes an unsettling white. He adjusts the digital monocle on his right eye.

"I do believe this is the item my clients requested," he says in a harmonic baritone.

"As I said. Can we wrap this up?" He leans closer to the blade one last time before straightening and sheathing it very carefully into a gel-insulated metal briefcase.

"Citizen Horn, as ever, you delivered the requested item in a timely manner." Oslo turns back to me, typing into his datapad. "You will note that the agreed-upon sum has been deposited into your Echo City account."

I pull up my own datapad to check. His right eyebrow goes up. "I trust everything is satisfactory."

"Yut," I mutter.

"Yut?" he says in curiosity. "Oh yes, legion speak. Denoting an affirmation, usually done to convey affirmative sarcasm to a disliked officer."

"It's called dog tongue," I say. "Not 'legion speak.' "

"Of course." He touches his chest. "In fact I studied it extensively. I suppose you could say I'm a bit of a military enthusiast. The traditions. The organization. 'Merrywater *ad portas*,' " he says with a smile, using the phrase that seven centuries of legionnaires have shouted in memory of John Merrywater, the American who almost turned the tide of the Conquering by invading Luna—a reminder that the enemy is always at the gate.

I let it go, reminded of something the Ash Lord said to my cohort as a valedictory speech. "Those you protect will not see you. They will not understand you. But you are the Gray wall between civilization and chaos. And they stand safe in the shadow you cast. Do not expect praise or love. Their ignorance is proof of the success of your sacrifice. For we who serve the state, duty must be its own reward."

Or something like that. Good branding. Works like a charm on sixteen-year-old gray matter.

"Now, what is next on your mysterious employer's list?" I ask. "The sword of Alexander? The Magna Carta? The blackened heart of Kuthul Amun? I know. The knickers of the Sovereign herself. If she wears any . . ."

"There will be nothing else."

"Between you and me, I doubt she wears—wait, what?"

"There will be nothing else, Citizen Horn," Oslo says, picking up the briefcase containing the razor.

"Nothing?"

"Correct. My client has found this business relationship most satisfactory, but this piece will be the final acquisition, completing their collection. Thusly will we conclude our affiliation. Your services will not be required in the future."

"Well, my bank account's sorry to see you go," I say, feeling a nasty hollowness knowing no job is waiting in the wings. It's the first time in three years I've not had one on deck. "But nothing good can last forever, eh?" I stand and offer my hand to the taller White. He shakes it gently, and I hold on. The platinum rings on my forefinger dig into his tissue-thin skin. "So you're still not even going to give me a hint about who I've been stealing for all this time?" He jerks his hand away and I narrow my eyes at him. "Just a hint."

Oslo stares at me intensely.

"Why did curiosity kill the cat?" he asks me.

"Is telling riddles part of the job requirement?"

He smiles. "Because the cat stumbled upon the anaconda."

I linger in the suite after Oslo has left, long enough to dull the bitterness of his words with a couple more glasses of vodka. Out the window, my city of towers writhes. She looks prettier in the dark.

Idly, I cycle through the contents of my address book, looking for a distraction. It's a sea of detritus: bodies I've explored, relationships I've stretched past fraying. And floating amidst that wretched digital sea, standing in front of the city that never sleeps, surrounded by a billion breathing mouths, I feel the dark creep of despair. I pour one last drink, willing the numbness to spread.

A half day later, after a nap and a sobering plate of Terran noodles, I meet my crew to disburse the funds, though I hardly feel like company, on account of the date. They're huddled in a booth in an uppity South Promenade bar on the fringe of Old Town, drinking vibrantly colored cocktails. Volga twirls a pink umbrella between massive fingers. The bar itself is located inside the gutted carcass of an old advertising dirigible that someone renovated in an attempt to commercialize irony. Seems to be working despite the wartime rationing. The place buzzes with soldiers, packs of slick, suited Silvers, new-monied Greens and Coppers. All the ones near the right levers to make cash when the free market opened, now surrounded by the gaggles that attend them like brightly plumed vultures. It's mostly midColors, and there's been more than a few nervous glances aimed at Volga. The big girl has ordered me something called a Venusian Fury. It's dark as its namesake, Atalantia au Grimmus, and tastes like licorice and salt. Something in it makes the back of my eyes buzz and my groin swell. "What do you think?" she asks hopefully.

"Tastes like the ass end of the Ash Lord." I push it away. She looks downcast at the table. In my haze, pity is slow to come, and dull when it does. I hate bars like this.

"You know what the Ash Lord's ass tastes like?" Cyra asks.

"Look how old he is," Dano says, taking a break from staring at a beautiful slip of a Pink at the bar, who looks nervously at his nasal piercings. His head is buzzed in popular fashion with Obsidian dragons. "Tinpot's been around long enough to try everything." I don't reply, trying to hold on to the buzz left over from Oslo's vodka. I'll need it where I'm going.

"Whose idea was this commercial shithole?" I ask.

"Not mine," Dano says, holding up his hands. "Not nearly enough bare tits in this place."

"It was mine," Cyra says defensively. "It was featured in *Hyperion Weekly*. You know, Eph, it *is* humanly possible to enjoy something different. Something new."

" 'New' generally means someone's just trying to make money off something old."

"Whatever. It's better than the black-hole dives you visit to pickle your liver. Least here I'm not worried about getting an infection just by walking in the door."

"Let's get this over with." I pull up my datapad so they can all see, and transfer the funds into each of their accounts. Sure, they'd see the balances change on their own pads if I'd just done it over the net. But there's something incredibly human and satisfying for them to see my thumb disburse the money. "All done," I say. "Six hundred apiece."

"Even for Limey?" Dano asks. "Thought she was getting half."

"What the hell does it matter to you?" Cyra snaps.

"The rest of us did our jobs without a bloody hitch." He goes back to looking at the Pink girl, who's talking with her friends. "No reason we shouldn't get a little bonus for that action."

"I need no bonus," Volga says.

Dano sighs. "You ain't helping the cause, love."

"What the shit is your damage?" Cyra glares at Dano past Volga between them. "Always jacking on about my business? Why don't you tend your own and focus on catching diseases from Pink slips."

I lurch to my feet. "All right, this was fun. Try not to catch anything."

"And he's out like a Drachenjäger." Dano checks his newest shiny chronometer. This one has rubies embedded in the hands. "Two minutes flat."

"When's the next job?" Cyra asks.

"Yeah, boss," Dano says. "When's the next job? Cyra's got bills to pay."

She flips him the crux and stares at me with more desperation than she probably means to show. It's pitiful. "So? Your man's got another job, right?"

"Not this time. We're all done."

"What do you mean?"

"What I said." Seeing rain slithering down the windows, I pop the collar of my jacket.

"Ephraim," Volga says plaintively. "You just arrived. Stay for a drink. We can order you something else?" She stares up at me with those big mopey eyes, and for a moment I consider it, until I hear a telltale hush of the patrons and turn to see two towering figures emerge from outside through the dirigible's metal door. Golds. They wear black jackets with legion epaulets, their shoulders eclipsing the heads of the other patrons. They blithely survey the room with entitled eyes, before one of them catches sight of Dano's Pink and strides to the bar. The others make room and he introduces himself without a care in the world. There's an iron griffin pin on his chest. Arcos spawn. Dano's eyes go down as the Gold's hand drifts to the Pink's waist.

"Boss . . ." Dano says, eyeing me warily.

I realize my hand has drifted to the butt of the pistol under my jacket.

Bloodydamn Aureate. We should have purged the lot of them, or exiled them to the Core. But that chance is gone. All for the war effort.

"Just one drink, Ephraim," Volga says plaintively. "It will be fun. We can tell each other stories. And share jokes, as friends do."

"It's always the same story!"

As I leave the dirigible in the gravLift, the warm laughter of one of the Gold youths chases me down into the night.

8

LYSANDER

The Gulf

T HE BAKING SAND WARMS MY FEET. They're smaller than I remember. Paler. And the gulls that career overhead much larger,
much fiercer as they spin and dive into the water of a sea so blue I
cannot tell where ocean ends and sky begins. Gentle waves call to me.
I've been here before, but I cannot remember when or how I came to
be on this beach.

A man and woman are in the distance, their feet leaving slender
paths that the waves, in time, slowly devour, step by step, then all at
once till they are gone as if they were never there. I call to them. They
begin to turn, but I do not see their faces. I never do. Something is
behind me, casting a shadow over them, over the sand, darkening the
beach and the sea as the wind builds to a feral howl.

My body jerks awake.

I'm alone. Far from the beach, drenched in sweat upon my sleeping pallet. A ventilator whirs rhythmically in the dimness of my room
and I shudder a breath. The fear fades. It was just a dream.

Above me on the bulkhead, the words of my fallen house glare
down at me, etched into the metal. *LUX EX TENEBRIS.* "Light from darkness." And spinning outward from those words like the spokes of a

wheel are the idealist poems of youth, the wrathful, slashing script of adolescence, when I was all blood and fury and ruled by wilder passions. Then, finally, the first fledgling steps of wisdom as I began to realize how terrifyingly small I really am.

My father never seemed small. I remember him and his immense calm. The smile lines around his eyes. His unruly hair, his slender hands, how they sat folded in his lap when he listened. There was a vast, settled peace inside him, a tranquility given to him by his father, Lorn au Arcos, who stressed duty and honor under the banner of the griffin. Lost things to this world. Though somewhere out there, the griffin still flies.

My memory is a formidable thing. In many ways it is my grandmother's great legacy, her teachings preserved in me. Despite that, my mother's face is a night shade in my mind, always roving in the chasms, slipping beyond my grasp. I've heard she was wild, a woman of vast ambition. But history is so often molded from tainted clay by those who remain. I know more of her from my grandmother's mouth than from my own memory. Such was my grandmother's grief after her passing that no servant was permitted to speak her name aloud. Who was she? The few pictures I've found on the holo-Net are all obscured, taken from a distance. As if she were a figment even cameras could not capture. Now time erodes her face in my mind like waves did the footprints in the sand.

I was young when my parents' starship went down over the sea. They say it was terrorists. Outriders from the Rim.

Only when I read the few poems my mother left behind in her notebooks do I feel her heart beat against my spine. Her arms wrapped around my shoulders. Her breath in my hair. I sense that strange magic of her that my father so loved.

"The night terrors again?" The voice of my teacher startles me. He stands looking into my room, Golden eyes dark pools in the starship's night-cycle lighting. His powerful shoulders fill the doorway and he bends at the neck, wary of the low doorframe. The engines hum soothingly beyond my small metal room. The place had space enough when I was a boy. But twenty now, I feel like a potted plant spilling root and limb from a cracking clay bowl. Books fill the spaces between my bunk, tiny closet, and lavatory. Salvaged, stolen, purchased, and found over the last ten years. My new prize, a third edition of the *The Aeronaut,* sits by my bedside.

"Just a dream," I say, wary of showing vulnerability in his eyes because I know how young the Martian still thinks I am. I swing my slender legs from the bed and bind my mess of hair behind my head with a band. "Have we arrived?"

"Just."

"Verdict?"

"My goodman, do I look like your valet?"

"No. She was much fairer. With better bedside manner."

"Adorable, pretending you just had one."

I raise an eyebrow. "You should talk, prince of Mars."

Cassius au Bellona grunts. "So are you going to sleep the day away, or get up and see for yourself?" He nods for me to follow; I do, as I have for ten years. I smell whiskey in his wake.

Once, the worlds called Cassius the Morning Knight, protector of the Society, slayer of Ares. Then he murdered his Sovereign, my grandmother, and let the Rising tear down the very Society he swore to protect. He let Darrow destroy my world and bring chaos to the Society. I can never forgive him for that, but neither can I repay the debt I owe him. He kept Sevro au Barca from killing me. He pulled me from the ashes of Luna and the chaos that followed, and for ten years he has protected me, given me a home, a second family.

We could be mistaken for brothers and often are. Our hair has that same luster of gold, though his is curled and mine straight. My eyes are pale as yellow crystal. His are dark gold. He's half a head taller than I, and broader in the shoulders and manlier in the features—a thick, pointed beard, a prominent bold nose, where my face is thin and patrician, like most from the Palatine Hill. I wish I did not look so delicate.

My name is Lysander au Lune. I was named for a contradiction: a Spartan general who had the mind of an Athenian. Like that man, I was born into something that is both mine and not-mine, a heritage of worldbreakers and tyrants. Seven hundred years after my ancestor Silenius au Lune conquered Earth, I was born the son of Brutus au

Arcos and Anastasia au Lune, heir to empire. Now that empire is a fractured, sick land so drunk on war and political upheaval it's likely to devour itself in my lifetime. But that is no longer my inheritance. When I was a boy, the day after the fall of House Lune, Cassius bent on a knee and told me his noble mission. "Gold forgot it was intended to shepherd, not rule. I reject my life and honor that duty: to protect the People. Will you join me?"

I had no family left. My home was at war. I was afraid. And, more than that, I wanted to be good. So I said yes and for the last ten years we have patrolled the fringes of civilization, protecting those who cannot protect themselves in the Reaper's new world. Roving between asteroids and backwater docks in the Asteroid Belt as the spheres change around us and war rages in the Core. Cassius brought us here in search of redemption, but no matter how many traders we save from pirates, or foundered ships we rescue, his eyes remain dark, and I still dream of the demons from my past.

I pull on a moth-eaten gray pullover and weave my way barefoot through the ship after Cassius, running my hands along the walls. "Hello, girl," I say. "You're sounding tired today." The *Archimedes* is an old fifty-meter Whisper-class corvette of the once-great Ganymede Dockyards, with three guns and engines fast enough to push her from Mars to the Belt in under four weeks at near-orbit. Shaped like a reared cobra head, she's made for scouting, raids. A hundred years ago she was top of the line, but she's seen better days. The larger part of my adolescent chores was scrubbing rust from the inside hull, oiling her gears, and patching her electrical innards.

But for all that tending, it's the *Archi*'s scars I love the most. Little beauty marks that make her our home. A dent under the kitchen's oven where Cassius fell and struck his head when drinking long ago—after news reached us of Darrow and Virginia's wedding. Charred ceiling panels made by the fire that Pytha started when she brought me a birthday pie when I was twelve and put the candles too close to a leaking oxygen pipe. Scratches on the walls of the razor training room. So many memories here woven together like those poems above my bed.

I enter the cozy, ovular cockpit. There is room for a pilot and two recessed seats for observation. Its original military lighting has been stripped out and replaced by warmer nodes. A thick Andalusian rug covers the floor. Several rows of mint and jasmine grow atop the console, presents I acquired for Pytha from a Violet's streetside botany shop in the Hanging Market on Ceres. Incense from the Erebian Mountains not far from Cassius's family home on Mars burns in the corner. Cassius and Pytha, our Blue pilot, peer out the cockpit windows.

Outside is the cargo hauler that drew us off our course to Lacrimosa Station. We were en route for ship repairs after last month's skirmish with Martian scar hunters when we received the distress signal from the Gulf between Republic space and Rim territory.

I told Cassius it was too dangerous to investigate so low on provisions.

But his heart guides us more than his head these days.

The ship out the viewport is a giant cube five hundred meters at the edge. Most of her decks are exposed to vacuum by design, while superstructure lattice holds together thousands of cargo containers. Her tag IDs her as the *Vindabona* out of the trade hub Ceres. She sits adrift and dark—a very odd, very dangerous thing in the Gulf. Several wild asteroids the size of cities float between us, ice crystals on their surfaces winking in the dark. We used one to mask our approach. The *Vindabona*'s civilian instruments would never detect a military ship like ours in this briar patch, but it's not the hauler that worries me. I scan the sensors for ghosts in the darkness.

"Well, she's a deepspace mulebitch, all right," Pytha murmurs in a monotone delivery that erodes punctuation and inflection. "Probably packing a hundred million credits of iron. Slag me but that's a crew I'd like to be on."

"Must you swear so early in the morning?" I ask.

"Shit, sorry, moon boy. Forgot to mind my fucking manners." Pytha is in her late fifties, with distant, pale blue eyes and skin the color of a walnut. Like all Blues, she still harbors the neurodevelopmental sculpting that enhances human-to-computer interaction but impairs communication outside her sect. She doesn't have the social niceties of the Palatine shuttle pilots.

My teacher grimaces. "Crew will make scratch," he says. "Captain might get a share to keep him loyal, but that's a hundred million credits of some trade lord's coin floating out there."

"A share, you say. What a novel idea for a captain to snag a share . . ." Pytha says.

"Pity you're a pilot and not a captain."

"Come now, Bellona. Between you and moon boy over here, you've got to have a dozen secret vaults. Why else do you think I signed up? Certainly wasn't your chiseled chin, *dominus*." She says the word sarcastically. "I'm sure you eagles have squirreled away some chit in hidden nests." Pytha snorts a strange little laugh to herself and looks back to the datastream as letters and symbols trickle past. The untrained ear would hear the Martian drawl in her voice and be done with it. But I catch the spice of Thessalonica, that city of grapes and duels that sprawls white and hot by Mars's Thermic Sea. Best known for the short tempers of its citizenry and the long list of deeds done by its most illustrious sons, the blackguard Brothers Rath.

That Thessalonican swagger is likely what got her expelled from the Midnight School and reduced to smuggling before her path crossed ours eight years ago. When Cassius learned she was Martian, he freed her from the brig of a mining city where she was imprisoned for a smuggling offense, and she's worked for us ever since. I've certainly learned new words since she came aboard.

Bald and barefoot, Pytha leans back in the pilot's chair, sipping coffee from the plastic dinosaur mug I won her in an arcade on Phobos years back. She's in gray cotton pants and wears her old sweatshirt. Her limbs are thin as a grasshopper's, the right bent under her, the left hanging off the side of the chair, which is shaped like half of a hard-boiled quail egg with the yolk scooped out. A second skin of stickers and decals from children's video games festoons its gray metal backside. The ship may belong to Cassius, but Pytha's left her mark.

"Sander, what do you think?" My teacher looks back at me.

I examine the ship out the viewport.

Cassius sighs. "Out loud."

"She's a VD Auroch-Z cosmosHauler. Fourth generation by my guess."

"Don't equivocate. We both know you're not guessing."

I wipe sleep from my eyes, annoyed. "She has 125 million cubic meters of hauling capacity. One main Gastron helium reactor. Built in the Venusian yards, circa 520 PCE. Crew of forty. One industrial docking bay. Two secondary tubes. Obviously she's a smuggler."

"Sounds like the human encyclopedia's got a turd up his nose," Pytha drawls. She pours a cup of coffee from her carafe and hands it back to me. I wish it were tea. "The last of the beans till we hit Lacrimosa. Sip wisely, peevish one."

I slip into the seat behind hers and take a mouthful of the coffee, wincing at the heat. "Apologies. I neglected to eat supper."

"I neglected to eat supper," Pytha repeats, mocking my accent. Born on the Palantine Hill of Luna, I have lamentably inherited the most egregiously stereotypical highLingo accents. Apparently others find it hilarious. "Haven't we servants to spoon-feed His Majesty supper?"

"Oh, shut your gory gob," I say, modulating my voice to mimic the Thessalonican bravado. "Better?"

"Eerily so."

"Skipping supper. No wonder you're a little twig," Cassius says, pinching my arm. "I daresay you don't even weigh a hundred ten kilos, my goodman."

"It's usable weight," I protest. "In any matter, I was reading." He looks at me blankly. "You have your priorities. I have mine, muscly creature. So piss off."

"When I was your age . . ."

"You despoiled half the women on Mars," I say. "And probably thought it was their honor. Yes, I'm aware. Forgive me, but I find books a passion more illuminating than carnivals of flesh."

He looks at me in amusement. "One day a woman is going to make a pretty meal of you."

"Spoken like a man who barely escaped the lion's jaws," I reply.

Pytha goes still and stares at Cassius for a long, awkward moment as her arithmetical brain endeavors in vain to divine whether he is offended or not. I sip my coffee again and nod to the ship. "To the matter, no legitimate Mars or Luna corp would send that poor girl out to the Gulf without escort. Not with Ascomanni about. Those

Julii-Barca Solar markings are false flags: wrong shade of red on that sun. Should be scarlet, but that there is vermilion. The Syndicate would know that. So, low-rate smugglers. Like Pytha said, probably hauling ore from some off-grid mine to avoid customs. And please, stop testing me, Cassius. At this point, you know that I know."

Cassius grunts, still stinging from the lion rejoinder. It was petty of me to say, and I feel lesser for having said it. Ten years recycling each other's air will make the best of men devils to one another. After all, that is why Blues were raised in sects.

"No bloody way that *vermilion* is an actual color," Pytha says.

Of course Pytha is as much an exile from her kind as we are from our own. I can't imagine why.

"Sounds more like the last name of a Silver," she adds. "Heh heh."

"Care to wager on that?" I ask gamely.

She ignores me. "Blackhell. You gotta be a special kind of stupid to wander into the Belt without legs to run or claws to fight. Nearest Republic gunship is ten million klicks away." She finishes her coffee and bites into the ion blueberry tail of a Cosmos Comet caffeine gummy. She offers me the remaining white tail, which I decline. "Suppose the distress signal was an accident? Didn't last long."

"Doubtful," Cassius replies.

It's too dark to tell if there are any carbon scoring markings along the outside of the *Vindabona*—the telltale sign of a forced breach. I don't find any, but that hardly disproves their existence. Pytha looks back at Cassius. "Do we risk hailing them?"

"Let's not announce ourselves just yet." Cassius looks back at me and speaks the word on both our minds: "Trap?"

"Perhaps." I overdo a nod to make up for my earlier barb. He doesn't seem sore. "Might be a pirate ship strapped to one of those asteroids. I daresay we've seen this one before. Emit a distress signal for bait, then sit back and wait. But . . . it's peculiar all the way out here. If it is a trap, it's a poorly conceived one. Who would run across it? No one likes the Gulf."

"So we should investigate." Cassius uses his instructor's voice.

"With caution," I confirm. "There may be souls aboard. But we needn't risk the *Archi* just yet."

"My mind exactly. So what do we do, my goodman?"

I smile and put down my coffee. "Well, Cassius, I daresay we should put on our dancing shoes."

Cassius and I float through space toward an oblong asteroid. It rotates lazily in the darkness. Veins of ice glitter and wind through her craggy skin as we coast into a rock formation at the edge of a shadowy canyon large enough to swallow the Citadel of Light. We arrest our motion on a jagged scree. My breath echoes in my ears. Darkness stretches under me, plunging into the fathomless depths of the asteroid. I doubt very much any man has ever set foot upon this cold chunk of rock, much less looked into its bowels. I feel it's my duty to give in to temptation and shine a light down into the canyon. I flick the switch on my forearm and a beam of light cuts into the darkness and is devoured by the lower reaches. There is no bottom that my eye can see. But at least now a man's eye has seen that.

"Turn that off," Cassius orders over the com.

"Apologies. Was looking for space worms."

"Biologically absurd," Pytha mutters from the cockpit. *"Organic tissue must have calories. What would they eat?"*

"Spacemen," I say with a smile.

"Spaceboys," Cassius corrects.

I'm certain that, had I been born in a different time, I would have been an explorer. Since I was a boy, I've had an insatiable itch for things remote and unknown. In the Citadel, I dreamed of sailing the violent light of distant nebulas and charting astral seas. The great philosopher Sagan once preached it was in our nature as a species to explore. Despite the modern chaos, we do live in a new age of innovation. Perhaps some brilliant boy or girl who has yet to take their first step will one day make an engine to carry us faster than the speed of light beyond our single star. Beyond the stain of man. Would all this chaos be worth that one innovation?

I often imagine what humans could do if there were no scarcity. Nothing to fight over. Just an unending expanse to explore and name and fill with life and art. I smile at the pleasant fiction. A man can dream.

Not wanting to bring the *Archimedes* into a trap, Cassius and I pushed away from her airlock toward the nearest asteroid in our EVO suits fifteen minutes ago. Now we reorient ourselves and push off again toward the hulking *Vindabona*. Rows and rows of cargo containers drift suspended between metal beams, bound together by wires and mesh netting.

Cassius and I use our shoulder thrusters to slow our approach, settling into the floating carbon mesh that pins in a row of green crates. They're stamped with Republic stars. With Pytha guiding us over the coms, we pull ourselves along the outside of the ship toward the central service airlock. There, I unscrew the paneling on the door's locking mechanism and hijack the console till the orange doors open silently. Cassius and I drift into the airlock. The outer door closes behind us. We each grip the metal rungs inside. Red light throbs down from the ceiling as the airlock finishes its cycle. Pressure slowly pumps into the room. Then oxygen. Finally the pull of gravity. We remove our razors from their holsters on our hips. A pair of lazy silver tongues of metal float in the air, two meters long, stiffening to just over a meter of sword as we toggle them to their rigid state. His is straight. I prefer mine in the slight crescent of my house. The red light becomes green and the interior door of the airlock opens with an asthmatic gasp. As ever, Cassius makes sure he's the first through before glancing back to make sure I follow.

The repair bay is empty except for tools and ancient EVO suits hanging from hooks. Pale lights embedded in the gray ceiling flicker, hurling shadows about the room. An indicator blinks green and so I retract my helm into a small compartment at the back of the neck and breathe in the scent of cleaning solution and oil. Reminds me of my early days with Cassius, hiding out in backwater transportation hubs, searching for a ship to carry us away from Luna. Away from the Rising.

That was a lonely time. The better part of me felt carved away as we fled Luna and I knew I would never again hear my grandmother say my name, never follow Aja along the garden paths to train before the morning pachelbel birds even woke. All the people who had ever loved me were gone.

I was alone. And not just alone, but hunted. I shove the memories in the void where my grandmother taught me to stow them lest they overwhelm me like they did her when she was a girl.

"Eagle to Mother Hen, we're inside. Level sixteen. No signs of life," Cassius says.

"Copy, Eagle. Do try to use words first this time instead of blades?"

"Unlike certain pilots I know, I have impeccable manners, Mother Hen."

"Captain," she stresses. *"Call me Captain."*

"As you say, pilot." Cassius lets his helmet retract and winks at me. His face is harder than when we first met. But every now and again there's that twinkle in his eyes, like a light inside a far-off tent, making you feel warm even though you're still outside. And I am outside. He thinks I don't see how wounded he is. How I'm a replacement for the brother Darrow of Lykos took from him in the Institute. Sometimes he looks at me and I know he sees Julian.

A small, selfish part of me wishes he just saw me.

I follow Cassius into the hall. The ship is barren and gripped by silence. Something here is amiss. Quietly we make our way through the ship, but before we've gone long, we find a smear of blood on the floor leading from a side passage to a central lift. We trace the blood to the starboard escape pod bay, and there, before the large doors, we find a massacre.

Gore congeals on the walls. Bodily fluids pool on the dented floor. The whole room redolent with the tangy scent of iron and sick, so much so that I would gag were I not conscious of Cassius's eyes on me. Red handprints streak the escape pod door, as if men were trying to claw their way out. Yet there are no bodies. I focus and try to view the room with the Mind's Eye—removed, analytical, as my grandmother trained me.

"The crew was killed here. Under a day ago," I say, examining the state of the blood. When I was a boy, my grandmother had Securitas investigators take me to murder scenes in Hyperion City to teach me the barbarism under the surface of civilization, under the manners of men. I bend on a knee and begin processing the scene. "Judging from the blood spatters, I would postulate that there were two assailants. Men or women of our size or larger, judging by their bootprints. No blast scoring or char indicates the work was done with blades . . . and hammers."

"Ascomanni," Cassius says darkly.

"Evidence suggests it." I take a sample of the blood on my finger and wipe it on the datapad built into a socket on my EVO suit's left forearm. "Brown, Red, and Blue DNA markers. Our smugglers. Several were killed and then dragged out. Others were still alive."

"You watching, Pytha?" Cassius asks.

"Yes," she says quietly over the com. Our suits feed her visuals as well. She's more sensitive to violence than we are. "No sign of ship signatures from the Gulf. But if it's all the same, will you please hurry it up? I've got an itch about this."

As do I.

The term *Ascomanni* is derived from the Germanic for "Ash Men." The first Vikings sailed down European rivers in boats of ash wood. And ash is what they left behind.

Once, the Ascomanni were just deepspace legends, dark whispers passed by traders and smugglers to new recruits in the shadowy hollows of asteroid cantinas or docking-bay watering holes. In the deep of space, so they'd say, there lurked Obsidian tribes who escaped the Society's culling of the rest of their race following the Dark Revolt hundreds of years ago. Hunted by my family's extermination squads and Olympic Knights, they fled into the darkness. For years they plagued the far colonies of Neptune and Pluto, remaining little more than myth to the Core.

But now, with the Obsidian diaspora from the poles of Earth and Mars, that myth has become reality. Bands of Obsidians, alienated by the new strange world, freed from military slavery to Gold masters—or exhausted from the Reaper's war—embrace the legend of their ancestors.

They've not so much left the Ice as they've brought the Ice to the stars.

Inside the lift where the blood trail ends, viscera smear the button for the thirteenth deck. Cassius presses it with the hilt of his razor. I feel the righteous anger building in my friend as we rise. It infects me.

The lift wheezes to a stop, shuddering as the doors part and reveal the hall leading into the thirteenth floor of the old vessel. Cheap white lights burn down at derelict halls, casting wicked, sharp shadows. Air ventilators with clogged purifiers rattle in the ceiling. Down the center of the hall, a red trail bifurcates the rusted metal flooring. Handprints smear the ground to either side of the trail like crimson butterfly wings. Cassius leads and I follow the trail, our razors held behind us at a diagonal as Aja taught us, our aegis arms held before us, bracers cold and inert but ready to spring into a meter-square energy shield at a moment's notice. My new plasma pistol is light against my right thigh.

Faded yellow signs on the walls indicate washrooms and crew quarters. We check the rooms as we go. The first several are abandoned. Unmade beds and overturned pictures and chairs remain as evidence of violence. The crew was caught sleeping.

Inside the next room, we find what's left of the crew. Corpses have been stacked in a heap against the far wall. A stagnant pool of blood expands from the pile and in it I see the reflection of a single terrified eye. I rush to the pile and pull the dead to the side to find six shivering survivors beneath the corpses. They're bound and beaten and tied feet to hands. I bend to free them but they flinch away, making inhuman, squealing sounds. Cassius bends to a knee and removes his right gauntlet so they can see the Gold Sigils on his hand.

"*Salve,*" he says in a deep voice. The prisoners calm, the sign bringing them courage. "*Salve,* friends," he says as their eyes search his face and see the Peerless scar there. A scar I've never earned.

"*Dominus . . .*" they murmur, weeping. "*Dominus . . .*"

"Peace. We've come to help you," I say as I ungag a paunchy Red man. One of his eyes is swollen shut from a gash at the eyebrow. He smells like urine. "How many are there?" I ask. His crooked teeth chatter together so terribly he cannot even utter a single word. I wonder if he's ever spoken to a Gold. I feel such pity for him. I rest a hand on his shoulder, intending to comfort him. He flinches back. "Goodman, *salve*. Peace," I say softly. "You are safe now. We have come to help. Tell me how many there are."

"Fifteen . . . maybe more, *dominus* . . ." he whispers in a thick Phobosian accent, fighting back tears. I look over at Cassius. Fifteen is too many without our pulseArmor. "Leader is . . . on . . . on . . . the bridge with the captain. Are you Moon Lords?"

"How did they board you?" I ask, ignoring his question. "Do they have a vessel?"

He nods. "Came from the asteroids, they did. Therix—our helmsman—fell asleep uplinked. Drunk." He shudders. "We woke and . . . we woke and they were in the halls. Tried to run. To get to escape pods. They punished us. . . ." His crooked teeth chatter together. I'm so close I can see the blackheads on his bulbous nose. The veins on his neck stand out from fluid redistribution from extended travel in low gravity. He's pallid and weak in the bones. I wager it's been half a life since he's felt the sun's warmth. "Their ship boarded through the cargo hangar."

"Explains why we couldn't see it," I say to Cassius.

He ignores me. "Why are you so far out here with full freight?" he asks the man.

"Shouldn't have been . . . shouldn't have taken the money."

"The money from whom?" I ask.

"The passenger. The Gold."

Cassius and I exchange a glance. "There's a Gold on board?" he asks. "Did they have a scar?"

"Not Peerless." The Red shakes his head, and Cassius breathes a small sigh of relief. "She came to the captain on Psyche. Paid us to . . ." He swallows, glancing over our shoulders as if expecting an Obsidian to appear there. "She paid us to drop her at an asteroid . . . S-1392."

"That's near the edge of the Gulf," I say. "Just outside Rim territory."

"Yeah. Captain told her nothin' was there, but she paid much as our freight. Told him we shouldn't get involved with Golds. But he didn't listen. He never listens. . . ."

"Did she give a name?" Cassius asks.

"No name." The man shakes his head. "But she sounded like him." He points at me, and I know Cassius has the same thought. Are the Obsidians here for the ship or the Gold?

"They might not be Ascomanni," I say. "Could be the Rising."

"Darrow wouldn't massacre civilians."

"In this war, two-thirds of the dead are civilians," I say sharply. "Have you forgotten the Sack of Luna by Sefi's Horde?"

"Not at all. Nor have I forgotten New Thebes," Cassius replies, referring to when my godfather, the Ash Lord, orbitally bombarded one of Mars's great cities after she fell to the Rising.

"Boys," Pytha's voice crackles in our ears, cutting through the tension between us. *"Boys, we have company."*

"How many?" Cassius asks.

"Three ships inbound."

I stand. "Three?"

"How the goryhell are you just telling us?" Cassius snaps.

"Couldn't pick them up because of the asteroid interference. They must have called in more of them to haul in the Vindabona.*"*

The crewmembers sense our unease and begin to shudder again in fear.

"What grade?" I ask.

"Military, third class. Two four-gun lancers, and an eight-gun Storm-class corvette. They're Ascomanni."

"How can you tell?" I ask.

"They have bodies on their hulls."

"It's a gorydamn hunting party." Cassius curses quietly. We could go toe to toe with one of the lancers, but a Storm-class corvette would rip *Archi* to shreds. "How long do we have?"

"Five minutes. Haven't yet spotted me. I suggest you get off that heap."

I rush to cut the remaining restraints off the prisoners. "Hen, I need you to pop off that asteroid and burn for the *Vindabona's* transfer tube," Cassius says. "We have people to evacuate."

"They'll see me if I make an approach," Pytha says.

"They might have guns, but we've got engines," Cassius replies.

"Copy."

"Can you all run?" Cassius asks the crew. They stare up at him without answering. "Well, you're going to have to. The Obsidians are still out there. You see them, you keep it together and get to the tube. Let us fight. You obey everything I say or I leave you to die. I need you to nod." They do. "Good."

"What about the Gold?" I ask Cassius. "They could still be alive."

"You heard Pytha," he replies. "We don't have time."

"I won't leave someone behind for those barbarians to keep. Especially not one of us. It is not honorable."

"I said no," Cassius snaps, almost using my name in front of the smugglers. "It's not worth the risk of all their lives for one person." He surveys the wobbling crew before us. "Everyone quiet. Stay together. Now follow me." Cassius, as always, is first out the door before I can reply.

The prisoners follow quick as they can into the hall back the way we came. I guard the rear, helping along a limping Brown. The bone of his right arm sticks out of a tear in his green jumpsuit. Cassius looks back to make sure I'm keeping pace. We load into the lift we rode up on to take it back down to the third level. But as the doors begin to close, I jump off the lift without a glance back at Cassius.

"Dammit, boy," Cassius says over the com after the doors seal and the lift carries downward. *"What do you think you're doing?"*

"What Lorn would do," I reply, walking back the way we came. He says we don't have time, but I know how careful he is with me, how cautiously he guards my life. "I'll be sensible. Make a quick reconnoiter."

He's quiet for a moment, and I know he's reserving his condemnation for later. *"Hurry, but watch your tail."*

"Naturally."

I adjust my hand on my razor and move back down the hall. I take efforts to calm my breath, but every corner I turn I expect to see a savage waiting with bloody teeth and hollow eyes. I feel the fear and remember my grandmother's words. "Do not let fear touch you. Fear is the torrent. The raging river. To fight it is to break and drown. But to stand astride it is to see it, feel it, and use its course for your own whims."

I am the master of my fear. I let myself sink into the Mind's Eye.

My breathing slows. A cold, distant clarity settles over me. I hear the rattle of air purifiers clogged by dust, the pulse of generators vibrating through the metal floor into my boots.

And then I hear them.

The low, quiet rumble of their voices drifts down the dark metal hall like a grumbling glacier. My hands sweat inside gloves. Everything Aja and Cassius taught me seems so distant now as the metal grating underneath my boots creaks. I've killed Ascomanni before, but never by myself.

At the end of the hall, I peer around the corner. I don't see the Obsidians. The commissary is round and holds several tables, the centermost of which has been laden with mounds of clothing. I'm about to move into the room when the mound moves and I realize my mistake. Three Ascomanni sit at the center table. Their long, braided hair cascades white and dirty down broad backs. Pale, scarred skin peeks out from under scrap armor. They speak in *nagal* and are hunched together eating and drinking the foodstores from the ship. Revulsion and fear swirl together in the pit of my belly.

Be the calm.

I lean back behind the wall and listen to their conversation. The savages' accents are thick, their voices sluggish and drunken. From Earth's North Pole. One criticizes the flavor of the man meat and longs to eat fresh elk. His friend says something I do not understand. Something about the Ice. Another is irritated that she claimed no slaves in the taking of the ship. She asks if she could buy the Sunborn from the first. He laughs at her with his mouth full and says she belongs to their jarl, body and meat. The Sunborn; the Gold.

I expect Lorn would kill them. My own pride would see me do the same, to prove to myself that I am greater than the fear I now feel. But pride is a vanity I cannot afford. My grandmother's lessons win out. Why fight when you can maneuver? I find a way around the commissary and continue my search, listening for any sound of life.

My pre-allotted time ticks away. I'll have to double back in two minutes. There's nothing but the Obsidian voices echoing down the halls and the unhappy rattle of distant generators. Then . . . I hear something. A faint creaking from behind a bulkhead. I find the door and clasp the narrow handle. It opens slowly, sliding back into its frame and squealing as it goes. I wince, praying to Jove that no one heard. I wait, poised with my razor in the hall for the Obsidians to come running. None do. I slip into the room.

It is filled with the rest of the crew. They litter the floor in mesh cages that constrict around their bodies. All lowColors. And hanging above them from the dark room's ceiling is a thin wire net that's been looped around a gas pipe. It sways back and forth and inside it, and hanging upside down as the wire cuts into her bare skin, is the body of a naked woman with Gold Sigils upon the backs of her hands.

9

LYSANDER

The Passenger

I RUSH FIRST TO THE GOLD.

Her body is contorted and twisted inside the confines of her prison. A bent metal chair lies beneath her, having been used to beat her as she hung in the net. Her right hand is a charred, burned mess from the welding torch that sits on a table. Blood seeps there, dripping onto the floor. The smell of burned skin and hair claws into my nostrils, making my eyes water.

She's dead. She has to be.

"Help us!" a Red woman whispers out of a bloody mouth. *"Dominus . . ."*

"Quiet," I snap, glancing back at the door. Dozens of pairs of eyes stare out at me from behind the cages. Each prisoner pleading with me.

I creep closer to the Gold, and as I reach to touch the net, her eyes flash open in the low light. Goryhell. I almost fall down. She's alive. Black engine oil has been slathered over her body, along with fouler-smelling things.

"Dominus . . ." a Brown hisses.

"Salve," I say to the Gold in a Thessalonican drawl. "I'm here to

help. My name is Castor au Janus." She watches me without speaking, giving no sign that she even understands. "I'm going to help you out, but you have to be quiet and quick. The Ascomanni are still outside. Do you understand?"

"Yes, I understand," she says. Hers is a rich Palatine accent. It startles me. The man was right. She's from the Luna courts as well. What is she doing all the way out here?

"Stay very still," I say. I stand beneath the net and slide my razor across the steel cable, cutting it from the ceiling. The girl falls into my arms. I expected her to lash out, but she stays still within the tight mesh. I see now how deeply the tacNet's cut into her skin. TacNets, or birdcages, are fired from compressed fiber cartridges and designed for police forces to engulf and constrict around a prisoner to harmlessly subdue them. But if you toggle with the contraction restrictions, you can eviscerate a prisoner to death. I set the woman on the ground and cut the wires one by one until she's able to crawl free. She lies there naked stretching her joints, teeth chattering with the pain.

I realize now that she's young, maybe even younger than my twenty years. I feel an overwhelming urge to protect her. I cover her body with a plastic tool sheet.

"It is well," I say. "You're safe now." I stand to go help the others.

"Stims," she manages through her chattering teeth. "Need stims."

I bend back down and produce a syringe from the dispenser on the right thigh of my EVO suit. It's one of my last. She snatches it from my hand and stabs it into the bicep of the burned limb. Her body convulses as the drug rushes through her system. She sighs with pleasure. "More," she demands. I glance at the other prisoners and produce my last two. She shocks me by injecting both at the same time. It's too much for her body mass unless she's built up a resistance to them, which inherently means something dangerous. There's something wrong here.

Filled with a manic energy from the stims, she stumbles to her feet. I spring back to catch her from falling, but she steadies herself using the table.

"We must leave," I say softly to the girl. "More Ascomanni are coming. We have to be gone before their ships dock. Help me with the others." Nodding along, she finds her clothing in a pile on the floor near the door. Still covered in oil, she dons the pants and a green jacket, fumbling with the zipper because of the drugs in her system.

"Sander," Cassius says in my ear as I bend to cut the Red woman from her cage with my razor. *"What's your status?"*

"I found the Gold, Regulus." I patch him to my visual feed.

"Copy." He pauses, seeing the others. *"Lysander . . ."*

"Boy," the Gold says from behind me. I turn. She's less than an arm's length away. "What docking tube are you using?"

"Two-B."

"Two-B?" She nods more to herself than to me. "I'll return it to you in four minutes. On my honor."

"Return what?"

There's a blur. I don't even see her strike as the meat of her palm collides with the side of my temple. I stumble, and something, maybe her elbow or knee, slams into my opposite ear and I go down, seeing stars. There's pressure on my hip, and I hear her footsteps going out the door. She's four seconds gone before I realize what she took. My razor. The one Cassius gave me on my sixteenth birthday. The one that belonged to Karnus. Its custom Bellona hilt is covered by a plain metal shell, but to Cassius it is priceless. Dazed, I lunge after her into the hallway. My legs go like rubber and I almost fall.

The lowColors shout in fear, terrified that I'm going to abandon them. I lunge back toward their cages, but I don't have anything to cut with. I can't use my plasma pistol. The wire is too tight to their bodies. Panic threatens to grip me. I tug on the severed strands of the Red woman's cage. *"Lysander . . ."* Cassius says. The lowColors are clamoring now, rolling around on the floor. *"It's too late."* I pull as hard as I can. The fiberwire of the net slices through my gloves and into my skin. Blood wells against the wire. *"Lysander! You have to leave them."*

"No, I can help them. . . ."

I groan as I pull with all my strength at the wire, using my legs as leverage. The wire cuts my fingers to the bone. And it doesn't even fray. There's a scream from the lowColors. I wheel around and see an Obsidian at the door. I grab my pistol and fire clumsily. The plasma bolt takes the Obsidian's head off from the nose up. Another one fills the frame. I fire and he ducks back into the hall.

"Lysander, get out of there!" Cassius says.

A scream wells up inside, but doesn't escape my lips. I stare down at the wailing lowColors, at the mothers and fathers I could have freed, their cries puncturing my fantasy of heroism and honor. They thrash on the floor screaming at me to save them, but I can't. The Obsidian death warble echoes down the hall.

Fear has come.

I run like a coward. Back into the hall, firing around the corner blindly. The Obsidian's chest melts inward as he swings his axe. I bend under it and slam into the far wall, where I use the impact to push off and struggle to my feet. The Obsidian's chest is burned through to the liver, but he stumbles toward me—a tower of sinewy muscle and scrap armor and the pelts of dead animals. Aja and Cassius both told me never to come within arm's reach of an Obsidian. They alone can break the reinforced bones of my kind. But there's no other choice. He swings his axe again, and I charge inside the blow, hitting the inside of his axe arm with the point of my elbow, jamming the point into his brachial artery. His arm goes limp, but the force of the collision knocks me sideways. I use the momentum to flow left, and drive my right knee into the genicular artery on the inside of his leg. He roars in pain and charges straight into me, slamming me against the wall. It's like the time I was kicked by one of Virginia's stallions. The breath goes out of me. His right hand grabs my throat and lifts me up against the wall, straining to crush my trachea. Cartilage crackles. I lower my jaw against his grip, but the world's going black. Bits of meat cling to his beard. The rancid smell of rotting teeth fills my nose. Twisting my body, I pull twice on the trigger of my pistol. The plasma enters under his rib cage at an angle and burns through his heart. His eyes go wide with shock and his body collapses, dead. I land and suck in air just in time to see the third Obsidian raging toward me down the hall.

I fire, miss, and run.

Darkened hallways and empty rooms flash past. I heave myself around them, gripping girders to tighten my turns around corners.

"The Ascomanni corvette's docked on 1C," Pytha says. *"Dead ahead."*

I skid to a halt. I hear them ahead of me, their tribal voices echoing as they move into the ship through the transfer causeways. Their boots rattle the metal. Each half again my weight, maybe more. They'll cut off the route to the lift. I turn back the way I came, checking my gun's display. The energy cartridge has seventeen pulls in it. I feel naked without my razor. But fighting isn't the answer today.

"Pytha. Hallway to lift 11A is closed. I need you to guide me."

"Take your next left," she says without missing a beat. Conscious that Cassius is listening, judging, I take the left. *"Two hundred meters."* I dash the distance, slow in my EVO suit. *"Maintenance lift is on your second right."*

I reach the lift and press the call button. It doesn't respond. A little sign's been affixed to the door itself, apologizing rather crudely for the broken lift by means of a talking phallus. "Lift's out," I say, making efforts to measure my breathing.

"Back twenty meters, left, stairs are right there. Twenty down."

"Back?" I ask, hoping I heard wrong.

"Now!"

I backtrack without running into the Obsidian and find the stairs to begin my descent. Two levels down the stairwell, I pause. I hear them. Their boots beat the stairs two levels above me. Through the metal grating I see their dark shapes, their milk-pale hair. The chant, called the khoomei, groans through the hall. It is a plea to Hel, Obsidian goddess of death, to receive her offerings. I clear the whole next flight of stairs with a single jump, racing down the levels as fast as I can. Behind me, like a dark avalanche, gaining, rumbling, and threatening to swallow me up, rush the raiders. Can't see their numbers. Can't hear what Pytha and Cassius are saying. My body is distant and numb and my mind still and focused.

I lose my footing on a rusted stair and nearly fall as the weight of the suit pulls me toward the ground. I stumble up, firing two quick shots with my pistol. I score a lucky hit. Someone grunts and a shadow of blood sprays on the wall as the green energy bolts hit meat, giving me time to reach the docking level.

I race through the metal door and close it behind me, cranking on the hatch as hard as I can to seal it. But the wheel stops and then turns against me as someone stronger on the other side begins to open it. I backpedal and fire three shots into the hatch, turning the metal wheel into red-hot slag and jamming the door. The muscle fibers of my arm tremble from the pistol's recoil. They'll be through the door in a moment, but I bought myself precious seconds.

"Hundred meters straight. Fifth left. Straight twenty meters. First right."

I follow Pytha's instructions, but as I turn to flee the door, I slam into someone and we both go down, hard. I roll as I fall and aim my pistol back up at my assailant. But it's not an Obsidian. It's the Gold girl. She's limping to her feet, bearing half a dozen new wounds on her oil-slick skin. Her jacket is in tatters. She carries my razor in her hand. It is bloody to the hilt. Clumps of white hair cling to the gore.

How she is standing is a miracle. At her stomach, layers of skin and fat pull back along a six-inch gash to the right of the belly button. Looks like an axe wound. She hunches there, listening to the Obsidians hammering on the door.

"Give me my razor," I say.

"Move." She lunges toward the door with her razor and sticks it through the molten metal. A raider on the other side screams and she draws the razor back. Blood hisses as the molten metal turns it to vapor.

"Where's your ship?" she asks, turning on me with wild, incandescent eyes. The door wheezes as the Obsidians knock half of it off its hinges. "Where is your gorydamn ship?" The Luna accent falters under the adrenaline in her voice, replaced by something very different. The wound in her gut is leaking blood badly.

"This way." I move to help her walk, but she flinches away. "Don't be a fool. You can barely stand," I say. Glancing back at the bending door, she relents with a hiss of air between her teeth and throws her arm around mine. We hobble fast as we can, putting the door behind us, passing through the cargo level, containers and cranes to every side.

We take a right. Cassius stands guarding the interior of the transfer bridge that connects our ship to the *Vindabona,* clad in his EVO suit and helm. He fires his pulseRifle over our heads at the pack that rounds the corner behind us. The distorted energy screams past my ears. There's a howl. I glance back and see an Obsidian's head disappear, neck spouting blood. Magnetically shot bolts as long as my forearm rip past us and embed themselves into walls. Then we're past Cassius and stumbling into the narrow causeway. He follows behind me, his pulseRifle roaring as he unloads the last of its battery into an Obsidian warrior who jumps into the causeway after us. The man's torso tears in half and spins backward, leaving his legs behind on the causeway. Cassius kicks the legs off the ship.

"Disengage!" he shouts to Pytha. Our bulkhead door seals, closing off the causeway as I spill with the Gold girl to the transfer bay floor inside the *Archimedes,* panting and soaked with sweat and blood. The girl leans her forehead against the metal floor and coughs in pain. Pytha pulls an emergency disengage from the *Vindabona* and we bank away. Cassius stares down at me. I feel his rage, despite his helm's smooth visage.

There's silence except for weeping from the crew we rescued. They're sprawled like us on the floor, huddled together, some in exaltation, others still in fear, not yet believing that they could possibly be safe. They're not.

"You idiot," Cassius says down at me. "What the hell were you thinking?" Before I can answer, he kicks my razor from the Gold's hands. He bends, as if to grab her face to look for the dread mark on her cheek, when the floor of the *Archi* opens up between us. He twists back and away as a fist-sized gray blur shrieks through and then goes out through the ceiling with a monstrous gasp of air. A hole has been ripped in the ship. Depressurization sirens scream. Red pulses from the overhead lights. Another railgun slug pierces our hull, slamming through the floor up through the body of the paunchy Red man we rescued, spraying us with his blood. Pytha shouts something in our coms. Pressure screams out of the holes. Then the cellular armor slides over the external damage and the mad gout of air stops. The sirens cease their wailing, but the warning lights continue to throb.

"Our engines are hit," Pytha says. *"Number one is at half power. Shunting energy from it to the shields."*

Cassius gestures to the gash on the Gold girl's stomach. "Cauterize that or she'll bleed out." He rushes through the survivors of the crew to the bridge. The Gold girl is losing too much blood. Her skin is pale under the black oil and her chest rises and falls with shallow rapidity. I lift her arm to get her to the infirmary, but she's too weak. The stims have overloaded her system. Her legs go out, so I loop my arm behind her knees and my other around her back and carry her through the narrow halls. The fierce face she wore when I first found her is gone. She's quiet and still, her eyes watching me, so distant from the chaos around us. I lay her down on the medical bed as the *Archi's* guns fire. The infirmary is small and understocked. Syringes tremble in their cases as we take another hit.

Those screaming faces of the lowColors.

The wails still chase me.

They'll all die.

The girl watches as I cut open her soiled shirt with medical shears. Two minor lacerations rend her skin above her breasts. My main concern is the axe wound. It's a deep and angry gouge six inches long in her lower left abdomen. What was she thinking, going back? What could have been so important? I clean the wound with an antibac spray and use the hospital-grade medical scanner to inspect her organs for damage. Her liver is lacerated. She'll need a real surgeon, and soon. All I can do here is cauterize the capillaries and load her with bloodsim. Flesh sizzles under the laser. She groans in pain. Once it's sealed, I apply a layer of resFlesh and strap on a compression pack. The ship shudders.

"Who are you?" I ask the girl. "What's your name?"

She does not answer as her eyes drift closed. *"S-1392,"* she whispers. *"Help . . . at . . . S-1392."* Her words trail away as she falls unconcious.

S-1392 is the asteroid she was heading toward. But what did she mean by "help"?

I examine her as if her face will hold the answers. The lashes of her eyes are longer than I might have expected. But even with the smear of blood and oil, I can see the stringy muscles of a fighter and a testament of old scars upon her skin. Too many for her young age. I trace my fingers over the six parallel scars that rake her lower back. Accompanying those scars are two old knife wounds near her heart, a terrible burn on her left arm, and the remnants of an old wound on the left side of her head that claimed the top corner of her ear. I thought of her as a girl when I found her in that cage. But she's not a girl. She's a predator in young skin. Who else would go back into that nightmare ship?

Why did you have to take my razor?

Did she leave something behind? I search her clothes, her body. There's nothing hidden. No false teeth. But I have a suspicion. I run my hand over her face. The cheekbones are bold and high and covered like the rest of her face with oil. I scrape my nails along her closed eyelids. The false lashes there are well made and applied with some sort of resin. My fingers drift to her right cheek. Dread twists my belly as I feel the skin there give.

I stand up and away.

I know what she is.

I suspected when she stole my razor, and then when her voice broke from the accent of the Palatine. Was she affecting that one? Was it a guise? I pick the corner of the odd patch of skin on her face till a thin layer of resFlesh—the same sort Cassius uses to disguise himself—pulls away from the cheek, revealing what lies beneath. Along her right cheekbone, slashing through the black oil at a cruel angle, is the pale mark of a Peerless Scarred.

10

DARROW

Liberty Eternal

S EVRO SQUIRMS ON THE WHITE CUSHION next to me as Publius cu Caraval, the Copper Tribune, leader of the Copper bloc, finishes the roll call. He's an elegant firebrand of a man. Middle-aged, small of stature, with a narrow, pleasant face, a large nose, cold eyes, and an ambivalence toward fashion that borders on antagonism. When he's not in his toga, he still wears the same drab suits he did as a public lowColor defense lawyer before the war. Since then, he's risen to become a voice of reason in the divided Senate, and an occasional ally of my wife's. They call him the Incorruptible for his punctilious nature and lack of vices.

Caraval stands on a small circular plinth before the tiered C-shaped marble steps that encircle the white and red porphyry floor. Small wooden chairs are set for each senator on the steps. Behind Caraval, recessed from the plinth, squats the unadorned Morning Chair of the Sovereign. Made of whitewood carved with simple geometric designs, the chair looks dreadfully uncomfortable and is without cushion—Mustang had it removed. She leans against one of the arms of the chair and watches the senators. They sit clustered by Color and political affiliation upon the cushioned steps—Dancer's Vox Populi to the left of the huge Liberty Doors that lead out of the Forum to the steps and the Via Triumphia. Mustang's Optimates sit to the right. Obsidian and Copper centrists occupy the middle.

Bored by the formality, Sevro lounges beside me in crisp military whites. He's staring at the ceiling, infatuated by the mural there. It is a romantic rendering of the Phobos Address, my speech that launched the Rising on Phobos ten years ago. I look young and radiant in paints of gold and scarlet and float on gravBoots, cape billowing behind me like a magenta storm cloud, flanked by Howlers, the Sons of Ares, and Ragnar, even though he wasn't exactly there. Sevro's jaw clenches.

"That doesn't look anything like me." He nods to his own image. He's right. The eyes of the rendering are blood-red and insane. His hair's standing on end. His teeth look like rows of shattered porcelain. "You look like a bloody saint plowed an angel and out you popped. I look like a deranged fucking mutant that eats babies."

I pat Sevro on the leg. Mustang catches my eye and nods up to the last of the Red Senators who have just entered the room. Dancer shuffles along at the head of the procession of my people to their seats. He feels my eyes and meets them without a smile. Even knowing he's my adversary of the day, it's hard not to feel fondness for him.

With the roll call finalized, I turn my attention to Mustang.

"A quorum being present, the floor will now hear the scheduled petition." She looks to me. "ArchImperator."

The sound of my boots on stone echoes through the Senate chamber as I go to take my place on the plinth facing the senators. I spy Daxo, who sits surrounded by his fellow Gold senators on the far right. He looks like a statue of some pagan god in repose, though I know he's still nursing as monstrous a hangover as I am. Only when the tension has reached its pinnacle do I finally speak.

"Mercury . . . is liberated."

The right half of the senators, along with the Coppers, led smoothly by Caraval, roar their approval.

"The First Fleet of the Republic under the command of Imperator Orion xe Aquarii met that of the Ash Lord over Mercury while the Second Fleet under my personal command launched an Iron Rain against the continent of Borealis. Through high cost, we prevailed." The highColor senators lead the room to their feet yet again, roaring their fanatical support for the war effort. The Vox Populi remain silent. And so, I notice, do the Obsidians.

"Now the Ash Lord is in retreat. He has recalled the greater sum of his forces to make a final stand at Venus. But soon we will follow. Brothers and sisters, we stand upon the threshold of victory."

It is a full minute before the renewed applause dies down.

"But we yet have a choice to make." I take my time, allowing the silence to grow again. "Do we allow this war to linger? To consume another generation of our young? Or do we press the enemy and grind them until the last of the chains have been shattered?" I speak over the applause this time, letting the fervor spread through me. "It has been a decade of war. But we can end it here. Now." I spare a look up to the viewing deck above, where the holonetworks have their cameras. My enemy will be watching this later with his daughter and advisors, his nimble mind dissecting my words, divining my plans based on the response of these senators. But more importantly, he'll be watching me. He must not see my exhaustion. Mercury was a great victory. We robbed him the Iron of his docks. But Venus . . . Venus is the prize.

Even here, amidst the thunderous applause of the right, I hear Lorn's words echo in the dark place of my mind.

Death begets death begets death.

"Brothers and sisters of the Republic, we are one choice away from a fully liberated Core. A free System from Sol to the asteroid belt. We would be the first men and women to ever see it. But it will be a sight not without cost." I pause and permit, for one small moment, the weight of these last years to show on my face. "Like you, I wish for nothing more than peace. I wish for a world where the machine of war does not swallow our young." I look to my wife. "I wish to live in a world where my child can choose his own destiny, where the sins of the past do not define the nature of his life as it has defined all of ours. Our enemies have held dominion over us for too long. First as slaves, then adversaries. And what stability, what harmony can we bring to the worlds we have freed while they continue to define us?

For the sake of our brothers and sisters on Venus and Mercury . . ." I look to Dancer. ". . . for the sake of the souls we have unchained, for the sake of our children, give me the tools and I will finish this war, once and for all."

They roar in approval.

I look to Daxo and, as we agreed, he stands to tower over his fellow senators.

"My noble friends . . ." His large hands splay plaintively outward. "I know you are weary. I feel the years of war in my bones too. I believe I had hair when this all began." There's laughter. "I know better than you the heart of the Peerless Scarred. They do not have the spirit for peace. It is not in their nature to accept this new world we have made. They must be defeated, by all measures at our disposal. My family has supported the Reaper since before he was known. My brother died for him. I have fought for him. And I will not abandon him now. Nor should you. The Optimates stand with the Reaper. And we propose a bill to the floor for a Resolution of Liberty Eternal, to draft twenty million fresh troops, to allocate ships from the Gulf, and to levy additional taxes to fund the war effort until the Core is free." Daxo sits back down and makes a pained expression in my direction and rubs his temple.

Publius cu Caraval rises from his seat when the applause finally fades. His short copper hair is parted on the side, not a strand out of place. "I was told I was brought into this world to serve. To move the invisible levers of an ancient and evil machine. We all moved those levers. But now we serve the People. We are here to liberate the dignity of man. Darrow of Lykos is our greatest weapon against tyranny. Let us sharpen him again so he can break the chains for our brothers and sisters in bondage on Venus." He touches his heart, bleeding empathy and resolution.

A chorus of senators declare their support, each shouting over the next. Mustang stands, hammering down her Dawn Scepter. "The resolution is registered by the Senate and now open for debate."

All eyes turn to Dancer.

He has not yet moved. Mustang analyzes his face. "Senator O'Faran," she says. "Nothing?"

"Thank you, my Sovereign." He picks at the edges of his toga in his nervous habit before rising to his feet. To this day he loathes public speaking. His voice is hoarse and halting, as far from Publius's as possible. "ArchImperator, my friend, my brother, can I first begin by saying how happy I am to have you home. There is no . . . greater son of the Republic." Many heads nod. "I would also like to personally offer you congratulations on the *partial* liberation of Mercury. Despite your methods, which I will get to in a spit."

I watch him warily, knowing what he intends, but not how it's meant to be delivered.

"You all know I am a man of war." He looks at his rough hands. "I have held weapons. I have led men. It's what I am. And like most of you, I am also a mortal in a war of giants." He looks at the Golds, the Obsidians. "But I have learned that giants can be felled with words. Words are our . . . salvation. So I stand here before you armed only with that voice." He pauses, grimacing to himself. "And I want to ask you, what age do you want to live in? One where the sword leads and we follow? Or an age where our voice can sing louder than an engine can roar? Was that not the Song of Persephone? The dream of Eo of Lykos?"

There are murmurs of agreement from his supporters.

An inner bitterness wells as he insinuates my deviation from Eo's dream. She was mine and I lost her to them. But each time she's mentioned, even in reverence, it seems to me as though she's been dug from the ground and paraded for the crowd.

"Senators, we have no power in and of ourselves," Dancer continues slowly. "We are just vessels. Men and women chosen to speak for the People, by the People, to channel their voice to protect the People. Darrow, you helped give the People a voice. For that, we are in your debt.

"But now you refuse to listen to that voice, to obey the laws you helped make. You were given an order by the Senate, by the People, to stand down over Mercury. You disobeyed that order. You released an Iron Rain." He looks to Sefi. She sits several seats down from Sevro on the guest benches, watching with an unreadable expression. "Because of your impatience, a million of our brothers and sisters died in a single day. Two hundred thousand Obsidians. *Two hundred thousand.* A number that cannot be replaced." The words are heavy as they fall, and I see the solemn anger of the Obsidian bloc, the same anger I've felt from Sefi since that day. "Not only did you do this, but you illegally pillaged elements of the Fourth Fleet that guards Mars to add to your assault on Mercury. Why?"

"Because it was necessary to—"

"One million souls."

I knew thirty-seven of those souls, and somehow that number seems larger than one million. "A man once said that a war fought by politicians will be lost by everyone," I say bitterly. "Harnassus and Orion supported my plan. Your legions have protected you this far. But now you question them?"

"Our legions?" he asks. "Are they ours?" Before I can answer, he lumbers forward, wrangling control of the conversation with all the grace of an old bear.

"How many of us have lost loved ones to war? How many of us have buried sons, daughters, wives, husbands? My hands are raw from digging graves. My heart shatters seeing genocide and starvation on planets we claim free. On Mars, my home. How many more must suffer to free Mercury and Venus, planets now so indoctrinated that our own Colors will fight against us for every inch of ground we take?"

"So as long as Mars is free, you're content to call it a day? Leave the others to rot?" I ask.

He looks me in the eyes. "Is Mars free? Ask a Red from the mines. Ask a Pink in Agea's ghetto. The yoke of poverty is as heavy as that of tyranny."

Mustang interjects. "We have a solemn duty to rid the worlds of the stain of slavery. Your own words, Senator."

"We also have a solemn duty to make those worlds better than they were before," Dancer replies. "Two hundred million have died since House Lune fell. Tell me, what is the purpose of victory if it destroys us? If we are stretched so thin that we cannot protect or provide for those we bring out of the mines?"

There are no weapons in the room, save those of Wulfgar and his Warden, but Dancer's words do damage enough. They rattle the Senate hall. And he's not finished.

"Darrow, you stand here asking us for more men and women, more ships to wage this war. So I ask you, and pray to the Old Man who guards the Vale that you can give me an answer, when will this war end?"

"When the Republic is safe."

"Will it be safe when the Ash Lord falls? When we have Venus?"

"The Ash Lord is the heart of their war machine. But he rules with fear. Without him, the remaining Gold houses will turn on each other within a week."

"And what of the Rim? What if they come and we've smashed our armies to bits to kill one man?"

"We have a peace treaty with the Rim."

"For now."

"Their docks are destroyed. Octavia saw to that. The Starhall analysts believe they could not attack us, even if they wanted to, for another fifteen years," Mustang says.

"Romulus does not want another war," I say. "Trust me on that."

"Trust you?" My old friend frowns. "We have trusted you, Darrow." I feel the same anger in him that I saw when he learned of what I did to the Sons on the Rim. "So many have trusted you. For so many years. But you're in love with your own myth. You think that the Reaper knows better than the People."

"You think I want war? I loathe it. It's stolen my friends. My family. It takes me away from my wife. From my child. If there were another path, I would take it. But there is no path around this war. The only way is *through*."

He watches me for a moment.

"I wonder, would you even know peace if you saw it?" He turns to the senators. "What if I told you, what if I told all of you there *was* another path? One that has been hidden from us?" Caraval frowns and leans forward. Sevro glances my way. "What if we could have safety not tomorrow, not a decade from now. But right this very moment? Peace without another Iron Rain. Without throwing millions more into the guns of the Ash Lord?" He turns to my wife. "My Sovereign, I invoke my right to present a witness to the Senate body."

She's caught off guard. "What witness?"

Dancer does not answer. He looks expectantly down the corridor to his right. At the end of it, a door opens and a lone set of heels click against the stone floor. In hushed silence, the senators crane their necks to see a tall, imperious woman of later years striding out of the corridor into the Senate hall. She stands a head taller than the Republic Wardens, excepting Wulfgar, as she passes on the way to the center of the floor. Her eyes are Gold. Her body serene and slight, despite her height. Her hair is spun behind her and caged by gold mesh. A gold collar in the shape of an eagle encloses her neck. Her gown is black and covering every bit of skin from her neck to her toes. And upon her regal, bitter face is a single curved scar.

I glare at the woman. She has been shadow to my life ever since I beat her favorite son to death in a simple stone room sixteen years ago. Now she comes to stand before the Senate.

"What is the meaning of this?" Mustang demands, rising from her chair to dominate the room. Dancer does not back down.

"This is Julia au Bellona," he says against the rising furor. "She brings a message from the Ash Lord."

"Senator . . ." Anger flushes Mustang's face, and she takes a violent step forward. "That is not your place! Foreign diplomacy is the province of the Sovereign! You overstep."

"So does your husband, but do you scold him?" he asks. "Hear what she has to say. You will find it illuminating." The senators shout their desire to hear Bellona out. Dread enters me. I know what Julia will say.

Mustang is trapped. She looks down at the woman, both the remnants of two great Gold houses that destroyed one another in their feud. Of their families, only Cassius remains. If he is still alive somewhere out there. "Say your piece, Bellona."

Julia looks up at Mustang with utmost distaste. She's not forgotten how Mustang sat at their table with Cassius and then turned her back on them.

"Usurper," she says, refusing to use Mustang's honorific. Her eyes look upon the senators with aristocratic disdain. "I traveled a month to stand before you. I will speak plainly so you understand. The Ash Lord tires of war. Of seeing cities turned to rubble." She continues over shouts of protest. "During the Siege of Mercury, emissaries, including myself, were sent to the *Morning Star* to seek audience with your . . . warlord." She glares at me. "We asked for an armistice. He replied with an Iron Rain."

"Armistice?" Mustang murmurs.

"And why did you request an armistice?" Dancer prompts over the whispering senators.

"The Ash Lord, and the War Council of the Society, wish to discuss terms. . . ."

"What terms?" Dancer presses. "Speak plainly, Gold."

"Did the Reaper not tell you?" She looks at me and smiles. "We requested a cease-fire in order to discuss the terms of a permanent and lasting peace between the Rising and the Society."

11

DARROW

Servant of the People

THE ROOM BURSTS INTO A CHAOS of thrust fists and rippling togas. Only the Obsidians do not move. Sefi watches the reaction with a neutral expression, unreadable as ever. Mustang turns on me in a fury. "Is this true?"

"He never wanted peace," I say coldly. Sevro is rocking in his seat in an effort to keep himself from strangling Julia au Bellona in the middle of the Forum.

"But he did send emissaries?"

"He sent provocateurs. Her and Asmodeus. It was a ruse that I did not warrant worth the time of this body."

Mustang can't believe what she's hearing. "Darrow . . ."

"Asmodeus was on your ship and you did not report this to us?" Dancer asks, incredulous. Someone betrayed me. Someone in the Howlers. How else would he know? "Next you'll say the Fear Knight himself was in your mess hall."

I fix my gaze on Dancer. "The Ash Lord burned Rhea. He burned New Thebes. He'd burn every city left to win back Luna. He wants the home we've stolen from him."

Dancer shakes his head. "You had no right."

Caraval and those Coppers who cheered me watch with uncertainty. Mustang has not moved from her chair, nor can she. Whatever she says will be dismissed as a wife defending her husband and might indict her as well. If they think she knew, she'll be impeached, possibly worse. Which is the very reason why I hid this from her.

My star is falling. If she holds on, it will drag her down too. Better to stay quiet, my love. Better to play the long game. I know better than to struggle. A Red senator lurches up from her seat and rushes across the floor. For a moment, I think she means to speak in my defense. Then she spits at my feet. "Gold," she says. Wulfgar eases forward to dissuade any others from breaking protocol.

For years I waited for this day to come, but as the Republic grew in strength, it never did. And I suppose I tricked myself into thinking it wouldn't. But now that it's here, now that I feel the blind hate rising and see the unpitying lenses of the cameras in the viewing deck above, I know how words will be lost on them. The noble newscasters will sanctimoniously peel at every decision, every secret, every sin, and stream them across the worlds, feigning duty, but delighting in the moral bloodshed, masticating my bones, cracking them for the marrow of ratings and feeding their vulture appetite for gossip.

I'm not surprised, but I am heartbroken. I don't want to be the villain. Wulfgar looks back at me pityingly, as if wishing he could carry me away from this public shaming. Sevro is standing from his seat in a rage.

"You fucking backstabbing little rat . . ." he says to Dancer.

"How can we trust you with our armies," Dancer booms, "when you disobey the Senate? When you lie to the People?" He does not give me time to respond. "My brothers and sisters, there is no place in our Republic for warlords or tyrants. They are the death of demokracy. Our seven hundred years of slavery stands testament to that! But tyranny did not just spring up. It bubbled up slowly, as the leaders of Earth watched and did nothing. We must choose. Is our Republic ruled by its voice, or by its sword?"

He sits, his work done. Amidst a roar of approval that spreads to more than just his usual supporters, Dancer of Faran, the hand of Ares who pulled me from the grave to make me a weapon, buries me under my own designs. And across the room, like a noble old olive tree neither flame nor axe can fell, Julia au Bellona watches me with hate in her gnawing eyes. Slowly, as if a long-forgotten promise is finally being delivered, she begins to smile.

Publius cu Caraval stands in the chaos. Only by Mustang hammering her scepter on the ground can she quiet the senators enough for the Copper to speak. If anyone could find something to say to defend me, it would be him.

"I do not share all the convictions of the Red senator. There cannot be peace while there is no justice. But in one matter, I fear he strikes the mark. You have overstepped, ArchImperator. You have forgotten your oaths made to serve the People." He turns to the senators, summoning firm courage to overcome the betrayal. "I propose a vote to remove Darrow of Lykos from high command and to place him under house arrest pending a trial for acts of treason against the Republic." Applause follows this. He looks back at me dramatically. "And I propose a temporary cessation of hostilities with the Golds of the Core so that we may decide ourselves between war and peace."

The sanctimonious bastard.

There is little Mustang can do. At her instructions, Republic Wardens come to escort all non-senators from the room. I let Wulfgar guide me out. Over the heads of his men, I see my wife watching me from her chair, fear in her eyes because she sees the rage in mine.

Outside the building, the world is quiet and untouched by my humiliation. Republic Wardens stand illuminated by the warm glow of blue lamps as we collect our weapons. Lesser bureaucrats thread their way across the plaza, tending to the affairs of a government responsible for ten billion lives. Dusk is over now and the sky is black. Autumn leaves roll across the white marble expanse.

"Darrow, you are not to leave the city," Wulfgar says to me. "Do you hear me?" He puts his hand on my shoulder again. "Darrow . . ."

"Am I under arrest?" I ask.

"Not yet . . ."

"You need to step back," Sevro says, his fingers tightening around the razor at his side. Wulfgar looks down at Sevro, who comes barely to his sternum, and steps back in respect. I descend the stairs away from the Forum, heading for the landing pads in the North Citadel. Sevro catches up to me. I stop and look back at the Forum as a loud cheer leaks out the open door.

"Some little shit told them," Sevro says. "I should carve Caraval's balls off. Treason? They can't actually arrest you, can they?"

"They might not put me in Deepgrave, but they'll lock me up for as long as they think they don't need me. Long enough for the Ash Lord to make his move."

Sevro sneers. "The Seventh Legion will have something to say about that. Should I call Orion? The Telemanuses? Kavax should be on his way back from Mars. . . ."

I look back to the Forum. Inside, Mustang will be attempting to repair the damage done. But with Copper lost, she won't have the votes to protect me. There's nothing more I can do here. This isn't my world. I knew it before, and Dancer just reminded me. The man says all I know is war. And he is right. In my heart, I know my enemy. I know his mettle. I know his cruelty. And I know this war will not end with politicians smiling at each other from across a table.

It will only end as it began: with blood.

"No, Sevro. Summon the Howlers."

12

LYRIA

SlingBlades

I FLEE THE GUNFIRE THAT killed my brother.

My baby brother, who I helped raise, who I made a notch in the doorframe for every time he sprouted a bit taller. Used to joke he was a weed so tall his head would one day touch the sky. Now I leave him in the mud.

Each heartbeat is a sledgehammer. Tears stream so thick I can barely see. Mud cakes my burning calves. The plastic homes flash past. There's more sounds now. More gunshots and the warbling of energy weapons. They've come by land too. I hear the squealing of hovertrack sleds. A fire's started near the southern fence. I see four-wheeled land vehicles there and men with floodlights and torches. They carry guns and slingBlades.

Our lane is still quiet as I make it home. As if in denial about what the night brings. I burst in through the front door. My sister still sits at the table, wearing her new shoes. "What happened? Were those gunshots?"

"It's the Red Hand," I say just as the monsoon siren begins to wail from the antenna array behind our home. They didn't make a siren for the Red Hand.

"No . . ." she whispers. "Where is Tiran?"

"He's—" My throat constricts. *Gone.*

"Gone?" She tilts her head as if she doesn't understand the word. "What do you mean 'gone'?"

"They shot him."

"What?"

I feel myself shuddering. Losing control of my own body. "They shot him." I'm sobbing. My chest heaves. I feel my sister's arms around me. Holding me. "He's dead. Tiran is dead."

Not just dead. Mutilated.

"Get Da," my older sister says, ghostly pale. She grips my head. "Lyria, get Da up. We have to go."

"Go where?"

"I don't know. But we can't stay here." I nod, still dazed. She shakes me. "Lyria, do it now!" How can she be so calm? She didn't have to see Tiran's head dissolve into fragments. She pushes me toward the bunkroom.

I find Da awake and staring at me, as if he already knows. Did he hear about Tiran?

"You know what's happening?" I ask. He barely nods. "I need you to help me with your arms." Tiran usually lifts him from his bed into his wheelchair. I'm not as strong.

I slip my hands under my father's armpits. "One . . . two . . . three . . ." For the first time since Mum was buried in the deeptunnels, Da says something.

"No." It's more of a moan than a word, but it is unmistakable. His eyes are wide and emphatic. Shakes his head and repeats it, "No." His eyes glance down at his body, then shoot toward his chair. He's right. There's no way we'll escape the Red Hand with him on our backs. Or that chair in the mud. Not without Tiran.

His milky eyes watch me. They see me now. That's what breaks my heart. He could have seen me sooner. He could have looked at me instead of draining his life away into the HC. Why now? Why when we have so few seconds left? I wrap my arms around him. I kiss him on the forehead, staying there, smelling the musk of his skin and greasy hair, remembering what he was.

With a heave, I hoist the old man from the bed toward his chair. I sag under his weight, nearly falling to the floor. The muscles of my lower back seize up, but I manage to twist my body and lever him into his chair. He lands roughly on his hip. More groans. "Hold on, Da. We have to say goodbye." I push him into the front room, where my sister and her children are readying to leave.

Through the doorway, my sister has gathered her little ones. "I need you all to hold hands," my sister is saying. "And don't let go of each other no matter what. That's very important. Stay together." She looks at me. "Lyria . . . Liam's still at the infirmary."

"Dammit." How could I forget him? Conn starts crying.

"It's all right, love. It's all right," Ava says. Ella is silent and pinned tight to her breast, swaddled in blankets. My sister won't be able to make it to the center of the camp and back, not with her children.

"I'll fetch Liam," I say. "You make for the jungle. We'll meet you there."

"The jungle?" she asks. "You'll never find us in there. The east guard tower . . ."

"There's trucks there," I say. "The north looked quiet."

"Then meet us there, at the north. Then we'll go together to the fishing boats. We can go downriver." A distant explosion rattles the plastic home.

"What about Da?" she asks. He sits in his chair watching us impassively.

I shake my head once.

"We can carry him . . ." my sister says.

But we both know we can't. We wouldn't make it twenty meters dragging him and the children. I look at the terrified children, then at my sister.

"Children," I say hollowly, "come kiss Dada for luck."

Ava understands. Her calm cracks. In the tears, I see the scared little girl who wept in her bed when our mother passed. The one I'd have to sing to sleep even though she was older.

"I don't want to leave Dada," Conn cries.

"I'll bring him," I say. "You all just have to go on ahead. Now kiss him." Believing me, the children rush to kiss my father on the cheek. His eyes brim with tears as they dart back and forth. My sister bends and kisses him on the brow. She stays there, trembling, before stumbling back. Conn holds on to him, not letting go till his mother rips him violently away and moves them toward the door. "The north watchtower," she says. "Be there soon."

"I will."

"Lyria."

"Yes?"

"Bring me my boy." We hold each other's hands, a life full of wedding skirts, births, and love reduced now to a single second of fear. And then our hands are parting and the door closes and she's swallowed by the nightmare outside. Through a crack in the plastic, I watch her run, clutching Ella to her breast and dragging her two boys along into the dark. I stay behind with my father in the hut, listening to the world ending beyond the thin walls. Some part of me thinks that if we stay here, the storm will pass us by. The plastic will somehow keep the Red Hand and their guns and slingBlades out. I want to tell Da it will be well. That I'll see him soon. It's the most present he's been in a year, looking at me, knowing this is the last time he'll see me. I kneel so that we are eye to eye, and clutch his face in my hands. This is the man who tucked me in at night. Who would sit me on his knee at Laureltide and tell stories of mining glories and pitvipers and fights. He was as vast as the sky itself. But now, he is a broken man watching helplessly as the world swallows his children.

"I will see you in the Vale," I whisper to him, our foreheads together. "I love you. I love you. I love you." Then I throw myself away from him. In three steps I am out the door.

Leaving him behind is like tearing a part of my body away.

My eyes sting with tears, but a cold clarity fills me. I have to get Liam. My sister is already gone. The camp's given over to madness. Gammas fleeing their houses. Flames in the distance. Two ships roar overhead through the black sky. The rattling of automatic guns, and the occasional whine of an energy weapon. Screams careen in from everywhere, swirling and swarming around me. I sprint diagonal between the homes, weaving my way through Gamma township to the central infirmary. I collide with a man full on and spin down into the mud, taking his elbow to my face. It barely jars him. He stumbles back, carrying a child, then rushes on. I know him. Elrow, one of my father's headTalks from years back. He doesn't even look down at me.

Struggling back to my feet, I find the infirmary with its door locked. A peaked white plastic building stained on its fringes by mud. Waiting there in the rain like a girl in a white dress. I hammer on the doors. "Let me in! It's Lyria. Let me in!" I kick the doors twice before they unlock from the inside and open. Three men and a woman stand in their yellow nursing livery, holding heavy medical instruments intended for my skull. I hold up my hands.

"Lyria!" Janis, a Yellow doctor and head of the infirmary, shouts. "Let her through!"

"Janis, where's Liam?"

"In the back." Janis guides me through rows of cots filled with terrified children and infirm patients till we reach my nephew in the back. He's sitting in his bed with his hands wrapped around his legs, sightless and listening to the horror outside. "What's going on out there?" Janis asks.

"Red Hand," I say. "Dropships and trucks."

"They're here?" she asks. She can't believe it. "But the Republic . . ."

"Damn the Republic," I say. "We've got to run. Liam . . ." I wrap my arms around the little boy. He's so thin he could be made of glass. His hair's an unruly explosion of red, like mine, but more closely cropped, and his mannerisms are all hesitant, like a boy asking a girl to dance at Laureltide. I kiss him on his head and wrap him snug in the little blue jumper I brought for him. I pull the hood up on his head so his little pale face is all that peeks out of it. "It's well. It's well. I've got you."

"Where's Mum?" he asks in a small voice.

"Waiting for us. But you have to come with me."

"Is she all right?" he asks.

"I need you to be brave. Can you do that? Can you be like the Goblin? When he followed the Reaper to the Dragonmaw? Can you do that for me?"

"Yes," he says, nodding his little head. "I can." I heft him from the bed and move to the door. Janis blocks my way.

"It'll be safer here," she says. "It's a hospital. Even they have to respect that."

I stare at her, dumbfounded. "Are you bloodydamn bent in the head? You need to get everyone and get out."

"Lyria . . ."

I don't stop to reason with her. I shoulder past and burst out of the infirmary, running with my nephew clutched to my chest. The gunshots are closer now. Rough voices yell to one another. A woman's screams are silenced with a wet thump. I weave through the gaps between the houses, heading for the north watchtower. Doors are broken off plastic hinges, young men run about with arms full of food and tokens and HCs and a thousand things less precious than the life I carry. Liam's little pale arms cling around my neck. Someone screams "Gamma" and points at me. Terrified, I duck into an alley and lose them in the shadows.

The guard tower is abandoned when we reach it. Its spotlight stares directly into the sky. The Republic soldiers who were there have fled. Somewhere a dog barks. My sister is nowhere to be seen. "Ava," I call quietly, hoping she's in the shadows waiting for me. No one answers. Then men's voices come from between the houses behind me. They followed me into the alley. I rush through the gate. A muddy field stretches all the way to the dark jungle. We'll never make it. To the right is the camp's dumpsite, and beyond that the river.

"Ava," I whisper again. The feet are closer. I pull Liam to the side and scramble into the shadows of the rubbish heap. I dive to the ground at the top of a mound and slide halfway down the other side. I tell Liam to be quiet and crawl a little back up the mound to look at the path I fled. A tide of Gammas from my township rush through the gate toward the jungle. I know all of them. I don't see my sister among them, so I stay silent and hunkered down in the shadow of the rubbish. But as the sounds of their footfalls fade into the night, a terrible fear of being left behind fills me. I'm about to rush from my place to join them, when I see the glimmer of something near the treeline. I want to shout at my kinsmen. Save them. But it's too late.

The glimmer becomes a hundred. Like the jungle itself is grinning and baring its pale teeth. My kinsmen scream as the men in the jungle come out to murder them in the dark with slingBlades.

I flee the screams, push deep into the dumpsite. Metal scratches my thigh as I run up a mound. I lose my balance and pitch sideways, tumbling down. Crash hard into the refuse, barely shielding Liam. He's crying against my chest. The sweet scent of rot makes our eyes water something awful. A rat skitters across my arm. I push myself up and gain my feet, cradling my little nephew, leg stinging from the wound. Insects throb around my bare calves in thick clouds, biting and crawling. Heat from decomposition pulses up from the garbage. I find a hiding spot and huddle low underneath the remains of a broken industrial washer. Liam's shuddering in fear, small body racked by silent sobs. I set him down. My arms are numb from carrying him. Men rove near the path now, close to where we entered the dump. Their flashlights slash at the darkness.

I flatten myself to the garbage and push a dirty finger to Liam's lips. A light beam goes overhead. The mosquitoes buzz around his face, casting shadows. I tighten his jumper so only his nose and mouth are showing out of the hood. Water from the rain slithers and drips through the garbage as the men speak to each other. The voices are like my father's, like my mother's, like my sister's and brothers'. But now their tongues sound cruel, all hard and dark and sharp-edged. How can Reds do this to their own kind? One comes close enough for me to see his painted hands. It's not paint that covers them, but blood, dried and cracking.

The flashlights move on, men speaking amongst themselves. I'm left with fear. Where is my sister? Was she found? I pray she pressed on to the boats. I don't know what to do, where to go, so I hunch there and peer out at the dark shadows moving along the path. With the flashing of flames from inside the camp, I catch their faces. They're boys. Some no older than fourteen, with fledgling scraps of beard on chins. Lean and gleaming with sweat. Shouting to each other, they peer into trash heaps, bent like hungry wild dogs.

Liam's small hands clutch together. In permanent darkness, he can only hear the wounds these angry young men have carved into the night. He trembles. I brush rainwater from his face, wishing I had the power to take him from here, to stop this.

"You're so brave, Liam," I whisper. *"Goblin brave, you are."*

"Where is Ma?"

"We're going to meet her. She'll be at the boats, I reckon. Since you've been so brave, I've got something for you." I reach into my pocket and find the chocolate that I kept from dinner to give to him. I press it into his hand.

"Thank you," he says. As he eats, I hear whispers in the darkness near to us. I ease up and see several sets of eyes catching moonlight from beneath discarded water containers. A family in hiding. A little girl raises her hand to wave to me. I wave back.

We're not alone.

We can survive this. Somewhere out there Ava is waiting for us. We'll go to her soon, I just need a breath. But then I smell the fire.

13

LYRIA

First the Screams

IT BEGINS AT THE EDGE of the dumpsite near the watchtower and soon spreads as more Red Hands light small blazes till a wall of fire rolls toward our hiding place. The air dances and writhes as tongues of smoke slither through the garbage, licking at my feet and legs. Liam screams in fear. I haul him up and clamber from our hiding spot. I run from the flames, but I'm hacking. Can barely breathe. Can't see, eyes streaming with tears. I stumble over mounds of garbage. Legs sliced by metal and glass and feet sinking in mire up to the knee.

Then, faintly, I hear the voice of a young girl calling to me through the smoke. It drifts to me like nursery song. So small and gentle. And then I see her in the chaos of ash, waving her arm frantically for me to find my feet.

I stumble up and follow her voice to find a seam in the smoke where I can gulp down clean air. There's others running ahead of us. Twenty, forty manic souls stumbling through the garbage, away from the flames, all bound for the river, where the fishing boats are moored. I clear the smoke and heave for air on the edge of the dumpsite.

Other refugees stream ahead of us through the brush, going toward the boats.

Cradling Liam, I join them and spare a look back. A pillar of smoke rises from the burning dump, a smear against the orange dawn. The sun rises over the camp that was once my home.

Ahead, mothers run with children and tattered scarves flowing behind them. Young men stumble on, all earthly possessions left behind, carrying elders or wounded friends. It's not just Gamma. Not just the collaborator clan. I rush with the masses through the green underbrush toward the flowing river. Weeds slap my shins. Mud clings to my feet. We're so near the river. Almost free of the night when I hear a scream ahead of us. Then a second.

In the muddy plain beyond the brush, a woman has fallen to her knees. Her children behind her. Her hands outstretched, begging for mercy. The refugees have stopped, making a staggered line. I can't see past them. Before me, an old man falls to his haunches and sits in the mud, staring emptily ahead.

In Lagalos, when the headTalks wanted to clear a tunnel of a pit-viper infestation, they would light fires and force the pitvipers from their hiding places among the gears and nooks and crevasses. Now we're the snakes. The Red Hand lit fires to force us from our refuge in the dump to bring us here. Barring our way to the boats is a staggered line of twenty young men covered with soot and sweat and carrying automatic weapons. Their hands are covered in red to the elbows. A lone woman stands with them. The same I saw kill Tiran at the shuttle. Her rusty hair is streaked with white. Half her face marred with terrible scars. The other half is worn beauty. She wears an armored vest and carries a slingBlade brown with blood. She says something to a man, who lifts his gun.

Time is stuck with us in the mud.

I push Liam behind me. There's a crack. Something hot and salty sprays my face. I wipe my eyes, hands coming away red. I see the old man sitting in the mud wobbling now. His head strangely lopsided. His body shudders again. Only in the back of my mind do I realize metal is doing this to him. Another bullet rips through him and he pitches sideways, howling. The children shriek and try to run. Metal shreds them, kicking their heads back, contorting their bodies into a manic dance. I push Liam down. Something hot and hard punches me in the shoulder. I'm off my feet and sprawled in the mud. Cool veins of shock trickle through my arm as I suck mud through my nose.

This is not real.

This is happening to someone else. I roll onto my back.

The sounds of the guns fade as I stare up at the blue sky.

I'm rising into it like I did the first time I saw it with my own eyes. Up. Up. Toward a single silver teardrop.

Flying closer.

Closer.

The teardrop glimmers hopefully. Is it the Old Man who watches the Vale? Has he come to take me home to be with my father? My mother? Tiran?

The teardrop divides, becoming three. Or maybe it was always three. And maybe I'm not sinking into the sky. Maybe the sky is falling down on me. I hear in the distance the whisper of angry metal. It's a ship. Three ships. They leave vapor trails in the sky. One fat. Two thin and quick. "The Republic!" someone shouts a million kilometers away. "The Republic!"

Heartbeat concussions ripple through the earth as missiles fall. *Whump. Whump. Whump.* The fat ship litters the sky with little sparkling seeds. The seeds begin to fall. Faster. Faster. Coming together like a flight of swallows, then splintering apart a thousand meters above us. One roars straight toward me, a hot stream of metal and vapor. It slams into the mud. A demon of metal in the shape of a man. His armor is orange. His helmet shaped like the face of a snarling canine. He lifts his left fist and points it toward the raider firing line. Sound and fury erupt. Currents of distorted air shriek over the mud. Men run for cover or melt. Then he's gone, back into the sky, trailing a war howl through an electronic speaker. *"—elemanus!"*

"Lyria," Liam says, touching my leg. He follows it up till his hands find my face. He's alive. Covered with mud, but alive. "Lyria, are you hurt?" he says through tears.

"I'm here," I say. I sit up and clutch him with my right hand. "I'm here." I hold him and sob among the corpses. "I'm here."

Something is wrong with my left shoulder. It hurts more than anything has ever hurt. Blood leaks from it and a splintering pain threads its way down my throbbing arm. We're in a soup of broken, squirming bodies. The Red Hand are dead or fled to cover to fire up at the sky. The two bone-white Republic ships fire at the Hand trucks and landed transports. Steel men whip through the air.

It's too much. Too loud. I take Liam away from it, following the few survivors of the massacre to hide amongst the reeds in the riverbed.

There, hunkered in fear, we listen to the battle. A dozen others survived. They flinch when a bomb goes off. But I sit in silence, rocking back and forth, watching bugs go out over the water. My sister is safe. Her children are safe. We'll see them soon and share a smile. Liam and I will be with them soon. "Look!" someone beside me shouts, pointing up. The knight with the canine helmet plummets from the sky, trailing smoke. He lands with a splash in the river thirty meters from us. We all watch the water. He does not reemerge. I look around at the survivors. Not one moves.

He's going to drown.

"We gotta help him," I murmur through chattering teeth. Cold despite the heat. No one looks my way. I say it louder, "We gotta help him." Still no one moves. "You gutless slags." I tell Liam to stay put and I stumble to the water, wading out into it until it's at my neck. Deeper than I thought. I won't be able to lift him by myself. I curse and look around. Spotting a long length of rope tethering a half dozen of the fishing boats together, I wade back to the boats and unravel the rope, then press back into the depths as the boats drift apart. The current tugs at my waist like a bad dancing partner, threatening to pull me downriver. Soon the water's over my head. I dive down, looking through the murk for the fallen knight.

I can't see him.

The silt is so thick I have to surface twice before I find him by luck when my right foot kicks a piece of metal. I trace my feet over the armor, barely able to find the outline of the man. I tie the rope around his leg as best I can with my wrecked shoulder and kick my way back to the surface, trailing the rope behind. When I make it back to the shore, a group of Reds waits to help me, all brave and heroic after I do all the bloody work.

Ten sets of hands tug on the rope till, with a great heave, we manage to drag the knight free of the water and into the shallows.

We hunch over him in the mud. The orange armor is filthy and charred at the abdomen from where something hit him in the air. He's a giant. Biggest bastard I've ever seen. His helmet alone is nearly as large as my torso. The great gauntlets of the armor could squash my head like a pitviper egg. Water pulses out of the holes in the metal. I run my fingers over it, expecting it to be hot for some reason. It's cold and faintly iridescent.

"Look at the size of him," someone gasps.

"Has to be a bloodydamn Obsidian."

"No, they wear white feathers. . . ."

"Is he dead?"

"Blast hit his generator," an old man says. I think his name is Almor. He was a drillBoy for Delta years ago. He kneels in the mud beside the knight, running his hands over the metal. "PulseShield is off, but means he got no oxygen down there. Could be drowned."

"We got to get him out," I say.

"Anyone know how this shit works?" a woman asks, pulling on the helmet. It doesn't budge.

"Should be an emergency release or somesuch," Almor says. He fumbles at the jawline. "Here." With a hiss, the faceplate pops loose. Water pours out. The old man pushes the faceplate back till it bends into itself, revealing the knight's face. He's no Obsidian, but he looks carved from granite. A red beard covers his heavy jaw. His head is bald and titanic. And a slim scar stretches down his right cheekbone. His nose is smashed flat and his eyes are small and ringed with delicate eyelashes. He's a Gold. The first I've ever seen with my own eyes. The first any of us have ever seen.

"Is he breathing?" Almor asks.

No one moves toward the knight. Still gutless. I lean over the man and put my ear to his nose. Just then, he spasms. I lurch back in terror as he vomits water. As he hacks, I sink back into the mud, bone tired. Overhead, the sky is torn to shreds as more supersonic ships come from the sky and descend to save the camp.

The Red Hand will retreat, but Camp 121 is burning.

14

EPHRAIM

Anniversary

I N A SMALL CORNER BOOTH in a shady back room of a cesspit, two slags are slouched drinking out of dirty glasses like pervy old gargoyles. They look up as I make my way through the neon-green demondust smoke that wafts from the burners of two Red mechanics.

South of Hyperion City Center, hundred sixty klicks from the maple-lined boulevards of the Promenade, towers the brutalist Atlas Interplanetary Docks. There are seven main towers to the AID, each inhuman in its size. Atlas sees one billion travelers pass through his halls every Earth-standard year. But for every new oligarch and old-blood Gold that lands here, there's a flood of space mariners and interplanetary immigrants and passengers. All these weary travelers crave restaurants, casinos, hotels, and whorehouses before taking transit to whatever their final destination on Luna might be.

It's a tumor that won't stop growing; that's why it's called the Mass.

Behind me, through the open doorway, electric signs and high-resolution digital flesh fishhook the eyes, pulling travelers from their trams or private aircars. Jerking them headlong into the vestibules of commerce to pump blood and cash into the veins of this hinterland city. It's the sort of place you go to forget about your life. But, in the irony to end all ironies, it's where mine began.

The bar looked different back then. I was two years out of the legion and had come to the Mass to burn a few credits with some squaddies from Piraeus. Two drinks in, some idiot spilled a glass of spiked milk down the back of my neck. I swung around to teach the prick some manners, but one look at that goofy face and baggy suit, I started laughing so hard I couldn't raise a fist. The man stared back at me with a milk mustache and wide, apologetic eyes. Who the hell orders milk in a place like this? The man was young, simple, and two years into the legion from some Earth backwater. We sat and talked in that corner booth and closed the place down. Rest was history.

He was my refuge. My small-town boy with a big heart and a bigger laugh. Jove knows what he saw in me.

"I beg your pardon," I say to the slags in the corner booth. They eye my rumpled suit, wondering if I'm lost.

"Wajoowant?" the Brown one asks. He's a Terran bastard by the look of his thick thighs. His loamy eyes narrow.

"I reserved this booth, citizen," I say.

"Deey don't take reservations here. Slag off."

"Sit there," says the larger man, a Gray with a sour look. "And shut it 'fore you get carved up." He points to a nearby open table and flashes a curved ionKnife the size of my forearm. It shimmers blue as he activates its charge.

"And you're gonna do the carving?" I ask wryly. "You don't look like you can even stand." He stands.

"Please, bitch. I used to own little sleets like you in Whitehold," the Gray says. By the look of his knotted forearms, he could easily break me to kindling. I should just move on.

"Whitehold?" I scoff. "That's odd. I thought they sent pig sodomizers to Deepgrave." Both stand, blades shimmering in the low light. I stumble backward, too late in realizing my tongue's drunker than the rest of me.

The Gray's about to come and try to open me up with that cutter of his when he sees something behind me and stops dead. There's silence in the bar. Something fiendishly unique has just walked through the door behind me. And anything unique enough to *this* sort of crowd could only mean one thing.

She came after all.

I turn to see a Gray woman my height, but built like a snub-nosed boxer with the physical dimensions of a concrete building block. Freckles, made dark by her time under the harsh Mercurian sun, maul an ugly, broad nose, while her hair, shaved on the sides of the head, shoots up from the top of her head like a surfacing great white. Her military uniform is all black, but every eye, wary bartender to dazed whore, scans the red flying-horse standard on the forearms of her jacket and the matted wolfcloak that hangs from her left shoulder. Pegasus Legion, Howler Battalion. One of the Reaper's own.

The woman strides past me up to the men blocking our path to the booth. "Move." They dip their heads politely and back away. She sits down and pours two shots of what remains of their whiskey into the glasses, wipes one glass for herself, and nods to me. I join her as she tosses them a gold Octavia. A hundred-credit Lune crescent. Still the currency of the day, despite the Rising's sad attempts to mint new legal tender. "For the whiskey, citizens."

They skulk away and conversations slowly start again throughout the bar. The woman looks back to me, flinty eyes searching.

"Holiday ti Nakamura, the Howler. In the leathery flesh," I say.

"Ephraim ti Horn. The dumbass with a death wish." She jerks her head at the two thugs. "What's your damage?"

"The usual. Would you like a thank-you for saving my ass?"

"Don't thank me yet; night's young. Besides, the Obsidian with the railgun over there might be a bit too much for you to chew."

"Huh?"

"Far side, second booth. Big girl with the bulge under the armpit." She jerks her head to a shadowy booth where a large shape is hunched in the shadows over a drink with an umbrella in it. In the haze from the vodka and pills, I didn't even notice her there. "You're slipping, Eph," Holiday says as she warily sniffs the whiskey bottle.

"Dammit." I sigh. "I'll be right back."

"Do you need help?"

"Only if you have tickets to the zoo."

"What?"

"Don't ask."

I stalk across the bar. Volga hunches sheepishly as if she can sink into the shadow of the booth so I won't see her. She gives up when I snap my fingers at her. "Outside."

Rain drips sluggishly down from the green awning over the bar's entrance. The bar itself is in a block of restaurants and drinking holes directly abutting a multilevel thoroughfare. Past the small retaining wall is a precipitous drop down into the concrete canyon between the buildings. I push Volga in the chest. "You stalking me now?"

"No . . ."

"Volga."

"Yes," she admits. "I am worried about you."

"Worried about me? You're the one who can barely catch a cab without me."

"I tracked you, did I not?"

"So I taught you something at least. But not how to mind your own business, you dumb giant."

"You seemed sad. . . ."

"Not your problem. You got enough of those, don't make me one of them."

"But we're friends. Friends look out for each other." She nods inside. "Who is that? Her cloak . . ."

"That's none of your damn business."

"But . . ."

"We're not friends, Volga." I push a finger in her chest and stare up at her bluff face. "We work together. Business associates. That is the totality of our relationship." She stands there as if I've struck her. I sigh in annoyance. "Go home. And stop following me just because you don't have your own life." I don't have to tell her twice. She hunches her shoulders against the rain and disappears up a flight of stairs to the taxi level above.

I head back inside, where Holiday has made some progress on the bottle, but her chair is shifted, like she's just gotten out of it. Did she listen at the door?

"You know her?" she asks.

"No," I snap.

"Right. Well . . . It's good to see you, Eph." She traces the rim of her glass with a callused finger. "To be honest, I'm surprised you came."

"Ouch. Thought I wouldn't care anymore?"

"Thought you wouldn't remember Trigg's birthday."

"And I thought your messiah master wouldn't let you off the leash for some R&R. Don't you have a parade to attend?"

"That was yesterday. But you knew that."

I shrug. "Well, this place has gone to shit."

"Yut. I preferred the tiki torches to whatever this is . . ." She trails off and gestures to the green lighting and myriad lowlifes.

I snort. "Maybe we're just getting too cultured. Still, has to be better than the Mercury sand belt."

"Hell yes it is," she says heavily. She's never been a looker, but the latest tour has been hard on her. Still, most of the wear seems on the inside. She sits at the table with the weight of the planet pressing her down into the whiskey bottle.

"You fall in the Rain?" I ask. She nods. "Saw the newsreels. Looked like a shitshow. What's one of those like? A Rain?"

She shrugs. "Good for weapons contractors. Hostile to the human experience for everyone else."

"To the returning hero and her perspicacity." I raise my glass.

She tips her glass to me. "To the malignant underachiever."

We click our glasses together and down the liquor. It's cheap enough I can taste the plastic of the bottle it came in, ration fare. My glass is refilled before it reaches the table. We do another. More after that. Drinking till it's murdered proper. Holiday examines the remnants of her last glass, wondering how it came so soon. She reminds me of all soldiers who've come home from the war. Worlds unto themselves. Tense, eyes constantly assessing. She awkwardly tries to make conversation, because she knows she's supposed to. "So . . . what's new? You still contracting?"

"You know me. Kite in the wind." I swish and swoosh my finger through the air.

"Which corp?"

"You wouldn't know 'em." She doesn't smile. I wonder if it hurts her to see me as much as it hurts me to see her. I was afraid of this. Of coming here. Sliding back into it all.

"So, you're living good and easy."

"Only thing easy is entropy."

"That's funny."

"It's not mine." I shrug. "I stay busy."

"There are other ways to stay busy. Meaningful ways."

"Tried that." My hand instinctively drifts to my chest where the scars from the Gold are hidden under my suit jacket. I notice her watching my hand. I drop it. "Didn't take." Her datapad buzzes on her arm. "On call?" I ask. She silences it without looking down.

"Grand theft's gone up. They've got a task force now. The Sovereign is tired of this city's culture being plundered for the highest bidder."

"The Sovereign, eh. How's old Lionheart? Still giving out Amnesty passes to murderers and slavers?"

"That still under your skin?"

"Grays: short in life, long in memory. Forget that little jingle? Tell me, does the new task force have a pretty insignia? I bet they do. Maybe a flying tiger or a lion with a sword in its lustrous mouth?"

"You were the one who chose to leave the Rising, Eph."

"You know why I left."

"If you didn't like how things were going, you could have stuck around, made a difference. But I guess it's easier sitting in the cheap seats, throwing bottles."

"Make a difference?" I smile nastily. "You know, when the Hyperion Trials started, I thought there'd finally be some justice. Honest to Jove. I thought the Golds would finally pay the bill. Even after Endymion, even after what they did to my boys . . ." I touch my chest again. "But then your Sovereign got cold feet. Sure, some Society military brass, some high-up psychos from the Board of Quality Control got life in Deepgrave, but more got full pardons because she needed their men, their money, their ships. So much for justice."

Holiday holds my gaze, willful.

After Trigg died on that Martian peak, I joined the Rising. More for revenge than anything else. I wasn't a believer. Eventually they put my Piraeus and legion-honed skills and understanding of Gold culture to use hunting Peerless war criminals down. Used to call ourselves "scar hunters." Just another slick name.

I know I shouldn't press the politics with her. She's as thick in the head and set in her ways as ever. Just another grunt seduced by the pretty demigods. But the booze is making me care.

"You know, every time I saw a Gold slaver walk free for the sake of 'the war effort,' it was like watching them spit on Trigg's grave. Aja might be dust, but men and women just like that bitch walk the worlds because the people holding your leash couldn't follow through. Shoulda put a Gray as Sovereign. At least we finish shit."

I drain my glass for emphasis and feel like an idiot talking head on an HC show. Cute empty words and flashy maxims.

"You know I can't help you if you're caught on a job," she says.

And like that, I'm dismissed because she's always right, and I'm always just running my mouth. "Public urination is a victimless crime," I say with a smile. I pull out a burner and light it.

"I meant what I said last time."

"About the Hyperion Chimera match? I'd have lost a fortune on that bet. Embarrassing spectacle. But fauxWar is unpredictable, neh? Karachi is a safer bet."

"The offer is still on the table, Eph. We could use a man like you. Come back. Help us unwind the Syndicate. You can save lives."

"I am saving a life. Mine. By staying as far away from your masters as humanly possible. Shame Trigg didn't get the same chance."

She watches me through the smoke I blow in her face. "I don't want to do this anymore."

"Be more specific."

"This." She looks around the bar. "This isn't for him. It's not even for me. It's for you. So you can sink in it and let it rot you. That's not what he would have wanted."

"What would he have wanted?"

"For you to have a life. A purpose."

I roll my eyes. "Why'd you bother to come? I didn't make you."

"Because my brother loved you," she says sharply. She lowers her voice. "He would have wanted more for you than this."

"Then maybe you shouldn't have gotten him killed."

The old Holiday wouldn't hit me. "It's been ten years, asshole. You have to let him go or it's gonna eat you up."

I shrug. "What's left to eat?" I didn't deserve her brother's love, and I sure as shit don't need her pity. I flag down the bartender and he comes over with another bottle. Holiday shakes her head as I pour myself a glass.

"I'm not coming back here next year."

"So sorry. Will miss you. Break the chains, and all that." She stands and stares down at me, about to say something spiteful, but she swallows it down, enraging me because I can smell the pity. "You know what just rubs me raw?" I say up to her. "You look down at me because you're in that little uniform and you think *me* cheap. But you're the one too stupid to realize you're wearing a collar. You're the one he'd be ashamed of."

"The only good thing about him being dead is that he doesn't have to see you like this. So long, Eph." At the door, she glances back down at her datapad and a shadow of fear passes over her face from what she sees there. Then she's gone into the rain.

Two glasses later, I abandon the bottle and stumble out of the bar and onto the sidewalk. Rain drips its way through the labyrinth of city above and below, growing fouler by the level. I go to the edge of the sidewalk and peer over the rusted metal rail down into the airway thoroughfare. It's a thousand-meter drop to the Mass's fetid ground level. Flying cars and taxis blink through the gathering fog. From the sides of hulking buildings, advertisements seep miasma stains of neon greens and violent reds into the air like rainbow pus. On a digital billboard, a six-story Red child is wandering alone in the desert. Lips cracked. Skin burnt absurdly. His foot strikes something in the sand, and eagerly he begins to dig and lo, he discovers something buried. A bottle. Feverishly he twists off the top and takes a drink. He laughs with delight and holds the glistening bottle up to the sun, where it sparkles and beads with divine drops of perspiration. The word AMBROSIA sparkles onto the screen, a little wing-heel logo in the corner.

A distant roar comes from the sky as a large passenger ship leaves its berth at AID, aimed at the invisible stars. I drink from my bottle, wishing I'd never left Hyperion for the Mass. Wishing I'd gone to a Pearl club and found a Pink to swallow my attention. Holiday was right about one thing; this just picks at the wound. But if I don't pick, then it feels like it didn't matter. And if didn't matter, then neither do I.

I pull my datapad out with one hand, almost dropping it over the rail, and pull up the last video played. Security cam footage. A wintery landscape fills the air in front of me. Careless raindrops punch through the holo. Trigg is stranded on the bridge to a landing pad that juts out from a mountainside like a waiter's arm bringing a tray. A huge Gold in blue armor charges him as he runs back to the Reaper. She plunges her blade through his spine out his stomach and hoists him in the air like a street vendor's kebab. Then she hurls him off the side of the bridge. My love spatters against the rocks beneath. His blood darkens the white snow.

I hurl the datapad down into the abyss, tears and rain blurring my vision. The railing is slippery against my hands as I find myself climbing it. Standing on the edge, looking at the cars beneath and the darkness beyond them. I feel the pain just as sharply as I did ten years ago when Holiday called me. I was in the Piraeus Insurance offices. Didn't even make a sound when I hung up. I just took off my uniform, ditched my badge, and left that office for the last time.

I could leave that quietly now.

But as I lean forward to go over the edge, something stops me. A hand gripping the back of my jacket. I feel my feet slide out from under me as I'm jerked off the rail back onto the sidewalk. I land hard on the wet concrete, the air rushing out of me. Three pale-faced men in black leather dusters and chrome glasses stare down at me.

"Who the fu—"

A fist the size of a small dog sends me to darkness.

15

LYSANDER

From the Depths

In the cockpit, Pytha has gone silent, now locked into the ship's battle sync. Her eyes stare distantly as her mind and the ship's computer function as one. "Better start thinking about how you want to die," Cassius says to me as I slide into the observation seat behind Pytha's. "One engine's down thanks to you playing Lorn. This is worse than the astral dump on Lorio."

"Nothing's worse than that." I look at the sensor displays and the data readouts. "Never mind." We're being pursued by the three craft. Not slapped-together pirate ships, but military vessels. Doesn't matter that they're old. Their engines seem to be in prime shape. Pytha's returning mid-range fire with our own railguns. Can't see the drama of it—it's all displays and sensor readouts in here. I feel the familiar shudder in the ship as her munitions funnel out of their magazines into the magnetic firing rods and race across space toward our pursuers. How many more shots till we run dry?

"Can we lose them in the asteroid field?" I ask.

"Not dense enough," Cassius says.

"Can we set down?"

"They're too close."

"Can we—"

"No," he says. "Can't hide. Can't run. Can't fight. Dammit." He slams his hand on the console. "You should have listened to me."

"I'm sorry, Cassius."

"Don't use my name. We have guests on board."

"She's unconscious."

"That crew isn't. You want one of them trying to collect a Core bounty while we're dodging Ascomanni?" He shakes his head, marveling at my stupidity.

"I wasn't going to stand by and let those savages eat one of us."

" 'One of us' . . . "

"My grandfather would have tried to save her."

"Course he would have. He'd have gutted a hundred lowColors to save one Gold life. Today, you killed how many . . . a dozen?" I see their mouths frothing in fear. Their eyes wide like a dying horse's. All white. "Was it worth it? You could have helped them," he says sorrowfully. "But you went for her! One person!"

I take the punishment. It's earned. But he'll forget today. It'll be diluted by time. For me I know it will not. My memory will trap me with those screaming faces even as I lie on my deathbed. I will see their cracking nails against the mesh. Smell the urine on the deck. And I'll wonder how many I could have saved if I'd had more sense.

Our ship shudders again as another projectile hits us. Our kinetic shields send it ricocheting off into space. If they were aiming to kill, they'd use missiles, but they're aiming for our engines. "They want us alive," I say.

"Of course they do. They saw that we're Golds. They'll rape us and kill us when they get bored of it."

"And they'll eat us," I say. "These ones are cannibals." He catches the fear in my voice. "How long can the engines last if we overburn?" I ask, knowing the answer, but knowing too where I need to push him.

He glances down at Pytha. "Not long. Maybe an hour, two. Then we're dead metal. But where would we go? Nearest asteroid city is five days out."

"The Rim."

"The Rim, he says. You forget your last name? My last name?" He lowers his voice, looking back down the hall. "Your grandmother ordered the destruction of one of their moons and their docks."

"So they say."

"They think I personally stomped in the head of Revus au Raa."

"The Ascomanni won't follow if we make the Line. They fear the Rim more than we do."

"There's a reason for that."

"The chance they'll have a warship even six days away from where we enter is negligible." Our ship shudders again. Pytha jerks in her seat. Blood dribbles down her lips. She's bitten her tongue. Her mouth guard wobbles on the console. I pry open her teeth and push the thin slip of plastic in. "I made a mistake in there. But this is a matter of probability. We can slip over the Line, shed the Ascomanni, fix our engines, then . . ."

"No ship has crossed into Rim Space in ten years. I won't risk starting a war."

"Then what's *your* plan?" I ask.

"We turn around and fight. We can get inside one of their ships. Turn the guns on the other corvettes. I've seen men do it."

Fight. Of course that's his answer.

"We're not those men," I say. His warrior vanity looks wounded. "And we don't have a launch tube on the rear of the ship. We'd have to pivot the ship starboard. And then we'd fire back into a fusillade of railgun fire. And if we make it through that, adding their current velocity to the velocity of the spitTube we will hit their viewports with . . ." I pull from my memory the detailed report and analysis my grandmother had me make on Darrow's mathematically suicidal assault on the *Vanguard*. ". . . potentially nine times the velocity used to breach the *Vanguard*. Our bones will be indistinguishable from our urine."

"Really?"

"Care to wager?"

"Shit."

"What about S-1392?"

"The asteroid?"

"It's the one the Gold bought passage to." I reference the sensors. "It's two hours away. Three hours closer than the Line. Before she fell unconscious, the girl said that help was there."

His eyes narrow. "When exactly did you have time to have a conversation with her?"

"In the medical bay."

"We don't know who she is. We don't know where she's from. Do you even know what kind of help she meant?"

"No," I confess. "But opportunities multiply as they are seized."

"Don't quote Sun Tzu at me like it was your idea. Her 'help' could be anyone. It could be the gorydamn Ash Lord himself."

"That would be a boon for us."

"For you, maybe. Your godfather would skin me alive." He stares at the Obsidian ships on the sensors. "She used your razor. Did she have a scar?"

If I say yes, he won't go to S-1392. He'll try to fight.

"No. No scar," I say. Then I feel the guilt building. My brain has always been faster than my conscience.

Our ship shudders again, harder this time, and the displays show damage to our starboard thrusters. Cassius winces with each shudder of the hull. It wounds him to see the *Archimedes* bleed.

"Slag it." He grips Pytha's shoulder. "Pytha, set course for asteroid S-1392. Increase engine output to fifteen percent over the redline. I don't care if they melt together." In her sync, she does not respond, but the ship does. I sit down as the *Archimedes* rumbles around us. The gravity pulls on my body as the compensators strain at the sudden acceleration and the *Archimedes* races for the asteroid. The Obsidians fall behind our sudden acceleration, but slowly they begin to match.

The die is cast.

While Cassius prepares the ship for potential boarders by outfitting the rescued crew with weapons, I return to the medbay to check on the Gold to see if I can draw any more information from her. She's unconscious still. I watch her for a moment, feeling more protective than I should for a stranger. Tenderly, I cut the rest of her clothing away and begin to clean the oil from her skin with alcohol scrubs. I drape a medical blanket over her to protect her decency. When I look up, her eyes are open and seem to have been watching me for some time. I feel color rising in my cheeks, fearing that she'll think I was doing something untoward. But her gaze is softer now than at our first meeting. Less animalistic. She looks at the razor on my hip.

"We're bound for the asteroid," I say gently. "You said there was help there. What sort of help?" She tries to speak, but her words are too weak to come out. *"Salve,"* I say, looking at the new layer of res-Flesh I used to cover her scar. "Save your strength." I set a hand on her shoulder. "I should check your wound. May I?"

She makes a small nod with her head. I pull the blanket to the side and examine the angry flesh. My cauterization was sloppy. I find a fresh bandage inside the cabinet and return to her wound. She flinches as I apply disinfectant cream. To soothe her, I recite one of my favorite verses from my mother's library.

> *"As from the darkening gloom a silver dove*
> *upsoars, and darts into the Eastern light,*
> *On pinions that naught moves but pure delight,*
> *So fled thy soul into the realms above,*
> *Regions of peace and everlasting love. . . ."*

The girl's fallen unconcious again by the time I finish the verse, and this time I let her alone. All those lives for her. As I leave, I smudge oil on her face to help mask the resFlesh covering her scar and hope that I've not lied to Cassius in vain.

At full burn we manage to close the distance to the asteroid in under two hours. The cabin is now bathed crimson by the warning lights as our last engine overheats. Our inertia carries us forward, but the Ascomanni are closing, eating up the distance between our ships. Soon they'll reel us in with magnetic tow beams and burn through our hull. We sit in silence. Pytha's un-synced with the ship now. Our guns are twisted scrap. Our shields are gone.

The whole ship vibrates as the largest of the Ascomanni craft locks onto our hull with a tow beam, slowing our velocity. Cassius unfurls his razor and I cradle mine. My hand is sweaty. My chest tight and my mouth chalky and dry. I sit with my legs crossed on the floor in silent meditation, letting the fear flow into me so I can be its master when its authors burn through our hull and enter our halls.

Cassius turns to me as he tightens the screws on the gauntlets of his pulseArmor. We've both discarded our clunky EVO suits for pulseArmor breastplates and arm gear. "We meet them at the door. I want you to stay behind me. There's not enough room in the corridors for us to fight side by side. If I fall, make sure they do not take you alive." He looks to Pytha. "I mean this since . . ."

His sentence drifts without finishing. I follow his eyes to the RAD sensor display. It warps sideways. The display's pixels disintegrate into a dancing pattern of blue and black static. Pytha squints. "Someone's jamming the nav."

"Can't be the Ascomanni," I say. "They don't have tech enough to compromise our instruments."

"Who then?" Pytha asks.

"Oh hell," Cassius murmurs. "Oh goryhell." I follow his eyes out the viewport to the large, seemingly benign asteroid in the distance. S-1392. Pytha enlarges the visual display. Shadows cloak half the asteroid. The surface is dirty pearl white and riven with impact craters. The shadows stir. Something moves in the dark distance, streaking out from the bowels of the asteroid. It comes into space like a black eel squirming its way from the recesses of a dark sea cavern, flowing out of shadow, eyes glinting with pearly menace. But this eel is not made of flesh and blood. It is made of metal, painted black, and marked with a three-headed electric dragon on its sides.

It is a warship.

In this empty expanse, where no warship has flown for more than a decade, a first-rate destroyer races toward us. One point three kilometers long, brimming with weapons and high-grade shielding. And flanking it are two torchShips of an unfamiliar design. From their hangars depart three squadrons of strange fighter ships that look like deep-sea horrors.

They close the distance in half a minute and speed silently past us to shred the Ascomanni ships without even the formality of a radio broadcast. The fighter squadrons deliver elegant death as they lace the Ascomanni with railgun fire and spit off missiles that crackle silently over the blast-scored hulls of the raiders till each vessel vents oxygen and shivers apart to float dead and quiet into forever space. The engagement lasts less than a minute.

Debris pings against our hull.

Pytha's voice trembles. "What was that?"

A blinking red light on the com signals an incoming direct transmission from the destroyer itself. It lurks in the distance, not approaching us. Beside me, I sense Cassius's unease. "What kind of ship is that?" Pytha asks. "Lysander?"

I stare out the viewport. "I don't know."

But Cassius knows. And there's a feeling about him, like he expected this. Like this was some inevitable end. I'm beginning to understand. "You lied to me," he says. He looks over to me with heartbreak on his face. "She had a scar. Didn't she?"

I accept his anger and meet his eyes. "She did."

He thinks I have killed us. And maybe I have. But as long as we breathe, there will be more opportunities for escape. We've jumped from the fire into the frying pan.

"Open the transmission," he says.

Static crackles through the open channel until a cold voice calls out from the deep in an accent not heard on the streets of Mars or the halls of the Luna since the Rim closed its borders a decade ago. The long, lazy vowels that linger in the back of the throat hail from the volcano moon of Jupiter. The same moon that House Raa, leaders of the Rim, call home.

It is the accent of Io and the Lords of the Dust.

"Attention, Archimedes," the disembodied voice says. *"This is the Rim Dominion Destroyer* Charybdis. *Your communications equipment is neutralized. Any deviation from present course will result in the destruction of your vessel. Any resistance will result in the destruction of your vessel. Stand by for boarding."*

The com goes off. Silence sits with us in the cockpit.

Desperate, Cassius grabs the com. "Charybdis, *we are not in viola-*

tion of Rim Space. Repeat, we are in neutral territory. This is a violation of the Pax Ilium. Repeat, we are not in Rim Space." No response. Cassius hurls the com in anger. Pytha flinches as the plastic shatters against the metal bulkhead.

"Better our own kind than Ascomanni," I say, though I'm disquieted by the fear I see in his eyes and Pytha's. We can reason with them.

"Reason? Bring me the faciem, Pytha." I look at him and wonder if his fear is warranted. "Lysander, get my box and yours and put it in the vault." He pulls his House Bellona ring from the chain around his neck and pushes it into my hand. "Make sure there's nothing that could lead them back to who we are. Holos, weapons, rings—everything goes in the vault. And Karnus's razor. That cover you have on it won't fool them. Hide it or we're dead."

I rush through the halls to the living quarters, where I collect Cassius's oak box in which he keeps his family heirlooms, the meager remaining inheritance of a man who once could have ruled Mars. I fetch my own box, a large ivory vessel that carries the last relics of my past. I deposit both boxes in the hidden vault in the wall behind the ship's oven. I frisk my body to make sure I've not forgotten anything. Grudgingly I take my grandmother's ring that hangs around my neck and Karnus's razor and push them into the box.

By the time I've returned to the cockpit, Cassius has opened the faciem, which we bought in a black market on Ceres. Set in foam is a honeycombed thin gray mask, a vial of smelling salts, a chemical ice pack, and a missing holster for the painkilling stim syringe, which we emptied weeks ago to fill our field kits. "You don't happen to have any extra stims?" he asks me.

"I used them on the Gold. Don't you?"

He shakes his head. "Gave them all to the prisoners."

"Goryhell," I mutter, looking at the mask's honeycombs. "Cassius . . ."

He laughs and lets a bit of his old roguish smile break through. "It's fine, my goodman. Pain's just a memory."

"Are you spacemad?" Pytha asks flatly. "You can't use that monster without stims."

"I can check the hold," I say. "We might have missed a pack. . . ."

Cassius shakes his head. "No time."

Pytha's horrified. "Lysander. Don't let him . . ."

I meet Cassius's gaze. "I'll hold you down."

Cassius glances down into the mask, a distant, forlorn look in his eyes. The same look he had when we had to pay for engine parts by collecting a bounty on a former Gold Tribune. It asks how it came to this. So far from what he thought he would be.

Sparing a gentle smile to us, one that belongs to another time, a gentler version of himself, he brings the mask to his face till only his eyes are visible. He tightens the plastic latch at the back so it is secure to his head.

"Don't let me take it off," he says.

"Coral hold?" I ask.

"Mantis lock. I'd break your arms in a coral hold."

I obey. Sitting behind him, I wrap my legs around his midsection and loop my arms around his biceps, then under his armpits, and clasp my hands together at the middle of his spine. "Pytha, you flip the switch." She creeps forward.

Muttering to herself, he grips the activation knob on the side of the mask. "On you."

"Do it."

Pytha twists the activation knob on the mask. There's a sibilant hiss as the three hundred needles built into the plastic of the scrambler mask spring forward into the skin, bone, and cartilage of Cassius's face. He jerks once. Twice. And then a gurgling scream escapes from beneath the mask like seething steam from a kettle. His muscles knot and clench rock-hard as he thrashes back into me, twisting so viciously with his arms that I think my own will break. He screams babbling, incomprehensible curses as he rolls, kicking out and almost catching Pytha in the shin. She jumps back. The mask mercilessly pumps artificial filler into his face, grafting imitation bone onto his jaw and forehead and eye sockets. In twenty seconds, the mask's indicator blinks from red to yellow and the worst of Cassius's convulsions begin to fade. We're on our sides breathing heavily. He mewls and drifts into shallow insentience. The indicator blinks green. I disentangle myself from his arms. There's a stabbing line of pain down my forearm that insinuates a stress fracture.

Pytha rushes to Cassius and gingerly unlatches the mask. His face is a bubbling mass of angry, swollen flesh. Like a wax figure strayed too close to flame. Bit by bit the swelling subsides under the anti-inflammation pack that Pytha applies.

When she pulls the pack away, our handsome friend is gone, replaced by a thuggish visage with a primitive forehead, a bulbous, veiny nose, chipped ears, and a slack mouth with engorged, lazy lips. The Peerless Scar is gone, recessed into this new Bronzie visage. Pytha wipes tears from her eyes.

She looks up at me in recrimination and jerks the smelling salts out of my hands to crack them under his nose. "You're prime, *dominus*," she says to him, cradling his head and wiping the vomit from his face as he comes to. "Easy as sin. It's all over now. It's all over." He sits up with her help and together we watch out the viewport to see the destroyer opening its docking bay to swallow us whole.

16

DARROW

The Den

I STAND UPON MY TOWER as a hard rain falls.

Before me, the steel skin of the Eternal City yawns into the night. Amidst the reaching towers and bloated stadiums and buzzing complexes lie dark pools of shadow where the Jackal, and the years of war that followed, left their mark. Now, with the radiation scrubbed and pulsedomes removed, arthropodal construction ships from Sun Industries drift with lazy purpose there, hauling and ferrying workers and metal.

Hyperion may be rebuilding itself, but the southern cities were all but destroyed by the Ash Lord's forces under his mad Minotaur, Apollonius au Valii-Rath, before the latter's capture and imprisonment in Deepgrave.

My people *do* suffer. But Dancer's false peace is not the answer. In my youth I was consumed with the fever of war. I don't feel that fever now. I only feel the cold weight of duty, and the fear of what it will do to my family. A ship glows as it approaches the top of my tower and sets down on the landing pad.

A thickset Silver man with a bald pate walks down the ramp. He wears a high-collared white velvet jacket. The eyeball of a Gold glints from a ring on his heavy hand.

"Quicksilver," I say. "Thank you for coming."

He grunts and shakes my hand. His lone companion, a Sentinel drone no larger than a child's skull, floats behind him, chrome hull shimmering in the rain. A red eye pulses in its center. I watch it warily.

"I watched the socialists tear off your crown. That was an embarrassing spectacle," he sneers. "Matteo's men tell me they've concluded the debate. The Obsidians abstained. Just sat there. Caraval and the Coppers went with the Vox. Your arrest warrant will be issued within the hour. They're voting on the armistice soon."

"Then you know what happens next."

"History is a wheel. And all mobs are the same. Full of small men with big appetites. Only way they grow is by eating men like us." He squints at me. "You could end the Vox Populi tonight. Storm the Senate. Put them in irons."

"They're still my people," I say defensively.

"Do they know that?" I don't answer. "The Vox Populi are a cancer. There's only one way to deal with cancer. Cut it out. I told your wife that years ago."

"We agreed to demokracy."

"Yet you're here. Aren't you?" he asks with a laugh. I haven't missed the hypocrisy. "Change isn't made by mobs that envy, but by men who dare. Fitchner knew that. And so do we. Even if they spit on us."

I look down at the bald man, remembering the first time we met on Phobos, how much I hated him. He's a strange creature. Full of malice and selfishness and rigid ideology. Not a man I thought I'd ever trust. But he pulled himself up from obscurity on sheer will. He founded the Sons of Ares with Fitchner. He rebuilt the Republic from my wars. Without him, Luna would be a land of craters and ash.

"You're leaving. Aren't you? Good," he says.

"Good?"

"What help is the Reaper in a cage?" he asks, nodding up to the sky. "We need you in the wild." I didn't ask his advice, but it reinforces my conviction all the same. He was Fitchner's friend. I wish I could talk to the man now. Just once. Would he agree with what I plan?

"I need your help."

"You know I always help my friends. Probably why I keep so few of them."

"You might want to hear what it is first."

"You'll never make it to your ships in orbit with the Wardens after you," he guesses. "You need one of mine."

"I need the *Nessus*." He flinches. "And I need it to look as if it's been stolen."

"Why the *Nessus*? What are you planning?" He grunts at my silence. "Never mind. I'll put it in dry dock for repairs. You know where it is."

I nod. "Thraxa is already waiting in the dock."

"So you knew I'd say yes."

"I hoped."

He laughs. "Bring my ship back in one piece, eh? She's Matteo's favorite."

"Sir," a concerned voice says behind me. I turn. My archLancer, Alexandar au Arcos, Lorn's eldest and brightest grandson, stands behind me. He's a smirking prodigy. Blade-thin with long white-blond hair and fair skin. Standing no higher than his breastbone is another of my lancers, my niece Rhonna, Kieran's headstrong eldest daughter by his first marriage. Twenty, with a buzzed head and a flat nose. She's only been a lancer for a year, but is eager to prove herself Alexandar's equal.

They duck their heads against the rain as it soaks into their black Pegasus Legion jackets. Alexandar eyes the drone behind Quicksilver with disdain while my niece eyes the man himself. "They're all here," Alexandar says.

I look back at Quicksilver. "If the Vox find out you helped me . . . You might be safer on Phobos."

"And watch as the mob steals my towers and my companies? I have security teams for a reason. I rebuilt this moon. My fight is here. Shame. You'll miss my birthday."

"Here's to making the next one." We shake hands and he departs.

"What you've heard is true," I say.

Thirty-seven Howlers stare at me through the smoke haze from their glowing burner tips. A savage's miscellany of psychopaths and hooligans, my pack is a scattermash of rejects that Sevro and I have collected over the past ten years. After losing twenty on Mercury, our official number is one hundred and eleven, but most have been dispersed throughout the Republic by Sevro to carry out my directives. Those who do not have homes on Luna reside within the Den, an ink-black skyscraper I liberated from the ownership of the Shadow Knight. Holiday nods to me from the back, the last to arrive. She looks like she's been drinking. Sefi sits to the side with our ten Obsidians. With her senators abstaining from the vote, I wasn't sure she would come.

"What you talkin' 'bout, boss?" Min-Min, my munitions expert, says through her nose. Her metal legs are up on the table. Sunken Red eyes watch me neutrally from her dark face. Her dusty mohawk is flattened to one side, and the haggard lines of her cheek are deep in the low light. "This emergency meeting shit's a bit gritty, doncha think?" Her robotic wolfhead ring taps against her beer bottle. "We just got back."

"What's he talking about?" Victra asks incredulously. Her long arms are crossed over her pregnant stomach and her jagged hair is pinned back by a clasp. She looks furious. "Do you actually live under a rock, Min-Min, or just look like it?"

"Oh, slag off, poshy. I was knee-deep in the Mass. Had this righteous Obsidian brute sandwiched between me thighs."

"Have you not looked at the news at all today?" Pebble, one of my oldest companions, asks. Her fleshy cheeks are flushed from her hasty arrival. She and her husband, Clown, were halfway to a Mare Vaporum resort for a vacation with their children when Sevro called.

"Naw." Min-Min sighs. "I'm analog, baby. Last thing I need to bloodydamn see is more sensationalist smut about psycho slags on Mars raping and burning. Doesn't do me well." She smooths her mohawk. "Not at all."

Sevro throws his datapad at Min-Min so hard she almost takes it in the face. She catches it and turns it over, muttering under her breath. Her eyes grow wide as she sees the headlines. "Bloodyhell."

"What I would like to know is which one of you snitched?" Victra asks.

"Yes, please stand up so we can stab you in the spleen," Sevro says. "Only way Dancer could have been tipped is if one of you chatted about the emissaries. If you talked to a whore, a docker, your bloody-damn mother, now's the chance to own it."

No one stands.

"I trust everyone in this room," I say, knowing it's what they need to hear. But it's not true. The leak had to come from someone in this room. Sefi? She did not exactly support me. Is she really so tired of war? "However they found out about the emissaries, it wasn't from one of you. You all know by now of the peace accords that the Ash Lord has requested. The Senate will soon agree to an armistice, a temporary cease-fire to negotiate the terms of a possible peace. I believe this is a ploy of the Ash Lord."

"Damn right it is," Sevro says.

"He knows of our division at home and is using it to gain time to regroup his forces around Venus. You all know what I fear by now." I pull up a holoMap and walk along it, dragging my fingers through the asteroids. "I fear dragons. The Raa are coming. Maybe not today. Maybe not tomorrow. But one day Romulus *will* attack. We must consolidate control over the Core before that happens. If we leave the Ash Lord alive, we will be caught between two enemies. We will not win."

"They'll never fight together," Victra says. "They might hate you, but I know Moonies. Even the hostages Octavia used to keep are born hating the Ash Lord. *Never forget. Never forgive.*"

"They do not have to fight together," Sefi says. "They only have to fight against us." With the heavy casualties the Obsidians faced on Mercury, I know she doesn't relish that prospect. Then why didn't her senators vote to support me?

I continue. "The Senate is evidently concerned that I am a liability to the peace process. They have called me a warmonger. As of now, they say I am no longer ArchImperator. Soon, I believe, there will be a warrant for my arrest."

"Might already be one," Sevro mutters under his breath.

"Dancer's a bastard . . ." Rhonna says. When she lived in the hidden city of Tinos, he was like an uncle to her. Her fists clench in anger at the betrayal.

"No. Dancer is a good man. He's doing what he thinks is right with the tools he has," I say. "It's our turn to do the same."

"What are your orders, bossman?" Min-Min asks. "You hiccup and the whole Seventh will storm the Senate and crucify any Pixie who looks at you funny."

"Damn right," Clown agrees. "The Senate is more corrupt than the Syndicate. I say you go in there and dissolve it. Have new, clean elections."

"And what?" Pebble asks her husband. "Darrow rules as an autocrat in the meantime? Don't be ridiculous. The Republic's done if that happens." She looks to me plaintively. "Can't Virginia do anything? Surely she won't let them place a warrant for your arrest."

"Of course she can't do anything," Victra replies. "Majority rules unless she uses Emergency Powers. But she does that, and the Vox Populi will cry tyranny and vote for impeachment. You seen the streets lately? The mob will back them, especially if they think they can end the war. No one cares about Venus."

"She's the Sovereign," Rhonna says.

"Which has one-tenth the power it once did. The silly lion helped write the laws that stripped the Sovereigncy of so much of its power. I told her not to. . . ." Victra sighs. "Idealists never learn."

Holiday stirs uneasily at her place on the wall. "You can't really be thinking of violence, Darrow. If you mobilize the Seventh, then the Home Legions will be ordered against them."

"By whom?" Victra asks. "What general would go against *us*?"

"Wulfgar," Holiday says. "And he'll be the one coming to arrest you, Darrow."

"Patriotic idiot," Min-Min mutters. She turns to Sefi. "Can't you rein him in, big lady? Aren't you their queen or somesuch?" Sefi doesn't even look her way. Her eyes are locked on me.

"Please," Victra says. "Half the people in this room have their faces on coins. The rest have statues. Whatever army they send against us will become our army. One look at Sefi and Darrow and they'll piss their pants." Does she not see how Sefi is watching me?

Victra looks up at me with a grand smile. "Darling, I say we all attend the peace talks. Make it a bit of a party. And once that sanctimonious prick Dancer is put in a cell, we give the Ash Lord our diplomatic reply and send him the head of Julia au Bellona back in a gorydamn box, mouth stuffed with grapes. Or her eyes stripped out and replaced with snake heads. Or Dancer's testicles, whichever you find more thematically appropriate. We can vote! 'Tis a demokracy, after all."

She smiles at the heads nodding along with her, but more than half in the room look nervously at their hands and each other. They're hesitant to go against the Senate. No one wants civil war. Holiday gives voice to their dissent. "I've followed you through hell, Darrow. Don't ask me to follow you through this. I believe in the Republic. We have to put our faith in something. If you march on the Forum tomorrow, you march without me."

"Loyalty gone just like that?" Victra asks. "A mercenary after all."

"And I thought you was hard, Holi," Min-Min says. "Pfah. You're getting peaceful in your menopause."

"Shut up, Min-Min," Pebble says. "She's right."

"That's a load of shit," Sevro snaps. "If they try—"

"Enough," I say, seeing Sefi's growing displeasure at the bickering. "Holiday is right. Gold fell because they let themselves be consumed by civil war. I won't let our Republic fall in the same way. I know how fond we are of escalation." Grins from some of my longest-serving Howlers. "But not this time. The Seventh stays in their barracks. We're not disbanding the Senate. The peace accords will continue. They'll take months."

"So you're, what . . ." Victra says, looking to Sevro, then me, aghast and more than a bit disappointed. "Going to let them arrest you?"

"No, love," Sevro says softly, looking back to me. Our conversation on the shuttle to the Den was short and to the point. "Not quite."

"The Ash Lord is no fool," I say. "Dancer and the Vox Populi are being played. He *wants* me to use the Seventh. He *wants* me to dissolve the Senate and seize power. It would fracture the Colors and allow him to pry them away, by offering stability."

"That's a stretch," Victra says.

"I know him. I will not break the Republic. And I will not be a prisoner. Which is why I am leaving this moon tonight." They look to each other in confusion. "The question is: who's coming with me?"

Sevro steps forward to stand at my side even as the rest of them look at me blankly.

He did not agree with my plan initially. He wanted to stay on Mars and dare the Senate to arrest me at the center of the Seventh Legion barracks.

"To where?" Holiday asks.

"You're running?" Victra almost spits.

"I'm not running. But if I tell you, then you are party to conspiracy," I say. Not to mention, the plan's details will leak like word of the emissaries. I look at each of them, wondering again who betrayed me. "You will be outlaws. Some of you have doubts about this. That, I understand. You followed me to Luna, to Mars, Earth, and Mercury. I will not pressure you now to compromise your oath to the Republic. We are family. We *will* survive this. But if you think your duty is here, it is time for us to part. Vale willing, we will see one another again soon."

For a moment, no one moves. Then Holiday walks around the table to stand in front of me, her face wracked with guilt. "I've followed you everywhere, but I can't abandon the Republic."

"I'm not abandoning it," I say.

"I know you believe that, sir, but I'll remain behind. You may not think you're starting a civil war. But there will be hell to pay. My Sovereign will have need of me." I feel no anger toward her despite the accusation in her voice. We shake hands.

"Watch over my family."

"With my last breath, sir." She thrusts her fist into the air in the Rising salute. "Hail libertas." And in a smaller voice, "Hail Reaper." She departs the room.

Sevro sneers at her departure. "Any other cowards?"

Seeing the doubt Holiday's departure has brought into the room. Colloway xe Char, my best pilot, sighs and lights a burner. His slender body is laconic, his skin a deep ebony and covered with cerulean astral tattoos. He blows a smoke ring, then stands sleepily into it, brushing his blue-black hair from his eyes. "I didn't eat cockroaches to sit at home while you have all the fun." The pilots of Warlock Squadron follow him, including Min-Min. My lancers, Rhonna and Alexandar, join her, followed by a flood of others. Clown can hold back no longer. He bursts to his feet.

"I'll go with," he says. "Darling, you stay with the children."

"Like hell," Pebble says, joining him, though I see the doubt in her eyes.

Sefi and the Obsidians are all who remain.

"Sefi, are you with me?" I ask.

I see her answer before she gives it. Unlike Wulfgar, she doesn't worship at the altar of the Republic. She carries the welfare of her people on her shoulders. When Ragnar died, that was her inheritance.

Slowly, she stands. "I care nothing for Venus or Mercury," she rumbles. "They are not worth Obsidian blood. We have carried the Rising on our backs, and for what?" Her eyes scorch the room. "For Gold to still sit on high? For the rest of the Colors to hate us, call us monsters? For us to speak, and for you to hear nothing?"

"There are still Obsidians left in slavery," I say, though I've seen this coming for some time now. The Obsidians have borne too much— Golds targeted them in the Rain above all others. "Your brother's master still lives," I say. I remember how Ragnar put her hand in mine as he died. I thought the bond would last forever, but I have felt the cracks for years now as I asked more and more from her people. "The Ash Lord made him a slave. Kept him in a fighting ring and made him kill like a dog."

"My brother was a living god." The Obsidians with her nod reverently. "But he is dead and in the mead halls of Valhalla, singing songs before Allmother death. On this middle plane, only I speak with him now." She closes her eyes. Her second eyes, the ones tattooed in blue on her eyelids, stare at me each time she blinks. "And he tells me that my duty is not to Darrow Morning Star. Not to my vengeance. But to my people."

The worst part is I don't know if she is right. If Ragnar were here, what would he do? He dreamed of seeing his people free, and now they are. But they throw their sons and daughters into our war. Is that freedom? Have I used them like a Gold?

I have.

"You dumb yeti," Sevro snaps. "You think the Peace will actually last?"

"No peace lasts, even the wind knows. But I am queen." She looks at me with her black eyes, and as much as I need her, I cannot fault her. I think our spirits are so well matched that she would come with me if she did not carry the burden left to her by her brother. But she does. "If I march with you, Darrow, all Obsidians march with you. I will not. It is time others fight their own battles."

"Sefi . . ." Sevro says desperately, his voice strained, knowing how much weaker we will be without them. "Please."

"I am sorry, halfman. I have spoken." She covers her heart. "Darrow. If we do not meet again in this world, I will save a seat for you in the mead hall beside Ragnar and my kin."

We watch them go, knowing the strength they take with them. And for the first time in a decade, the Howlers are without the Queen of the Valkyrie. I feel somehow as if Ragnar's spirit has finally departed, and it leaves me without his protection.

When the last has left and the door has shut, Clown turns to me.

"So, uh, boss, are we going to rejoin the fleet?"

"No, Clown," I say, trying not to let the loss of the Obsidians steal my confidence. "We're not going to rejoin the fleet. Not going to raise men on Mars. Not going to waste time wrangling with politicians. We're going to Venus to find the Ash Lord and cut off his head."

"Now, that's what I call diplomacy," Sevro says. He laughs maniacally and jumps atop the table, boots shattering a coffee cup. "Who's up for some blood?" He howls hideously, his old mania vibrating through the room. Min-Min shoots up from her seat and howls. And soon the room wails with the cacophony of two dozen maniacs pretending we do not feel the hollowness of the howl absent so many of our friends. As Sevro rages atop the table, I watch Victra motionless in her seat, her hand on her newest child, watching in horror as her husband pretends he's young again.

The doubt creeps in, and I feel so very old.

17

LYRIA

Debt

THE BLUE SKY MOCKS the dead that lie in the mud.

The soldiers and medics that came in the second wave of Republic ships laid the bodies of the dead out in the grass beyond the east wall of the camp. Once those bodies were full of life, but now they're little more than empty husks of skin and bone. The spirits that made them have fled to the Vale of our ancestors. I feel like my spirit has already joined them. A hollowness in my bones as I walk the grass looking for my sister.

Here and there, survivors weep over the bodies of loved ones. A woman makes animal screams over her dead child as others search for their own. My people are taught that this life is just a road to a place we are all going in the end. A place washed in light and love where the very air is thick with laughter of lovers meeting again. I can't see that world. I can only smell the burned bodies. I only see the pale legs smeared with soot. Cracking with dried blood. And everywhere, flies. Fat with blood, they buzz and hover in thick clouds over the dead.

I walk alone, having left Liam with the medics. My arm's slung up; the shoulder throbs despite the meds they've given me, and the skin tickles at the resFlesh bandage holding the wound together. More support ships cut across the midday sky, banking around the columns of thinning black smoke.

I found Tiran where they shot him, facedown in the mud. Bootprints chewed the ground around him. I couldn't even hold him to my heart one last time. His body was a ruin I could not bear. I sicked up and fled, gathering just enough courage to return to our house to see if my father somehow managed to hide.

He did not. I have no parents left.

Now I look for my sister in the killing field.

With every body I pass, I feel the window of hope closing. Knowing there's only so many left. So many steps more till my world falls apart. But I hold on to the stubborn little voice in my head that says maybe she escaped. I pray before I look at each new face, and feel sick as I breathe sighs of relief when it is someone else's mother, someone else's sister dead on the ground.

I'm reaching the end of the last row. She's not here. I don't see the bright blue of her new shoes. Fifteen bodies left. Ten. And then I slow. Heels sinking into the mud. Stomach raveling into knots. The frantic wingbeat of the flies fills my ears and I'm swallowed by horror.

"No. No."

A thin body lies on the ground. Its throat has been hacked through to the spine. Red hair encircles her head in a filthy halo. It's not her. It can't be her. But her children lie beside her, their pieces twisted like broken toys. And one of her shoes hangs loosely on her foot, covered in mud. The other foot is bare. Her lifeless eyes stare at the sky. Eyes that saw my mother birth me. That used to look down at me with perfect love as we lay in bed together under the covers, whispering of boys and the lives we would have. Eyes that fell in love, that watched four children come from her flesh into the world, made cloudless and empty by some angry young man with a hunk of metal in his hand.

I feel the mud on my knees. My hands.

I claw at my sister's body.

Someone shrieks in the distance like they're on fire. And it's long after the medics pull me away from my dead sister and her dead children, long after they stick a tranquilizer into my shoulder, that I realize the screams are my own.

"You must avoid any undue exertion, citizen," the Yellow is saying. "You're lucky to be alive. Keep the wound clean. I'll put your information in the system so the medics at your next stop know to recheck it for infection." I stare through her, watching an iridescent beetle the size of a thumbnail settle on my exposed knee, several inches below where the paper medical smock ends. Its pigment darkens to match my skin.

"Next stop?" I ask, looking up at the medic. She's hard into her forties. Sulfur eyes peer out from a mess of freckles. A white-filtered medical mask covers the rest of her face. Despite the sweat on her brow, she's clean. From a city. Do we disgust her?

"They're taking you and your nephew to a regional medical center," she says. "You'll be safe there."

"Safe," I echo.

She squeezes my good shoulder and then Liam's. "There was a doctor," I say. "Janis."

"I'm sorry. None of the medical staff survived."

She leaves and I lean back in the bed and look down the row of cots. Hundreds of us are clustered beneath the awnings. My pants and the tattered remnants of my shirt are crumpled in a bag at the end of my bed. Liam adjusts his hold on my hand. He hasn't let go since I woke up. I don't know what to say to him.

I'm spared the choice when we're both eclipsed by a shadow. It blocks out the light from the nearby doorway. A man comes through the mosquito netting, drawing the eyes of the doctors, one of whom rushes to him and scoldingly points at some animal that follows him in. The man pushes the animal back out with his foot and then closes the netting. But *man* isn't the right word. No bloody way. On the riverbank, he looked like a statue. Moving, upright, he looks like a god. The Gold's thighs are broader than my da's chest. His hairy hands hang at his sides like giant, swollen mallets. And his head is bald and shiny with sweat and looks made for knocking down doors. Liam hears his footsteps and begins to shake in fear.

"Are you the one known as Lyria?" His voice soothes like the distant rumble of a clawDrill.

"Yes," I manage with a dry tongue. "Who are you?"

His eyes, a dark gold, are small and close together. They glitter in a friendly way as he smiles and pushes himself awkwardly through the cramped confines of the medical tent till he's at my bedside. "I am a man who owes you a great debt, little one. Yes indeed. A great debt. You saved my life."

"Wasn't just me."

"Oh, but it was. I spoke to the Reds at the riverbank, and they told me what you did, despite your wounds. How you swam to the depths for a stranger." He kneels. "I have many that I love who I will now see again, because of you. So I thank you, child, with all my heart." His hands swallow mine. He kisses my knuckles.

"Who are you?" I ask again.

He frowns. "You do not know me?"

"That a crime?" He's taken aback by my tone.

"Telemanus," he announces grandly. He leans back, pleased at the recognition in my eyes. "I am Kavax au Telemanus. Eaglebreaker. Praetor of the Republic."

From my side, Liam gasps. "The Kavax who slew Tiberius au Bellona? And flew with the Reaper to Luna? And cut off Atalantia au Grimmus's leg?"

The Gold hadn't noticed Liam, so low is my nephew to the ground, but now he puffs up his chest like a regular Helldiver, delighted to have his reputation precede him. "I can see this child is very wise." He spares a look at me. "Though I was not alone against the Ash Lady. My daughter was with me." Looking down at my little nephew, Kavax slowly realizes that Liam, with his unfocused, foggy eyes, is blind. The change in the Gold startles me. His voice softens and he kneels so that he is not so far away from my nephew. "And what is your name, young knight?"

"Liam, of Lagalos, *dominus*. But . . . but I'm not a knight. . . ."

"That is a good name, Liam. It is an Old Earth name from the Irish Isles and means warrior, protector."

"Does it?" Liam asks.

"It does indeed. Your people, the first Pioneers, brought more than flesh and blood with them from Earth." He smiles. "I knew a man with such a name and he was very brave; but I fear you are wrong. You are a knight." He puts a hand on Liam's head, startling my nephew. "See . . . yes, you have a hard head. A fighter's head. Just like mine. Do you want to feel my head? I've been told it is the hardest this side of Romulus au Raa." With care, Kavax lowers his head and places Liam's hand upon his great dome.

"You're a bloody plant!" Liam exclaims in shock. His hands reach along Kavax's head to find the end of its dimensions.

"Liam! Mind your tongue." I pray this massive man doesn't take offense. But he just chuckles.

"I am big enough for most things," Kavax says with a grin. "But when I'm not, I call on my friends like your sister here. And we are friends now, little one." He pulls a small silver fox pin from a pouch. He sets it in my palm and closes my hand around it. "If ever you want for anything, show this to any Republic soldier or employee and they will find me, and I and any of my family will do what is in our power to help you. You have my word."

"My family . . ." I say.

"What of them?" He looks around. "Do you want me to fetch them? We need family when we are wounded. It is important. Tell me where they are, and I shall bring them to you."

"They're gone," I manage in a small voice, not having any other words to describe what happened. Their absence does not feel real. But it creeps on me, a dark loneliness.

"Oh." Kavax knows what I mean. His shoulders sag. "Oh, child." I let him take my hand between his own. He leans close enough so I can smell the smoke in his beard and the oil he uses to shape it to a fine point. "I am sorry."

"She said she would protect us . . ." I whisper.

"Who?"

"The Sovereign . . ."

He's silent for a long moment. "I know it may be impossible to believe now, when everything is dark and broken, but you will survive this pain, little one. Pain is a memory. You will live and you will struggle and you will find joy. And you will remember your family from this breath to your dying days, because love does not fade. Love is the stars, and its light carries on long after death."

I can think of nothing to say, so the Gold, called away by an assistant, leaves me there in the bed under the crinkled sheets in the small tent in the middle of a place that never felt like my home. Leaves me there as if his words were a gift. But what the hell use are words? How will they protect us? Feed us? Give us a future?

I will go where the Republic tells me to go. Likely another camp. But without my family this one will be empty of its soul. I don't want that life. I hate this planet. There's nothing holding me here. I suffer enormous guilt for thinking of it like that, but I can't stay here. I'd rather die.

I need more. For Liam. For me.

"Liam, stay here," I say, lunging up out of my bed.

"Where are you going?" he asks in fear. His hands reach for me.

"Just stay. I'll be back."

"Lyria, no . . ."

"Liam!" I snap. He reels back from me. I sigh out the anger and kneel, taking his face in my hands. "I promise I will never abandon you. You're my heart. Be brave, and I'll be back."

I pull my pants from the plastic bag and jump into them. My shirt is bloody and in ruins, so I leave the medical smock on. I can't find my shoes, but there's no time. The nurses are moving toward me. I duck out the mosquito netting before they can block my way. The mud is warm between my toes as I race from the tent without shoes. I sprint fast as I can past soldiers and medics and mourning Reds till I reach the muddy landing strip where traffic controllers wave orange batons at landing shuttles. They look at me like I'm stark mad. I clip past.

No one stops me till I reach the Telemanus shuttle. A brooding black vessel shiny as the belly of a pitviper, with a dancing red fox on its upright wings. It's as tall as any six trees stacked end over end. At the top of a ramp, Kavax speaks with another Gold and a Yellow. Two Gray soldiers with the same strange canines on their chestplates block my way to the ship. Each a head taller than me. One grabs my wrist, easily pulling me against his chest.

"Lord Kavax!" I shout. "Lord Kavax."

He cannot hear me. My voice is too small. The roar of the engines too loud. The soldiers are pulling me away without effort. I call out till my throat is hoarse. But it's not Lord Telemanus who hears me; it's the animal that sits at his side. It looks like a dog with glossy red fur, but it's nearly as large as Liam and has pointed ears and a narrow snout streaked with white. At the sound of my futile shouts, the animal quirks its head, turns to look my way, and then lopes back down the ramp toward me. Only then does Lord Telemanus turn. He follows his pet down the ramp, confused knights and attendants trailing in his wake. Finally he sees me.

"Off," he barks to the soldiers. "Hands off the girl."

They release me, and I push off the one who bruised my arm to stumble in front of Kavax. He towers above me, his eyes quizzical beneath tangled eyebrows. I pant for breath and pull my medical scrubs back into place.

At full height, I barely reach Kavax's belly. In the tent, he seemed kind and human. Here, before hundreds of eyes, he's untouchable. He pitied me earlier. That is why he stood by my bedside. But what am I to him? They say all Colors are equal now, but we all know that's a load of snakeshit.

"Take me . . ." I stammer.

"Up," he thunders. "Speak up. Hard to hear you up here, little one." He chuckles to himself as his pet threads through his legs. There's a watchfulness to the creature. A brain examining me.

"Take me with you," I say in an angry voice.

He doesn't understand. "With us?"

"Yes. With you."

"Child, we're not staying on Mars. We're bound for Luna."

"Lovely. Then you can get me off this rock."

"But . . . this is your home."

"Home? It's a grave."

Kavax frowns, not knowing what to do. A tall, plain-faced Gold in her early forties, who wears a beautiful cloak the color of a storm cloud, drifts to the man's side. Beneath the cloak, she wears cloth instead of metal. Her eyes are not as kind as Kavax's, but dreamy and distant. She carries a large datapad with her medical equipment. "What is it, Father?" she asks.

"The girl wants to come with, Xana. This is the one who saved me."

"Oh, heart." Xana looks pityingly at me. "Father, you know she cannot."

"Please . . ." I beg.

"It's against the immigration regulations," Xana says. "We can't ignore them."

"If . . . if you can't take me . . . at least take Liam. Take my nephew. He deserves to have a chance at life."

Again, Xana shakes her head before her father can respond. "We're bound for Luna. If we take you, everyone will want to come. And the moon is already backlogged for years with refugees."

" 'Everyone' didn't save your da."

"Sorry." She looks past me to the refugees at the tents who stand and watch. "It's an impossible precedent to set. There is a system in place that the Senate designed. We can't simply go against it because we want to. You will be taken care of. You will be protected. It's to your benefit. . . ."

"Protected? Like last time?" I snarl. I know I should rein in my temper. But my face is numb with anger. Tears leak out of my eyes. "You pulled us up out of the mine. You stuck us in this camp. You said it would be for six months, but two years later we're still slagged in the mud. Two *years*. You abandoned us, Gold." I jab a finger up at them. "The Sovereign abandoned us. And now my family is dead. My father, my sister, my brother, my niece, my nephews, because you lied."

"I'm sorry, child," the woman says. "But it's a bit more complicated than that."

"It actually is that fucking simple: the Rising took everything; now it owes me."

"The answer is no." She sets a hand on her father's shoulder. "Come, Father. There's been news from Luna."

"What news?"

Xana looks back at me. "It isn't meant for all ears."

Kavax's eyes are apologetic as he turns to say farewell. I shake my head. "Lord Kavax, you said if I ever needed anything, you would do your best to give it. Are you a liar too?"

"I am sorry, little one. If it were in my power . . . There are regulations. We must obey them. Stupid Senate. I have friends here. I will tell them to come help you. Have patience." He kneels and picks a piece of mud from my trousers. "Farewell." He leaves me at the bottom of the ramp. "Come, Sophocles." He pats his leg, but the animal does not join his master. He's fixated on me. Tail swishing back and forth. "Sophocles?" The animal plods silently down the ramp to my side. He sniffs the air as if it were heady with a delicious scent. And then he lunges. I yelp, thinking he's going to bite me, but instead he's stuck his snout into my pants pocket. Sniffing, he rummages around till he's found what he's looking for. He trots happily back to his master. "What have you got there, my little prince?"

Kavax takes two pieces of candy from the animal's mouth, one green, one purple. The large man's eyes go wild and wide as he tastes the purple. "Grape! It is a sign," he breathes through his white teeth. "A sign!" Xana turns back to see what's happened.

She sighs. "Father . . ."

"Quiet, skeptical child. Sophocles has given Lyria his blessing." The big man holds up the candy to his daughter and comes back to me, his hands gesticulating wildly. "There is magic yet left in the world." He tosses the candy to the animal. "And Sophocles has found it."

"Father."

"Has Luna changed our house, so?" he asks. "Must Sophocles remind us of our Martian honor?" His daughter does not answer. "Apparently! She comes with because . . . because . . ." An idea finds its way from his huge head down into his eyes. He points at the silver pen on my hospital gown. "Because she is now a valet of House Telemanus."

"A valet?" Xana and I ask in unison.

Xana sighs. "Are you going to make the entire village our employees?"

"Just this one. Sophocles has chosen, and House Telemanus does not leave one of their own behind." He puts a heavy hand on my shoulder. My knees almost buckle under the weight. He doesn't notice. "Does that meet your judgment, daughter?"

Xana smiles, surrendering to her father. "I'll add her to the registry. Customs won't like it."

"Well, then they can suck my beard . . ."

"Now you sound like a Barca."

". . . telling me who I can and cannot hire. Uppity, Pecksniffian Pixies." Kavax waves his hands at his men. "Underlings, on your feet! Find her nephew. A little blind knight with a mole on his nose that looks like chocolate. You cannot miss him. Bring him here." He punches his palm with a fist. "We depart with haste."

I stand in shock, not understanding even though I heard well enough. But the soldiers are moving past me, following orders, and Xana is going back up the shuttle ramp into her ship, leaving me alone with her father. I can't believe it is actually happening. We are leaving.

After he watches his daughter disappear into the shuttle, Kavax kneels so he can look me in the eye. "Don't mind Xana. She thinks her duty is to protect everyone from themselves."

"I didn't have anything in my pockets. Did you put the candy in there?"

He turns to me with a mischevious smile. "Sometimes, little one, it's best if the worlds think you a little mad." He winks. "Inspiring what they'll let you get away with."

He extends a hand to me. My fingers wrap only around his index and middle fingers, but he's gentle as a bird despite the calluses, and he pulls me along with him to walk up the ramp into his ship. At the top, before we enter the craft, I stop and look back at the camp. A strange quiet presides. The fires have died. The bodies are being buried. And amidst the tents at the edge of the landing strip, my nephew's head bounces in the breeze as he's carried to us by a fair-haired Obsidian.

I feel Kavax's hand settle on my shoulder and I think of my sister and father and mother and all my family that has lived and died and been swallowed by the ground of this planet. The sadness in me is a well without a bottom. But it is right that I leave. Without my family, this place is just mud and memories. I look up at the sky, knowing my brothers and Ava's husband are out there, somewhere. Several stars are visible even at the height of day. I wonder if my sister looks at them too from the Vale. I know she does. And I know I must live life for the both of us.

"Thank you," I say to Kavax through the tears.

He squeezes my shoulder. "The worlds are very big and you are very small. Do you think you are ready, little one?"

"Yes," I say with a trembling voice. "Yes, I am."

18

EPHRAIM

The Duke of Hands

I SUFFER THE SPLINTERING HEADACHE and telltale nausea of a concussion as I come to. Wish I could say it is a new sensation. There's water trickling nearby. The shuffling of feet and murmur of voices. I'm sitting in a hard chair; metal binds my wrists at the small of my back. The stink of ammonia is like fire ants in my nostrils. I blink groggily and open my eyes.

A table sits before me. Lying in the center is a silver bonesaw. My blood runs cold. Screams echo in memory.

Past the table, an insidiously beautiful man with slender legs, alabaster skin, and eighty-thousand-credit designer cheekbones stands amidst a half-completed highrise. He looks interminably bored. His shark leather boots tap impatiently. His long overcoat, tails falling to his mid-calf, is the color of a rainy midnight street. His tailored pants are black, and so too is his high-collared silk shirt, held together with an onyx clasp. To top off the dashing absurdity of him, his feathery hair is blown straight up like a lazy pink candle flame. Rose-quartz eyes twinkle as he looks out the window into the darkness.

Men linger in the shadows of the unfinished highrise. They wear black leather duster jackets with collars to the ears and tails to the boots. Fleshware glows softly in eyes and jaws and around bald heads covered with bright tattoos.

I feel a deep nauseating fear in my belly as an Obsidian nightmare walks from behind me into my field of vision. He's one of the biggest men I've ever seen. With beetle shell eyes and white hair unbound to his waist, he leans against a concrete support beam in a chrome suit. His face is bloodless. His eight-fingerered hands the size of dinner plates and wormed with blue veins, tipped with immaculate, razor-sharp nails. He flicks a package of ammonia inhalants onto the ground.

"The thief is awake," he says in a low, intelligent voice.

"Thank you, Gorgo," the Pink says. He turns his attention from the darkness and approaches carrying a thin cane with him, twirling it as he goes. The shaft looks like real ivory, but at the sight of the onyx octopus handle I blanch, swallowing down my fear. He sets the cane on the edge of the table and sighs down into his seat.

I grimace. "Well, this is ominous."

The Pink is not amused.

"We are not acquainted, Mr. Horn, but we are a genus in common." Though he is slender, his words are seductive and heavy. It's not my first tangle with his sort. Just as Obsidians are bred to be killing machines, Pinks are made to be fucking machines. Both can be very persuasive. There's levels to them too. Obsidian have their Stained. Pinks have their Roses. Just as rare, about as expensive.

I swallow dryly watching the Pink trace his nails over the tabletop. Idly, I wonder what Gold he used to be a sex pet for. I'd ask, but the little flesh monkeys don't like that very much at all.

"We are both thieves," he says. "But there are two subspecies of thieves in this world. The first thinks anything that can be taken should be taken. This thief believes in anarchy. The second subspecies is one who believes that not everything should be stolen. That some things must be sacred. This thief believes in order. My question, then, is which subspecies are you, Mr. Horn?"

"I'm afraid you've got your wires crossed," I say, stretching my neck. "I'm not a thief. I'm an insurance investigator."

"No. That is what you were. But I wasn't asking that."

"Look, I know we all look like—"

"Ephraim ti Horn." He interrupts softly and without breaking eye contact. "Born 707 PCE at Courneuve Hospital in Evenstar, Hyperion. Current residence at 777 16B Salt Place, Upper West Promenade Level 17. Known associates: Volga Fjorgan, Cyra si Lamenis, and Dano . . . *Sunshine*?"

"I told him it was a shitty name. But it was between that and Starfall." No one laughs. "Tough crowd."

But this isn't some street shakedown. They've got resources and money. My name's not much of a secret. But knowing my address? That information costs more than a couple drinks at a dark dive. And knowing my birthplace? Only one damn soul on Luna knows where I was born, and Holiday wouldn't touch these people through decontamination gloves. Only way they'd know is if they had my old legion records. That's some deep data.

I look back at the octopus cane.

The Pink watches me for a dreadful moment, and I remember a rumor I once heard in the Rising that during the Battle of Luna some of the platoons used Pinks as human lie detectors in the fields when they couldn't get their hands on tech. Makes sense. They're all about the subtle shades.

"Yeah, you got my name right. Golden laurel to you," I say. "But I'm no thief."

"Disappointing," the Pink murmurs. "Very disappointing." He looks back down at the bonesaw. "It tires the mind, these telarian games. All these street pretenders weaving their webs, forgetting they are the flies, not the spider. Since you evidently cannot answer a complex question, I will ask a simple one. Mr. Horn, where is my sword?"

A knot forms in my throat.

They're going to melt the flesh off my bones.

"Your sword?" I frown. "Sorry, citizen, I'm more of a gun man. Unless you were talking euphemistically about your cock. In which case, it might be in that one's mouth." I jerk my head to the one he called Gorgo. The monster's black eyes have not left my face. "He looks like he swallowed more than mead and roast beast in his time."

The Pink bursts out laughing. His men do not. They glance at Gorgo in dead silence. "What do you think of him, Gorgo?"

Gorgo smiles, revealing a mouth full of gold-plated teeth. "Humor seems to be his survival mechanism, my lord. Under the current circumstances it may indicate suicidal tendencies. Shall I punish him?"

"Perhaps later," the Pink says. "For now, I am enthralled. Mr. Horn, you delight me. It's been too long since someone took a chance at making me laugh. Good comedy is always such a risk." He wets his lower lip with his tongue. A slow, intentional motion that might be for my benefit, or simply a learned sexual methodology taught to him in the Garden of his youth. "Do you know who I am?"

"Give me a hint."

His lips curl back from his teeth. *"Ave Regina,"* he says hoarsely in Latin. As the syllables vibrate from his lips, a ghostly, Byzantine tattoo crown appears on the skin of his forehead in ink that moves almost like the tentacles of an octopus sprouting spiked thorns. The centerpiece of the crown is a black hand.

"Do you know who I am, now?" he asks as the voice-activated ink begins to fade till his skin is clear and pale porcelain again.

"Yeah," I say numbly.

"Then say my name, Mr. Horn." He raises an eyebrow. "Will you make me tell you twice?"

"You're the Duke of Hands."

"How clever you are!" He leans back in his chair. "And do you know why they call me that?"

"I've heard rumors." I eye the bonesaw.

"Excellent. Gorgo here is of the conviction that we should hurt you to loosen your tongue. It always comes to savagery these days. More efficient. But now that the Territory Wars are behind our little underworld, I was hopeful that you would be cultured enough for a civil conversation."

"You've an interesting definition of 'civil.'"

"It's all relative. So, since now you know who I am, and all attendant threats are implied, is it safe enough to assume we will be honest with one another?"

"Suppose there's a first time for everything."

"Good," he says. "Good. That makes it simpler." He claps his hands together and stands. "You were here during the Battle of Luna, yes?"

"All three years."

"Fighting for the Rising?"

"For part of it."

"Change of heart?"

"No. I just saw enough body parts separated from their owners." I don't feel like going into the politics of it like I did with Holiday.

"Then you would have witnessed the Rape of Hyperion?"

"Liberation, you mean. Made you fellows rich." He stares at me till I clear my throat. "All right. 'Rape of Hyperion' is much slicker sounding."

He continues. "After the Sovereign died but before the Ash Lord's counterattack to relieve the marooned legions and Peerless, Hyperion lay black. During that time, the Hyperion Museum of Antiquities was looted by soldiers who had promised to protect it, by citizens who thought only of their own pockets. As the moon steeled itself against the next wave of war, those cretins absconded with the combined heritage of man. A heritage shared by all Colors.

"As you know, all commerce that flows through the black markets of Luna is my province. My domain, as given to me by my queen. When I discovered a trove of stolen treasures being hawked by ex-legionnaire baboons, I looked at it as my duty as a citizen of Luna that they be returned to their rightful place. Now I find that the crown jewel of my donation, the Sword of Silenius, has been stolen . . . again. Our ears told us that it was a very particular sort of heist. One that only a few freelancers would be capable of executing."

"Well, there's not many of us left," I say. "You're dressing them all up in dusters and giving them juicy contracts to steal for you."

"Out of chaos, us. Thieves of order," he says, and traces his finger along the table in one elegant movement. It reminds me of the time I took Trigg ice-skating. He didn't move with the elegance of this man's finger, and that was what I loved about him. There's no honesty in elegance, not in the elegance of humans at least. "When you took my sword from the museum, did you know from whom you were stealing?" the Duke asks.

"I did not."

"Lying," Gorgo says.

"Convince me," the Duke says. I don't know where to begin. "Would you be more eloquent with a grenade in your mouth? I have some on board." He nods back to the yacht idling on the landing pad beyond the construction floor.

"Do I look like an idiot?" I ask. "If I'd known, I'd have walked away. Shit, I'd have shot the man who asked me to do it. There's a difference between bold and stupid. I know which side this falls on."

"Do you?" the Duke asks. "Your reputation says otherwise. It reads as if you have a . . . death wish."

"That again . . ." I roll my eyes and feel a stabbing pain behind them.

"Four of your heists in broad daylight. Nearly always public spectacles."

"I work for middlemen. Arbiters. Occasionally they leave out details about the job. In this case, important details like whose protection the sword was under." I lean forward, selling hard because my life depends upon him buying what I'm selling. "I don't rat. And I don't play with the Syndicate. Man has to have a code."

Any moment now I expect to feel a carbon hard wire around my neck. Or the nip of one of those Martian pitvipers Syndicate thorns love to import just for play. The last thing I'll see is this pretty jumped-up ganglord reclining in his chair like he's king of the universe, when he used to be little more than a sex toy. All this new money expects everyone else to have a short memory. Wish I did.

But the wire doesn't come. Neither does the bite.

"In the Gardens, they teach us body empathy as well as the art of shadow dancing—a proportional mimicking of body language to make the subject at ease," the Duke says. "It facilitates emotional bonding. It makes me ghastly good at sniffing out liars." He seems to disdain his schooling, but he leans back till he's a shadow version of me. Shoulders slouched, legs out, a perfect replica. "You, my dear, have a dishonest face, so it's easy to tell when you're telling the truth."

"So you believe me?"

"I do."

I hesitate. "Then I can go?"

"What a pleasant world that would be. Although you were ignorant in your crime against me, it was, as you know, also a crime against the Queen herself. So I'm afraid you don't just walk away from this." He smiles sympathetically. "I'm the sort of man who would let you go if it was just between us. I see how frightened I've made you. To be honest, that's often punishment enough. But I fear this isn't just between us any longer. Others know. The Duke of Hands has been made into a fool. I can't have that." He leans across the table, a vein pulsing in his temple. "Can't have that at all. In words of Old Stoneside, 'Mercy emboldens evil men.' You and I have the misfortune of floating amongst a sea of evil men. A debt is owed. A debt must be paid."

I can't even think of anything to say. The ramifications of his words cause a spike of fear to go straight into my chest. They're going to hurt me, badly.

"Please, don't fret. It won't be anything inequitable. If you'd crossed the Duke of Legs, you'd be wobbling around on those grafted metal prosthetics the rest of your life. And if you insulted the Duke of Tongues, you'd be gibbering like one of those Lost City black-teeth—he is much crueler than the last one. But I'll only take your least favorite hand." He smiles as Gorgo slips forward. "Promise."

Now comes the garrote. A thin wire looped around my throat from behind by Gorgo, not enough to break the skin or trachea, but enough to let me know they will if they need to. It immobilizes me. "Which hand will it be?" the Duke asks. "You owe me a debt. Choose." I rear back against the garrote, but Gorgo's fingers are the size of potatoes. "Choose."

Sense abandons me. My mouth is dry, my body shaking.

"The . . . left," I manage as they ease off the wire.

The Duke nods to his thugs and they grab my left arm. I stare in horror as he picks up his bonesaw and turns it on. The razor-sharp sawteeth vibrate. Sheer panic grips me now. The memory of flesh peeled from muscle, how the fat separates from bone, and the screams of friends. I watched, once, and all I thought was, *Thank Jove it isn't happening to me.* The guilt returns. The sound of my friends shouting to each other in a bombed-out Endymion building. *"Don't rat! Don't rat!"* The fear and sight to come of metal teeth gnawing through my body. The grisly, butcher-shop look of naked muscle. I search frantically for something to haggle with, but there's nothing I have that he wants. I feel a desperate, pitiful sob building in my chest that I don't let out. The Duke lowers the bonesaw toward my wrist. The teeth buzz like insect wings. I grit my teeth and close my eyes.

"There is a way to keep this hand," he whispers. "Tell me where the sword is."

"I don't know! I sold it to my broker already."

"Tell me his name."

"I . . . can't."

"Why not?"

"I told you. I don't rat," I say coldly. The way it comes out of my mouth soothes me. I'm less afraid, because I have a reason now to let them take the hand. A conviction.

Forgot what that felt like.

"I could carve through your ribs." He twirls the bonesaw. "Take your manhood. Carve off your toes. Turn your eyes to jelly. You'd tell me then, if I really wanted to find your broker." He's going to do it now. Gorgo's cologne fills my nostrils. "Tell me who he is!"

I glare up at the Duke. "Get to it, asshole."

He stares down at me, then laughs. "Gorgo, I believe you owe me a diamond." He turns off the bonesaw. The garrote around my neck disappears. I look up to see the Obsidian shuffle forward, rummage through an alligator skin billfold and pull out a teardrop diamond that he sets in the Duke's hand. The Duke slips the diamond into his pocket and smiles down at me as the Obsidian eases away. "I've been tearing Luna apart for someone like you, Mr. Horn. A man with a code."

"What?" The adrenaline floods out of my body, leaving me as limp as empty clothes. "What are you talking about?"

"Oslo said you were bright. Odd. A White prone to exaggeration."

I blink dumbly. I didn't say his name.

"You know Oslo?" I ask.

"Do I know Oslo? Ha! Your broker has often served as an intermediary between the Ophion Guild and the Syndicate. If you had betrayed him, well, that would have been the end of Ephraim ti Horn. But instead, treasure awaits. You see, the master of thieves"—he touches his black jacket where his heart allegedly beats—"happens to be in need of a thief of chaos. And who better than one recommended by Mr. Oslo and tested by me? There is something of particular significance I would like to acquire. This, my dear Gray, was the final part of your audition. And congratulations. You passed with flying colors."

I blink up at the madman. "The sword. You had me steal the sword . . . from you?"

As an answer, a gleaming smile splits the man's face.

I sit there, my body shivering from the adrenaline leaving the system, still not entirely sure he's not going to snatch my hand and saw it off. "You're a special kind of asshole," I mutter.

"You've clearly never met the other Royals." He touches his chest in offense. "I'm the tender one."

"The Syndicate has enough thieves," I say. "Why do you need me?"

"Are any as good as you?" he asks, attempting flattery.

"Three, at least. The Figment, Zendric . . ." I shake my head, wishing I had taken Holiday up on the job offer. "I told you, citizen. I don't mess with the Syndicate. You boys play too hard. Whatever job you want me to do, use your men." I glance at his thorns and Gorgo in particular. "I don't wear a collar."

"We all wear collars," the Duke says, tapping his forehead where the invisible crown lies dormant. "Some are more comfortable than others. And now it's your turn, Mr. Horn." He pulls something from his pocket and sets it on the table. They call it the Queen's Kiss. A black iron rose that can bribe Watchmen, open doors, and intimidate even senators of the Republic. It is the warrant of the Syndicate's ruler, and those few dark creatures who carry it do so at her bidding.

"This is not a request. The debt is still owed. By you, the Obsidian, the Green, and the Red," he says quietly. "Now, I assume a man with your reputation, with your . . . history, is prone to vendettas. I warn you against thinking of this as an onus set upon your shoulders, and instead counsel you to look at it as the greatest opportunity of your lifetime." He points out the window with his cane. "You have a chance to become more than a thief. With the Syndicate, you can ascend. You can rule. Serve me well and this world can become your playground."

His silken words are lost on me. I don't want to ascend. Could give a shit about their games or their ridiculous delusions of grandeur—they're just another gang with better than average organization and accounting. Sooner or later, they all eat themselves. But even though I might stand on a ledge and think about jumping, that doesn't mean I want to get bonesawed to death. That's what will happen if I say no. Or he'll go for my team first. And I'll hear the screams all over again. I think of Volga standing there in the rain looking like a lost puppy.

"I'll do it," I mutter. "Now, what's the prize?"

The Duke of Hands laughs merrily. "Glad you asked! My darling, we're stealing the most valuable thing in all the worlds."

19

EPHRAIM

Pernod

M Y ASSOCIATES STARE AT the Queen's Kiss on my glass coffee table. They have not moved since I set it down. I examine the drooping clock in the painting on the wall. One of my favorite Dalís. With the original lost or destroyed, even a forgery of *La persistencia de la memoria* is a treasure. This one I stole from a robber-baron Silver in the Mass. Time stands as still in the room as in the painting.

"This is a lark, isn't it? Another one of your games, Eph," Cyra finally says, waving her hands in her animated way.

Dano chuckles to himself from his place on the formofabric couch next to me. He's sprawled on it like a drunk cat, leg over the armrest. Overcompensating his slickness like we all don't know how insecure he is about being fifty kilos soaking wet. He smothers his spent burner in the coffee-cup-turned-ashtray on his stomach and lights another. The smoke slithers into the air, stained green and purple by the AI lover advertisements that writhe out the window on the building adjacent mine.

Cyra sneers at him. "Is this a joke to you too?"

"Lass, life's a joke," Dano whispers as smoke comes out his nostrils.

"Wonderful. It's all a joke. And we're the damn punchline." Cyra stares at the untouched vodka lemon I poured her, trying to come to grips with the tale of my night with the Duke. I want her to drink it. Shit, drink four of them, woman. She's a damn stress when she's sober, and only mildly tolerable when inebriated.

It's the late hours of the evening, dark cycle. A sluggish late summer rain falls on Hyperion. And I'm stuck between a madman with a buzzsaw and a job that will certainly kill me. I feel a sense of resignation. This is the end of the line. What the Syndicate asks is impossible. This business is so far past their paygrade I thought the Duke was joking.

We're going to die. But dying pure and quick on a job is better than dying slow at their hands. Now, just have to convince my crew. If I don't, anyone who doesn't play along will have an octopus in their mouth and their body in a gutter by morning.

"This is your shit, Eph," Cyra says. "They came to you. So, fine. You take the contract. I'm not interested. Never wanted to tangle with those psychos. If you're smart, you'll realize you shouldn't get involved in this shit either. This is *big*. Too big."

"You are not out," Volga says without any malice. "Ephraim needs our help. He helped us. You are in."

"Slag that."

"Yeah, I'm with the grass ass for once," drawls Dano, burner dangling from the corner of his mouth. "This is manic, and not in a sexy way."

Volga leans forward. Cyra involuntarily flinches. "Dano, you would be in Whitehold or dead if it weren't for this man. Cyra, where would you be if Ephraim did not pay your debt to that data shark? I would still be on Earth, loading boxes and collecting loans from sad men so I could eat." I watch her with an unfamiliar warmth going through me. I hurt her outside the bar, but still she has nothing but love for me. Why? "We will help him because he helped us."

Dano claps his hands. "Bloodydamn fine speech."

"Cut the yapping, you mutant," Cyra sneers at Volga. "No one owes anyone anything here."

"They know who you are, Cyra. They know who we all are," I say into my Pernod. It's a drink from the days back when I used to care, emerald green with the taste of licorice. Trigg loved them. I knocked back a pair while waiting for my team to arrive, watching the news recycle clips from the Reaper's dismantlement at the hands of the Vox Populi. Lionheart couldn't do anything to stop it. Made me feel warm and fuzzy, seeing the king and queen get caught with their pants down.

"They want my team. It wasn't a request."

"What if we refuse it?"

"We refuse the Queen's Kiss, we're dead," I say.

Cyra has a burst of inspiration. "We can leave town. Set up farside in Endymion. There's plenty of work there."

"I'm not going to Endymion," I say sharply.

"Eph . . ."

"No, actually it's a grand idea. Their Endymion outfit will be waiting to welcome us to the city. Show us the sites. The Crescent Orb, the Tridian Palazzo, the Ephor Spires." I put a finger gun to my head and pull the trigger. "Then they kill us."

"We can go off-planet."

I sigh. "The Duke of Legs has men in the docks. They'll kill us in transit."

"Then we don't fly commercial. We charter a ship farside out of Eridan Interplanetary. I can wipe the transit records. Or get us documents for Earth or Mars."

"Cyra, you *might* have enough money to charter a ship. But to buy vintage Solar Republic passports with hologram veracity and magnetic coding on this timetable?" I ask, knowing how dearly she fancies her sparkling new condo in the Sordo District. One of the new Redache glass buildings. Gaudy shit. "After the down payment on your haunt, how much do you have left?"

"It's none of your. . . ."

"Your mortgage has a bigger appetite than Volga, love. And those diamonds you're wearing aren't exactly sale items. From Gustave's?" Her face pinches. "Don't get tight, I'm not going through your receipts. But new money all shops the same." She looks embarrassed, but I keep punishing, because I need her to know there's only one way out. "So . . . after the diamonds, the mortgage, the server farm in your spare room, I'd say you have maybe fifty thousand in your account." By her expression I know it's less. Lady loves to spend. "Gods. You don't even pay taxes and you're broke!"

She's not done trying. "We could combine our money. Dano. How much do you have?"

"Me?" Dano looks up from his datapad, where he's texting one of his warm bodies. "Rooting in the wrong mine, lass. I like fliers and Pinks too much to gather commas in the old account. Sin's a hungry slag. What about you, tinman?"

"I'm dry," I say.

"Tables leech you?"

"Something like that."

"You're a mess of degenerates," Cyra mumbles.

"I have money," Volga says from the window.

Cyra wheels on Volga. "How much?"

"All of it."

"All of your share?" Cyra asks, incredulous.

"Yes."

"From all our contracts?"

"Yes." Volga hesitates, embarrassed. "Well . . . I must eat. And I eat much more than you . . . smaller people. And I like beer. And I pay my landlord each cycle change. He says I am the best tenant." She blushes. "And . . . and sometimes I go to the Cerebian. You know. The zoo? I like the popcorn and the animals. And the people are all so happy. Especially the children. But I go in the middle of the day, so tickets are cheaper," she adds quickly at the end to mitigate the gross expenditure.

"Volga!" I feign astonishment. "You're out of control. A regular hedonist."

"I know," she mutters, shaking her head at herself. "I know."

"I'm joking, Volga. You're as parsimonious as a White."

"Thank you," she says, beaming, then squints. "Parsimonious. That is a fine word."

"That should be more than enough money," Cyra chirps. "With that much we can get a real starrunner. Maybe even buy a used—"

I toss the last centimeter of my Pernod into her lap.

"What the hell," she sputters.

"You're a horrible person," I say. "That's Volga's money."

"Kinda slagged up, Cyra," Dano says.

"Because I want to live?"

"I don't mind," Volga says. "I will share."

I know she's been saving the money from our jobs to buy herself some acreage on Earth. All those dreams of Luna, and now she wants to start a refuge for carved animals that have been discarded by their masters. She told me one night when she was drunk. She wants zebracores and griffins and all other manner of beasties that will probably eat her in her sleep. She doesn't remember, but I do, and I'll be damned if I let these other two take her piece.

"Yes, you do mind, Volga. Or I mind for you. It doesn't matter if we had ten million credits to spend. Wherever we go, they'll find us and kill us."

"There's another option," Cyra says. "We could take it to Republic Intelligence."

Dano sniffs the air obnoxiously. "Odd, Eph. A prime spot like this having the smell of rats."

"I'm not a rat," Cyra says.

"You smell like a rat. Know what we'd do to rats in Lost City?"

"You little ruster . . ."

"What did you call me?" he says, sitting up at the word.

"I'm not a rat. . . . I just don't want to die an old woman at the bottom of the sea. Deepgrave is what'll happen if we try this."

Cyra pushes at her temples with shaking hands.

I lower my voice to Cyra. "Headache?"

She nods. "Forgot to bring my stuff."

"I've told you a dozen times. You gotta lay off the cyberplay." I pull my silver dispenser from my jacket and choose a zoladone. "Earth knockoff, but it should do the trick." She takes the pill greedily and leans back in her chair.

She snorts and downs her vodka. I pour another for her. "Better?"

"No!" She rubs her eyes. "Why us?" she asks me. "What did you do? I know this is because of something you screwed up. Someone you owe."

"Not this time."

Volga could blow all this open if she says I met with a Howler right before getting picked up by the Duke. She saw Holiday's wolfcloak. But the big girl stays quiet.

"You're gonna do it?" Dano asks me. "You wanna do it."

I decidedly do not want to do it.

"It's the heist of the century," I say with a smile. "Look on the shiny side. The Syndicate has never broken its own rules. Not once. If we acquire the prize, there's no reason to believe they won't pay us the commission. *Eighty million credits.*" Dano whistles. Volga doesn't react. Cyra looks numb. "And if we survive to spend it, we don't have to steal anything ever again. Buy an island. Buy a star cruiser. You're free. Nothing can touch you. Not even this war."

That sells them. Cyra leans back to rub her temples and sip her vodka, in the shallow, warm waters of the zoladone high now. She stares at the black rose. No larger than my palm, it feels bigger than the room. Pulsating evil. "What's the timeline?"

"A month."

She stares placidly at me and nods, the zoladone cooling her blood. Dano's more animated. He pauses midway to lighting another burner. "This gets better and better."

"A month is not long," Volga says.

"We need four months to plan this," Dano says. "A year . . ."

"I know. Apparently that is nonnegotiable. We got a month. Less, actually." No one interrupts. "We were given three specific locations and times when the prize will be in public. We just have to pick the juiciest."

"How do we have this information?" Volga asks grimly. "This will not just affect us. It is important to know."

"They've got their tentacles everywhere." I shrug. "Your guess is as good as mine. Question, Cyra." I snap my fingers to bring her attention back from her high. "How long would it take for you to don your black hat and pillage some data from Epirus and Leomant?"

"The accounting firm? Depends on their firewalls. That's some high-grade software. Why?"

"Because I need to know who pays whom. We need an inside man."

"Bloodyhell . . ." Dano says, eyes fixed on his own datapad. "The Senate has just issued an arrest warrant for the Reaper."

We look to each other, sharing the same morbid thought. A game is afoot and we are pieces on the board. I look out the window to Hyperion and wonder what is about to shake my city. But in the back of my mind, I care more about the collar on my neck and who really holds the leash.

I take the holocube that the Duke of Hands gave me and activate it. The pale light washes out the contours of my crew's faces. The three locations glow in the air. I sit back in my chair, knowing they believe deep down we can pull this off. They're young enough to have never failed. To never have been captured. But the chance for success is so small, so absurd, that I know we are gallows bound. Yet it seems a dignity to take that chance, to grasp it for all it is worth and not fall under the hacking of the blade of a bonesaw, not off the ledge of some thoroughfare, but on the stage, heart pulsing, feet racing, all the variables falling into place one last time.

The game is afoot. And finally, I begin to smile.

20

LYSANDER

Dragons

I'M BLIND WHEN THE COMMANDOS storm the ship. Their stun grenades emitted white flashes that activated every photoreceptor cell in my eyes. Though we surrendered, they beat us beyond sense. I take several rifle butts to the back of my head and finally reel sideways as one bloodies my nose.

They grab my hair and slam my head to the ground. A boot presses down on my head as they frisk me and cuff my hands behind my back with magnetic shackles. They latch a second metal cuff around my right ankle and jerk the two shackles together so that I'm hogtied, blind, and bellydown on the floor. Something tight slithers around my neck and constricts.

With six seconds of ancient method, they strip my humanity away.

I feel them dragging me. Slowly, indistinct shapes coalesce, though a pulsing blue afterimage remains in my vision. They carry the crew we rescued out of the ship with me.

I see one of them screaming uncontrollably and holding on to a metal panel. A soldier stomps on his hands till they break. The blood leaks down my throat from my broken nose. There's horrible choking from someone nearby. Thick, asthmatic barking from animal throats and a blitz of commands.

Stay down.
Slag the floor.
Hands behind your back.
Nose to metal.
Nose to metal, gahja!

This is my fault.

Not the choice to lead us to the asteroid, but my hubris or vanity or misguided honor, whatever it was that led me off that lift, into the corridor, wasting seconds and then making the gamble that might now cost us our lives. And for what? Out of loyalty to a Color so devious they destroyed themselves? It was such an illogical chain of decisions of which I am ashamed.

A wet, mucus-filled mouth snaps centimeters from my face.

Scaled paws and serrated talons scratch the metal deck. I twist myself and see point-blank the four-legged *kuon* hounds—insectoid-canid hybrids. There are three of them; bred for war. Chitinous black shells along their torsos ripple gray as they move. Spines of needle-thick translucent hair stand on end upon their backs. The Gray houndmaster jerks the beast back from me. Its bark is deafening, its eyes yellow and compound. I shudder away from the hound, trying to master my fear.

It's impossible.

My grandmother's lessons and Aja's meditations flee as my heart slams in my chest, and boots against the deck match the beat as a second squad moves up into our ship. A terrifying old Gold woman in a brown cloak with a bald pate and a laconic drawl issues orders to the soldiers around her to search the ship for bombs and other passengers. A Blue woman, one of the crew we rescued from the *Vindabona,* finds the chaos more than she can bear. She panics and tries to run.

They let her go, perhaps as sport, perhaps to set an example, and after her tenth step, the small metal cuff on her right ankle blinks green and detonates. The lower ends of the tibia and fibula explode. A flash of sizzling light cauterizes the wound. She screams and spills to the ground, leaving her foot behind. Leg wheezing smoke. The kuon hounds are released and pin her on her back, one tearing into her thigh, the other biting her right wrist, before waiting for the next command. The houndmaster looks to the old Gold woman. She gives the command herself.

"Yokai." The old Gold looks to the largest of the kuon. *"Hakaisuru."*

The largest kuon lunges like a rail slug out of a barrel and the Blue woman's face disappears into its maw.

"Stop!" I shout, trying to rise up.

A steel-toed boot disabuses me of my empathy.

When I come to in a small pool of my own spit, I see the world sideways. The boot is still on my head. Nausea wraps me in a hot cocoon. There's weeping to my right from the lowColors we rescued. Two of the hounds are still hunched over the Blue woman, snapping and snarling as they feed on Blue bones brittle from a youth spent in low gravity. I force myself to watch and see what my mistakes have wrought.

Cassius meets my eyes from his place on the ground nearby. His face is unrecognizable but the cool look there gives me strength. *Patience,* it says. I focus on breathing, on allowing everything else to rage around me, and control myself.

A bored young Gold with a hollow, pale face stands with her boot on Cassius's head and her *hasta,* a long razor, balanced just above his spinal cord. Pytha shivers in fear beside me, listening to the hounds feed.

"Do not be so maudlin, *gahja,*" the woman says to Pytha, pulling up her head by the hair so she must watch the kuons feed. "It's just carbon."

I dare to steal a look at the *Archi.*

They've pulled her into a large hangar with a pulseShield sealing the open bay to space. We lie in front of our home, surrounded by a cadre of Peerless Scarred. They're tall and severe. Their bodies elongated by the low gravity of their birth. Their hands and faces pale from their long absence from the sun, but callused and battered by the harsh elements of their volcanic plains and ocean moons. They wear loose-fitting storm-colored cloaks. Arrogance earned fills the room, radiating from them. Gray legionnaires inspect the outside of our ship with Orange techs. Guarding each of us are several Obsidian slave knights. Not the freeColors of the Republic, but the indoctrinated slaves of an imperial system. In their minds, they serve the gods. They wear tribal cloaks, carry axes, and wear thin gray metal collars like the one they strap on my leg. Buzzing about the rest of them are half a dozen other Colors—mechanics and support staff. It's like watching an ant colony.

I've not seen such harmonized efficiency before, not even when watching Luna's preparations for the Rising's siege. The old Gold woman bends in front of Cassius and looks him in the eye. She doesn't like the fierce look she finds there. She lets him go and turns to me.

"The young one," she rasps. She stands looking down at me as one of the Obsidians pulls me to my knees by my hair. Her cruel eyes are the color of bitter sulfur, set in a face calloused and riven with age. Lips like two whispers of shed snakeskin pull back from small teeth and receding gums. "You tread near our ink, *gahja*. Why?"

"We're traders," I manage with little dignity, but I meet her eyes as best I can, hoping to merit some degree of respect from her for my obvious mettle.

"*Why?*"

"Ascomanni came. . . ."

"Why were you in the Gulf?"

I fight back the quick answer. The frightened answer. And I follow a memory back to a room in the Citadel where I listened to my father whisper to himself as he read beside me so many years ago. I smell the bitter aroma of his tea, recall the crisp fibers of the cellulose pulp between my fingers as I turned the pages of my own book.

"We . . . seek sanctuary," I say, back now in the room with the Gold woman.

"Sanctuary?" The Gold masticates the word.

"Under article 13, clause c of the Compact: 'Any full Aureate Citizen of the Society may, when life and property are threatened, invoke a right of temporary trespass on government, private, and military space to seek sanctuary from pirates and illegal elements.'" The words are verbatim those in my small copy of the Compact I owned as a child. I look into her dead eyes, seeking common ground, but standing my own. "The Core may have abandoned order, but it was my understanding that the Rim still obeyed the laws of our Ancestors. Am I mistaken?"

Her face is a desert. No emotion. No life in the creases and crags. Only a barren foreboding. Without blinking or moving her gaze from mine, she takes a gnarled thumb and slowly presses it into my right eyeball. I lurch backward, more struck and horrified by the casualness of the violence than by the pain it brings. Then she pushes harder, gripping my head with her other hand. I thrash. The capillaries pop, the tissue stretches inward, the nail cuts in.

"You are spies."

I gasp. "We are not . . ."

"Who paid you to cross the Gulf, *gahja*? Do you have sensor equipment in your ship? What is your name? Your mission? These are things you will answer."

"Venator!" a Gray calls from the ramp. "It's her."

She removes her thumb from my eye and I gasp at the release from pain. Even in the haze of pain, I notice what they call her. Venator. The woman is some form of elite policing unit. She twists her turkey neck to look up at the Gray. "Her?" she rasps. "She's in *this* ship?"

"Yes, Venator. She's in their medbay. Wounded direly."

"At last. Does she have a storage device on her?"

"I don't know."

"Find out." She speaks into her datapad. "Break radio silence. Send a direct transmission to subQuaestor Marius. Tell him we have a small, flat stone in our possession and ask for instruction." The woman turns to the Peerless behind her. "Is the Storm Knight back with his squadron?"

The Storm Knight I knew is dead, killed by the Reaper himself above the Great Barrier Reef on Earth. They must have a new order of Olympic Knights out here. How antiquated they suddenly seem, seeking to replicate the glory of what once was. And yet some boyish part of me is glad that the order has not yet fallen.

"They're docking presently, Venator."

"Can they be stalled?" she asks quietly.

"He's already out of his cockpit. They'll be here in minutes."

She makes a bitter face. "Seek him out. Tell him his sister is here, before he finds out from another. And summon a medical squad." She turns back to me and Cassius, measuring us, wondering about our part in this, but not yet lifting us from the deck. It's then I notice the onyx implant on her hand. A snake slithers around the webbing and up over her knuckle to devour its own tail. A relic from an earlier war. *Krypteia*. The secret police and intelligence agency of the Moon Lords. My grandmother claimed to have purged them all after Rhea burned. Who is this woman?

There's a reverent silence when a Peerless Scarred in his mid-twenties with shoulder-length white-gold hair streaked black marches into the hangar wearing the kit of a fighter pilot. Gloomy, narrow eyes brood within a pale, beardless face that bears the vestiges of beauty underneath a depository of brutality. Large lips, long eyelashes, the rest scars and scowls and crooked cartilage. He wears all gray, and on the helmet in his left hand is painted the image of a dragon cloaked in cloud and lightning. As for ears, he has only his right. Three men in gray follow him. The man's eyes darken further as he sees the kuon hounds chewing on the remains of the crewmember. The force of him is so raw, so true and uncalculating, that he seems as pure as a natural element. Undimmed by compromise, untamed by society. He makes me feel trapped, impure, and suddenly so small as I realize men like him can exist.

The old woman stands before him as if facing down a thunderhead.

"Diomedes," she says.

"Venator Pandora, where is she?" His low voice is a product of hardship, but it is the name that shakes me from the spell he's cast. *Pandora*. I thought she was a Rim myth. Their greatest assassin. *The Ghost of Ilium*, withered and aged, but breathing still.

"On the ship. The medics are bringing her out," Pandora rasps. Diomedes storms past her up the ramp just as the Yellows bring the Gold girl out on a gurney. They stop as he approaches.

"Little Hawk," he says tenderly. He kisses the girl's face and pushes his forehead to hers, nearly weeping. "Little Hawk. I thought you were for the dust."

"Diomedes," she says in a low voice, barely audible from my place on the deck. Nearly delirious from the morphone, she reaches up to caress his face as I strain to see it better. "My joy. What . . . how are you here?"

"Where else would I be?" He smiles slowly. "When a sister is lost, a brother seeks. Father sent me, Seraphina."

Seraphina . . . I know the name, just as I know her brother's. I glance over at Cassius. The names have not been lost on him, and any hope that was in my friend expires.

"Father . . ." she murmurs.

Diomedes nods. His voice tightens. "Pandora is here as well."

"No . . ." the girl says with a start. She turns to see Pandora standing at the bottom of the ramp. Her eyes widen in fear. "No."

"Rest now," Diomedes says. "All is well."

She pushes against him. "Where is Ferara? Hjornir?"

"Ferara and the rest of the traitors are in the hold," Pandora says. "Breathing. Which is more than I can say for your crow. He told us your return vector after I took his teeth."

"You old bag of bones . . ." Seraphina claws to get off the gurney.

Pandora looks to a Gold krypteia who shakes his head as he exits the ship, carrying the girl's meager belongings. "Where is it?" Pandora asks, coming closer to the girl. "You didn't come all this way for nothing. Is it in your teeth? Your belly?"

"I found nothing," Seraphina says bitterly. "I was wrong."

I glance at Cassius, wondering if this makes more sense to him than it does to me. What errand would send her into the Gulf? What would make this girl violate the Pax Ilium? A trespass that would most certainly mean death . . .

"Be still, Pandora," Diomedes warns. He tries to calm his sister, pushing her down into the gurney. "Seraphina, Father sent us to bring you home. Both of us. Now you must see the surgeons." But she won't listen. Even now she's trying to rise from the gurney to get at Pandora. He motions to one of the medics, and they dart forward to plunge a syringe into her shoulder. Slowly the fight leaves her eyes and she sinks into the gurney. The medics try to lift it back up, instructed by the krypteia, but Diomedes stands in their way. An awkward standoff ensues between Diomedes's men and Pandora's.

"My lord, she must be questioned," Pandora says. "If she found something . . ."

"What could she find, Pandora?" he asks. "What is my father afraid of?"

"Nothing, my lord. But diligence must be done. Your father . . ."

"Is not a sadist. He desires his daughter back, alive. A state uncommon to those you question. I don't blame you for your nature, Pandora. You serve my father well as a huntress. But if you wish time alone with my sister, you must first pass through me." Her eyes search him and he smiles. "In your day, it might have been a question. But your day has passed. She is under my shield." She nods acquiescence. He looks at the kuon hounds, then the rest of us before his eyes settle on Cassius. "As are the rest of the prisoners until our Sovereign renders his judgment."

"He'll want them interrogated. They could be spies."

"What a gift you have, to know my father's mind so many leagues away." The words cow her. "We make for home. Recall the rest of your pickets."

"Is this fleet no longer mine either?" Pandora asks. "Do the powers of an Olympic Knight stretch so far?"

Diomedes blinks, caught off guard. "No. Apologies. You are right, of course. I overstep." He bows deeply, and stays bent.

"Forgiven," the old woman sighs. He straightens, turns from her to lift his sister from the bed to carry her from our ship into theirs. When he's gone, we're left alone with Pandora's men.

"Shall we take them to the white tanks, *domina*?" a soldier asks.

She contemplates it. "No. You heard the Storm Knight. Put them in the cells."

Spared from torture, I should be overrun with joy. But as they drag me away from Cassius and Pytha into their ship, fragmented facts coalesce into shape: the scar, the razor, the brutal violence of the girl, the warship, the dragon sigils, and now the names. I knew the lineage of my own house going back to Silenius the Lightbringer before I was five years of age. I knew the rest of the major houses by seven.

But even an average child of the Palatine to some lesser prelate would know the names Diomedes and Seraphina. And even a street urchin on the wharfs of Venus would know their father. So long as there are men, his name will be remembered. The man who allied with the Reaper to break the Society in half. Sworn enemy of my grandmother and my godfather—Romulus au Raa, Sovereign of the Rim Dominion.

This is his ship, his children, and we are now under his power.

21

DARROW

There Will Be Violence

W E GATHER GEAR QUICKLY, raiding the Den's armory for provisions. I watch the city move outside the window as I pause inside the concrete and metal room. Two Red Howlers push a crate of specialized combat armor out the door behind me. "So you know how we're marching into almost certain death?" Sevro says from behind me.

"I wouldn't say that," I reply without turning.

"If we're to go to Venus, slip past their orbital checkpoints, planetary patrols, and the Ass Lord's own private army, I need something from you."

"Name it."

"I need to see my girls before we go."

I feel a pang of sympathy. "That's not a good idea."

"Neither is yours. They cancel each other out."

"I want to see Pax too. . . ." I try not to think of his face. Of the betrayal that will be in my son's eyes. "But the Wardens will look here first, there second."

"You got Lionguards there," Sevro says. "Wardens won't get past them. It's Augustus House territory." It's a good point. "The others can

get the *Nessus* from orbit and we'll rendezvous. No time wasted . . ."
He looks at me hopefully, and I know whatever I say, he's going to go.

This constant pull of duty and family. We bear it together, but he
bears it naturally. I feel I'm not the father my son needs. I should not
leave before telling him I love him. But still I'm afraid to face him.
The memory of him in the dueling grotto staring up at me lingers.

"All right, but I go with you."

"Well, I should hope so, dipshit. You've got a son to kiss goodbye."
He claps me on the shoulder, hoists up a drum of ripWing ammunition, and shuffles away. I look out at the window and wonder if Mustang has figured out my play. I wish more than anything that she
were not the Sovereign. That I could have her with me. But our duties are different, and they're what we chose for ourselves. I return to
stuffing supplies in a rucksack.

"You know what is funny to me?" Victra's reflection joins mine in
the window. Her jade earrings are brilliant in the pale light. "They
think you know what you're doing."

"You think I don't?"

She snorts her answer and looks at the Minotaur helm in Pebble's
hands as she passes us.

"There was always a contingency plan to assassinate him," I say.
"This isn't some ad hoc stupidity. The pieces are aligned."

"Haven't you tried to kill him before?"

"A few times, but not personally." A pulseFist is jammed into the
sack.

"I've tried three times," she says to my surprise. "Assassination is
probably the only enterprise where private industry is not more efficient."

"I have a plan," I say. In goes a backup razor.

"Of course you do." She pauses. "Darrow. Have you stopped to
think what happens if you die?"

"You saw what happened in the Senate, Victra. I'm not the Rising
any longer. It's evolved past me. I am obsolete. And that's a *good*
thing. Virginia is more important than I am. Hell, Dancer is more
important than I am. My purpose is singular—to remove the threats
to the Republic. The Ash Lord is irreplaceable. If I kill him, then the

Saud and Carthii and the last great houses will destroy each other in the power vacuum."

"Atalantia will still be alive."

"Atalantia is not her father," I say. "She's more Aja than her father. A soldier. Not a general." I place four ion detonators in the bag.

"You always did want to be a martyr. Didn't you?"

"What I want doesn't matter," I say curtly. "This is about responsibility. The Republic can't survive with war always snapping at its heels. This division is because I took too long. I told them to trust me with the war. And I haven't won it yet. But I can, and I will."

"Fuck the mob. You don't owe them anything."

I smile at her. "I wish I could agree with you."

"Darrow . . ." She comes close so no one can overhear her. "Have I ever asked you for anything? Then you'll know how much I mean this: do not take Sevro with you. As a favor to me. Tell him to stay here."

"He won't."

"He will if you tell him to."

"No, he won't." I pause my packing, look at Victra's pleading eyes. "We both know I would have to knock him unconscious and leave him here hogtied." She shrugs her shoulders, suggesting she would be fine with that plan. "I can't do that to him."

"But you can take him to Venus? Where he's likely to die?"

"I can't manipulate him," I say. "I won't. Even if I do, we both know he'll be right behind me in another, slower ship."

"Then I'll put his leg in a bear trap."

"He'll just chew it off."

"True." She makes a small, judgmental sound and leans forward to kiss me on the lips. She lingers so I smell the bitter flowers of her perfume, and for a moment, so close and quiet, we are in a different world, in a different life. Then she draws back to look at me. The gold of her irises is brilliant even through her narrowed eyelids. "I love you, Darrow. You are the best friend I have. You are godfather to my children. But if you do not bring my husband back to me, I will leave this blasted moon, return to Mars, and you will never see me or my children ever again."

"I'll bring him back," I say. She looks doubtful. "I promise. But you have to promise me something in return—"

"You know I hate politics," she interrupts, guessing my game. "Those rats hate me. Even Daxo's little band." She sighs nonetheless. "But I'll help the lioness. If she lets me."

"Thank you," I say, meaning it more deeply than she probably knows. Three more ammunition cases and a big knife disappear into the rucksack. I cinch the opening closed with finality.

"Yes, yes. You're lucky you're so pretty."

I join the rest of the Howlers on the roof and watch Sevro say goodbye to Victra. She clings to him in a desperate way I've never seen. Should I leave him? Could I? I don't know if I could go the distance without him, but seeing his head clutched to his wife's chest, I feel the trauma of what I'm doing not just to him, but both our families. It feels like the world is doing this to us. But is it the world, or is it me? The way I am built? A breaker, not a builder after all.

Soon Sevro is with me, wiping his eyes despite the falling rain. I'm about to say something, a feeble attempt at making him stay behind, but he's already past me. The Howlers follow him. They make a pack in the rain-stricken night, ducking their heads against the wind as they cross the roof toward our waiting ships. Absent are the howls. The jokes and ribbing. The city throbs with light, but my men are quiet and dark. I look out at the writhing cityscape and wonder if the Republic Wardens are already on their way.

It is two hours by shuttle to Lake Silene. The hour is late and the house quiet by the time we arrive. My family's Lionguards salute as we pass across the grounds. I feel their eyes on my back. They will know what I am about, and they'll notify Mustang. Sevro goes to the room of his children, and I go to Pax's. I sit for a moment watching him sleep, thinking I should not wake him. The lie I tell myself is that I should protect him and just leave. The fear is that I cannot face him. But I must, or what sort of man am I?

Gently, I touch his shoulder. "Pax."

He was already awake. "Father?"

"Put your shoes on." My son dresses and follows me sleepy-eyed from his room to the garage. It smells of rubber and engine oil. I walk to the row of hoverbikes that sit resting on their flipstands. "Which one is yours?" He points to a rickety hunter-green bike as long as a man. Three saber-like manifolds jut out from the front of it. A pale leather seat sits midway along the narrow, wasplike fuselage.

"Your mother lets you ride this?" I ask in mild surprise.

He's wary of me, of my tone. "Yes, Father."

I sit on my haunches. "She says you built it yourself." He nods. "That's incredible. Will you tell me how?"

"Why?"

"I want to know. It's not something I can do."

He grins suddenly and bursts to life with explanations of RPMs and thrust and stabilizers and adapting mismatched components. I sit back on my heels watching him, falling in love with my son all over again. His mind is more curious than mine. More delighted by the nuances of knowledge. An overwhelming desire to protect him rises up in me. If only he could hold this joy for the rest of his life. I wonder if my father thought the same of me before his cause swallowed him up.

"How did you even think to build it?" I ask him.

"I watched the mechanics, and I asked questions. It's all scrap parts. Dorian au Arcos has a bike. His mother let him ride when he was seven. So I asked Mother if I could get one too, but she said I could if I built it myself. She wouldn't give me any money, so I had to collect the parts from the scrap garages."

"In Hyperion?" I ask.

"No!" he laughs. "It's too expensive there. I could never afford it. Niobe took me to Tycho City. They've got lots of racers there at the track. So they cycle through models fast and I was able to get a good deal."

Mustang was clever in that. How hard it is to teach children that their parents' money is not their own. I remember how Romulus au Raa raised his children—without servants and holo access until sixteen. Mustang was as taken by the idea of it as I was.

"Where'd you get the money?" I ask.

"Aunt Victra."

"She gave it to you?"

He frowns. "No, she lent it to me."

"Really? Wait. At what interest rate?"

"Sixty percent."

I burst out laughing. "Well, that's one way to learn a lesson." He frowns again. It's startling how quickly I can affect his confidence. I'm used to soldiers, not children. I set a hand on his shoulder. "How much did you borrow?"

"Five hundred credits."

"How much do you owe now?"

"Eleven hundred."

"Never get in debt. That's the lesson your aunt is teaching you." He nods sagely. I rise to my feet and trace a hand along the bike's fuselage. I should leave, but I don't want to. Not yet.

His eyes are fixed on its fuselage. "I made it for us to share," he says quietly. He takes the ring of magnetic keys and pulls one off. He hands it to me. I hold the key in my hand and look down at him. I feel like I've been punched in the heart.

"You want to show me how it rides?" I ask.

A grin splits his face.

We roar along a narrow path through the trees, curving back and forth, going deeper into the forest till the path spits us out into a hidden cove. Pax drives us out over the lake, the bike hovering a half meter above the water. Near the center of the lake, I tap his shoulder and point to one of the many archipelagoes. We land the bike there and dismount. He joins me in sitting on a log and we look back across the lake to the house where our friends sleep. Earth hangs overhead. The water laps against the log. My son picks at the moss that grows between us.

"You're leaving again," he says. "Aren't you?"

"Yes. I wanted to say goodbye."

He's silent for a long moment. "I don't want you to go."

"I don't want to go either. But I have to."

"Why?"

"I wish I had an easy answer for you, Pax."

He stares at the reflection of Earth in the water. "Why can't you send someone else?"

"Some things you have to do yourself."

"It's not fair." He shakes his head and I notice the silent tears streaming down his cheeks. "You just got back."

"You're right, it's not. But one day, you will understand what it means to be responsible for the lives of others." I try to put an arm around him, but he pushes away.

"It's not fair. Not to me. Not to Gran. Not to Mother. She needs you here. She won't say it, but she does. You don't know what it's like when you're gone. You don't care."

"Of course I care."

He crosses his arms. "If you cared, then you would stay."

I want more than anything to give him what he wants, what he needs. I feel the erosion of my credibility in his eyes. And I wish I could explain how he is right—a father should be there for his son. My father should have been there for me. I hated him for leaving us. For dying on the scaffold in his failed rebellion. "I'll come back," I say.

"No." He shakes his head and looks away. "You won't."

As I drive us back over the lake and feel his heart beating against my back, I sense the yawning distance growing between us, the stretching of the years and the passing of time and life we can never have back, and I know there's one thing I can do to stop it. Stay.

But I won't. I can't. And I hate that this is who I have to be. Worse. I hate that this is who I've allowed myself to become, but still not enough to change. Not enough to surrender.

The last I see of him is as he goes up the stairs into the house. The heel of his shoe pauses on the last stair, as if he's going to come back, as if there's a last thought of love on his tongue. But the shoe disappears into the house and he's gone and I'm left in the thunderous silence of the garage, wondering what happened to the life I imagined when I first saw him on that beach in my mother's arms.

I wipe my eyes and put the key in my pocket.

In the hall upstairs, I still hear Sevro speaking to his girls. We were all meant to be here together for a month upon our return. So much is in shambles. I leave Sevro his last moments with his girls and walk back out of the house, across the wooded lawn to the landing pads.

"Were you going to say goodbye?" a voice says from the darkness. I look under the bough of a cypress tree and in the shadows see the moonlit face of my wife. She sits on a stone bench, watching me, her hands folded on her lap, her guards nowhere to be seen. She wears a purple silk jacket with a high collar that's open to the base of her neck. Circles ring her eyes.

"I was going to call you from orbit," I say.

"When you were out of my reach."

I hesitate. "Yes."

"I see. It is the only way to maintain that I was not complicit in your treason. Reasonable, I suppose."

I walk toward her and, feeling awkward towering over her, sit on the edge of the stone fountain nearby to face her. Water bubbles out of the half-broken face of a winged cherub, leaking out his eye and ear through a crack.

"It's not treason," I say.

"Yes, it is. Euphemisms only go so far. You're leaving me a mess. Dancer will seek my impeachment."

"He needs two-thirds of the vote for that. He might get the majority for a peace vote, but never an impeachment."

"You think they'll really believe I didn't know you were leaving? You're my husband. They think we share everything." My wife, I've often thought, can be two people. One is her, full of life and light and awkward innuendos and snorting laughter and imperfection. The other is the imperious lion. In her face, I feel the shadow of Augustus, my two great enemies, her brother and her father.

"You're leaving tonight with the Howlers?" she asks.

"Holiday already told you?"

"Where are you going?"

"I can't tell you that."

"To Mars?" I say nothing. "To Orion on Venus?" Again, I do not answer. "The Vox Populi think you're going to storm the Senate with the Seventh."

"I don't want a civil war."

She looks toward the landing pads. I reach for her hand. She pulls it back.

"What is the point of this—marriage—if there's no faith between us?" she asks. "No trust? I know you love me. I know you love our son. But love isn't enough. You can't hide things from me just because I'll disagree with you. This war isn't your burden to bear alone. It is shared by all of us." She looks over at me. "But maybe you think you're meant to die. Maybe you think you're supposed to follow her."

I feel sudden pain for my wife.

"This isn't about Eo."

"No, it's about you praying for storms, believing that when they come they'll bring you peace." She shakes her head, on the verge of tears. "I already lost my mother, my father, and my brothers. I will not bury you." She snorts. "And if you die out there, I won't even get to do that. You'll disappear, like you never existed. Claimed by space or our enemies. And Pax will grow up without a father. It's like you want me to shut myself off to you. Is that what you want?"

"If I don't end this, how many more will die?" I ask.

Her face hardens and she pulls back from me, standing.

"And how many will die if you do leave. The Republic is cracking. If you reject its authority, it *will* shatter. The laws that you mock have protected demokracy for ten years. *Ten*. Without civil war. Without assassination and coups. But if you spit on those laws, you tell the worlds that the laws themselves do not matter. Stay here with me. With your son. Together we can change Dancer's mind or stop him. We can finish this the right way."

"There's only one way to finish this."

"Your way." I say nothing. Her lips make a thin line. "No. We tried your way. Now let's try mine." She touches the datapad on her wrist. "Wulfgar. Bring the Wardens."

From the distant sky comes a mournful sound that most would mistake for the wind. But I know the noise military gravBoots make on full thrust. I burst to my feet. "Mustang . . ."

"I'm sorry, Darrow. You made this choice. If you will not listen to your wife, you will obey your Sovereign."

I pull up my com. "Sevro, we have to go! Now! Wardens inbound."

He does not answer. The com is jammed.

I push past my wife and sprint toward the landing pad. The roar of gravBoots fills the air above me now, rattling through the pine needles. High-intensity light shines down on me. I feel an intense burning on my neck as someone in the air opens up with a beam weapon.

"Halt!" an amplified voice calls from the air. "In the name of the Republic, halt!" I tear across the grass, almost to the landing pad. There's a concussion in the air behind me. I whip my razor off my arm just in time and tense my body. The birdcage hits me like an Obsidian punch in the spine. I slam to the ground as the fiberwire constricts around me. Before it pins my arms to my side, I activate my razor. The blade severs the net and I scramble to my feet as ten Republic Wardens slam down onto the turf in front of me in full armor. Five Colors are represented. Their sky-blue capes droop in the humidity of the summer night. Wulfgar lets his helmet slither back into his armor. His white hair flows over his shoulders.

"'Lo, Wulfgar," I say, gaining my feet.

"Darrow."

"Out for a midnight stroll?"

He smiles. "The night air soothes the spirit." My eyes rove the knights as they move forward. Wisely, they keep their distance and stay in an arc instead of encircling. There are Obsidians and Golds in their ranks. I mark them first, but I'm wariest of Wulfgar. There's a pained look on his face. They came prepared, wearing new-model pulseArmor and carrying nonlethal weapons except the razors on their forearms. I'm keenly aware of the thinness of my leather jacket, the nakedness of my bare hands and exposed head. Wulfgar looks at the razor in my hand. "Perhaps we could walk together, Morning Star? Your spirit could use soothing."

"My spirit's light as a kite," I say. "Seems everyone else is the problem."

"I've been given orders by the Senate *and* the Sovereign to place you under arrest."

And the Sovereign. I resist looking back at my wife.

"So you're with them then. You want to barter with the Ash Lord."

"I am with the Republic, Darrow. As are you. Do not claim I betray you. No man is above the law. And the law will find you inno-cent. The People would not let the Reaper be punished. You will rise stronger than ever."

"Is that what you think?" They'll put me in a cell. I feel the Jackal roving through the back of my mind. Hear the dinner plates echoing through the stone. I told myself long ago that I would never be a prisoner again. To have my choice robbed from me, to have my body constricted . . . I cannot fathom allowing any man or woman to ever strip me of my liberty again.

"You really think the Ash Lord is ever going to accept peace?" I ask. "You're sharper than that. You saw New Thebes. Death for forty kilometers."

"It is my duty to uphold the New Compact and obey the Senate. Just as it is yours. That is what I know."

He's too starry-eyed to see there's a vast gulf that separates his idea of the Republic and the corrupt reality of what it's become. "I thought you might say that." I nod to my ship. "You're going to have to move, Wulfgar."

"I will not."

"You don't want me to move you." I take a step forward. The knights ripple back. Their cloaks roll up into compartments in the back of their armor.

"Darrow, stop," Wulfgar says with a laugh. "We're in SI-7 pulseAr-mor. You've got a leather jacket."

"So?"

His voice softens. "Think what you risk." He nods back to the house. I look back for Mustang. She stands on the edge of the clear-ing, letting the law do its own work. "Would your son be proud?" He steps forward, voice plaintive. "Would he understand?"

His nearest man is ten meters away. I'll never close the distance before they put me down. "One day he would," I say. I'm buying time for Sevro to join us. I'm not sure they've clocked him back at the house.

Wulfgar's face hardens as he sees I'm not going to come with him. "Out of respect for who you are, I will ask you one last time to come peacefully."

"And if I don't?"

He opens his hands. "There will be violence."

Sevro must be out in the darkness somewhere. Even with him, the odds are not good. But the odds will be far worse if I let them take me into custody. I'll be at the mercy of bureaucrats and they won't let me out till Dancer's peace is made and the Ash Lord's trap sprung. Or my men will break me out, and start a civil war.

"Have it your way." I toss my razor to the ground.

"On your knees."

I obey. Three Wardens come forward, a Gold, an Obsidian, and a mechjob Red. They carry a metal electrical collar and train their weapons on me.

I look past them to the rest of Wulfgar's men. "Which of you served with me on Earth?"

"I did, sir," a young, pale Gray woman says. "Eighth Legion, Second Cohort. I followed you through the pass of Kardung La against the Minotaur and again through the Gates of Paris."

"And who served with me on Mars?" A Gold and a Red nod solemnly to me.

"And who serves with me still?" I ask. They look to one another.

"Remember your oaths," Wulfgar says, his left hand drifting to the razor on his arm. "Stand fast!" The men coming to arrest me look back for instructions.

"Hail libertas," I say past them.

"Hail Reaper," two of the veterans answer. They step back from the line and turn their gravRifles on their own. The air thumps and two Wardens are punched twenty meters through the air. The rest wheel toward the new threat.

"Put him down—" Wulfgar roars.

The half-second distraction is all I need. I grab my razor from the ground. It hardens into a slingBlade. And there, at the center of three Wardens, I hack off the barrel of the Gold's rifle, as well as several of his fingers. I slash backward and sever the ligaments in the sword arm of the Obsidian. The Red I finish with four alternating thrusts delivered to kneecaps and wrists. They don't get a shot off. In three seconds, three Wardens fall screaming to the ground. Injured but alive.

Then the air erupts from the firing line.

I use the Gold as a human shield, catching him as he stumbles back from the wound I gave him, and rush at the remaining men as my two veterans sow chaos. I fling my razor out at an Obsidian's pulseRifle. The razor wraps around the muzzle as he pulls the trigger. I jerk it sideways and nonlethal charges spray down the line into his armored companions, slamming two to their knees. I retract the whip, severing the muzzle from his rifle, then cut off half his hand as he reaches for his razor. Another man is shot by my Gray ally. Wulfgar flings up his aegis, and the pearlescent energy shield blossoms from his right arm. He takes the fire of the Gray behind their line and launches toward her with his gravBoots. The edge of his aegis melts through her bare skull, sheaving it in two. She falls dead. Wulfgar bowls into the Gold veteran, their armor making a terrible clang. Their rifles tangle and their razors flash out.

I'm hit in the left shoulder with a glancing energy round as the Wardens try to keep their distance to use their nonlethal munitions.

The nerves from shoulder to elbow go ice cold. I roar in rage and kick one of their Reds so hard in the chest he's lifted off his feet. Someone hits me from the side with the shoulder of their armor. My teeth clack together. A birdcage is fired a half second later. Instinct saves me. I see the blur and slice it in half midair before the round can expand. I whip my razor around the foot of an Obsidian as he flies upward on his gravBoots to escape my charge and get a better angle to shoot down at me. I let him carry me up off my feet, then I retract the razor, ripping off his foot. I fall back down amongst the men below as he sputters sideways, screaming.

As I land, I throw my razor at a Gray leveling a rifle at me from ten meters off. It goes end over end and spits him through the shoulder, piercing his armor and jutting out the other side. I grab a razor from the body of a downed Red and roll to my feet just as a razor emerges from my left bicep as if my body is giving birth to a meter-long tongue of grisly metal. The Obsidian woman on the other end tries to stake me to the ground, but I pull sideways and let the blade go through the meat. Then I turn on her and exchange a fury of blows, but don't have time to finish her off before the remaining three Wardens charge from the left. I spin backward and toward them, so that I alter the angle to face one man on their flanks, his body blocking the others. I slap his blade to the side and stab his left shoulder, then his right elbow. Neither a killing blow. His razor drops.

I spin and slap my razor in Lorn's Whirlwind movement, creating chaos for the last two Wardens, and moving so fast they seem stuck in mud. I forgo killing blows and hack off two hands, one right after another, razors still clenched in their grips. Then I fire the gravity gun point-blank at a Gray who just gained his feet. He shoots backward into a tree, cracking branches as he goes.

I turn on Wulfgar as he pulls his blade from the Gold's sternum. She's dead on the ground.

"Darrow . . ."

I fly at him in a fury. He is a warrior of the ice. Sold as a child, he fought in the pits as a gladiator and rose by the strength of his sword arm. He fights with wild, hacking power, but I am the last student of Arcos. I grind the taller man back, our blades a kinetic shower of sparks and blood-hungry metal. Reverberations gnaw through my hands. My breath is measured; my feet sound against the grass. I'm going to win. I see his balance go several sets before it happens. Two slashes at the legs, a jab at the knee, then the armpit, using the momentum of his blade's deflections to move my blade to its next attack. I slash sideways at his bicep. He twists and moves back, shoulders extending too far out from his center of gravity. I pursue, leading with my blade rigid and aimed for his sword shoulder. Then there's a wail from behind me. An energy round, the cool blue of a stun weapon, slams into the armor of his thigh. It's absorbed harmlessly, but it pushes him sideways into the path of my thrust.

Resistance pushes its way down the blade to the handle. Blood follows.

Wulfgar steps back. His legs sluggish. His eyes confused and blank as he teeters there. The blade has entered through his mouth and out the back of his skull. Blood spills down into his beard. His teeth click against metal.

He falls to his knees, and there, dead, stares on at me down the length of my blade.

Instinctively, I pull the blade from his mouth. Then the realization falls upon me with all its weight.

"Darrow!" Sevro sprints from the house toward me, a multiPistol in hand. He stares in horror at the body of Wulfgar. "Darrow." I kneel in front of the fallen knight. The rage that gripped me when my blood was high gives way to crushing sorrow.

No. No. No. Wulfgar . . .

This is not what I wanted.

Wulfgar's head bubbles blood into the summer grass. His wounded men, those who can, rise to stare at him, at me. I step back from their eyes, seeing not anger in them, but utter confusion and betrayal. The only others dead besides Wulfgar are the Gold and Gray who fought for me. I stumble back as I realize the horror I've made.

"Darrow . . ." I hear Mustang's voice behind me. She stands weaponless at the edge of the fray. She drifts slowly toward me. "What have you done . . ."

This death will reach beyond this small plot of earth and rattle the Republic to its foundations. Wulfgar carried the luster of Ragnar's legend with him. He was a hero. More than that. He was a symbol, and not just to the Vox Populi. The people will hate me. Especially the Obsidians. I've taken one of their favorite sons, one of their great bridges to the Republic, and cut him down in the grass.

What did I think would happen?

Sevro looks back at me, his eyes red. "Darrow, more will be coming." He grabs me when my own legs won't move. "It's time to go. Reap. Come on." I look over at him and see the fear in his eyes.

Amidst the bodies, Mustang looks a ghost of herself. Ten years of building, and one night has broken it all. "I'm sorry," I say. She stares at me, finding no words for her horror, and I let Sevro pull me away.

As we lift off from the landing pad, I stand looking out from the closing passenger ramp and see my wife standing amidst the ruin I've left behind, and beyond her, in the shadow of a conifer pine, my son watches me leave the killing field behind.

PART II

SHADOW

A fool pulls the leaves. A brute chops the
trunk. A sage digs the roots.

—Lorn au Arcos

22

LYSANDER

Io

W E HURTLE LIKE A black thunderbolt over a pale waste of silicate dust and sulfur dioxide frost in a starship adorned with electric dragons. Out the breath-fogged window, a yellow-green sulfur plain stretches toward the dark side of the moon, broken only by lava floes, volcanoes, ash plumes, and mountains. They do not rise in chains according to the humors of tectonic activity, but in isolated, violent surges out of the moon's crust, so that they look like leprous old giants wading through the stained sea.

Each day, 3600 rems of radiation—enough to wither a man's DNA in hours—bombard the moon that was once one of the driest objects in the Solar System. But now, six hundred years after the first ice was carved from Europa and transported to Io, she has become the breadbasket of Ilium—as the Jovian Moon Lords prefer to call their cluster of moons.

Despite the fear I feel at my incarceration, I can't help but be enamored by the testament to human will.

The Conquerors were not daunted by Io's temperament. Wise as they were, they did not try to change her face, but instead created bold bubbles of life upon her surface. Out the small dirty window on the other side of the passenger aisle, I glimpse a chain of agricultural domes, docks, and skeletal tramways. There, botanical enterprises manned by lowColor slaves produce enough food to feed Ilium and, with Titan, feed the rest of the Rim.

Io is a contradiction, and so, I know, are its inhabitants. Something I must keep in mind if I am to find some means of escape for my friends.

The ship jerks against sudden turbulence. I lose hold of the plastic cup that I've brought up to the edge of the metal muzzle that's affixed to my head. It drops to the floor, spilling the water across the deck. The guard stares at the water running along the floor planking with dull, mole eyes. He is disgusted by the waste and my noises as I lick the mesh of my muzzle, desperate for any last drop of moisture for my swollen mouth. He moves on, the magnets in his boots securing his rangy legs to the deck despite the turbulence from the atmospheric entry.

"May I . . ." My dry throat closes around the words. "May I have another cup?" I rasp out, eyes on the man's boots, trying and failing to keep the desperation from my voice. This one's name is Bollov. He has an unyielding disposition, a tremor in his right hand. He likes power and teaching lessons to spoiled Corish Pixies like myself and Cassius. I wish I knew why; perhaps then I could dismantle him. My grandmother once told me, "A new wound can take a body. Opening an old one can claim a soul."

I observe the small exchanges between the guards, the idle chatter in halls or as the watch changes; but these Rim dwellers hoard their emotions. Better to guess the thoughts of a lizard than those of Bollov. My head pounds from the dehydration headache that I've been nursing for thirty-four days. My sleep has been restless, filled with visions of the crew I abandoned.

The water deprivation is civilized torture, and I know deep down Pandora yearns for something more barbaric. It seems only Diomedes's protection has staved off that course. Could he be a potential ally? Pandora is certainly not. She's a savage. Two days into my capture, the old woman visited my cell. For an hour she sat cross-legged on the floor and watched me, saying nothing until she asked if Seraphina brought a datacube onto the *Archimedes*. I told her I didn't know of such a cube. She left without a word and I've been unable to discern just what the datacube could contain.

Since that day I've been given just enough water to survive, but no more. My muscles ache like they've seen hard gravity. My gums are swollen, mouth like chalk. Every day she would return, watch me like an old, evil owl, and make the same request. I'd give her the damn datacube if I'd seen one. It doesn't matter to Castor au Janus, the persona supported by our ship's logs. Cassius is Regulus au Janus. We're Martian traders from New Thebes who were on the Rim ferrying water to blackmarket ore miners.

The fact that I still have my skin must mean they haven't found our vault yet.

"Please," I implore Bollov. "Just one more cup."

"That *was* your cup, *gahja*." Their word for outsider. Derived from the original Japanese language that was the native tongue of the Raa, before the arrival of a South African strain of Golds. "Waste not. Want not." Bollov moves on.

Beside me, Cassius hunches in his seat, his arms sealed in metal cuffs and locked to his chest, with just enough room to bring his cup to the steel mesh muzzle that's wrapped around his head. He'd share with me, but he's already gulped his down. A thin chain connects the jaw of his muzzle to a belt around his waist, so he's hunched in permanent supplication, even when he walks. Together in the tan prisoner uniforms, we look like a pair of pre-Neanderthal hominids. But my friend is alive, and that is all that matters.

This is the first I've seen him in the month voyage from the asteroid belt to Io. Based on Jupiter's current orbit, these new ships of theirs are faster than they have any right to be. I crave to see their designs, their new engines, but my world has been a steel cube three meters by three by three. I almost wept when I saw Cassius waddling toward me in the hall before we boarded this shuttle, his face still as ugly and bulbous as the day we escaped the Ascomanni.

Despite the joy of our reunion, a pall hangs over us. We don't know if Pytha is alive. If this is how they treat Golds, it makes my heart ache to think what misery her life has become. I've not stopped thinking about how I could have averted this. How I could have done better. What action would I adjust? What different move would I make?

"Give him another cup," a voice tells Bollov from behind me. Coming up from the storage hold of the dropship through the prisoner section is Diomedes au Raa. His hair is loose and falls around the shoulders of a gray scorosuit, a hooded body-fitting polymer suit with electromagnetic radiation shielding and water reclamation pockets. His storm cloak flows behind him and seems alive with mutations in the color.

"If you're so afraid of Pandora, set it there and go on." The guard does just that, leaving the plastic jug on an empty seat. I nearly pitch sideways to steal the whole thing, but I wait patiently as Diomedes opens the jug and pours me another portion, hoping to impress upon him that we are of the same breed. He gives me just one cup to replace the one lost. There's little mercy here, but even amongst the guards, there's been less callous cruelty than in the Interior since our imprisonment.

"Thank you," I manage. The lukewarm water gives new life to my throat.

He looks down at me without a smile and then moves away toward the main cabin.

"Why was she in the Gulf?" I ask. He stops and I wish I had read his psychological profile in Moira's SIB database when I was younger. I remember he was secondary heir to his older brother Aeneas, who died at the Battle of Ilium. He's risen to the challenge of being an heir, it seems. No easy task. I would know.

"Shut up, Castor," Cassius mutters to me. "Take your gift and be silent."

I don't shut up. Whether Cassius wants to admit it or not, these people are our kin. And if I do not stir the pot, the only opportunities will be the ones they choose to give us. That is unacceptable.

"She was in the Gulf for a reason," I say to Diomedes. "And without permission from your father, it would seem." Diomedes turns back, measuring me with a blademaster's gaze: eyes then hands then scars. "Do you even know why? Or is that Krypteia jurisdiction?" His silence speaks for him. There it is. A chink in the emotional stoicism of the man. I appeal to what seems his strongest sense, that of a soldier's honor: "If you are truly thankful that we saved Seraphina, save us. Do not let us see Io. We're traders, that is all. We thought we stumbled upon salvage. All we've seen is a hangar, cells, and this ship. If we see anything beyond this ship, we both know we will never leave. Let me and my brother and our pilot go back from where we came. Escort us to the edge of your space and send us on our way. That is what is honorable. Life for life."

"My brother is a child," Cassius grovels to the knight. "Forgive his mouth. It tends to run. He didn't grow up amongst his own."

Diomedes walks back to me and cocks his head as if I were the most curious of bugs. "There are no eyes like yours beyond the Belt. You are a pretty boy. Aren't you?" I don't reply. "How old are you, Martian?"

"Twenty."

"Your brother is right. You speak like one of our children." With an easy show of strength, he grabs the chain attached to the back of my muzzle and pulls it so hard I'm lifted off my feet. My neck bends painfully. "A lesson is needed. I will teach you."

"Don't . . ." Cassius says from behind his muzzle.

Diomedes presses something on his datapad and Cassius's muzzle buzzes with electricity. Shaking violently, Cassius falls back into his seat and I'm dragged by my chain through the prison unit into the loading bay. Diomedes shoves me into the center of the floor doors and presses me to my knees into the worn intersection of a painted red X. He does something behind me I can't see, though I hear the click of metal and feel the evil fingers of fear slithering through my stomach. *It's a test. Slow your breathing. Do not be afraid. Stand astride the torrent.*

He talks as he works.

"When I was a boy, I remember the envoys the Core would send.

Slippery Politicos in their slick suits, fingers laden with gaudy rings."
I glance back and see him unspooling a cable that's now attached to
the back of my harness. "All they wanted to see were the *seas* of Europa. The *mountains* and *towers* and *dockyards* of Ganymede. Always,
though, they had to come see my grandfather. To pay homage to
Revus au Raa, because power lies where honor reigns. But you could
smell the derision when they came to my home. They called my family savages behind our backs, safe under our shields. Rustics. Dusteaters." Trailing the cable behind him, he walks to a red button protected
by a plastic case on the wall. It takes every ounce of courage I have to
remain kneeling in the center of the door and not to scramble to
safety. He smiles at my inability to tame my fear. My hands shake.
"They were startled by my grandfather's hospitality. The respect he
showed them. The gentle way in which he spoke, even as the Codovan and Norvo gnashed their teeth over Rhea. They mistook grace
for weakness. Abused his kindness. Then Fabii learned the lesson I
am about to teach you."

"I don't have an oxygen mask," I say.

"No. You do not."

With that, he slams his hand against the red button and the steel
doors beneath my knees retract, leaving me kneeling on open air. My
stomach rises up into my throat as I plummet out the belly of the
craft, legs thrashing, holding my breath against the poisonous air.
Wind roars through my ears. Then a horrible pain erupts at my waist
as the cable snaps taut and arrests my fall, digging into my skin and
jerking me upward. My head snaps down into the restraining vest so
hard I feel metal puncture my skin and nick the bone of my forehead,
sending flashing lights scattering across my vision. Blood streams
into my eyes and I swing up, pressed to the belly of the craft as it
races across a sky stained with acid-yellow clouds.

My body lurches into shock from the temperature. I'll die from
the heat well before I gasp for oxygen. I close my eyes as needles of
fire stab into my brain. Sound and fury swallow me, pain as my body
slaps against the hull. And just as my lungs have depleted their oxygen, I'm dragged back into the hangar by the chain and tossed onto
the floor. I gasp for air and it's some time before I can open my eyes.

My body aches and my skin feels alive with fire. Diomedes stands over me, his dark eyes still and quiet, no evil in them, no malice. "Have you learned the lesson, *gahja*?" he asks. It is a lesson in respect.

"Apologies," I manage.

This is met with a satisfied look from the man. "Forgiven," he says, hoisting me up by my bonds. "Welcome to Io."

23

LYRIA

Foxwalker

"**B**LOODYDAMN." I CURSE AND draw my hand back from the rosebushes. A small drop of blood beads where the thorn pricked me. I suck the blood away and stretch myself deeper into the bushes, feet spread wide so I don't lose my balance in the low gravity as I scoop up the fox shit with my trowel. Body still hasn't wised up to its own weight here. I reach the scat this time, taking a clump of dirt with it, and finally dump the waste into the blue plastic container Dr. Liago gave me for sample collection. Sophocles has been mad as a box of snakes since we arrived on Luna last week, trying his best to kill the lovely pachelbel birds that fill the trees of the Citadel's gardens.

He was well mannered on the return trip from Mars when I was introduced to him by Kavax and told my duties by Bethalia, the terrifying old general of the army of Telemanus servants. Sophocles spent most of his days trotting around the ship with Liam and me, following along dutifully behind Kavax, or curled up in his master's chambers, but now he catches one whiff of the pink birds and he's nearly pulling my arm out of its socket to claw furrows in the trunks of trees.

Dr. Liago, the Telemanuses' personal physician for fox and human alike, can't figure out what's wrong with the beast. Which leaves me picking up fox shit samples three times a day. Tedious, but compared with the muggy hell of Camp 121, it's not a shabby life. I'm paid a good wage, fed three square, given four spare uniforms, and sleep in a climate-controlled bunk room. There's no mosquitoes, and no fear when I walk the grounds late at night in the dark cycle. I go out most nights to look at the stars and watch ships come and go on the Citadel of Light's landing pads atop the Palatine Hill to the northwest. The last time I can remember feeling this safe was nestled between my da and mum watching my brother Aengus dance with the lasses at Laureltide as Dagan glowered to himself.

Kavax has been just as kind to Liam as to me. He put Liam in the Citadel school with the children of the other employees who live on the grounds. They board near the north wall in dormitories set in a small forest of cypress. Even though the school is within the Citadel walls, it's still twenty klicks north of the Telemanus estate, so I only manage to catch the tram to see him three times a week. I stop in at nighttime before they put the children to bed. Each time I have to leave, he clings to me, not wanting me to go. Breaks my heart every time. He says the other kids are kind. But he's one of the only Reds there.

"Righto, you little beast, time's up. Back inside," I say, turning back from the bush. "Sophocles?" He's gone. I search the sycamores and the elder shrubs. He slipped his leash again and ran off somewhere toward Lake Augustine. There's no sign of him. "Dammit." If he kills more pachelbel, I'll be in for it with Bethalia.

I walk the gravel path that winds through the Esqualine Gardens in search of him. The gardens sprawl around the base of the Esqualine Hills, where the manicured stone estates of old Gold families sit inside the Citadel walls. They are now filled with the Sovereign's most powerful supporters—chiefly Houses Arcos and Telemanus.

Little ponds and streams are nestled at the bases of the hills, amongst tranquil copses of rosebushes. It looks like a storybook painting of the Vale. But this garden has some deep shadows and the men and women who walk here are empire breakers.

It is early autumn now in Hyperion, a season far kinder than the grueling summers of Boetian Plains. Something of it reminds me of the tunnels of Lagalos, how dew would bead on the outside of the metal doors all throughout our township in the early mornings. *You'd love it, Tiran. The way the fog catches on the walls and cloaks the Palatine spires. Just like one of your storybooks.*

No. Don't go there. Don't think of them. I bite the inside of my cheek till I taste blood to draw me out of the quicksand of memory.

It's morning. The small datapad on the underside of my wrist reads 7:32 A.M. Earth Standard on the sixteenth day of the bright month of October. Sixty degrees Fahrenheit and cloudy with afternoon showers. The datapad is unlike anything I had in the mines, let alone the camp. Sometimes I lay in bed staring at the slowly turning hologram of Mars before drifting off to sleep, guiltily wondering if I should miss it. I don't. If anything, I miss Lagalos.

My body still has not welcomed the low gravity here; I feel more trapped on this moon than I did on the three-week journey from Mars. I felt it the moment I stepped off the shuttle that took us down from orbit and missed that first step down from the ramp. The lethargic gravity is at odds with the manic pace of the ships in the blue sky overhead, the constant flow of important people on important tasks. But the worst is the protocol and judgment from the other valets.

I thought Kavax would forget about me as soon as I boarded his ship; instead, he took a liking to me, hell knows why. He had me sup with him every breakfast, first teaching me the intricacies of Sophocles's dietary and care requirements. But those lessons were forgotten when he gave me a book of lullabies that Sophocles requires sung to him before bedtime. I had to confess that I could not read more than half the words. He stared at me as if I had thirteen heads.

"That will not do," he roared. "Not at all! Stories are the wealth of humanity! My wife would not forgive me if I denied you the key to that wealth."

He took to giving me lessons after every breakfast in his stateroom. But they were abandoned after Xana burst into the room in a panic. I learned later that she had just heard news of the Reaper's demotion at the hands of the Senate, his murder of the captain of the Wardens, and his disappearance from Luna.

Heavy shit.

The news has turned the moon into a madhouse. Protests clogged the boulevards on the day we returned. A crowd of hundreds of thousands flowing like a tide of Cimmerian ants, calling for the Reaper's arrest, the Sovereign's impeachment. But they were met violently by a mass of the Reaper's worshippers. The Watchmen had to disperse the clashing mobs with heat beams and gas.

Does me good to know I'm not the only one who's lost faith in the Sovereign.

"Sophocles!" I call out again, following a narrow track of gravel past the base of another estate. "Sophocles, where are you?" I feel watched. He's playing games again. I crouch low and move off the path in between two sycamores to search the bank of the lake. A black swan stares at the shore. There! Jutting out from behind a tree trunk is a bushy red tail, swaying in the breeze.

I creep forward, minding the twigs under my new shoes. Quietly, carefully. The tail moves with excitement. I burst around the tree, and Sophocles pounces on me in a flurry of red fur. Laughing, I let his weight take me to the ground, where he licks my ears till I have to wrestle him off. His cold nose pokes at the side of my neck. I reattach his collar.

Then I hear a strange *pop* through the trees. I walk toward the sound. In a small clearing, I find a concrete block of a Gray warden speaking with a slender Copper with a familiar face. Though I crouch barely twenty meters away, I can't hear either man. It's almost like magic. The Gray shoves a finger into the Copper's chest as if scolding him. The Copper looks away, my direction.

I dart back into the trees, hauling on Sophocles's leash. Whatever was happening wasn't my business. I pull Sophocles along the path back to the Telemanus estate. At the side door, I'm moving so fast I run straight into someone and almost fall down. I look up into narrow, cold eyes. A woman with a face like tree bark stares down at me. She's Gray and built thicker than any man in Lagalos. I've seen her twice before, always quiet and in the shadows of things. The servants say she's a Howler, and before that, a Son of Ares. Her eyes turn to me as if she could sense me watching. A chill goes down my spine at standing so close to a bloody Gray. I feel like I'm back in the mine as I mumble apologies. She steps past me and continues down the hill.

Feeling twice as small as I did before, I pull on Sophocles's leash and make for the estate.

I find Liago curled over his botany desk like a long length of old ivy. He's an old Yellow, maybe seventy? People age slower outside the mines. They use crèmes on their faces. Injections. Laser therapy. Makes some of them look positively deranged. In the mines, you wear your age proudly. You got white hair? Bloodydamn fine for you. Must be quick on your feet. Proud thing, that.

Liago seems to agree very much with my people. His face wrinklier than my father's knuckles. All crags and fissures and little patches of scaggleweed facial hair. The top of his long-jawed head is crested by great plumes of white hair. Nimble hands prod the base of a slim, violently orange flower. He doesn't hear the howling of the kettle on his small electric stove.

"Dr. Liago?"

"Lyria!" He wheels around. An odd piece of tech secured by a clear plastic strap around his head covers his right eye, magnifying the pupil hilariously. "By Jove on high, you scared me half to death, sneaking around like that."

"I'm not sneaking. You're just deaf as a rock."

"What what?" He doesn't wait for an answer. "You people are so light on your feet." He looks me up and down. "But not for long. You're looking pudgier by the day!" His voice takes on an annoying conspiratorial tone. "Found the key to the cupboards, did we?"

"The valets say you're mad as a sack of cats," I say very quietly. "And your head is jealous of your ears because they stole all its hair."

"What what?"

"I asked if you want me to pour your tea?" I ask sweetly.

"My tea?" His eyes widen. "Yes. I was meaning to get that. Like it extra hot, you know! And pour one for yourself too. It's my favorite green tea from Xantha Dorsa. Martian, like us. You like tea, yes?"

"I've had tea with you four times."

"Really? Of course you have. It was a test." He stares at me shrewdly, though I'd wager a good pair of boots that he's thinking about what sort of jam he'll have on his midmorning toast.

"Can't today," I say. "Bethalia would lash me. Got extra duties."

"Nonsense. She runs you ragged. Spare a moment with me." He winks. "She's got a soft spot for old Liago. I can get away with murder."

If anything, it's the other way around. Liago dotes on the old Pink like a lovesick drillboy, sending her flowers he designs personally for her. *That would have done the trick on you, Ava. Personal flowers.* I let Sophocles off the leash to sniff around the floor and I bring Liago his cup of tea, glancing at my reflection in the shining silver surface of one of his medical machines. My cheeks do look a bit plumper. Not a bad look, that.

"What's that?" I ask, gesturing to the flower Liago's bent over. Its stem is pale white and slender. A deep violet stains its buds, which are shaped like human dancers.

He looks lovingly down at the flower. "This? Oh, my dear. This is my pride and joy. Thirteen years it's taken me to perfect the supple grace of her genetic code. And a lifetime of research. Which is why my greenhouse back in Zephyria is littered with infant renditions. It's the echo of a woman I once knew."

I tilt my head and draw close to the plant. "It's lovely."

"It's poisonous," he says. He smiles when I don't recoil. "I designed it to sense kinetic reverberations in the air. Reach out . . . touch it gently."

"How poisonous? Enough to make me sick up? Or will I get a rash?"

"A rash? Ha! Death, this one courts." Now I flinch. "Don't you trust old Liago?"

"No farther than I could throw you."

"What what?"

"You first, Doc."

With a lone finger, he touches the stem very carefully. Its pale, fleshy skin ripples indigo and a deep purple. The plant arcs into his hand, like a cat being scratched. Sophocles watches from the floor, cocking his head. "It invites gentleness," Liago says. "But if you rush your hand upon it . . ." He takes a length of unsliced cucumber from the remains of his breakfast and hits the plant. Small spines erupt from the feet of the dancer buds and the cucumber begins to shrivel and blacken, filling the room with a rotting stench. Sophocles backs away.

"Cellular death!" he announces.

I laugh in genuine delight. "Wicked. What do you call it?"

"Nyxacallis."

I sigh. "Is that Latin?"

"It means Night Lily." He's lost in thought. I'd ask him who the woman was if I didn't recognize the pain on his face. Maybe that's why I'm so fond of the old bat. He's the only one in the Telemanus estate who wears his pain in his eyes. Rest are all playing games.

"So you brought me another sample?" he asks after a moment. "Let's see." He opens the plastic container and takes a deep, satisfied whiff of the scat before slipping out of the greenhouse to a small silver machine in his lab. I follow behind. After a sample has been inserted, numbers and symbols flow from a small holoprojector in the machine into the air.

"What's that?" I ask.

"Those?" He's confused. "Of course, curious cat. How would you know? Those are chemical notations. That is skatole, hydrogen sulfide, mercaptan, and that . . . that is carbon. That is in every living thing that is, was, and will be. It's in me. It's in you. It's in the Night Lily." He watches me grasp the idea. "You know what I like about you, Lyria?"

I glower, knowing it's with pity that he looks at me. The same pity that fills the eyes of the other servants, and has driven me to isolation. They pity my manners, my poor haircut, and pity that my family was butchered. Here, surrounded by so many people, I've never felt more alone. More alien.

"Not really," I mutter.

"What do you mean 'not really'?" he says, aghast. "What kind of way is that to think about yourself?"

"I mean, no one's talked to me like you have, except Lord Kavax, and some of the dockers. Everyone else talks slag behind my back, but they're too scared to lay it out plain eye to eye, because they've never been in a tumble."

Liago clucks his tongue, thinking he's not like them, but in a way he is. I've seen how he watches me when I leave, when I enter. Like I'm going to explode into tears at any moment.

"Those little uppity pups." He wags a finger at me over his tea. "You're proper Martian. I've been too long here on this moon. Ten years, only a little back and forth. Everyone's uppity. Putting on airs. I bet that's what Lord Kavax sees in you. A breath of home. It's what I like about you as well. So don't you worry if the others don't like you right away. It's their own insecurity at the wretched creatures they've become. . . ."

He puts a hand on my shoulder, like I need fatherly advice. "With all you've been through, the last thing you need to worry about is being popular." I recoil. He can shove his advice right up his drill exhaust. But before I can tell him that, Sophocles darts out from under the table, snarling horribly. I almost piss myself. He pounces up onto one of Liago's tables, knocking over beakers and test tubes, sending them shattering to the floor as he springs up toward an open window where a small pachelbel sits. The bird titters and flies back out the window. Sophocles hits the wall and slides down. "Out!" Liago shouts, looking in horror at his broken supplies. "Get him out of here! And don't bring him back till I find out what mangles his wits!"

Later that afternoon, I leave Sophocles with Kavax and collect more treats and shampoo from the huge warehouse that supplies most of the Citadel with food. I spare a few minutes to smoke burners with the Reds who work the forklifts and stocking rooms. All are Martian, since Houses Telemanus and Augustus hire exclusively from home.

Security reasons. Most of the older men and women were with them before the Rising.

"Any chance they found out what's what with Sophocles?" one of the Reds asks. "Heard he's gone mental."

"You would too if they cloned you twenty-odd times," says an old woman named Garla, exhaling burner smoke.

"Cloned?" I ask.

"Aye," Garla says. "No one told you? Only ever been one fox in House Telemanus. Sophocles is seven hundred years old. This just happens to be his twenty-first life. He's like me. Fourteen generations in service to the fox." Her bandy legs dangle off the edge of a box of coffee stamped with Mars import markings. She pulls a chain from around her neck. "Kangax, the father of our liege, gave this to my own da." She tilts it to me. The other Reds roll their eyes. It's a monster cast in gold. "One of those wild carved beasties, a griffin. Kangax put a price on the head of a wild griff that was terrorizing their Zephyrian lands, and me father, just a docker like me, went into the mountains and shot it dead with a longbarrel scorcher." I reach to touch the griffin, but Garla pulls it back and stuffs it in her shirt.

"So he got the bounty?" I ask. I'm at ease with these people, with their bluntness and the dirt under their nails. Some of their accents are even spot on for Lagalos.

"Aye. Bought out his contract and lost it all in a year."

One of the other Reds laughs. "Got all high and uppity. Forgot he was a ruster."

"Shut your bloodydamn gob," Garla snaps. "And don't use that word round me, hear? Ruster." She spits. "That's a slave word." Her voice lowers and she shrugs at me. "Da liked to gamble. But Kangax hired him right back. No bad feelings. He was a good man. And Kavax is a good one too." The others nod along. "Even if we just lug boxes and clean up shit, it's our job to protect him here in this bloodydamn viper nest of a moon. All of us. Remember that."

24

EPHRAIM

Kobachi's Tech Emporium

Volga, Cyra, and I unload from the taxi onto the buzzing Hyperion street. The sliver of morning sky seen through a gap in the overhead bridges and buildings of the city above is as bright and blue as the dresses girls wear to the summer races at the Circada Maxima. This dilapidated deep level of Hyperion is naked under the high sun. Ancient buildings, moldering signs, forgotten by the progress above. Grafitti of upside-down pyramids embedded with screaming mouths score storefronts and alley walls. The Vox Populi seems to have an endless supply of paint.

On a building-side HC a newscast blares. A fatally serious Copper reporter drones on about the hunt for the Reaper after his murder of the ArchWarden. Hacked the man down in cold blood, they say. Sounds about right for the bastard. I might like booze, but power's his cup of poison. The Colors are shocked, appalled that such an affront to the Republic could occur by their great hero. But after seeing the fall of one empire, I know enough to see the cracks in the foundation of this one.

I suck back a burner. With our preparations for the heist under way, we've been running eighteen hours a day. The first several days were strategic, scouting the viability of the three posited locations for the heist that the Syndicate provided. Once we picked one, I told Gorgo, our Syndicate liaison, the only way the task could be done proper was with a military-grade gravWell. I half told it to the Obsidian as a bluff to test the limits of his reach, but the Syndicate beast looked unfazed and kept smoking a burner over his espresso at the highrise café where we met. Said he'd run it by the Duke. He did. Said it would take two weeks. Guess dancing with the devil means you get hell's resources.

I pull my wool overcoat tight against the early autumn chill and notice Volga staring up at a residential skyscraper with a sliver of green foliage on its roof.

"What would it be like to live up there?" she asks. "A garden atop the clouds."

"After this you'll find out," I say.

Cyra snorts. "Don't tease the crow. Even after this dreadnought of a payday, all of us together couldn't buy that penthouse."

"How much do you think it costs?" Volga asks.

Cyra shrugs. "Hundred million, maybe more."

Volga shakes her head at the number, stunned on a primal level.

"There's your Rising for you," I say.

We cross the street after an automated grocery truck trundles past, and make our way across the fissured concrete to a small shop underneath a gaudy, glittering holosign proclaiming, KOBACHI'S TECH EMPORIUM. WON'T TAKE A BYTE OUT OF YOUR WALLET. Another sign underneath flashes: NO RUSTERS. NO CROWS. NO EXCEPTIONS.

Volga pauses outside the door. Cyra goes right on in. I pause and consider Volga for a moment. She kept my secret from the others. But the last few days she's been sullen. "Want to see inside?" I ask.

She looks at the sign and shakes her head. "No, thank you."

I sigh. "What's wrong? You been slumping along like a wounded puppy since we took this job."

She relents and looks at me hesitantly. "Are you not worried? Worried that this will hurt the Rising?"

"Life's a mountain, Volga. Nasty, steep, covered in ice. Try to move it, you'll go nowhere. Try to help someone else, you'll fall right down with them. Focus on your own feet, and you just might make it up and over." I reach up to clasp her muscled shoulder. "Now come on."

"It will be trouble."

In response, I flash the black rose in my interior coat pocket and grin. "Pale lady, today we're the trouble."

The interior of the shop is a dim jungle of gadgets and secondhand gizmos so thick they seem to grow into the humid air. Amidst floating indigo signs, obscure relics hang on hooks beside knockoff datapads and ocular implants. A good half of the store has been given over to biomodifications. Two teenage Greens with heavy tattooing and liberty spike hair sift through plastic packages containing discounted neurolinks. Idiots. After the darkness of the Society, this new generation is so desperate to plug in, to know everything instantaneously, that they put the whole holoNet in their heads without giving two shits about the consequences. The teenagers eye Volga nervously as she comes in.

Cyra's already snagged a cart and is getting to work on her datapad's shopping list. Volga stands behind me, eyes darting around like a puppy given leave over a butcher's shop. They settle on a holoExperiental station that several kids have gathered around. "Go on, feast your eyes," I say. She gives me a careful smile, then, taking huge care not to let her broad shoulders knock over a rack of metabolic implants, lumbers over to watch. A Blue kid is sitting in a chair, nodes attached to his head. A projection of what he's seeing with his closed eyes dances in the air above him. His friends watch excitedly, waiting their turn. They peer back as Volga's shadow eclipses them. One of Kobachi's employees, a gangly young Green, monitors the experiental over a tray of nasal caffeine inhalers. The Red's flying a Colloway xe Char mission—the fantastical first where the dashing ex-pirate personally relieved House Saud of ten tons of gold bullion they were moving from their Luna banks to Venus in a caravan. They put a hell of a bounty on him after that, and made him famous.

The employee blanches when he sees Volga. "No crows," he says, gesturing to the sign. She looks down at him, embarrassed. "Can't you read, girl?"

"Yes, I can read," Volga says in a small voice.

"She's with me," I say.

He doesn't turn. "Look, if she was a ruster, she'd steal shit. If she was a Brown she'd clean shit. But she's an Obsidian: they break shit. I don't make the rules, brotherman."

"Kid," I say. I nudge the employee. He turns his bloodshot eyes to me. His pupils are huge on some designer drug, his armpits dark with sweat. "Watch your fucking manners." He swallows, seeing the Omnivore pistol hanging on the holster inside my jacket. "Where's Kobachi?"

"In the back."

"Get him for me. Tell him it's Ephraim."

The Green just blinks at me.

"Before I grow a beard."

"Keep up, pops. Already called him." He taps the scar on his right temple where his neurolink went in. His eyes narrow rebelliously. "Told him a tinman was waitin'."

A few minutes later, I spy Kobachi peeking out the crack of the door leading to the back of his shop, where he does his repairs. He catches me spotting him, then ducks away before reappearing grandly, extending his arms in welcome. He's a little mechanized gecko of a man. In his deep sixties, his sleepy green eyes embedded with sensors and magnification lenses. Bald headed. In patched-up overalls with multiscrews and other tools sticking out of the belt on his tiny hips. Dull metal implants rise up out of the pale flesh covering his skull.

"Ephraim, my dearest friend," he says in a thin voice as he comes up to me in the cluttered aisle. He hasn't yet seen Volga past the stacks of music equipment. "What joy to see you again. Such a fright you gave Kobachi." He leans closer. "I thought you were the Watchmen come back with cruelty on their minds. Such nasty, nasty customers, your kinsmen. All extortion and bullying and demanding the severest discounts. Sometimes they even demand . . ." His voice falters. ". . . *refunds*."

"Refunds," I say. "The horror."

"I know. *I know*. But such times we live in. No protection for the small-business owner. Only taxes and extortion. Such is to be expected from leaders who have never run a business!" He waves to a floating sign that says NO REFUNDS. "But is it too much to ask for a literate militarized police?"

"At least they weren't too upset about the shit knockoff lenses you repackaged in Sun Industries wrapping. . . ."

He gasps. "Repackage! Insidious accusation! And this, from a dear friend."

"More like insidious business practices. Those lenses you fleeced me for scratched my cornea. You're as bad as Roduko."

"Roduko! How dare you." He sets his reedy hands on his hips and can't find them because of the bulk of his tool belt, so he settles for crossing his arms. "Kal ag Roduko is a two-bit Terran hustler without a kilobyte of consideration for his customer. Profit. Profit. Profit. They're all the same."

"Immigrants or Silvers?"

"Either! Both! No care for being an institution in the Bazaar. It's all about what they can extract from their customers."

I smile, genuinely amused at the small man. He's the most useless hustler I've ever met. But somehow, someway, he's remained on this corner for forty years, like a benevolent fungus resistant to any and all change. Hell, I keep coming back even though a quarter of the commercial goods I buy here are guaranteed to break after a week's use. But maybe that's just because the turnover rate on everything else in Hyperion is manic. Gotta respect a fungus like Kobachi. Especially one that files off serial numbers and wipes digital signatures. Best ghost tech for fifty kilometers. Even if the toys occasionally break.

He smiles at me now, a toothy, obscenely disingenuous one that seems to grow every time he smells credits in my pocket. "What can Kobachi do for you today? Virility implants? Infrared ocular sensors? Zero-gravity acid applicators? Or will you be wanting something more . . ." His smile grows till it reaches his ears. ". . . expensive."

"Actually, custom is the game of the day."

"Crow! Mind your hands!" he shouts past me. I turn to see Volga frozen mid-reach toward an iridescent glass globe with floating electrical wires inside. She sheepishly steps away from the item. Kobachi wheels on me, eyelids pinched in anger. "Kobachi thinks it is not just

Wardens who cannot read." He waves to another sign that has an X drawn over an apelike monster that is supposed to be an Obsidian. "No crows. No exceptions."

"Volga likes toys," I say. "Volga is going to look at toys. And you're going to mind your manners, Kobachi. For once."

"This is my shop—"

"And you're happy to have us here," I say, producing the iron rose from my pocket so that only he can see it. He blanches, as if I were holding death in my coat pocket. "Aren't you?"

"Very happy," he says quietly, but the look on his face says otherwise.

"Glad we understand each other." I pocket the rose and clap him on the shoulder. "Now, that custom order."

He grunts and leads me to the back of the shop, which is filled with a large workbench stacked with half-completed projects. "So this is what it looks like back here," I say. He looks at me with an altogether different set of eyes now that he's seen the rose. He keeps glancing at my pocket.

"I was not aware . . ."

"It's a new arrangement. And not permanent."

"Silly Gray. It's always permanent," he says quietly. "They never let you go. You don't want this, my friend." I dismiss his words with a shrug. I don't need him to know what I'm feeling. But I know he's right. After so many years of watching the Syndicate's tentacles stretch from the Lost City up to high Hyperion and out to Endymion and the other spheres, I know they never let go of something valuable. After the Fall, they decided they wanted the whole ecosystem. That's what caused the Territory Wars between them and the old gangs. There's few of them left anymore. Even old Golgatha fell hard.

"Is this all you have?" I ask Kobachi. "Gorgo will be disappointed." The name affects Kobachi. His knees begin to shake so badly they almost knock together. He touches a button underneath the workstation. The back wall retracts into the ceiling, revealing a secondary room stocked with a treasure trove of gleaming titanium, slick plastic and steel—weapons, drones, data slicers and all manner of illegal military tech. He smiles with pride, despite the fear that the Syndicate has put in him. So *this* is what pays his rent. I laugh. "Kobachi, you old dog. I didn't know you had so many secrets."

"A better compliment, there is none." He begins rattling off his catalogue of weapons. "For close work, the R-34 Widowmaker with ion pellets. Of if you're feeing like something discreet, a wrist-mounted Eradicator. Or . . ."

"I've got a gun," I say.

"A plasma pistol?" he scoffs. "Clumsy weapon. Loud. Indiscriminate. Hardly an improvement over—"

I pull out my gun.

"An Omnivore-540," he whispers. "Semiautomatic railgun. Titan Arms. Powered by a rechargeable ion cell to drive the round along patented parallel reactive conductors. Adjustable internal diameter, multicaliber friendly, with"—his voice goes hushed—"an autonomous forge in the magazine." He smiles dreamily. "Metal goes in. Death comes out."

"No need to get dramatic."

"Only twenty thousand were ever made. Where did you find one this side of the Belt?"

"A man's gotta have his secrets."

"I will buy. How much?"

"Not for sale. What I need is one of these." I walk to a rack of glistening titanium hunterkiller drones, with silent engines and a neurotoxin deliverer concealed in their front faceplates. It is an assassin's machine. "How small can you make it?"

25

LYSANDER

Lord of the Dust

OUR DROPSHIP SETS DOWN in a fortress carved into the heart of a lonely mountain. The gray stone juts up out of the frozen Ionian waste like a tombstone, while the hangar, cut into the top of the mountain just beneath gun bartizans, is vast and scored black from ages of passing ships.

A coterie of masked legionnaires and a tall Gold woman of mature years greet us. She's lean, with withered patience, a pinched mouth, and a methodical, droll disposition. Her hair is chopped short, a cut that looks self-administered. Vela au Raa, sister of Romulus and his favorite captain during his war against my grandmother. Her mech units made hell out on the smaller moons, and gave me a fair amount of respect for guerrilla warfare as I watched from afar on Luna.

My neck aches from the injection site of the antiradiation drugs they pumped into me after my brief exposure. Nausea swirls. I watch Vela greet Seraphina with a chilly touch of their foreheads.

Seraphina does not look like the girl I rescued. The grime and blood are gone, the girl replaced by a woman who walks with a storm in her veins. Her lips are full, her nose slightly hooked, her dull Gold eyes sleepy and large, with thick eyelashes. Her hair is buzzed and notched on the right side. She is not beautiful by the standards of Luna's courts. There's something too feral about her. Something wild beneath the laconic movements and unsmiling face.

Little Hawk indeed.

Cassius catches me watching Seraphina. "What did he do to you?" he whispers, hunched in his manacles.

"Educated me." I grimace and play off the horror.

"I told you not to run your mouth." He eyes my wind-burnt face. "Gods, man. You look like a lobster."

"I feel like one too. Cooked and buttered."

He looks at the Golds preparing to lead us into the fortress. "Follow my lead. Every word here counts."

I try to breathe out the sibling peevishness. It clings in me, but not enough to convince me that he's wrong. If my little flight out the ship taught me anything, it is that Cassius knows these people better than I do, for all my studies.

The halls of the fortress are bare rock, like the hangar, and seem to have been carved crudely by clawDrills. Errant marks abound. Protection glyphs riddle the archways, like wood eaten by termites. The place is abandoned except for Romulus's soldiers and the fortress's other two breeds of denizen—robed Obsidians with bare feet and bald heads, with iron pyramids emblazoned on their simple gray robes, and several White hierophants who wear strange perruques made of coarse blue-black hair. This is a remote installation. A fortress that's been left to molder. Why are we here and not in Sungrave?

Romulus is trying to hide something. Is it simply his daughter's indiscretion? Or is it that recording Pandora asked about? What did she think Seraphina was bringing back? What could be so valuable to spark all this?

There is no furniture in the warroom of the fortress. Huge pillars support the uneven domed ceiling, and at the far side wait a coterie of shadowy forms.

My heart beats faster as we draw closer to a great stone throne made for a man larger than a Gold. I search the shadows, expecting the infamous warrior to be lounging upon it. But Romulus au Raa, twenty-third Lord of the Dust, Sovereign of the Rim Dominion, does not sit upon the throne. He sits at its foot, cross-legged on a thin cushion, wearing only a gray scorosuit.

His cheekbones are high, the lines of his jaw long and leading to surprisingly sensual lips riven with two scars. His hair is dark gold, streaked with gray and tied behind his head in a simple bun, through which pierces a stick of black wood. His right arm was lost in the Battle of Ilium and never replaced. A sliver of his bare chest, moon pale, shows as the collar of his suit falls open from his quiet labor.

He makes adjustments to a dissembled black hasta in his lap. Longer than the razors of the Interior, it stretches to two meters in its active, rigid form, resembling a lance. Silver figures are etched into the metal. It is not their ancestral sword, Starfire. That was lost at the Reaper's Triumph when his father's corpse was robbed—its owner now a great mystery.

I find myself admiring his poise.

There is an intensity to his quiet, like a lone cold stone sitting in a still pool of water. A humility to his bearing and expression that I did not expect, and in some way makes me feel as if we stumbled upon an ancient creature in his private garden, one who has seen the shaping of worlds, the sundering of empires. I feel calm, but very, very small as the myth earns flesh. Unlike me, he stood before the Reaper but did not surrender his moon. He gave an arm and a son to protect it.

The Obsidians push us to our knees.

An ugly Gold in his mid-twenties with a crisp dark goatee and close-cropped hair emerges from the shadows beside Romulus, watching us with intelligent, mismatched eyes. He looks like a spider smuggled into human flesh, all knobby joints and spindly appendages, lending him a covetous air. His forehead and jaw are overgrown, and the skin and coloring possess the anemic quality of a skinned rabbit, except on his neck where there are several small brown splotches.

The famous fiend, Marius au Raa. I knew him when he studied at the Politico Academy on Luna as a hostage. I remember him a boy of thirteen, quiet, resentful of the parties and as disdainful of his peers as they were of him. I duck my head, worried he might recognize me.

He does not.

His eyes linger a moment, then pass on, absorbing us all as he ignores his sister and brother to exchange a few hushed words with Pandora.

When Romulus has sealed his razor's casing again, he breathes a long, sonorous note of air from his nose. Marius touches his shoulder. "Father, they've arrived."

"And they've brought *gahja*," Romulus says.

When he finally looks up, I am struck by his gaze. The left eye is missing. In its place is a smooth globe of blue marble. Romulus eases himself to his feet and greets his son Diomedes. The younger man must bend at the waist so that their foreheads touch in their fashion. "Son." He turns to Pandora. "Pandora, you have done well. Please."

She nods stiffly and rises from her deep bow. "Only my duty, my liege."

He smiles at his sister, Vela. "The Ghost never changes."

"I would not know what to do if she did."

"Thank you, Pandora." Romulus sets his hand on her shoulder. "I wish I could tell the Moon Council what you have done. The Rim's greatest servant deserves more than just my meager thanks."

She nods obediently. Before her master, gone is the hound, replaced by a pup. The adoration is shared by Diomedes and the rest. I feel it seeping into me. Only Cassius seems immune. His eyes rove for some means of escape, as I should be doing.

At last Romulus comes before Seraphina, who kneels, her shaven head bowed, her eyes fixed on the ground. Her father lifts her chin and kisses her on the brow. "Seraphina. My burning one. How I missed you."

"Father." She looks up at him with absolute love on her fierce face. "I didn't know if I would see you again." Has anyone ever looked at me with such love? He presses his forehead against hers. After a moment, he pulls back and looks at us.

"You bring *gahja*."

"They're friends," Seraphina says. "I was set upon by Ascomanni. . . ."

"I heard," Romulus says, sparing a look to Pandora. "Let me see their hands."

With the help of the guards, our hands are shown to him; he looks down at our palms. "You are not Scarred. So why do you both have the calluses only a life with a razor could give?"

Diomedes glowers down at us, as do the others.

"My name is Regulus au Janus. We're water traders. I was once a warrior by necessity," Cassius admits. "I never earned a scar; my family wasn't well placed enough to earn me admission into the Institute. But I served Augustus, as all our family have. When my home was taken by the Rising, I picked up a razor and fought . . . until Mars was lost, then I fled with my brother, Castor."

"So you accepted exile over death," Romulus says. "I see."

He looks back to his daughter. Cassius glances at me to make sure I continue my silence. "Why did you not tell me where you went, child?" Romulus asks his daughter.

"Would you have let me go?"

"No. When you disappeared . . . I thought you had died. When I discovered that you went to the Interior . . ."

"You wish I had?"

The words wound him. "No . . ." Vela and Marius seem to disagree. "I would have moved the worlds to bring you home."

"But instead you sent your dog to hunt me down," Seraphina says. "She killed Hjornir. *Hjornir*, Father. You've known him since he was a child. You taught him how to hunt. All he ever wanted was to serve Gold, and that bitch pulled out his teeth."

"He was a slave who disobeyed his master," Romulus says.

"Did you tell her to torture him?" Her voice softens. "Did you?"

"I did," Marius says from behind his father.

"You?" Seraphina hisses. "Of course it was you."

"Do you expect a concession of regret, sister?" he asks with soft malice. "I daresay the fate of your pet should be on your conscience. Jeopardizing the Pax Ilium for a flight of fancy? What if the Slave King and his Horde had caught you? War would follow."

"You might try sounding less pleased about it, brother," Diomedes says. I note the tension between them, filing it away for later, and glance at Cassius. He's eyeing the razor Romulus left on his pallet.

Seraphina spits at her brother's feet. The greatest sign of disrespect on a world barren of natural water. "I weep for a world where a worm like you could order a man like Hjornir to the dust."

Marius does not rise to meet her anger, he just sighs.

"Did I raise a dog?" Romulus asks her.

Seraphina's face reddens. "No, Father."

"Then don't act like one. Your brother is my Quaestor. And his service has been faithful. I would have questioned Hjornir myself had I been there." Seraphina looks away from her father in disgust. "He conspired with you to break a legal treaty. He was a *traitor*."

"Then so am I."

"Yes. You are," Marius says. "Strictly speaking."

"Boy . . ." Romulus stares at his son till the man lowers his head in apology. He turns back to address his daughter. "You broke the peace. A peace that has protected our moons for ten years. You went against your Sovereign. You went against your own father. *Why?* What could you possibly seek?"

"The truth," she says passionately.

"What truth?"

"The truth of what happened to our docks."

This gets Cassius's attention, and mine.

Diomedes blinks. "What mystery is there? Fabii destroyed them for his Sovereign." Unlike the utter destruction of Rhea, my grandmother cannot claim responsibility for the destruction of the Ganymede Docks. She gave no such order. Roque au Fabii's reasons for crippling the far worlds died with him. Or did they? I lean forward in interest.

"So you've been listening to Mother's fantasies again?" asks spindly Marius. "And did you find anything?"

"No," Seraphina says, hanging her head. "Mother was wrong."

I catch the slightest movement of Romulus's lips, so slight all but a Pink and a boy raised by my grandmother might have missed it. Relief. Interesting. He feared she would bring something back. "You wanted war so badly?" he asks his daughter.

"I want justice," Seraphina says. But she has noticed something else, and echoes my own thoughts. "Why did you not bring me to Sungrave? Why here?"

"All of Io believes you are on a mission for me," Romulus says. "That is what I've claimed. If the council discovered the truth—that you went into the Gulf of your own accord—you would be executed for treason. I brought you here to protect you."

"Then where is Mother? Why is she not here?"

"I think you know why," Romulus says. "She used you, child. She would have had you spark her war. But as I told her, you cannot draw blood from the stone. There is no mystery. No conspiracy. Fabii destroyed our docks. Anything else is the fantasy of a warmonger." Romulus steps back from her. "Now what am I to do with you?"

"Let me return to Sungrave. Let me serve the Rim."

Romulus looks down at his daughter, but his eye is fixed on the past, heavy with the weight of age. He lost his firstborn daughter in the Reaper's Triumph. His son Aeneas at the Battle of Ilium. How much more will he lose? he wonders. I know because I have seen that same look in Cassius's eyes. The same weight in his spirit.

"If only I could," he says to her. He nods to the robed Obsidians. They seize Seraphina from behind. She struggles in vain against their huge hands.

"Father!"

"Were I stronger, I'd bring you before the Moon Council. But I don't have the heart to watch you meet the dust. You risked a war. You broke the law. Now this place is your home. Living quarters have been installed for your comfort. But it has no communications equipment. It has no transports. The nearest outpost is three hundred kilometers away. The Sohai I leave behind will be here for your safety. But they will have no kryll. No scorosuits or radiation shielding. If you attempt to leave on foot, the dust will devour you in a kilometer. This is the fate you made yourself."

I don't know these people, but I feel a keen ache seeing family trauma as Seraphina begs her father not to do this, for her brother to stop him. But they're right, it was not her place to risk war.

Diomedes looks pained. "It is this or death. I am sorry, Little Hawk. It has to be."

Face torn with betrayal, Seraphina is dragged cursing from the room. Cassius and I are left on our knees, a sick feeling spreading through me, as I realize that we too must be forgotten. All those weeks in the cell just to face the same end. For me. For Pytha. For Cassius.

"What of the *gahja*?" Diomedes asks his father.

"They could be the Slave King's spies . . ." Marius murmurs. "Interrogate them."

Romulus paces before Cassius and me.

"You saved my daughter's life. For that, I give the gift of my thanks and my son has given you the gift of reprieve from torture. By the calluses on your hands, I know you are men of weight, and so I awarded you the dignity of my attention."

"We're your guests—" I begin, prepared to launch into a long spiel about honor and dignity. But he speaks over me.

"Guests are invited. You cannot stay. You cannot leave. So the only right I can afford you is a swift end." He turns to Pandora. "Behead them, put their bodies into their ship, and then cast it into Jupiter."

"Diomedes," I say, hoping I gauged him right.

There's a small hesitation in the large man. "They saved Seraphina's life," he says.

"And to keep her alive, there must be no witnesses to her return except those we trust," Romulus replies.

I search for some clever gambit, straining for an outlandish conceit that might save us. Something out of the Reaper's own book. Cassius is preparing to launch himself not at Diomedes, but at Romulus himself, to try to take a hostage. I know the current of my friend's mind, and how I might help him using my body as a shield against Diomedes. I'll likely die for it. But he'll have a chance. The tension builds first in his muscular neck, then his toes as he finds purchase on the stone. And just before Cassius is about to fling himself forward, the ground rumbles under our feet. Diomedes steps back from us.

"What was that?" Diomedes asks. "Volcanism?"

"No." Romulus puts a hand to the ground. "A missile strike."

Vela pulls her datapad and snaps several questions into it. "Romulus, we have incoming vessels. Our escorts are down."

"Impossible," Marius whispers. "No one knows we are here."

"Evidently someone does," Romulus replies. "How many ships?"

Vela blinks hard at her datapad. Romulus is forced to repeat himself, "How many?"

"Ten warhawks."

"Ten?" Diomedes repeats, startled by the number.

"And more chimeras."

"How could they get past the orbital defenses?" Marius asks.

"They didn't come from orbit," Romulus murmurs. The Golds all tense at the implication. Vela takes control.

"Pandora, have your Krypteia stall them in the hangar." Pandora salutes and heads toward the hallway, flanked by her men. Vela turns to the rest of the bodyguards. "Protect your Sovereign."

But then Romulus begins to laugh.

"Father?" Diomedes says, sparing a confused glance at Marius as their father sits back down on his cushion and sets his razor on the ground. "What are you doing?"

"Waiting . . ."

"For what?"

"Isn't it obvious? Your mother."

26

LYSANDER

Wrath of the Mother

D IDO AU RAA, WIFE of Romulus au Raa and mother to his seven children, enters the warroom as if she has the intention of tearing it down from the inside. She stalks at the head of an armored column of cloaked Peerless Scarred dressed for war. Orange goggles cover their eyes. Dark ugan wrap around their faces. Unlike Romulus and his sons, they carry heavy weapons and wear battle masks and skipBoots. I see not a single Obsidian or Gray amongst them. This is a Gold affair. Cassius and I crouch together, momentarily forgotten. We search for some passage from the room, but there's only one door.

"Hello, wife," Romulus says from his pallet.

"Husband," she says, voice muffled as she strides in front of her men toward Romulus's smaller coterie. She wears a tan cloak, underneath which is dust-colored light karatan armor with radiation shielding and a hood. A kryll covers her face, orange reflective goggles cover her eyes, and around her head is wrapped a cloth ugan, like a Bedouin rover of Old Earth. A long black rifle is strapped to her back. She removes a new item every third step, till at last she pulls free the ugan, pulls back the hood, and a thick tangle of graying dark

hair falls about her shoulders, framing a masculine, strident face with ridgelines for cheekbones. Gray-gold eyes flare out from behind thick rows of dark eyelashes and heavy, sleepy eyelids like those of her daughter. There is a duskiness about her, and a warmth to skin raised in Venusian seas, close to the bosom of the sun. "You said you were going hunting. But you didn't say your quarry was *gahja* and errant daughters." Dido clucks her tongue.

"Perhaps it should be duplicitous wives," Romulus replies. He scans the soldiers behind her, eyes settling on a towering young Gold who bears a striking resemblance to Romulus himself. The man has an iron fist the size of a grapefruit embedded in the sternum of his armor. Doesn't leave much of the man's temperament to the imagination. "Bellerephon, you too?"

"You've held us at bay long enough, Uncle." The young man's voice is reptilian and amused. His eyebrows are thick as catepillars atop a dramatic face with a hooked nose. "Debts need repaying."

Romulus looks back at his wife. "Is this really what we have come to?"

"It is where you have brought us. Now, where is my daughter?"

"In the upper reaches." Romulus sighs. "You'll find her scarred from her travels."

Dido nods and motions to three eager young lancers. They depart at a run. She turns to her two sons. "Hello, children. I see your father has employed you in his schemes. Marius, I wish I could say I'm surprised, but you've always been a general offence to me. If ever a child deserved to be forgotten in the desert . . . But Diomedes, you disappoint me. Skulking about in the night on ill errands is the duty of an assassin, one of your father's Krypteia, not an Olympic Knight."

"Mother," Diomedes says, nodding his head and dutifully receiving the kiss she puts on his brow, not knowing what to do. "Why are you here?"

"To voice my dissent."

He eyes the men behind her. "And the men?"

"To ensure that dissent is heard," Bellerephon says.

"I wasn't talking to you, cousin," Diomedes snaps. He steps toward his mother. "I know you and Father have had your differences, but this . . . this is beyond the pale. It is unforgiveable."

"So many things are unforgiveable." She shrugs. "I'm only visiting my husband. But why do I feel I've caught him with his hand on the water jug? Has he a paramour here? Come out, paramour!" She frowns. "No? None?" She makes a show of looking around. "None at all?"

"Are you quite done?" Romulus asks.

"Oh, Romulus, I've hardly just begun." She fans out her cloak and folds her legs to sit across from him. Cassius waits with me in the shadows of the pillar, watching the door. There are too many Golds to escape.

"Wait," I whisper to him. "Let them sort it out." It pains him to sit and watch, but the new Golds are our only hope.

"Did you fire upon my escort vessel outside?" Romulus asks.

She shrugs innocently. "I remove obstacles from my path."

"And my Krypteia?"

"Sorted."

"You raise a hand against your Sovereign," Marius hisses. "Have you both finally lost your wits?"

"No," Dido sneers. "I have not lost my wits, you venomous, loathsome toad. You have lost yours, if you ever had any to begin with."

"Mother—" Diomedes begins.

She holds up a single finger. "Mother is speaking." She looks back to her husband as her large son lowers his head. "Did you think you could keep this a secret? From me? From the council? Shutter my bright child away and I would be none the wiser or worse about it?"

"Must we do this in public?"

"What have we to hide?" She smiles. "Do you know why she even went into the Gulf?"

"Because you sent her after your folly."

This catches Dido off guard.

"You knew. But did not arrest me?"

"You are my wife," he says as if that answers everything. I watch for some sign of affection to take hold of her. Even on Luna, their love was something of fable. Romulus and Dido, the star-crossed lovers who burned a city for their love. But the years, it seems, have dimmed their star. And now Dido pulls back away from Romulus, a look of disgust spreading across her face.

"Then you are a coward."

"Perhaps. Are you more angry that I have faces you cannot see, or that I showed you mercy?" Romulus asks, amused.

"Where is the man I married?" she whispers. "The man who could carry a world on his shoulders? I look for him, but all I find is this withered, cowed creature you've become. If you were an Iron Gold, you would have sent me to the dust."

Romulus sighs, unaffected. "All this Venusian prattle and bluster . . . You're wading in the shallows, my dear. Shall we cross the Rubicon?" He looks past her to address the fifty Gold who've followed her into the room. More pack the hall outside. They watch from behind filtered reflective goggles, their cloaks making them look like devilish bats gathered in the shadows. "Children of the Dust, you stand before your Sovereign uninvited, wearing weapons and hiding your eyes like Horde filth. Remove them and kneel."

They do not.

"I said kneel."

Not a man moves. "There we have it," Romulus says. *"Alea iacta est."*

"You are a Sovereign, not a king, my love," Dido says, her humor fled. "You have forgotten that, as did the old Luna bitch." My blood stirs at the mention of my grandmother, even if her words are true enough. "Forgotten that you are expected to serve the will of the Moon Lords from Io to Titan. As you cloister yourself here, men *loyal* to the Rim seize control of Sungrave. They move against your Praetors in their ships, your Imperators in their barracks. By dawn, patriots will have control of Io, and I, as its Protector, will serve until such time that a new Sovereign can be elected."

He smiles ruefully. "You may seize Io, but you cannot hold her. The people will not forget your birthright. A *gahja* till I made you my wife."

"Don't you start with me too. . . ."

"The blood of *my* ancestors watered this moon. Their hands shaped her. She is ours and we are hers. You are not a Raa, no matter your brood. I make you a Raa." He leans forward, baring his teeth. "Ganymede, Callisto, Europa, they will all fall upon you, and then Norvo and the rest of them will come and you will have spent your life and mine for nothing."

"Perhaps."

"Seraphina brought back nothing."

"Is that a fact?" She stands to look down at him. A dozen of her men come forward. "Romulus au Raa, you are under arrest." I wait for her to say the word "treason," as does Romulus, but it never comes. "Bellerephon, seize him."

Flanked by his men, Bellerephon steps forward. Diomedes's hasta snaps up from his waist and forms into a two-meter-long lance. He points the long black length at his cousin. "Aevius, Bellerephon, as much as I love you, take another step and you will be for the worms."

"Come now, cousin. Don't be truculent," Bellerephon says. But Diomedes does not relent.

"Son . . ." Dido says. "Your duty is to the Compact. Your father has violated it . . ."

"By protecting Seraphina?"

"For other sins."

"You have evidence?"

"Forthcoming."

"Insufficient." He does not move.

She sighs. "Disarm Diomedes. Kill anyone who isn't dragonblood." Dido's men hesitate, looking to Bellerephon for confidence. He nods them forward and they move as one toward Romulus and his defenders, their long razors held in two hands above their heads. Diomedes lifts his rigid razor to his lips. He closes his eyes and kisses the metal. Then his eyes open, and the spirit behind them bears no kindness.

When Diomedes moves, they begin to die.

He skims diagonally across the front rank of his mother's men with such possession of his body that it seems he were another species entirely. One made of wind and wrath. He sidesteps two of their thrusts and removes the head of the one he called Aevius, and exchanges two parries with a thickset woman before pulling a second, shorter razor called a *kitari* from his belt, and skewering her stomach and ripping sideways through half her rib cage. Aevius's body hits the stone and the woman stands there trying to stuff intestine and mesentery back into her abdomen before collapsing to her knees, bubbling screams from her mouth. Bellerephon and Diomedes crash together at the end of Diomedes's assault. I watch in awe, and glance at Cassius. I thought he was the greatest Gold swordsman left. By the look on his face, I know now that presumption was shared and mutually shattered the moment Diomedes moved.

Sparks fly from the long razors of Diomedes and Bellerephon before they separate, both of far greater skill than the men around them. The other Golds encircle Diomedes, about to close on him from his flanks when his brother Marius lunges forward clumsily and sheathes his blade through the eye socket of a rangy Peerless. He's slashed in the side of the head by Bellerephon. He reels back, like a child struck by a father, losing his right ear and very nearly his right eye. Flesh flaps open. Bellerephon kills two of the bodyguards as Diomedes takes one more of his lot. Vela is about to throw herself into the fray as Dido's other men shoulder their rifles to gun the unarmored Raa down.

"Hold!" Dido shouts, stopping Bellerephon and Diomedes from cutting one another apart. Bellerephon draws back to her side, warily watching his cousin.

"No hand touches my father," Diomedes growls as more Peerless encircle him. His eyes stay on Bellerephon, the most dangerous of the traitors. Marius and Vela tighten to make a hydra fighting formation, their spines pressed together as blood sheets down Marius's neck. Clearly no warrior, he looks ridiculous amongst the rangy killers, like an overgrown glass figurine trying to dance with boulders. Despite their earlier friction, Diomedes angles himself to protect his younger brother.

Diomedes points his gore-covered weapon at his mother.

"You would kill your own mother?" Dido asks, stepping past her men toward him till the tip of his razor rests against her right breast. She leans into it. Blood wells through her tan armor. "Me. Who carried you in my womb. Me who nursed you on my flesh, on my milk." She leans forward, centimeter by centimeter letting the blade enter into her body. "Me who pushed you into this world."

"Enough," Romulus says coldly. "You waste our blood. Let them take me. I have nothing to hide."

Only when Romulus sets a hand on Diomedes's shoulder does his son lower the blade. At her brother's instruction, Vela lets her own weapon clatter to the ground. Once the rest of Romulus's men are unarmed, Dido's come forward warily and bind Romulus and his kin.

It ends as fast as it began. If this were a coup of the Core, Romulus and the rest of us would have been mowed down from the door. Fast and clean, with blame placed where it does further good—that is how my grandmother dealt with her rivals. It is how she told me I should deal with mine.

Seraphina enters with her mother's men as her father is escorted out. Her eyes follow him with deep sadness. Dido bends by the dead Golds and tips a finger into each of their blood and spreads it on her Peerless scar as a Rim sign of respect. "See that they are sent to the dust with all honors," she tells her lancer.

"Seraphina," Dido says. The women embrace.

"Tell me you found it."

"I did. You told me no one would be hurt."

"Diomedes." Her mother shrugs as if that explains it.

I stand up behind the pillar. Cassius joins me hesitantly. "Shall we try this again?" I ask.

He winces. "Let me guess. You want to talk. Go on. Use that silver tongue."

"With pleasure."

We step out together from our hiding place. The women turn to us. Their men rush forward with their razors. Cassius and I are knocked again to our knees.

"We get the gorydamn point," Cassius mutters when one grabs his hair.

"The infamous *gahja*," Dido says with a laugh. "Hiding like mice."

I look at Seraphina. "We never had a proper chance at introductions. I am Castor au Janus. This is my brother, Regulus. Pleased to finally meet you. Now, considering I saved you from being a three-course Obsidian feast, would it be terribly rude of me to ask for a bath?"

"They saved my life," Seraphina says in amusement.

"Saved your life?" Dido is annoyed. "I did not send you because you are a woman who needs saving. But still . . . My goodmen, I do not believe my husband showed you proper hospitality. Men of the Rim can be so blunt. Prithee, excuse him and let me amend the oversight." She has her men unclasp the muzzles and opens a foil packet of wafers from a pocket on her armor and breaks a wafer in half to give to us. She pushes the pieces into our mouths, but we're too dehydrated to swallow them down until her men push canteens to our cracked lips. "You are now my guests. And guests need not kneel."

27

DARROW

Deepgrave

WE FLY LOW AND FAST over the bucking sea. A storm has risen over the Atlantic, heaving up mountainous waves of cresting foam. With a howl of joy over the coms, Sevro leads his squadron through a wall of water. They look like sea lions, their scarab-Skin oily and glistening wet as they weave above and through the churn, red beacon lights blinking from the heels of their gravBoots.

I dive into a wave, Thraxa au Telemanus to my right, and rip back up toward the dark sky.

It is liberating to be an outlaw once again. Octavia was right. Legitimacy and reign come with heavy burdens. But so too has my emancipation. With Wulfgar's death, I ignited a wildfire across the Republic that has shifted popular opinion against the war and my wife. Even incorruptible Caraval raves for my arrest. For the last month, we've been holed up in an abandoned military base on Greenland, preparing for this mission. From the too-small cot in the cold barracks, I've watched Mustang give speeches in the Senate and fend off calls for impeachment. If it weren't for her summoning Wulfgar and the knights personally to her estate, she would be out of office. Somehow she clings on.

In the pale light of the old holoCan, she looks so pure, so above the tarnish that Wulfgar's death has put on my soul. I can't help but feel I've sullied her too with the blood of a good man. I project an air of jocular confidence to my men. Many of them knew Wulfgar. But at night, when the winds sweep in off the sea to howl against the concrete bunker, I'm plagued by the demons the world has given me. Even more so by those I've made for myself. I can only fall asleep to the sound of her voice.

They say Republics are naturally eager to devour their heroes. I always thought my Republic was the exception. Now, Copper and Red holoNews pundits, who once objected to the ArchWarden being an Obsidian, have made Wulfgar a martyr. They rail for my capture, declaring me a menace to peace. A warmonger. Useful once, a liability now. It wounds me, but not as much as it wounds Sevro. He blames himself for Wulfgar's death, and has shrunken inward, growing sullen in the absence of his family. Fearful, I imagine, that his daughters will believe those who say we are wrong.

We may not ever be welcomed back.

There's nothing worse for a soldier to imagine—that there will be no home to return to once the violence is over, no way to become the men we want to be. Instead, we're trapped in these violent guises, guises we only ever had the courage to don because of how much we love our home. Is this all we'll ever be? Is this what I've made Sevro become forever?

Republic Intelligence searches for us. I know many of those men and women. They're no fools. But they search deep space for signs of my passage to Mars and Mercury, thinking I would retreat either to my homeworld or the legions, where the populace or military would rally around me. They still don't understand me. The only thing that lies in the tunnels of Mars or upon the desert planet is the possibility of civil war. Were I to consolidate power, I would make Mars or the legions choose a side. I would rend our fledgling Republic in two. Exactly what I believe the Ash Lord intended. No. The key to Venus and to the end of this war isn't with my army. It lies beneath the waves of Earth.

Our quarry, a lonely deep-sea trawler, glows on the horizon.

At the mercy of the waves, it rides a giant swell up and then disappears behind the range of foaming water. For a moment, I think it's capsized. I bank up above the water, gaining altitude till I see it riding down the slope of a wave. It is one hundred meters from stem to stern. And as I descend upon it, I see its red paint has long since given way to rust and the gnaw of the sea. Huge yellow plastic crab containers at the back of the ship rock uneasily against their restraints. Men in yellow coats labor desperately to add extra lashings to tie the loose containers down. Another wave catches the ship and it rocks hard to port, throwing one of the men into the sea and snapping his safety cable.

"Mine!" Sevro says. There's a chorus of challenges and the game is afoot. His squadron surges forward, some diving under the water, others bowing upward to retrieve the sailor. Breaking free of the pack, Alexandar au Arcos skims tight to the surface of the water, then recklessly close to the hull before slicing down into the water just before Sevro does. A moment later Alexandar resurfaces on the far side, spiraling in the air like a surfacing dolphin, dragging the sailor up by his severed safety cord. He lowers him roughly onto the deck and lands dramatically on a knee to a chorus of boos on the com.

"*Superior genetics for the win,*" he crows. "*Be not ashamed, geriatric friends.*"

"*Shut your gob, Pixie,*" Sevro mutters in defeat.

Sevro and the rest of his squadron emerge from the water around the boat and land with Alexandar amongst the terrified crabbers. Most of the crabbers are Red, with a scattering of Obsidians and Browns taken to the sea to make their living. I slow my speed and descend less dramatically to land nearer the pilot's cabin. The captain, a bearded Brown with a continental-sized paunch, stares at me from the open hatch, his magnetic boots steadying him against the rocking of the ship.

"Plebian, are you the captain of this vessel?" I ask through my helmet in as haughty a Venusian accent as I can muster. He just stares at me, eyes fixed on the dull gray Society pyramid on my armor's chest and on the demonic visages of the scarab masks. I am the world he thought gone forever, now returned. "Kneel," I growl. The man falls to a knee. More Howlers land—only the tallest of our number, to complete the illusion—till there's twelve of us clad in the military accoutrement of a Society commando squad. Our helmets, our masks for the day, remain on.

I feared resistance in the crew and am relieved to only see terror. They fall to their knees, eyes downcast in fear of their returned overlords. Only the two Obsidians amongst the crew stare up at us in hatred from under their water-repellant hoods.

"We're just crabbers," the captain mumbles, trying to come to grips with his new reality. "Nothin' military on board . . ."

"Silence, whelp. You will address me as *dominus*. This ship, like you, is property of the Ash Lord. Prithee, Captain, assemble your men in the cargo hold and none of you will be liquidated." I eye the Obsidians amongst his crew. "Any attempts on the lives of my men will result in the decimation of your crew in its entirety. Defiance is death. Do you understand?"

"Yes?"

"Yes, what?" Thraxa snarls.

"Yes . . . *dominus*."

I feel a dark pit open in my gut and motion my men to take command of the vessel.

We commandeer the boat and deactivate their radio and satellite communications and consolidate the crabbers into the cargo hold with jugs of water. Pebble welds the doors shut in case they feel a flush of patriotism coming on. Soon, the rest of our number come with Colloway on his pelican. It floats above the water on the port side of the crabber and drops the submersible we took from our weapons cache on Luna's orbital docks. The submersible lands with a huge splash. Then the pelican sets down on the exposed deck of the crabber. Some of the lowColor Howlers—Winkle, Min-Min, and Rhonna—disembark carrying gear. The rest of the support staff, including my brother Kieran, are on Baffin Island, waiting with our escape vessel.

Winkle, a nihilistic, sleepy-eyed Green, is our lead cyber operations officer. His face is a pincushion of piercings and fashionable digital tattoos. He's particularly fond of monsters, and a blue dragon perches on his neck, its tongue slithering up his chin. His hair is acid green and defies gravity.

"Fuck. I'm already fucking seasick," he says, lugging his equipment out. "I'll never be able to work on this fucking floating tetanus trap."

"Rough ride, Winkle?"

"Char flies like a madman." He sniffs the air. "Ugh. Smells like an asshole after Venusian stew. Thraxa, doll, will you take me off this deck and to the coms." Thraxa leads him away to the bridge. "Never thought I'd miss the gorydamn desert. . . ."

I hop up into the ship and find Colloway finishing his landing protocols. "You hit turbulence?"

"Manmade," he says. "Winkle talks too much."

I laugh. "How's the sky?"

"Civilian traffic only. If the Republic knows we're here, they're waiting till you go down."

"That's comforting."

"I aim to please." He winks. The older man is so handsome it's easy to see why they make toy figurines in his likeness.

I hop off the craft and watch my niece bring Thraxa battery packs for her power hammer. No more than a third Thraxa's weight, Rhonna looks a child even amongst the smaller Howlers. I had a mind to leave her behind at the Den, but she won't be in harm's way today. Had to give her a taste of action before the more dangerous Venus leg of the mission.

"She's still bitter about the Iron Rain," Pebble says to me at the base of Colloway's ship.

"Well, pouting isn't going to make me put her in the sub."

"She just wants to prove herself."

"And she can, when her life and someone else's isn't at risk."

"She's as old as we were when we fell in our first Rain."

"And look at all the dumb shit we did." I glance over at my friend. Her cherubic face looks younger than her thirty-three years. Bright, optimistic eyes look out from cheeks as flushed as they were when she rode back with Mustang after besting House Apollo. Without malice, but possessing incredible fortitude, Pebble has faced more battles by now than even Ragnar ever saw. Seems just yesterday that Cassius was mocking her at the feast before the Passage, along with Roque, Antonia, and Priam. We see who got the last laugh.

"You know, Pebs, if Sevro is the father of the Howlers, you just might be the mother."

"Ha. I think that's the nicest thing anyone has said to me all year, boss." She wrinkles her nose as, across the deck, Sevro and Clown cackle to each other as they compete to see who can urinate farther over the side of the boat. "And what . . . interesting progeny we have."

When we've reached our coordinates at six in the morning, I follow the rest of my men out onto the deck. My muscles ache from the hard gravity of Earth. It's been some time since I labored in a gravity gym. The air on deck is crisp and clean, the ocean calm as it laps against the rusty hull. Rhonna leans against the starboard railing with her arms folded, in a mood at being left with the support platoon on the crabber. I join her as the others make their preparations.

"Remember to keep an eye on the jamming array," I say. "Last thing we need is for one of the crew to get free and send out a signal."

"Yes, sir."

"And make sure Winkle doesn't snort too many amphetamines."

"Yes, sir."

"Don't worry, my goodlady," Alexandar says, walking past with Milia. She's a Gold from my army at the Institute who joined the Rising with the flood of minor Martian houses that declared themselves for Mustang after the Ash Lord nuked New Thebes. Alexandar and Milia are an odd pair. Milia looks as if she's been recently resurrected, with pale skin, sunken cheeks, and the most nihilistic temperament I've ever met in a human. While Alexandar wouldn't have been out of place as one of Antonia's pretty concubines. That fine jaw and the white-gold hair that flutters behind him like a comet tail. Even I find myself resenting the boy at times. On the outside, he's the picture of all I ever hated. "I'll make sure I bring you a trophy, so long as the decks are clean and scrubbed. I want them shiny enough to eat off of," Alexandar says with a grin.

Rhonna glowers at him.

"Can't believe you're taking that gilded shit," she mutters. Her jealous eyes follow the Howlers going over the side. My brother was heartbroken when she signed up for the legion training at sixteen. She was assigned to a unit in the thick of fighting on Mercury, but by merit of her examinations I had pretext to bring her onto my personal staff as a lancer. She was not pleased.

"Rhonna, you're just too short to pass as a Gray. We're a Society commando squad. If you're not six feet, you're staying on the ship. Same goes for everyone."

"Not Min-Min."

"Min-Min is staying in the sub. Besides, she's a veteran."

"You don't think I can handle myself. Do you?" She jerks her head at the Howlers. "The rest of them think that I'm only your lancer because you're my blood. They think I'm just dead weight."

"No one thinks that."

"Colloway literally said that to me."

"Colloway is an asshole. Listen, if you weren't my blood, we wouldn't be having this conversation. You'd say, 'Yes, sir,' or I'd get a new lancer. You can't have it both ways. Suck it up. Do your job, and you'll get your chance."

Her jaw works. "Yes, sir."

I find Sevro watching me from the other side of the ship. "What?"

"You remind me of my father more every day."

"I don't know if that's a compliment."

"Me neither." He snorts. "I want to say again, for the potentially posthumous record, that this is a shit idea."

"Do you have another way onto Luna?" I ask.

"About a dozen that don't include releasing a psychopath."

"A dozen which you, me, Thraxa, and Pebble all picked apart. I thought you agreed to this."

"It's important the mutts think we're synced up," he says. "But I still don't like it. Didn't you learn anything from the Jackal?"

"The Jackal didn't have a bomb in his brain."

"I still say we should steal a Gold ship," he says stubbornly.

"And how would we find one?" I ask. "Patrol the inner orbits and pray any fully-rigged ships of war we see don't outgun us? If we do manage to board, fight our way through a battalion of space legionnaires, they'll frag their codebank as soon as we board and transmit a distress signal. That means we show up at Venus, which is guarded by the totality of Society naval power, injured, depleted from corridor fighting, with nothing but our pricks in our hands. And after all that, we'd still need an army once we land there."

"Then we stop by Mercury and pick up some legions."

"Which of our friends will we have to kill then?" I ask sharply, and nod to the water. "This psychopath is our key, our army, and our escape plan."

He lets me finish, unimpressed. "I once saw a man try to ride a shark. . . ."

"Where the hell did you see that?"

"Europa."

"When?"

"Callin' me a liar?" He glares at me. "Point is we won't be able to control him."

"Then we kill him."

"That's my job."

"Sure, if you down more guards than me. If I win, I get the honor."

We shake on it.

Outside the door to the submersible, I pause, hesitating before ducking into the narrow hatchway. Once I was a creature of tunnels and caverns. I felt safe in close confines. The Jackal twisted that nature in me. My body itself remembers the cold walls of his table and rebels against me every time I approach narrow spaces. I hide my fear from my men and slip through the hatch.

Thirty minutes later, the submersible sinks into the sea. With the Obsidians absent, we've had to combine my unit heavy knight with Sevro's Ghosts—Alexandar, Clown, Thraxa, Pebble, and Milia. Their multiRifles carry nonlethal spider venom munitions for meat targets and electrical rounds for armor. Ink black in their scarabSkin, they're packed behind me in the passenger hold. It'll be a tight fit on the ride up with our cargo. Min-Min steers the submersible from her seat in the nose with her hands in gel controls. Through the reinforced forward viewports, there's nothing but gray water. As we dive deeper, out of reach of the sun's rays, the hull creaks. The pressure builds and the water blackens as the ocean squeezes us into its fist and drags us down and down.

It takes us an hour to reach the abyssal plain at the bottom of the sea. A halo of lights around the front of the submersible illuminates the sand of the ocean floor. Out there in the darkness, three Poseidon-class Republic submarines patrol the Porcupine Abyssal Plain that stretches from the west coast of the British Isles to the slopes of the Mid-Atlantic Ridge. Up on the deck of the crab trawler, under protection by Rhonna and the others, Winkle is embedded deep in the cyberscape, linked in to the Republic's Starhall mainframe through a back door Theodora had her men prepare for him. The location of the sentinel submarines blinks on a holographic display to the right of Min-Min's navigation controls. The nearest one is two hundred kilometers southeast, patrolling in a circular arc around her charge.

We creep along the bottom of the ocean, undetected. Designed for future war on Europa, this prototype—stolen by Sevro last week—was built with sonar-resistant skin in a Republic lab on Earth. He disguised the theft by detonating explosives in the warehouse. I had Winkle issue a false press release from the Red Hand taking credit for the sabotage. By the time the authorities clear the rubble and the Red Hand disavows, we'll already be on our way to Venus and they'll think this was all the work of Society commandos and their Securitas agents. So I hope.

Fifty kilometers from our destination, we enter into the drone defense grid and cut our lights. Up on the boat, Winkle accesses the drones via the mainframe and puts the data acquisition from the drones on loop. We pass through the defense grid.

Clown shifts uncomfortably between Milia and Thraxa. "If Winkle's wrong and they spot us . . ."

"Shut up," Sevro mutters.

"I'm just saying dying here at the bottom of the sea, caged by lung-crushing pressure, is not how I expected to go."

"How did you expect to go?"

"Well, smothered under tits, actually."

"Thraxa, I can't reach my husband. Hit him for me?" Pebble says.

Clown holds up his hands. "A joke, darling! All I'm saying is that this is essentially a metal coffin." Milia looks at him with sullen eyes and Clown smiles awkwardly.

The thought of this being a metal coffin makes my skin crawl again. But no torpedo comes and we press through the grid. After this, Republic cyber forensics will discover Winkle's back door and we'll be severed from the Republic's information network. It's a hard price to pay, but worth it if it gets us onto Venus. I only hope Theodora isn't incriminated. With her position in Starhall's intelligence bureau, she's too valuable to my wife to be spent on me.

"You hear that?" Sevro asks. I strain my ears, hearing nothing at first, then something like a heartbeat. It vibrates softly through the hull of the ship. The heartbeat grows louder. Thickening, multiplying till it sounds like a wooden stick dragged down a rib cage. Then we see it through shadow and silt.

Our quarry.

Deep in the darkness of the ocean moves a huge, humped behemoth. A shadow that glitters with lights upon its dark crest. The lights bathe its metal carapace in pale blue. I've seen it on schematics before, but in the metal flesh, it's a dreadful sight of an older age. The prison is like a giant primordial crab crawling along the abyssal plain. A dome ribbed with intake vents and docking stations and barbed with antennae monopolizes its cephalothoric bulk. The dome sits upon a legion of barnacle-covered hydraulic metal legs that thump against the sand as they drag the station across the ocean floor. Several long umbilical tubes hang from the belly of the dome to suck refuse and litter into her recycling processors and incinerators. Inside her belly, she holds trash of a fouler sort.

For four hundred years, Deepgrave Prison has crawled the abyssal plains of Earth's oceans, sucking up the sins of Old Earth and punishing the sinners of the Society—murderers, rapists, terrorists, political prisoners. Now, war criminals.

One of Mustang's many reforms in her first days of power was the abolition of the death penalty in the Republic. Informed by revolutions of Old Earth, she feared that it would be abused to mete out fraudulent justice to deposed or innocent Golds and mark the Republic with a stain of genocide that could never be washed out. But she couldn't pass it while the Jackal was alive. It would be seen as nepotistic. The day she pulled Adrius's feet, she abolished capital punishment. All the war criminals, all the oppressors, slavers, and murderers whom I would have hanged, are here.

And now I've come to free one of the worst.

Min-Min guides our submersible through the legs of Deepgrave, banking us up to the underside of the dome. The hull shudders violently as she engages the magnetic couplers and the submersible's top hull locks into place, creating a pressurized seal between our thermal drill and the prison's hull. The drill whirs above us as energy from the engines funnels into the drill's heat coils.

When the drill has finished, it retracts back and shifts sideways into its cooling sheath. Sevro waits several minutes for the heat to dissipate before cranking open the top exit hatch of the submersible. On the other side of the hatch, the circular block of hull from the carved hole is suspended by a gravity well built into the submersible's penetration system. From the cockpit, Min-Min reverses the gravity and the block floats up into the station.

"Hats on," I say, donning my scarabSkin helmet. My vision goes dark and then the heads-up display flickers to life, brightening the confines of the submersible with its spectral amplifiers. The vitals and names of my friends appear above their heads.

I step toward the hatch to go first, but Sevro puts a hand on my chest. "Trying to get a head start?" I ask.

"Don't be so competitive, boyo."

Milia and Clown go in front of me to take point, shouldering their multiRifles. Thraxa follows, her pulseHammer magnetically coupled to a holster on her back. Min-Min swings out of her pilot seat and tosses one of her drones into the air. Small as a thumb and matte black, the projectile races up the hole. She surveys through its cameras and gives us the thumbs-up.

"Playtime."

The two point Howlers climb the ladder up to the hatch and then go weightless as the gravWell grips them and eases them up through the hole. Sevro removes his hand from my chest.

"Your turn, princess."

Using the schematics stored in Starhall's data vault, I chose the water filtration room as our point of entry. It's dark, full of noise, and entirely automated. Huge machines suck in seawater and desalinate it for the use of the guards and the prisoners. I call up the map on my HUD and a blue waypoint flares to life, marking our target's cell. White footprints glow on the display, illustrating the path we chose.

I shoulder my rifle and lead them up out of the desalination plant. We move in silence. A station mechanic's breathing is amplified by my helmet. He glows like a humanoid coal through a hulking photo-electrical oxygen splitter. I move forward, crouched. Then Sevro runs past me and slides to round the corner first. There's the soft sound of a spider venom round hissing out the narrow barrel of his short-stock rifle. A body crumpling. Sevro hogties the man with plastic restraints and comes back around holding up one finger.

"One."

Leaving the desalination level behind, we move through the lower bowels of the station like a silent nocturnal animal made of fourteen legs and arms. The station relies on its external defenses, which would eviscerate even a heavy assault force of the Ash Legions, but on the inside, the security systems were made to keep men in, not out.

We subdue several workers sipping coffee from thermoses as they set to their morning work, Sevro and I racing each other to be the first to hit them with our spider rounds. He's better with firearms than I am, and it's already four-to-one in his favor as we pass through heavy reinforced security doors so thick they appear to have been made by some ancient race. They're old and rusted, like the rest of the bones and shell of this dilapidated crab station. Only the sinew is new. Glowing biometric scanners. Sun Industry drones. Crowd-suppressant gas nodules in the ceilings. All neutralized by Winkle's access into the mainframe.

We activate our ghostCloaks and slip into the open door of a guard station outside the massive doors to the high-security Omega Level. The guards gab to one another over tin breakfast bowls and drink Terran coffee spiced with chicory. To ensure loyalty to the Rising, most of the guards are from my planet. While the political officers are mostly Reds, and wear the Vox Populi inverted pyramid badges sewn into their uniforms to declare their affiliation to the proletariat, the bulk of the guards are still Grays.

Once, I hated Grays. Ugly Dan and the rest of the tinpots that lorded over Lykos left a foul impression. But years on, I respect their discipline, their devotion to duty. And I pity them. For centuries they've been the frontline soldiers and battlefield pawns of Golds in house warfare. And now they toil for our Republic.

I remind myself of the endgame: this will end the war. It must.

What will they do then?

Not more than three steps behind the breakfasting guards, I stand in the doorway, a rippling translucent shadow in the ghostCloak. From inside the cloak, the guards are distorted like a child's crayon rendering. For them it's another tedious day of gloom in a six-month shift. They're counting down the hours till they can spend their mandatory thirty minutes in the UV beds to get their vitamin D, and smoke burners in the common room and watch porn experientials on their holoVisors. A thick Gray man with a bulldog neck sniffs the air. He's in a black uniform, a member of their tactical response squad. He should be a lurcher, but we couldn't spare specialists down here. They're needed on the front lines.

He grunts. "Does it smell like wet dog in here?"

"Warden's pooch don't leave the roost no more."

"Someone oughta shoot that poor little shit, out of mercy. It smells like it's inside out."

One of the guards looks appraisingly at the contents of his bowl. "Smells like rotten algae to me."

The man in the black sniffs the air again. "It's definitely dog."

"Sorry. That's just me," Sevro says. The guard turns in his seat, tracking the sound to the door, where the casual eye might think us a fault in his vision or a premonition of a migraine, but his fixed gaze sees us for what we are. His cracked lips part no wider than a finger's width when two spider rounds hit him in the neck.

A barrage of puffs and a dozen rounds punch into the flesh of half a dozen men as they try to stand from their chairs. They tremble on the ground as the paralytic agent spreads through their bodies. We deactivate our ghostCloaks and take over the section station, piling the men in a corner. They'll have a devil's headache this time tomorrow and might lose their sight for a few days, but they'll survive. "Six–three," Sevro says to me. Pebble and Alexandar set up to receive guests if an alarm is raised. The rest of us press into the Omega Level.

The lion's share of the prison's general population is housed in levels high above this one. They have communal cells and labor in crews every day from six A.M. to six P.M., hand-sorting the refuse sucked in by the umbilical tubes for recycling or incineration. There's sanity in an honest day's work. I would know.

But here on the Omega Level, those who were sentenced by the Republic courts for crimes against humanity languish in solitary confinement, never to see another face. Never to hear another voice. Or feel anything but the touch of the cold metal. They are given water and an algae protein gel through a tube in the wall and allowed to exercise in the common area for fifteen minutes every other day. But when they exercise, they do so alone. No prisoners with which to share their burdens. Just an echoing mausoleum of cold, faceless cell doors without window or crack or key. I've heard that the guards will sometimes play a holo for them in the center of the floor, but if they do, it is triumphant moments of the Republic.

The Republic might be above murdering its prisoners, but its morality is not without teeth. It wasn't what Mustang had in mind when she abolished the death penalty, but Publius cu Caraval has blocked every resolution for prison reform for the past six years. Some say it's because he's beholden to campaign contributors. My suspicion is that he lost more to Gold than he lets on. For my part, I agree with him. These men and women chose to put themselves above their fellow men. So let them now be separate. Forever.

Most of my enemies lie in the ground. The rest I put here. Boneriders fill some of these cells. The Jackal's own. I only wish we'd been able to throw Lilath in this pit instead of giving her the easy way out by shooting down her destroyer till it crashed into Luna's surface. In coming down here to free one of them, I wonder if I am becoming the traitor that the newsreels say I am.

We pause outside a cell door. "Is everyone going to behave themselves?"

"Are you, bossman?" Clown asks. "You almost cut off his head last time."

"Almost," I say. The sight of the Gold in the dark hall on that Luna night, his bare face covered in Howler blood, has not left me. Sometimes I wake from sleep thinking he's outside my door, waiting to come in. Waiting to kill my family. "Sevro . . . are you going to be civil?"

He shrugs.

"Good enough."

I disengage the lock. The door whines and the blue light encircling the handle goes dark. Steeling myself, I crank the handle and haul back the door, stepping out of the way of my men with their raised rifles. We're hit with the smell of algae and feces. The cell is a dank concrete box. Empty but for a toilet, a plastic sleeping pallet, and a shirtless, gaunt man. He faces away from us, asleep. His spine like a fossil in dust through sun-starved skin. Greasy white hair spills off the side of the pallet. He turns to look at us with black eyes sunk deep in a tattooed face. I take an involuntary step back, seeing my time with the Jackal in the man's body.

"What the hell? That's an Obsidian," Sevro says.

"Winkle, the package is missing," I say. "Are you certain he is in cell O-2983?"

"Positive. I'm looking at the roster now. He's stated as present in his cell. No medical intake info or labor duty. This is bad, bad, bad, bad."

"Yes, thank you."

"Then who the hell is this?" Sevro asks. The prisoner stands very slowly. He's no giant like Sefi. He stands barely six and a half feet and is as thin as Alexandar. He's past fifty, with a deeply receding hairline, a filthy beard, and more tattoo ink than I've ever seen on a man.

He watches us with intelligent, curious eyes. Not holding himself like a warrior, but as if he were a sinister mathematician studying string theory on a holoboard. A set of tattoo spirit eyes stare at me when he blinks. The only men who wear that ink are shaman of the Ice. And most of them are women.

Sevro steps toward the Obsidian, gun raised. "Who the hell are you? Answer, shithead."

The Obsidian smiles with his eyes, looks at the gun, then to Sevro's mask, back to the gun, then gestures to his mouth with a single finger. He opens it wide. Sevro shines a light inside. "Gross." He steps back. "Someone cut off his tongue." And that's not all they took. What I first took for a receding hairline I see now is a half-completed scalping. It makes the front of his head look indented, like the bottom of an egg.

"His hands . . ." Thraxa says.

"Let's see your hands," I say.

He cooperates without protest. Embedded in the back of the knotted hands are the crescents of the Obsidian caste. Black. Not the bleached white of a prisoner. "You're not a prisoner." He finds my eyes, even through my opaque helmet, wags one finger and then sketches a shield over his heart. "Guard?" He points a finger at me. Yes.

"You get lost?" Sevro asks.

The Obsidian thinks, then makes a fist and pounds it into the small of his back, like he's being stabbed. I watch him with greater interest. Why was a guard stabbed in the back?

"The prisoner 1126. Did he do this to you?" Thraxa asks. The man wags a finger no. "Do you know where he is?" No.

"Winkle, can you track 1126's implant or collar?" I ask, turning back to my task.

"No. It's not on the system."

"What do you mean it's not on the system? He can't have left the damn station. He's a prisoner of the state. He's on code black, no transfer. No one in history has escaped from Deepgrave."

"Your dad did," Clown says to Sevro.

"That wasn't exactly an escape," Sevro mutters under his breath. "I swear to the Vale, if that slimy shit has been out in the worlds all this time . . ."

"Do we really need him in particular?" Clown asks. "We got our pick of sociopaths."

"Boss . . ." Thraxa says.

"We'll have to take a look around," I say. "We need to find him."

"There's two hundred guards here," Sevro says. "Can't sneak around not knowing where we're going. If the alarm goes, shit will get mortal, fast."

"Boss . . ." Thraxa says.

"I know it's not ideal—" I say.

"Not ideal?" Clown interrupts. "The alarm goes, the subs will know we're here and we'll never get back to the trawler."

Underneath my scarabSkin, my son's key dangles from its chain, cool and heavy. I didn't leave him to tuck tail and run at the first sign of friction.

"Do you want to leave empty-handed?" I ask, my tone even, but the implication lacerating. They shake their heads.

"Boss!" Thraxa shoves me hard from the side, almost knocking me down.

"What?"

She jerks her head to the Obsidian. "I think he knows how to find 1126."

28

DARROW

Prisoner 1126

W E LEAVE THE OMEGA detention block behind and follow the Obsidian guard, now wearing an ill-fitting uniform he pulled off one of the subdued Grays. The pants come only to his lower calf, leaving exposed a strip of runic blue tattoos and pale skin. The jacket is a better fit. I'm wary of the man, despite his claim of being a guard. He was in that cell for a reason. Still, he's our best option here.

Tight behind him, our heavily armed pack ascends up exposed switchbacked stairwells with precipitous drops to either side. Beyond the stairwell is a dingy coliseum where the central processing facility sprawls. Prisoners toil at conveyor belts, sorting the trash from the seafloor. Guards patrol through their ranks with stun batons. High above this, hanging in clusters from the ceiling like the rusted eggs of some giant metallic spider race, are the cellblocks.

On a newer level, we glide over metal floors buffed smooth as glass. We pass myopic cameras and closed doors and the echoing coughing of prison guards abed in their barracks. The sound of a morning news program from Old Tokyo drifts through the halls. I miss a step when I hear my wife's voice. Just the holos.

We snuff out somnolent guards without breaking pace. The Reds and Grays don't stand much of a chance, but the rare Obsidian guard is taken down with extreme caution. Some can fight for a minute with three rounds of spider venom in their veins. In passing, I muse how it would be easier to kill them, but then shudder afterward at my own reptilian coldness. These are my *people.*

The guard certainly has no qualms as we lay waste to his colleagues.

What did he do to end up tongueless and imprisoned? Something either very good or very bad.

True to his word, the Obsidian leads us to the warden's quarters. The door is locked from the inside, beyond Winkle's control. Sevro kneels to melt through the lock with a plasma charge. As he lays out the components to his charge, the Obsidian sighs impatiently, steps past him, knocks on the door, then steps back. Inside, a dog begins to bark.

"Shut up!" Someone on the other side of the door screams in vain at the dog. There's a thump and a yelp. The barking stops. Behind me, Thraxa grunts. I look at the Obsidian and he motions for me to wait. Metal unlatches and the door pivots backward into the room, leaving me standing sternum to nose with a cadaverous, gecko-eyed Copper with a long-slack mouth, a cup of coffee in one hand, and the bunched folds of his black and gold silk robe clutched closed at his waist with the other. Sevro grumbles and disarms the plasma charge.

Staring at the asp-black sternum of my scarabSkin, the warden gibbers something unintelligible. His mug shatters on the metal floor and spatters coffee over his bare calves and the festive brocade of the Venusian rug that he now backs onto. I jab two rigid fingers into his right brachial plexus and then his femoral nerve to stop him from running. He stumbles back from the nerve strikes and I bend to fit under the door and follow him into the room.

A dog, some kind of terrier, barks and growls at our approach, backing away and leaving a trail of urine across the floor. Following my team in, the Obsidian walks toward the dog, crouches down, and holds out his hand. The dog approaches with its tail between its legs. When the man makes a whistling sound, the dog spurts timidly forward to lick his bony hand.

"Warden Videli cu Yancra, I presume?" My helmet's speakers distort my voice to a gravelly rumble. The door clicks shut behind my men.

"Yes . . ." he says, shaking from the pain of my light assault. But he's not a stupid man. He looks up with quick, adaptable eyes at our combat gear, at the Obsidian, where his eyes linger in fear and confusion before returning to me. "Whom do I have the pleasure of addressing?"

"We're wearing masks for a reason, dumbass," Sevro says. He walks behind the warden and pulls out a chair for the man. "Sit. Hands where we can see them, my goodman." The warden fumbles to find a chair and sits down. Sevro takes a seat behind him on the edge of the table and puts a hand on his shoulder.

I sit across from the warden and pour him a glass of water from a decanter as Thraxa spins her hammer at the door and Alexandar waltzes about the room thumbing the warden's possessions with a practiced eye. The warden looks to his bedside several times. The Obsidian fetches the warden's datapad and gives it to Sevro.

"Your men aren't coming, pleb," I say. "And lucky they are for that."

"What do you want?"

"Surely you haven't forgotten how to speak to your masters." Sevro slaps him hard on the ear. "You will address us as *dominus*, you quivering whelp."

The warden looks over at the Obsidian, then back to me. I'm not sure who he is more afraid of. "I can help you, *dominus*. It would be my honor. Just tell me how."

"You have a man in your charge. Prisoner 1126. He is not in his cell, even though his collar places him there. If the prisoner had been there, *cuprum*, we would be gone from this place and you would still be lord of your little fiefdom. But he is gone, and so I am here wondering whether to make your crown out of your toes or your fingers." I lean forward. "Where is prisoner 1126?"

He pales at the mention of his charge.

"He's dead. He died a year ago. Took his own life by starvation."

Sevro and I look at the Obsidian. He shakes his head.

"You trust him?" the warden says. *"Him?"*

"Seems you're the one who took his tongue," I say. The Obsidian points at me. "So yes. Did he see something you didn't want him to see? Say something you didn't want him to say?"

"No, he—"

"Liar, liar, prick on fire," Sevro says into his ear, and lowers his multiRifle to rest on the warden's groin.

"Prisoner 1126 is dead!"

"My goodman, if he had died, then you would have simply entered it into your logs and his cell would be filled with another deviant. So, pray tell, why was his beacon there?" I pat his leg. "I'll answer for you. It was there in case you were visited by Republic inspectors. It was there to cover up your graft."

"No," the warden says sharply. "I would never . . ."

"Be able to afford a carpet like this on a warden's salary?" Alexandar asks. He toes the carpet. "Venusian silk. Dyed with crustacean extract. Really ties the room together. Perilously fine taste, my goodman."

"What's the price on something like that?" Sevro asks.

"At least forty thousand credits," Alexandar answers.

Sevro coughs. "No shit?" He takes the pot of coffee on the warden's table and dumps the coffee inside on the carpet. If the man is angered, he hides it well. "Oops."

"Warden, warden, make it stop," Alexandar moans.

"A little *cuprum* weasel like you might fancy yourself a special sort of conniving," I say. "An entrepreneur harvesting an inefficiency in the system. What a waste it must seem to have Aureate sons and daughters locked in little metal coffins, with all their hidden bank accounts and vaults languishing out there in the worlds. What a waste that someone should not profit."

The warden looks up at me tactically, searching for some angle. He will see a giant in black armor and stare at a reflection of himself in the pitiless, insectoid eyes of the helmet. Submission is his only option, and it wounds his pride. It's no backwater bumbler who finds himself warden of Deepgrave. This is a high post.

"Prisoner 1126 paid you to leave solitary, didn't he?"

"Yes," the warden says smoothly. "He made improved arrangements for his incarceration. The Omega Block is . . ."

"A dungeon," Thraxa says.

". . . taxing on the psyche. But he is still here."

"Your testicles thank you for that," Sevro says, nudging his gun deeper into the man's groin. The warden flinches. *"Ya hara,"* Sevro coos—Venusian argot for "poor thing." "Does that hurt?" he adds. The theater is for the warden so there is no doubt in his mind that we are from Venus. That it was Society operatives who broke out one of Deepgrave's most hated charges. At the very least, I hope it throws a wrench into the peace talks. Mustang may puzzle it out, but if it gets back to the Ash Lord, he can't know I was here.

"I wonder, what if we were to report your graft to the noble Republic after our departure?" I ask the warden. "No matter how clever your Copper accounting, your actions will be discovered. Your trial will be a public farce, to set an example of how their Republic is intolerant of corruption." Sevro snorts at that. "To proclaim the circularity of justice, you will be sent here to serve your sentence."

"How long do you think you will last on the other side of the bars, pennyfingers?" Sevro asks. "How will you sleep, how will you shower, how will you eat knowing the monsters you once lorded over are now watching, waiting?"

I lean forward, allowing his imagination to work its worst magic. His composure falters for a moment and I see my chance: "When they come for you in your cell, I want you to think back on this day when I sat here before you and I want you to wonder if there was not something you could do to erase it all." I lean forward. "Because, warden, I'm here to tell you that there is something you can do."

His eyes light up. "Name it, *dominus.*"

"Take us to prisoner 1126, and then, when we escape, carry on with your life. Do not report the escape or our presence here to the Republic. Do this, and it will be our little secret. What do you say?"

"I'd say yes if I were you, goodman," Alexandar says, leaning back in a divan. "A life as an Obsidian's pet is no life at all." As if on cue, the old Obsidian bends to pet the dog again. I'm beginning to like the skinny man.

"I'll take you to the prisoner," the warden says uneasily.

The dog follows us, keeping its wary distance but never letting the Obsidian out of its sight as the warden leads us to a newer part of the facility. From a guard station, he extends the ramp over the divide to a suspended cellblock. We cross, and as the great doors to the block open, music trickles out.

The interior of the cellblock is a globe with a central communal area and the cells in three levels accessed by walkways and a stairwell. Sevro pushes past the warden. "What the blazing shit . . ."

It's not a prison. It's an improvised paradise. Thick layers of expensive carpets cover the steel floors. The walls are painted eggshell white. Golden roses and ivy grow along the walkways and crawl along the guardrails, fed by UV lights that hang from the ceilings. The cell doors are open. Three cells are filled floor to ceiling with books and datacubes, another with bottles of wine, another with camisoles and robes, another with a refrigerator and a portable generator and a stove, another with a garden of tomatoes, garlic, and carrots, another with hulking iron dumbbells and tension bands.

The communal floor is one great lounge. Hookahs stand like emerald scarecrows amidst a sea of pillows and blankets. Two collared Pink prisoners, a slender woman and muscular man, sprawl there naked, bruises mottling their bodies. Empty bottles and other casualties of debauchery litter low tables. And amongst all this, a powerful man sits in a chair with his back to us, playing a violin with feverish hummingbird strokes, bathed in the light of a UV lamp, naked but for the dull metal prisoner collar. He skin is tawny, darker than that of his younger brother. His golden hair is long and coiled and splays down his broad back. Lost in reverie, he does not hear us enter.

"Apollonius au Valii-Rath," I say.

The man stops playing and turns around. If he's surprised to see us, he doesn't show it. It's as if we materialized out of the fever of his song. For me, there is pain in seeing him sitting there twisted around, the equine nose, the sensual lips, the dark eyelashes and hot-coal eyes. He is a twisted simulacrum of his younger brother, Tactus— a man I cared for despite his darkness because I saw in him a glimmer of something good. But this is not my friend, no matter what blood they share. If there ever was light in this man, it was long ago snuffed by the hungry shadow inside him.

"What's this?" he says, eyes searching our masked faces. His amused baritone smooth and quick as thick wild honey down a hot knife. "A deputation of devils come to my acropolis with calamity on their heels? Have you come to kill me, fiends?" He twirls the violin to hold it by its neck like a weapon, his voice becoming pugilistic. "I venture you'll not find it pleasant."

"He's bloody mad," Sevro says over our coms. The man was always touched, a lover of violence and vice, but there is a mania behind his eyes more precarious than was there when I last saw him standing bruised and proud before a Republic court.

"Apollonius," I say again. "We've come to take you home."

The war criminal's eyes narrow. "At the behest of whom?"

"Your brother."

"Tharsus?" His eyes widen as he slides out of the chair like a grand saltwater crocodile and faces us without any shame for his nakedness. Long white scars from razors cover the lean muscles of his torso. The two nearest his heart are from me when we met in the hallway outside my bedroom in the Citadel. "Tharsus is alive?"

"He's waiting for you on his flagship, my lord," I lie. "We've come to ferry you to your fleet."

Apollonius looks down at the ground and a shudder of boyish joy goes through him. He looks up with a predatory smile. "Magnificent. Soon we will join him. But first, debts." He glides toward the warden. Thraxa takes a protective step up to my side. "Warden, warden, warden. Recall for me, for my memory has a tide unto itself, did I not promise you something upon the genesis of my incarceration here?"

"I've done what you asked," the warden says to me. "Honor your end of the bargain."

"I speak to you, warden, not my brother's minions."

"I do not recall what you said, prisoner. I receive many threats."

"Lies! A punctilious race such as yourself does not forget. You squirrel facts away like nuts in winter. Never too many nuts for a meticulous little creature . . ."

"I've helped you, *dominus*."

"Ah. Now you say *dominus*. . . ."

"If it weren't for me, you'd still be in the hole sucking algae from a pipe."

"Sucking from a pipe." He smiles. "A vibrant thought, that." He strokes the man's face. Sweat beads along the warden's receding hairline. He's terrified of Apollonius. "You should choose your words with more care, frail creature." He takes the man's sweat from his brow and tastes it. "As I suspected. You taste like coins."

"He's going to kill him," Thraxa says over my com, her worry bleeding through.

"Serves the dog-kicker right," Sevro mutters. The Obsidian leans against the doorframe, his head motionless but his eyes darting back and forth between us as if he knows we are speaking on private coms.

"Lord, we need him alive," I say.

"Why?" Apollonius asks neutrally.

Because he will keep this quiet, you psychopathic shit. "He has a biometric monitor on his heart. He dies, the whole place locks down," I lie. "We're on a timetable before their drone systems reactivate. *Yalla.* We need to go."

Apollonius steps close to me and stares into my mask. I wave Thraxa back.

"What is your name?" he asks.

"Artullius au Vinda."

"I do not know an Artullius," he says. "Take off your mask."

"Can I shoot him?" Sevro asks.

"Then we'll have to carry him with this Terran grav," Alexandar says.

"I'll carry the shitheap," Thraxa replies.

"He's not supposed to be this big," Alexandar mutters. *"Bastard was supposed to be eating algae for the last six years. He looks like he's been eating whole cows. Musta put on fifty kilograms of muscle."*

"I'm going to shoot him, Reap," Sevro says. *"He's on to us. And he's a pervert."*

"Don't shoot him," I say.

I close the remaining distance so that Apollonius and I are eye to visor. He's slightly shorter than I am. "Six years is a long time for new men to make their mark," I growl out of my mask. "I've been paid for your breathing body. And I will deliver it to your brother. Hardly matters to me if you're unconscious and drooling or traipsing about like a gorydamn Pixie. So, shut up. Get dressed. Or I break your nose and drag you in like the Martian dog you are."

He stares at me for three pumps of the heart and then breaks the spell with a pleasant laugh. "Venusian?" he asks.

"Venusian," I confirm.

"I hate Venusians. Are you Carthii?"

"Saud."

Beside me, Thraxa's hand has settled on her hammer.

"Then you live the day." He smiles. "How I've missed my people, even you clam eaters. Gold has an unyielding manner, no?" He sniffs the air, throwing the Obsidian a disdainful look, and turns to rummage through the pillows till he pulls out a white kimono brocaded in purple and gold. This he ties around the waist with a silk sash and bends to kiss his sleeping Pinks farewell. They do not stir, likely under the effects of some narcotic. He brings his violin with him and returns to us barefoot.

"Shall we?"

We prepare to leave the warden behind in the cellblock, having no more use for him. Alexandar and Sevro open the cellblock door and go through. Thraxa and I follow with Apollonius. Then he lunges backward away from us.

By the time I turn around, he's already standing with the warden, his huge hands wrapped around the smaller man's head, tilting it back and forth, exploring its contours with his fingers. The warden is frozen in his grasp. Apollonius looks over at me with the bored insolence of a dog taking a shit on a carpet. The warden screams as Apollonius presses his hands against his eyeballs. Apollonius's muscles ripple. His veins engorge. Before I can rush to separate the two, there's a meaty squelch. Blood sprays Apollonius's face as the warden's eyes puncture and explode in their sockets. Alexandar gags. Apollonius lets the warden fall to the ground and looks blithely up at me as the man screams and paws at his face. The Gold brings a bloodied thumb to his tongue.

"Just like coins."

I stare at the squirming warden, appalled.

"Sevro, shoot him."

A fusillade of darts hiss past my shoulder. Two hit Apollonius in the face. He laughs and pulls them free from under his cheek. Sevro and Alexandar shoot again and Apollonius swats the darts with his hand, where they stick in the meat. Silent, he charges Sevro like a joyous, blood-soaked bison. I lower my shoulder and tackle him from the side, hitting him just under the ribs and lifting him off the ground, arms gripped behind his knees. We crash to the carpets. He's a better wrestler than I am and I'm caught off guard by his immense strength. He rolls around me like an anaconda till I'm on all fours and the back of my head is against his sternum as he stands, pushing from the ground with his legs, cranking on my neck, straining my spinal cord as his thumb knuckles try to dig up into my Adam's apple. I choke, unable to breathe, but claw up at his face and stick my thumb into his nostril and try to bury it up his nasal cavity. His grip doesn't slacken. I'm going to pass out. Then the Obsidian guard is there. He hits Apollonius in the side of the head with a hookah and I manage to wrench myself free. My scarabSkin mask comes off in the Gold's vise hold and he crumples to the carpet as I stand, winded and red-faced over him.

Looking up at my naked face, Apollonius begins to laugh again, slow drunken sounds from his diaphragm as the venom finally overwhelms his body. He spreads his arms wide on the ground, covered in dark blood like some evil primordial squid. Sevro runs up and punts him in the temple, more for good measure, and the man's eyes roll behind his heavy eyelids as he drifts into blackness.

I stand panting over Apollonius.

"Thank you," I say to the Obsidian. His eyes search my face, knowing now who I am. He shrugs in amusement and looks back at the warden. For a moment I think he's going to take his revenge and bash the Copper's skull in. Instead, he tosses the bent hookah to the ground.

"Bloodyhell," Sevro says. "The warden?"

Thraxa's standing over the man. "Unconcious, lucky for him."

"Corrupt, now blind." I grunt. "Something tells me he's got the money for a new pair."

"Goldilocks, you prime?" Sevro asks. Alexandar hunches at the door. He wavers, then lurches to undo his mask, managing to get it off before he throws up inside it.

Sevro jumps away. "Idiot."

"Sorry," Alexandar says, face pale. He avoids looking at the mangled warden and puts his mask back on.

"The Minotaur, felled by a hookah." Sevro kicks the hookah and pats the Obsidian on the shoulder. "Wicked swing. Looks like our deal with the warden's off. . . ."

"Why? Blind or not, he wakes up and reports this to the Republic, he spends the rest of his life in a cell. Something tells me he's gonna bite the bullet."

"Hell of a gamble," Sevro says. "His men might go around him. . . ."

"You think they're not on the take? When in doubt, depend on self-interest. Take Thraxa and Alexandar and double back to the Omega Level to help Pebble and Clown transport the other prisoners. Thraxa and I will take this piece of shit to the sub. Go."

He pauses, looking darkly down at Apollonius. "This is shit," he mutters so only I can hear.

"Tell me something I don't know."

"I won 6–3. Time comes, I kill the prick." He jerks his head at the Obsidian. "What do we do with . . . hey! What's your name?" The Obsidian stares at him in annoyance and points to his mouth. "Nevermind. Tongueless it is." Sevro looks back at me. "He's seen your face."

The Obsidian waits patiently as I look him up and down. "Want a ride?"

29

LYRIA

Rust and Shadow

O N MY LEAVE DAY I wake up early and eat cold cereal in the commissary before anyone but the maids are awake. I dodge past their little packs of cleaning robots in the halls. With a week left in the bright month, the sky is bruise blue and leaks lazy rain. I make my way down the Esqualine Hills to the southern tram hub, which I take to the main station, on the eastern side of the grounds. Under the Silenius Arch, I show my leave pass and security ID to the Gray Lionguards there. I wanted to bring Liam, but it's a school day, and I'm worried the sounds of the city will overwhelm him.

"First trip to Hyperion?" the sleepy Gray asks at the station check-point as he examines my pass. Lines of first-wave commuters from Hyperion pass through inspection on the other side of the station. He's taking too long. He'll find something wrong with the pass. I keep my hand on my billfold in my pocket. How much do I bribe him? I should have asked one of the maids, but you can't count on a straight answer from any of them. They'd lead me astray for a laugh. More guards watch a holoprogram inside the guard station. "Seeing the sights?"

"Yes, sir."

"Skip the Circada. Lines are dreadful."

"I have a flexipass." I hold up the shiny silver pass the steward handed out to all the Telemanus servants.

"Ripper," he drolls sarcastically. "That'll get you in but it won't let you cut the queue. Tourist sites are flat out. Martians everywhere." He eyes me like I would a mosquito in 121. "Any fourth-class IDs are subject to full-spectrum assessment upon return after 22:00."

"I'm second class. . . ."

"Only on Telemanus grounds," he corrects, referencing my pass. "Extra-Citadel clearance is a different protocol. Savvy?" I nod. "Enjoy our moon, citizen."

I board the rain-slick train and huddle near a window, bundling tight my overcoat against the chill. The train sets out from the Citadel with only six other passengers. It cuts across trees and the low-lying autumn fog that buffers the Citadel from the city, rising up and up toward the jungle of lights and metal that is Hyperion. I remember seeing the city from the sky for the first time. It was magical then, thinking there were so many people in the worlds. Now, thinking of the riots and protests, it puts dread in my belly.

I disembark at Hyperion Station and push my way through the mass of commuters that cluster on the platform to board the train for its return journey to the Citadel. There's Greens and Silvers in the crowd, but most are Coppers. All buttoned up against the chill in expensive identical overcoats and scarves and dark broad-brimmed hats. I beg their pardon as I push through them, but they don't hear. Glowing earbuds fill ears. Holocontacts flicker in eyes. I use my elbows. I'm so short I can't see my way through and almost get trampled when a speaker pings. *"Train doors closing. Mind the pinch. Train doors closing . . ."*

Hyperion Station reminds me of Lagalos. It is a huge stone cavern of bustle and echoing noise, full of travelers from the farthest reaches of the Republic—scarf-wearing, leather-skinned Reds of Terran latifundias. Waifish Blue lads from some orbital flight school in snappy black jackets. Biomod manic Lunese Greens listening to thundering music from shoulder speakers, all stirred into a pot like one of Ava's stews. I pass glittering shops with moving advertisements showing expensive-looking things on expensive-looking Pinks.

At a map vestibule, I accidentally touch the screen and the holo flips sideways, showing a pitviper's scrum of travel options. It's dizzying and I'm not sure how the bloodydamn ticket machines work. The Yellow behind me is tapping her foot impatiently.

I feel a sudden panic. I stick out like a blistered toe. I want to flee, go back to the Citadel, watch holoflicks in my bunk. Kavax took Sophocoles with him to Lake Silene for the day for some secret meeting, so I don't have any duties.

No. Hyperion is the jewel of the empire. I look up at the carvings on the stone of the station. *Ava, you would have killed to see this.*

I owe it to her to give it a chance.

Overwhelmed by the transit maps, I leave the station and head out on foot. I can trust my feet at least, and the GPS in my datapad. Only a five-kilometer walk to the gallery. Half the distance Liam and I would walk from camp to the strawberry fields.

Along the way, I stop outside a little café on a glittering boulevard. Groups of Brown janitors in gray jumpsuits pluck at trash with metal claws. Vox Populi protesters are beginning to gather in a square to hear a man speak. Off the side of the tree-lined walkway, past flowering shrubs littered with trash, is a huge drop to the city levels below. Over the edge, apartments stretch as far beneath as they do above. My gut churns, having just realized I am kilometers above the surface of the moon.

Fliers trundle along in aerial boulevards like migrating beetles. Beneath them is a layer of pollution and fog. Lights glow beyond that. A whole other city concealed in the murk. *It's manic, Da. Would make even you look away from the holos. Might even give you a smile.*

I go into a nearby café, feeling a bit heady from the vertigo. Confused by the huge menu, I order a coffee and pastry. It's the first money I've ever spent outside 121, and the coffee alone costs a quarter of what I make in a day.

The Brown cashier sighs when I pay with bills instead of dataCreds and makes a show of rummaging through the cash register for change.

Once she hands it back, I move to sip my coffee in the corner. The coffee is good, sure, but the pastry overwhelms me. Buttery and flaky, with chocolate and nuts inside. *Woulda sold two of your children for a bite of this, Ava. See, I can enjoy myself. I'm a regular citizen.*

I watch out the window at the pedestrians but still feel so alone. They're part of this world. That's how they can afford these coffees every day. They have skills. Went to school. Know computers and advanced things. I'm not like them.

All's I know is to be a servant. Before that a slave. I imagine myself sitting across from a big man in a suit at an interview like they show in the holos. He'd ask my skills and I'd tell him I know how to tend silkspiders to keep them free of beetles, and how to put them to nest at night. I know how to bribe mine tinpots, how to haggle down an ounce of sugar, how to listen to rumors so I don't get stuck by a 121 gang.

"Ruster smarts, my goodlady," he'd say. "But we don't need that around here. Have you tried janitorial?"

The museum is fine and clean and cluttered. The Dawn of the Space Age wing is packed. Full of ancient spaceships donated by Regulus ag Sun himself. I have to push through a group of Grays and Blues to even glimpse half the relics. Through a crook in a woman's elbow, I recognize the winged heel of the Silver's company logo. The same that was on our tents and our food packets and our water purifier. The same as on the robots that replaced us in our own *unprofitable* mine.

The History of the Conquerors exhibit is closed; Warden barriers block it off. A flock of Coppers in front of me titter like jungle he-lions about there being some sort of terrible theft a few weeks back. Through a gap in the tarp that covers the front of the exhibit, I see several Greens are installing hardware in the floor as a crew of Oranges and Reds fix a marble arch where CONQUERORS has been burned over with COCK SUCKERS.

I smile to myself.

I skip the wing devoted to the Rising—little Conn and Barlow would have wailed in disappointment—and instead join the line for the Liberty Wing. There I find a room of concrete that stretches several stories high, narrowing at the top to let in a thin stream of light; a million Red Sigils litter the floor. Small as thumbs, made of flexible metal just like those on my own hands. Each taken from the mines that the Jackal of Mars liquidated. They call it the Hall of Screams.

It's grotesque and cold and I want to flee it. But I stay. Of all the art here, this is the straightest in the eye you can look at the horror. A man barely older than me falls down weeping, clutching one of the Sigils. He's alone, but Reds behind him kneel to comfort him till there's a thick cluster around him and they're all weeping and I'm wiping my own eyes and looking away, wondering if I should join, but feeling too awkward and too moved to actually do it. Where was this love in Camp 121?

A pair of towering Golds stand on the far side with their young son, watching the display. They're a handsome couple. Their eyes somber, respectful. But I want to shout at them. Tell them to slag off. This belongs to us.

Then the iron tinkles as their son slips from his mother's grasp and walks out onto the Sigils. His shoes rattle the Sigils together. The sound bounces against the concrete, rising level by level, the noise growing with each ricochet till it reaches the top of the room's cold concrete throat.

The clustered Reds stop and stare.

Made nauseous and claustrophobic from the Hall of Screams, I push my way out of the crowd, trying to find a place to sit down and recover. All the coffee shops are filled, so I aim for a small park outside the museum. I squeeze between a slow-moving gaggle of airy Blues, past jabbering Greens, the Colors all clustered together on the broad white steps that lead up to the museum. Carefully, I brush past a dreadful Gold woman who is stopped in the middle of the walkway, talking on an internal chip. A Red with eccentric piercings bumps into me, eager to get ahead. "Sorry, love," he mumbles, and carries on, sliding through the crowd, trailing smoke from his burner.

Someone shouts behind me on the stairs. I turn around to see the Gold woman wheeling about in a frenzy, her eyes scanning the crowd till they settle on me. She points a long, jeweled finger. "You." I look behind me to see who she's talking to. "Thief!" She pushes in my direction and I realize she's coming right for me. The people around me lurch away. I have the urge to flee, but I stand rooted to the spot on the sidewalk. "Watchmen!" the towering woman shouts. "Watchmen! Where is it, you little ruster?" the woman sneers down at me. Easily a foot taller than me. A hundred pounds heavier. More, despite how thin she is. She looks like an emaciated gold salamander wrapped in a fur coat, but her large eyes glitter like two evil gems. "I know you took it."

"I didn't take shit," I snap. She grabs my arm and yanks so hard I feel my shoulder grind in its socket. My feet come clear off the ground.

"We'll see about that. Watchmen!"

"They're coming," someone says.

I look around in confusion and squirm sideways so that she loses hold of my rain-slicked jacket. "Don't let her leave." A female Green and an old Silver man step into my path. The Silver grabs me and holds my arm until two Watchmen push their way through the gathering crowd. Grays. A spike of fear goes through me. They wear blue cloth caps and gray uniforms with titanium badges with a blindfolded woman holding the star of the Republic. The younger of the two tells the bystanders to move along as the oldest cranes his neck to look up at the Gold, nodding respectfully. "Is there a problem, citizen?"

"This one's a thief."

He looks at me calmly. "What, her?"

"The little urchin stole my bracelet! Took it right off my wrist."

My eyes widen. "Like hell I did."

"I saw her try to get away," the Silver declares. "I detained her till you arrived."

"It was a diamond and lyrconium bracelet. Incredibly expensive. I was talking on my com and she pickpocketed me. Slippery little fingers."

My tongue is struck dumb. "Hold your head still, citizen," the older, fatter Watchman says. A clear optic falls over his left eye from the thin plastic headset he wears just beneath his blue beret. "Gotta scan you in."

"But I didn't do anything. . . ."

"Then you've got nothing to hide."

"Did either of you see this happen?" the younger Gray asks the Green and Silver.

"Saw the ruster bump into her."

"No. Just heard the shout."

"I didn't do anything!"

"Shut up or we'll haul you in for running your mouth," the younger Watchman says.

"Citizen, stop moving your head." I hold very still, biting back a tinpot insult. The Gray's eye flickers with light from the optic's projection display. A kaleidoscope of faces streams against his pupil. "She's not in the Archive," he tells the other. "Where are you from, citizen?" He motions me to put my finger in his DNA sampler. I feel a small prick of a needle. He frowns at the results.

"Martian, obviously. Talks like she's got mud in her mouth," the Gold says. "Just arrest her already. I want my bracelet back." She gestures to the buildings around. "Can't you call up a camera feed?"

"Private property. Not linked to the Archive, so we'd need a warrant."

"Ridiculous bureaucracy. Streets have turned to scum. Theft on the Promenade! If you'd stop heeding those plebeian senatorial scarecrows and just do your jobs . . ."

"Citizen, please," the older Watchman says. He looks around at the Reds amidst the bystanders, probably wondering if they're Vox Populi. Wrong eyes see and this turns into a riot. "Are you Martian, girl?"

Breathe. Breathe. "Aye. I'm Martian."

"You're not in the Archive. Where is your transit permit? Do you have it on your imbed ID?"

"What?"

"Do you have *any* ID?"

I reach quickly for my pockets, where I keep the Citadel ID. Both Grays step back, their hands dropping to their sidearms. The younger one pulls his and I stare down the metal barrel, two meters from my face. "Don't move!" I quiver at the order, a gene-deep terror of Grays with guns racing through me. "Hands out of your pockets! Hands out of your fucking pockets! Do it!"

I freeze, whole body locking up and trembling. I'm too frightened to even pull my hands out. Hostile eyes stare at me, loathing me, validated that I've fulfilled some twisted fantasy of theirs. "Pull your hands out! Slowly! Slowly!" I pull my hands out. The older Gray sees Reds and Browns watching from the crowd. Several are speaking into their coms. One steps our way. The Gray lowers his gun, a flicker of fear in his eyes. The younger Gray doesn't see the onlookers and rushes to slam me against a nearby wall. He shoves my hands out and kicks my legs apart. With a baton, he scans my body then pats me down and then cuffs my hands behind my back with magnetic shackles. I don't know what to do.

"No shooter or bomb," the young one says, still not seeing the older one's trepidation. "No bracelet either." He takes my ID out of my pocket and steps back. "Lyria of Lagalos." He pauses. "Eh, Stefano, look at this."

"Then she must have an accomplice," the Gold is saying.

"Did see another Red . . ." the Green pipes up.

"I saw him too. Gang member, no doubt. Tats, piercings. Look, Officers, can I just give you my testimony or card?" the Silver asks, glancing at a timepiece. "I have a meeting. . . ."

"Rico, take their testimony and IDs." The older Watchman's com crackles. He holsters his weapons. "We'll need a wagon at Promenade Level, 116th and Eurydice. Send crowd suppression. Got some Vox watchers. Could escalate." To me, "You can turn around, citizen."

Hands behind my back, I shuffle awkwardly around. Rain's started falling again. I shiver. The younger Gray looks over my ID. "Citadel staff, eh?" I nod. "Janitorial?" Then he notices the fox sigil to the right of my name. "Telemanus personnel. Second-class clearance. Look at that. That's why she's not in the Archive."

I'm not sure if it's a question.

"Probably stole the ID too," the Gold says.

The older Watchman wheels on her. "Citizen, *please*! Look around you."

"Do you not know who I am?" the woman sneers. "I'm Agilla au Vorelius, Officer. That's right. Why aren't you trying to find her accomplice? She has one. They run in packs, you know. Little savage offworlders gone wild. Nowhere is safe. What's your name? I'm going to report you to my dear friend Senator Adulius. You'll be guarding water filtration plants on Phobos with one com call." She leans forward, her bright eyes narrowing as she reads his badge. "Officer Gregorovich."

The older Gray pales. "Citizen Vorelius, we're taking her in. . . ."

"Taking me in?" I howl. "I didn't do—"

"Shut up," he tells me with an instinctive shove. I'm so angry and scared I just stumble and stare at the ground. "We'll take her in and perform a full investigation and get feeds from all the cameras, after we get a warrant. If she helped steal your bracelet, she'll pay."

"Good. Good. You should report it to the Telemanus steward. They should know they have a thief in their midst. Not that that would bother Martian warlords. But she should at least lose her job. Must keep the streets clean."

That terrifies me more than the Grays.

I'm led away as a battered gray flier shaped like a loaf of bread with Hyperion cyan stripes sets down on the street. They open the back up. It's filled with rows of rough-looking bastards, most tattooed low-Colors, drunks and vagrants.

"What'd she do?" an old Red shouts from the bystanders.

"Move along, citizen," one of the Grays orders.

"Bullshit!" someone else shouts. A bottle smashes on the ground near the officers. "Fuck you, tinmen!"

"Get her in."

"Slag you . . ." I hiss, resisting as the Watchmen try to push me into the back of the jail wagon. I feel like a child throwing a tantrum. My face has gone numb. One of them pulls out a stunbaton.

"Get in with your pants pissed. Or get in without your pants pissed. Comply, citizen."

Flinching, I step up into the bed of the flier and let them push me into a seat between a ragged old Pink with chattering black teeth and a drunk Obsidian with vomit and blood on his flashy racing jacket. My shackles clank as the magnetics lock me into my seat. A deep animal fear rises up in me. I tug at the shackles. "Please. Please don't . . ." There's shouts now outside. The sound of sirens and more bottles breaking.

"Officers," someone says on the street before they shut the doors. A slim Gray man in an overcoat approaches them. He has a forked goatee and a bad limp in his right leg.

"I'm afraid there's been a mistake," he says. "That girl's a friend of mine."

"The pickpocket?" the older Watchman asks, glancing at the gathering crowd.

"That's a ripper!" The stranger laughs. "If she's a pickpocket, I'm a worlds-renowned art thief! Known her family going on eight years. We were out for a day on the town. To take in the sights. First stop was the Liberty Wing, then Hero Center—tedious, I know. Wanted to show her a bit of my past. Make sure this flashy new generation knows the sacrifices our kin made back in the day."

"Your past?" the old Watchman says. "Were you a Son?"

The man shrugs as if embarrassed. "We all do our part. Worked the Watch first." The massive Obsidian beside me snorts phlegm out of the bowels of his nose and spits it at my feet. His cracked teeth smile at me and he whispers something in a language I don't understand. His breath smells like a Flush tube. Meanwhile, the Grays rattle at each other in military lingo while I watch on, utterly lost.

"What cohort?" one of the Watchmen asks.

"*Cohors XV.*"

"Serenia Center?"

"Crater town itself."

One of the men whistles. "A smokejack in the flesh."

"Then you were a first responder. . . ."

"So they say."

"Was there too," the old Watchman says. "Was Thirteenth then."

"Helluva day," the stranger replies.

"Helluva day." The men shake hands.

"Philippe," the stranger says.

"Stefano," the older Watchman replies. "That's Rico. He's a jackass."

"So, what's the flak, Stefano? My friend there looks like she's about to be that crow's lunch. And you look like you're about to be the mob's."

"A citizen says your friend stole her bracelet," Officer Rico says peevishly, annoyed at being left out of the conversation.

"Her bracelet?" The stranger named Philippe laughs. "Did you find it on her?"

"No, but . . ."

"Then why's she in the wagon? *Rusters ad portas?*"

The older one nods. "Citizen threatened to cause a fuss. Threatened to call up the pyramid. Connected, you know."

"Ah." The stranger lifts his eyebrows. "A Gold, then?"

Stefano looks ashamed. "You know the story."

"Same gears, new oil."

"So it goes."

"So it goes. How long till your pension?"

"Three. They bumped them all back five years."

"Bastards."

"Yut. New recruits ain't up to scratch. Reds and Browns . . . even an Obsidian. It's fuckin' madness. No discipline. So they're keeping the old dogs in the kennel."

"Criminal."

"So it goes."

The stranger steps close and drops his voice. "Listen . . . I know you got a job to do, Stefano. I know that. But look around you. Fuse is lit. Cart her away and Vox goes boom. I vouch for this little lady. Told her mother I'd watch out for her. She's the right sort. It'd get me killed if I had to go back and tell her parents what's what. You know Reds: small Color, big temper. And you take her to the station, this all gets messy. Especially since she's done jack all. Any way you could forget to log this one in?" He looks back at the crowd. "Save everyone a headache."

"Stefano . . ." Officer Rico starts.

"Quiet, squib." Officer Stefano looks at me, back to the street, and then at the other older Watchmen who brought the wagon and nods. He jumps in the back of the wagon and disconnects the magnetic coupling on my shackles. I follow warily out the back.

"I owe you a chit," the stranger says. "Damn fine of you."

"Don't know what you're talking about."

The stranger sticks out his hand. *"Semper fratres."*

"Semper fratres."

The Watchmen shut the wagon and stride off into the crowd, shoving any lowColor that gets too close. The wagon levitates back into the air and merges back into the air traffic, leaving me standing with the stranger. The crowd, robbed of its martyr, evaporates as quickly as it gathered. Some come to ask if I'm all right. I nod, still rattled.

"Pretend like we're friends," the man says as he guides me away. "They're still watching."

"Why'd you do that?" I ask him when he sits down on a bench to have a smoke. I take one from him and he lights it with a flame from his pinky ring.

"It was another Red who did it," he says. "Saw the kid make his move."

"Why didn't you say something right off?" I ask hotly.

"I don't know you," he says. "Trouble starts easy these days."

"Looks like it," I mutter.

"Are you always this . . . aggressive with people who take time out of their day to help you?"

"No . . . I just . . . I'm sorry."

"And no point in my coming to chat with that Gold hovering like a feral wasp. They've got nasty stings. Easy way to get into a quagmire."

"Quagmire?" I ask.

"Messy situation," he explains. "Philippe." He sticks out a hand. His voice is lighter, more playful than it was with the Watchmen. He has a wicked face and smart eyes that look bored by most things they've seen, but they focus on me intently.

"Lyria of Lagalos."

"Martian?" He laughs. "Well, then I'm relieved they didn't ask how the devil I knew you. Martian. Ha. That's a rip. Could have undone it all." He rubs out his burner and gets to his feet, about to leave.

"Why'd you help me?" I ask again.

"You look like someone I used to know." He pauses. "And I hate that highColor piss. Flexing muscles, as if they haven't already had their run. You have a lovely day now, Lyria of Lagalos. Mind your tongue when talking with tinpots. That Stefano was a nice one. Most are all twitchy as flies these days with all the terrorists and Vox fire-starters."

He walks off.

"Wait!"

He stops. "Yes?"

"I owe you," I say, reaching for my billfold. "You mind me, I mind you. That's how it's done."

"You want to pay me?" He's offended. "Heavens no. Don't cheapen the serendipity, love." He pauses as people pass between us. He seems to be contemplating something. His hand rests on his sternum, touching something under his shirt. "Well, damnation," he says with a sigh. "You do look like a lost thing. How long have you resided in our fair city?"

"It's my first day."

He coos. "You poor little rabbit."

"I'm not a rabbit," I snap.

He laughs. "True. Your teeth are much bigger. So, day one. And what have you seen?" He snatches my brochure when I hold it up. "Piteous child. You'll stand in line all day. Well, just so happens I need to walk. It's for the knee, you see. Old wound. How about you thank me by giving me some company and lending me an ear so I don't have to talk to myself the entire time. It's an even trade, I think."

I hesitate.

"I promise you a splendid day of revelry and fraternity."

He's got mischievous eyes. On the whole, I trust those more than I do kind eyes. Those are the ones that pity me. "I can do that."

"Splendid." He turns to walk away. "We're going now, Lyria of Lagalos." He pats his leg. "Hop, hop."

I find Philippe hilarious. We walk and talk across the Promenade level, stopping at the unpopular but beautiful Pallas Gallery to see glass sculptures that look like Laureltide dancers frozen in time, and at the Cerebian Zoo, where kangaroos and zebras and other extinct creatures have been brought back to flesh and blood by carvers. He introduces me to caramel and cardamom popcorn and flavored ice. We smoke burners amongst lamplit trees in Aristotle Park and watch loose dogs chase mourning doves that gather to drink at the fountains. Philippe narrates as if I asked him to. He has a way with words, using many I don't know, and some in ways I'm not familiar with. There's something worldly about him, something cultured, so cultured that he mocks the uppity manners of the ladies in the furs and jewelry that I at first thought so intimidating.

Ava, you'd love this man. Nothing like the stupid boys of the township.

He also seems to want to know me. Not *about* me like everyone else, but about what I think. I ramble on, forgetting to feel self-conscious, and he watches, touching that something beneath his shirt.

He might be older than my father, but he's got something youthful about him that makes me smile. He hides something, a deep sadness maybe. And sometimes I catch him watching the trees or a fountain like he's been here before with someone else a long time ago. When he does this, he always touches his chest.

I wonder who I remind him of.

I lose track of time, forgetting that the sun doesn't set at the end of the day here. When I say I should get back to the Citadel, Philippe demands to escort me after we cap the day with a dinner at a little Venusian place he knows. I hesitate despite the growling in my stomach, about to make an excuse because I've never been to a real restaurant, and I'm self-conscious of my terrible coat, and I'm fretting I won't be able to afford it; but he twists my arm. Damn well he did. The little Venusian place is the finest place I've ever seen. Napkins and plates as white as hardboiled eggs. Silver utensils. Music trickling from a Violet zitherist playing underneath an ivy gazebo that looks out at the Citadel and the mountains to the north.

"Pains me to think you've lived a life without oysters," Philippe says, slurping one down.

"Well, you haven't ever had fried pitviper eggs."

"An acquired taste, no doubt."

I shiver as I slurp down another oyster. I chewed the first one and almost retched, but now I know to take them down all at once, I'm beginning to like them if I sauce them with enough vinegar. Or maybe I like that I like them. I feel very important when the waiter comes and asks if we'd like anything else and I say, "That's right, another flight please."

"And two more martinis," Philippe demands. "Insidiously dirty, you charmer."

The waiter blushes and patters away. I watch him go, dreading what this will all cost when I could barely afford a coffee. Philippe tosses his empty shell into a pail. "These don't hold a candle to true Venusian crustaceans, but with the war, Earth does its best."

"I heard trade might reopen with the Peace," I say knowingly. Heard that bit from one of Quicksilver's men who visited Kavax couple weeks back.

"Ha! The Peace won't last. It never lasts. Golds can't handle conditional victory. They simply must have it all."

"Vox Populi might pass it without the Golds."

"And how do you know that?"

I shrug, knowing I've said too much. "I hear things."

He examines me. "Doesn't that bother you? Making peace with the slavers?"

I consider it, relieved he didn't ask where I've heard these "things." "I don't know."

"I'm sure you'd know if it bothers you."

"That senator . . . Dancer O'Faran. He was the one who freed my mine."

He whistles. "That's something."

I nod. "Took me a while to remember. But if you saw how he

looked at us . . . He just wants to make things better. Here and on Mars. Seems all the Sovereign thinks about is her personal score—finishing things with the Ash Lord. And the small people get left behind. She hasn't even been to Mars in six years, and the place is a . . . quagmire."

He smiles at the word. "And what about the Reaper?"

"I don't know." I shrug, drunk and wanting to talk about something else. "It's like he's one of them now."

"A Gold."

I nod, thinking of my brothers in the legions, wondering if I should tell Philippe about them. No. I don't want the pity to ruin the night. "I just want it to end," I say. "Just want that life we were all promised."

"Don't we all. Ah, the oysters!"

We finish the next flight, and, after the two martinis, Philippe gets the bill without me noticing. I make a show of scolding him, but inside I'm thanking the Vale and feeling stupid for worrying so much about it.

Tottering drunk, we stumble away from the restaurant arm in arm, singing a Red ballad Philippe insisted I teach him about a boy so charming he seduced a pitviper. Though Philippe's at least thirty kilos heavier and two hands taller, he's drunker than I am.

"Red constitution, damnably impressive," he says with a sigh, sitting down midway through Hero Center despite the light drizzle that falls from the cloud layer. The dimness of the light makes it feel almost like a Martian night. "Must rest the leg. It aches so."

We sit together on a bench in the middle of the Hero Center's plaza. Statues ring the expanse. My favorite, Orion xe Aquarii's, towers seven stories high over a riot of red maples. The notoriously curmudgeonly Blue stands with her hands on her hips and a parrot on her shoulder. The largest of the statues is at the center of the plaza. At night, lights in the ground blaze up to illuminate the Iron Reaper: a Red boy ten times the size of a real man stands chained to two huge iron pillars. He is not grand. He is half starved. His back is bent. But his mouth is open in a roar. The chains seem to crack and snap. The columns are shattered and in their shards are more shapes and icons and screaming faces. Philippe strokes his necklace as he leans back looking at the statue.

"What's that?" I ask him after a moment. His eyebrows rise. "Under your shirt. You been stroking it like it's a pet all night."

"Hm?" he sits up straighter and takes out the necklace. The size of a small egg, it is the face of a youthful man with curly hair and a crown of grapes. "A little something given to me by a special some-one. It is Bacchus. Lord of frivolity and wine. My kindred spirit."

"Who gave it to you?" I ask. "Sorry. I got shit for manners."

"Dispense with thy manners, my darling. I'm too drunk for them." Still, he pauses, his face losing its natural amusement, replaced by a darker, more intense emotion. "It was a man. My fiancé."

"Fiancé?"

"That a problem?" he snaps in a clipped, new voice.

"No . . . I just . . ."

"Because I know lowReds are primitive little shits 'bout that sort of thing. Part of your mine conditioning. The nuclear family! No efficiency in homosexuality. A waste of sperm, declares the Board of Quality Control!"

I glower. "We're not all like that." Da was, though.

"No," he says with a little, airy laugh, himself again. In that moment, I understand him. All the big words, all the dandy eccentricity, are a shield. There's pain beneath, and for a moment, he trusted me enough to share it. "I'm sorry, love. I'm terribly tight. Easier to see only ahead when you're terribly tight." He sighs and watches water drip down the Reaper's statue. Birds huddle in the armpits of the monument.

"What was your fiancé like?" I ask softly.

"*Husband.* I hate calling him fiancé. Cheapens it. He . . . was a good man. The best. Nothing in common with me, except an infatu-ation with the lord's wine. Our private joke. He's gone now. But you probably guessed that."

"I'm sorry."

"We all have our shadows." He smiles bravely.

"My family was killed on Mars," I say, surprised to find myself speaking the words out loud. So many people have asked, and dug, but I sealed them off because how could they ever understand? That sadness in Philippe understands me. In his eyes, I don't feel pitied. I feel seen. "I was in one of the assimilation camps. We were there too long, and the Red Hand came."

"What were their names?"

I make a small, pained sound. "No one's asked that."

"Then I'm honored to be the first to know."

"My brother's name was Tiran. My father's name was Arlow. My sister was Ava. Her children: Conn, Barlow, and Ella. The littlest one . . ." My voice catches. "She was a baby." I try to smile. "But I got my nephew out, and I got brothers alive too."

His silence is that of a man wrestling with something inside himself. The battle plays out in the muscles of his jaw and the shifting of his hands against the bench. After a time, not knowing which side has won, I follow his eyes to the Iron Reaper.

"Know what I see when I look at that?" he asks. "A thief." He laughs. "Suppose that's blasphemy to you. He's your great hero. Your messiah."

"He's not my messiah."

"No?"

"No."

"It's incredible," he says, looking at me.

"What is?"

"Everyone is so loud these days. But you, you're silent when you've all the right to scream. Luna isn't made for silence. Neither am I." I say nothing. With him I don't feel a need to, and maybe that's why I told him about my family. It was a secret I wanted to hold close because I didn't want the pity. I don't want to demean their deaths or prostitute them for attention. "What do you see?" he asks of the statue.

"Rust." I pause. "And shadows."

We walk to the train depot in silence. Steam from the heat of the friction on rails billows from the tracks. "Thank you," I say, "for everything."

"The pleasure was all mine, Lyria of Lagalos." He pauses, considering his words carefully. "I know Hyperion may seem too big to reckon. And the people here grander than you. But don't let them make you feel small." He pokes my chest and smiles wryly. "You are a world entire. You are grand and lovely. But you have to see it before anyone else does." He smiles at me, a little embarrassed. "You have my pad number. Don't be a stranger, little rabbit." He kisses my forehead paternally and turns into the rain. "Till we meet again." He hops twice like a rabbit before his bad knee buckles comically. He grins back at me. I can't help but laugh.

In my bunk back in the Citadel, with the covers tight around my neck, I curl up, too tired to pull up the holo of Mars, and think it marvelous to have finally made a friend.

30

DARROW

The Nessus

WE EXTRACT OUR PRIZES from Deepgrave without incident, taking ten other high-value prisoners from the bowels of the station with us in our submersible. Even though they're paralyzed and bound, the press of their bodies and the stink of their unwashed flesh, stacked in the back of the cramped cabin, is nearly more than I can bear. Stealing only Apollonius would have broadcast our intentions. Now, if the warden doesn't live up to his end of the bargain, the Ash Lord and the Republic will think it a general jailbreak. I only hope our nonlethal methods and our access into their system doesn't give us away too quickly.

Despite the success of the mission, I feel trapped. Imprisoned by the proximity of the scum. Apollonius lies atop the pile of fallen warlords in his kimono, like some dread corpse king. In my chest, my heart is made heavier by the dark, silent eyes of my friends hunched in the red light of the submarine—knowing they feel the same weight, that we are all party to some unspeakable deed. Thraxa, who has always held overwhelming guilt for the evil works of her own Color, stares balefully at the prisoners. Were this to go wrong, were these Golds to stand again at the head of their legions, all their evil would rip fast as a wildfire back into the world.

"Sir . . . I want to apologize," Alexandar whispers carefully to me so the others can't overhear. "I was already seasick, from the waves on the trawler, and when I saw the eyes go . . . well, it was mawkish of me. Not to the level I hold myself, and I hope you don't think lesser of me for it."

"Ragnar would puke in null gravity," I say. "Nothing to apologize for."

He nods, not hearing me. It must be a heavy burden, being the eldest grandchild of Lorn au Arcos. An impossible standard to follow.

Sevro wonders why I like the youth. For all the entitlement, all the arrogance, a deep vein of insecurity runs through Alexandar, and I feel a powerful protective instinct toward him. He wants to be good. If only he didn't want to be famous as well.

He reminds me only too much of Cassius.

"Sir, I know it is base to ask. But I wonder if we could keep *it* between us?"

"You worried about Rhonna mocking you?" I ask. "Trust me, Alex. It's not her you have to worry about." I look over to Sevro, who is eavesdropping on the conversation with a nasty little smile for Alexandar. From the back of the submersible there comes a bark. I wheel around to see the skinny Obsidian smiling down at his lap. A small snout pokes through his fingers.

"Don't tell me you brought the warden's dog," Sevro mutters. The Obsidian grins wickedly and opens his bony hands to show us the terrier hidden between his legs. "Dognapping? Careful, mutts, Tongueless here is a bad, bad man."

When we surface back at the trawler, I struggle to hide my agitation and wait for my men to exit first and help load out the prisoners one by one before exiting at the last to gulp down fresh air. Yet even the brine of the sea and the cool wind of the Atlantic cannot wash away the feeling that I've made some irrevocable mistake.

I can't let the Howlers see my doubt, so I emerge out of the submersible with a grand smile, and laugh to Rhonna at our catch of the day as they lay the prisoners lengthwise on the deck and shackle their hands and feet together under a clear and endless sky. ". . . and he puked over my boots," Sevro says, finishing his story of Alexandar's embarrassment to Rhonna and the support crew's delight. Alexandar tries to laugh it off, but his cheeks are bright red. "And then we kidnapped a dog! Did you meet Tongueless? He's a riot. Tongueless, come say hello!"

After loading up the Golds onto Colloway's pelican, we cut open the door previously sealing the crew in, and leave the crab hauler via the pelican, flying north to our departure base in the frozen wilderness of Baffin Island. There, the *Nessus*, a stolen Society *Xiphos*-class frigate of war, lies cold and quiet under camouflage tarps in the shadow of granite escarpments. As we made our preparations for Deepgrave in Greenland, my brother Kieran hid here with the rest of the Howlers, getting ready for our departure.

They wait for us out in the snow in thermal cloaks to help load up the prisoners, watching the parade of blindfolded Golds with the solemnity of funeral mourners. I share their disgust. This dirties all of us. Compounded with the death of Wulfgar, it has darkened the mood perceptibly. I don't imagine it will brighten as we near Venus.

On the snow, Sevro and I look up at the *Nessus*. Painted snow white the entire length of her hundred-meter hull and crested on her starboard and port with the winged heel of Quicksilver, she's got some of the prettiest lines ever to dart between spheres.

"This beauty puts a rocket in my pocket," Sevro says. "What'd Quick want for her?"

"Nothing."

"Man doesn't get that rich asking for nothing." His eyes follow the last of the prisoners up the ramp. "We should keep the youngbloods away from them. Half those rich shits could talk their way out of a black hole. Especially Rath."

"They were sentenced to solitary. Solitary is what they'll get."

Sevro nods to Tongueless, who is standing near the ship's portside battery, wriggling his bare feet in the snow, arms spread wide. His spirit eyes stare off into the wilderness as a storm gathers its breath.

"What you want to do about that box of fun?"

"We'll send him to New Sparta with the rest." He grimaces. "What, you want to bring him with? We don't know anything about him."

"I like his fiber. I mean, he knocked a Peerless out with a water pipe."

"He has to be over fifty! Jove knows how long he's been in that cell and why he was there in the first place. It's a risk."

"He saved your ass. And we'd still be wandering around down there with guards up our peckers if he didn't play guide." He chews his lip. "To be honest, it'd be good for the pack to have an Obsidian around the table. They're feelin' a little light in the breeches."

By the look in his eyes, I know he's not just talking about the pack.

"Your call," I say. "His choice. But you tell him where we're going."

"To certain death, general mayhem? Who could resist?"

As if hearing us—impossible from the distance—Tongueless turns. He smiles, then looks up at the Quicksilver heel on the ship.

Sevro was right about the *Nessus*. She is a pretty thing. And a killer straight from the Venusian shipwrights. While the Republic might have a vast numerical superiority in ships and resources at her disposal, the new line of Core capital ships puts Victra and Quicksilver's fledgling Phobos Shipyards to shame.

Quicksilver's men captured the *Nessus* two years ago after she was damaged during a Gold raid on a Republic supply caravan to our main fleet around Mercury. Instead of alerting the Republic Navy like he should have, Quicksilver seized her, citing arcane salvage laws. When Republic lawyers tried to claim her for the war effort, Quick won the court battle and retrofitted her to serve as his personal interplanetary shuttle.

Which is why I need her.

Kieran waits for me in the *Nessus*'s lower garage as I stamp snow off my boots. He stares after Apollonius as Thraxa drags his limp body to the brig. The warden's dog waddles behind Tongueless as Clown leads him to the galley to put some meat on his bones. "'Lo, brother," Kieran says, frowning at Tongueless, wondering where he came from. I greet my brother with a hug. He jerks his head after the hooded Gold. "So that's that prize, eh?" In his mid-thirties, my brother is skinny as a rail, freckled, and terminally optimistic. He smells like chlorine today.

"The Minotaur of Mars in the flesh," Sevro says.

Kieran blinks from under a tangle of red hair. "He's big. The dog his?"

"No, it was the warden's," Sevro says.

"Sure." Kieran nods, as if it makes perfect sense. "And the Obsidian?"

"It's complicated. How's the ship?" I ask. For the past five years, Kieran's served as the head of the Howlers' engineering department.

"She's tip-top slick and ready for immediate launch." He grins. "There's really nothin' to fix. We been swimming half the time. You should try the pool, it's like the Vale itself. There's even a sauna."

"You been swimming?" Sevro says jealously.

"What about the stores? Trust you didn't put much of a dent in them."

"Just the whiskey." Kieran does a little dance. "She's stocked for a tour of the Solar System, brother. Those Venusians will drool over what Quicksilver's got in the holds. Gotta say, it's some fair bait. You certain they'll take it?"

"They had bloodydamn better," Sevro mutters. "Otherwise we just jailbroke a bunch of savages for nothing."

"Tharsus has a legendary appetite," I say. "He'll bite." I unzip the front of my scarabSkin. Steam and stink pour out into the cold garage. Sevro undoes his own. Kieran steps away, snorting. "We'll depart in the morning."

Sevro grunts, his scarabSkin now a crumpled shadow on the metal floor. He's naked underneath. "Since we're not going anywhere, I'm going to eat."

"Shower first," Kieran says. "For the sake of the men."

"Don't be so dramatic. Ass sweat never killed a soul."

"That's not a fact," Kieran calls as Sevro saunters away. "You can't verify that." Kieran picks up his discarded scarabSkin with a wrench. "I'll wash this before it infests the ship. Last time, he brought sand-mites back in his hair. Gave the Obsidians the worst rash. Guess we don't gotta worry about that now." He pauses. "How'd my girl do?"

"She was fine." We watch Rhonna sort gear from the pelican into bins on the far side of the garage near the starShell bays. Kieran scratches his neck, leaving grease stains.

"You know when we were kids and you'd sometimes tell me ghost stories? I hate ghost stories. Scared the piss out of me, thinking Golback the Dark Creeper was going to come from the cracks in the floor and eat my teeth."

"Golback!" I say. "I thought you loved Golback."

He shudders. "You wanted to tell 'em, so I let you tell 'em. Point is, and it really wasn't that good of a point . . . I don't like asking for things. I know you're sharp and all, but can I say something that will prolly be blinding obvious to you?"

"Course."

He looks back at his daughter trudging through the snow. "Was talkin' to some of the boys, and we all agree this is bound to get a little mad. I mean, shit, Wulfgar's already dead, and we just broke into a maximum-security prison. I'm with you, brother. I gotta be. But I don't want my daughter coming with us."

"Then she won't. And you're not coming either."

"Darrow . . ."

"This isn't a debate, Kieran. You've a gift with the gears, but you're not meant for a firefight. And that's what we're driving into."

He knows what I mean. I don't want him to die.

After the prisoners are sealed in their cells, my men slink off to the showers and then to the galley for a hot meal. I gather several of the support Howlers together in the garage to tell them they won't be coming with us. Rhonna is amongst them. Kieran shuffles awkwardly in the corner as I give them each assignments here on Earth to aid the Howlers that will be returning from the field. They'll need a network to help them hide and reorganize. Afterwards, Rhonna confronts her father and me.

"So this is what all the girls who wanted to be Helldivers felt when they were told they needed a prick for the job," she says. "Respectfully, I deserve to come with."

"And how do you figure that?" I ask. "I don't see a wolfcloak. You're putting the engine in front of the ship, lass."

"Don't call me that. You lied to me. You said I'd get a chance to show my fiber."

"This is your chance. What you do in New Sparta will be just as important—"

"Bullshit," she snaps.

"Say that again?"

"Rhonna, don't swear!" Kieran says. "He's your commanding officer."

"He's my bloodydamn uncle!" She sticks a finger out at me. "I'm not a support trooper or a spy or a *lass*. I trained for three years for armored cav. Sucked mud at Hog's Tooth. I was third in my class in basic, second at HT. There were only four other Reds there. And still everyone said I was only there because I was your niece." She sticks a thumb in her chest. "I am a Solar Republic Drachenjäger. A mechman. I did that. I had sockets put into my bones." She shows us sockets in her forearms that attach to the three-story mech she was trained to operate. "After the PT and the bloodydamn nerve-melding, I got a spot with the Twenty-fourth. Was finally about to slag some slavers, then you show up, pull me from my unit and prove everyone *right*. And for what? So I can carry crates? Stay behind while my unit goes to war? Wait for the lads to return?"

"So it's about you?" I ask.

"I just want to do my part. It's my war too."

"You think any individual can survive on their own in a war? You're part of a unit. You have to trust every member of that unit. And right now, I don't trust you not to get someone else killed. So you can either obey, or find another outfit." I might admire her spirit, but not her control. "Do you hear me, *lancer*?"

For a moment I worry she's going to spit more bile at me, but she regains her composure and snaps to rigid attention. "Hail Reaper."

She storms out and Kieran breathes a sigh of relief.

"Thanks for the help," I mutter.

He grins up at me innocently. "Looked like you had everything under control."

Exhausted and feeling my temper getting a bit raw, I follow Kieran's instructions to Quicksilver's stateroom on the third level. Sevro's commandeered the captain's lounge's speakers to blast some sort of classical rhyme ruckus that would have made Ragnar's ears bleed, and Clown is whining loudly about someone stealing the blankets from his room.

The noise cuts off as I shut the door to my stateroom. For the first time in seventy-two hours, I'm alone. The room is certainly not as the Venusian shipyards intended—military austerity replaced by luxurious walnut and oak. On closer inspection, I see that there are holoprojectors built into the furniture. I turn on the ocean feature and soon waves crash against rocks on the walls. Sea stretches in every direction. I half expect Lorn to step around the corner. I sniff. The room smells like brine from the olfactory feature. "Not bad, Quick. Not bad at all." The ceiling has turned cornflower blue and a gull flies overhead, reminding me of the beach I visited with Mustang on Earth in that breath before the war began in earnest. When I held my son for the first time and thought only of the world I would make for him. It breaks me to see how far I have turned from that path.

I peel off my own scarabSkin and liner and shower under scalding water in the marbled bathroom. Alone, my thoughts wander to my son. I try not to think of his eyes when I flew away, my razor soaked in Wulfgar's blood. Overcome, I grip the key around my neck. At the bedside, I find a slim holoframe beside a bottle of Lagavulin 16. My wife and son float in the frame, smiling at me. Quicksilver must have had it sent. The picture was taken by my mother on the steps down to the water at Lake Silene. Another memory of theirs I never shared. Feeling hollow, I slip into bed and let the tears come quietly in the dark.

In the morning, the pelican, carrying my brother, Rhonna, and the support Howlers, departs south for New Sparta, Africa, and we head to the stars, rising up from the mountains, fresh covered with snow from the night's storm, and ascend gradually into orbit. To blockade a planet is nearly impossible. You'd need the whole Republic fleet to even have a chance at it. The *Nessus*'s advanced stealth hull hides us from the orbital scanners, and by the time we are visually detected, we are already pushing for deep space. With these engines, nothing will catch us.

As Earth shrinks behind us, I watch it on the holoscreen, staring not at the oceans or the mountains or the glittering cities under the slow-moving veil of night, but at her moon, where my child will be tucked away in his bed and my wife will be in her office poring over documents until the small hours of the morning. I feel the distance grow between us, and I wonder if this is what it is like to be a bad father—always finding a reason to be gone, a reason that, no matter how virtuous or shining in the eyes of a child, will seem empty and false in the memories of the man he will soon become.

31

EPHRAIM

Kites

A WEEK AND A HALF after my first encounter with the rabbit, Kobachi finishes his custom work four days behind schedule, and three before the main event. Pisses me off because he's slagged with my timetable. Would not be nearly as troublesome if it weren't for the sudden increase in security in Hyperion. Something has happened, something they don't want the general public to know. There's no news on the HCs. Nothing but the political war between the Sovereign's Optimates and the Vox Populi as they masticate each other in the press on the merits of the Peace. Half the fleet from Mercury is coming home, so the talking heads say, because the Senate is terrified the Reaper will rally the whole Armada and return to dissolve their power. Meanwhile we're on overdrive adjusting our plan to ensure the increase in security doesn't slag all our hard work.

Kobachi is making some last-minute adjustments, bent like a nearsighted hierophant over his workbench. I ease my nerves by smoking half a pack of burners in a crusty formFab chair. I go through correspondences from contractors on my ghost datapad, my tenth in the last month. Even using Syndicate freelancers, everything has to be done piecemeal so no contractor can point a finger my direction if this blows up in our faces. Which, despite the thoroughness of my plan, seems to be the outcome we're racing toward. I feel like I'm the only one who knows it. Cyra and Dano are both infected with the excitement of all the new gear, while Volga sulks around like someone stole her favorite toy. Whenever I ask about her mood, she puts on a brave smile and says it's nothing. Knowing her, she's having second thoughts about the job. But doubts have never stopped her from following me before.

I smile when I see a message from the Obsidian beast himself: Gorgo has the gravWell. I'll be damned. I feel like a kid who wished for a lizard and woke up to a dragon sitting on the lawn.

I look at my watch. I'm to meet the rabbit at Aristotle Park at two in the afternoon, and it's already pushing one. Cyra and Dano wanted me to make the plant on the girl the first day out. They worried I wouldn't be charming enough to ensure I'd see her again. Too many variables, they said. Cyra knows computers, and Dano knows angles, but leave the human condition to me.

We kept correspondence since I last saw her. It started facile. Sharing little jokes, musings on the superciliousness of Luna's jewel-bedecked denizens. It was a bore at first. She was just a child realizing she could mock the world. I expected the vitriol to continue to pour out. But the more comfortable she grew, the kinder she became and the heavier the black, gnarled weight in my stomach grows. In some ways she reminds me of Trigg. Small-town, good heart waltzes into the big, rotten city; and here I am, the welcoming party. Some people just have shit luck.

I look at my watch again, annoyed.

"Kobachi. Almost done?" He doesn't answer. "Hey, gecko, I'm talking to you."

Kobachi starts and peers up at me, his eyes magnified by the lenses. "Quite. Quite. Come have a gander." He shuffles to the side to make way for me. I pick up the small metal drone from the table, turn it over in my hands and match it with the Bacchus pendant already around my neck. Perfect replica, but a bit heavier. "The face is just as you requested. Sweet and gentle, lively and compassionate, but the devil's behind the eyes, eh?"

"Will it work?"

"I bet my reputation on it."

"Not just your reputation, Kobachi." I pat him on the cheek and slip the pendant around my neck, shoving the other into my pocket. I head to the door. "The Syndicate will cover the expenses."

I change into Philippe's clothes in Kobachi's lavatory and fix his beard to my face. I apply the makeup for my fake scars and insert the blackmarket retinal forges, which turn my eyes a gray so pale it could almost be white. I twirl an extendable cane out before me in front of the mirror and work my face through the gamut of emotions to check for creases in the makeup and resFlesh scars. "A pedestrian's penchant for circumambulatory locomotion is the pedantic paroxysm of a pleonasm of peremptory drivers and sometimes leads to imperfectly preventable parricide." I repeat the phrase four times till I have Philippe's pretentious multisyllabic-adoring accent down pat. Satisfied, I check the Bacchus pendant one last time and tuck it away. The cool metal slips under my shirt and waits against my skin. It's uncommonly heavy. Will she notice? I stare at myself in the mirror. My pupils huge in the low light. I sink into the darkness in them, remembering how the Gold spit Trigg with her razor. Holiday's words slither back.

What would he think of me now?

I reach for the zoladone dispenser and activate the blighter on my collar.

After catching a taxi to Aristotle Park, I find the rabbit waiting for me underneath an old sycamore that's seen at least five Sovereigns. She's watching squirrels chase each other along the boughs. "Finally!" she says, bursting to her feet and looking up at me with those big rusty eyes. Her hair is more fashionable now. Straightened and hanging to just below her ears. I liked it better the other way. In the reptilian chill of the zoladone, I vivisect her. The city is already changing the girl. The hair, the silver nail polish, the faux-leather black jacket she wears with purple lights on the sleeve—eroding the romantic rustic mystique I built around her. The city never infected Trigg, except for those coral earrings and that sad jacket. Least she still talks like she's from a mine, for now. "'Lo, geezer, I was startin' ta think you'd been hit by a bloodydamn train. I'm almost an old maid here."

That's not what she was thinking. She was thinking I'd ditched her. That's what you always think when you're alone. That you'll always be alone, and any present company is an aberration.

Cold inside, I feign a smile and touch my leg. "A thousand apologies, love. No, a million! My leg, the old limb, has been the black death of me today."

She pales and looks at my cane. "Oh Jove, I'm sorry . . . was only a jest."

"You couldn't know."

"You should have messaged me. I could have met you. . . ."

"An old tinman's rust should never jeopardize a lady's enjoyment of an afternoon as splendid as this."

"You should have told me," she says crossly. "We don't have to walk the park. . . ." We'd planned to stroll the park and take a taxi to the wharf to see the water of the Sea of Serenity—an idea I couldn't get her to drop. But to go to the water, we'd have to cross through a security checkpoint, and checkpoints have advanced sensors and my Philippe credentials are hardly unimpeachable. Say what you want about the Republic, whoever created their ID system was a razor-smart bastard.

"We could find a café if that would be easier for you," she says. "Or maybe go to the stalls and get a picnic on the grass?"

"No, the wharf would be lovely!"

"Philippe . . ." She crosses her arms. Subborn little rabbit.

"Well . . . only if you insist." I emphasize a sigh of relief. "I believe you've saved my life this time. The water makes my leg ache so. Are you sure you don't want to walk? I could grin and—"

"We're having a picnic," she concludes. "And that's the end of it."

"Then I insist on shopping with you, paying for everything, and escorting you properly as I do it. Young Lyria . . ." I proffer my arm. She smiles, delighted by the courtly manners and how dashing she must look in her new black jacket; she slips her arm in mine. We cross the park, where lowColor children fly their kites through the twilight sky—slate blue stained with fingers of whorehouse pink—and my sight lingers on indiscreet lovers who lie in the deep shade. The rabbit's eyes seek out families playing and lounging along the edge of a pond.

In the market, we amble through stalls of foods from four planets and ten continents. Fatty strips of beef bubble over charcoal grills. Seafood simmers in oil. Squid steams in marrow vapor. Vegetables, flash-frozen and shipped from Earth, like all the rest of it, glimmer wetly in clear plastic. The air is soupy with the scent of cloves and Martian cumin and curry, making my mouth water. We choose two foils of Pacific sweet fried cod, a plastic bowl with olives swimming in oil, European Gruyère cheese wrapped in South American prosciutto and baked in a flaky pastry, and for dessert a pint of jasmine ice cream and custard-stuffed dates. We lay the spread on the grass and eat while watching the children's kites bank in the sky.

"I like watching them," Lyria says about the children.

I mutter something neutral.

"All they know is that their parents love them and they like kites. Do you like kites?"

"Who doesn't like kites?"

"I don't imagine the Sovereign likes kites."

"No?"

"No." She takes on a pompous, hilarious Martian Aureate accent: "What are these bits of paper, floating in yonder air? For what efficacious purpose do they exist? The betterment of man? I think not. Put the paper toward the troops! The string to the nurses! The children to the munitions plants!"

I smile, but with a half dozen milligrams of zoladone in the veins, I can't find it in me to laugh. "Children fly them on Mercury, you know. From the parapets and rooftops. Thousands of kites in midsummer."

"Have you seen it yourself?" she asks.

"Just once. On a work trip for a former employer."

"That must have been beautiful," she says dreamily.

I feel the sudden need to quash her enthusiasm. "But they use glass string and angle them to cut each other's kites out of the sky till there's only one left."

"Why?"

"What's more human than competition?"

"Thousands of losers and one winner? That's so sad."

I snort. "Sounds like something Volga would say."

"Volga?"

I realize my mistake. "A friend of mine," I say instinctively.

She snorts. "You have friends besides me? The nerve." She smiles. "Really, I'd love to meet her. Volga. That's an Obsidian name, isn't it?" She looks apprehensive at the idea.

"Lamentably, she is no longer with the living," I say, and as I say it, I feel like I'm not with the living. Not tethered to any of the people around me. All these lies to this girl, and for what? Money? My life? I settle back against a tree to close my eyes, hoping Lyria forgets the name and lets the subject die.

"How's the Telemanus family coping with the peace talks?" I say to distract her. She's caught off guard. I've never asked about them before.

"They think Caraval is playing both sides. And that Dancer can't control the Vox like he thinks he can."

"Interesting."

"Something's happened." She squints. "Something bad. I'm not sure what, but it was on Earth. They've been sealed up in the Sovereign's wing for days."

"Hm." I let the subject die, lest she become suspicious.

Despite everything, it feels good to lie down and ease the ache between my shoulder blades. I've not been sleeping well in my apartment. I never do when it's a bright month. Up all bright night pacing back and forth in front of the smoke glass, racing through burners and watching that Gold bitch kill Trigg again and again on my holocube. The two of them are doing their little dance across my gray matter, and the Reaper watches, huddling with Holiday as Trigg dies and dies and dies, for him. For their messiah.

What would Trigg think of how this has all turned out?

Seven years ago, Luna was a war zone choking on dust and debris, her sky groaning with bombers. But today there are children laughing, children born who've never seen those bombers or the mechanized legions that once prowled the cityscape. The sky is warm and friendly. The air cool. The girl beside me breathing shallowly. And I feel, despite myself, at ease enough to drift to sleep.

"I've been thinking about what you told me," the girl says suddenly. I look over at her from under my shades. She's on her back, her eyes closed, shirtsleeves rolled up so the autumn sunlight can warm her dark forearms.

"Oh dear. Whatever did I prattle on about now?" I ask.

"About seeing myself before others see me."

"Oh, that. Forgive the proselytization, I was quite well sorted."

"You weren't that drunk," she says. Her eyes are open now and watching the kites. "I've never really been alone before. I mean, I have my nephew, Liam, here. But he's so done up in the Citadel school that I hardly see him. And when I do, it hurts both of us. Reminds us of who isn't here." I turn on my back and look over at her, propping myself up with an elbow. "So when you said I have to see myself before anyone else does, I look and I . . . well, I look and I don't see anything." This is hard for her, but she steels herself and goes forward. I find myself admiring the resoluteness in her face. The zoladone must be fading on account of the food in my gut. "In Lagalos, I was always minding my family. Watching my little brothers so Mum could sleep. Stitching my big brothers' clothes together with my sister. Patching boots. Then they sent me to school to learn how to work a silkery. Didn't much change after the Rising. Kept on minding my job, my family. And when we got out to the camps, it was the same. Only my brothers left and soon I was minding my father and my jobs and my sister's little ones."

I wish she would stop telling me her story. I can tell she's kept this pain locked in a dark little chest inside her, just like I did. But I'm not the good person she is. I want her to be a little nasty creature. Want to see the ugliness I know everyone's got inside them seething out of her eyes, spewing out of her mouth. But all that comes are little tears.

We're not alike.

I hoard my pain, because no one will understand it. She's just been looking for someone she can trust. Someone to share it with. Not me, stupid girl. I don't deserve it. But she keeps going, and I feel heavier and blacker on the grass, wishing I took more zoladone.

"When the Red Hand came, I thought I'd be braver. You know, get a gun like they do in the flicks. But everything felt so fast. And I felt so small. All I wanted to do was sink in the mud." She wipes her eyes and returns her arms to guard her chest.

"And you feel guilty for being here, when they're not," I ask quietly.

"Yeah."

I hesitate. "Don't you think they're waiting for you in the Vale?"

"I don't know. I hope so."

"And if they were watching you, would they be proud?"

She considers, looking up at me with glassy eyes. "I hope so."

We linger in the park till our ice cream has melted. I walk with her back to the tram depot so she can return to the Citadel. We hug farewell, and as I planned, I take off my necklace and fix my face with compassion, but the words don't come as smoothly as intended. They stick in my throat.

"Philippe?"

"I want you to have this." I push the locket into her hands. "To wear it. It's always brought me strength."

"I can't take that. . . . Your fiancé . . ."

"Gave it to me so I'd remember wherever I went I had him with me. But I don't need a pendant for that. But you should be reminded that wherever you go, you're not alone. We're friends, aren't we?"

"I think you're my only friend."

"And what do friends do? Friends help each other. You carry my shadows. I carry yours for a spell." I take an imaginary necklace from her neck and put it on myself and buckle my knees like it's a great weight. She laughs. "Maybe then we'll both be a bit lighter when next we meet."

"Do you think he's watching you? Your fi—your husband. Not from the Vale, course. I know you lot don't believe. But from somewhere?" She stares up at me from under her mop of red hair.

"No, I don't."

"I think you're wrong. I think he's watching you. And I think he's smiling and got a twinkle in his eye." She bundles her coat and heads to the depot, but turns around and runs back to me to give me a small kiss on the cheek. "You're not alone either, Philippe."

Sweet little rabbit, if only that were true.

32

LYSANDER

The Rending

SUNGRAVE, THE GREATEST CITY of Io, surges up out of a white, frozen plain riven with fissures venting heat from subterranean magma. We fly toward it looking out the forward windows of one of Dido's chimeras.

Carved into Io's highest mountain, the eighteen-kilometer-high Boösaule, Sungrave is a city of black stone obelisks and spires that rides the shoulders of the mountain range. Centuries ago, after the use of Lovelock engines was deemed inefficient for Io, great mirrored lasers carved much of the mountain and part of its attending 540-kilometer-long range into a city of jagged towers. The builders followed the draconic predilections of their great progenitor, Akari, bringing creatures of childhood fables and ancient campfire stories to life in the stone.

A necropolis of animalistic spires flecked with topaz, zircon, and myriad nesosilicate rocks looms above us, blocking the sky like the petrified remains of a great dragon host. They perch rank upon rank along the Boösaule's crest, some of them encompassing whole peaks, legs straddling frosted valleys, their wide wings buttressing their great heights as they crane their stone necks up as if to drink the gases of marbled Jupiter. Duroglass windows glitter with internal light, like scales. And deeper in the heart of the mountain, where long ago Red drillcrews dug out the interior, lies the city itself.

The city, like all the other mountain cities of Io, draws its energy from the tidal heating caused by the war of Jupiter's gravity on Io against the gravitational pull of Europa and Ganymede. The cities of Raa need no helium-3 to survive or power the pulseFields that shield them from radiation and Io's poisonous air. That is why they survived my grandmother's siege ten years ago—their shields could resist bombardment longer than the helium-3 power generators of the Sword Armada's ships could keep them in orbit. Still, I expected Io to be a desolate backwater, beset by rationing and scant starship flight; but the ship that captured the *Archimedes* was brand new. As are many of the trade and war vessels that flow into Sungrave's high stone docks like itinerant gnats.

I look over at Cassius and feel his unease.

How were those ships built? On what dock?

New Olympic Knights, new ships, a new generation. The Rim has not been sleeping. And now, if they gain Seraphina's evidence, they will awaken.

The scent of foreign incense fills my nose as the steam from the caldarium walls filters soundlessly up from the hypocaust beneath the floor into the dim room. Two sets of hands knead the knots of tension from my shoulders and legs. The bruises inflicted by Pandora's men are now faded pools the color of sulfur on my shoulders and jaw. Somewhere in the steam, Cassius bathes alone in the solium, a large pool sunken into the rough-cut stone. Since Dido's wafer, time has passed like a dream, my body flushed again with the life of water and food which Dido's men gave us on the flight to Sungrave.

As a child, I surrendered to the disappointing reality that I would never see fabled Sungrave in person. It would be too great a risk to send the heir to a place where he might be captured and held for ransom. But I am heir no longer, and my eyes are greedy for all Sungrave's sights, to see her depths, her botanical complexes, her great mountain cisterns filled with Europan water.

It is so different here from my home on Luna. Not just the acrid air and the dim sky, but the unforgiving stone, the Spartan decor—empty rooms, no chairs, and an incredible adherence to cleanliness and martial virtue. Seraphina gave me an all-too-brief tour after we arrived and I was taken to my quarters, but in her presence I noted less of the city than I would like. My eyes would drift to the back of her proud neck as she led me through her childhood corridors, like she was a black hole, pulling all light, all attention into her, not just from me, but from the servants, from the guards. She is much loved.

Little Hawk, they call her affectionately. Barely twenty. Not a Praetor or a Legate—those titles must be earned—just a woman of worth and promise. Yet despite her mother's consolations, the guilt of her actions against her father seems to weigh heavily on her. She said little before depositing me in my quarters and disappearing before the door had closed.

When the Pinks have finished their massage, they scrape the oil and dead skin from my body with strigils, flattened bronze hooks, which they put into a clay pot for some recycled use. Nothing here goes to waste. One offers me a pipe of dried tharsal root. Head already woozy from the steam, I decline the mild hallucinogen. Then the slaves ask me how I would like to take them. Their legs are eerily long from the low gravity of their home. Their skin, unblemished by the sun, is burnished and smooth and without hair. The hair of their heads is thick, the male's silver, the female's a black so deep it shines blue near the lamps. She's older than he is, with quartz eyes and the frailness of a small bird. But her mouth is truculent, her eyes not so empty as they should be. They startle me when they meet mine, and the spell the warmth and their hands cast is broken. She sees me.

A deep revulsion, physical and intellectual, twists the lust into a knotted, blackened thing.

I can't look at them as my ancestors did, as consumable treats.

One could argue for the necessary industry of Reds or the cultlike military religion instilled in Grays, or the efficiency and neutered emotions in Coppers, but this . . . Pinks were not needed to make my grandmother's world function. They were built for lechery, subjected to centuries of systematic breeding, abuse, psychological and sexual domination. Chemically neutered and twisted inside so that their suicide rate is eleven times higher than that of any other Color.

Gold is to blame for that. Gold lost its way.

And now this Pink woman looks at me with eyes too ancient for her face.

"What's your name?" I ask her.

"This one's name is Aurae," she says.

I gently take the Pink's hand from my thigh. "That will be enough, Aurae." The male Pink looks awash with shame, thinking himself not beautiful enough; but in the woman, I see a small tell, a spasm of relief at the corners of her eyes. Then she feigns shame like the other one. Strange.

"We shouldn't insult them," Cassius says from the pool. "Come, join me. There's enough room for the two of you." The Pinks rise to obey.

"Like the Brothers Rath, are we now?" I ask.

He sighs. And motions for the Pinks to leave. They do. My eyes follow Aurae out the door. I ponder her relief. When they've left, Cassius casually taps his ear to show that we're no doubt being listened to. Of course I know that. Does he forget where I grew up? "I think we deserve a little fun, Castor. Water torture, enduring that family squabbling, the beatings . . ." He laughs. "Besides, they're slaves, and you're not their savior. Romantic as you find the notion to be."

"You know, not everything you say to me has to be a lesson," I say.

"If you didn't need them, I wouldn't teach them. Anyway, looks like Pytha owes me fifty credits." He sighs contentedly to himself and leans his broad shoulders back in the bath.

"What for?" I ask, unable to not take the bait.

"Friendly wager. She couldn't possibly believe you were still a virgin."

"What?"

"A virgin. It's when a man or woman has not . . ."

"I hardly think that's any of your concern. I'm not, as it is."

He closes his eyes against the steam. "Then why turn them away? You sure it's not because you're afraid she's watching?"

"Of course not," I say sharply. Is Seraphina watching?

He chuckles. "See? Pent-up sexual aggression."

"Just because I believe in actual romance instead of plundering the virtue from merchants' daughters and buggering everything that moves like a gorydamn Gaul does not mean that I should be shamed."

"'Like a gorydamn Gaul?' My goodman, you curse like you're ninety."

"And you're a hypocritical fornicator."

"Gods, you really haven't been laid, brother."

"Will you stop talking." I throw one of the strigils at him. He ducks into the water before pulling himself out to join me on the tile bench. He nudges me with his shoulder after a spell to lighten the mood—difficult considering we both know they're analyzing us now, attempting to peel back our story to see if we are spies. Neither one of us is convinced the brotherly spat is just for show, though that might be our excuse.

"Seraphina told me Pytha was alive," I say, trying to change the subject.

"My guards said the same to me. But don't get too comfortable. We're not guests here. When when the coup is over, our heads will likely roll."

"You don't think it will succeed?"

"Tell me you didn't see the doubt in the daughter."

I nod. "I didn't think that was the reason for it."

He laughs. "Don't be so easily impressed by a rogue century of Peerless. Dido's sharp, but she's Venusian. The Rim won't forget that. The minor Lords of Io will be coming from all over the moon, loyal to Romulus. And if they don't finish her off, the Lords of Europa and Ganymede, likely even Callisto, will do it. Not to mention the Far Rim. They like their Romulus out there."

"And what about their evidence?"

"Did you see her bring anything back?"

"No."

"Well then, either she hid it well, or it was a bluff."

I know without him saying it that he blames me for our current predicament, but it was his decision to investigate the *Vindabona*. His decision to take away everything I had as a boy and then act like he was my savior.

He lives in a fiction, espousing a moral code to justify killing his Sovereign, turning his back on our Society, but I know why he really did it—because she let the Jackal kill his family. The sanctimonious morality came long afterwards. This noble Morning Knight is built on a foundation of self-interest. And now, because he trusts no Golds, he decides we will anger our hosts in hopes they will want our services, when instead he should swallow his pride and see if their hospitality is genuine, as I do.

He has little faith in our Color. I'm losing all mine in him.

I feel a despicable little creature, thinking all this of Cassius. Whatever his motives, I know his love for me is genuine. The nights of listening to music in the rec room of the *Archimedes* as he falls asleep holding his drink can't be washed away. Neither can the protective warmth I felt all those times when Pytha and I helped him back to his bunk when he was so drunk he could not even stand but he could murmur Virginia's name.

"I miss home," I say in an attempt to find some common ground to ease the tension that's grown between us these last months, before the *Vindabona* even.

"Mars?" he asks, and I know he means Luna. And I do miss that place, the libraries, the Esqualine Gardens, the warmth of Aja, the approval of my grandmother, stark and sparse though it was, the love of my parents. But most of all, I miss sitting in the sun, eyes closed, listening to the pachelbel in the trees. That was peace for me. That is where I feel safe.

"But I was thinking of the *Archi*. I've never had to miss her before. Two days on Ceres. Three on Lacrimosa . . ."

"She's a good ship," he says. "I'd give two years' haul to be under way in the rec room with a tumbler of whiskey right now and a good concerto on the holo."

"Playing chess?"

"Karachi," he corrects. "We played chess all last year."

"More like I taught you to play all last year . . ."

He rolls his eyes. "He wins five in a row and suddenly he's Arastoo in the flesh."

"It was seven, my good man. But I'll relent and let you play Karachi, even though it's a game entirely devoid of reason and mathematical skill."

"It's called reading people, Castor. Intuition."

I make a face. "My only condition is we listen to Vivaldi and not Wagner."

"My goodman, are you trying to kill me? You know I abhor Vivaldi." He laughs. "Not that it matters. Won't be able to hear a note over the sound of Pytha whining about immersion games or how it's not her turn to cook."

We grin at each other, indulging the fantasy that once seemed so commonplace, but now so nostalgic and impossible.

"Oh, don't look so maudlin," he says. "We'll return to the *Archi* with Pytha in surly tow. We'll be sharing a whiskey and burning black matter once this is sorted." We both know it is a promise he cannot keep.

I see by the melancholy look in his eyes that we are united in understanding that something between us is breaking and neither one of us knows how to stop it. Even if we leave Io behind, we can never go back to the way things were, to the private world we shared.

I have outgrown it. I have even outgrown him.

33

LYSANDER

Alien

I'M DEPOSITED IN MY ROOM to change for dinner with the Raa family. The room, like all Ionian rooms, was made with attention to geometrical energy. It is perfectly square, without frivolous comfort and with no furniture except for a thin sleeping mat on a slightly raised platform. A small window looks out onto the heavy darkness of a night nearly a billion kilometers from the sun. I doff my robe and stand naked before the window, pressing my nose to it, appreciating the chill of the rock on my bare skin, and imagine I am floating in the cool waves of Lake Silene. I wonder if the Reaper's child now climbs the stone stairs there from the shore to Silene Manor and his waiting parents. Do they warm themselves by the fire pit? Sleep in the room I slept in when I was a boy, where all Lunes have slept since the children of Silenius? A deep anger fills me, but I push it into the void.

All is silent in the room.

Not the busy silence of space, where air purifiers hum and engines tremble through the metal. It is the silence of stone and the silence of darkness that stretches into an unseen, unending frozen landscape. A cavernous, alien silence.

Those crewmembers on the *Vindabona* will be dead by now. It's the only mercy I know to hope for. How long did they last?

Two lonely lights glide across the plain in the distance, too low to be aircraft. Hoverbikes? Where are those two souls going? What errand do they attend? Are they lovers? Friends? Then a score of lights burns out of the blackness behind them, chasing them across the expanse. I lean forward in excitement as bright orange tongues of flame lick out from the pursuers and the two leading lights vanish in blossoms of white fire.

Two more fall to the coup. It seems it is not as peaceful as Dido would like us to believe. Cassius is right, yet again.

All across the city men will be dying. Silent squads will arrest loyal members of Romulus's faction. The cells will fill. Guns may rattle. Razors drip with blood. All balanced and gambled on the promise of the evidence Seraphina brought back.

I know coups, and am little impressed by them. They're more common than weddings in my family. These Rim rustics hold their noses at Golds of the Interior, at my family and the "bitch on Luna." But they're little better.

Then I remember Seraphina. How she stood before her father, and the sadness I saw upon her face when she realized his intent. Torn between the love of her people and mother, and the love of her father. What choice would I make?

I see my own father in my mind's eye and try again in vain to summon my mother. I reach for her, but my fingers rake nothing but shadow, and I feel, in no small way, that her absence is my fault. I did not study her enough. Did not love her enough. And so, she will never hold me in her arms, never kiss me upon the brow. As if she never existed.

My thoughts are interrupted when a jammer activates with a static pop behind me.

I swing around to see a pair of amber eyes staring at me from the shadows of the sitting room. "Jove in hell!" I flick on the glow lights to reveal a woman sitting on my sleeping mat. She watches intently as I scramble to put my robe back on. "Seraphina?" She's at home now, her prisoner jumpsuit gone, and wears the garb of the Io. A gray wool cloak held together with a charcoal sash. She peers up at me, amused.

"Do all Martians have such dreadful hearing?"

Her eyes rove as I pull tight my robe. She wears rubber-soled slippers and two heavy rings—on her left middle finger a dragon eating a lightning bolt, on her right a simple iron Institute ring of House Diana's stag's antlers. I should have guessed she'd be a hunter.

"Are all Moonies as rude as you?" I look at the door, and know it made no sound, and, more impressively, neither did she. Must have come through the walls, then. A secret door. "Are you lost?"

She frowns. "Lost?"

"Well, you do seem to be in my room."

"Your room?" Her sudden laugh is surprisingly girlish. Then the drawl comes back. "You are in my city, *gahja*. On my moon. There are cameras in the stone. What does it matter that I watch you through the camera or here? This is more honest, no?"

"Well, it is entirely eerie either way," I say with a smile. "Most inhospitable."

"If I remember correctly, you are a watcher too. I saw you looking at me on the table. . . ."

"You were injured," I say. "I was checking your—"

"Tits?"

"Your wound. The one on your—"

"Breasts."

"*Stomach*. You're clearly still insensate. Took a knock on the head, turned a bit mad. Or do your kind all talk like gutterborns?"

"I have manners," she says with a smile. "The dust is a hard teacher." She hurls a package at my face as she stands. I barely catch it. "Clothing. Yours was soiled from the journey."

"Charitable of you." I open the package to don the clothes. "Our pilot," I say. "You said she's alive and well. I want to see her."

"No."

"No negotiation? Very well." I thumb the clothing she brought. She doesn't turn away or leave. "Do you mind?"

"Mind?"

"Yes, I'd like to change now."

She cocks her head in challenge. "I have seen naked men before."

Unlike her own, mine was a solitary upbringing. "A Sovereign is an island," my grandmother would say.

"It's just carbon. Are you ashamed of your body?" she asks. "Or perhaps you are embarrassed you do not know how to use it?"

"So that's why you sent the Pinks. So you could watch?" I find myself unusually pleased by the revelation. "Why so curious?"

Her brow wrinkles. "Were you injured? Is that why you turned them away? Does your manhood not work?"

"That . . . is absolutely none of your concern. Thank you for your interest, however. It works just fine."

"I am sorry," she says. "I did not mean to offend."

"Well, you're quite accomplished at it. Compliments to whoever taught you."

"Would you be at ease if I were naked again too?" Even under the folds of her loose tunic, I see the subtle rise of her breasts, the length of her muscled legs, and . . .

I cough and shake my head. She waits patiently till I have a small, annoying epiphany. "Do you always toy with your guests?"

"Sometimes." She smirks. "You do look a little like a toy. All that hair and those dandy little limbs."

"Dandy?"

"Dandy. And your nose has only been broken recently. Are your eyes real?" She leans in. "You didn't have them carved like a Corish Pixie, did you?" I don't dignify the question with an answer.

"You're not going to leave, are you?"

"Why would I? Everyone is busy preparing for supper. I am bored. You are entertaining."

"Very well then." I drop my robe to the floor, intending to embarrass her. She doesn't look away. She scrutinizes.

"You have more scars than most Pixies," she says after a moment.

"Because I am not a Pixie."

She surprises me with a laugh and counts my scars till she finds one curious. It is a long, thin scar, like a necklace around my neck. "Who gave you this one?" Her pale fingers brush against the scar, and impossibly I hear the howling of the wind outside my window. And in the darkness there and in my mind, he lurks, the Reaper's beast, the demon of my childhood. Instinctively, I put my robe back on and sit on the ground. She looks suddenly apologetic.

"A man gave it to me when I was young," I say, chastising myself for losing control of the memory. Some demons never leave. Grandmother wanted to laser the scar off. I convinced her to let me keep it.

She joins me on the floor. "A lover?"

"No."

"Did you kill him for it? For hurting you?"

I shake my head.

"Why not?"

"Like I said, I was young. He was not."

"Did you find him and kill him later? You are a man now."

"No."

"Why not? If he hurt you and remains alive, then he is your master. That is why I slayed the Obsidian warchief who beat me on the *Vindabona*."

"It's in the past. The past doesn't define me." I repeat Cassius's words like they were my own. How many times did he tell me this? How many times have I failed to believe him?

"Stupid *gahja*." She taps my forehead. "Nothing is past. Everything that was, is. That scar is a story of your subjugation. Slay the man who gave you that, and it becomes the story of your liberation."

"Did your father teach you that?" I say, angry that she would preach to me.

Her eyes turn cold and flinty, sensing the accusation.

I'm suddenly achingly aware of the difference between us. She might be the child of a Sovereign like me, but she is a soldier. She was raised in gladiatorial academies amongst sinewy killers on a moon that breaks down your DNA if you step outside without at least three centimeters of high-grade radiation shielding. She has a scar from the Io Institute. There is none more brutal. The students don't kill as much as Martians or rape as much as Venusians, but the games can last for years in temperatures that freeze your blood before it drips from a wound.

What have I done but read and run all my life? I suddenly feel indicted by my own banter. Like I'm a dog barking at a wolf who knows very well that I'm not from the wild, but lets me bark because it *entertains*.

"Apologies," I say carefully.

"Forgiven," she replies. "Yes, my father taught me that scars are why our ancestors were able to shape the worlds. As Golds, we were born as perfect as man can be. It is our duty to embrace the scars our choices give us, to embrace and remember our mistakes, else we live believing our own myth." She smiles to herself. "He says a man who believes his own myth is like a drunk thinking he can dance barefoot on a razor's edge." The smile disappears as she perhaps remembers her father's face when he was led away by her brother. And I see clear as day the true war that rages inside the girl. It softens me to her, because it feels a reflection of the same war inside of me. I fight back the urge to touch her hand.

"You think me wicked," she says quietly, her eyes fixed on the window. "Betraying my own father . . ."

Why does she care? "Families are . . . complicated."

"Yes. They are."

A silence grows between us, and in it we share an understanding that goes beyond words.

"You are strange," she says finally. "Your friend is a killer. But you, you are gentle."

"I'm not gentle."

I'm suddenly conscious of how close she is. How aware of her body I am. The space between us vibrates and trembles with something raw, newly woken and terrifying to me. I feel the heat in her breath, the cold petals of her pale lips, and the lonely fire in her dark eyes that would pull me into her and consume me. I would let it, and that frightens me more than her family. More even than the death that awaits me if she learns my family name.

She feels the same tension between us, and breaks it by turning away. "Marius says you are spies. That it was not by chance that you found me."

"You don't seem to put much trust in what Marius thinks."

"He is a reptile, but not a fool."

"I care more about what you think."

She considers. "Anything gentle that lives long, hides its stinger well." She turns to the wall to make her exit.

"Why did you take my razor?" I say, feeling a sudden flash of anger at her. "All those people died because I couldn't get them out."

"I know," she says quietly. "But that is the horror the Slave King has made."

"That's not good enough."

"I did it for the greater good. You will understand."

"Your mother doesn't know you're here, does she?" I ask her, nodding to the jammer on her belt. "Why did you really come?"

She hesitates as if she doesn't even know.

"You saved my life. I . . . wanted to see if yours was worth saving."

"And?"

"I have not decided." She looks at me with strange pity. "You play with things you don't understand."

"Your mother made me a guest. I'm protected by old law."

"My mother is not my father." She pauses. "Give her what she wants. For your own sake."

"What does she want?" I ask, but the wall has already parted, and Seraphina has slipped into its shadows. Cassius was right.

We are not guests here. We are prey.

34

DARROW

Apollonius au Valii-Rath

I FINISH MY MORNING LAPS in the pool on the fourth deck of the *Nessus* in the early morning. The swimming is part of the physical therapy to recover from the razor through the arm I suffered in the fight with the Republic Wardens. My body is a history of aches and pains. Not even in my mid-thirties, I've already had three cartilage replacement surgeries for my knees alone.

The swimming makes the arm ache like hell, but also helps displace the feeling of claustrophobia that has crept in during our second week in deep space in our push toward Society territory. That and razor training with Alexandar help keep my mind from my family.

After dressing in my stateroom, I find Sevro in his quarters. He's lying on his bed watching a video of Electra when she was a baby. The little girl floats in the air above him, silent and dour even as an infant, as Victra dresses her in a high-collared vest. Sophocles's tail swishes in the air, blocking the camera's view. I hear Kavax laugh in the background. It's been two weeks without communication to the outside world. It's eating at Sevro.

"You still not out of bed?" I ask. "Lazy bastard."

He squints over at me, eyes still swollen with sleep. "What's the rush?"

"Apollonius. We agreed to talk to him this morning."

"Oh, that." He looks one last time at his daughter and turns off the holopad. "Sure we can't keep him on ice a few weeks longer?"

"I wish. We'll be in Gold territory in five days. Time to see if he's on board."

"And if he's not?"

"Then you get to space him. And we burn for Mercury."

Pebble finds us in the hall on our way to the chute down to the fourth deck. She looks tense. "We have a problem."

We find Colloway hovering over a holoDisplay in the sensor room on the second deck. Clown stands behind him with his arms crossed, foot nervously tapping. "What's going on?" I ask.

"Tell him what you told me," Pebble says.

Colloway rubs his temples. For as much sleep as the man gets lazing around on the recreation room's couch and playing immersion games, he looks exhausted. "So, you know this ship has an internal monitoring system that detects our thermal signatures."

"Sure."

He brings up the blueprint of the ship. Human-shaped figures glow red amongst the decks. I see Winkle's cool signature on the bridge, Thraxa's hot signature as she trains endlessly in the gymnasium. Sevro chuckles and points to two thermal signatures side by side in one of the staterooms. "Looks like someone's going to Bone City. Who is that?"

"There's twenty-four of us," Colloway continues, counting off the figures one by one. Many are still in their bunks. "Ten Golds in the cells."

"Then what's the problem?" Sevro asks. "We got shit to do."

"Last night I couldn't sleep . . ."

"You mean you were perving on people."

"So I synced into the ship and I saw this." He rewinds the blueprint to the middle of the night. "Count them."

"There's twenty-five." Sevro squints. "Shit. How did you just notice this?"

"There's no reason for me to sync when we're on autopilot. It's a waste of my time," Colloway says in annoyance. "It looks like they're masking their signature, staying near the engines or wearing a thermal blanket."

"They could have been on the ship before it was stolen," Pebble says. "Could be a dockworker or one of Quick's servants."

"If it's a docker, then they could sabotage our life support systems or melt down the helium core," Colloway says. "That would be—and I say this as understatement—cataclysmic."

"A gorydamn grandma in the com center would be as dangerous as a *Stained*," Clown says. "If they transmit on our coms, the whole gory system will know where we are. Society and Republic. We're slagged! They'll find us, obliterate us, and our molecules will drift through space for ten million years."

I turn to Clown. "You done?"

"Not really."

"You're done. Get Alexandar and Thraxa and meet me in the armory."

Ten minutes later, Clown, Alexandar, Thraxa, Sevro, and I shoulder our multiRifles. I toss them green clips of ammunition. "Spider only," I say. "I want the stowaway alive."

By eliminating the known thermal signatures one at a time, Colloway manages to track the signature of the intruder back from the galley to the engine room. The open room spans all four decks at the back of the ship. Metal walkways switchback down from the top and extend out amongst the machinery. The lights won't turn on. Thraxa and Clown guard the bottom exit while the rest of us come down from the top, searching level by level. Our helmet floodlamps chase the shadows away as we comb through the machinery. Sevro signals me as he kneels. He shows me a wrapper for a Venusian noodle bowl. There's more litter in an alcove on the third level, along with a holo-Visor and a bundle of blankets.

There's a patter of feet on the level below. "Rat?" Sevro says with a grin.

"Go," I say. Sevro and Alexandar jump off the side of the metal walkway and land on the one below. There's a thump and a laugh.

"Darrow, you better come down here," Sevro calls up.

"It's definitely a rat, a *bloodydamn* big one with freckles," Alexandar adds. I take the stairs and find Alexandar and Sevro standing over a small woman who sits on her haunches. Her face is illuminated by their floodlamps.

"Rhonna?" I sputter.

My niece grins up at me. "Sorry, Uncle, got lost on the way to the shuttle. Is this New Sparta?"

"What the hell are you doing here?"

"Stowing away," she says. "Can I stand or are you going to shoot me?" She looks in annoyance at Alexandar's rifle. Unlike Sevro, he still points it at her. She stands.

Sevro chuckles. "Got some big iron balls on you, don't ya?"

"That's the general idea."

"I gave you an order," I say, trying to calm myself down as Thraxa joins us.

"Yeah. You can put me in the brig if you want, but I think the cells are all filled up. Or you can let me do my job. If Sir Pukealot here can have your back, so can I." Alexandar glowers in embarrassment. "By my count we're two weeks in. No way to turn back now, Uncle. You're stuck with me." She's right.

"You think this is about me?" I ask. "You just broke your father's heart."

Her jaw tightens. "It's my life. Now, can I join the rest of the crew and get to—"

"Alexandar. Shoot the dumbass," Sevro says.

Alexandar grins. "With pleasure."

Her eyes widen. "No, not him. Anyone but—"

Alexandar grins and fires his spider poison round into her thigh. She spins down, grunting in pain. Her fingers curl as the paralytic spreads. "Ouch."

"Leave her," Sevro says when Thraxa tries to pick her up. "You'll be able to move by tonight, shithead. Clean up your filth and find a bunk. Tomorrow you scrub the latrines in every bathroom. Starting with mine. Real shame for you because curry is on the menu tonight." He bends down. "You sad you ain't with a Drachenjäger squad? A mechman? Please, we eat those little bitches for breakfast. You're lucky to be in our glorious presence." He leans in even closer. "You want respect? Earn it."

"The nerve of her," I mutter as we head out into the hallway.

"Least she didn't come through the viewports."

"Poor Kieran. You should have seen him ask me to leave her behind."

"Was a bit harsh, don't you think?" Thraxa says, catching up to us.

Sevro grins. "Listen, Thraxa, kids are like dogs. Some whimper, some bark, some growl. You just gotta find the right language and then speak it back at them."

Alexandar smirks. "You can speak to dogs?"

"I talk to you, don't I?"

Min-Min lounges in the brig guard post forward of the cellblock with her rifle leaning against the wall when Sevro and I arrive to talk with Apollonius. Her bandy metal legs are up on the console, a coffee cup balanced precariously on her hydraulic joint as she watches a holo comedy about a Red moving in with a Violet and Gray in Hyperion City; hijinks ensue. She scratches the coarse whiskers on her neck and looks back at us. "'Lo, bosses."

"How are the little devils today?" I ask.

"Quiet as mice." Min-Min keeps one eye on the projection and laughs as the Red tries to reach the top cabinet in their apartment's kitchen to get the whiskey the others hid from him. "That's some racist shit," she says. "We're not all alcoholics." The smell of whiskey wafts up from her coffee. "Tongueless is on his conjugal visit again." I look down the hall to see the old Obsidian sitting cross-legged looking into one of the cells.

"How many is that?"

"Comes every day."

Our collection of "escaped prisoners" is a motley assortment of devils. Half are men and women the Howlers labored to capture personally over the last ten years—all ten are Venusian. It seems a blasphemy that we've been the ones to free them. I feel the silent anger in the Howlers at mess, in the ship's gymnasium, even when they pass in the hall. Not anger toward me or our mission, but as though this is some grand joke that existence plays on us. We circle around again to see the same faces, the same ships, the same battles. Again and again. Around and around. It's the very reason I need to kill the man at the axis of the cycle, around which this all spins.

Tongueless sits on the floor of the hall, the warden's dog asleep in his lap, watching Apollonius play his phantom violin through the one-way glass. The old Obsidian has cut his hair short and trimmed his beard to a fine goatee. He looks an altogether different man, sophisticated even in the military fatigues. His dog wakes and growls as we approach. Quieting only when Tongueless strokes him behind the ears.

Apollonius is naked in the dim light of his cell. His clothing folded neatly on the floor. It disturbs me, watching him rocking there playing his phantom instrument, his golden hair pouring down his shoulders, eyes closed, face a monklike mask of concentration. A bandage is affixed to his head over a shaved patch from Winkle's surgery.

I want him dead. Gone from the worlds. He's taken two people I love and tormented another as a boy. The thought of setting him loose again makes me sick.

"Do you fancy the evil violinist, Tongueless?" Sevro asks.

The Obsidian looks up at us with his dark eyes and shakes his head. He makes a motion of the violin and points to one of the tattoos on his arm of an old man with a long beard and a harp in his hands. It is the Norse god of music, Bragi. "Is he that good?" I ask.

Tongueless nods. He taps his ear and then his heart, as if to say he wishes he could hear him play again. "Not happening," Sevro says. Tongueless nods, accepting that, and stands to leave us alone with Apollonius.

I watch him go and wonder what he'd say had he a tongue. He's unique amongst the Obsidians I've met. The way he moves is elegant, cultured, like he's accustomed to finer things. He's quickly become a new favorite in my pack, owing to his craft in the kitchen. Men don't ask questions if you feed them well. But I'm beginning to suspect there's more to the story about how he ended up in an Omega cell than simply getting on the wrong side of the warden's temper.

"Why does he always have to get naked every time?" Sevro mutters, drawing me back to Apollonius. "Go on. Let's get it over with."

I deactivate the opacity on Apollonius's side of the glass so that he can see us in the dimly lit hall. He's nearing the end of his song. Rocking and thrashing out a crescendo, then a slow, silent denouement. And when he has finished, he leans back to look at us, an amused smile on his lips.

"Did you like my sonata?" he asks, not waiting for us to answer. "Much approbation is granted Paganini as the great violin virtuoso of the pentadactyl period. Well, before the coming of Virenda, of course. But for sheer Orphian transcendental rigor, I've long maintained a true master must attempt Ernst's Variations on 'The Last Rose of Summer.' The fingered harmonics and left-hand pizzicato are facile enough, but the arpeggios are a Herculean labor."

"I don't know what any of that means," Sevro says.

"A pity for you to have such narrow concerns."

"You're dying to tell us when you first played it, aren't you? I know you folks can't resist a little brag," Sevro mutters. "Well, go on. Impress us, Rath."

"I mastered it when I was twelve."

"Twelve? No!" Sevro claps his hands. "What genius! Reap, did you know that we had a psychotic virtuoso aboard?"

"I had no idea."

"The mastery of music is its own reward," Apollonius says. "The process by which one's heart is entwined with masters of old. You do not know the toil, nor could you suffer it, and so you will never know the reward of understanding it." He leans forward with slit eyes. "But by all means, dismiss it if you cannot comprehend. Art survived the Mongols. I wager it will survive you."

"You're hardly a patron of the arts, from what I've heard," I say. "You broke Tactus's violin when he was a child. Not very inclusive of you."

"So full of nuance, families. Would I understand your relationship with your brother?" He gently plucks out several strands of hair and uses them to tie the wild of his mane into a ponytail. "Have you pulled me from my cage just to put me in another? Seems a cruel irony for a man who prides himself on breaking chains."

"I hardly think your suite on Deepgrave was a cage," I say. "Did well for yourself."

"Not so stark as your prison was, I admit. The Jackal was a bizarre creature, pregnant with pain, wasn't he? Much like his sister."

"You're lucky we haven't spaced you, after what you've done," Sevro sneers. "But talk about Virginia again. Go on. We'll see how good your violin sounds in vacuum."

Apollonius sighs. "My goodmen, enemies we may be, but let us not pretend we are bands of troglodytes warring over fire. We are sophisticated creatures who met in conflict under the agreed-upon terms of total war."

"You're not sophisticated. You're a monster wearing a man-suit," Sevro says. "You boiled men alive."

"My brother boiled men alive. I am a warrior. Not a torturer."

"Your brother, you. What's the difference?"

Sevro looks at Apollonius and reduces him to a gestalt of all the men who have hurt him over the years. He has suffered the likes of Apollonius his entire life.

He forgave Cassius for me, once, because he knew the hope of our rebellion balanced on the fragile notion that a man could change. I suspect he's worried that I believe the same for the man before us. The Goblin stands close to me now, as if to protect me from the prisoner, despite the sheet of duroglass.

But the deepspine truth is that he's really trying to protect me from myself. That's why he came.

He need not worry: I will never trust this man. Cassius was a man who lived for an ideal; Apollonius is too bright and too narcissistic to live for anything but himself. But even that can be useful.

Apollonius sighs. "Please don't insult me by claiming you still labor under the notion that you alone in history are an innocent army. War summons the demons from angels. I've seen Gold scalps hanging from Obsidian battle armor. City blocks naught but powder and meat. Or would you have me forget the atrocities you wrought on Luna? On Earth and Mars? Hypocrisy is not becoming of either master or hound. Especially ones who ally themselves with Obsidians."

"The men who did that were punished," I say, knowing that it isn't true. It was two whole tribes that sacked Luna after Octavia's death and ravaged its citizens—low- and highColor alike. Too many to prosecute without losing Sefi. Compromises were made. Always compromises.

"I was an agent of war, like you," Apollonius continues. "We played the same game. I lost. I was caught. Punished. And I used the devices nature and nurture provided me to lessen the blunt impact of incarceration. The great hilarity is that, in many ways, I owe you a debt of thanks." Sevro grunts at that. "Solitude can be the best society. You see, I encountered a perilous choice when I faced your tribunal and received the terms of my sentence. A choice that helped me define myself.

"After life imprisonment was handed down with clean white gloves, a syringe was left for me in my cell by which I was to erase myself from existence. Left by you, Sevro? No matter. The more cowardly examples of my kind did choose this expedient death, finding the shame of losing an empire more than their hearts could bear. Your late friend Fabii, for example. They caved to their own despair. Do any now sing their songs? Does anyone speak their glory?"

He lets the silence answer.

"I knew it was my duty to my own legend to survive this trial. But I was still crippled by my own devices. Imagine me as a great fully-rigged man-of-war. Four masts, great bulwarks of oak and five score cannon. All my life I have sailed smooth seas and waters that parted for me by virtue of my own splendor. Never tested. Never riled. A tragic existence, if ever there was one.

"But at long last: a storm! And when I met it I found my hull . . . rotten. My planks leaking brine, my cannon brittle, powder wet. I foundered upon the storm. Upon you, Darrow of Lykos." He sighs. "And it was my own fault."

I war between wanting to punch him in the mouth and surrendering into my curiosity by letting him continue. He's a strange man with a seductive presence. Even as an enemy, his flamboyance fascinated me. Purple capes in battle. A horned Minotaur helmet. Trumpets blaring to signal his advance, as if welcoming all challengers. He even broadcast opera as his men bombarded cities.

After so much isolation, he's delighting in imposing his narrative upon us.

"My peril is thus: I am, and always have been, a man of great tastes. In a world replete with temptation, I found my spirit wayward and easy to distract. The idea of prison, that naked, metal world, crushed me. The first year, I was tormented. But then I remembered the voice of a fallen angel. 'The mind is its own place, and in itself can make a heaven of hell, or a hell of heaven.' I sought to make the deep not just my heaven, but my womb of rebirth.

"I dissected the underlying mistakes which led to my incarceration and set upon an internal odyssey to remake myself. But—and you would know this, Reaper—long is the road up out of hell! I made arrangements for supplies. I toiled twenty hours a day. I reread the books of youth with the gravity of age. I perfected my body. My mind. Planks were replaced; new banks of cannon wrought in the fires of solitude. All for the next storm.

"Now I see it is upon me and I sail before you the paragon of Apollonius au Valii-Rath. And I ask one question: for what purpose have you pulled me from the deep?"

"Bloodyhell, did you memorize that?" Sevro mutters.

The man before me is not the man I saw before the tribunal all those years ago. His vanity has remained, but now it is a hardened, sharpened sort. Once, he was a vulture of the Society. Instigating duels for fun. Throwing orgies that would last for days. He and Karnus au Bellona were even longtime drinking companions. He'd been looking for a reason to exist, to escape the nihilism of tedium. Then war came.

"You say you have dissected your mistakes," I say. "Let's put that to the test."

"I welcome all tests."

"Goryhell, do you ever shut up?" Sevro asks. "Just let us get a verb in."

Apollonius folds his hands in his lap, waiting patiently.

"Tell me, if you can, how you found yourself in Deepgrave," I say.

"The man who thought himself a king discovered he was but a pawn. I angered the wrong man. Magnus au Grimmus. *The Ash Lord.* But you know that, don't you?"

"I was curious if you did."

He smiles to himself. "I was the first Martian to fire at Lilath au Faran's ship over Luna, you know. I helped save Luna from nuclear holocaust. And I brought him ships, legions, and, along with the other great Martian houses, political capital to offset House Saud on Venus. But he resented me because I would not bend the knee like those Pixie Carthii. I was his ally, not his servant.

"I never saw the knife coming. When he proposed a mission to cut off the head of the Rising, I volunteered eagerly. He let me lead a division of my knights; one century of ten that were to penetrate the Citadel and kill you and your families. With the Carthii we were to be a thousand Peerless Scarred. What a sight it would have been! Not had such a pure force been assembled for a single mission since the Battle of Zephyria. It was to be a coordinated attack.

"My century infiltrated Luna. But it wasn't until we were pressing through the Citadel that I realized we were alone. No other century was on the grounds, let alone the moon. We'd been played as fools by the Ash Lord. By the Carthii. Our support did not answer on the coms, but the Ash Lord's voice did speak. It was a prerecorded message. . . ." He pauses, modulates his voice to a baritone rumble, " 'The seed of Valii-Rath will die with you and your brother. You will be forgotten. Lost to the stars. Farewell, Minotaur.' I knew I was to die, so I made the effort to do so in glory by taking your head. I failed." Apollonius shrugs. "But you knew much of this. You interrogated me, my men. So, again, I ask, why liberate me?"

"Is it not obvious by now to your supreme intellect?" I ask. "There is only one thing you and I share. A common devil. I've pulled you from your prison to offer you the most precious thing I can offer a man like you: revenge."

"Revenge? Do tell."

"Like you, I seek the head of the Ash Lord. The difficulty is parting it from his body. In that, I require your assistance."

He's suspicious. "I have no army, no weapons, nothing left to give but blood and bone. How can I benefit you, Darrow?"

"It's not what you have. It was what was stolen from you." My smile is cold and hard. "Part of what I told you in the cell was true. The Ash Lord did not kill your brother. Tharsus is alive."

Apollonius is stunned. "How . . ."

"You know the answer. You've wondered if it was possible. Tharsus sold your life for your title of paterfamilias of House Valii-Rath. For your monies. Your men. Your ships."

"I see." The charm of the man vanishes. "If I agree to help you . . . what trust can there be between devils?"

"This isn't about trust. It's about leverage. That bandage on the back of your head is from a particular procedure involving a cranial drill. There's a quarter ounce of high-grade explosive embedded in your gray matter as well as a neural chip to stimulate your ocular nerve." I activate the detonation timer on my datapad. Numerals appear on my datapad, but also in Apollonius's vision, via Winkle's biomod. A ten, then a nine, then an eight . . . "You have seven seconds to give me an answer. Yes or no."

Six. Sevro grins.

Four. Apollonius stares blankly.

Two. I back away from the glass.

"Very well." Apollonius smiles, though his anger has not abated. "I accept your proposal. But I have demands."

Thirty minutes later, we watch Apollonius devour a two-kilogram steak in the *Nessus's* officers' dining room with the patience and manners of a well-bred crocodile. Each bite-sized piece is dipped into the *jus* and chewed laboriously before being washed down with a thick Bordeaux from our stores. When he has finished, he leaves several ounces of the steak unattended, as well as a thumb of the red wine, and has only a spoonful of the iced lemon dessert that he requested made for him by Tongueless. He leans back in his chair and blesses my lieutenants with an expansive smile as Alexandar takes his plate away. Apollonius levels his gaze at Alexandar.

"You're a pureblood-looking boy. What is your name?"

"Alexandar."

Apollonius eyes him with interest and then gestures to Sevro and Colloway. "Does it not rankle you to serve such genetic inferiors, Alexandar?"

"I've now seen sharks fly and lions bark." Alexandar laughs. "A lecture over genes from a Valii-Rath." He leans forward, Apollonius's plate still in his hands. "It would have been a severe pleasure to see my grandfather educate you on the merit of *your* genes."

"And whom do you call kin, Alexandar?" Apollonius asks.

"Lorn au Arcos."

"Well now! A griffin in the flesh." Apollonius is impressed. "Blood of the Conquerors still in your veins makes you an endangered species. You must have been there when my baby brother was gutted by your grandfather on Europa. You would have been in the seed of youth. Eight, nine? Tell me, did the violence excite you?"

"It educated me on how to kill Valii-Rath. In that, it proved most satisfactory."

"One could say we have a blood feud between us, young man."

"Please," Alexandar says with another laugh. "I wouldn't give your lowly house the dignity of my attention." The insult finds its mark. Sevro shoos him out of the room with a fraternal slap on the backside.

"Apollonius," I say quietly. "If you insist on provoking my men, we will have a problem."

"Provocation is the nature of predators like us, Darrow." He looks around. "But of course, where are my manners? Apologies for offending you." He waves his hand to the walls. "This is not your moonBreaker. Nor a dreadnought or a destroyer. The officers' mess is much too small. A torchShip perhaps? Smaller?"

He's a sharp one. "It's a frigate. *Xiphos*-class."

"So they're finally deployed. What a curious ship for a warlord, and custom tables . . . What a curious exodus from Deepgrave. If one didn't know better, a sagacious intellect might suspect that something is foul in the state of the Republic."

"This is a black ops mission," I say. The less he knows, the better. "The *Morning Star* is a little less than discreet."

"Indeed," he says. "Now, I think it is time you tell me about my brother and what has befallen my house in my absence."

Sevro smiles. "I'm going to enjoy this."

"Your house is a shadow," I say. "Your brother may have bought his life. But it was at a steep price. He is a political puppet. Your destroyers and torchShips have been given to your enemies, the Carthii of Venus. Your coffers have been drained into the Ash Lord's own pockets. Many of your legions have been disbanded, the men conscripted to serve the Ash Lord. Your house is small yet again. Everything you built on the profit of war is gone. . . ."

"Except my name." A great darkness has built in his eyes.

"Give it a year," Sevro says. "Men forget."

"How do you know all this?" Apollonius asks skeptically.

"One of your family lawyers defected several years ago."

"And where is he now?"

"Slipped in the shower," Sevro says. "Our people found him in thirty-four pieces. Atalantia likes her assassins to make a statement."

Apollonius smiles pleasantly. "And what of my brother? Has he sat idle as the house of my mother and father was pillaged by that Lunese brute?"

"The lawyer said Tharsus has given himself over to vice," I say.

"Oh, how typical of him." He picks at his nails. "If my house has fallen to disgrace, what is my utility to you? In six years, I imagine the defenses for Venus have quite changed. I have neither information nor means."

"No. But your brother does."

I throw a holo of Venus into the air above the table. The verdant planet with two polar ice caps is ringed with metal and military ships. A great dark spot mars the center of one of Venus's oceans. Starhall thinks that is where the Ash Lord resides, but his confidants are far more discreet than those of Valii-Rath.

"This is the latest image of Venus from our spy telescopes," I say.

"Unlike Luna, she is self-sustaining. Farmland, teeming oceans, and vast mineworks. But the rigors of war are demanding. All production is geared toward the war effort. There is no trade. That means no ships in or out."

"There is trade from Mercury. . . ."

"No longer. Mercury's skies are mine," I say.

Apollonius's eyebrows float upward. "Indeed? Respect. How did you bypass the defense platforms?"

"With an Iron Rain," Sevro says.

"What a price you must have paid. What a price." He looks around the table. "Is that why you must risk life and limb for this desperate gambit, because you shattered your army?"

I ignore him. "As you can see, there is an extreme military presence on Venus. The engines of this ship and the stealth capabilities could conceivably run the blockade to escape Venus if we need to, but not to land there. We need you to help us land."

"As I said—"

"Your brother may have tamed his spirit to survive. He may have bent a knee to the Ash Lord. But what is one thing that a brother Rath cannot tame?"

Sevro looks at Apollonius's plate. "His appetite."

"The rigors of war have forced even the wealthy to ration. But your brother has plunged himself into debt with his taste for blackmarket goods, and his appetite has not declined. Sevro . . ."

He pulls up his datapad. "Ninety-nine boxes of Earth wine, two hundred bottles of baiji, two hundred bottles of brandy." He grimaces and says in a small voice, "One hundred thirty-seven bottles of Earth whiskey. Four bottles from Mars." I look back at him, noting the low count of Martian whiskey. Sevro remains assiduously looking down at his datapad. "Two hundred bottles of arrack. Two hundred bottles of schochu. Two thousand kilograms of beef, five hundred kilograms of lamb, four hundred snails, three kilograms of hummingbird tongues, three kilograms of caviar, and twenty imaginary Pinks of Quicksilver's personal stock."

Slowly, Apollonius begins to clap.

"Yes. Yes! Now, that is the Reaper I remember! Tharsus will not be able to resist. Avarice is his nature. He will have a broker beyond Venus, likely Bastion station. I suppose that destination may prove inconvenient." I nod. "Then I will need a facial construct to alter my features and a com station with access to the main antenna array to contact the broker. But landing on Venus does not kill the Ash Lord. He lives in a fortress."

I point at the dark spot on the map. "Republic Intelligence's working theory is that he hangs his crown in the darkzone. Can you confirm?"

"There was talk of a cloaking device to absorb radio and lightwaves," Apollonius says. "I see our engineers have made progress. That is the location of Gorgon Isle, his fortress. It is four hundred kilometers from my island. But you will need an army to breach his defenses." He looks again at the narrow lines of the room. "And something tells me you have no army."

"But you still do," I say. "The Ash Lord couldn't have taken all of your men. And I wonder. What do you think will happen when we land on *your* island and *your* legionnaires see that Apollonius au Valii-Rath, the Mad Minotaur himself, has come home? He does not return as a prisoner of the Rising, but with a platoon of loyal commandos."

I take his Minotaur helm from a bag and slam it on a table.

"I am *not* mad," he growls.

"The indomitable Minotaur," Sevro tries.

"Better." He strokes his helm. "You would put me at the head of a legion?"

"No," Sevro says, dangling the bait Apollonius cannot resist. "Think *bigger*, Rath."

"A coup . . ." Apollonius says suspiciously.

"Tharsus will give us the information we need, then your legion and my men will launch a joint attack on the Ash Lord's fortress. When he dies, Carthii and the Saud will scramble to take his throne for themselves." His lips curl at the mention of his Carthii enemies. "But to the Conqueror go the spoils. Your Praetors will return to fight for you. Your men will defect en masse when they hear you are alive. And in these cells beside you are ten blood family members of

Houses Saud and Carthii, five from each. You will use them as bargaining chips in the ensuing struggle. We will leave Venus, but you will stay and once you have consolidated control and crowned yourself Tyrant in the Ash Lord's stead, you will contact the Sovereign of the Republic and issue a conditional surrender."

"And what do you believe the terms of this surrender would be?"

"You agree to end the war, to give us your rivals, including Atalantia au Grimmus, to be tried in Republic courts for war crimes. You give orders for the legions on Mercury to surrender. You rule Venus for the rest of your life—as you see fit."

"And what would stop the Republic from killing me when it's all over?"

"Me—and you can hold your own people hostage with the Saud atomic arsenal."

"Well, this is magnificent for you. Isn't it? A coup with minimal Republic loss. Enemy gutted from the inside, and the only cost is that I betray my species."

"Species?" I ask. "You're one of a kind, Apollonius," I purr.

"The Gold betrayed you, Apollonius. The Carthii helped the Ash Lord put you to rot. And because of that, you're a footnote. A man in another man's army. I'm offering you a chance at revenge against those who sent you to your death. And a chance to dwarf the Ash Lord in the memory of humanity. We both know you don't care about Gold. So let me help make you the last legend of a crumbling age. The Minotaur of Mars."

"And Venus," he says with a smile, picking up his war helm.

Sevro and I linger in the conference room after Apollonius is escorted back to his cell. "Do you think he knows that they'll never unite behind him?" Sevro asks.

"No. He's insane. The Golds all know it. Saud and Carthii might have bent a knee to the Ash Lord, but they'll never surrender their homeland to a Martian brute. But if we set him loose, he'll tear Venus apart from the inside. We will descend on a fractured Venus. The Ash Lord wanted to give us a civil war. Fine, I'll give the bastard one right back." I take a sip of the wine he left behind. "And if, somehow, Apollonius is able to unite them, we release the video of this little conference and his own men might just kill him for working with me."

Sevro grimaces. "Pops would be proud of this one."

At the mention of his father, I touch Pax's key under my shirt.

"What's that?" Sevro asks.

I take it out. "Pax gave it to me."

"What's it for?"

"A gravBike he made. When I said goodbye, he told me I wouldn't be coming back." I look over at him. I know I should have put words to my regrets sooner. "I'm sorry I made you leave your girls. About Wulfgar."

"You didn't make me do a damn thing." He pats my leg. "Let's just make sure all this is worth the price we're paying."

"It is," I tell myself. "It has to be."

35

TEARDROP IN
THE DOOR

Banquet

"Y E GODS, IT'S AMAZING. Better than a Rose spa," Alban, the
second valet to Kavax, says as a slender human-shaped robot
massages his back with fifteen translucent fingers sprouting from
four hands. The robot's face and body are opaque white plastic. Beneath, a blue light pulses like it's got a mechanical heart beating beneath its assembly-line shell. Is this what replaced my da in the mines?

The personal traveling staffs of Houses Telemanus and Augustus
lounge in a sitting room in Regulus ag Sun's tower. Electronics and
consumer goods litter the room—basket gifts for all the staff, even
me. He's the only man I've ever heard of who gives gifts to everyone
else on his birthday.

So what does Quicksilver want for this basket? I turn the attached
card over in my hands. *Lyria of Lagalos*, it reads in flowery gold cursive, *For your unsung service to the Republic. August wishes, Regulus ag
Sun*. Bribe or not, I cherish the card and rub my finger over the em-
bossed winged heel.

"As if you've ever gotten a massage from a Rose," one of Niobe's
valets says.

"I did one time, you know. Didn't even have to pay."

"Liar. You've silver dripping out of your ears."

"Don't I know. Oh gods, yes, robot, that is the spot."

"Harder, sir?" the robot asks in a hollow human voice.

"Always! Ow! Ow! Not that hard, are you trying kill me?"

"Impossible, sir. The First Law of Robotics states—"

"I know what it states, you toaster."

I sip my ginger tea, wishing Philippe were here to lend his wry opinion. My own is not needed among the servants. I'm still an outsider to this little club of valets. Most, except Alban, are in their forties or fifties and have served since they were younger than I am. Their parents served and their parents before them, just like Garla and the docker Reds.

Everything in Quicksilver's tower is shiny and sparse and silver and white, except the racing ships that roar out sound from a holographic projector on the far side of the room. Some valets and political staff sit there in tuxedos smoking or tapping away importantly at their datapads. Bethalia enters from the hall, speaking with Quicksilver's steward and the Sovereign's, a happy, plump man with quick fingers. Looks a bit like a giddy pig surprised to find himself in a tuxedo.

We're here for Quicksilver's birthday. It was a sight as our caravan taxied in through the air to his skyscraper dock. Spotlights carved the November dark-cycle sky. Onlookers with cameras filled dirigibles and rooftops. I watched out a staff compartment window from one of our armored ships as the Sovereign and her son exited onto the silver carpet with the Telemanuses. For a moment I felt like I was back with my family watching the HC from half a billion kilometers away. The Augustans looked mighty fine. But I resented them all the same. This is their life. Galas and parties. I feel guilty for that resentment. I owe so much to Kavax.

The guilt dissipates when I remember the feel of mud. The sounds of the flies on my sister's body. They'll never hear that sound. None of these serious, pompous servants have heard that sound. I think of Philippe, feel the weight of his Bacchus pendant, and take comfort in the fact that I'm not alone.

My datapad vibrates on my wrist. I hesitantly approach Bethalia and wait till she notices me so I don't interrupt her conversation.

"Yes, Lyria?"

"Kavax pinged me. Should I go in to the banquet?"

She adjusts my collar absently. Unlike the men, the women don't wear a tie. Our collars are stiff and high, and without undershirt. "Yes, but they're not at the main party. Cedric, could one of yours guide her?" The other servants watch me jealously as I leave the room. I grin back at them for a little fun.

One of Quicksilver's security captains, a tall dead-eyed Gray, guides me through the halls past Lionguards. The woman has no interest in talking with me, so I return the favor. We divert to a small lift and take it down to a quieter level that's more darkly lit by lights that run along the ceiling. Water sweeps under the glass floor. Strange shapes swim through it. I try to stop and get a better look, but the valet tuts at me, so I hurry along behind her. She leads me in to a large ivory door where several serious Grays in tuxedos with Augustus Lion pins on their chests loiter outside, weapons bulging under suit jackets. Two Obsidian men watch me from the shadows. I eye them warily, still terrified around their kind. They scarcely seem human.

"She's here for the fox," the valet says.

"You class two, citizen?" The Gray at the door makes me show him my ID, another pushes open the door for me. Kavax's voice is the first I hear.

"Come, now, Victra. Dancer is not so bad a creature. . . ."

"He's a pompous, churlish, three-inch backstabbing rat," a woman drawls. "A little rust-livered rat that has half the Senate eating out of his germ-infested hands."

"You do not have to defame the man's honor," Kavax says. "He's still our friend."

"You big idiot. Socialists don't have honor, they have psychoses."

The woman speaking is half naked. A pregnant Gold with jagged white-blonde hair and a profoundly scandalous black dress with green spikes on the shoulders and a neckline that plunges almost to her navel. Trying not to look at her is like trying not to look at a burning house. A dozen people join with her in intense conversation in a sitting room with a glass-domed ceiling. Several servants bring them coffee and liquor. I spy Sophocles and pat my leg. He looks blankly at me, comfortable on Kavax's lap.

"Hear, hear," a rotund bald man says through his jowls. He holds whiskey in his fist and has a ring with a Gold eyeball in it. Quicksilver in the flesh. A picturesque Pink man sits at his side, gently holding the stem of a wineglass. "Sadly, the diagnosis is terminal for that lot."

"Does he really have six blocs?" Kavax's wife, Niobe, asks a grandmotherly Pink.

"The Coppers have not yet decided," the old Pink says, glancing at another woman, who stands with her back to the room, looking out the window at the glowing city.

"So we have six blocs and they have six. And the Obsidians still won't talk. Who would have thought that war and peace comes down to Copper?" Kavax rumbles. "I warned you of this . . . demokracy." He spits the word.

"Caraval told me in my office this morning that Dancer promised him a bill on lowColor and midColor reparations," the old Pink says.

"Reparations . . ." the pregnant woman says with a laugh. "It was a fine Republic. A bold Republic. Until it went bankrupt in its eleventh year because of socialist lunacy. They take the Senate, they'll gut the war effort to pay for their agenda. Or they'll raise taxes."

"Or?" the old Pink says with a smile. "They'll do both."

"I'm already being taxed into oblivion," Quicksilver says. "How much more blood do they think they can draw from this stone?"

"I think you're doing quite well enough," Daxo says from behind his brandy.

"Well enough?" Quicksilver asks hotly. "Who the hell made you arbiter? Not enough you're blocking my acquisition of Ventris Communications *and* curtailing the mechanization of mines, now you want to define when a man, who built a business *and* a resistance army with his own two hands, has done well enough. I had less trouble making Tinos than getting a bill through your quibbling Senate."

"Monopolies are bad for the people. . . ."

"Government is bad for the people." Quicksilver makes a disgusted sound. "More regulations are bad for the people. You raise taxes, I have to raise prices, little people get crushed."

"Regulus ag Sun, defier of tyranny, guardian of the . . . little people," Niobe says. "How noble you are."

I pull out a bit of duck liver that I carry with me as a lure for Sophocles. He stares on at me and lowers his head willfully to drink out of Kavax's mug. Damn fox. He best not make me come get him. I'll die if they notice me. Some already have. I've been too long in the room.

"I say we kill Dancer," the pregnant woman says. "I've ten men that can make it look like an accident. Ten thousand that can make it look like an example."

The old Pink looks at the servants bringing them drinks. "Really, Victra? Some digression."

"I'll buy a holobillboard above Hero Center. I don't care—and don't act like they aren't your creatures."

"You don't mean that, Victra," Niobe says.

"Why not?"

"Because it's murder, and he's a hero of the Republic. Akin to Darrow and Ragnar." She grimaces. "Maybe more so these days. You can't kill him. He's the voice of Red. If he's murdered, the mob will storm the Citadel. We'll have an uprising, and not just here. Mars would disintegrate."

"The Ash Lord would have a laugh at that," Kavax says.

"Father is right. Might be his intention," Daxo adds. "Darrow certainly thought so."

"Ridiculous," the pregnant woman says. I've just realized who she is. Victra au Barca. "Politics is such a bore without a little murder. Honestly, I don't know how you people sit in the Senate listening to blowhard softbodies yammer on about universal welfare at a time of war. I'd cut my gorydamn ears off."

"Dancer is going to take the Senate," the woman at the window says. My heart skips a beat. I know the voice. Virginia the Lionheart turns around. My heart rushes under my sternum. Years of anger, resentment, now compromised by the subtle beauty of her, by the rolling power of her calm voice. The muted magnetism strikes me dumb, even as I realize she is barefoot. "He will take the Senate when we vote next week," she repeats. "It's not a matter of if. It's only a matter of when. Caraval will fold. He's just drawing this out to get a deal for his people."

"And the Obsidians?" Niobe asks.

"Sefi will not meet with me."

"What does that mean?" Victra asks.

"I don't know. But we must assume it means we don't have their votes; so Dancer will have the majority needed to ratify the peace accord. Seven blocs to six. Then I'll veto it. No senator will sit across the negotiating table with that Bellona. It will pit the executive against the legislative. . . . I'm afraid Darrow was right, this is a ploy by the Ash Lord to distract us. But Dancer will have to keep his flock of senators from straying, while I just have to mind myself. Who do you think will cave first? Me or a few senators?" They laugh. "His momentum will run upon the mountain and founder. Dancer is smart enough to know this. So the question that keeps me up at night is: where's the twist? How will he break the impasse?"

Her eyes settle on me and I feel their massive weight, knowing I look like I'm eavesdropping. The others follow her gaze and suddenly all are staring at me. "Lyria . . ." Kavax says, rising. He brings me Sophocles, who claws as he's handed over. "This little man needs to go piddly. Go on now, lass." My cheeks are aflame. The most powerful people in the Republic staring down a ruster of Lagalos.

"Now can we please talk about who the hell stole my ship?" Quicksilver rumbles. I finally let out the breath I'd been holding. I grab Sophocles by the collar and rush out of the room. My blood is pumping so loud in my ears I can hear no more of the conversation. The door shuts behind me. Directed by the valet, I follow a trail of golden footprints that appear on the floor toward the garden and mull over what I heard.

Sophocles suddenly growls, his hackles rising as a small chrome globe no larger than my fists held together floats toward us in the center of the quiet hall. One of Quicksilver's drone sentries. Sophocles snarls at it as it draws closer. The drone floats politely upward to wait for me to pass.

"*Good day, Lyria of Lagalos,*" it says.

"Good day," I reply with a laugh. Sophocles sniffs the air, less impressed, and then squats and takes a piss right in the center of the floor. A light on the drone glows red through its silver carapace.

"*Bad,*" it says, and shoots a thin line of rancid liquid onto Sophocles. He yelps and darts down the hall. I'm pulled right along with him.

"*Have a splendid day, citizen,*" the drone says.

"Damn robot," I curse as I catch up to Sophocles.

In the garden, I free the fox. He sniffs under bushes searching for the perfect spot. I sit down, still thinking of the Sovereign. I've seen her from afar, but never been seen by her. Under her gaze I felt she could hear all my evil thoughts. All my anger toward her and the Republic. She may have been larger than life on the HC. Brilliant, perfect. But never once did I think about her as flesh and bone.

She was tall, beautiful. But that's not the impression she left on me. No, the Sovereign is *tired*. What would it be like, I begin to wonder, to be responsible for so many lives? *Is that what you felt, Ava, when your children ran with you in the mud?*

"Who are you?" a voice asks. I jump and look to see a boy in a tuxedo sitting on a rock amidst the garden's trees. A holo plays in his irises. I recognize his strange eyes and his dusty gold hair, and for a moment I think I'm looking at the Reaper himself. But he's a child, one I've only ever seen on the HC and from a distance. I look at the ground.

"Lyria, sir."

"The foxwalker." I'm surprised he knows me. "I'm Pax."

"I know, sir." It's a false humility, introducing himself. He's the most famous boy in the Solar System. The bloodydamn First Child. Head's as bare of sigils as his father's.

"*Sir.*" He wrinkles his nose. "Don't start with that." I bend awkwardly at the waist, forgetting I should bow even though he's a boy. "Or that!"

"Sorry."

"Can't be helped, it seems. Were you lot watching the race?"

"The race?" I ask. He taps the corner of his eye. "No. I mean the others were. Don't know slag about races."

"Really? Well, time for an education, I think!"

"I really should just—"

"Oh, Uncle Kavax can stand a moment without the beast." He smiles sincerely. "Please. It'd be nice to talk about anything but politics. Mother makes me sit in on those little councils of theirs. Had to listen to Senator Caraval for two hours yesterday. That man can bloodydamn talk."

I flinch.

That is not *his* word.

He pats the bench beside him. I awkwardly join, fearing what Bethalia would say if she walked in, but I can't very well say no. He switches the feed from his eye back to his datapad and then into the air. Ships suddenly fill the garden. The cherry racer is still out in front, darting between three star constellations suspended above the Hyperion cityscape. A pack of other ships follow in a tight line. "The Circada Maxima," he says over the roar. "I begged Mother to let me go, but she said it would be bad form to miss Quick's birthday. And a security risk." He points at the cherry racer. "That's Alexia xe Rex. Best pilot in the Solar System."

"I thought Colloway xe Char was the best," I say.

"The Warlock? Psh. You're brainwashed already. Pity." He examines me with a wide smile.

"I heard Char has one hundred and twenty-six kills."

"If we're counting kills as skill . . . sure, he's good. Class to himself. But he's a gunslinger. Rex is a ballerina. Both outliers. Both artists, but . . . here, here, watch this turn. Most'll ease up on the accelerator so they don't crash into the wall. But they lose speed. She'll cut her rear engines, shunt power to her starboard thruster, and then pump the energy back to the rear, all without stalling or blacking out. Watch."

I watch him.

He's not like any boy I've ever known. He's aware of himself. Who he is. Who his parents are. I think he knows how nervous I am. So he goes out of his way to be kind, cheery. But if he really was so chummy with servants all the time, he'd be watching in the break room, not skulking here in the garden. But in the race he loses the self-consciousness and the boyish energy bursts out, reminding me of my brothers.

We watch as the cherry racer speeds toward a huge white pylon. Behind the pylon is a floating wall on the edge of the racecourse. All the other ships slow to take the pylon turn. But Rex's banks around the pylon, arcing like a kite on a tight line, and then rockets back the way it came, rounding the obstacle in a blink. "Hohoho," Pax cheers. "That's flying."

His enthusiasm is infectious and I find myself cheering with him as the cherry racer speeds across the finish line several minutes later, the rest of the pack trailing far behind.

"So?" he asks.

"She's good," I admit. "But I still like Char."

"Because he's handsome."

"No."

"But he is."

"Maybe you think he is. . . ."

"Funny. Then why?"

"My brothers are in the legion. Infantry. Anyone who takes Society rippers out of the sky has got my love."

"That's a damn good reason." He winces. "Sorry, not supposed to curse. Don't tell Mother. It's not genteel."

"I'd be too terrified to tell your mother anything," I say, trying to hide my bitterness with a smile.

"She can be a fright, can't she? She's really the kindest person you're likely to meet."

Sophocles has done his business and is staring at me impatiently. "I reckon I should get Sophocles back."

"That's right. Kavax might start weeping from separation anxiety."

"Kavax is a great man."

He looks horrified. "No, of course he is. He's my godfather. Well, co-godfather? I think him and Uncle Sevro arm-wrestled for it. There was cheating. Anyway, I was just japing. Where are your brothers stationed?" he asks, joining me on my walk back.

"They're in the Eighth," I say. "They were on Mercury."

"Harnassus's Own," he says knowingly. "He's ArchLegate. A Red general. They're in the dune cities doing aid work, I think."

"They said it was classified."

He nods. "Our secret? You haven't talked to them?"

"Most of the satellites are down. Too expensive."

"Because most were blasted out of the sky." He says it like it just happened naturally, not like his father led ten million men in warships down onto the planet. I want to hate him. I have hated him. I hated him when he walked by his mother's side on the silver carpet, and when I saw him on the news with all the photographers and journalists swarming. But it feels wrong now to have hated him. He's not so different than Liam—just a boy with circles under his eyes who misses his father and has to hide in a garden to find a moment's peace.

"May I ask you something, Lyria?" he asks awkwardly. "I don't know how to ask. . . ." *Then don't.* "I know where you're from. And I've always wondered, because my grandmother and father won't tell me much. What's it like? The mines?"

There it is.

I keep walking. "How did you know I was in the mines?"

"Father says it's important to know everyone's name and something about them. Not like a fact or something to memorize. But something real. I go over the new staff members so I can better understand them, and Kavax mentioned you offhand the other day. Said you saved his life, so I looked up your dossier. . . ."

"My dossier?"

"Your history."

I stop walking.

Then he knows about my family. Suddenly the attention makes sense. It's guilt. Pity. All over again I feel sick and viciously angry at him in his perfect tuxedo with his white teeth and parted hair. Who is this little spoiled brat to try to bring my grief back to the light of day just so he can live like a peeping neighbor through *my* pain? My family didn't die so he could learn a lesson or satisfy his curiosity.

"What was it like . . ." I murmur, turning on him and feeling the anger coming. *Temper, temper,* Ava would say.

"Yes. They keep me in a bubble here. I want to understand."

"Understand?" He steps back from me and my cruel eyes. "Little Gold wants to hear about the nasty shit? The cancer, the pitvipers? Maybe you wanna go on about how they force us to marry at four-teen so we can get to breeding. Or how mine guards rape us for meds. They did that, you know, boys and girls. Don't show that on the HC for all you highColors."

"I'm not a highColor," he says. "I'm a Red too. . . ."

White anger flashes. "The fuck you are. You're just as Gold as your da is."

His face falls and it feels good to see it, to know I can hurt too. I turn away from him, pulling Sophocles along on the leash. They all want a part of it. A part of pain that's not theirs. Nod their heads. Wrinkle their foreheads. Now they want to pity it, gorge on my pain. And when they're done or bored or too sad, they whisk themselves away to stare at a screen or stuff their fat faces, thinking *How lucky I am to be me.* And then they forget the pain and say we should be good citizens. Get a job. Assimilate. Maybe the Vox are right.

They planted us in stones, watered us with pain, and now marvel we have thorns. Slag them. Slag the lot of them.

Stewing mad, I return Sophocles to the guards outside the confer-ence room door, too sick in the stomach to face the hypocrites, and go back to the break room. I get so nauseous from all these lowColors buying the snakeshit myth that they matter, pretending they're im-portant because they shine shoes and carry capes and clone bloody-damn foxes. In moments I am back outside, smoking burners on a balcony, touching Philippe's pendant and trying not to cry.

I watch the cold, ancient light of the stars and wonder which of them are already dead out there in the blackness. I miss my sister, my family. And though I speak to them still, all I want in all the worlds is for them to speak, to answer. Some proof that the Vale is real. That they are not simply gone into the dark.

But they do not speak to me.

When the Augustuses and Telemanuses have finally had their fill of partying and conspiring, we depart. I slump along with the procession with my head down, crushed with guilt, not just because of how cruel I was, but because I know a little prince with his feelings hurt will go and tell his mother and I'll be sacked within the day. I feel Bethalia's eyes on me and know she knows. I'm just as the other servants pegged me: a rusty bitch with mine manners and no place in their fine company.

The valets carry the gifts Quicksilver's given to our masters into the shuttle's staff entrance. I follow behind with Sophocles's kit and my own basket, now almost forgotten, in my arms. I see Pax and a mean-looking Gold girl about the same age, saying farewell to their important mothers. Both the Sovereign and Lady Barca are going back to the Citadel along with most of the staff for more meetings, and I'm bound for Lake Silene with the Telemanuses, Sophocles, and the children for the week.

I wonder if they'll sack me now or wait till we reach the manor. Probably wait. These Golds hate causing a scene. Pax sullenly says farewell to his mother. She bends to ask him something. He shakes his head and leaves abruptly. On the passenger ramp to our shuttle, his eyes meet mine and he looks down and turns away.

In my seat in the staff cabin, I look back over the frantic rant I typed to Philippe while smoking on the balcony. He hasn't yet replied. Odd for him to take so long. Did I scare him off with my ranting? *You bloody fool. He's sick of you already.* I want to send a message apologizing, but that would look even more desperate. I glance down the aisle up to the passenger cabin. Sophocles sits in Kavax's lap. Pax takes a seat across from the man.

Where will I go when they cut me? What will I do? Would Kavax send me back to Mars, pull Liam from a school he's beginning to love, from friends he cares about? The thought of disappointing him crushes me. I should have just kept my mouth shut.

I look back out the window as our ship rises up, signals its lights in a salute to the Sovereign's more heavily guarded caravan, and banks off to slither through Hyperion's skyscrapers, heading north to Lake Silene.

The buildings burn with lights and are as dense as the trees of the jungle outside 121. Water slithers along the ship window, distorting the lights and making the night seem like it's bleeding blue and green. Our escorts' own lights blink rhythmically to the right of our ship. A strange red light blinks beyond them, against the skyscrapers.

It goes on. Off. On. I squint and then discover it is not outside the shuttle. It's a reflection. I look down, and through my suit's jacket, a red light throbs. "What's that?" one of the valets asks, leaning to get a look from across the aisle. "Lyria . . ." I pull Philippe's necklace out from the neck of my jacket. Bacchus's silver face stares up at me. His gentle mouth pulling upward into a laugh. His face split in a grin. The eyes themselves blink red.

The face of Bacchus begins to shudder and tremble like an animal is inside. Startled, I drop it and the silver splits in half along a tiny seam. From the seam, out of a hidden compartment, a dull metal disk the size of three thumbnails spins up into the air inches from my face. It hisses, then darts away from me, down the aisle fast as a bullet. It reaches the front compartment before I even know what happened.

No one noticed but the servant. "Bomb!" she shouts.

The cabin bursts into chaos. Servants ducking, spilling drinks. Bethalia rising from her seat. Lionguards standing to protect the passenger cabin. I try to stand but my legs are ghosts of themselves. They won't work. They crumple under me and I fall down into the aisle, head angled toward the front of the ship. Other servants collapse along with me till bodies litter the floor.

"Gas," someone behind me gurgles. My own voice won't work.

Lionguards start falling as they rush to the passenger cabin. Lights flash in the ship. Gas masks fall out of overhead compartments. But everyone has breathed it in already. Bodies are falling in the aisle, slumping in chairs.

I've lost all feeling. Kavax swings wildly at the disk, smashing apart the walls in a frenzy to destroy it. But he's slowing, growing lethargic before he becomes the last to fall to the ground. Then there's a high-pitched scream from the device and a pulse, like air being sucked in. The lights go out. Filtration units silence. Engines tremble no more. The drone falls to the floor.

And we plummet from the sky.

Buildings and lights and moving advertisement screens and avenues of ships flash past out the window. Our dead vessel spins sideways. Limp bodies flop and fly around the cabin. I slam against the sidewall, nose to the window, and see us passing through a layer of smog. We tilt again and I'm thrown back into the aisle. Glasses and datapads and gift baskets whirl around the cabin. Then the ship jerks to a stop and gravity reverses. Debris and people float through the ship. There's buildings outside the windows, half-constructed and missing their façades.

My body hovers upward along with cracked datapads and the gift baskets. Then the suspension of gravity vanishes. Everything slams back down. The ship jerks downward again and crashes into the ground. Out the cracked window, I see a retracting door closing over the ship, shutting us off from the light of the city.

We lie in graveyard silence.

Then a metallic sound echoes outside the hull, coming from the servants' passenger door. Something whirs and a stone-on-bone reverberation goes through the ship. A teardrop in the door begins to glow.

36

DINNER WITH DRAGONS

Guests

WE ARRIVE FOR DINNER after the Raa family has been seated around the low-lying table in a warm stone room that looks out through a glass wall over the plains and an escarpment of uncarved mountain. Oxygen-making ivy creeps along the walls and the domed ceiling, emitting a pale luminescence from white floral bulbs. More than a dozen Raa are in attendance. Rangy and austere even in their own home, they wear handmade rough fabrics of earth tones and sit rigidly on thin cushions around an ovular stone table, at the center of which is a single floating orb of blue light. The table is the only furniture in the room, and the ivy the only decoration.

Cassius and I join, both wearing dark Ionian kimonos and cloth slippers. There were no mirrors in my room to see how the clothing hangs. Ionian Golds believe mirrors promote vanity and obsession with the self. It's a crime for even a lowColor to possess one. "Of course they don't want mirrors," Aja would say. "I've dogs handsomer than those Rim dusteaters."

To be fair, the Raa family is not beautiful by Luna standards. Their faces are too long in the jaw, as though someone took the clay of their visages and pressed them between a vise. Except for Dido, their skin is incredibly pale, their eyes slightly larger than desirable, their hair darker. On Luna they would seem dour, cold creatures without proper refinement. But Seraphina's words ring true. The absence of courtly behavior and affectation has a brutal purity to it. Grandmother despised most of the fops at court, and while I know she was not fond of Rim Golds, she did respect their stubborn fidelity to the old ways. It is the reason why she had my godfather obliterate Rhea: the hardest iron cannot be bent, only broken.

The serenity in the Raa's movement and the dignity in their conversation are more impressive to me than all the carver-enhanced visages and pompous exchanges of Luna's upper echelons. The family is not eviscerating the work of a new artist or lampooning a socialite for some faux pas. Instead, as we join, a quiet conversation debating the moral high ground between the Cyclops Polyphemus and the warrior Odysseus is under way.

"Poor Polyphemus," says a young girl with wispy hair and dark-ringed eyes. "All he wanted to do was to eat his supper, but Odysseus had to come in and put out his one eye. He didn't even have one to spare like Father!"

"To be fair, Polyphemus did eat two of Odysseus's men," Seraphina says, sparing a smile for me as I sit. "He's a lesson on how not to be a bad host."

There's an empty space at the table beside her where a silver flower rests in place of a table setting. Probably for her sister, eleven years dead but still remembered every dinner. It is not the only empty seat. Though their patriarch is missing, we're joined by the rest of Romulus's brood. I'm introduced to them. Young Paleron, a thirteen-year-old silent boy. His laughing delight of a sister, Thalia, the Polyphemus sympathizer, who can't be more than nine, and is utterly besotted with the color of my eyes. And Romulus's mother, Gaia, a desiccated old harridan with larva-pale skin who drinks heavily and smokes bitter-smelling weed from a long pipe, which she clutches with spider-leg fingers. She does not touch her food and speaks only to the children in a wandering, frivolous voice.

The rest of the table is filled out by Seraphina's cousins, including

Bellerephon the Bold and his wife, a slender woman with large eyes and a trident diadem of House Norvo of Titan. The well-married man stares at us with pale eyes set in a sullen, cruel face. His long body is hunched like a praying mantis waiting for supper. Despite the earlier violence, Diomedes is also in attendance. He sits serenely at his mother's side and seems the favorite object of the children's adoration.

"The heroes of the hour," Dido says with a smile to her family. "May I introduce Castor au Janus and Regulus au Janus. The men responsible for bringing our Seraphina back to us." Two bowls are handed to us. Dido stands, takes two pinches of rice from her own bowl, and drops one into Cassius's bowl and one into mine. Her family follows the same custom, each walking over to us to share from their own bowls, even Bellerephon, who flicks the rice with boorish contempt. His wife smiles apologetically. Last in line, Seraphina meets my gaze as she honors the rite and returns to her seat.

I wonder if her mother knows she visited my room or if her claim of her mother's ignorance was a deception in itself. I didn't tell Cassius. He would think it some devious manipulation. Perhaps it is. I've not stopped replaying the exchange in my head.

With rice before us, the meal is delayed as per ancient custom, to demonstrate that the Golds are not slaves to the whims of their hunger. My stomach rumbles, but I dare not touch my rice. A Violet with short-cropped hair enters the room carrying a slender harp. He plays a gentle melody and is joined by one of the Pinks from earlier—the woman with the ancient eyes and truculent mouth, Aurae. She sings "A Memory of Ash," a quiet, famous dirge written after my grandfather burned the rebel moon of Rhea in the First Moon Lord's Rebellion. No one ever accused the Moon Lords of having short memories. Without the buzz of the cosmopolitan cities of the Core, it must be hard to forget.

When the Violet and Pink have finished, they depart the room to light applause.

Diomedes's eyes follow Aurae in a way that he should hope no one in his family notices. I file it away for later.

The main course of the meal is served without further delay by minute Browns in dusky gray livery. Their eyes never rise higher than the knee of any Gold, but they are treated with politeness by their masters; thanked for their services and addressed by name. It's a civility I've seen in the halls and the hangars and the bathhouses amongst the Colors from the top down. Each Color within their sphere. There is no undue rudeness, coarseness, or cruelty from Gray to Brown or Gold to Gray. I find it uniquely admirable, especially when I notice the children are not served by the Browns, but must get up and fetch their food from a cart at the far side of the room. Servants are earned with a Peerless Scar, I remember. The Browns skip Cassius and me as well until Dido motions them to serve us. "We'll forgive the guests their naked faces, for now."

A small bowl of flowered water sits beside each place setting along with a white linen towel. Recalling my lessons from my grandmother's steward, Cedric, I dip my fingers and dry them on the towel.

The fare itself is as simple as the clothes: roasted fish from Europa with hearty seasonings of salt to mask the lack of pepper at the table. Flatbreads, hummus, plain rice, and roasted vegetables steam in unadorned bowls, which are passed around and served without utensils. The rice is in abundance, but the cuts of meat are meager in size.

"Regulus, the *Archimedes* is your ship, yes?" Dido asks.

"She is."

"A sleek flier, who has seen more than a few years. Older than Gaia even."

"Hmm?" Gaia asks, looking up from her pipe like a disheveled barn owl.

"I said his ship is *almost* as old as you. You remember the line, I'm sure. A GD-17 Whisper-class frigate."

"Who is whispering?" Gaia asks. "No whispering at the table. It is rude." She goes back to her pipe and stares up at us suspiciously through a bramble of eyebrows as if we mean to do her great harm. I've seen enough of intelligence to know how hard it is to hide. The woman does a fine enough effort for this backwater, but her guise wouldn't last the length of a gala in the Luna courts. The dancing faces worn there are the best in the worlds. Deception, the language of life. But it seems Gaia has everyone at this table convinced she is senile.

Interesting woman.

"Your ship is a rare craft for simple merchants," Bellerephon says coolly. He traces a finger along the stone table. The man's a brutish clod with the petulance of a child. Devoid of mystery, a man must have dignity. I find the lack of either boorish. "Hard to see how it would be come by legally."

"I'm not sure I like your tone, my goodman," Cassius says. "But the pressure on your moon has befuddled my ears. Perhaps you might clarify so we might have no misunderstandings." Again with the antagonism.

Bellerephon scowls at him. The rest of the Raa family look on with the faint amusement of people far too comfortable with violence to care much about verbal ripostes.

Seraphina raises an eyebrow and eats her fish.

"He means nothing by it," Dido says smoothly. "Do you, nephew?"

"Nothing at all." He stares on at Cassius.

"I won her in a bet six years back from a new-money Silver who couldn't hold his amber," Cassius explains now with a smile. "She was liberated from Rising sympathizers."

Diomedes gracefully removes the bones from his fish with a single pull and shows Paleron how to do the same. "Regulus, you said you served," he says without looking up.

"I did. I was a centurion within the Augustan legions during the Martian Civil War."

Diomedes looks up. "Then you fell in the Lion's Rain?" Respect fills his voice. The rest of the table listens raptly. Mention a battle and their ears perk up like a kennel of dogs hearing a can open.

"I did."

"What was it like?" Seraphina asks.

"Hell," Cassius says, disappointing them with his answer. He might not have fallen in the Reaper's Rain, but it cost him his entire family, save his mother.

It's a clever game Cassius is playing. By saying he's an Augustan man, he's one of the only Core Golds with the same sense of betrayal the Rim must have felt after the bloody Triumph and the failure of their rebellion. A dangerous gambit. He might claim to know the same people. And some of them might have sought refuge here.

"Did you know the Reaper?" Diomedes asks Cassius. I don't mind being relegated to the background. Grandmother thought talkative men the most hilarious of creatures, so busy projecting that they never notice anything until the jaws of the trap close around their legs. The key to learning, to power, to having the final say in everything, is observation. By all means, be a storm inside, but save your movement and wind till you know your purpose. It's a pity Darrow and Fitchner au Barca were better students than the last generation of Gold.

"I did not know him personally, no. He was Augustus's lancer," Cassius answers. "Peerless don't socialize with men like me." He taps his scarless face.

"Then you've come up in the world," Bellerephon says.

"Did you ever see him fight?" Diomedes asks.

"Once."

"They say he slayed the Storm Knight of Earth and defeated Apollonius au Valii-Rath in single combat. They say he is a true blademaster, the heir of Arcos. That not even Aja au Grimmus could stand against him now." The dark spirit in me bucks against that claim. I almost break my silence.

"They say many things," Cassius replies.

"What was your measure of him?"

Cassius shrugs. "Overrated."

Diomedes booms a laugh.

"Diomedes is the Sword of Io. A blademaster," Seraphina says proudly. "One of six left in the Rim. He also studied with Arcos on Europa—became a stormson."

I feel a spike of envy.

"Lorn taught me how to fish with Alexandar and Drusilla," Diomedes corrects. "His last student misused his gifts." The understatement of the millennium. "He had no desire to make better warriors, only better men."

"In that he succeeded." Seraphina smiles at her brother. "One day, Diomedes will test the Reaper for himself."

Bellerephon watches as Diomedes humbly returns his attention to his younger siblings. I smile at his jealousy and watch Diomedes with growing respect. We eat in silence for a time. I nurse the small fish on my plate. Cassius is already finished with his. Always a man of appetites. I'm more practiced than he in the art of self-deprivation at the dinner table.

Doesn't feel so long ago that I was a knobby-kneed boy sitting at my grandmother's dinner table when she turned her long neck to me and peered down that peregrine nose, and, in a kindly manner, inquired if I intended to sleep outside in the gutter instead of in my bedchamber, because by virtue of the fact that I'd eaten three whole tarts I'd clearly abdicated being a man in favor of being a little pig. It was two days after my parents had died. I seldom eat sweets any longer.

Cassius makes a show of looking around for more food.

"Pardon the portions," Dido says with the faint hint of apology. "They're more conservative than you're accustomed to, I'm sure. We're in the midst of a ration cycle."

"Thought you were sitting on a breadbasket here. And Europa is just one big sea. Or did you already eat all the fish?" Cassius asks.

I wait in trepidation. This line of inquiry is dangerous. An innocent observation that will lead inexorably to a casual inquiry about the new ships we've seen and the state of their docks and their stores of helium-3. I fear him asking that question.

Dido smiles obligingly. "On the contrary, the fisheries and latifundia have never been more productive."

"Then a lack of ships, I warrant."

"Many were destroyed by the Sword Armada," Dido admits. "And there were . . . lean years. But no. Not a lack of ships or helium-3. In fact, it was disruption of agriculture on Titan last month that forced us to part with more of our bounty than anticipated."

It isn't natural for her to tell us so much.

"A daughter of Venus must have found this place . . . strange," I say diplomatically, trying to pull Cassius away from his obvious end-game.

"Ah, so you know my lineage. Aren't you a well-studied merchant?" she says.

"You're rather famous," I reply, playing the overwhelmed youth. I spare a glance at Bellerephon, who has not stopped watching Cassius since he sat down at the table. Something is wrong here. I can sense the sharks beneath the surface. "Even on Mars we know of Dido au Saud."

"I doubt my father would let me still claim his name." She leans forward. "Tell me, am I as famous as my husband?"

Seraphina tenses at mention of her father. She's barely touched her food, and looks uncomfortable, furthering my unease.

"Few are as famous as your husband," I say to Dido.

Her mouth pinches. "How diplomatic."

"But on Mars, 'Romulus and Dido' is still a fairy tale."

"A fairy tale. If only." She smiles at that. "When I came here for the first time, I was a foolish little sun creature raised in the court of Iram. A *gahja* through and through. I fell in love with a pale wisp of a knight and thought our life would be a poem. But once I arrived here, I felt the darkness, the cold my mother warned me about. I missed the sun and hated this place. Hated my husband's austerity. He would fret over water left in a glass. A crust of bread uneaten. But then I learned one of Io's many lessons: here, by darkness, by radiation, by hunger, by thirst, by war, we are always at siege. It is not like the world of my birth, where life grows on every rock and men eat until they vomit. On Io, scarcity makes us strong. It makes us value what we do have."

She looks around at her family with a warm smile.

Seraphina clarifies. "Father set a decree three months ago that rations are in effect until reserves are back to appropriate levels. No Gold may eat more, as measured by weight ratio, than the agricultural Reds do."

I'm startled. "You mean to say even you follow the ration limit?"

"Why wouldn't we?" Seraphina asks, confused. "It is law."

"Qualis rex, talis grex," Dido says.

"As the king, so the people. But you have power," I say, intensely curious. "You can do what you like." Cassius shoots me a not-so-subtle look. He wants me to shut up and eat my food, leave the games to him, but my curiosity gets the better of me. My tutors called the Moon Lords impractical isolationists. But there seems little here but practicality."

"An errant claim. Romulus and I believe it important to teach our children to be more than just powerful." Dido slowly picks the meat off the bones of her fish with her fingers. "Gold was meant to be an ideal, to inspire. Don't you agree?"

Why does she bait me?

Cassius's eyes tell me to be careful. And so do Seraphina's. "I'm just a merchant," I say with a humble shrug. "My family wasn't like yours."

"Oh, please. Don't be ponderous, boy. Peerless aren't the only ones with opinions. Pray tell, do you agree? Speak plainly or don't speak at all. Were we meant to be more than just force? Weren't we meant to inspire?"

"Yes. But then we forgot it."

"See! An opinion." She looks over at Cassius. "You really should let him have a mind of his own, my goodman. Sighing like that when he speaks his mind? Not good to quash the naturally inquisitive." She turns back to me. "Now, Castor, it's been ten years since we purged the Sons of Ares from our moons and eliminated the last of the Slave King's terrorists. Out of curiosity, how many rebellions and terrorist attacks do you think Ilium has had in the last year?"

"Forty-three," I say instinctively, based on the ten-year annual average of reported incidents before the Fall. Seraphina's eyes narrow at the precise number.

"Two," Dido replies.

"Just two?" Cassius asks in suprise.

"A shooting and a bomb. The hierarchy has not changed. Do you know what inspires this loyalty to the Compact from all Colors? Honor. Honor in work. Honor in morality. Honor in principle and family. Our rules are harsh, but we obey them from Gold to Red.

Romulus eliminated the rigged quotas in mines and the latifundia, has begun to phase out the Obsidian gods, and makes each man understand he is part of the same body. He has replaced subjugation with participation. Given a reason to sacrifice for the betterment of all. And it starts with us at this table, the head of the body."

"Each man and woman given liberty to pursue achievement, with the best of his virtue and abilities, and rise within the station for which his flesh was made—a sacrifice of the Self for the preservation of All." I murmur the words of the Compact like scripture. "Admirable."

"Yes," Seraphina says, her eyes warmer to me than ever before.

"Why did you not carry on the fight? Why become traders?" Diomedes has been nursing the question, waiting for a pause in the conversation. The timing is awkward.

"You mean fight for the Ash Lord?" Cassius asks, sipping his wine. "I think not. His daughter murdered my friends at the Triumph."

"What of you, Castor?" Dido asks. "Don't you want revenge for your family?"

I feel Cassius's gaze on me, the weight of expectation as I regurgitate his lessons, his maxims. "What good would it do?" I answer loyally.

"Is that your answer . . ." Dido nods to Cassius. ". . . or his?"

How many times have I lain in my bunk on the *Archimedes* lonely, fantasizing of strength, of revenge? Of sailing home and taking back my grandmother's scepter, her chair, and putting Darrow and his rabid wolves in chains? I always thought it a fantasy, something that could never be. But now that I see how much strength is left in Gold, how much of the old virtues, it grows harder to see it as the vain, idle fantasy of a little boy any longer.

Gold is not dead.

"Is that why you want war?" Cassius asks. "For revenge?"

"In part, yes," Dido replies. "To avenge the wrongs the Slave King has done us. But also to heal the chaos that he has made. His Republic has had ten years to create peace. They've failed. The time is right for the Society to be rebuilt. We have the will, the might. But we need the spark. That is why I sent my daughter to the Gulf. To retrieve that spark. Thanks in no small part to you, she brought it home." She pauses a moment to smile with no kindness in her eyes. "But now, I fear it is missing."

Finally, the twist. The reason behind all these innuendos and games.

"Is that an accusation?" Cassius asks warily.

"Oh yes, my goodman."

"That's why you went back into the *Vindabona* . . ." I say to Seraphina. "But you didn't bring anything back with you."

"I brought your razor," she says.

My heart sinks in my chest. I missed it. I've walked straight into their trap. They've been toying with us, with me. And here I was admiring their civilization like a gorydamn anthropologist.

"And where is your razor?" Dido asks. "We're dying to know."

"It was lost," I say.

"Our hull was punctured and the razor pushed into space before the cellular armor could close the breach," Cassius explains.

"Is that so . . . Regulus?" Dido leans back. "The fish has left a foul taste in my mouth. I think it is time for dessert." She motions to the servants and the door to the room opens. Two Obsidians with bulging pale arms enter carrying a load between them, which they set in the center of the table.

It is our safe.

37

LYSANDER

Prey

"THE SAFE WAS WELL HIDDEN," Dido says. "But of course our men are nothing but thorough. Fortunately, the krypteia who discovered it was one of mine."

"If you are so thorough, then you know what sort of safe that is," I reply before Cassius can speak. The safe might hold our damnation in our family rings, but it also is our only leverage. It can't be lost. "It is a halcon-7. It has four inches of rolled steel with an analog tumbler lock instead of a digital mechanism, which makes it impervious to electronic incursion. More importantly, it has three Sun Industry military-grade plasma charges embedded on the interior wall faces of the safe. You drill, it will detonate at a temperature of three thousand degrees Fahrenheit. But of course you know that, or you would have already opened it."

"Indeed," Dido says. "Personally, I would very much like my daughter's efforts not to have been spent in vain." She holds up a finger as I'm about to reply. "And I would be wary if I were you at further insulting my intelligence by claiming your razor is not inside this safe. I bear insults poorly." Then her lips slide into an enigmatic grin. "But open it for me, and we can be friends again. I am a most generous friend."

I glance at Seraphina.

"Is that the only reason we're alive?" I feel foolish for letting her lower my guard. A strain of grandmother's malice pulses into me, despising her attempts at manipulation.

"Castor, let the adults speak," Cassius says slowly, his eyes fixed on Dido. "The safe can be opened, for a price."

"A price?" Seraphina laughs in appreciation of his boldness.

"We are merchants, after all," Cassius replies.

"What is your price?" Dido asks.

"For the key to your war, I offer a bargain. Give us our ship. Give us our pilot, and any surviving crewmembers of the *Vindabona*. Give us our freedom. And once we reach safe distance from Io, we will send you the combination."

Dido wags a finger at him. "Are you trying to make a fool of me? Castor left out a feature of the halcon-7. Didn't he? Clever boy. A secondary detonation code. One that can be given in place of the real code. One you could supply me with when you are cruising toward the Belt."

"And why would I want to destroy what's inside?" Cassius asks. "We take no issue with your war. Only your value of our lives."

"Yes." She runs a finger over her lips. "Why indeed?"

The silence grows to terrible length.

"On my honor, I'll send the proper combination," Cassius lies. He'd rather die than let them have their war.

"Your honor." Bellerephon laughs at a private joke. "Be thankful we do not peel you like tank shrimp."

"They are guests," Diomedes says sternly. "They have eaten our bread, supped at our table. No guest in the history of our house has been violated. Not even Fabii and the Reaper. Not even the Ash Lord after the Burning of Rhea. Do not disrespect your ancestors."

Bellerephon rolls his eyes at his cousin and turns to his aunt. "Aunt Dido, we don't have time for this. Vela is already rallying legions at Karath." If Vela escaped, then Cassius is right again. The coup is not concluded. "The Codovan will be coming too. Our allies are nervous. Some won't stand by us if Vela attacks. We need the evidence."

Dido opens her hands to us. "You see my predicament. There is no time for your proposal. One option remains, and that is to trust me. Have I not been a good host? Have I not shown honor?"

Does she think we're so stupid?

Cassius smiles. "You have my terms."

Seraphina looks to me. "Castor, no harm will come to you . . ."

"My brother speaks for the both of us," I reply.

Dido leans back in her chair and nods to a Brown by the door. "Tell Pelebius to bring in his pet."

"Have you a new creature for the children?" old Gaia asks in delight. Her wrinkled neck cranes in anticipation as an old Violet with a black mustache limps into the room. "Oh. Vile." She frowns as he carries in a glass jar filled with noxious yellow liquid. Something stirs within, but I can't yet make it out. The Violet stands ominously at the end of the table.

"It is said that a life is made great by sorrow and joy." Dido stares at me, then Cassius. "But you men are cursed. You will never really understand life because you do not know what it is to bear a child. To push a life from your flesh. To have two hearts beating inside you at once." She looks at the empty seat beside Seraphina. She takes the flower there between her fingers. "To have had seven hearts beating beyond you, carrying your hopes, your dreams. And when one of those hearts stops . . . you feel it as if it were your own."

She crushes the flower in her slender hand and lets the mangled petals drift free one by one to settle on the barren bones of her fish.

"The story of their life ends. All those dreams gone. And you begin to forget them. You begin to loathe yourself for time ill-spent with them. For your grief stealing the joy their life brought as their memory begins to fade."

More Obsidians enter the room and stand behind us.

"My daughter, my Thesalia, was not made in my image or Romulus's," Dido whispers. "She was a birth of air. A sweet girl. A vessel of all my joy. Eleven years ago Thesalia went with her grandfather Revus to see Mars and attend Augustus's summit. She wanted to see the Valles Marineris. The Olympus Mons. Eleven years ago she watched her grandfather die and felt fear as her head was caved in by a Martian boot. My joy vanished that day, and as a family, we swore vengeance upon all those responsible. Roque au Fabii, Lilath au Faran, Aja au Grimmus, Adrius au Augustus. Antonia au Severus-Julii. Octavia au Lune." Dido's lips curl. "And Cassius au Bellona."

38

LYSANDER

Gruesli

Cassius bursts from his seat, diving across the table to try to reach the access pad on the safe. The Obsidians grab him and wrench him back. I lunge for one of the knives on their belts, but Bellerephon stands and in one fluid movement whips his razor diagonally across the table. The thin black metal snaps around my arm. He jerks me sideways and I spill down, set upon by Obsidians. Bellerephon's fingers move over the hilt of his razor to recall the whip to rigid form. He'll take my arm.

"Bellerephon," Seraphina snaps. "Not that one."

He says nothing but flicks his whip free of my arm and recalls it back across the table. It slithers like a snake across plates and spilled rice. The Obsidians shove me into my seat. They've wrestled Cassius back to his. "If you hurt him, I won't give you the combination," I say quickly. "Seraphina, he saved your life. You're in his debt and he's under your promise of hospitality."

"Void because of your lie," Dido says.

Diomedes, who has sat like some paragon statue this whole time, watching the drama unfold, now frowns. "Mother. I know the face of Bellona as well as any man. That is not him."

"Oh, but it is . . ." she says. "The razor of a Bellona is in that safe. Concealed under a shell of titanium."

I look to Seraphina, hiding my horror as I realize what gave us away. When she opened the razor to hide her evidence inside it, she must have discovered the false cover and seen the eagles on the handle underneath. She knew all along.

"Did you think we do not know the technology of our enemies?" Dido asks Cassius, gesturing at her own face. "You may keep your Silver-spawned enlightenment; here we have masters of the old ways, of flesh and bone." She gestures to the Violet and his jar. "You may begin."

The Violet shuffles up to the table and, with a pair of tongs, reaches into his jar. From the yellow liquid he draws a tiny horror. A hideous spider-legged slug with corpse-pale skin and a belly riddled with small, hungry apertures. "This is a *gruesli*," Dido says. The creature squeals like a burning worm and writhes in the air over Cassius's face. He flinches away. From its apertures, thin tentacles push past layers of pallid flesh toward his face. "The gruesli eats masks, you see. You are not the first spy to breach the Gulf."

The Violet lowers the creature onto Cassius's face. Black stingers spurt from the tentacles into his skin. It wraps its legs around his head and sucks, shuddering with an orgiastic sigh as my friend gurgles beneath its flesh. I watch in cold terror as the creature feeds till it is engorged and lethargic and the Violet pulls it back up with tongs, to reveal, under a mess of puncture wounds and thin trails of blood, the swollen face of my handsome friend. He blinks through the layer of grime up at Dido as the Obsidians haul him up to face our hosts. Blood and milky fluid drip into his beard.

"The truth, at last," Dido says.

Cassius laughs and rebelliously spits blood from his mouth. "Cassius au Bellona . . . at your service."

I look to Seraphina for help, but there's no ally left in the room. She loathes Cassius as much as the rest of them.

"You didn't just take my daughter. You took my brother," Dido says.

"Marcus," Cassius says. "The Joy Knight."

"Your sworn brother. Your fellow Olympic. You cut him down before you killed Octavia."

"He was a bastard."

"Yes. But he was my blood," she whispers. "I will give you one last chance to open the safe."

Cassius grunts. "So you can have a war that will send mankind back to the dark ages? Funny. You don't look stupid."

"These are the dark ages," Seraphina says. "We will bring order back."

"Says the little girl. Have you ever seen a city after orbital bombardment?"

"I saw Ganymede after the docks fell from orbit," she replies bitterly. "I've seen horror—starvation. A whole city frozen."

"You haven't seen war." His heavy eyes strafe the rest of the Raa. "You all think you're the chosen people. The keepers of the flame. Please. You know how many have thought that? You're just like the rest. Too vain to realize the flame has gone out. The dream of Gold was dead before any of us were ever born. You want a war because you think the Rising is vulnerable? Because they still battle the Core? You don't know Darrow. You don't know his people. If you attack, you lose everything."

"The Slave King has already fallen," Dido says, smiling at Cassius's confusion. "Of course, how could you know? He has become an outlaw. His own mentor and wife have turned their backs on him. The Obsidian Horde is thinned. The remainder stirs with discontent. Their Senate devours itself and debates peace with the Pixies of the Core. They are flailing, scattered, and weak."

"The Ash Lord has sought peace?" I ask.

"It seems war has softened his resolve. He is craven, and will be dealt with once we have retaken Mars and Luna. Rhea will be repaid in full." Dido turns her eyes to me. "They say your family is cursed, Cassius. How lucky you are to have a brother survive the Jackal's purge. Which one is he? Theseus? Daedalus? They would be his age by now. . . ." She looks back to Cassius. "It doesn't matter. If you do not give me the combination, I will let our dragons suck the marrow from his blasted bones."

Cassius looks over at me with love and sorrow in his eyes. He's been searching for this for the past ten years. A chance at redemption. Denying her war is that chance. It crushes him now to know the price it will cost. But he will pay it, I realize. Even if that price is my life.

"I swore to protect the people. That is what I will do. No matter the cost."

"And do you share your brother's insanity?" Dido asks me.

Cassius would have stayed to free the prisoners on the *Vindabona*. He wouldn't have run at the first sound of Obsidians like I did, because he is a hero, and I am not. Whatever hate I have for Darrow, whatever hope these Gold have kindled in me, I cannot betray Cassius now. I love the man too much. But it breaks my heart to know that the masses he would die for would have his head on a spike if they could.

"He speaks for the both of us," I say again.

Dido makes a small noise of disgust. She leans back, realizing the impasse, quick eyes searching for a way around it. "Diomedes. A bloodfeud needs resolution. Will you do the honors?"

"No," the stoic knight replies. She turns on him in confusion.

"What?" Dido asks, caught off guard.

"You heard me, Mother."

"He killed your sister."

"They are our guests."

"You're joking."

"You blathering idiot . . ." Bellerephon hisses. "They're enemies of our blood."

"They are our guests. If you want blood, draw it yourself."

"Let him alone," Seraphina says, standing. "It is his right to refuse. I will do the deed."

"No," Dido says.

Seraphina flinches. "You doubt I can?"

"Yes. Sit down." She ignores Seraphina's wounded expression and looks down the table. "Bellerephon, do what your cousin will not."

"With pleasure."

The man uncoils to his feet, long legs taking him around the table till he stands looking down his crooked nose at Cassius's bloody face.

"Beware, milky," Cassius says with a feral grin. "I am a student of Aja au Grimmus."

"And I am the son of Atlas au Raa. Sixth shade of the Shadowfall. Slayer of Petro au Bretta, the Desert Spear." Bellerephon's eyes glitter with delight as he gathers phlegm and spits it onto Cassius's face. It drips down Cassius's cheek, running diagonal with his Peerless Scar. "This is a blood feud. The blood of my grandfather and my cousin is upon your hands. Hear me now, you wretched worm. We are devils to one another. In the name of House Raa, I, Bellerephon au Raa, challenge you to single combat in the Bleeding Place till one heart beats no more."

"Very well, my goodman," Cassius replies with a brilliant smile. "I am delighted to accept."

39

EPHRAIM

Lions' Den

I T SOUNDS LIKE THE DAMN WORLD is ending. Clustered outside the downed Gold shuttle in the center of our trap, Volga, Dano, and I look up and feel the fear. Two escort ripWings chase after the downed Augustan ship. The blast door above us locks closed as the first round of gunfire pelts its reinforced surface.

The shuttle plummeted a kilometer through the city, drawn downward faster than the speed of gravity by the fleet-grade Sun Industries gravWell. The machine gripped the shuttle as soon as the EMP Kobachi built into the custom drone went off inside the shuttle. We almost lost the ship twice on the descent as its rotation made it drift out from the gravWell's projection radius. Dano wrangled it back by increasing the gravity to four times Earth grav.

Aside from the shuttle, the gravity beam pulled down a deluge of rain, seven fliers, a forest of shrubs from balconies, several clotheslines, and three shattered hoverbikers who died by smashing into the floor at nine hundred kilometers per hour. All that haul lies in a broken bone and metal soup around the shuttle in the garage of the half-completed Lower West Hyperion Hospital. Dano kicks one of the shattered hoverbiker helmets away from the breech we've burned into the shuttle's hatch. The head is still inside.

My stomach knots up. I'm back in the block war.

Digging through debris. Boots stomping over rubble and bits of men. Gasping like a dying fish, lungs starved from thermobaric burrow bombs that eat the oxygen out of the air.

I tear my eyes from the disembodied head, thankful for my helmet so my crew doesn't see my horrified face. I didn't take the zoladone tonight, afraid that the stomach cramps would knock me flat. I'm already feeling too much.

The blast door shudders above us as the escorts pour more munitions into it. Soon it will buckle. We've four minutes before a rapid response team of Hyperion's counterterrorism Watchmen deploy from the Twelfth Cohort headquarters.

Already, there will be armored bodyguards jumping from the escorts, searching for some other way into my metal trap.

I stare into the mirage of heat as our breeching device burns a hole in the hull. Volga, armored in a military-grade chestplate and helmet, pulls the breecher off and slams a steel and lead battering ram into the metal. It caves inward on her third swing. She tosses the ram aside and moves into the ship. The green magazine globe of her plasma rifle's barrel glows as she primes the generator. Dano goes in next. I follow with the Omnivore in my trembling hands. If even one of the nasty bastards inside didn't get knocked flat by the anacene gas, this could turn into a bloodbath.

Trigg run through on a Gold's razor.

Men crumpling like cans to powerHammers.

Ozone and burning flesh as the Gold skins my team alive.

My hands shake harder.

The ship is upside down and black inside. It looks like a party gone wild, all the revelers having drunk themselves to insentience right where they stood. Bodies, still buckled in their crash webbing, hang upside down in chairs from a ceiling that was once the floor. Others are sprawled atop each other in a living carpet with eyes that shine like fountain coins up at me. We pick our way through the arms of servants and leather-faced killers in tuxedos. The anacene-17 has made the muscles in their bodies, including their eyelids, unresponsive. Only their lungs and hearts still work, allowing them breaths so shallow they look dead.

There's no movement.

My heart slams in my chest. We push for the forward passenger compartment in search of the prizes. As Dano bounces around the ship with a gymnast's ease, Volga and I climb over the body of a titanic Gold with a red beard and almost step on a fox the size of a large child. It lurches up at us, snarling. I shout in surprise and kick it as it lunges. It flies down the aisle and onto Dano's leg as he hangs with one hand from one of the upside-down passenger headrests. He screams and falls down.

"Get off me. Get it off!"

He flails, falling to his back, and points his gun at the animal's skull, ready to blow its head off. Volga pushes the weapon aside and pries the fox's jaw open to free Dano's leg. *"I'm gonna kill it!"* Volga ignores him and grabs the flailing fox by the scruff of its red coat and locks it in the cockpit. We hear it slamming against the door as I haul Dano up.

"What the hell was that?" Dano shouts into his com. Blood dribbles down his leg.

"Shut up. Work."

Amidst a thick human shield of bodyguards and Golds, we find the prize.

"He's here," Dano says triumphantly as he limps forward. *"The little shit is bloodywell here!"*

He says it like he doubted it. He's not the only one. The intelligence was too good. The plan too big. The stakes too high. The players far too nasty. Yet it's all slick and clean. Even I smile when I see the prize.

The boy hangs suspended upside down, paralyzed and wrapped to his seat in crash webbing. Blood leaks into his hairline from a long gash on his forehead. He's smaller than I expected, no giant like his father, but still at ten he's almost Dano's size. He's dressed in a tuxedo with a gold lion clasp at his neck instead of a tie. His eyes stare at us in terror. Limping and muttering curses to himself, Dano roughly cuts the clasp off, pockets it for a trophy, and then starts cutting the crash webbing as Volga keeps her gun on the paralyzed bodyguards. We pull the boy from the seat. Dano hoists him over his shoulder and carries him out of the ship as Volga and I find the secondary prize three seats up. The slender Gold girl has a hatchet face and deep-set, angry eyes. Unlike the boy, she shows no fear, just absolute, unmitigated hatred. She's promising me a slow death with that look as I cut her free of her crash webbing and cut the bleeding sun brooch from her jacket. I can't resist patting her on the head. Volga puts her over a shoulder and departs the ship.

I stand alone in the dark vessel, listening to the thunder of their escorts against the blast door. Littered around me are the powerful and mighty who thought themselves untouchable. Thought themselves gods. A dark, unexpected thrill shoots through me as I realize I've humbled the lot of them.

I step atop the giant who the fox was protecting. The massive man has big iron on his hip. A razor just like Aja's. My boots smudge dirt and biker blood into his tuxedo. A Telemanus. I recognize him now. I turn to regard the cluttered cabin, wishing they could see my face and know that a lowly Gray has driven them to their knees.

"Reap what you sow," I say in a thick Red Martian accent. "Give my regards to your masters, my goodmen."

With a deep and courtly bow, paying all homage to Gold manners, I hop off the Telemanus and dip my gloved hand in a pool of blood gathered around the head of a wounded bodyguard. I press the hand into the wall, leaving a blood-red handprint.

Blame placed, I walk toward the passenger compartment.

Time for the part I've been dreading.

I find Lyria lying amongst three other servants who had the misfortune of being unbuckled from their crash webbing. One has a broken neck. Lyria stares up at me in the darkness. To her I'll be a masked shadow, unrecognizable, with a glint of metal in hand. But I feel as if she and she alone can see through the mask. She'll know that Philippe did this to her. And she'll tell them. I can't have them piecing it all together. My life will be over.

Make it clean.

I point the Omnivore at her head.

My hand shakes. Sweat trickles into my eyes inside the humid helmet. She looks up at me blankly. Even in the darkness, she can see the gun. She accepts it. There's no wild fear in her eyes, just sadness. Resignation. *Pull the trigger. Pull it, you son of a bitch.*

What is wrong with me? I've killed men in cold blood before. I was all professional when I explained the plan to the others. It needs to be done.

"I'll wrap it up nice and neat," I said.

You can't pull a testimony from a corpse.

Pull the trigger.

It will be quick. She'll feel nothing. I told myself I'd do it without the zoladone. That I'd sack up. I'd own this.

I close my eyes and see her little smile to herself back in that restaurant as she ordered that last flight of oysters. It was like seeing a child laugh at an adult's joke. So proud to feel accepted, but still self-conscious, wondering if their ignorance will be found out.

Why did she have to smile like that?

Like him.

Fuck it.

I pull the trigger.

Nothing happens. I look down at my gun. The safety is still on. I almost throw up. I'm shaking, backing away from her, my stomach all tied up in knots, disgusted with myself. *Idiot. Shoot her. Shoot her.*

I can't. Not twice. I holster the Omnivore and turn to leave.

I'm halfway out the door when I stop. I'm a bastard to leave her here alive. It's worse than shooting her. The Lionheart will peel Lyria apart. They'll think she's a traitor.

What are you doing, Eph?

What are you doing?

I watch myself from a distance as I rush back toward her. She's light as child. I carry her out of the ship and join my friends at the bottom of the ramp, where our junker hovercar waits. Dano sits on the hood with a pistol in hand.

"What the hell is that?" he says. I ignore him. He blocks my way. "This isn't part of the plan."

"Shut up and get in the car."

"The hell's your damage, you old flit? Lose your stones?" Dano reaches for his pistol. "I'll do it for you. Wait in the car like a good little—"

I level the Omnivore at him. "I will shoot you in the fucking head. Get in the car." I step forward. "Now, ruster."

"What . . ." Dano steps back in terror, but not of me. I turn to see a hulking mass emerge from the hole in the ship. All shoulders and thighs, the Telemanus with the red beard slumps there, held up by his hands on the door, his legs butter from the anacene. His eyes filled with hate. I drop Lyria and raise my pistol. The anacene slows the man; he fumbles for his razor before giving up and lunging forward like a drunk bear. He hits me in the sternum so hard my vision flickers black. My gun flies from my hand and I'm lifted off my feet. I slam down into the floor, skidding into a wrecked flier.

From the concrete, I watch as Dano pulls up his gun and shoots the monster twice in the chest. The bullet goes through his tuxedo and slaps into the ship. It doesn't stop him. Stumbling, the Gold reaches Dano. He grabs the top lip of Dano's chest armor, holding him still as the Red claws desperately to escape. Then the Gold swings a lazy punch. It hooks in from the right, casual, almost like an afterthought. The reinforced knuckles cave in the side of Dano's skull. His head lolls, ear touching the opposite shoulder. A white root of spinal cord juts upright into the air.

Drenched in Dano's blood, the giant hurls Dano's corpse to the side and turns his horrible bulk to me. He takes an awkward step and is blasted sideways as Volga fires through the windshield of the aircar. The plasma stream hits the Gold in his side, melting through his arm and hurling him off his feet into the ship's hull.

Volga rushes to me as I try to stand. There's a dent the size of a grapefruit in the center of my chest armor. Several broken ribs scream as Volga hauls me to my feet and drags me into the car.

"Torch the body. Get the girl . . ." I say through gritted teeth.

Volga stands over Dano's body and holds down the trigger on her rifle. Concentrated energy melts through Dano's corpse, leaving a steaming heap of crackling tissue and oozing bones. She rushes back to Lyria. The Red girl issues horrible moans from her paralyzed throat toward the big Gold man on the ground. Volga throws her in the trunk. She grabs my gun from the ground as I stare out the windshield as the Gold, impossibly, pushes himself up to his knees. The flesh of his right side melts off the bones, anacene pumps in his blood, but he's still trying to stand. *"Paxxx . . ."* he roars. The room vibrates as ships try to pound their way in through the roof.

"Drive!" I shout at Volga. "Drive!"

She jumps into the driver's seat and slams on the pedal. As we shoot away into the darkness of our escape route, we hear the door finally give and crash down into the garage. Volga drives at breakneck speeds through the half-constructed hospital, faster than Dano did in our practice runs. We weave between support beams and equipment as I stare out the back of the car, watching in terror for pursuing airborne knights.

I hold my chest and wheeze.

Like an egg. Dano's head caved in like an egg.

After a kilometer of switchbacks and vertical elevator shafts leading to connecting buildings, we reach the staging ground in the abandoned canning warehouse and pull up in front of a makeshift clean room—metal frame pipes with plastic sheets enclosing it. I half-expected a dozen Syndicate thorns to be waiting for us with heavy weapons and Gorgo at their head. But they want to stay as far away from this shitshow as possible. Our headlights illuminate Cyra standing nervously with the two needle-thin contractors I met two nights ago. They wear operating smocks, one a Violet, the other a Yellow.

"Where is Dano?" Cyra asks as she comes to greet us from her mobile station. A dozen holograms from cameras she placed fill the air around it. On the holos the hospital is swarming with soldiers come for the boy. The cameras inside the garage have gone black.

"Dead," I say.

"How?"

"Gold."

"Shit. Shit. Shit," Cyra says under her breath as Volga drags the children out of the back of the vehicle straight into the clean room, where she loads each onto a table. Inside, the Syndicate technicians move with haste. They slice open the children's clothing till they are naked. No. Not children. They're killers in training. I know what they'll become. Golds that pop heads like eggs.

Without even thinking, I pull out my dispenser and pop several zoladone in my mouth and crush them between my teeth. They fizz and I feel the cool fire spread against my tongue and the inside of my cheek, radiating into my blood vessels and carrying the warmth down into my body, sending chemicals to my brain to kill the fear and the pain in my ribs. I exhale a calm breath and look back at the car where Lyria lies inert.

I turn my attention to the technicians. We're on schedule, but the schedule doesn't feel fast enough anymore. I shouldn't have wasted time in the ship getting Lyria. Dano's neck breaks again. I grimace and glance at the holograms. A flight of armored soldiers is landing around the hospital just four buildings from where we stand.

"Hurry up!" Cyra says to the Syndicate men.

"Don't distract them," I say. "Recheck the detonators. Then get out of here."

I don't have to tell her twice. Cyra's hoverbike whines as it departs through the escape tunnel. Only when I'm sure she's gone do I go back to the junker. I haul Lyria out and move her into the backseat of our clean car, a ten-seat taxi that sits next to the other rides. I take out our bags and dump our changes of clothes onto the floor, then lean back in to speak with Lyria. Her big red eyes stare up at me.

"You've been drugged with anacene-17. It will last another hour." I consider the Telemanus. He was four times her body weight. "Maybe less. We're going to meet some very bad people. When the drug wears off, do not speak, do not move. If you do, they will kill you. Afterwards, if you behave, I will take you wherever you want to go and give you enough money to start a new life." On the zoladone my voice sounds like a robot's. It's a lie I'm telling her; she'll be hunted forever, but I'll still give her a running start. She deserves that at least.

"Do you understand?" She can't blink or move. Hate is all she can manage. "Good."

I stack a bag on her face and cover the rest of her body. Even beneath the zoladone, I know I will hate myself later. I know the look in her eyes is one I'll never forget. Add it to the pile. I strip my gear and toss it into a metal barrel and dress in one of my black Kortaban suits.

"Volga, strip and burn," I say when she emerges from the clean room. She dumps corrosive acid into the barrel after she's stripped her gear.

"Found it," the Yellow with a metal sniffer nose says inside the clean room. "Right shoulder blade." The Violet, this one with multi-hued chimeras tattooed onto either side of his neck, finds the mark, and soon two wicked-looking drills whir to life. Metal burrows into skin. The children whimper through numb mouths as the Syndicate contractors dig out the imbed tracking devices with forceps. Tears tumble out of the children's paralyzed ducts. The men toss the bloody little chips into a container.

"They're babynaked and ready to roll," the Violet says.

"Double-check for radiation stains," I say, gingerly feeling my ribs. "Don't be sloppy." After they've finished, the two operators shove the children into plastic smocks and then drag them out of the clean room. The knights on the hologram jump into the garage through the hole punched by the ships. The operators leave the children with us and depart in their own vehicle, taking it through a subterranean tunnel that links with abandoned tramways. Volga takes both children and loads them into the back of the taxi, laying them parallel on the seats as gentle as a mum tucking her kids in for a nap. She lingers there looking down at them.

"Volga."

She jerks her head up to glare at me and slams the taxi door hard enough to rattle the glass. "Fuck you too," I say calmly. I leave her to go activate the timer on the explosive charges outside the clean room. Thirty seconds starts ticking down. I activate the charges in the junker car, toss another next to the barrel for good measure, and hop in the driver's seat of the taxi as Volga tosses one of her charges into the clean room too. I follow the path of the Syndicate operators down into the tunnels.

"If you gotta leave the field, do it in style," I mutter without heart. Soon as the old drill instructor's words are out of my mouth, the concussion of the charges going off shakes the tunnel. A second set of charges goes off a minute later at the tunnel's entrance, collapsing it behind us. We drive in silence, Volga pinched in the seat next to mine.

The high of the heist died with Dano. Neither Volga nor I expected to survive this. And now that we have, the weight of living comes crashing down on the big girl. She rolls down her window and closes her eyes, sticking her hand out into the wind like it's a dolphin riding the waves. She sits six inches from me, but we might as well be worlds apart. Cold, fetid air from the tunnels rolls through the car. We pass ramps going down deeper into the undergrid of the city. The tension works its way out of my jaw, but the sight of Dano's blood on the fists of the Gold oozes through my skull. Volga links her datapad with the taxi and turns on Ridoverchi.

As his piano plays a gentle melody and we carve our way through the darkness, tears stream from her eyes, but not from mine.

PART III

DUST

Pulvis et umbra sumus.

"We are but dust and shadow."

—House Raa

40

LYSANDER

The Bleeding Place

CASSIUS IS LOST IN THOUGHT, staring up at a dragon carved into the stone of the antechamber. Its snout is long. Its greedy maw open and lined with uneven teeth. The bold knight that faced down the Raa family has departed, leaving behind the tormented, reflective soul I know. The wounds where the gruesli pierced his face are swollen and red, but he's shaved his beard and looks younger than he has in years. Only his eyes are old.

"What are you thinking?" I ask. He does not seem to hear me. The distant voices from a hundred throats whisper from behind two black doors down a set of stone stairs just beneath the dragon's gaze. Our Gray guards give us space, allowing us to speak. "Cassius?"

"It was a flower," he says quietly.

"A flower?"

I realize he is far from here. "A white edelweiss. That was the last thing Father gave me before he died." He pauses, eyes still fixed on the dragon. He rarely speaks of his family. "It was a proud day," he says slowly. He spares a look at the guards. "You were too young then. Mother kept you at Eagle Rest. But the rest of us were in Agea on the Citadel steps, where Augustus used to give the Perennial Address.

The Sovereign summoned us there for a council of war. Augustus's ships were two days from Deimos. The sun was high in the sky; you could feel the energy of a storm in the air. Wind had already come. Rain was following. I remember smelling the flowering judas trees from the steps. And . . . for once, our silver eagle flew from the flagpoles of the Citadel, where all my life I'd only ever seen lions. It was to be the end of a corrupt Mars and the beginning of our era.

"We had the numbers. We had the right. And once we defeated Augustus, we would have Mars—something Father never coveted, so I knew he would treat her well. But I was ashamed. After I lost the duel to Darrow, my father told me he was disappointed. Not that I had lost. He was ashamed at my selfishness." He grimaces. "My petty pride. The carvers mended me and I put myself to one purpose: redemption in his eyes. I begged the Sovereign to let me lead the legions sent to trap Augustus at the Dockyards of Ganymede after Pliny gave us the intel. She sent Barca along to ensure I did not fail. I didn't. I returned to Agea dragging Augustus behind us in chains. I found redemption in her eyes. But I didn't have Father's till we stood on those steps and he saw how I'd changed.

"He was to meet the Augustans in orbit with our cousins and sisters. I was given the rest of our family forces to defend Agea. You've never known pride like it, Castor. The shining faces. The laughter. The hair and pennants kicking in the wind as two full generations of Bellona strolled out from the summit in armor under the sun.

"He turned to me at the foot of the stairs and told me he loved me. He'd done it a thousand times before. But it was different. 'The boy has fled,' he said. 'In his place, I see a man.' It was the first time I felt I deserved his love, to be his son. I realized how lucky I was, how blessed I was to have a father like him. In a world of terrible men, he was patient, kind. Noble in the way the stories told us to be as boys."

I glance to see if the guards are listening. Their faces from the bridge of the nose down are covered with duroplastic breathing units. The flinty eyes that peer out from beneath the gray hoods give nothing away.

"He took an edelweiss from a pouch in his armor and pressed it into my hands and told me to remember home. To remember the

Olympus Mons. To remember why we fight. Not for family or for pride, but for life.

"The flower had grown near his favorite bench on a ridgeline there, just beyond the outbuildings of the Rest. He'd climb to that ridgeline every day before the sun set, to find peace, from us children, from work." He smiles. "From Mother. Sometimes, if I was very lucky and quiet, he would let me walk with him, and we'd talk or just sit and watch the eagles visit their nests in the crags. It was the only time I remember being truly happy. Not craving something more.

"Julian was mother's favorite, but Father didn't play that game." He smiles. "I know he was not happy with the venal creature I became in the years before the Institute, or the bitter one thereafter, but there on the steps . . . when he pressed the flower into my hands, I knew I'd finally become the man he always hoped I would be."

There are tears in his eyes.

"What happened to the flower?" I ask gently, not wanting to break the spell.

"I lost it in the mud." He looks back to me in shame. "I didn't think it would be the last time I would ever see him." He's quiet, wrestling with something larger than the fear of the coming duel. "All of them are dead. All those shining faces, dimmed. Their laughter . . . just silence. I want to see them again. . . ." He almost says my name before catching himself. He looks to the door. "Hear them. Feel Father's hands on my head. But I won't. Not even when I die. The Void is all that will greet me."

"You won't die today, Cassius. You can beat him," I say, knowing that even if he wins, our lives are likely forfeit. "You are the Morning Knight. You are still that good man as . . . our father saw. And you are not meant to be the last Bellona."

"My brother . . ." He smiles and rests a hand on my shoulder. "Sometimes I forget how young you are. I'm not afraid that I won't beat him." He looks up at the dragon, past her teeth and into the hungry darkness of her throat. "I'm afraid because this world is all that is. Karnus was right." He smiles at a private joke. "But who knows, perhaps the darkness will be kinder than the light." He looks down at the black doors and listens to the voices beyond them. "No matter what fate waits beyond those doors, do not acquiesce. If they have their evidence, they have their war. It is our duty, even if it is our last, to prevent that war. To protect the people."

"It's not our Republic to protect," I say.

"That's Octavia speaking, not you. Of course it is ours to protect."

"Why? It's a broken place that betrayed us. The people you want to save are being ground into the dirt. Dido is right: the Reaper has failed." I pause. "Choices were made," I say slowly, choosing my words with care so he does not feel assaulted. "Though I may not agree, I understand why you made them. The Sovereign let the Jackal massacre . . . our family. She was a tyrant. I know that. The Society was corrupt. But look what's replaced it. The people on that ship— I see them every night and I think what I could have done better. But they didn't die because I chose to help a Gold first. They died because of Darrow." I hesitate. "You opened Pandora's box. Now you've spent these years trying to justify the choices you made." I lower my voice. "Guarding the orphan you created. Patrolling the trade lanes you endangered. Maybe this is your chance, *our* chance, to put things back together. Not by hunting pirates out in the middle of nowhere, but by restoring order."

"You want to give them their evidence. Their war."

"I do."

He steps very close to me so only I can hear. "You open that safe, you're dead too. You won't have a chance to fix anything soon as they find out who you really are."

"That's a chance I'm willing to take."

"Stop thinking with your cock. Seraphina doesn't give half a shit about you. She's bait that Dido is dangling like a piece of meat."

I snort. "It's not about her, Cassius."

"No, it's about revenge, isn't it? Your revenge."

"You took yours," I say quietly. I watched him stand over my grandmother as she bled to death. I watched him kill Aja, the woman who was like a mother to me. "You don't sleep. You drink. You preach and hunt pirates. We've never been in one place longer than a month. You think that is because you're protecting me? You think it's because you have a sacred duty to save merchants who chose to risk the Belt to line their own pockets? Stop lying to yourself for one gorydamn moment and admit that you made a mistake! You let the wolves through the door. Being a 'good man' won't fix what you've done. Neither will suspending yourself in a state of constant motion. There is no atonement except killing the wolves, shutting the door, and reestablishing order. That is how we make things better than they are now. It's how we can fix the worlds."

Even though I know the intransigence of my friend, I hold out some boyish hope that my words will arouse some sense inside him. Instead, inexorably, his eyes harden, our world darkens, and I know our fellowship has ended.

"I had you for ten years. She's had you for a breath. Is her spell is so complete?"

I feel pity as I see him realize he has failed. Not to protect me, but to convince me that he was right. That the pain he caused me was just. If he could convince me, me of all people, then perhaps he thought he would convince himself and know beyond all doubt that what he did was good. I've robbed him of that hope and any chance for his heart to be at peace.

Ten years of brotherhood evaporate in a breath.

We stare at one another and see strangers.

He snaps his fingers at the guards. "We're done here." They come forward and I step aside so they can lead him away down the stairs to his death.

At the bottom of the steps, he stops. "This duel isn't for me. It's for you. If you love me at all, you will let me die."

Beyond the black doors, down a narrow chasm of gray rock, lies the Bleeding Place. It is a circular amphitheater carved into the stone of the mountain. Amongst sculpted lotus flowers, stone dragons, slick and pearly with condensation, hang down from the dark ceiling as if to drink the blood centuries of Raa have spilled here to satisfy quarrels. Servants finish scraping yellow and green moss from a section of tiered benches carved into the rock. The benches encircle a white marble floor. At the center of the floor, the Sigil of Gold has been emblazoned onto the pale stone. Hundreds of Golds stand to watch from the stone as the brilliant son of Mars goes to meet their pale champion. Many are Ionian, but I see a Codovan crest, a Norvo, a Felix, and scores more. A dozen moons are represented, and not just Jupiter's. I'm guided to a bench in the third row where the Raa family sit more than thirty strong, despite the gaps in their ranks from those imprisoned along with Romulus in the Dust Cells.

The Rim obeys the old customs.

I look anywhere but at Cassius as a Chance, a young girl of the White caste carrying a white bag, leads a Justice, an old blind woman with milky eyes and translucent hair, onto the fighting floor. One day the little girl will grow old, and, if she reaches a state of transcendence, she will summon the courage to chemically blind herself and become a Justice herself. It is the ultimate honor of this hierophant race. Raised in monastic sanctuaries, they endeavor to divorce themselves from their humanity and embody the spirit of justice. Though many Whites in my grandmother's Society aspired to more worldly and profitable heights.

The duelists bend to their knees as the frail hierophant whispers blessings to them and touches her sacerdotal iron rod and laurel branch on each of their shoulders. Cassius stares at the floor, maybe still in that day on Mars with his father. When the Justice has finished her benediction, she is led to her bone chair at the edge of the marble by White adjuncts.

Chance pulls the string from the bag and litters white sand onto the floor until a large, unbroken circle is formed around the two men. I remember seeing the blood fill the white sand when I would go to the Bleeding Place as a boy to watch young Peerless fillet one another over perceived slights. Seems just yesterday I saw Cassius, bold and young, cutting his way up through the duelists of Luna. I always thought the practice stupid. A vain exercise of pride.

I'm numb to it now, replaying my conversation with Cassius over in my head, torn between honoring him and honoring my own conscience.

Someone slides into the empty place on the stone next to me. I turn to see Seraphina. Her eyes surprise me with their sympathy. Is

Cassius right? Would that sympathy vanish if the safe opened and she knew who I was? Would she let me die? Of course. Our ancestors have loathed one another for centuries.

"I'm sorry you must watch this," she says.

"If you were, you would have stopped it," I reply. "It wasn't just me who saved your life. But of course, I assume you think gratitude a coward's conceit."

"I said I was sorry you must watch. Not that he must die."

"He didn't kill your sister or your grandfather, no matter how absurdly you wish to twist it. He arrived after the massacre. And he was following orders from his Sovereign."

"He partook. Blood is on his hands."

"And so his will be on yours." I tire of looking at her. The slight imperfections, the heavy eyes, the sullen mouth, which I found so alluring, are now ugly and small.

She stares on at me. "The Reaper took your family when you were a boy, Bellona. Can you forget? Can you forgive?"

I remain silent because I don't know the answer.

Dido watches Cassius on the floor from amongst her family. Farther down, ancient Gaia sits smoking her pipe, still playing the fool. And past her, separate from the family, Diomedes sits with a clutch of Olympic Knights. They wear all black. Peerless steal glances at him, each with their own judgment of his honor for not being the one to challenge Cassius. He's the only Raa here who retains any of my respect. The knights alone have not taken a side in the coup, as ordered by Helios au Lux, ArchKnight of their order.

The Olympics sit in the gulf between a divided room. I discovered from eavesdropping that half of the powerful Golds in here were called to Sungrave from their own mountain cities or moons before the coup began, under the false auspices of an emergency summons sent out by Dido under Romulus's warrant. They have been disarmed and held prisoner by Dido's men since they arrived. No armed Obsidians or Grays: lowColors are not allowed in this place.

Duels are sacrosanct. Propriety and manners imperative in the audience.

We'll see how long that lasts.

Dido stands and raises her hand for silence. Her allies quiet respectfully, but as insult, her husband's allies speak on with one another and turn their backs to express their antipathy. It infuriates Dido. "You know the face . . ." Her words are drowned out. "You know the face of . . ." Romulus's men speak even louder. At her side, Seraphina watches with faint amusement. Diomedes does not help his mother. Nor does the ArchKnight Helios. Bellerephon looks to Dido for instruction. She flicks her hand for him to begin and sits down with her jaw set in anger.

The knight slams his razor on the ground. Once, twice, till the room is silent.

"Cassius au Bellona, I see you." Bellerephon stalks around the ring, his razor trailing behind. "You wretched buzzard. You spineless cur. You conspired to kill my grandfather and liege. You sought to kill my cousin in the flower of her life. You betrayed the Compact of Society and aided the Slave King of Mars. You came here in disguise, intent on mischief." He smiles. "For these insults you shall whimper and bleed."

Even Romulus's men are silent and stare down at Cassius. All know how he betrayed the Sovereign, even if they did not claim her as their own. Coincidence bringing Cassius into the Rim beggars belief. So they require little to convince them that Darrow sent him here for some nefarious purpose. Cassius knows this. And so does Dido. Absent her evidence, she uses this to quell the dissent over her coup.

"I came of my own accord," Cassius says to deaf ears. "I have no affiliation with the Republic."

Bellerephon laughs. "Liar."

"Bring evidence if you think me a liar and try me. No? Then you have no evidence, and you resort to bloodfeuds for justice. An absurdity in itself. But what can one expect from Rim rustics? No one ever taught you manners." He chuckles. "As for the bloodfeud: it I do not dispute." The Peerless meet the concession with hungry silence. "The blood of children and many more is on my hands. I expect no mercy. I ask only that if I fall, honor my bones and send them to the sun."

Bellerephon spits boorishly on the ground. "You will have no honor. Your corpse I will feed to my hounds so they might shit Bellona. But your eyes I will put in a jar so they might watch as I feed your brother to the dust."

Seraphina makes a disgusted sound. Amongst the Olympic Knights and much of the room, the proclamation is met with sharp disapproval. Helios makes a motion to Diomedes, who booms out an affirmation. "You will be so honored in your way, Bellona." This maddens his cousin and Bellerephon almost flies into the crowd to strike at Diomedes to finish their earlier affair.

I feel Dido's eyes on me, and I know Cassius was right. Again.

Of course this is all for me. They think I am the weak link. That, to spare Cassius's life, I will give them what Cassius will not. Fools. They see my slender hands and naked face and believe me weak. Dangerous game, judging a blade by its scabbard. I stay seated, silent, watching as Bellerephon shouts at Chance and gestures to the bit of elm she holds in her hand. "Break the damn stick, girl, before I do it for you."

Startled, Chance bends the elm, and as it snaps, the duel begins.

The men do not lash into one another, but pace in a circle, measuring. Seldom have the forms of the Core and the Rim met in duels, at least after Revus forbade any Ionians from dueling on Luna. Most of the Rim houses followed his lead.

As is old custom, neither duelist wears armor, though Cassius is allowed an aegis: a small shield generator embedded in a metal vambrace on the back of his left forearm. In his right hand, he carries a coiled razor. They could have given him their unfamiliar, longer hasta, but instead gave him a razor of the Interior.

Bellerephon's hasta slithers on the ground behind him like an oiled snake, nearly three meters long in whip and two meters in lance. In a scabbard on his left hip he carries the short kitari thrusting sword.

Hardening his razor into its lance form, Bellerephon raises the wicked black blade. Hands above his head, the weapon pointed toward Cassius so that Bellerephon looks like some strange, pale scorpion with its long stinger wagging in the air.

It is the Shadowfall stance of the Rim's razormasters.

"He's a shade?" I ask Seraphina. She does not answer. Her eyes devour the scene with excitement.

Cassius observes the alien stance warily. He holds his blade rigid and at his side with one hand in the summer hold of the Willow Way. His aegis he holds tight to his chest, ready to activate the shield. I blink. And by the time my lid pulls back from my pupil, Bellerephon's blade has spun in his hands, changed to whip form, and now slashes at Cassius's face.

Cassius bends back. Too slow. The whip slices a chunk of scalp off the front of his forehead. Blood sheets down his face. Bellerephon uses his momentum to spin with his whip forward, lashing it into another strike toward Cassius's leg. His attack relies on the length of the hasta and his height to send the black blade falling down in a frenzy of incredibly swift blows. It reminds me more of Darrow than Aja or Cassius.

Blinking the blood out of his eyes, Cassius falls back under the onslaught, bending and circling and deflecting as the ground sparks from the metal whip. His own whip is useless against the longer reach of Bellerephon's, so he uses it in rigid form for defense and relies on his aegis to turn away most blows. Time and again he tries to close the distance, but while Cassius is stronger, Bellerephon is the quicker of the two, more accustomed to the gravity here. He shuffles his feet instead of lifting them. Each time Cassius attempts to close, Bellerephon slides back, calls his razor to rigid form, and nearly spears him through the stomach.

The two men part, their world tiny and furious. Their bodies tell them to flee the metal and break out of the horrible confines of the circle, but their minds tether them together and again they lash out. It has been years since Cassius has faced a man like this. I'm not sure he has ever faced Shadowfall in an actual duel.

Each is a master of their craft, using their litany of tricks hard learned over the years. Each probing, testing, then locking into a furious spate of exchanges, arms a blinding flurry, the whips nothing but blurred movement. Blood sprays across the white marble and into the stands, where it spatters the face of a young child three rows back. I can't even tell which man is wounded until Cassius stumbles away, a flap of skin and muscle folding over a long laceration all the way to the bone of his left shoulder. Blood pours out. Bellerephon seizes the moment and presses his attack.

"You can stop this," Dido says past Seraphina. "Give me the code and he lives."

"He doesn't need my help."

Despite my words, I watch in fear as Cassius falls back before Bellerephon and the momentum tips in the Rim knight's favor. I thought Cassius invincible. Part of a story that could never exist without him in it. They can't see the grandness of him. They can't see the warmth, the pain, the regret, the love. All they see is a vessel for their hate. They stare down at him pitilessly, thinking his death their right, even those adversaries who despise Dido's coup.

In the circle, Cassius can barely see for the blood in his eyes. He has no time to wipe them clean. He's losing too much from his shoulder and now is pressed against the edge of the circle. His heels scrape the sand. Bellerephon lashes at him, maintaining his distance, but Cassius continues to turn away the whip with his aegis. The metal cracks into the small energy shield and bounces back, sending blue sparks hissing through the air as Cassius activates it milliseconds before each blow lands to prevent the shield from overheating. Smoke already rises from the battery pack.

Bellerephon batters Cassius down, blow after blow, till Cassius is on a knee, the whip raining down on his smoking shield. Bellere-phon's whip arcs in a high overhead strike. Cassius raises his arm yet again to deflect. But then his aegis winks out. The whip slashes down onto Cassius's raised left arm and coils tight around it. Bellerephon could rip off Cassius's arm from the elbow down, but he's caught in the middle of his acrobatics, expecting to meet the aegis again and for the whip to bounce back. He loses half a second.

Now, Cassius attacks. He uses the Snapping Branch gambit.

Springing forward with his thick legs just as he jerks on the whip with his arm, he pulls Bellerephon off balance toward him. With his left hand, Bellerephon desperately brings his kitari up to block Cassius. But Cassius bats the small blade to the side with his razor, and then cuts diagonally at Bellerephon's right arm, which holds the hasta. His diamond-hard blade cleaves through the bone of the man's arm like it's pudding. An open artery sprays a single spurt of blood two meters long. Cassius spins with his momentum, and cuts in the other direction. The metal severs Bellerephon's remaining arm at the forearm.

Both limbs spin to the floor. Bellerephon totters, looking at the weeping red stumps and the pale bone poking out from the meat, mouth opening and closing like a stunned dog's.

I almost surge to my feet in a joyful shout as Cassius sets his hand on Bellerephon's shoulder and guides him gently to his knees. He looks up at Dido. *Prime show, my friend. Damn prime show.*

"Do not waste a man like this," Cassius says. "He bled for you. He doesn't have to die. Release me and mine. Agree to our terms, and his life will be spared."

Dido glowers down at him. Not for a moment does she entertain the idea of sparing her nephew. A cold heart beats in that chest. "Bellerephon?" she asks. "Your fate is yours."

"*Pulvis et umbra sumus.*" He shivers. "Akari, bear witness."

Honor calls him to the dark. What a waste of a man.

But there is something beautiful in it all the same.

His body shakes and I marvel at the life's worth of discipline that goes to keeping himself erect on his knees. The pale Raa knight looks to his family, his slender Norvo wife, and up to the dragons of his ancestors on the ceiling.

Cassius hacks his head off at the spine.

Beside me, anger roils from Seraphina as her cousin dies.

"This is your fault, my son," Dido says to Diomedes. Amidst his knights, watching his cousin die in his stead, he looks stunned and stricken with guilt almost as immense as my relief. Bleeding from his forehead and shoulder, drenched in sweat, Cassius manages to smile at me, knowing that I could have given in to Dido but did not. He raises chin and lifts his voice for all to hear. "I am Cassius au Bellona, son of Tiberius, son of Julia, Morning Knight, and my honor remains."

It is over.

He has won. The matter is settled, though I don't know what shape the next moments will take. And then I look over at Seraphina, readying to console her on the loss of her cousin, only to see implacable Dido's face unchanged, her hand in the air, her fingers snapping together.

"Fabera," she calls.

My hope sinks and Cassius's face falls as a young hawkish woman with a bald pate hefts her razor and jumps from the second row over the heads of those sitting on the benches beneath. She lands on the edge of the white marble and paces toward Cassius, her long razor rigid. She spits on the floor and enters the circle, where she crows her challenge to Cassius, her name and her right as cousin to open his veins.

"It's over!" I say in protest to Dido. "The feud was settled with Bellerephon!"

"His feud is with House Raa," she replies.

There is a part of me that wants to rail against her and decry her hypocrisy, but the look she gives me is so reptilian that it activates the colder part of my own blood. The shock disappears and I work to understand. "Do you support this?" I ask Seraphina.

Though surprised at her mother's action, Seraphina says nothing. "Don't look to her," Dido snarls. "I preside here. That *creature* murdered my daughter. He killed Revus!" The room cries for blood. Then, very softly, Dido leans toward me. "But I can forget. I can forgive. And you can end this. Open the safe."

Dangerous woman.

I look down at Cassius and let my silence answer. Dido sighs. "A pity. Fabera, honor House Raa."

She is not a shade, but she is fast and knows this gravity. She lunges at him with her razor, roving and probing like she's hunting boar. Knowing he's losing too much blood, she tries to draw out the duel, but Cassius continues to charge and close. She's more agile than Bellerephon, but not so powerful. Cassius manages to pin her against the rim of the circle, where they exchange a dangerous series of slashing parries. She scores two cuts on his right leg, but has no time to savor the moment. I see her die two seconds before it happens. Cassius flows into the Autumn Wind movement as easily as if we were sparring together with blunted weapons on the *Archi*. He strikes three times at head level, locks blades, pushes against her so she counters his force, then he pivots right and slides his blade overtop hers in a leverage position so the tip enters her forehead and pushes through her brain before coming out her throat and through her jaw. She dies before she hits the ground. He slides his blade from her skull, flicks off the gray gristle coating it, and limps to turn and face Dido.

"I am Cassius au Bellona, son of Tiberius, son of Julia, Morning Knight, and *my* honor remains."

Dido snaps her fingers. "Bellagra."

Another knight jumps down.

"Seraphina, you're going to lose another cousin," I say, knowing that this execution wears on her.

Diomedes does not retain his composure. "Mother, enough."

"Bellagra, honor House Raa."

The knight surges toward Cassius. This one was not the same quality as the first two and dies quicker than Fabera. Cassius parries a weak blow and splits the man down the middle. His halves twitch on the floor and leak his life's blood into the Gold Sigil. But something strange has happened. Despite the condemnation of the Olympic Knights, the room roils with volunteers. Each death decays their manners and resolve and reaches into the crowd with forked rootlike fingers to enrage and poison another soul—a lover there, a cousin, a friend, a drinking companion, a brother in arms. From Dido's allies to Romulus's, the anger boils. It dawns on me then the cruel stratagem the woman has devised. I don't doubt that her hatred of Cassius is real. But they do not waste in the Rim. Each death is a down payment for her war. Absent her holodrop evidence, she uses my friend to boil the blood, to distract, to bind her allies and foes together in anger. And the more Raa that fall, the more her position solidifies, the more the blood of the Rim is raised against the Interior and not against her coup.

This is the depth of her conviction, a willing sacrifice of her own kin to reveal whatever truth hides within our safe.

I witness Dido at long last: the immensity of her resolve, the cruel-ness of her intellect, and I am terrified to think that I ever was so arrogant as to presume her Romulus's inferior simply because I'd heard his legend more. She reminds me of the woman who taught me all I know—more passionate, less subtle. But a shade of my grandmother dwells in this woman. At her side, Seraphina sits with a weary expression that seems to say she understands all but will suffer it because she must.

But I cannot watch my brother suffer much longer.

There will be no end to it.

No mercy. Just death, and for what?

Cassius limps to his feet, again standing over the body of his foe. The floor is littered with them. "I am Cassius au Bellona." He pants for breath, barely able to go on. "Son of Tiberius . . . son of Julia." He squares his shoulders and summons his pride to lift his voice. "Morning Knight, and my honor remains."

"Mother! Stop this madness!" Diomedes cries out. "He has won. How many of our blood will you throw away?"

"As many as honor demands," she says. "Save your kin, Diomedes."

He does not rise.

"A pity," Dido replies. I feel the words coming before they leave her lips, because I saw Seraphina's legs bouncing, her fingers tightening the laces on her boots, and I saw Dido notice the glances shared between us at dinner. Now the woman turns to me, only one card left to play and she plays it well. "Seraphina, honor House Raa."

41

LYSANDER

Heart

Seraphina bolts upward like a kuon released from its leash. She leaps, clearing the heads of those seated beneath us, and pulls free her razor before she lands on the killing floor. Diomedes watches in fear for his little sister. But the Golds clamoring for their chance to face Cassius now sit back down in disappointed silence. They think the matter settled. Seraphina is the executioner.

Cassius bleeds and sweats, his golden curls matted to his forehead. His knuckles sliced and savaged by metal. Blood soaks his shoes. His body is shaking from pain as steam trails off his flayed skin and open meat, but still he stands, using one of the discarded hasta for a crutch, watching neutrally as tall Seraphina lopes into the circle. This is his end. But there's nothing glorious about it.

All I feel now is dread.

The same dread from that day when I watched my grandmother die and did nothing to stop it. Not even when I saw Cassius and the Reaper's pack finish Aja. I cannot hate him for his part. It was I who did nothing to protect those I love. And I do love him. In this moment, he is true and pure and, in a way, everything I wanted to be as a child. Tears, unwelcome and unfamiliar, leak out my eyes as Cassius looks at me and shakes his head. *Let me die,* he is saying. That is all he wants. Absolution in death. But it is the wrong absolution.

The wrong death.

Seraphina steps past the corpses of her cousins and nods to Cassius. "Bellona, would that we had met as equals. You deserve better."

"We all deserve the worms, Raa," Cassius replies. He wipes blood from his paling face. "Shall we meet them together?"

In reply Seraphina draws up into the Shadowfall, a shade herself, and Cassius sinks into the Willow Way.

Hoping to surprise her, and knowing he can't last for long, Cassius lunges forward with his remaining strength. It is not enough. She ripples into motion. Not as fast as Darrow, not as strong as Aja, but smoother than either could ever hope to be, sliding sideways easy as a bird's shadow over the sea. She blocks his blade with her hasta and spins her kitari from her belt and hammers the blunted handle into his knuckles. Cassius's razor slips out of his hand and skitters over the bloody marble. He hunches without a weapon, panting. Sluggishly, he lunges for another discarded razor, but Seraphina cracks her whip and sends the weapon Cassius seeks flying into one of the walls.

She stands over Cassius and allows him one last honor. My friend crawls to his knees. Pauses there, gathering his breath, and with a groan manages to gain his feet. Dazed, he looks around the arena, lost until his eyes desperately find me. He gives me one last smile.

One of thanks because he thinks that I have let him die for his cause.

But I watched Aja die. I watched Grandmother die. And I did nothing but huddle in fear. I stayed silent and obeyed when Cassius said follow because I was afraid by crossing him I would lose him and be alone. Here at the end of the worlds, in the belly of a mountain surrounded by enemies, what is left to fear?

I will not watch any longer.

I launch myself from my seat, sailing in the low gravity over the heads of the Golds beneath me to land on the white stone of the killing floor just outside the circle. Seraphina turns around at the sound, stunned. I hold out my hands to the guards, showing I have no weapons.

"Don't . . ." Cassius slurs.

"I won't let them kill you."

"Do not step into the Circle," Seraphina growls. "You have no right to this fight. His crimes are his alone."

I turn to face Dido and the host of Raa.

"I have every right."

I let the Martian drawl molt away from my voice like a tattered cloak to reveal my Hyperion heart beneath, and for a moment, I feel proud to represent the City of Light here, so far from home. Luna may never have been perfect, may never have been as noble as I thought it was as a boy, but it gave peace for seven hundred years. I tire of apologizing for it, of being afraid of my own heritage.

My days of running and hiding behind others are finished.

I will no longer fear my name.

"My name is Lysander au Lune," I bellow into the cold room.

I did not know what weight my name still had, but the seismic tremors that now shake the room bring chills to my flesh and deep, powerful pride. Hate my grandmother all they like, the blood in my veins came from Silenius the Lightbringer—greatest of our kind. It is the myth of my ancestors these people wrap themselves in. The first Raa elected Silenius Sovereign. They bowed to him, as did all Raa thereafter until this generation. Seraphina almost drops her razor. Her jaw hangs open. Dido curses under her breath and leans back in her seat, unable to comprehend it. Diomedes stands, a look of childish awe on his grave face.

Cassius watches in silence, his heart breaking in his chest.

"I am the blood of Silenius the Lightbringer, son of Anastasia, son of Brutus, grandson of Lorn au Arcos the Stoneside, and Octavia the Sovereign of Man. I was born upon the Palatine, west of Hyperion, at the heart of Luna and the City of Light. I may know little of the Rim, but even in the heart of empire, they spoke of the honor of House Raa. Of the Moon Lords, chief among them the Ionian Golds. Where has it gone? Has it deserted you? Has it fled after the tremors of war? You may have lost it, forgotten it, but I have not forgotten mine. And *my* honor will not let me sit idly as this travesty unfolds." I feel Cassius's agony, but I cannot look at him.

"Your bloodfeud is sated by any measure. The Bellona have been wiped from the face of the worlds. Do not fall prey to the very cannibalism that allowed the Rising to flourish. This man, this *Gold,* is not your enemy. I am not your enemy. The Slave King is." I turn in a cold fury to Dido. "Bring me the safe."

42

EPHRAIM

Lucky You

WE PULL OUT OF THE RAIN onto the fiftieth floor of an abandoned building on the outskirts of a reconstruction zone. I turn off the music and look out through the windshield. Lights glare down from the level above. Exposed electrical lines and ventilation tubes snake through the building. In his chrome suit and a black high-collared duster, Gorgo waits in a grand old dilapidated green armchair beside an industrial lift, smoking burners. Purple smoke slithers in a halo around his gigantic head.

"Never thought I'd be happy to see him," I say to Volga, but I don't get out of the car.

"Will they honor the contract?" Volga asks. I check the account. Twenty-five million sits in the balance, put there when the operators confirmed we had the prize. We get the rest on delivery.

"Don't know."

"You told the others they would."

"No shit. What else would I say?"

I look back into the passenger compartment. The prizes are twitching under the plastic tarp. The anacene is wearing off. Hyperion is about to be thrown off its axis. The Syndicate is making a play. Can't even begin to guess what they want. But I wish I could see Lionheart's face when she finds out. She pardoned Gold rapists, slavers, murderers. Now comes the bill for stabbing the rest of us in the back. And she'll find, as the rest of us have, that she can be touched by this war as well.

I should feel driven by righteousness, but instead I feel dirty sitting here with my human cargo. A man has to have a code. When did mine begin to include kidnapping children?

"They can't very well break their own rules," I say, trying to convince myself.

"Are they broken if no one knows?" Volga asks.

"When did you become a philosopher?"

"I am wise. You are smart. This has always been our way." She sets a comforting hand on my shoulder.

"You stay here, wise one. I can carry them myself." I get out of the car. Volga follows. I look at her and she looks back willfully. "All right, together then."

"Yes, together."

We haul the prizes out of the car. I lean in and lift the bag off Lyria's head, positioning myself so that Gorgo can't see her hidden in the back. "Remember, rabbit. Silence is golden." I set the bag back and leave her in the car. I let Volga carry both the prizes over her shoulders to Gorgo. He stands as we approach, eclipsing me by more than a foot and a hundred kilos. His black shark eyes drift back and forth between us and the prizes.

"Right on schedule. The Duke awaits." He puts out his burner and motions for us to stop. "No weapons." I put my pistol on the chair and Volga sets her plasma rifle down. Gorgo pats my arms, torso, balls, and legs with his huge hands.

"You enjoying that?" I ask.

Wordless, he slides the stiletto out of my boot and takes four more knives out of Volga's jacket. "Really?" I ask her. She shrugs. Gorgo finds two more knives in her boots and an acid shooter strapped to her calf. He stacks these with our other weapons and seems amused by the collection. "Little crow likes toys. Would you like to be one of mine?" She ignores his predatory smile.

With the children in tow, we take a lonely lift up to the fifty-second floor, where the Duke waits for us amongst a host of Syndicate thorns. They stand in the shadows of the half-constructed highrise, light from their burners catching on jewelry, platinum smiles, and chromejob eye implants. At the far side of the floor, a sleek luxury yacht rests outside on one of the highrise landing pads.

The Duke applauds as we approach. "A debt was owed. A debt is paid!" He wears a jet-black asp skin jacket with long, calf-length tails. His lipstick is violet tonight and he sits behind a plastic table with a steaming pile of half-eaten crab claws and two bottles of wine.

"Punctual. Well dressed. And devastatingly handsome. My dear Ephraim. You are a treasure." He eyes Volga. "You brought a body-guard this time. How precocious of you."

"She's luggage detail."

The three Obsidian men behind him stare at Volga. All are ice Obsidian, probably ex-legion, and wear dusters and their bright white hair long and unbound. The biggest is a head taller than Volga and has emerald piercings in his chin. He grinds the haft of a chrome pulseAxe into the concrete floor.

"The prizes, as agreed upon," I say flatly. The night's exhausted me, Dano's death robbing me of any humor. Volga hands over the prizes to two thorns, who lay them down on the table. The Duke pulls the hoods off the children's faces and coos to himself.

"My, my, my. The Queen will be pleased. See, I told you, Gorgo. He's pure quality. Syndicate material." Gorgo shrugs. "Gorgo here did not think you were up to the task. He thought you would run. Fly to Earth, Mars, but no, I said. A man's reputation is his life's work. It is all he has. And you have lived up to yours. That gravWell . . ." He shudders. "Patent Ephraim ti Horn."

He looks down at the children, focusing on Pax.

"Hello, little prince." He bends to inspect the boy more closely. "You may call me *dominus*." He rears back and slaps the boy across the face. Volga twitches. A red welt forms on Pax's cheek. "Weep." He slaps him again. "Weep." Pax stares on at him, trying to be brave. "Weep." The Duke's voice loses the affected polish bit by bit, till it sounds like an animal inside him is trying to escape. "Weep. *Weep. Weep.*"

The sight of it disgusts me, but I stay rigidly still, afraid.

"My Duke . . ." Gorgo says. The Duke looks up at him, murder in his eyes. Gorgo stares back evenly but says nothing more. The Duke slaps Pax again and tears finally leak out of the boy's eyes. The Duke shudders with pleasure and tucks back the pink locks of hair that have fallen over his eyes. He takes a teardrop on the tip of his finger and licks it off with his eyes closed. "Tastes like justice."

His men laugh. Volga's trembling with anger. Poor girl looks like she's going to lurch forward and strangle the man. I shake my head at her, but her eyes are fixed on the Duke.

The man's voice softens to a coo as he bends to stroke Pax's face. "There, there, little prince. Do not weep. Shhh. Consider me an ambassador, welcoming you to the real world. The rest of us have been here for some time. But do not worry. You'll soon learn the rules." He turns to his thorns. "Put them in my yacht. No rough play. We mustn't damage the Queen's merchandise. She has quite a plan for them." The men haul the children up and take them away. Volga's eyes follow them till they disappear into the ship.

"Apologies," he says, the polish back. "At the root, I am a creature of *severe* passion."

"I expect the rest of my payment now," I say, eyeing the thorns behind me. They've crept closer. My voice sounds dead even to my ears.

"Yes. Yes." He makes a dismissive gesture to a thorn. My datapad vibrates as the funds transfer.

"Thank you," I say, checking the number. "It's been a pleasure doing business."

"That's it?" the Duke asks, raising his plucked eyebrows. "Am I a payday so summarily dismissed? I thought our fraternity ran deeper. I even saved you a bottle of La Dame Chanceuse. I was hoping we could drink it together."

"Now?"

"Yes, now. A toast to a success for the ages. A triumph for the little men."

"It's been a long night. I'm not thirsty."

"My darling Ephraim, where did the rogue go? Where is the bluster, the charisma? Dirty deeds deserve sweet reward." His fingers run along the edge of the bottle. "If I didn't know better, I'd think your scruples were rankled."

"You hired a professional," I say. "If you want a social companion, I suggest you call up some Pink entertainment. I hear they're splendid company." His smile disappears. "Thank you again for your time, my good Duke." I turn to leave. Volga doesn't turn with me.

"What will you do with the children?" she asks.

No. No. No. I turn back around. The Duke's eyebrows float upward. "It speaks."

"She's passionate too," I say. "Means nothing by it. Come on, Volga."

"Not at all!" The Duke beams. "It's a fair question for the curious crow after all the sweat and ill deeds. What if I told you I was going to give them to the big brutes behind me to play with as I was played with my entire life?" the Duke asks. "What would you do?" Volga doesn't answer. "What if I said I was planning to feed them to ants? What response would that elicit? Violence, perhaps?" He smiles. "Yes, I think so. Morality is a dangerous thing for a thief to possess in company such as this."

I pull Volga's arm. Would be easier to tug on a house.

I'm about to say something when a pipe clanks behind us near the stairs beside the elevators. The thorns wheel around with their weapons as a bolt of red hair disappears down a stairwell. The Duke snaps his fingers and his Obsidians are loosed. Their long legs cover the distance in two breaths and they fly down the stairs. My blood runs cold. *You stupid girl.*

Gorgo blocks our path to the elevators.

"Did you bring company?" the Duke asks me.

"No."

"Are you certain? There are motion detectors on all the entrances. Your flier was the only one allowed in. Who did you bring with you?"

"No one. My crew's gone to ground."

"Sit." I'm about to object, but Gorgo shoves me into the chair in front of the table. Two Obsidians wrestle Volga down. One shoves an industrial laser cutter in front of her face. The red beam wavers close to her eyes. She goes still. In the distance, we hear the muffled sounds of scorchers going off. I feel myself darkening.

I let a rabbit into the wolf den. Now they tear her apart.

The Duke waits, staring at me, a single vein pulsing under his right temple, until one of his Obsidians returns. I hold my breath at the sound of boots approaching. When the man finally comes to the Duke's table, I can breathe. Miraculously, he's empty-handed.

"It was a ruster," he rumbles. "She escaped."

The Duke stares at him. "A. Red. Escaped. You. Belog?"

"We had her cornered. She dove into a ventilation shaft. She's likely pulp."

"A ventilation shaft?"

"We could not fit. It led down. Harald and Hjerfjord hunt. They will bring her head back by its bone tail."

The Duke continues to stare at the brute until the Obsidian lowers his eyes in fear. He glances plaintively to the other Obsidians, but there's no pity in their arctic eyes.

"I am . . . disappointed in you, Belog."

"Yes, lord."

"Do you know what the Queen would do if she were disappointed?"

The Obsidian glances at Gorgo, who is baring his crescent of gold teeth. "Yes, lord."

"Fortunately, I know how difficult it is for a bear to catch a mouse. So many holes for them to run to. So I will forgive you, but I fear a debt is now owed. How will you pay?"

The Obsidian looks forlorn; slowly he extends his left hand. The Duke slaps it lightly. "The left. Very good. How old was the girl?"

"Young. Twenty winters."

"Distinguishing features?"

"She wore a tuxedo."

"A tuxedo." The Duke looks at me, then back at the Obsidian. "Go help your brothers, Belog." The Obsidian bows and rushes back to the stairs, disappearing into the shadows. The Duke turns to Gorgo. "Wake the baron of this neighborhood. Criminsky, isn't it?" Gorgo nods. "Put out a bounty on a Red bitch wearing . . ." He looks at me again. "A tuxedo."

Gorgo steps away. The Duke looks back to me, tapping his lacquered nails on the table. "I am also disappointed in you, Ephraim. . . ."

"She's not—"

One of the Obsidians slaps my right ear. But a slap from one of them is like getting a door slammed on your head. I pitch sideways to the ground for the second time of the night. They straighten me back in the chair. "Who was she?" the Duke asks.

"I don't know."

"Are you lying to me? I do hate liars."

"Why the bleeding hell would I bring someone else here?" I shake my head so I can see straight. "I know the rules. . . ."

"Yet you broke them. I said only bring your team. And you didn't even bring all of them. As if you were afraid of me. As if I wouldn't keep my word! As if I need to lie!"

"I never bring my team to a drop."

He looks at Volga in amusement. "Except your luggage hauler. But do not fret; since you took it upon yourself to disobey me, I took it upon myself to help you follow the rules." Gorgo returns from his call dragging a woman behind him. It is Cyra. They've brutalized her. Face one large contusion.

Volga lunges forward. An Obsidian slams Volga in the back of her head with the haft of one of their axes. She goes woozy and tries to get up. He and another thorn kick her legs out and stand on her back so she's belly-down on the floor. "Volga, stop," I tell her numbly. The Duke watches me with neutral expression.

"Is this how the Syndicate treats its contractors?" I say.

"No. I am no slaver. Respect is given until a debt is owed." The Duke smiles. "After all, what is a man without a code?"

Cyra looks up at me helplessly through the swollen mess of her face. I never liked her, not that I liked Dano that much more, but it makes me sick what these psychos have done to her.

"Let her go. She's done nothing to you."

"On the contrary, she has betrayed a friend of mine."

"Who?"

His eyes glitter. "You, darling."

"What? What are you talking about?"

"Your friends are cheap," Gorgo says. "I approached the Red man, but this one . . . she came to me of her own volition. Offering to spy on you, for money. Every smoke. Every drink. She scurried to me and chittered in my ear like a little, greedy pet wanting a snack and a pat on the head. Wants to be a thorn, this one."

Cyra can't meet my eyes, and I feel sick knowing it is true.

"You were our friend," Volga says to her.

No, she wasn't.

"I assume the Red girl you brought from the ship was your insider?" the Duke asks. "Lyria of Lagalos. The one you fooled into carrying Kobachi's drone?"

I never wanted the Syndicate to know about Lyria. Cyra did tell them everything.

"Yes."

"And then you saved her life? Your professionalism is suddenly quite indicted, Ephraim." There is no smile on his face now. "Why save her?"

"You asked me if I was a thief of order or one of chaos," I say slowly. "I get the groove. This is your world now. Your rules. She performed a service—a debt was owed. She deserves to get paid."

"That. Is a good answer," the Duke says. "But she is not a thief. And she is not your friend. She is a slave in all but name, and will run back to her masters. So, I am afraid she must die." He waits for me to object, but I know it's useless. The only thing I can protect now is my life and Volga's.

"I suggest we kill him too," Gorgo says.

"Oh my. Are you now the Duke of Hands, Gorgo?" the Duke asks. "No? Then shut your mouth." Gorgo smiles coldly at him, but says nothing. "You have complicated things, Ephraim. But the Syndicate honors its contracts. You owe nothing. You are free to leave."

"What about her?" I ask, looking to Cyra.

"She has shown a duplicitous nature. She cannot be trusted. If she spoke so quickly to us, who else might she speak to? But . . . she wronged you, not me, therefore her fate is in your hands. Acid, axe, fire, fist. Choose the one-way ticket."

"Ephraim . . . I'm sorry," she says pathetically through swollen lips. I can't hate her. I'm too tired to hate her. "Please . . ."

"Volga?" I ask. She shakes her head. "Just let her go," I say to the Duke.

"Thank you," Cyra whimpers. "Thank you. Volga, I—"

"Don't talk to her," I snap.

The Duke raises an eyebrow. "Very well. Gorgo, you heard the man. Let her go."

Gorgo grabs Cyra by the hair and drags her to the edge of the highrise. She kicks and screams when she sees what he's about to do. "Ephraim! Ephraim!"

I do nothing.

Gorgo throws her off the edge of the highrise like a sack of trash. We don't even hear the impact. I imagine her lying in a messy pile of meat fifty stories below. Like Trigg on that mountainside.

I watch the Duke, my ears filled with the scream of memory.

"Let the Obsidian girl up," the Duke says. Released by the thorns, Volga stumbles to her feet, more angry than afraid. "Only that one was loyal in the end. I appreciate loyalty. So her life is my parting gift to you. A proven, true friend. You are lucky. Such is more than most thieves can manage."

I face the Duke and swallow back the bile.

"Then I thank you for your patronage, Duke. I trust our business is concluded."

"For today."

I turn and help Volga limp away.

"Ephraim," the Duke calls. I pause, fearing another twist. "I wonder, where will you go now?"

"To sleep."

"Alone? A pity. But after that . . . ?"

"Don't know. Haven't thought that far ahead."

"You have money now, all for yourself. Money enough to retire. To do whatever you like. But I know you, and you're not the sort to gather dust. You need this life. Need it to feel alive. To feel anything at all. We always want *more*—people like you and me. The Queen can give you what you crave. I can give that to you."

I spare a look at Gorgo, then ask the Duke, "Are you offering me employment?"

The Duke smiles. "Amongst other things." He gives a card to Gorgo, who brings it to me. A datapad number is printed in white on black. "When you grow bored. I'm always looking for a helping hand."

Gorgo holds on to the card with his long nails as I try to pull it from him. The card tears in half. He flicks his end at my face. I gather up the pieces and put them into my pocket and Volga and I walk away, doing everything in our power not to run as fast as we can. In the back of my mind, I wish rabbit a swifter end than Cyra's. Rat or not, the Green was one of mine. And now a debt is damn well owed.

43

LYRIA

Street Prey

M Y SHOES POUND WET PAVEMENT. The sound of the scorchers echoes in my ears. The weapons chewed the ground
around my feet as the Obsidians rushed me in the industrial tower.
Scarier than the bloodydamn Red Hand. There were three of them in
black. Their hair white as bleached bone. They moved faster than the
dogs of Camp 121, pushing off walls and support beams like there
was no gravity. I thought I was dead, cornered on a level with only
open air behind me.

I saw an open ventilation duct. Didn't even look to see if it had a
bottom before I dove in. The sheet metal vaporized behind me from
their weapons. I fell ten levels before I managed to jam out my legs
and hands to halt my fall. The friction shredded the skin from my
palms and dislocated my shoulder. But I managed to slide down the
rest of the way, just as my brother Aengus taught me in the vents of
Lagalos.

For the first time in my life, I'm glad I'm small.

When I reached the end of the air duct, I kicked my way out,
found a construction ladder down, and then limped off into the
streets of the reconstruction zone. Still, the Obsidians follow.

I can't outrun them, so I jump into a dumpster behind a tenement complex and push rotting trash over myself. Rats the size of toddlers and cockroaches the size rats should be scurry around me, biting my back, my arms. But I lay corpse-still and listen to the Obsidians howling to each other in their alien tongue. They're searching the streets. A searing line of pain works its way down my left forearm. I must have cracked the bone in the fall. Someone's coming. I hold my breath.

The top layer of skin on my hands oozes blood. I wince as I clutch the shiny pistol I took from outside Philippe's car. I was too terrified to turn around and use it on the Obsidians. I've never even held a weapon before. Could I shoot a man? Who were they anyway? Who did Philippe deliver the children to? The Pink one was the boss, but I didn't hear his name. If only I'd caught Philippe's—his real name.

I hate the bastard.

His crow shot Kavax. They killed Kavax.

Are they going to kill Pax and the girl? *Don't let them die. Don't let it be my fault. Please.*

I shift in the garbage. Flies buzz up in my face. The smell brings me back to the dumpsite outside 121. I feel Liam pressed against my chest, his little heart beating so fast. It's too much. I fling myself out of the garbage bin, swatting the flies off me in a panic. My shoulder stabs with pain. I kneel there in the street amongst burner butts and feel the tightness in my chest fade as the rain soaks through my tuxedo jacket.

Think, Lyria. Think.

I have to run. But where do I go?

The Sovereign will think I'm in on this, and they'll kill me or put me in a cell for the rest of my life. I can't go back to the Citadel. But Liam . . .

Only shadows populate the streets. Cold rain has been falling since we left Quicksilver's. My teeth chatter together. I think of Kavax's kind face, how he said that Sophocles chose me. How I was a sign of magic. Bloodydamn lie.

I'm poison. All the time I was in the Citadel, I resented them. I loathed the Sovereign. That's why the children were taken. Because I was rotten. I was stupid enough to trust a Gray.

I tuck Philippe's pistol inside my jacket, pick a direction and start moving, sticking to the shadows. I jog as much as I can, but my shoulder hurts so bad I have to rest every three blocks or so. I reach into my jacket to clutch the pistol and duck into a doorway when several hoverbikes roar down the street. On the backs, men in shiny beetle-black helmets scan the shadows. I fall to the ground and start shaking like an addict and scratch under my nose like I've just done black dust. One of the hoverbikers pauses, ten meters away, then rips off down the street, thinking me a junkie.

I can't linger here. They'll flush me like they did in the dump at 121. I gotta go up. Carefully, I leave the shadows and push on, searching for a lift. But all the tenement houses here are stunted buildings underneath the foundation lattice that supports the highrises. Those that are connected to the highrises are fortified and secured with huge doors. I pound on several, but they won't let me in. So I follow old elevated tram tracks, looking for a station. Might be a lift near one. Up ahead, I hear a nostalgic sound through the rain—a zither. Reds. They might help me.

Underneath the tram is an abandoned, derelict station skinned in graffiti. A tent city of vagrants has sprouted up around it. Electronics glow from inside the tents and men gather around a burning barrel for warmth.

"Oy, what've we got here?" a man asks, spotting me. "You lost, little lass?" He's from Mars by the sound of him, and I know right off I've made a mistake.

"'Lo, brother. There a lift near here?" I ask. "I'd settle for stairs."

"What would a little thing like you need to go up for?" another Red asks, this one from Mars too. "You'd look better going down." I step back from him.

"Some nice silk, that," another says.

"Fancy silk. Gamma silk."

"Righto! Have we got a Gamma on our hands, lass? Teeth all clean. Hair all nice."

"What's your name, lass? Where you from?"

"None of your bloodydamn business," I say. "But if you want to point me on my way, might be some chit in it for you."

"Might be we just take that chit."

"Why you holdin' your arm?" one of them asks. "You fall from the sky? Aerial accident?" His teeth are black and crumbling from demondust. He's got the black tip on his nose, the cartilage eroding between the two nostrils. "Come here, let us take a look at it." Two of the men on the outskirts of the group have started inching toward me from the sides. I back away; my shaking hand drifts into my jacket.

"You wanna mind yourself," I say thinly. "My people will be looking for me."

"We're your people, lass." Memories of Red Hands in the moonlight seep into the moment. "Come on and get warm by the fire. We got some swill and some dust if you wanna see angels, sister. We'll show you that. All the sights of the Vale."

"You warm each other up," I snarl. "Touch me and I'll burn your bloody balls off."

"Nah, nah, mouthy one," the one with the teeth says. He's been slowly walking toward me. "That's not what a lass's mouth is for, doncha know?" I pull the pistol out of my jacket and point it at his balls. The men recoil but the one with the black teeth just laughs at the trembling barrel. "Nice scorcher, that! Classic lines. Where'd you get your hands on a piece like that? Master give it to ya?" As he waits for an answer, his eyes flick up. It saves my life.

I wheel around and see a man lunging toward me from behind. I fall back and pull the trigger. The gun is silent and without recoil. His leg explodes as the metal slug tears into it. The skin of his thigh peels back like the flesh of an overripe peach. His severed leg kicks back across the pavement, hissing steam and blood. He screams, looking at the stump, and falls. I wheel on the rest of them with the gun. They cower like children. I step toward them, heart raging, wanting to kill every last piece of shit. The man on the ground moans in pain, clutching his mangled stump, and I feel sick.

I turn and run from them till my legs are numb.

Shaking, I collapse between two crumbling tenement complexes. Dogs bark and babies scream out open windows. My stomach lurches and I sick up all over the trash. When my stomach has emptied, I fall back on my ass and shake. The man is going to die. I was going to kill the rest of them. I toss the gun away, disgusted.

There's a loud roar and the sound of a crash from the street.

I crawl to peer out of the alley and see a street stained by the green sign of a tenement complex. A hoverbike idles in the center of the street. A huge man gets off the back and pulls off his helmet. White hair flows down his back. He can't be more than twenty, though it's hard to tell with Obsidians. The man stalks toward a person he just shot through the leg with a harpoon reel from the front of his bike. Faces watch out the windows of the complex. The Obsidian picks the person up with one hand and draws a pointed hammer from a holster on his back. I look away and almost throw up again when I hear the wet sound of the skull caving in. The faces disappear from the windows and the bike roars away, dragging the red-haired body behind on the harpoon reel.

I pick the gun back up.

If I stay on the streets, they'll find me. I look up and see the rails of the old tramway. If I can climb up there, I can move without being on the streets. But someone might see me. I gotta risk it.

My fingers are bloody by the time I climb the cracked concrete support column up to the tramline. There's a depression between the rusted rails that I can scramble along without being seen from the ground. It's all that saves my life. As I work my way along the tramline, more bikes search the streets. Like the whole underbelly of Lost City has woken to try and find me. Who are these people?

Over the next hour, I pass several public gravLifts, but they're all guarded by men in black coats with chrome nightshades. Finally, exhausted and shivering, I find an abandoned stairwell beside a derelict gravLift. It's unguarded.

Feral dogs snarl at me, their eyes glowing from under the covered stairwells as I make my way upward toward the lights of Hyperion ninety levels above. As I ascend level by level to brighter, more reputable zones of the city, fliers speed through the air in the avenues. Surface cars and trams rattle on crisscrossing bridges.

I duck my head when I feel eyes on me and keep a white-knuckled hold on the pistol inside my jacket. Now that I have it, I don't ever want to be without it again.

I stop glancing up at the smog layer above. It seems no closer each time I do. This city wasn't meant to be crossed on foot. But there's no one to ask for help, and even if I did find Watchmen down here, I'd be too frightened to approach them. Not after last time. Who would believe my story? And who's to say they aren't on the payroll of the man Philippe works for? Remembering that Pink's smile chills me as much as the rain.

Slick, pretty, but rotten underneath. Just like the rest of this forsaken city.

I'd do anything to be home. Not in the Citadel. Not in the camp. But in the mine. My family around me before the world started chewing us one by one.

Ava, why did we ever leave?

I speak to her as if she had the answers. But it only raises more doubt. In the Citadel there's a pair of other mothers desperate to find their children. Children I lost.

My legs burn. Each step harder than the last. It seems a life ago when I thought this gravity easy. Back when Philippe and I walked the whole Promenade. Was all of it a lie? Even the pain I saw in him?

I make it to the next level. Then the next one after that. It's anger keeps my ass moving. Anger at Philippe for using me, at the men who thought I was their prey, at myself for trusting anyone on this bloodydamn moon.

I'm almost there. The stairwell grows cleaner. The graffiti is covered up by gray paint. There's more lights. More cars. More sounds of a healthy city—sirens and advertisements. The stray dogs are on their lonesome now and wag their tails at me as I pass. I'm just beneath the smog. I can see the neon stain of holo advertisements through the gray clouds and a checkpoint up guarding the entrance to the Promenade levels above the smog. If I keep going up, I'll have to pass through it. I could stay a level below—there's shops, lights, people milling through the streets.

I look out at the city in the rain. My breath clouds in front of me.

I could disappear.

I could find a way to run.

But if I do, then what of it? I'm like Philippe: just another canker. I'd never see Liam again. As the rain seeps through my saturated tuxedo, I keep coming back to my sister's face the moment we parted in 121—the fear in her eyes, the trust when she begged me to protect her son. It shatters all that's left of me to know I did that to someone else. Helped a man steal their children. Watched the man who brought me out of hell die on the floor. I lean against the concrete barrier to catch my breath.

The sounds of the city warble all around me. But I feel so very far away. I hear the laughter of my nieces and nephews, I remember the smile on my father's face when he'd find me wearing his boots. I ache for my mother, who deserved so much more than to wither and die from the inside. I miss my brothers who went off to war, and I see again my sister perched up on that rusty antenna looking out over the camp and dreaming of stars she would never reach. And I feel anger—a consuming, furious anger—building in my chest at the people who would destroy families, hunt their fellow humans.

The Sovereign didn't protect my family, but I'm not her.

I force my legs to climb the last stairs to the first Promenade level and walk toward the fenced checkpoint. I swallow my fear of the Grays behind the duroglass. My hands rest atop my head as best they can with my injured shoulder. A weapon-warning siren warbles as a scanner flickers blue light over my body.

"Weapon detected. Weapon detected. Weapon detected."

Two Watchmen atop the guard posts aim their rifles at me. *"Stop, citizen!"* a voice says over a speaker. *"On your knees or we will shoot!"*

44

LYRIA

Lionguards

I SIT IN A WINDOWLESS GRAY ROOM with an untouched cup of coffee on the table in front of me. The shiny black lens of a camera watches me from the wall. The checkpoint Wardens who confiscated Philippe's pistol were incredulous when they heard my story. Rightfully so. They say it ain't on the news. They haven't gotten a dispatch from central. All they got is the words that tumble out my gob in a chattering mess.

I've not seen anyone since they left.

I'm half asleep when the door slams open and a soldier fills the frame. She's a stocky Gray with exhausted, narrow eyes, wearing black combat armor etched with a pegasus in flight over the Roman numeral VII. A drenched animal pelt hangs from her left shoulder. I stare at it in fear as I remember colliding with her chest in the hallway at the Telemanus estate. She smells like oil and wet dog. Two soldiers with roaring gold lions on their chest armor come in after her, one an Obsidian, the other a Gold, but she's clearly in charge. "Lyria of Lagalos." The words are a demand, not a question.

I nod, frightened by the hard-looking group. Their faces look carved of cracked city concrete. The stocky Gray is a Howler. One of the Reaper's own. And the other men have sworn their lives to the Sovereign. To them, I'm a terrorist.

"I hear you've been spinning quite a tale."

"Who are you?" I manage.

"My name is Holiday ti Nakamura, special envoy of the Sovereign. Muzzle her." The men come around the table. I push backward instinctively. They grab me. One slams a fist into the side of my neck. My legs turn into a puddle. Black throbs in my vision. Something metal is shoved against my face. The fingers of the device crawl around my head, pulling taut even as a rubber appendage pushes into my mouth and expands till my tongue is pinned to the floor of my mouth. I hyperventilate. "Through the nose," the Gray woman says. She snaps her fingers in front of my face. "Breathe through your nose, girl, or you'll pass out. Breathe."

I listen to her and suck oxygen down through my nose. "Shell her."

One of the men pulls a plastic vest down over my head. My vision is still spotty as my head emerges out the top of it. He pushes my arms together in front of me and I groan in pain from the pressure on the dislocated shoulder, then the vest inflates, wrapping around my body, pinning my arms to my chest. Once it's inflated, armor hardens on the outside as the polymer darkens.

"For your protection," Holiday says. She leads me roughly by my muzzle out the door. A dozen heavily armed Lionguards with the red planet globe on their left shoulders, Martians all, wait in the rain in front of a warship bristling with guns and blazing with lights. Their rifles are up, their mechanized helmets scanning the buildings around. Several shadowy figures circle overhead. The local checkpoint Watchmen eye the Lionguards with awe and glance out the windows at the shadows in the sky. The Watchmen are under guard by more Lionguards and have had their weapons taken away. A Red Watchman with a Vox pyramid sewn onto his uniform nurses a split lip and sits handcuffed. A shattered datapad lies on the ground beside him. Holiday addresses the Watchmen.

"The information you heard tonight is classified. Divulging even a word of it will earn you charges of treason against the Republic. A second shuttle is on its way to collect you for debriefing." She looks at the bloodied Vox Red. "You ever wanna do anything more than sort trash in Deepgrave, I suggest you comply." She turns back to me. "When I say run, you close your eyes and run. Understand?"

I nod.

"Package ready for boarding," Holiday says into her mouthpiece. "Blackfire? Ocelot?" There's a murmur from the com clipped to her ear. She looks at me and slings her rifle from her shoulder and primes the charge. "Three. Two. One. Run."

Three strobe lights sizzle white-hot light from the top of the ship, blinding out my vision before I clench shut my eyes. They pull me along at a run. I feel rain, the concrete, then the metal deck of a ship under my shoes. My vision returns, stained green by the shuttle lights as the soldiers funnel into the back with me. The shuttle jumps upward, the back ramp still open. When we're a hundred meters from the ground, more of the Martians float up on gravBoots and land inside the craft. Only then does the ramp close.

The warship's engines roar and they shove me into a seat. The men don't set their weapons down. The Gold and the Obsidian both touch razors on their forearms. Out the cockpit windows I see the shadowy figures are still escorting us. I glimpse inky-black helmets shaped like the stuff of deepmine nightmares and thick black armor as they fly through the rain.

"Company yet?" Holiday asks the helmeted Blue pilot.

"Sky's clear, ma'am. Civi traffic diverted. We'll be in gov alt in ten seconds." My ears pop. Then it's silent except for the engines. Everyone is edgy. Are they worried about another attack from the kidnappers? How far could their reach possibly extend?

"Distance to Citadel?"

"Fifty klicks."

Something beeps in the cockpit. "Incoming bogies. Atmospheric rippers," the pilot says. "Descending from a skyhook. Barca markings."

"How many?"

"Fourteen rippers. Two gunboats. Shall I call SkyLord support?"

"That damn woman," Holiday mutters. "No. Alert the Citadel but tell SkyLord to hold. I was ordered to keep this quiet; a dogfight over the city ain't exactly whispering."

The Blue carries out her commands as the co-pilot speaks into his headset. "Attention Barca aircraft, this is the HAF *Pride Seven,* you are in violation of Republic Government space and a Sovereign's warrant. Deviate your course immediately to civilian altitudes. You have ten seconds to comply."

They're not deviating. I see them now through the cockpit. Little black dots small as flies in the distance, hovering in a line to prevent us from reaching the Citadel.

"Incoming transmission."

"Nakamura," a woman's deep voice growls over the com. *"Should have known she'd send you. Cut your engines and deliver me the Red terrorist."*

A Blue hands Holiday a remote com. "Victra, the witness is under arrest. Do not interfere with Republic jurisdiction. I've been authorized by the Sovereign to deliver her using any and all means at my disposal. You don't want this trouble."

"Darling, I am the trouble."

Two streaks of light rip across the darkness from her ships, missing the cockpit by bare meters. *"They took my daughter. My daughter."* I shiver as I realize who is on the other side of the line.

"You want the whole damn Republic knowing about this?" Holiday snarls. "They'll make the Sovereign step down. Divert your ships. The witness is being taken in for questioning so we can get your daughter back. You're wasting time."

"Questioning?" Victra laughs. *"More of Virginia's half measures. Look what that has given us. It's my turn."*

"If you fire again on this ship, you risk killing the only lead we have. She came to us. We're going to the Citadel."

"You idiots lost my child. I will get her back. With words, or with iron. Your choice. Give me the Red, or I will come and cut her out of the belly of your ship. You have ten seconds to comply. Victra out."

Holiday is worried. "Was that broadcast coming from the ships?"

"No, ma'am."

"Pilot, full speed straight down their throats." She turns to her men. "Weapons hot. Return fire only. She's not in the gunships. She's airborne." She swings out her rifle. "Expect Gold boarders." The men hop to their feet and point their guns back at the closed ramp. Something slams into the ship. Then three more collisions against the hull. Our ship roars through the air toward the wall of ripWings, closer, closer. Warning shots across our bow. "Faster," Holiday says. The ceiling sparks and glows as someone drills in through the outside. The Lionguards cluster around the sparks, guns pointed up. "Faster!"

We punch through the line of ripWings. They bank to follow us. I see the Citadel glowing in the distance. The ship cracks as it breaks the sound barrier. The sparks rain down from the ceiling on me. More Augustus vessels rise up from Citadel landing pads to greet us. With them ascend dozens of men in armor, at their head a huge figure in pale blue fox armor. Niobe au Telemanus has come to war.

45

DARROW

Venus

ONCE UPON A TIME, Venus was the evil sister of Earth, swollen from solar dust to similar shape and size. But while Earth was blessed with water, sweet air, and a temperate disposition, Venus had a more quarrelsome spirit. Her surface, cruel enough to melt lead, was marked by interminable days and nights, each numbering 243 of her sister's. Under her foul breath, nothing could live, nothing could grow, nothing could move but winds of carbon dioxide and torpid clouds fat with acid rain.

And then man came from the blackness and drank up the hydrogen of the gas giants and breathed the fresh breath into her skies. The ensuing rains fell to cover eighty percent of her surface in oceans. With high-altitude mass drivers, man scalped away the withering atmosphere and cooled her surface. With asteroids hurled from the asteroid belt and mass drivers at her equator, he spun her out of her torpor and into an agreeable dance, her days now like her sister's. Mankind dressed her in green and blue and she waited, eager and fresh, for the humans to come down from their floating cities to join her in her new dance, which had been four and a half billion years plus ninety in the making.

House Carthii of Luna was the first to arrive.

Now, for the first time in my thirty-three years, I dare to see Venus in the flesh. Her clouds are thin and clutch her mottled blue body like the tails of a tattered nightgown. Diadems of ice and snow dust her poles. Emerald islands rise from her temperate blue seas. And about her neck is cinched the might of Gold, a Byzantine necklace of ships and orbital dockyards, sparkling with landing lights and loaded with half-completed frigates and destroyers all made from Mercurian steel. Around this necklace glide dark-hulled ships painted with the crowned white skull of the Ash Lord inside the pyramid of the Society. There are far fewer ships than intel suggested. Most must be on the far side of the planet.

"Mm, into the mouth of the beast," Alexandar says from beside me on the bridge. "'Then, even then, Cassandra's lips unsealed the doom to come: lips by a god's command never to be believed or heeded by the Trojans.'"

To my other side, Rhonna sighs in exasperation. "Can't we damn well go five bloody minutes without commentary leaking out your ass?"

He chuckles. "Like you'd know what to do with the silence."

"Anything would be better than you quoting Nilton."

"Milton, for your edification. Only that wasn't the blind Englishman. It was the Attic."

I turn to look at them and they shut up, Rhonna into a moody silence, Alexandar into a luxurious one. He finds a scuff on his black chest armor and pulls out a silk handkerchief to wipe it off. "Lancer, which fleet is that?" I ask Rhonna.

She shakes off her irritation, steps forward and pulls an image from her datapad into the air and magnifies the hulls of the capital ships. "It looks like the First and Third. There's the sphinx of House Carthii, and the dogs of Cerana, their bannermen." Alexandar makes a polite sound of disappointment. Rhonna scans the image in frustration, not understanding what she got wrong. "Shut up, Alexandar."

"I said nothing."

"Alexandar? Do you know the answer?" I ask.

"First, Third, and Eleventh."

"Eleventh?" Rhonna asks.

Alexandar continues smugly. "Cerana is no longer with the Third. Intel suggests that the Ash Lord has continued his reform in fleet management, and his favoring of smaller, independent forces with greater local autonomy. House Cerana was spotted operating in Martian orbit three months ago without additional support. Starhall believes there are now at least twelve main subdivisions within the Societal Navy." He pushes his long hair from his eyes. "The lattermost fleets of course being of smaller size. The rest of the fleets are likely concealed behind the planet, as per the Ash Lord's modus operandi."

"How many capital ships are in the Eleventh Fleet?" I ask, becoming annoyed with him.

"Estimates say two destroyers, six torchships, ten frigates, sir."

"Correct."

"Thank you, sir."

Rhonna goes into a dark silence. I turn to her and say quietly, "What do you think I'm going to say?"

"That I should read my briefs."

"Yes. But why?" She doesn't answer, but looks over my shoulder at Alexandar.

"Rhonna, the first rule of war is to know where your enemy is. How can you know where he is if you do not know how many he is? Say you spot one torchShip with Cerana dogs in the asteroid belt. How can you decide your course if you don't know how many ships she travels with? How many variables are at play for ambushes and counterattacks?" I lean close and nod back to Alexandar. "And more importantly, don't let him bait you."

"Yes, sir."

"And you . . ." I turn back to Alexandar. He freezes as I pull a holo from my datapad showing the ship's bridge. I rewind it and replay the self-satisfied smiles he was giving Rhonna when my back was turned. I make him watch it three times till his pale cheeks are rose red. "Don't be such an asshole. It's why there's war in the first place."

"Yes, sir."

From his perch in the pilot's chair above, Colloway chuckles in amusement, though still no smile. He's never been fond of Alexandar, or many Golds for that matter, but he takes particular joy in seeing my dashing lancer humbled. It doesn't happen often. Except for his mouth, the boy would make Lorn proud. He'd like everyone to think his gifts are Jove-sent, but not a moment of his life since I met him has not been spent studying or practicing the martial arts. Sometimes Lorn would let him sit in on our secret lessons in Agea. He would bring his sister's hazelnut bread and watch with wide, enamored eyes.

I motion Alexandar closer. "I want you to keep your distance from Apollonius."

"With all due respect, sir, the man has a bomb in his head."

"He's a madman. He meant it when he mentioned the bloodfeud. Won't throw a gauntlet because he knows I'll stop it. But he still might take his chance if you turn your back."

"He won't. He knows you'll blow his head off, and I rather think he likes his head."

"He'll probably wager that he's safe. That I won't sacrifice the mission in order to avenge your death."

"Of course you would." A slow look of pain grows on his face. "Wouldn't you?"

"Of course I would," I say, catching Rhonna's eye. She knows I'm lying, because unlike Alexandar she does not suffer the shared delusion of grandeur under which all Golds secretly live their lives: that they are the chosen one, and their time is nigh. Rhonna would expect me to put the mission above her. With that single look between us, I see her in a fresh light.

"Sorry to interrupt the school lesson, but we're being hailed by planetary security," Winkle says from the sunken communications pit. His white padded chair is tilted back. The ambient light from the holographic controls that float in front of him bathe his spindly arms in a radioactive green. He's done this dance before, as we've already passed through three levels of security with the codes received from

Tharsus's buyer, the first coming at Bastion station, then twice more from Gold patrols and sensor drones as we plunged deeper and deeper into the maw of the enemy orbit. Aside from our contact with the Society, we've been on a coms blackout.

"Last code," I say. "Prep the engines for max burn if it doesn't work."

Into the mouth of the beast indeed.

After passing through planetary security, we touch down beside five older assault frigates on a quiet landing strip set into the shoal of Tharsus's island in Venus's equatorial seas. Helmeted sentries in observation obelisks watch the ship settle onto the concrete and then look back with disinterest over the night water. "That's it?" Sevro mutters. "Five frigates? I thought there'd be at least a dozen."

"There's probably more off-island," I say.

"And if there's not?"

The Howlers assemble in the hold near the disembarkation ramp, where they finish donning their armor. Pebble and Milia escort Apollonius from his cell. He doesn't look a prisoner, dressed all in black and wearing a purple cloak that we found in Quicksilver's closets. Sevro went on ahead of me and now sits on one of the parked gravBikes, sharing an apple back and forth with Tongueless, who takes small, delicate bites. Sevro glowers at Apollonius as a Howler tightens the screws on his armor's backplate. "You remember what happens if you get clever, Apple?" He squeezes the fruit till it explodes in his grip. He wipes the pulp and juice on Apollonius's black jacket. "A little promise from me to you." Tongueless frowns at the smashed fruit.

"How is your wife, Barca?" Apollonius asks after a brief pause. "A magnificent woman. Tharsus and I shared her sister several times, of course—a venemous appetite, Antonia—but I cannot say I ever had the exquisite pleasure of the elder Julii. From what Tactus told me, she was like an eclipse of the sun."

The Howlers between them back out of the way, but Sevro doesn't move.

"No insult meant. A mere compliment on a fine, if incongruous, coupling."

"I have a collection you'll be contributing to very soon," Sevro replies, tapping his knife on his boot.

I'm wary of the Gold. He's gotten us to the surface and honored his end of the bargain thus far, but how long will that last once he's reunited with his brother? They're a strange and sadistic pair. Even Tactus, the most faithful of the brothers, couldn't be trusted farther than you could spit.

I motion Tongueless over. He's gained almost fifteen kilos since we found him in that cell. Clown and Pebble have started training him in the onboard simulator for starShell piloting. He's not good, but he's certainly not bad. I was hesitant when Sevro suggested we bring him on the mission, but we need another tall body, and he knew his way around the weapons locker better than he knows his way around our kitchen. In a way, that's more disconcerting, but I had Winkle put a security measure in his suit as an insurance policy.

"Inside the darkzone we won't be able to transmit to the tech in Apollonius's skull," I tell Tongueless now. "I want you to watch him. If he steps out of line, you waste him." I gave the same instructions to Thraxa about Tongueless and Apollonius. The Obsidian pulls one of Sevro's knives from his belt. He must really be making an impression. Casually, as if it were encoded into his DNA as a passive trait, he twirls the blade through his fingers. He smiles and nods.

"Goodman," I say quietly.

"Fascinating conceptual model," Apollonius says, looking at my Howlers as I join him. "So many disparate genuses working with autonomy. I wonder, if not for the Golden monster, how long would it take for you to eat each other?"

"Well, hope you end up being around to find out," I say. I turn to the Howlers and see Sevro watching my conversation with Apollonius. "All right, ladies and gentlemen, helmets up." The friendly faces of my tallest Howlers disappear behind the cold masks of pulseArmor, replaced with the faces of the demons. My men wear none of their menagerie of trophies, or their wolfpelts. And the armor, which often is violently painted per the owner's preference, is a Society commando squad's matte black with an iron Minotaur on the breast. "You fascists look like you'd raze a village and liquidate the local populace with particle beams."

"Ready for a genocide, sir," Clown says, snapping to attention.

"Remember, run silent. Stay tight. We're Golds returned with the heir." I turn to Apollonius, who alone wears no armor, and grin. "Let's go meet the family."

The ramp lowers and we stare down the barrel of an anti-aircraft partical cannon with a Gray in the firing chair. Twenty other Grays and a clutch of armored Obsidians stand at the base of the ramp with their weapons casually shouldered, expecting to see a crew of motley pirates and not a garage full of heavily armored Golds.

"On your knees or you will be fired upon!" their leader shouts.

Apollonius steps forward into the floodlights, his hands held out. "Vorkian, is that how you welcome your master home?" he asks.

A dark-skinned Gray with buzzed bright white hair and a face carved from old boot leather steps out from the ranks. *"Dominus . . ."* She falls to her knees, but cannot lower her eyes. "Is it you? Is it really you?"

The men behind her fall to their knees before Apollonius even gets halfway down the landing ramp. "It seems the Void is not ready for me yet. For it is I, Apollonius au Valii-Rath, liberated from the depths and returned to command you, good Vorkian."

"Who are they, sir?"

"Have you so long been idle that you fail to recognize *loyal* friends, Vorkian?" He looks back at me and smiles. I ready to blow the bomb in his skull. "They are my liberators."

"Sir, forgive me. I did not know you were alive—"

Apollonius holds up a hand, cutting her off. "Endeavor only to serve me now, and forgiveness you may one day find. Will you serve me, Centurion Vorkian?"

"I never left your service, sir. But your brother . . ."

"Yes, I hear he has been busy despoiling the house of my mother and father. Where is the idle libertine?"

"Swimming, sir." Vorkian's face darkens in disgust. "With his entourage."

"Magnificent. I am known to enjoy an aquatic fete." Apollonius's teeth glimmer. "Smile, Vorkian, the end of ignominy draws nigh. For we have glory to claim once again. Tell the guards and servants they are to retire for the evening to their barracks and quarters. There you will stay and rest, for this is a family matter."

"Some of the men do not know you, *dominus*. They're the Ash Lord's toads."

"Can they be overcome?"

"Yes. The loyal stand ready." Her men nod their heads.

"Good. Pass the word. Take the Ashmen to the barracks, douse them with engine grease, and light them on fire. Then cut off their heads and arms and feed them to the crabs."

"With pleasure, *dominus*."

Vorkian and her men jog off into the darkness as we press into the main house. Green foliage consumes the place, jungle vines creeping on walls, trees leaning over walkways. Our path carries us into the complex through the glass doors at the base of a glass pyramid. We pass more guards, who, alerted by Vorkian, kneel at Apollonius's arrival. Two are dragging a Gray officer beaten half to death.

"Minotaur Invictus," they say to their dread lord, and carry on their dark task. Soon, the complex is a ghost town.

"There should be more of them," Sevro mutters under his breath.

We find a man swimming laps in the back of the complex, where the roof extends out over a rocky cove. The ocean water is lit from beneath with lights. Four other Golds lounge by the side of the water on divans, sipping wine and eating from small plates. Two are naked, the others wrapped in silk robes. Three Pinks flit about, distributing flutes and rubbing sore muscles.

When Tharsus has finished his laps, he slides through the water to the edge and pulls himself out. He's naked and less muscular than Apollonius, all arms and legs and a newly grown belly paunch. He goes to his towel, but picks up the glass of wine there instead. Hard to imagine he is one of the only Boneriders to escape capture. Last time I saw Tharsus in the flesh, he was trying to purchase Sevro's corpse from Cassius. He stands, slouching to sip his wine while he fondles the breast of one of the Golds playfully. She swats at him with an annoyed laugh, but then acquiesces to a deep kiss.

He dribbles wine over the Gold woman's stomach till it collects in her navel. He stoops and she moans softly as he licks it out. The Pink who had been massaging the woman's feet slinks away. None have seen us. We scan for signs of any guards.

"You said that ship carries Frankian wines?" a muscled Gold man wearing nothing but a diamond necklace says in surprise.

"Indeed," Tharsus says.

"It looked like an assault frigate. Wherever did you find it?"

"Stolen from Quicksilver himself by my audacious armada. Treasure, my goodman, lies in the stars."

"Ever the mogul," another sycophant adds. One of the Pinks hands him a flute.

"We must throw a fete of bacchanalian proportions," the muscled Gold says. "The new rationing restrictions are draconian. We're practically nibbling on the crust of bread. I feel like a Raa."

"You're as ugly as one," Tharsus says.

"I daresay, a party is a charming thought, Gregarius," the woman says. "If Tharsus can control his appetites long enough to save some for the rest of us."

"We can invite the Ash Lord," Tharsus adds, reaching for his com.

"Oh, that old hermit," the woman replies. "I daresay it will take more than a fete to lure him from his shell." She shudders. "What if he brings Atalantia and her *concubine*?"

"Vorkian," Tharsus says into his com. "Vorkian, where is the damn wine? That ship landed twenty minutes ago. I'll have you scourged if you make my guests wait any longer."

"Don't you mean *my* guests?" Apollonius says, stepping onto the shadowed patio. We follow behind him, keeping our eyes out for unaccounted guards.

Tharsus wheels on us, unable to make out our faces.

"Who is that? How dare you wear armor in my presence. Vorkian?"

"Not Vorkian," Sevro says.

"Who are you!" Tharsus demands.

"Don't you recognize your own blood, little brother?" Apollonius asks, stepping into the light. Tharsus goes sheet-white and steps back. Sevro joins Apollonius in the light and retracts his helmet.

"Hello, boyo. Long time no see. Still want my rib cage?"

Tharsus stares at him in abject horror.

"Ares!" one of the Golds hisses, still holding her glass. The rest stare at Sevro in confusion. In that moment, they taste a small bit of the fear their slaves endure every day. The Pinks gawp at the sight of us. Grins split two of their slender faces. They rush off, knowing what comes next.

"Take Tharsus. Kill the rest," I say, pulling the railgun from the holster on my right thigh. I squeeze the trigger. The muscled Gold's head explodes. Tongueless fires. The woman whose navel Tharsus drank from holds a hand up as if it can stop a toroid of superheated hydrogen moving faster than the speed of sound. Her hand disappears. The lower half of her jaw goes with it. One of the Golds charges us and Tongueless shoots him as well. A huge bloody hole opens up as the plasma eats out the other side of his chest. His body carries on. Sevro shoots his leg out and he spins sideways to the ground to mew and die.

Tharsus springs sideways into the water. "Mine," Sevro says. He shoots his stunFist into the water to the left of Tharsus. The electricity crackles through the wet conductor and electrocutes the man. He spasms in the water and then floats to the top. The rest of my men pour onto the patio, securing it. The last Gold uses the body of the first Gold I killed as a shield and searches frantically for a weapon.

"Apollonius, stay," I say. But he ignores me and slips forward, blocking my shot. The hiding man sees him coming and makes a break for the water of the cove. Apollonius tackles him from behind. The two wrestle on the ground until Apollonius rolls the man sideways, then snaps his neck with a single twist. He stands slowly from the corpse, watching in amusement as Sevro dives into the pool to retrieve Tharsus's body.

With Tongueless's help, Sevro hauls him out of the water and onto the ground.

Apollonius rejoins me. "I told you to stay," I say.

"Would Athena stay Odysseus's hand when he returned to Ithaca? No Color is immune from my wrath." He pours wine over his brother's unconscious face. "Tharsus. Run away from the light. No time for dreams. Back to the land of the weary living."

Tharsus's eyes open. He spits up water. "Apollonius?" he whispers hoarsely.

"Hello, brother. Did you miss me?"

46

DARROW

The Brother's Wrath

After the patio is secured, Tharsus sits with a robe around him in a chair apart from the bodies, his initial shock having given way to beleaguered contempt. "Apalling company you now keep, brother," Tharsus hisses to Apollonius, who sits across from him.

"Means to an end, Tharsus. Means to an end."

"And you brought them here. To my home."

Apollonius slaps his brother gently across the face. "My home," he corrects. "I am the heir of Valii-Rath, not you. I know you haven't forgotten that. Or else I doubt I would have been a prisoner for so long."

"I tried to rescue you," Tharsus says convincingly.

"Did you, dear brother?"

"I spared no expense. Hired mercenaries, spent half my spies . . ."

"Sorry, Tharsus," I say. "There was one assault made on Deepgrave, and it was not for Apollonius and not from you."

"Slag you, halfbreed," Tharsus says, spitting at me.

Apollonius slaps him across the face, this time so hard he tumbles out of his chair. He waits for him to find his seat again. "Manners, brother; when at the mercy of your enemies, petulance demeans your entity."

"I reserve manners for people, not slaves," Tharsus says. I stare down at him without pity. Apollonius has a measure of majesty about him, but Tharsus is a deviant with long eyelashes. His beautiful face no more than the evolutionary adaptation of a predator.

"You're confused, dear brother," Tharsus says with a manic laugh. "Lost in the tumble of your own mind without me to help you sort it right." He smiles softly up at the bigger man. "Now, I shudder to think what they want, what they've promised you. But they don't care for you as I do. When they get what they desire, they will cast you aside." He looks at Sevro. "Mongrels without code or custom."

"I might be a halfbreed," Sevro says. "But at the end of the day, you're still a bitch, and I've still got two ears." He pulls the bootknife, grabs Tharsus's hair, and cuts off his left ear. Tharsus cries out in pain and Tongueless steps toward Apollonius, but there's no need. Apollonius watches with dispassion as Tharsus thrashes.

"Apollonius . . ." Tharsus hisses.

"I told you: mind your manners."

"Mother was right. You're mad!"

"I am not *mad*," Apollonius growls, and steps forward. Tharsus reels back in sudden terror. But Apollonius's anger dissolves as fast as it came. "I am not mad," he says quietly, then breaks into a broad smile. "I simply lust for life and the thrill sport of war. Why should I deny myself the delight, when these two descended to offer me the ultimate play?" He sighs. "I know it is difficult for you to see me again, dear brother. Why, how easy it must have been when quarrelsome me was languishing in the abyss. But it was not easy for me. Neither the isolation nor the boredom nor the fear that my great strand of life would be cut short before the time of my glory. But do you fathom what the deepest, darkest lamentation was?" He leans forward. "Do you? It was the fear that my dearest, loving brother, my partner against the world, was complicit in my incarceration."

"Complicit? Ridiculous."

"Irrefutably complicit."

"That's a lie," Tharsus says. "They've filled your head with bilious dreck."

"Is that so?"

"Dreck. Bold and grotesque."

"Come now, Tharsus. Do you really think I don't know your tells by now? You could never hide them from me."

"Apollonius, I would never betray you. . . ."

Apollonius smiles. "You should be honor bound to a bloodfeud against Grimmus. Why would the Ash Lord keep you alive if you were not his creature? Did you think he would bring you to his side? Tharsus, the Pink drinker. Tharsus the Torturer. Tharsus the Vampire of Thessalonica? The Jackal might have treasured your cruelty, but these others see you and they laugh at you like the drunken jester you are. They think you a little nasty adolescent with blessed genetics, but, point of fact, you're an adolescent with an army. So they kept you and let you distract yourself with idle playthings and helped themselves to that army. You let Grimmus give it to those clameater *Carthii*." His lips curl back over his large teeth. "*My* army. The Ash Lord played you like a fool, brother. You knew. Admit it." He leans forward. "Admit it."

"Yes . . ." Tharsus says. He looks down in shame. The blood flow from his ear now a sluggish trickle. "It is true. I knew." He looks up with hopeful eyes. "But I had no choice."

"No?"

"I had to survive!"

"Why? For a facile existence of wetting your prick in myriad holes? You pathetic little deviant. You are not a child any longer." He snatches his hair and finally Tharsus's rebellious façade cracks. The hint of terror he let slip earlier gives way to a storm of it.

"Don't kill him," I say. "We need him to get into the darkzone."

"Kill him?" Apollonius looks back at me, seeing my apprehension. "An ear is just an ear. But a life." He shakes his head. "He's my brother." He looks back to Tharsus. "My brother who betrayed me. My brother who left his beloved kin to rot." He squeezes his hair, pulling tighter. "My brother who wished to be an only child."

"I didn't . . ."

"Didn't what?"

"I didn't want to die . . ." Tharsus says pitifully. "He said he would kill me if I didn't comply. But if I did, the Valii-Rath name would live on. Mother and Father gone . . . I didn't know what to do. . . ."

"Of course you didn't. You need me," Apollonius says soothingly. "You need your big brother." He releases his hold and gently strokes Tharsus's hair. "All this time by yourself. All these decisions. What horrible loneliness your ambition has brought."

Tharsus closes his eyes, sinking into the touch of his brother.

"I am sorry. . . ."

"I know."

"If I could take it back . . ."

"I know. But amends must be made. A pound of flesh taken." He strokes Tharsus's face as the younger man's eyes, filled with tears, open to look at him in terrible fear. "No, not from you, brother. There's only two of us left in all the worlds. And what pleasure would there be there in witnessing the rise of our house if I am alone? I forgive you, my darling." Tharsus looks like he doesn't understand. Apollonius leans forward to kiss the tears from his brother's face. "I forgive you, Tharsus. For your sins. For your nature. For everything."

Tharsus bursts into drunken tears.

The display does not warm my heart. It shows the vile, maggoty innards of this family. I feel tainted being here with them, breathing the same air, and want nothing more than to be done with this. To be home with my family, to feel real love, not this weird tapestry of domination and cruelty they've woven. Poor Tactus. What chance did ever he have?

Sevro looks sickened by the display, and I feel heartbroken knowing I've taken him so far from his girls, from Victra, into this pit of devils. Maybe Victra was right. Maybe I should have left him behind. Then Wulfgar's blood would not be on his hands, nor mine, and we would not have to share air with these men.

"Thank you, Apollonius," Tharsus says. "Thank you. But why are you here? Why with . . . them?"

"Because our pound of flesh must be taken from the man who

turned brother against brother. Soon, the Ash Lord will die. That is the cause that binds the Reaper to me. And you, my beloved, will deliver him to us."

"How?" Tharsus asks.

"You'll gain us an audience," Sevro says. "Get us in nice and tight."

"But . . . the Ash Lord hasn't had an audience in three years. He reigns in solitude."

"Three years," I repeat, not believing it. "That's absurd."

"Nonetheless, it is true."

"How the hell is that possible?" Sevro asks.

"There was an assassination attempt, so the rumors say."

"By whom?" Sevro presses. One of Victra's? None of mine got even close.

Tharsus looks perplexed. "I assumed by you. No? If anyone wishes to see him, they must go through his daughter, Atalantia." He looks to his brother, something passing between them, some unspoken knowledge that I don't like. It was a risk in letting them reunite. Men with unspoken bonds like the one Sevro and I have are always the most dangerous. "But Atalantia has vanished," Tharsus says.

"What does that mean?" I ask. "A woman like that can't just disappear."

"It means I don't know where she is. If the Carthii or the Saud know, they aren't telling me. I've been frozen out."

"Is the Ash Lord cloistered on Gorgon Isle?" I ask, hoping Republic Intelligence was correct about the darkzone. "At least tell us that."

"Yes." Tharsus nods. "But you cannot approach the island without a summons. The place is a fortress." Sevro looks over at me. "The air around the island is restricted to House Grimmus aircraft for two hundred kilometers. It will be defended by an army. His Ash Legions. You'll never get in."

"Not unless we bring an army of our own," Apollonius says with a smile.

47

LYSANDER

Teeth and Tears

I RUSH TO CASSIUS AS DIDO sends her men to bring in the safe. He's fallen to the floor. Color has fled his cheeks. I shake him. "Cassius . . . wake up!" Holding him now, I feel how limp he's gone, how much blood of his has stained the white marble. "Stay with me," I whisper, checking his pulse—so faint I can barely feel it. "Cassius!" His eyes open a sliver.

"Julian?" he murmurs.

I hestitate. "Yes," I say. "Yes, it's Julian. Stay with me, brother. Stay with me."

He blinks up at me, clarity coming to him. "Lysander." I smile, happy to be seen. "Lysander, what have you done?" Tears leak out of his eyes. "What have you done?"

The accusation puts me on my heels. Robotically, I turn to Dido. "He needs a surgeon."

"And he'll have one when I'm satisfied."

"No, he'll have one now. His life for the safe."

"Already making demands? Perhaps you really are a Lune after all."

Seraphina kneels to feel his pulse. *"Mother."*

"Very well." The woman motions her attendants to collect the man, but Diomedes steps in their way.

"The Olympic Order will take custody of him."

"Do you not trust me?" Dido asks.

He ignores her. Seeing the worry in my eyes, he says, "Our surgeons will do what they can. If he dies, it will not be by their hand." I nod in thanks. The stoic man motions two Olympic Knights to carry Cassius out. They hoist him up and pass unmolested through the crowd to disappear through one of the stone doorways.

He will survive. He has to.

Lost in thought, I flinch as the safe slams to the ground in the center of the blood-soaked marble. Dido's men back away from it. "Your turn, young Lune," Dido says. "Prove who you are." I pass Seraphina without looking at her on my way to the safe, conscious of the hundreds of eyes that watch and judge not just me, but the worth of my blood.

I bend before the safe and numbly turn the dial through the combination. My hands are shaking so severely I have to try twice until the tumbler thumps inside the safe. The lock unlatches, then the secondary lock, and the door swings open. I back away, Cassius's words echoing. *What have you done?*

I've made a choice. The right choice.

I move so Seraphina can replace me in front of the safe. She carefully sets my ivory box and Cassius's oak vessel atop the safe. The sigils of our houses stand out in the dim light on the wood and ivory. "It's in my box," I say.

Seraphina reverently opens the lid. Inside she finds my grandmother's House Lune ring. She shows it to her mother before moving aside my mother's book of poetry. Her fingers glide over the worn green leather edges of the poem book as though she can feel what's inside before lifting up Karnus's razor. She produces a small tool, unfastens the screws smoothly on the bottom of the hilt, and pops open the mechanism. The holodrop is stuck to the chemical impulse unit like a lone drop of morning dew. She deposits it in the receiver plate of the holoprojector Dido's men have brought into the room and steps aside to make room for her mother. Something makes her look back at the box and the crescent moon there.

I hate her eyes lingering on it. It feels somehow shameful that my family's last relics are held in so small a box, bare now for the world to see.

"I did not want this path to be taken," Dido says to the Moon Lords in a grand, sweeping voice. The sort great statesmen and tyrants all seem to possess. "This violence. This coup against my own husband . . ." She shakes her head wearily. "It is a travesty." There are whispers of agreement there. "You all know I have labored for years to convince Romulus that the Pax Ilium was made under false pretenses. I have been ridiculed. Mocked that this obsession is a madness born of my foreign birth. Perhaps the hot blood of Venus is not gone from my veins entirely. But I am a child of the Dust now. I know I am not above the law." The Golds frown down at her. "The actions taken by me and my men are not above the law. In fact, they were enacted to ensure that the law is followed. Which is why, when I have finished speaking, I will set myself at your mercy. Like my husband, I will set myself before an Olympic Trial and you may judge if I am mad, if you like. And if my actions are found treasonous, I will meet the dust. But until then, I ask you for your ears. . . ."

Greeted by silence, and a nod from Helios, ArchKnight of the Olympics, she continues.

"Ten years ago, the Dockyards of Ganymede were destroyed. A hundred thousand died on the station. Ten million Ganymedi died when the rubble fell upon New Troy. It was a calamity not seen in the Rim since the coming of the Ash Lord. We blamed Roque au Fabii and his Sovereign." She looks at me. "But what if I told you there was a hidden truth? Another man responsible for the newest in the long list of crimes against our people?"

She paces along the floor.

"Four months ago, I received word from a broker in the Core, who claimed to have information that would be of interest to me. The broker, a White of the Ophion Guild, represented an unknown seller who wished to exchange the data for information in our archives. The information was purported to be sensitive; they could not risk transmitting it for fear of Republic interception. Knowing my husband was required to uphold the Pax Ilium, and would do so regardless of the information, I acted of my own accord and sent my most trusted agent, my daughter, Seraphina, into the Interior. This is what she returned with."

She activates the holoprojector.

The audio comes first. The sound of metal dragged upon metal. Whimpering. Metal on flesh. Then the video appears in the air in the center of the room over our heads with ghostly radiance. It shows the bloodied deck of a starship, a grand one judging by the size of the bridge. The mutilated body of a dead Gold woman is being dragged by her hair by a pair of huge pale hands covered with tribal runes. They could only belong to an Obsidian woman. The hands pry open the Gold's mouth, pinning her teeth open with a curved wedge of ceremonial bone. Fingers jam roughly into the Gold's mouth and pull her tongue forward with a pair of iron prongs. Then, with a hooked knife, the hands saw at the base of the tongue till it comes free with a grisly sucking sound. The hands pierce the tongue with an iron barb and push it along to join the dozen others already hanging there on the Obsidian's belt. Racial indignation rises in me. The Peerless at our sides watch without flinching.

This is the true face of the world. The darkness beneath civilization that my grandmother warned me about. I have known it, felt it, and, in absence of her guidance, watched it leak through her fallen empire.

The Obsidian leaves the corpse behind and walks past the body of a second fallen Gold. At her feet, the epaulets of an ArchPraetor are flecked with blood but the body is seemingly unmolested. The face of Roque au Fabii is pale and bloodless. The Obsidian joins a coterie of battle-scarred women in spoilt armor who form a crescent around the forward viewport of the bridge. White hair stained with blood and soot hangs down their backs. In front of them kneels the dread woman Sefi, the powerful sister of Ragnar Volarus. She clutches a battle-axe and gazes out the viewport as the ship slides across space toward a mottled blue and green moon. Two armored Golds stand beside her along with a stocky Asiatic Gray looking out at the pride of Ilium—the Dockyards of Ganymede. Two hundred eleven kilometers of metal, bolts, dry docks, engineers, refineries, assembly lines, ingenuity, and dreams and labor. One of the two great dockyards of humanity, before the Republic's fledgling shipyards over Phobos. All suspended above the pale splendor of Ganymede's equatorial seas and at the mercy of her enemies. Not of Fabii and his Sovereign as the worlds have believed for more than a decade, but of the Rising. Of the despised Slave King.

"Men built this?" Sefi asks in awkward Common.

"It took two hundred fifty years . . . it's how old the first dock there is," says the Gold woman at her side, the traitor, Julii. The Gray comes forward to whisper something to the second Gold, a man. He stands with his back to us, but I would know him by his shadow or even the faint whisper of his hoarse voice.

His helmet is off. His armor was once white, but now it is scored with pulseblasts, razor marks, and viscera. He's slouched, his weight leaning on the rigid slingBlade at his side. He seems an old man, but the side profile of his face is scarcely older than mine is now. How could he do all this before his twenty-third year? Even Alexander of Macedon would marvel at the Slave King of Mars, a creature as grand as the empire he broke. His image glitters in the eyes of the hundred Moon Lords.

The Reaper turns to look back with stony eyes at someone in the bridge pits, but the Julii sets a hand on his shoulder. *"Share the load, darling,"* she says. *"This one's on me."* She raises her voice. *"Helmsman, open fire with all port batteries. Launch tubes twenty-one through fifty at their center line."*

The Peerless around the Bleeding Place stand in silence, their faces illuminated by the pale fire that tears into their lost dockyards.

The docks were never meant for war. Her ships were to defend her. What horror that her greatest child, the *Colossus,* would return upon the brink of independence to destroy her.

Tungsten iron rounds shear through metal bulkheads like hail careening into wet bread. The dockyards die in silence. Oxygen vents. Spheres of fire gasp and drown in space. And dead metal drifts off, pulled inexorably to Ganymede's bosom.

As the destruction rains, the Reaper turns from the viewport, his face a death mask of grief and pain, and I feel as if I hear his heart beat across the years, across the space, and know how far he's come from the man he wanted to be.

He reminds me of my godfather.

While the room disintegrates into fury, I marvel at the boldness of Darrow's charade, even at the shrewdness of his cruelty. In the last moment of his victory, he saw an opportunity to win a war against the Rim that had not even begun, and he took it with as bold a maneuver as I've ever seen. But it is certainty I feel, not respect or horror. This is the man I once idolized. An unpredictable gambler of savage intellect with a limitless capacity for violence. I respect his capabilities, but I do not respect the man. And here, in the wake of his destruction, I understand beyond a shadow of a doubt that to protect mankind, the Reaper must die.

Dido, it seems, was not mad after all.

"The Slave King betrayed us," Dido says, lifting her razor high till the bitter blade trembles in the air through the projection of the dying docks, the metal shiny and opalescent, like a strand of tears frozen in time. "The Pax Ilium is broken! When his tattooed, mechanized horde is finished with the Core, they will come for us. Your families. Your homes. You see it! You know it. So now, my noble friends, I call for war."

The Moon Lords look to old Helios, who sits with Diomedes. The old man stands slowly to his dignified height, the picture of dignity and cold resolve. He pulls his razor from his hip and extends it into the air. "War!" cries their Truth Knight.

"War!" thunder the eleven others, unsheathing their blades. While they thrust them into the air, Diomedes barely lifts his hand.

With the Olympics having spoken, a fever spreads through the assembled Moon Lords. A host of razors unfurl and shine in the dim light, the teeth of so many dragons. Seraphina looks at me. Finally she has what she's sought. With a look of religious satisfaction, she unravels her razor and, like her mother, like her brother and generations of kin, she lifts it into the air.

"War," she says softly, as if declaring it only against me.

48

LYSANDER

The Boy and the Knight

I N THE BEDLAM THAT FOLLOWS, I'm spirited away by Diomedes and a coterie of his men. They take me back to my room and push me inside.

"Diomedes," I say before the door closes. The knight turns. "Cassius, I want to see him. I need to know if he's alive."

"It is not safe for you in the halls."

"I helped you."

"You are still a Lune. Whether he lives or dies is up to him."

"And your surgeons."

Realization dawns. "Do you think we would not care for him? He showed his honor. I will stand vigil myself and send word when I know his fate."

"Thank you."

He hesitates. "He betrayed your grandmother, yet you travel with him. . . ."

"He saved my life from the Rising. I am bound to him."

"I understand." He nods, his first sign of respect to me. "But if he dies, you will be free of him. Then to what will you be bound, Lune?" He leaves me with that and shuts the door. It locks from the other side. I pace the cold stone, unable to think of anything but Cassius on the floor asking me what I've done. I feel the walls closing in.

I retreat inward. Forcing myself into the Willow Way, imagining my breath as the breeze that moves the branches and sways the grass and kisses the water. A second movement of breath now comes, which moves the lavender and pushes the bees and tinkles the wind chimes of summer at Lake Silene. A third movement is that of fall. The fourth breath that moves the curtains and twists the flames in the braziers and brings the snow of Hyperion in through an open window and makes Cassius's cape dance in the wind is that of Luna's winter.

Deep in that distant pool of memory, I see him again for the first time.

The young Bellona stands with his back to me, looking out at the Citadel grounds beyond the balcony. Sun glints off the gold tip of the Legion Pyramid headquarters in the distance. His hair is coiled and shines with scented oil. Snow melts there. His coat is dark blue with feathered silver epaulets and a silver fringed collar. He wears a silver razor on his hip and silver buckles on his boots. He looks like a storybook knight, and it makes me distrust him.

Though capable, he is a petty, spoiled creature who lured my favorite House Mars student onto the bank of a river and there betrayed him. Why? Because he could not absorb what Grandmother extols as the highest lessons of the Institute—the bearing of loss. If the loss of a single brother in the Passage broke him, what good would he be under the grind of war?

"So you are the favorite son of Tiberius," I say in the memory. He turns around to appraise me. In a white cashmere jacket with pearl buttons, holding a book of mathematics in my hands, I stand no higher than his waist. A condescending smile spreads across his lips. "*Salve*, my goodman," I say.

"Lysander, isn't it?" Cassius asks without attention to protocol.

"It is." He waits for me to say something more. I do not.

"Well, you're an eerie little creature, aren't you?" He leans closer, his lively eyes narrowing. "Jove, you look eighty and eight all at the same time."

"My grandmother is wroth with you," I say.

His eyebrow arcs. "Is she now? Have I done much to be wroth about?"

"You have killed eleven men in the Bleeding Place since summer. And your villa has been a constant source of debauchery and media fodder. If you were attempting to encourage the stereotype of Martians as warmakers, you succeeded most admirably."

"Well . . ." He flashes a smile. "I do like causing a stir."

"Why? Does it make you feel important? *Alis aquilae*. The words of your house. 'On eagle's wings.' I suppose an air of self-satisfaction is natural amongst the apex predator of the sky. Who would contradict them?"

His face darkens. "Careful, little moon boy. You may wag that tongue all you like on this hill. But on Mars, that's how men meet their end."

I blink up at him, knowing I have nothing to fear. "Does truth disconcert you so?"

"Call me a pedant for manners."

"Manners. Well, if it's manners you wish to discuss, I can call Aja in and you can debate the particulars with her. They are different on Luna."

He wags a finger at me. "Using the claws of others is not brave, nor is it the same as having claws. I would have thought you of all people would know that."

I'm not sure what he means, me of all people, so I fight the instinct to shrug, knowing it a foul habit, and incline my head to dismiss his puzzling insult. "One day I will have claws and I will learn to use them, my goodman. Until then, I do believe the claws of others will suffice."

"Goryhell, you're a terror." He watches me a moment. "I've decided to like you, little moon boy."

"Thank you," I say. "But do not be offended if I withhold similar sentiment. I told Grandmother the other Martian would be better."

His mood swings to darkness once again. A feeble trait to be so protean. "Which other Martian?"

"The orphan," I smile. "Andromedus."

"Darrow . . ."

"Yes. He *was* ArchPrimus. Was he not? He stormed Olympus. Unheard-of quality, despite his parents being of such . . . humble acclaim. The Andromeduses were Martian, bannermen of House Aquillus before they tried their hand in the Belt. Your bannermen. Did you know them?"

"House Aquillus?" He smirks. "Haven't even heard of it."

"It is in eastern Cimmeria. But of course he takes nothing after them in features either. He's inordinately . . . durable and clever. Most importantly, he inspired loyalty. You, despite your natural gifts, did not."

"I won't be lectured by an unscarred brat, no matter his last name. You're not even supposed to know about the Institute yet. Little cheat."

"You prove my point. You have no humility. Andromedus would be better."

"Better for what?"

"Now, Cassius, didn't Lady Bellona teach you patience is the utmost virtue?" A young woman wearing my house colors but speaking with an Agean brogue leans at the doorway to my grandmother's office, smiling nastily at Cassius.

"Virginia," he says with a strange, Pinkish smile.

"Hello, handsome." She smiles sweetly at me. "Lysander, did you write any poems for me today?"

I blush and suddenly wish I were as tall as Cassius. "None of worth, I fear."

"That's not what Atalantia told me."

"She's much too . . . forgiving."

"Well, I'll be the final judge of their quality. Shall you read them to me after supper?"

"Aja was going to take me to see the falcons at Gosamere," I say.

"May I come?"

I nod despite knowing Aja will be annoyed.

"Wonderful, I do love falcons."

"Eagles are better," Cassius says. He looks her up and down admiringly and in an objectifying manner with which I immediately take umbrage. "Heard your man went off to play with ships."

"Subtle," she says. "In any matter, I don't have a man."

"Well, not for long anyway. Karnus has been enrolled. Perhaps my brother will have a better go at him than yours did. Where is that Bronzie miscreant these days anyway?"

"How should I know?"

They stand in awkward silence.

"The Sovereign's waiting, Cassius. . . ." Virginia gestures him to follow and winks at me. "Tell Aja not to leave without me."

"I will . . ." I say distantly.

The memory evaporates as I open my eyes.

The room is quiet, and so far from home.

Cassius's blood has dried on my hands and begun to itch. I wash them in the basin in the corner till the spigot tells me I've reached my daily ration of water. I pump the spigot once more. "Daily ration exceeded," it drones again. My hands are still pink. I sit back on the sleeping pallet and wait, focusing on slowing my breath till I slip into a shallow slumber.

I wake at the sound of my door opening, hoping instinctively that it is Seraphina. But why would it be?

The Pink, Aurae, stands there nervously, her hands clutched together, her eyes on the ground. There's blood under her nails.

"Dominus." She bows. "The Storm Knight sent me."

"Is Cassius alive?"

She shifts on the soles of her gray slippers.

"Is he? Be plain."

"No." Her eyes flutter up to meet mine. "He has passed."

I say nothing for a full minute. "When?"

"Not long ago. I am sorry, *dominus.*"

I drift to the window. The darkness and cold outside creep in. "That long? I didn't even feel him go." It was while I was sleeping.

The roar of my crumbling world drowns out the woman's voice. This is not how it was supposed to end. I thought I had saved him. That I would have a chance to show him that he was wrong. To help him realize the mistake he'd made choosing Darrow and convince him that there was still good he could do in the world. Still peace he could bring. Somehow I thought our lives would go on together, and one day he would follow me as I follow him.

Instead, he's gone into the void.

His last moments spent thinking I betrayed him and stole his redemption.

I'm weightless there against the stone, floating and, at the same time, crushed by the weight of my choices and the impossible question I ask myself: what would I have done differently? In some other world, the Pink is still talking. "I was told that he died of exsanguination."

"I understand," I hear myself saying. *Stand astride the sorrow. Do not let it touch you.* "Thank you, Aurae," I say. "May I see him?"

She looks back at my guards, and I realize they are not the same Diomedes left. These are Dido's men. "I'm afraid that is impossible, *dominus.*"

"Why?" She looks at the ground. "Answer me."

"His body was taken by schoolmates of Bellerephon to . . . desecrate in the Waste. Diomedes went to pursue them."

"So he sent you."

"I have his trust."

"I see. Is there anything else?"

"No, *dominus.*"

When the door closes, the composure shivers. First a crack, like a plate of glass struck by an errant pebble. The crack stretches and spreads and proliferates till the whole plate of dignity shatters all at once. My legs cave from under me as I think of how Pytha will suffer from this news. A single sob escapes. It is alone in the room. No sound follows it to give it company or comfort. Just one long lament of a wounded animal and I am quiet, rocking there on the cold floor with my knees hugged to my chest like that distant child who heard from Aja that his parents had perished. Her dark arms held that boy as he trembled. Her whispers soothed his heart. This stone is cold like that stone. This pain is deep like that pain. This moment like that moment. Only now, with the passing of Cassius, there is no one left to hold the boy; all that was left of him is dead, and the life of the man must begin.

49

LYRIA

Enemy of the State

THE BARCA BOARDERS ABANDONED their attack on the shuttle soon as the Telemanus and Augustus forces from the Citadel threatened to overwhelm them. Now the knights guide us to an elevated landing pad atop a spire in the Citadel of Light. The soldiers drag me from the assault ship out into the rain.

I lower my head, afraid to meet anyone's gaze. These are not the Grays who guarded my mine, or the Reds who came to 121, or the ones who pulled their guns on me in the Promenade. They're colder, harder creatures. I look up at the night sky and glimpse the stars through a break in the cloud layer. The air is cool, wet with rain. I try to feel it all, to mark these sensations, knowing a cell is where I'll spend the rest of my days. In the mine, I thought sky was stone. And after a month in Camp 121, I forgot the stars were there. But now as I know it is the last time I will see and feel them, I wonder how I ever survived without them.

I'm escorted deep within the Citadel till we reach a pale wood door. Obsidians larger than any of the Telemanuses stand to either side. Holiday drags me through the doors into the room and shoves me into a chair in front of a long table made from a single slab of black wood. Across the table, under the golden angels on his bald head, Daxo au Telemanus's huge eyes dissect me. He wears a violet tunic with a golden fox lapel. Next to him on the table sits a small aquarium filled with water and a maggot-colored animal. A carved creature with spindly legs and a gelatinous torso that reminds me of the mud leeches in the river outside 121. I shudder.

A spoon clicks on china. I tear my eyes from the monster to look at Daxo's companion, the elderly Pink woman I saw with the Sovereign at Quicksilver's. Elegance in beige robes. Her gray hair is spun up above her head like a frosted rose and held together by a simple silver clasp. Her motherly eyes, set in an old, distinguished face, watch me with a more human interest than Daxo has ever looked at anything.

No one speaks. My fear deepens.

After a moment, Daxo peers at his datapad and uncoils himself from his chair to walk to the balcony door. He opens it just as a streak of metal slams onto the stone parapet outside. I flinch as Niobe, fresh from the sky, walks in smelling like mine brimstone. Her armor is slick from the rain and leaves puddles on the floor as she stalks past her taller son into the room. Her snarling foxhead helmet stares at me with electric blue eyes before slithering from her face into the collar of her armor. *Bloodyhell.*

The pleasant, welcoming wife of the man who brought me from Mars is gone. Replaced by a violent warlord. Bags gather under her eyes. And her neck fat pushes against the collar of her too-tight armor. It's been some time since she wore it, I know.

"Take off her muzzle," Daxo tells Holiday. The woman undoes the metal arms around my mouth and extracts the plastic tongue depressor. I gasp air in through my mouth and work my tongue over the raw spots the plastic made on my gums. Holiday undoes the imprisoning armored jacket. I exhale in pain as my dislocated shoulder jostles.

"Lady Niobe—" I say quickly.

"Do not speak," she says, barely able to look at me.

"Is Kavax—"

"Silence!" she roars. She slams a metal-clad hand down on the table, cracking the black wood. I reel back. "You will speak when spoken to, or Jove help me, I will . . ." Her words falter and she steps back. Her son reaches back to comfort her. I tremble, not just from fear, but from the inability to explain, to put into words how sorry I am. Rain patters against the windows. A fire crackles in the corner and I shift, unable to meet their eyes.

"Is Kavax alive?" I ask.

There's no response. "Barely," Niobe whispers. "He may still die."

"Lyria of Lagalos." Daxo leans toward me, his chair creaking under his immense weight. His voice alone is twice the size of me. "Your life, such as it is, depends on what you say in the minutes that follow. Do you understand?"

"I understand. I got information. I saw them, the people that did this. I can help you."

"Good. The truth is your only refuge." He nods to Holiday behind me. "But . . . if I discern you are lying or being less than forthcoming, other measures will be taken." His hand brushes the aquarium. The creature inside slams against the glass, seeking the heat from his skin. "Invasive measures."

"There was a man named Philippe . . ." I begin.

Daxo holds up a hand. "We're aware of what you told the Watchmen about this *Philippe*. But horse before the cart. Are they alive?"

I nod.

"Thank Jove," Niobe murmurs. "Were they hurt?"

"Not badly."

"Where did you last see them?" Daxo asks.

"In an industrial building. After they slagged the shuttle, Philippe took us there and gave over the children to the others."

"Where were they taking them?"

"I don't know. I didn't hear." It's clear Daxo and Niobe don't believe that. I want to explain about Philippe, but their questions come in a sudden spit.

"Were they Golds?" the Pink asks. "These others."

"No."

"What Color were they?"

"Mostly Obsidian, Gray, thought I saw Reds, and a Pink."

"Obsidian . . ." Niobe says in fear. "We should tell Sefi."

"We can't tell Sefi," Daxo says. "Who knows what she would do with the information? They won't even meet with Virginia any longer."

"The Pink was in charge," I say.

"Could be a Society black ops," the old Pink says to Daxo. "Perhaps lurchers, or a Nightstalker." Daxo nods and looks back at me.

"Did they have Venusian accents?"

"No."

"Martian?"

"I don't know. Mostly Lunese, I think."

"Did you recognize any of them?"

I shake my head.

"Who was this Pink? The leader of the group that took the children?"

"Didn't hear his name. Listen, I tried to get closer to hear clearlike, but I nudged a pipe. And then they came stormin' after me."

"Who did?"

"The crows."

Daxo smiles in amusement. "You expect us to believe you outran Obsidians?"

"Didn't bloody outrun them. I jumped into a vent." I gesture to my shoulder and bloody hands. "What? You don't believe me?" They exchange skeptical glances.

"Where did this supposed *chase* happen?" Daxo asks. "The trail will soon grow cold. We must catch them before they go off-moon."

"They may already be gone," the Pink says.

"We should freeze all air traffic," Niobe says. "Search every ship."

"Across the whole moon?"

"What they did to your father . . ."

"Mother, I wish we could. But that would expose the whole affair. Virginia would have to step down. Her judgment would be in question. The vote is scheduled for next week. This must be dealt with in silence."

"It was in one of the reconstruction zones," I say quickly. "There were cranes everywhere."

"Which one?" Daxo asks. "Which zone?"

"I—I don't know. I've only been to Hyperion twice."

"She was picked up at an Alpha City checkpoint—21b, Senator," Holiday says.

"I initiated a search before you were brought in," the old Pink says. "Ten teams are scouring the area."

"All Martians?"

The Pink looks at Holiday for an answer. "Yes, sir," Holiday says. "Loyal men, all."

"Good."

"But we don't even know what we're looking for," Holiday adds. "And the longer we look, the more attention we're going to get. The Vox Populi will hear about it if we increase our presence."

"That is not an option," Daxo says harshly.

"They mutilated your father," Niobe growls.

"And we will find them," he replies. "With precision, not an army."

"Then we need to refine our search," the Pink says.

Daxo waves a hand and a map of the reconstruction zone grows out of the table in three dimensions. Thousands of buildings. "Show me the building, Lyria."

My eyes scan the hundreds of half-completed skyscrapers. They all look the same. "How am I supposed to do that? All these look the same. Wasn't exactly lookin' back at the building with crows after me."

"I told you what would happen if you did not cooperate," Daxo says.

"Gods, Daxo, give the girl a damn moment," the Pink says from her side of the table. "She's clearly been through an ordeal. Do you need pain medication for your arm, Lyria?" I nod in thanks. "Coffee with morphone," she says into a com. A moment later, a servant enters and sets the tray of steaming coffee down in front of me.

"My name is Theodora," the Pink tells me after thanking the servant. "I was the steward for Darrow of Lykos."

His steward? Then she knows the Reaper better than almost anyone. "Thank you," I say as I sip the coffee and feel the cool relief of the morphone as it dulls the pain in my shoulder.

"We're all people in the end. Good to remember that. See, this isn't just about getting the son of the Sovereign back. Pax is dear to all of us. Such a soft soul. You've met him?" I nod. "So you can understand how much we need your help. Now, can you remember a logo, a tram depot, a monument perhaps?"

"There was a tramway," I say. "Broken. I ran there when I escaped from Philippe. I was trying to find a way up out of Lost City."

"How far did you run? A kilometer? Two?" Daxo asks.

"Maybe four. Couldn't have been more before I found it."

He filters out all buildings more than four kilometers from a tramline. "I followed it along like this." I sketch a finger along the tramline toward the pedestrian stairs that lead up to the checkpoint. I remember the crumbling numbers crawling with lichen. "I started near station . . . 17, I think."

Daxo nods to Holiday and she steps away to radio teams to search the buildings in the area. "They'll have gone by now, so send the forensics teams." He looks over to Theodora. "I want satellite footage showing all ships entering and leaving that district."

"You're doing wonderfully, Lyria," Theodora says. "This is the only way to help yourself—by continuing to cooperate." I don't like the way she says it. "Now," she says with a soft smile, "when did the Society recruit you?"

"What? The Society? I wasn't workin' for anyone."

"You expect us to believe that?" Daxo asks. "My father brings you in, shows you kindness, shows your nephew kindness, and you betray us to the Society—or was it the Red Hand? Tell me the truth."

"I am."

"We have video of the device used to disable the transport before it fried the cameras," Daxo says. "Preliminary forensics tell us that it was a custom build made at great expense. Far beyond your means."

"If you have the video, then can you see my face?" I snap. "Did I look like a person who expected my necklace to burst into a bloody robot?"

"If you weren't complicit, then why did your *Philippe* take you with him?" Niobe says softly. Rain falls on the windows behind her. "Why not leave you behind? Or kill you? Why save your life?"

"Do I look like a lowlife thug smart enough to make fools out of the lot of you? No. So how the hell would I have a bloody clue? Ask him."

"Was it during your time in the assimilation camp?" Theodora asks. "Is that when someone contacted you, asked you for a favor, or promised you something so long as you helped them? Is that when you met Philippe?"

I glare at her. "I met him here."

"Is your name really Lyria of Lagalos?" Daxo asks.

"You know it is, or you wouldn't have let me work in your father's house."

Daxo watches me for some sign of duplicity, his hand stroking the aquarium again. "I've played this game since I was a boy, Lyria. Half-truths. Hidden hands. The Ash Lord is a master at this subterfuge, as is his daughter. It would not take much to massacre a Red camp. Even less to place one of his agents amongst the survivors. Wound her. Have her impersonate a Red of Lagalos, and then play upon the sympathies of my father so that you could slide into our house. Discredit the Sovereign's judgment just before the vote on the Peace." He looks me over. "You look a lamb, but perhaps a wolf lies under the wool?"

"I was born in Lagalos. I can tell you the name of every headTalk and Helldiver for the last thirty years. Try me."

"But of course you can, Society Intelligence trains its agents well. Perhaps you even believe you are who you claim to be. Perhaps they conditioned you. Your memories, your history, your grief for your dead family could all be a fiction."

"Slag you. My sister was not a *fiction*. And neither is Liam. You think he's a spy too?" I try to breathe the quick anger out, remember my sister, the smiles and warm embraces. "I am a Red of Lagalos. I am not working for the *slavers*."

"No, of course not," Theodora says. "The Society killed her mother. Isn't that right, Lyria? They denied her the medication that would have saved her life." I nod. At least she understands. I'd rather die than help the Society. "Her blood, along with so many others, is on their hands."

"That's right."

"And the blood of your family is on the hands of the Republic." My gut twists. "The Republic should have protected you." Her eyes glisten with empathy. She leans forward. She understands. "We liberated you from the mines, promised you a new life. And then we let murderers take everything from you. We hurt you more than the Society ever could. Didn't we?"

I wipe the tears of anger that fill my eyes.

"You're right to blame us," Theodora says softly. "You're right to blame the Sovereign. Their deaths are her fault. So it's only right you want revenge. Was it the Red Hand?"

"You aren't listening to me!"

Daxo takes over. "They died because of her. Your father, your sister, your brother, your nieces and nephews. You wanted to hurt the Sovereign."

"No!"

"To get her back because it was her fault. Her fault that they are dead. Her fault that you are alone. You blame her. Don't you?"

"Yes, I blame her!" The rage oozes out of me, dark and nasty. "That bitch brought us up from the mines and put us in a camp to rot. The Red Hand took everything. And she didn't stop 'em. She didn't even try, 'cause she had bigger shit to worry about. Like birthday galas and walks in the bloody gardens. They're dead because she promised freight she couldn't deliver." I stab a finger on the table. "But I'm not working for anyone. And I would never hurt a child."

My composure cracks as the last word comes out. I've bottled it up inside, this anger, thought I could keep it down and forget the pain. But it wasn't ever forgotten. Being closer to these people has made it worse. Philippe saw that something inside me is broken, and he used it. The Pink watches me with pitying eyes.

"Use the Oracle," she says softly.

"The Oracle," Niobe whispers.

"They have Pax and Electra," Daxo replies. "You saw Father. What do you think they're doing to them?" His mother's shoulders slump. "It has to be done. Holiday, hold her down."

The Gray hesitates. "Does the Sovereign know?"

"We are her council," Theodora says. "You told Darrow you would protect his family. When he returns, do you want to tell him you failed?"

Holiday's hands bruise my shoulders as she grabs me. Daxo reaches into the aquarium and pulls free the carved monster. Its legs claw at the air as he approaches me. The scent of its pale flesh is sweet, like candied almonds. Its scorpion tail is covered with a plastic cap and waves as it sees my exposed forearm. I shiver in fear, begging them to stop. They don't listen. I knew this would happen. I knew the Sovereign would have her men peel me apart. But it doesn't make the horror any easier. In Daxo's other hand is a small knife. He draws a shallow wound on the underside of my forearm.

"Stop!" I beg. "Please! I'm telling the truth."

"We will soon find out."

The creature lunges for the blood and begins to suck. Its cold, slippery legs hug my arm like the fingers of an old woman. I jerk in horror, but go nowhere under Holiday's hold. "Let us begin again," Theodora says. "Who—"

"What are you doing?" an angry voice says from behind.

Niobe sweeps into a bow. Daxo follows, his less deep. "Virginia. The girl is intransigent," he says. "We need what she knows." I crane my neck around and see the Sovereign standing at the door in a tunic of white.

"Did I say you could torture her, Daxo?"

He meets her gaze without flinching. "There's no need for you to see it. This is why you have us."

"Because I'm such a frail flower that I need bold souls to do my torturing for me?" She sneers. "Niobe, even you?"

"After what was done to Kavax—"

"Yes. And what would he say about this?" She waits. Then, whipping out her razor, she storms to my side and grips the barbed tail of the creature sucking my blood. She stabs it in the back of the head. It screams like a human child, tail thrashing in her hand. She flings it to the ground, where it crawls and finally shudders to death. She turns on Theodora. "I told you to kill all those monsters. Years ago.

Did you not hear me or is insolence now to be expected from my spymaster?"

"I preserved a litter," Theodora says. "To protect your family I would do anything."

"If Darrow were here . . ."

"I would look him in the eye and tell him I will not stop till his child is found, without apology and without remorse."

"And will you tell him that his child is lost?" Theodora is taken aback. "Oh, you thought I didn't know you helped him get into Deepgrave to release a war criminal who tried to murder my family in our sleep?"

"Virginia . . ."

"No." The Sovereign raises a hand. "I tire of being treated like a child by my own council because I have chosen to obey the laws. You're no different than Victra. You mistake morality for naïveté. Now get out. I don't want to look at any of you any longer. It's time I talk with the girl alone."

50

LYRIA

Mother

THE SOVEREIGN WATCHES ME from Daxo's vacated chair. I feel shredded and thin from the interrogation. The horror of the Oracle has not fled. I still feel its legs around my arm.

Only Holiday remains with us in the room. I glance at the Gray nervously out of the corner of my eye, knowing if there's pain to come, it'll be from her.

The Sovereign is dressed simply, her hair held back from her head in a ponytail. Unlike most Golds you see on the street, she doesn't wear jewelry, only a gold lion ring on her left middle finger for House Augustus, and an iron ring of a howling wolf on her right. She's younger than I thought she was when I first saw her. But her youth doesn't make her look vulnerable. It makes her look alive, powerful. No wonder a boy from the mines fell in love with her. I used to think it a betrayal. He should have stuck with his own. But how could he resist a woman like this?

"I apologize for that," she says softly. "They are . . . afraid."

I nod, barely hearing her. "Your son—"

She interrupts. "Why did you return? Whether you were working for someone or were simply used, you knew the dangers in coming back here."

"What does it matter?" I ask in frustration. "We're wasting time. Your son is out there. . . ."

"You think that fact is lost on me?" I shake my head. "Understand that you are a stranger to me. I have seen you twice—in Quicksilver's meeting room and again on the landing pad . . ." She saw me watching her there? I was a hundred meters away. What doesn't she miss? ". . . and both times you were listening and seeing more than appropriate. That and your dossier and testimony from Telemanus servants and their steward are all the information I have of you. They say you are angry, judgmental, and isolated. The picture of a terrorist. So, to your question: why do your motivations for returning matter? Because any information you give is suspect. If you want me to believe you, you must first make me believe *in* you. If you fail . . ."

"Then you torture me again?"

"No. I stop wasting my time. Why did you return?"

"Because it is the right thing to do."

She shakes her head. "Not enough. Try again."

I don't know what answer she wants. But I understand there's no point in bluntly answering her questions like I did the others'. She's not like them. So how do I reach her? How do I make her understand? I search her face and find no hint. But there's something we have in common. Perhaps the only thing.

"Your . . . husband was a Red . . ." I say haltingly.

"He is a Red," she corrects. "No matter what the Vox Populi say."

"If you saw my dossier and talked to Kavax, you know how I came to be here, on Luna. What . . . what happened to my family. And you know I brought my nephew with me and that he is in the Citadel school."

I touch the Sigils on the back of my hands self-consciously.

"If I ran, Liam would grow up without a family, thinking I was a terrorist. And he'd feel small the rest of his life. He'd think the evil's in his blood. That he deserves shame. And he'd believe what they say about us, about Reds—that one of us was worth more than the rest of us combined. About Gamma—that we're greedy in the blood." I shake my head. "I'd sooner rip my eyes out than let him feel that. I . . . I promised my sister I would protect him. And I will. Liam will be proud of who he is, who his family was, and the Gamma blood that runs in his veins. So throw me in Deepgrave. Kill me. My life doesn't mean shit. Your son's life does. The girl's life does. And if I can help save them, then Liam can hold his head up high." I pause. "And so can I."

She watches me without a smile. The moment stretches. I've not reached her. I'm not smart like them. I know it deep down. But then she smiles.

"That is something I can believe."

I breathe in relief and let my hands relax, not realizing I'd been clenching them into fists this whole time. "The key to this seems to be the man you call Philippe." She motions to Holiday. The woman opens her datapad on the table and waits for her instructions. "Where did you meet him?"

"On Hyperion Promenade outside the museum. I'd just come from the exhibits there and a Gold . . . a woman accused me of pickpocketing her. I hadn't. Think it was another Red. I got thrown in cuffs and they were haulin' me up when Philippe came and talked 'em out of it."

"This was Tuesday the seventeenth," she confirms.

"How did you . . ." Realization dawns. "My flexipass."

She looks at the projection from Holiday's datapad. Various angles of me touring the museum glow in the air. "On which side of the museum did you meet him?"

"The west entrance."

"That's our blackspot, yes?" the Sovereign asks Holiday.

The Gray nods. "The cameras there were scrambled with laser disrupters."

"Just like we guessed. Something happened there. It's likely the Red pickpocket was working for Philippe." I watch her mind work, wondering what else they've pieced together while I've been running for my life. "If Philippe talked the officers down, then there would be no incident report. But the officers would have bodycams. Holiday . . ."

"Already in Watchmen Central Command. Searching for officers on duty in the area." She pauses. "Shit. There's more than a hundred. If we had his name . . ."

"Officer Stefano," I say abruptly. "He was the older officer. From what he said, he was Warden Cohort."

The Sovereign looks at me in surprise. "Holiday . . . ?"

"Found him. Stefano ti Gregorovich, First Sergeant. He was on duty around the museum that day." Holiday glances sideways at me.

"Very good, Lyria," the Sovereign says. Holiday pulls up Stefano's bodycam and blurs through his day, starting in the precinct locker room, whizzing past interactions with vagrants and young hoods spraying graffiti of the Sovereign mating with a wolf, before coming to me. They speed through my arrest. And just when I'm loaded into the wagon, the camera distorts.

"Feed's dead for ten minutes," Holiday says. "His partner's too."

"So we have a ghost," the Sovereign says. "A gravWell, a blast door, zero DNA, Citadel intinerary information . . . this isn't some low-level operator. But at least it narrows the field. I don't think it's Red Hand, despite their mark—they don't have the resources. Did you go anywhere else with him?" I tell her the sites we visited. As Holiday works, the Sovereign continues. "And at what point did Philippe give you the EMP drone?"

"It wasn't that day. It was later on."

"Under what pretenses did he offer it?"

"Sorry? Pretenses?"

"Why did he give it to you? More importantly, why did you take it?"

"He said it was because we were friends," I admit in embarrassment. "Should have known something was wrong. Got security clearance training. I know we aren't supposed to take gifts, but . . ." I don't say it. But I think it. I was lonely.

"Don't blame yourself. If he knew to target you, then he knew your position in the Telemanus house well enough to know when on the itinerary you would be with my son and in the proper position for his plan to come into effect. That would mean he had access to your personnel files. He knew about your family." She grimaces. "He knew how to play you."

Play me. Like I'm not even a person. When I told him about my family, he already knew. It makes me nauseous.

"Got the feeds from Aristotle Park and the restaurant," Holiday says. Then she curses. "They're slagged." She throws them into the air from her datapad. A score of videos of me in the streets and the monuments appear. Philippe is there in his dark suit, but in place of his head and face is a flaming sphere of white fire.

"What is that?" the Sovereign asks.

"Blighter," Holiday says, surprised the Sovereign doesn't know. "New blackmarket tech. Giving the Watchmen a hell of a time. It uses a prism of high-frequency light waves to create an invisible mask around the user to slag facial recognition. Not as thorough as a jammer, but more range and more elegant with a fraction the power usage. Same breed as the ones used on Earth last month." A knowing look passes between them.

"Could they be connected?" Holiday asks.

"I really don't see how. Unless it's meant to draw him out. If that's the case, we can expect this to be public soon. If it's not public, then we know the ransom will be political, and I'm the target. Or Victra."

Holiday absorbs the consequences of that deeper than I can. She looks back at her screens, a shade paler. "He also paid at the restaurant with a ghost debit card. Anonymous account now with a balance of a hundred credits. The card was used only on that day, once at a tech vendor for a datapad, twice at museums, at a coffee shop, at the restaurant, and at a shop on Alemaide Street."

"What did he buy at the shop?" the Sovereign asks.

"Item 22342C. Cross-referencing with their online catalogue." She pauses. "A toy lion."

"He's mocking us." The Sovereign watches out the window as a ship passes, thinking. Since the questioning began, her face has guarded her inner workings. But now I see how afraid she is. I saw the same look on my sister's face when I told her the Red Hand had come. There's nothing like a mother's fear. I feel sudden pity for the woman.

"We found a Red at the scene of the accident. Dead. Body torched. Did you see any other accomplices?"

"He had a crow with him," I say.

"He had an Obsidian?" Holiday asks tensely. "What did he look like?"

"It was a she."

She parses the word. "A she?"

"Saw her from behind. Big, white hair . . . She . . . shot Kavax."

"Do you have any idea why he took you with him from the shuttle?" the Sovereign asks. "That's the one piece of this that doesn't measure up."

"No. He was gonna kill me. Had his gun to my face and all that. But then he didn't. He dragged me out and said he was going to set me free, give me some money to start a new life."

The Sovereign frowns. "The men that Philippe delivered the children to. Do you remember anything about them aside from what you already told us?"

"I couldn't see most of their faces. It was dark and they wore black. But there was one . . . a Pink. The boss."

"Is there anything else you remember about him? A name? A scar? A ring? Anything . . ."

"No . . . wait." I search my memory. "He had a cane."

"Were there any embellishments on it?"

I squint, trying to remember. "It was white, the length of it. The top was black. Shaped like a monster."

"A monster," the Sovereign repeats. "What sort?"

"I couldn't tell, but it looked like it had arms . . . loads of 'em."

The Sovereign pulls out her own datapad and throws an image of a fleshy, multi-limbed creature into the air in front of me. "Is this the monster?"

"I think so. Yeah."

The Sovereign stares at me. "You're certain this was on his cane?"

"Sure. I mean yes. Why? What does it mean?"

She doesn't answer. Holiday shifts in worry. "Ma'am . . ."

The Sovereign rises from her chair and walks to the window, where she stands for almost a full minute before speaking. "It's not a monster, Lyria. It's a cephalopod. An octopus. It is the symbol of the Syndicate." She turns back to face us. "The Syndicate has my son."

Dark fear seeps from her eyes into the room. And for the first time, she does not seem in control, not of this room, not of this world, not of the fate of her own son.

"The Syndicate . . ." I repeat. Even on Mars we've heard of the Syndicate. Reds will pay three years' wages for them to smuggle their families to Agea or Attica or even Luna. Many never make it.

"It's a criminal organization, a highly evolved one that ruled the underworld of Luna for years," the Sovereign explains. "When the Society fell, there was a civil war among them until a new leader bound the survivors together and then purged the rest of the gangs. She's known as the Queen. The man you saw was likely one of her dukes. In all likelihood, it is the Duke of Hands, her prince of thieves. As far as I know, you're the only person outside the Syndicate ever to have met him and lived. Your Philippe was likely a thorn."

"It can't be them," Holiday whispers. "They're just criminals. They wouldn't dare cross the Sovereign. . . ."

"They wouldn't have dared against Octavia, no. But they're not afraid of me. Just like the Vox Populi." She's quiet and looks at the door her council went through. "Maybe Victra was right. I invited this. I gave away all my teeth."

"Damn Victra. The Republic should never be the Society," Holiday says firmly. "Isn't that the point of all this?"

"What was it that Lorn once said? 'Mercy emboldens evil men.'"

"Why do they want your son?" I ask.

"Leverage . . ." She has an epiphany but doesn't share it. "Holiday, we need Theodora to contact Darrow. Call an emergency meeting of the Sovereign Council. Then find me Dancer. I want him in my office in an hour."

"What about the girl?"

The Sovereign looks down at me. "I will need you to testify. And there will be more questions. For now, my steward will see that you have food and a room."

Holiday motions me to the door. I'm dismissed. I want to wish the Sovereign well, tell her I'll be praying for her son. But I doubt the words will be well received. "I hope the gun helps," I say. "I didn't think about fingerprints till after. Mind was mud. But maybe some of his are still on there."

"Gun?" the Sovereign asks, turning around. "What gun?"

Holiday looks as clueless as her master.

"The gun I had when I came to the checkpoint," I say. "I stole it from Philippe's car. It's his."

The Sovereign wheels on Holiday. "Where are the Watchmen?"

"In holding."

"Send a team to the checkpoint. *Now*. Tell them to turn the place upside down."

"What's happening?" I ask.

"We weren't given a gun."

"I told them it was his."

"Well, they didn't tell us," Holiday says.

The Lionguard teams arrive at the checkpoint by air. We watch via their helmet holoCams as they search the building. They find the pistol stored in a boot bag at the bottom of a Watchman's locker. "That's a Vulcan Omnivore," Holiday says distantly. "They only made one line of them about sixty years back. It's a collector's item. Worth tens of thousands. One of them must have nipped it to sell."

I'm a second behind the Sovereign in noticing the strange tone in Holiday's voice.

"Running forensics," one of the Lionguards says over his com. A holo of the gun appears in the center of the Sovereign's conference table. My fingerprints show up on the barrel, trigger, and hilt. But a second set from larger fingers stands out on the battery pack.

"Filtering through the Index," Holiday says in a dead pitch. "Match found. Piraeus Insurance company register 741 PCE." She swallows. "Ephraim ti Horn, claims investigator." The swarthy face of a man in his thirties appears in the air. His eyes are narrow and mischievous, his mouth pinched in playful derision. He's much younger than Philippe, his nose smaller and his face thinner.

"Is this your Philippe?" Holiday asks.

"His nose is smaller. His cheeks are different."

"He might have worn prosthetics."

I lean forward toward the holo as she plays an interview clip from his personnel file. The man sits with his feet up on his desk, talking to the camera in a bored, Luna lilt. "*. . . it seems the case of the missing Renoir comes down not to the cunning of a cat burglar but to a mere case of bankruptcy due to moral putrescence. This is fraud. Plain. And. Simple. I recommend denying recoupment and throw the fucker in Whitehold.*"

"That's him. That's the bloodydamn bastard in the flesh."

Holiday lets out a heavy, wounded sigh.

"Do you know him, Holiday?" the Sovereign asks.

The stocky woman nods and laughs a sad laugh to herself. "You could say so. He's my brother-in-law."

51

EPHRAIM

Skyhook

I T IS MY LAST DAY on Luna. Still dark cycle, but the sunrise stains the east. I sit watching the fledgling dawn with a glass of vodka from the heated terrace of a hotel suite I've rented. Tomorrow Volga and I will take the private shuttle I chartered to Earth, where all enemies of the state go to disappear. Digital monitoring on the old planet hasn't quite caught up to Luna's. Mars was an option, but it's too unstable for my taste. I've been drinking since word reached me earlier that one of the Syndicate heavies killed a Red girl near the warehouse. I pour a glass of vodka for the little rabbit. Add a zoladone for myself.

She will have died bloody and scared in an alleyway. Hacked apart by hatchets and blades, just like her family. The ache of it in my chest fades as the zoladone spreads its cool, careless fingers through me.

Over the sprawl of the Mass and the flickering cityscape, I see Hyperion. Beyond her, a faint stain of pink that bleeds into a bruised sky littered with skyhooks and blinking satellites and the vein of starships from the AID that make their way into space.

Soon I'll be on one of them. Not soon enough.

Lionheart's killers, Holiday included, will be peeling Hyperion apart.

I look up as Volga trudges out onto the balcony. We came directly from our meeting with the Duke and paid cash for one of the suites at the penthouse level. They are sound-sealed and come with autonomous security systems as well as smoked glass for privacy. I reach under my armpit for the reassuring feel of my Omnivore only to grip empty leather. I'm naked without that gun.

I look back down at the city that has been my home since my mother spat me out, the youngest pup of six. I was just a government check to her. And to the government, I was just another dog for the pack. I never tricked myself into thinking my city cared about me, but I cared for it in a way I never cared for the Society. I fought to free it. I fought for it when Gold came to reclaim it. Now it changes around me. Old swallowed by new. And at the heart of the new is something I don't understand. Some wild, frenzied clamor for power, for riches—a war of all against all.

I played along, but it wasn't me.

The more I think about the Syndicate, the more I understand it was only natural that they would grow bored of running the petty crime of this moon. Of course they would reach for the next rung, for politics. I gave them a boost.

Why *do* they want the children?

I thought I could close the book on this job just like the rest. But this is different, bigger, and I can't fool myself into shrinking it down. Cyra and Dano are dead because I pulled them into this. Not just the job with the Syndicate, but this life. I look across the deck at Volga, who has her arms barricaded around her chest like bulwarks. My only friend. She wasn't a criminal till she met me. She was in love with the idea of the city. So many people from so many places. Then I pulled her into the shadows because I needed a guard dog. She'd be better off without me. *Everyone* is better off without me.

In the grip of the zoladone, the idea is served cold, wrapped pristine in logic.

Sound from the holoNews trickles from the suite's living room out onto the balcony. A rainstorm is coming for Hyperion. The Reaper has been spotted on Mars and Obsidians are disappearing all over the Republic. There's been no news of the kidnapping on the holos. Nothing but a blip of how a government ship went down from mechanical failure and that all on board survived.

The silence is part of the game.

The Sovereign is compromised. They have her son. But she keeps it a secret to keep Dancer and his ilk from getting the upper hand on her. So what will the Syndicate demand as ransom? That is the trillion-credit question.

"Do you regret it?" Volga asks.

"Be more specific. Selling children? No. Love that. Being mocked by a psychopathic crimelord and now hunted by sociopathic Golds? Fun stuff. Or maybe having our colleagues butchered in front of us?" Feeling the tension in my neck and bubbling in my brain, I pull out a second zoladone and roll it around in my palm. I'm about to down it to feel the sweet numbness, when Volga knocks it out of my hand and takes the dispenser off the table beside me.

"Volga, don't be a twat."

"No more."

"Give me the dispenser. Volga . . ."

"I am tired of you walking around asleep. Tired of seeing you numb. It's too easy for you. Feel bad, pop pill. Snort dust. Drink booze. Feel good."

"Do I look like someone who feels good?"

"No." Her big lips curl. "You feel nothing."

"Give me the dispenser."

"No."

"Volga, you pale shit. Give me my dispenser."

"You are not my master. Come take it if you want it," she says with a shrug. I lunge up for it, and she pushes me to the side so I trip over one of the chairs and crash down, a blinding pain going through the old wound in my right knee. She doesn't apologize when I crawl up from the chair.

"Give it back."

"Fetch." She throws it off the balcony and it spirals down into the aerial traffic beneath. I rush to the edge and watch it disappear from sight.

"You little monster," I mutter.

Her nose flares wide. She pushes me again with her left hand, her huge strength sending me stumbling back. My cracked ribs lance with pain. I can't breathe. She comes after me and hits me in the chest again, knocking me off my feet. I fall hard on the marble balcony, shoulder blades smacking into the stone.

"Do you feel anything now?" she asks.

"Oh, fuck . . . off." I cough.

She puts a boot in my stomach and begins to push down. "Now?" With my right hand I reach into my boot to grab the stunner there. I jam it into her leg. Her skin underneath her pants crackles as it burns. She grimaces in pain, her eyes going dark as the pain summons the bloodlust hidden in her genes. "Volga . . ." I say. "Volga, no!" She lifts me up in a rage, easy as a pillow, and holds me with both hands, about to throw me over the edge of the balcony. I stare at the aerials hundreds of meters below.

"Do it," I sneer. "Go on. Do it, you monster."

The grip loosens and my world reorients as she sets me down. I sit there on the ground, breathing heavily. She collapses into the chair, almost breaking it, and stares at me with tears in her eyes. "I'm not a monster. I'm not." She looks up at me, her eyes puffy and swollen. "But you are. They were just children."

"You knew what we were trying to do," I say, rubbing my ribs. She definitely cracked a few more. "That someone could die. Now you cry about it because you can't handle the guilt?" I snort. "Grow up. You did the deed. Same as me. Now go buy yourself a spine and a good fuck with all that blood money. Jove knows you need both." She stares at me as if she can't believe what she's hearing. I don't know what else she expected. The deed's done. Time to move on. "Why'd you even go along with it if your panties were in such a bunch?"

"I did it for you!" she says in a pitiful voice. "I did it because you needed me. I've always needed you. You brought me here. You're my family. And I've never been able to do anything for you. Every time I try, you get angry. 'Go home, Volga. Fuck off, Volga.' But here. *This.* It was something I could do to help. I could have your back, like you have mine. I did not know it would be so hard."

She sits there trying to stop crying. Her huge shoulders heave up and down.

I don't know what to do. "Just think of the new adventures we are about to begin," I say distantly. "A tour of Africa. The seafood. The animals. The whores of the Barbary Coast!"

She looks up with puffy eyes. "Do you think they will kill them?"

"No. They won't kill them. You heard the Duke. No rough stuff. What use is a dead hostage? They'll want more money or something, I guess. I don't know. It doesn't matter. It's not our business."

"Not our business? We're a part of this, Ephraim. Part of the Republic."

"Why? 'Cause we live here? That's the sort of shit they want you to think so you go along thinking you got skin in the game. It's all a scam, princess. You're never fighting for yourself. You're always fighting for them. Lune, Augustus, Reaper, what's the damn difference?"

"Why are you like this?"

"Like what?"

"Evil."

I sigh. "I'm not evil."

"Then what are you?"

"Self-aware. You can't take care of anyone. That's not how it works. All you can do is take care of yourself. No one else is going to."

"I would take care of you."

I roll my eyes. "You think those children care about you? You think they would grow up into people who would care about you? To them, you're just a weapon."

"And what am I to you?" Volga asks. "If I was not a weapon, you would not keep me with you."

"Well, I sure as hell don't keep you around for the conversation."

By the look in her eyes, I know I've finally gone too far.

Something breaks. Something important. "Volga." My hand reaches out halfheartedly like she's falling as she takes a step back from me. But then I lower my hand, and she sees me lower it, and she turns and walks away. The door to the suite slams and she's gone, and I know deep down under the cool tide of the zoladone that this is how our story together ends.

Alone again. And better for it.

I leave the hotel room soon after Volga has gone. I don't go back to my spot, fearing Republic Intelligence or maybe Gorgo might pay a visit. Instead, I find myself in the street outside Cyra's apartment, staring up at the glass building that billows up into the sky like a piece of string on the end of an airduct. I wanted to see where Cyra lived. I don't know why. Maybe for closure. To see how she lived so I can understand why she put a dagger in my back; but I can't go inside. There's retinal scanners in the lobby, and the building has private guards.

So I stand on the street as the rain falls, looking up at the building, wondering which glass window Cyra looked out and will never look out again, and realizing I never understood who she was, not really. Not her. Not Dano. Because I kept them on the street looking in, and they returned the favor in kind.

I walk the streets, passing through steam coming up out of the sewers, through a forest of noodle vendors and fleshtech salesmen, all calling to passersby. They transmit a kaleidoscope of sex advertisements from holo broadcasters perched on their shoulders like metal gargoyles. I walk the old route Trigg and I used to take from the Promenade, past the Gravity Gardens, all the way south to seedy Old Town. I outstrip the path we walked together and continue into the early hours of the morning, long enough to witness the changing of the guard from the nocturnal men to those of the day. All of it bathed in the hazy pink of the long sunrise.

As the city wakes, I eat a breakfast of doughy cinnamon noodles and coffee at one of my favorite old stands on the edge of the wharf, and feed the seagulls like Trigg used to. Below, in the water of the Sea of Serenity, large scrubbing robots collect litter. Afterwards, I catch a cab to my storage unit. In one of the private rooms, another slender robot with forklift arms sets the metal box onto the table and leaves me. In the box are my ready bags. Two of them, both slick black leather. I'm surprised how much it depresses me thinking this is all I have of my life. A thief with nothing worth packing. Sounds like a bad joke. Maybe this is what I've been looking for. A chance to start clean. I've got nothing aside from stacks of hard plastic currency in the bags, IDs, several DNA sleeves, two suits, the two pistols, and a stash of backup zoladone pills. I pocket those, but I don't take one yet. Save it for the ride.

I take a cab to the private aerial skyhook, a floating star-shaped port for the rich and famous three kilometers above the city. It's suspended there on gravLifts, room enough for ten private yachts to dock. It's offensively expensive chartering a private ship, but I need to be armed, so commercial is out of the question. I'm deposited on the top level of the skyhook at the reception level. The taxi takes off the concrete runway and dips back down into the flow of terrestrial traffic, leaving me in a parklike expanse above the clouds. A fashionable Pink stands behind a reception desk in a white uniform with a tilted cap on her head and a fur coat. I shiver in the thin air.

"Good afternoon, citizen. Welcome to Zephyrus Trans-Terrestrial. Will you be checking in for your flight today?"

In my pocket, I slip one of the transparent DNA sleeves over my finger. I pretend to lick the finger and I swipe it through her sampler. "Ah, Mr. Garabaldi." She smiles obligingly as her computer registers one of my false IDs. "We're so pleased to have you today. The *Eurydice Wind* will be ready to receive you in thirty minutes. Your pilots are performing preflight checks."

"Am I the first passenger to arrive?"

She references the manifest. "Yes, Ms. Bjorl has not yet arrived."

"Notify me when she does."

"Of course. You may depart whenever you like after the preflight checks have been performed, but we welcome you to enjoy our worlds-famous services in the terminal until then." She pushes me a holoMap from her datapad. Mine catches it. "You'll see that we have two spas, a saltwater pool, alt reality pods, massage and pleasure staff on hand. We also have a game room, two lounges—the twilight and the sky. . . ."

I follow a bellhop who takes my bags to the well-appointed bar. A man plays a piano in the corner of the sunrise-washed room. I sit on the crème leather, my back to the windowbanks of clouds and eerie pink sky, my eyes on the door, waiting for Volga's immense bulk to fill it. Other passengers come and go. Most are Gold and Silver, and their conversations tinkle like spoons on rare china. Some are actresses I recognize, and one or two famous racers. Soon it sounds like the buzzing of gnats to my ears, claustrophobic, irritating. The cramps from zoladone withdrawal are starting. Still I don't take one.

After my third drink, Volga hasn't arrived. I retire to the ship, where I meet the Blue captain and flight crew and settle my bags in the sleeping quarters. The flight stewardess makes me a vodka litchi and I wait for Volga in the ship's lounge. An hour. Then two more.

By midday, I finally digest the fact that Volga is not coming. A loneliness settles in me. Not a pang, to which I'm accustomed, but the deep loneliness of knowing that this is it. This is the bottom. A two-bag life for one. The end of a friendship, set to the sound of the droning holoNews and the slam of a door. My newest vodka litchi seems suddenly very tasteless. The gravity in the cabin eerily absent. When booking, I had asked the captain to put on null grav for the preflight. I did that for Volga. It was something she missed from our first flight from Earth to Luna. No point to it now. I've always hated the feeling of space. I ask the stewardess to kill the null grav and tell her that I'm ready to depart. Ms. Bjorl isn't coming.

I head to the lavatory to relieve myself before the main engine ignition. I take antinausea medication and am about to go back to the lounge when I remember I should alter my destination now that Volga isn't coming, in case her conscience gets the better of her and she goes to the authorities. Goodbye, Africa; hello, Echo City. I climb the stairs to the flight deck. It's empty. Quiet. The flight crew that had been preparing me a meal in the kitchen is gone. I check their small bunkrooms. Nothing. This isn't good. I creep past the kitchen toward the cockpit and peer inside. The pilots are gone too. Nothing seems amiss out the cockpit viewports. The landing pad is deserted and it's clear sky beyond that. Still, something is wrong. I pull my snub-nosed pistol from under my armpit.

Have the Syndicate come back to finish me after all?

I move through the hall. The gun is slippery in my sweaty palms.

I clear the top level and look down the flight of stairs, listening for movement. Hearing nothing, I creep down the stairs.

In the lounge I hear something. Voices. Volga? I burst into the lounge with my pistol out in front to find two women staring at me from the leather flight chairs. "Holiday . . ." The word sticks in my throat like a shattered chicken bone. She sits with her elbows on her knees, in civi clothes. Black pants, boots, and a hunter-green leather jacket that looks like it's got some sort of concealed pulseShield generator sewn into the fabric of the left sleeve. A heavy railgun pistol is strapped into the holster on her right thigh. Woman is ready for urban warfare. And at her side, in new clothes and freshly washed hair, sits the rabbit, with blinding hate in her rusty eyes. Her arm's in a sling. "Ah. Shit . . ."

"Sit down, Ephraim," Holiday says.

I keep the gun on them and look down the hall for others they might have brought with them. They seem alone, but there's likely a squad of lurcher commandos waiting just inside the terminal. It's over. I laugh bitterly and point a finger at Lyria. "You're supposed to be dead."

"That'd be easier for you, wouldn't it?"

"How did you get past the Obsidians?"

She makes a face at me. "Magic."

I grunt. "How did you find me?"

"We are the State," Holiday says. "How long did you think you could hide?"

"Longer than a day," I admit. "Do you mind if I make myself a drink? Or four?" I ease toward the wet bar.

"Shut up and sit down."

I frown and look at my pistol. "I'm the one with the gun."

"I'm the one with a Stained in the cargo hold."

"Talk about overkill." I slump into the seat across from hers. I'm surprised to notice that I don't feel defeat or fear. If anything, I feel relief. I engage the safety and put my gun on the table between us, pushing it toward Lyria.

"You'll probably want to use that."

"Already got one," she says, pulling my Omnivore from her jacket and setting it on her knee. There's a fingerlock around the trigger. I smile in seeing it again.

"Escaped the Obsidians. Somehow prevented yourself from being skinned alive by Republic Intelligence. Now sitting here with a gun. Must be magic."

"Ephraim . . ." Lyria starts.

"Call me Philippe, if that makes you more comfortable."

"Slag you."

"Original." I lean back and cross my legs. "So, what happens now? Commandos burst in and drag me to an interrogation tank? Peel off parts of me to give to the Reaper when he gets home? Or will it be chemical torture? Experiential? Lock me in a holoimmersion for a relative century? Or do I have a one-way subaquatic ticket to Deepgrave?"

"This is the part where you tell us where the children are," Holiday says. "Then you tell us who you sold them to. What you know about the Pink with the cane. And how we can get them back. For your sake, I hope you know enough to spare yourself being booked for treason."

"Fortunately, capital punishment is no longer an option," I say.

"We might make an exception."

"How noble."

She leans forward. "You're gonna have to get used to the idea that you're going to spend the rest of your life in a cell, Ephraim. How big that cell is depends on what you tell me."

"Holiday, you've spent too much time in the military. You can't go at a man like that. Give him no means of escape. No incentive. Remember the Eleventh Legion? You were there. The Golden Basilisks." She remembers. "What happens if you surround an enemy force with no path of surrender or retreat? They fight to the death. And that's not good for anyone. Trapped by that dam, weren't they? Do you remember how we just kept firing into them? Eight hours to kill fifty thousand men because we didn't want to break the dam with bombs. Who knew it could take so long? I never saw the Reaper's face after that. But you must have. Did he like it?"

"This isn't a game, Ephraim," she says. "If you hate life so much you want to die, then be my guest. I'll give you the bullet to eat. But don't take two innocent kids with you."

"Innocent? Everyone keeps throwing that shit around. Their parents put them on the board. They didn't have to attend functions of state. They didn't have to parade them around like the paragons of progress. But they did. They made them the targets, not me. How many little kids do you think died in the Battle of Luna? I saw whole blocks disintegrated by Valii-Rath particle beams. Schools turned to dust by termite munitions with Republic stamps on them. Dead kids are the loose change of war. Don't come whining to me because the man and woman who started this don't want to pay out of their own pocket like the rest of us."

I've never seen her look at me with so much disgust. "What happened to you?"

"Life. Same shit that happens to everyone else."

"Trigg would spit on you if he could see this."

"Well, he died on your watch. Not mine."

Holiday looks blankly at me as if I've slapped her across the face.

All the days we met on Trigg's birthday, that truth hung between us, unspoken like some weapon of mutually assured destruction. And now that I say it, I taste ashes in my mouth. To use Trigg like this, as a weapon, is the ultimate perversion of who he was, what he meant to the both of us. But he followed her everywhere. And she led him to his death for a cause that doesn't even remember his name. Holiday can't meet my eyes. But Lyria shakes her head.

"That's not fair, and you know it."

"Save the speeches, love. You're just a little girl who thinks she's a hero. You don't know a thing about me."

"You're right. I don't," she says. "You've gone hard to make that clear. But I know my ma died of cancer in the mines. Ate her lungs right up. Pa thought it was his fault. That he couldn't get her the right meds. Saw it squeeze the life outta him. And by the time we got out of the mines, he was already dead. All he saw—the sky, the world—he hated, because she didn't get to see it. You think she would have wanted that for the man she loved?"

"Never been a slave. Wouldn't know."

"We were promised everything when they brought us up; then I lost my family. My *whole* family. You can whine about your nicks and scrapes, but you got no idea what that's like. Should I turn nasty because I saw evil done to them? Should I blame the worlds? I blamed myself. I blamed the Sovereign. And what luck did that get me?" She clears her throat, emotion welling. "You asked me if I believe in the Vale. I don't know. I don't know if it exists or if they watch me. But I know it doesn't matter if they can see us. What matters is that we can *feel* them. Remember them. And try to live to be as good as we were in their eyes."

I look away from her to the window where pink clouds twirl.

"Trigg might be gone, yeah. I know you feel robbed. But you gotta remember that he saw something to love in you, even if you can't see it. He saw you as a good man, Ephraim. So if you ever loved him, be a good man."

"That man never even existed. It was just something Trigg made up to make himself feel better."

"Then why did you not kill me in the shuttle?"

"I did. I pulled the trigger. The safety was on. It was just luck."

"You could have pulled the trigger again. But you didn't. You let me live."

"And look what happened."

"This man you're playing at. You sure he's not the one you made up to make yourself feel less?"

I feel everything now. As I stare out the window at the ships bound for orbit, I see Trigg in the waters of the Aegean Sea when we took our first vacation during his leave. I remember him playing his little guitar in the hammock behind our bungalow. He sounded terrible but I loved watching the sweat beading on his temples, the freckles on his shoulders, the childish laugh in a man the world kept trying to make hard. He was patient with me. Slowly breaking down the walls that had stood tall since my mother looked at me and said she loved me for the thousand credits a month. He proposed on that vacation.

All the good memories of him have been held hostage by the horror of his exit. Now the bars crack, the doors open, and they flood me. All I want is to say goodbye to him. To let him know he was mine and I was his. But sitting here, surrounded by the ruinous shit I've made, I still can't feel anything but anger.

I look at Holiday and I don't have anything to say. I can't apologize. The words just won't come out; just as she will never apologize for letting him die, not even to herself. But she sees the animal pain in me.

"He would have wanted you to fix this," she says.

"I don't know where they are," I say.

Holiday's more comfortable talking about the kidnapping than she is about Trigg. "Who was it?"

"Syndicate. My contact was the Duke of Hands."

She already knew. "Could you identify him?"

"Yeah. But I doubt he's in the census. He was a Rose. High, *high* end. Private stock of a loaded Gold. Start your search there. And there was an Obsidian named Gorgo, definitely military. Not fresh from the Ice." She takes notes. "What's your exposure, Holiday? What could they want?"

"You tell me. There's been no proof of life. No demands."

"They didn't kill them," I say. "The Duke said they were for the Queen."

"Did you meet her?" Holiday asks.

"No. Word in the game is that she's an Obsidian warlord from Earth. No one knows for sure."

"Really?" Holiday frowns. "Republic Intelligence has been operating under the assumption that she's a Red for more than a year now."

"A Red?" Lyria whispers.

"You think Obsidians would follow a Red?" I laugh.

"There's also a chance they're working with the Society," Holiday says.

"That seems unlikely."

"Why?"

"The Duke was a slave. He loathes the slavers. If he's working for the Ash Lord, he doesn't know it. Is this about the Peace?"

"Maybe." Holiday looks out the window nervously, or as nervous as a woman with a head like a cinder block can look.

"Expecting someone?"

"You should tell him," Lyria says. "He's got the right to know."

"Know what?" I lean forward. "Know what?"

"We aren't the only ones looking for the children. . . ."

"Slag me." I half stand from my seat. "He's back? The Reaper?" I look out the window, feeling the color drain from my face. "Ares?"

"Worse," Holiday says. "The Lady Julii is on the hunt. And she's out for blood."

"She's eight months pregnant. Forgive me if I don't shake in my boots."

Holiday smiles. "She attacked an Augustan shuttle over Hyperion in full war armor because Lyria was inside."

I stare at her. "I didn't know they made maternity armor."

"They do."

"Does she know it's the Syndicate?"

Holiday shrugs. "We don't know what she knows. And she's not sharing information. We caught some of her investigators breaking into the crash site."

I scratch my head. Fingers are getting itchy for a burner, stomach knotted for more zoladone. "Well, if that woman declares war on the Syndicate, the kids are as good as chopped. They'll start sending body parts to the Citadel in thorn-wrapped boxes."

"Which is why we are here and Republic Intelligence is not," Holiday says. "You know the Syndicate better than we do. We need you to come in and help coordinate the rescue effort."

"Not a chance. They have people in your government."

Holiday squints. "How do you know that?"

"We were given the boy's itinerary more than a month in advance. But they didn't volunteer any other insiders. Prolly didn't want to burn them. Which is why I had to recruit you. . . ." I look at Lyria. "If they know I'm helping you . . ."

"Body parts," Lyria says.

"If we're compromised, then you'll have to retrieve them," Holiday says.

I snort a laugh. "Fuck that."

"Thought you'd say that. I know you don't care about your life,

Ephraim. But something tells me you care about hers." She sets a holocube down on the table and an image of a cell appears with a woman hunched on a bench with her head in her hands. It's Volga.

"We found her at the Cerebian Zoo," Holiday says. "She was easier to find than you were. What wasn't easy was keeping the Telemanuses from killing her on sight."

"If you touch a hair on her head . . ."

"No. It's your turn to listen. Your turn to obey. If you do not do everything I ask, then I will give her to the Telemanuses." Lyria looks as surprised as I am.

"Don't hurt her," I say.

Holiday leans back. "So there is someone in there."

"She didn't want to do it."

"I don't care. You will bring me the children. Then you can have your friend back." She stares back at me without remorse. "This is the game you decided to play."

I look back at the holo and wonder how I ever could have been cruel to Volga. She followed me like a puppy from the day we met. All she gave me was love. She never even asked for it in return. Since she was born she's been a slave, a monster. Kicked down by everyone. Then she found me and I treated her just the same. I feel sick.

"There's a way," I say. "But I want a pardon for me and Volga."

"A pardon? After what you've done?"

"I want it in digital with a third-party negotiator."

"No pardon for the rest of your crew?" Lyria asks.

"They're dead. Why do you think I'm even talking to you?" So much for my code.

"What do you think, my liege?" Holiday says as she looks at me. She tilts her head. "She wants to speak with you." Holiday touches her datapad and the face of the Sovereign appears in front of me. Her eyes are a pure liquid gold that have seen fleets burning off the shoulder of moons and war criminals walk free on her warrant. I hate her without measure.

"Ephraim ti Horn."

"Lionheart." The informality irritates Holiday. "I want Volga released immediately."

"No."

"Then we have a problem."

"She will be released when I have the children back. I will have a binding agreement drawn up via the Ophion Guild."

"Amani," I say.

"Excuse me?"

"Ophion is in the pocket of the Syndicate. You go there with a contract for me, we have a problem. Use Amani." It's a very strange thing telling the most powerful woman in the worlds something she doesn't know. "And I want Volga to be pardoned on the event of my death."

"No."

"We both know how much you like handing out pardons. I know I'm not a Gold rapist or mass murderer, but in the spirit of the Amnesty, surely you can find it in your heart to forgive."

"Do you *want* to die, Mr. Horn?"

"Irrelevant. Volga deserves life."

She's not pleased by my intransigence. Tough shit. "The man she shot was like a father to me. He's still fighting for his life."

"Then I certainly hope you don't lose a father and a child on the same day."

She doesn't react. Her Gold calm is so perfectly preserved and haughty that I want to reach through the holo and throttle her. "Very well," she says. "Holiday will fit you with a transponder. When you locate the Syndicate base, you will signal with this transponder, and a strike team will arrive at your coordinates."

"The Syndicate will check for a transponder."

"It will be hidden."

"And they'll find it. Subdermal, isotope, they'll find it. These aren't street thugs. You might have noticed."

"Then what do you propose?"

"Give me a pad number, and I'll call it. Then your killsquad can track its GPS and fly in and murder everyone in whatever way gets you off."

She doesn't like it, but neither of us has much of a choice. "Very well, Mr. Horn. You have a deal. But I would like you to know one thing. If you attempt to escape, or if you defect to the Syndicate, know this as a certain fact: your friend will die. And be it on Mars, Luna, Earth, the Rim, or Venus itself, one night you will wake in the middle of the dark and find a shadow standing over you. If you are lucky, it will be me. If you are unlucky, it will be Sevro or my husband, and you will die shitting yourself in a foreign bed."

52

DARROW

Host of the Minotaur

IT WAS NOT LONG AGO that a Gray could boast of his allegiance to the Minotaur in a bar and expect his drinks to be paid for wherever the pyramid flag flew. But that was at the fevered height of Apollonius's warlord ascendance, before his betrayal and decline.

Now, a mere 911 men remain of a host that once numbered 250,000. The rest have found employ with House Carthii or House Grimmus. These men stay because they could not serve the betrayers of their master or because they have nowhere to go. Orphaned by duty. Severed from all ties of family by their service to their house. Devoid of any underlying patriotism, they float along through life, like the stubborn jetsam of a once-great ship that refuses to sink under the waves.

Once it might have seemed a dream to live out their pension days in peace on a Venusian island. But these men were not made for peace. The novelty of bedding local sun-browned Pinks from the coastal cities and swimming amongst the coral shoals of the Guinevere Sea is gone and they hunger for something more. I thought there would be several thousand, at least to assist us once we gained our audience with the Ash Lord. But there will be no audience, and this paltry remnant is all that we have.

Sevro, Thraxa, and I watch via holo from Tharsus's library as Apollonius addresses them. He looks out to his soldiers. They stand assembled on the ill-kept tarmac on the south side of his island. Tiny azure-shelled crabs skitter between the weeds in the cracked concrete. The uniforms of the soldiers are untidy. Their necks wreathed in hued shells, hair long in local braids. Apollonius spits on the ground.

"I fear a dread illness has fallen upon the house of my father and mother," he says, pacing before them with his proud shoulders hunched, his mane tied tight to the back of his head. Tharsus stands behind him like a scolded child. "An illness that has leeched the glory from our veins, the color from our banner. It was not brought by you." He looks at his brother. "That blame lies upon the shoulders of another. But it was nurtured by you. Sustained by your torpor. I look at you, and do you know what I see?" He scans the crowd of them with wild eyes. "Do you?" The wind gusts mildly from the early morning sea, rippling their uniforms. "I see . . . *Venusians*."

They shift in shame.

"I see clameaters. Men of war made into simpering sprites and disporting coxcombs. Where is the honor for your fathers and mothers?" he cries. "Where is the fury for your fallen brothers and sisters? The Ash Lord and his simpering allies, the Carthii, sent them to their deaths on Luna. Served us up to the Reaper like a Trimalchian feast. I watched as men and women you knew went to dark death. The Ash Lord betrayed us. It was no secret to you that I languished in the belly of the sea. No. It was known from our homeworld to Mercury."

He paces in venomous silence.

"Yet you let me rot. You let your brothers and sisters perish. And here I find you fattening yourselves like mulling kine, as if Calypso herself had besotted you with wine from her tits. Was your idleness worth the price of your shame? What would your fathers say? What would your mothers think?"

He hangs his head and I find myself admiring the drama of the man. He knows how to play a crowd.

"I look at you and I weep. Such shame is upon me that only Lucifer himself would know the depths of my pain. We have lost our halos, my children, fallen from the grace of heaven through the fabled clouds and landed here in a boiling hell of debauchery and defilement while our enemies laugh at what we have let ourselves become.

"But all is not lost. The unconquerable will, the need for revenge, the immortal hate, and the courage never to submit or yield are strong in my heart." He beats his chest so hard with his fist I feel it through the holo. "I will not rest till vengeance is mine, for I am Apollonius au Valii-Rath. Imperator of the Minotaur Legions. Man of Mars. Iron Gold. Today I ride forth on the wings of battle from this island prison to settle a debt and free myself from this foul affliction of shame. I ride to war. To glory. I ride for the head of the Ash Lord." He lunges forward and lifts his razor. "I would not ride alone. So I say to you, my darkest devils, awake, arise, and reclaim your glory!"

A roar answers him that chills the deeper part of me. I turn off the holo and stand quiet in the echoing silence of the library as an ancient clock ticks on the wall. Sevro runs a hand along his fresh-shaven mohawk. "That's our army?" he mutters. "They're the scraps you leave behind when you eat a rack of ribs."

"They'll do," I say.

"They'll do," he repeats. "On what do you base that? Apollonius? He's barking mad. Riled up for a suicide run. They'll get ripped to shreds out there, and we'll be left holding our pricks against a fortress. We didn't prepare for this."

"How do you prepare for a kick in the balls?" I say. "You don't. You suck it up."

"That supposed to inspire me? His men are past their prime." He glares at me. He's been moody ever since we landed and saw the state of the Valii-Rath holdings. "And they ain't the only ones."

"You trying to say something?"

"Obviously, because everyone else is sucking down your myth like it's milk from a cow's tit."

"Then say it. Go on. Thraxa won't mind." Thraxa looks awkwardly at her datapad.

"I've backed you this whole way. Someone mutters something, I knock them down and give them a good old speech. But you know why I've been loud as a mouse since we got here? I was waiting for you to realize how shit this is. They don't have the manpower. Apollonius is insane. This is not going to work." He crosses his arms and looks as if he's marveling at his own stupidity. "I didn't even want to come. It's been a month since we got any news from home. A bloody-damn month."

My anger flares. "Then why the hell did you come?"

"Because I don't want to raise your kid," he snaps. "I came to keep you breathing. And to keep the rest of them safe from you."

The words knock the anger out of me.

"You think you need to keep them safe from me?"

"Don't I? Look where you've led your best friends. Look how many gravestones follow us. And you know why that is?"

"Have a feeling you're gonna tell me."

"You take shortcuts. Straightest line through any field of shit, and trust that everything will be ripe and splendid."

"Seems to have worked out fine enough. We—"

"Hold on," he says, cutting me off. "Let me ask Ragnar if he agrees." He looks around. "Oh, wait. He's not here. Let me ask Pax. Oops. Lorn . . . oops. Pops . . ." He holds up his hands. "Can't ask him either. You're so hungry to end this that you're gonna gamble the whole mine on one half-assed hand."

"It's not half-assed," I say evenly. "It will work. You're being emotional."

He stares at me with wild eyes—my old Red eyes—and realization dawns in them. "Well, slag me sideways. You really are drunk on your own myth, aren't you? I didn't buy it when Clown said it. But you believe them all. You think you're a god. You can't die."

"Someone has to end this. You can be a father on your own time. Right now, you need to sack up and do your job."

"We shouldn't be here."

"All right, what do you have in mind instead? Run back to Luna with our tails between our legs? Turn ourselves in to the Wardens and watch as the Republic gets gutted by Vox Populi, then carved up by the Ash Lord and the Rim, whenever they decide to stop playing possum? That'll mean we broke out a gang of mass murderers for nothing. That means Wulfgar died for nothing. My voice loses its composure. That means we've fought ten years for *nothing*. And then what do you think happens when the Rim comes?"

"This plan is wasted," he says. "We should cut our losses. Go to Mercury with the fleet if we can't go home. I don't want to die for this fucker."

"I've heard your opinion," I say, trying to keep the anger out of my voice. "Thank you for giving it, Imperator. I've considered what you've said and I've decided the mission is still a go. I want the men fed and the starShells loaded onto the assault shuttle by 16:00. Make sure they stay out of sight. Last thing we need is his legionnaires knowing who they're fighting with."

I wait for him to curse me, maybe hit me. His own fear of not seeing his girls again is making him irrational, a coward even. But he just stares at me and then slowly raises his fist.

"Hail Reaper." He turns on a heel.

"Sevro," I say before he reaches the door, the memory of Roque's departure echoing. He stands there facing the wood. Looking at the back of my friend's scarred head, I feel the distance between us. "I'm sorry you don't agree with me. But I've told you everything I know. And I believe we have the initiative and the means to destroy their command structure."

He nods. "Course you do." He chews his lip. "After this, I'm done. I won't be like you. Won't be like my pops." He looks at me, his eyes protective and spiteful. "My girls will have a da. If that's selfish, I don't give a shit. Let someone else be Ares."

He leaves.

His words play at my doubts, but I don't have time or room for reflection today. I look over at Thraxa. "You have an opinion?"

"Nah. Ain't got the time. Shall I ready the men, sir?"

Two hours later, I stand in the shadow of the hangar bay where the Howlers make preparations on the *Nessus* and our ripWings. Over the clamor of loading gear and curses from Min-Min and Clown, I hear the distant roar of engines as the mobilized might, such as it is, of House Valii-Rath lifts off the tarmac. Forty ripWings ascend from the concrete like ducks off a pond, their engines burning indigo and their shadows languorous and long in the late afternoon light. They fly due south. With them rise the five long assault frigates and assault shuttles, packed with Gray shock troops in grasshopper suits. A tardy trooper rushes to catch the last shuttle, carrying a forgotten token of luck in his hand. The crooked elongated legs of the grasshopper suit pivot backward along a joint behind his knee, then propel him in an inhuman jump to clear the five meters into the craft, where his friends grab his hand and hoist him in.

Apollonius comes to say farewell. He looks at home in his armor. Unlike the stark, muted grandeur of modern Martian gear, his favors the baroque of the Core. At the center of the purple chestplate is his Minotaur. "Hail Reaper," he says mockingly. He closes his eyes and smells the air. "This is life, isn't it?"

"Your men don't know our presence?" I ask.

His eyes are still closed. "The dogs yap of masked men in the night carrying mischief." He opens his eyes and smiles. "Mercenaries. Ronin. Sellswords. By any name they do suspect, except the one that's true. But I would ask you to dissuade your diminutive accomplice from displaying any lupine flavors. My dogs do hate wolves."

"We didn't bring the wolfcloaks with us," I say. "We brought two alpha mega nukes instead." I search his eyes for some sign of duplicity. "My men don't like the fact that you're not coming with us."

"Understandable. All suspect what they do not understand. But we understand one another, do we not, Reaper? Betrayal from friends cuts far deeper than the sword of a foe. We are both the spawn of a war god. Favored of his children, and stand astride the shadow of our lost brother, Achilles." I make no sign of agreeing with him. He sighs. "If I am late, if I am naughty, destroy me." He taps the scar where the bomb went in. "But you and I both know I lead my men into hell's teeth. What commander would I be if I were not amongst them?"

That I can respect.

"In the darkzone your bomb imbed won't respond to our activation signal," I remind him. "As soon as you enter, it will be on a three-hour timer for detonation that can only be deactivated by us. If we die, you'll follow. If you leave the theater of engagement, it is also programmed to detonate." He listens quietly. "I'll see you at the way-point. If you make it, Gold."

He smiles. "I shall wait on you, Red." He extends a hand. Grudgingly, I take it. Sevro watches dourly from the ramp of the *Nessus,* no doubt misjudging my politeness for fondness. Apollonius releases my hand and backs away from me, singing loudly with his huge lungs as his Minotaur helmet rolls out of the neck of his armor to cover his head. The horns, long and twisted, stab into the sky. *"'Into this wild Abyss the warie fiend stood on the brink of Hell and look'd a while, pondering his voyage; for no narrow frith he had to cross!'"*

With that, he rips up from the tarmac on his gravBoots and bends across the sky to join his departing legions. Rhonna comes to watch him leave. "Sir, Colloway says the *Nessus* is ready."

"Are you?" I ask.

"Sir?"

"We need the *Nessus's* firepower, but she's got no maneuverability in atmosphere. She'll be a slow cow. Colloway will be of better use in his ripWing. That means we don't have someone to sync to the *Nessus.* Min-Min will be flying her. And she'll need gunners. You've trained with firing systems, I presume?"

She grins. "Damn straight."

"Good. Go find Winkle, he'll give you access to the gunner chamber."

She salutes. "Thank you, sir." She leaps forward and gives me a kiss on the cheek. "I won't let you down, Uncle." As I watch her run back to the ship, I wish I could say the same. But Sevro sowed doubt in me, and something else gnaws at the back of my mind. No one has seen the Ash Lord in three years. Why? He always led from the vanguard. What is he hiding behind that curtain of darkness?

53

DARROW

Wargod

"MINOTAUR-1 HAS CONTACT. *Engaging enemy,*" Apollonius says over the com.

On the sensor display inside my starShell, the curved edge of the Ash Lord's darkzone blots out the corner of the blue-hued map. The mass of gold dots from Apollonius's small fleet approaches the barrier. I listen to their com chatter as they detect hostile patrols and engage with full force. Two ripWings go down almost immediately; a third disappears into the darkzone. Apollonius's squadron pursues. Soon their signatures disappear. Their massed assault will eat up the attention of the Ash Lord's forces, and the bulk of the casualties. With the *Nessus*'s stealth hull, we'll come in the back door and rip straight for the Ash Lord.

"*Minotaur is inside the darkzone,*" Char says. "*Two minutes to breech.*"

Inside the firing tube in the port side of the *Nessus*, my soft body is cocooned in the vestments of war. Thermal skin, pulseArmor, starShell—a twelve-foot-tall mechanized armored suit. I'm like one of those layered wooden toys they sell down by the wharf in Thessalonica, the ones that are painted with the faces of rosy-cheeked Reds and Violets. I bought one for Pax when he was young. It was our first and only trip to Mars as a family. He sat in Mustang's lap, gasping each time he pulled apart the dolls to find yet another inside, looking to us hoping we saw the miracle as well. Seeing the joy in my wife's face, I was witnessing another miracle. One, for a long time, I believed I would never see again. Love so potent, so whole and true, that it hurts, because even when you convince yourself that it will last forever, you know enough of the world to see how things break and fade, but somehow, some way, you believe this love will be the exception. That it alone will last.

An ache fills my chest. Not just at the memory, but in thinking Pax was ever so young and innocent. It seems like it was just yesterday, before we were pulled back to Luna. Where did the time go? I ask when I know the answer. I spent that time. And I spent it worlds away from those who needed my love.

I sense the claustrophobia now and the fear of the coming violence beyond the hull. The *Nessus* roars over the sea escorted by Colloway's ripWings, my friends loaded in its spitTubes.

"Enemy contact. Six bandits inbound. They've seen us," Colloway says. *"Warlock Squadron engaging."* Colloway and his depleted Warlock Squadron race ahead of us to target the incoming patrols. They dance across the sensors, dots flashing in and out of existence.

"Bandits eliminated," Colloway drones, his normal insouciance replaced by the hard-edged voice of a master at his craft. *"Warlock-1 crossing into darkzone."*

I watch through the *Nessus's* holoCams from my starShell as the ripWings cross the threshold into the darkzone ahead of the *Nessus,* disappearing from our sensors to be swallowed up by the looming black curtain.

"We'll be deploying at their back door," I say over my com to my starShell squadron. "Expect a firestorm, regardless. We can't expect communications to work inside. You have full autonomy. Group up after initial threats are eliminated to reassess."

"Copy that, Howler 1," Alexandar says unnecessarily.

"How can you even breathe with your nose so far up Reaper's ass?" Clown asks.

"*I hold my breath,*" Alexandar replies. "*Far easier that way, my good-man.*"

"*No one can hold their breath that bloodydamn long,*" Rhonna says from her gun turret.

"*Ragnar could,*" Sevro says.

"*Well, Ragnar could lift a mountain with his gorydamn pinkie,*" Clown replies. "*And drink an ocean without needing to piss a drop, so powerful was his bladder.*"

"*What's the quickest way to a Peerless Scarred's heart?*" Pebble asks. "*Ragnar's fist.*"

Sevro cackles. "*Unlike mortal men, Ragnar didn't sleep. He merely waited.*"

They make me miss my old friend more than I can say. Seems so unfair Ragnar died without knowing that Tinos would be saved, and Luna would fall. "Remember today what the Ash Lord did to our friend," I tell my men. "Remember that he made Ragnar a slave. That he made him kill his own kind for sport. A debt is owed. Two Grimmuses have fallen. Two yet remain."

"*Atalantia au Grimmus. Magnus au Grimmus,*" they recite as a promise, and I hope Atalantia is here with her father so we can end their family's saga once and for all.

Tongueless drones the death rattle of the Obsidians. It fills my ears with righteous dread and I feel the bitter winter plains of Ragnar's homeland roll inside me. I wish I had my old friend here today. What I'd give to see him lead this charge on his old master. To see the Golds quake as they did before no other man.

"*Hyrg la Ragnar,*" Sevro snarls.

"*Hyrg la Ragnar,*" the men bellow back.

The *Nessus* plunges into the darkzone. The external cameras go black. My com silent with static. I am no father. No husband. I summon my anger. My hatred. I am Helldiver of Lykos. The Reaper of Mars come to rip the life from the last great warlord of Gold.

Yellow lights flash outside my suit on the firing mechanism's launch alert console; I stare at it hungrily. Desperate for it to turn green and release me. I perform preflight checks on my interior dampeners and pulseShield, power my gravBoots, charge up the particle cannon on my right shoulder and the railgun that makes a stump of my left arm. A whine from the particle cannon draws energy from my suit's main reactor on the suit's hunched back.

The light goes green.

The firing chamber's hooks push me forward into the mouth of the railgun. I clench my teeth together and lower my head. Then the hooks propel my suit into the clashing current and I launch forward at three times the speed of sound, punching through the darkzone, my heart in my throat.

I tear into a scene of death.

No time to orientate myself. Proximity sensors scream with incoming ordnance. A particle beam smotes the sky in front of me, a pillar of light as thick as a forearm and as bright as a sunbeam. The impulse sensors in the formaGel that surrounds my body communicate with the suit and bank me hard. I pass the particle beam and feel the heat even through the layers of armor. My evasive maneuver throws me into the path of an anti-aircraft battery's fusillade. Fist-sized shells detonate in clouds of superheated shrapnel. A shell detonates to my right, spinning me through the air, my pulseShield screaming from the kinetic energy transfer. I boost out of my spin, diving blindly toward the sea.

A bad start.

We've come out of the darkzone's veil directly into the teeth of the enemy perimeter defenses. So much for the back door. Beneath, atop a cluster of atolls garlanded with anti-aircraft batteries, six automatic turrets swivel on gyroscopes, filling the air with metal. The guns slam munitions into the underside of the *Nessus*'s shields. She vaporizes an atoll with her main particle cannon. Colloway's three ripWings are trapped in a frenzied dance with a squadron of enemy first-responder ripWings. Two of my starShells already smoke and limp away from the theater of fire, but ten others race with me down toward the atolls. No way to tell who is who in our uniform black. I race headlong toward the largest atoll, a towering pillar of rock crested with a particle cannon installation. Light crackles in its meter-wide barrel and then erupts upward at me. I weave right of the certain death and bring my smaller particle cannon online and draw a bead. I expand my left hand, building the energy in the battery. When I'm close enough I can see terrified parrots fleeing the island's canopy of trees, I clench my fist and my cannon roars. Lightning crackles from my right shoulder and slices a molten gash through the base of the gun installation. I sweep my closed fist back and forth, guiding the cannon and lacerating the installation's roof till I hit their power generator and the installation explodes. I bank up and see the Howlers destroying the rest of the gun installations.

When the last gun of the perimeter defense is silent, the starShells form up atop a rock formation on one of the atolls near the smoldering remains of a gun battery. Colloway's ripWings fly a thousand meters higher, the *Nessus* floating above them. She tears apart the sky as she fires at the main islands in the distance. But they fire back.

It sounds like the planet itself is cracking in half.

One by one, the Howlers land on the rugged escarpment with me. The three-ton starShells, with their apelike elongated limbs and armored carapaces, make them appear in the bright daylight like a dark band of crustaceous golems. They stare at me through the triangular duroglass face shields. Smoke billows from the shoulder of Tongueless's shell, but his flesh wasn't hit. Thraxa steadies herself as she lands; the nuke launch tube is still strapped to her back. Sevro is the last to land. He hangs above us on the cliffside, holding on to an outcropping of rock.

Our coms are down from the darkzone's interference, so I signal commands with a laser display on my armored chest. When I'm through, Sevro and I rocket upward from the island, gaining altitude to see the Ash Lord's hidden world in its totality.

A placid emerald sea littered with volcanic islands stretches before us. Twenty kilometers in the distance, at the epicenter of the Ash Lord's realm, lies a humped island with an impressive white spire atop its central rock formation. Reaching out from the island is a spine of towering jagged atolls and islets of shattered arms and legs that claw out at the sea. Pale sand, visible under the clear water, seeps around the bases of the islands like spilled marrow. Fire laces the islands from the *Nessus*'s gun batteries. Already the island's main antenna is melting slag, but a shield generator has activated over the main island and its spire, leaving only a hundred-meter unshielded gap above the waterline.

Distant thunder rolls across the water.

Thirty kilometers away, past the island on the eastern expanse of the darkzone, a war rages. I magnify my vision. Apollonius's rip-Wings twirl in a kaleidoscopic firefight with the Ash Lord's over the sea. Streams of red railgun fire and electric-white particle beams streak up from submerged gun installations and anti-aircraft batteries hidden in the crests of the islands.

Concussions from bunkerbusters echo as Apollonius's heavy, spider-shaped thunderWings make runs on the main islands. His ripWings have carved a hole in the defenders, and dropships filled with his legionnaires race through heavy fire across the no-man's-land of water to make landfall. Despite heavy casualties, he makes progress.

Then I see something terrifying.

On the second-largest island, about four klicks from the Ash Lord's spire, ripWings rise from a large airfield to join the fray. Three squadrons, thirty-six aircraft. Nearly two hundred more ships fill the airfield. Long metal buildings that look like barracks glint from the neighboring islands. Hoverboats are already speeding across the water, carrying pilots to their aircraft.

Seeing our presence to the west, an enemy squadron detaches from the wing from the airfield and slowly banks around to block Colloway's ships from attacking the rows of waiting ripWings on the ground. I glance up at his squadron of three. Warlock's going to have to earn his reputation today. Already long-range missiles streak between the craft.

Sevro and I lock eyes through our faceplates.

We have to eliminate the pilots before they reach their ships or we're all dead. I drop like a stone, Sevro on my tail, and land amongst my men. I signal them to follow me. We plunge into the water as the ripWings engage out over the sea. Railgun rounds eat into the water, but shatter on impact above us. We dive to twenty meters and head toward the islands like a school of metal sharks. Two torpedoes fall into the water and detonate, bucking us sideways.

Then, from the deep, I see something moving through the water toward us, a blur of metal no larger than a fist. It slams into one of the Howlers' shells and detonates, vaporizing half his body. More metal swims toward us from the deep. *Minefield.* I shoot upward out of the water, my Howlers hot behind, the mines screaming after them. A lance of fire streaks down from a belly turret on the *Nessus* and cuts the mines out of the air. Good shot, Rhonna! I could kiss her.

We surface just off the bow of one of the hoverboats. More than a dozen of them race toward the airfield. Two have already landed. I burst over to one and land on the deck just before the command cabin. Through a glass partition, I see the female Blue pilot and half a dozen Orange and Green crewmembers. I switch to the railgun implanted into the left arm of the suit and fire into the command cabin just as the pilot lifts her hands in fear. Superheated metal makes pulp of the men. Throughout the bay, my Howlers in starShells leap-frog back and forth between the fleet of hovercraft, massacring the command cabins. Thraxa wades into one against pulseRifle fire and slams a Gray twenty meters into the air with her powerHammer. She disappears inside. Light flashes from the interior. Sevro floats above another, firing down onto it. I burst forward through the shattered command cabin into the passenger hold of my own hovercraft, where two dozen uniformed Blues in flight gear stare at me in terror. Some are no older than Rhonna.

I pull the trigger and make meat of men.

Evaporated blood fills the air with a rusty mist as fragments of bodies twitch on the floor.

By the time I make it out of the hovercraft, their fleet is a ruin of smoldering, sinking wrecks. Sevro has marshaled the Howlers on the airfield island. I skip over the water and land next to him. "There's no bloody back door!" he says of the main island, popping his top. "Place is a porcupine."

"We'll have air superiority soon. Those frigates are pummeling them."

"Apple's boys can fly," he says with a laugh. "You see Colloway? He slagged half a bloody squadron on his own." We peer up and see black specks swirling around each other in the clouds above. They look so peaceful. So too does the beach. It faces out to sea away from the main island. Water laps against the feet of my starShell. Crabs skitter along the sand. And out in the bay, hulking wrecks of the hovercraft smolder and sink to the deep.

"Who is missing?" I ask.

"Grana and Vandros," he says quietly. Eight of our twelve remain. I try to pull up a battlemap, but static still distorts the sensors. It's infuriating how little of the battlefield I can see. But this is what Niobe teaches our children, what Sevro and I learned long ago: rely on tech and you'll soon be dead as your batteries are.

"Doesn't look like he's going to try a shuttle escape," I say.

"Course not. For once he overestimated us. Prolly thinks we have a whole fleet waiting for him to try and escape. Gonna make us dig him out."

"We should wait for Apple's forces to push inland on their side of the island," Sevro says. Tongueless and Thraxa land together after scouting the coastline. Pebble and Weed watch the interior of the island where the airfields lie beyond white rock hills and olive trees. Alexandar joins them with several Howlers.

"Can't wait," I say. "Chances are they got a signal out before we destroyed the array. We'll be dealing with reinforcements from the mainland soon."

"Then let's move our asses," Sevro says.

The air's a deadly place to be, so we move as a pack across the rocky island toward the coastline facing the main island, low to the ground, skipping thirty meters at a time. I send Tongueless, Alexandar, and Milia inland to demolish the ripWings on their landing pads. Plumes of fire rise over the hillsides from the airstrips before they rejoin us. In the sky we've had a drastic setback. The *Nessus* has lost its gun battle to the particle cannons on the Ash Lord's main island and has been forced to retreat to a lower elevation to seek shelter. And another of Apollonius's frigates has fallen from the sky.

Under the shelter of a ridgeline, Howlers help each other check their starShells as Sevro and I climb the ridge to look at the main island. A kilometer of open water separates the landmasses. Turrets line the rocky coast.

To our far right, Apollonius's force has pushed in and landed troop carriers on the main island. Hundreds of mechanized soldiers storm the beachhead on grasshopper legs, supported by heavily armored spider tanks and the remains of his air force.

Into the teeth of death, the last legion of Valii-Rath charges.

The first wave is mowed down by cluster munitions fired by drones and gun batteries on the high cliffs. The ripWings drop bunker busters and big guns fall silent. Ash Legions, caught unaware, now pour out of subterranean barracks. I see a flash of armor in the sky as Apollonius, flanked by bodyguards, exits a troop carrier midair and falls for the bunkers in the cliffs. His holobanner glows in the sky above him, three times his own size: the raging head of a purple Minotaur, inviting all to come dance and die. He lands amongst a squad of Grays and decimates them.

Clang.

I'm kicked in the chest. Falling from the rock formation, I collide with the sand below and stare up at the sky, dazed. "Sniper!" Sevro shouts.

Sevro lands next to me. "Reap, where are you hit? Reap?"

"Oh, goryhell, he's going to die!" Clown says.

"Shut up, asshole!" Sevro shoves him away.

Pebble kneels over me. "Darrow, can you hear me? Darrow."

"Ow," I say. They help me sit up. The armor-penetrating round pierced the starShell but was stopped by the pulseArmor underneath. The arms and legs of the suit won't respond. Pebble and Weed help me activate the ejection port. The mech splinters apart and I crawl out, still dazed from the shot. There's a dent in my pulseArmor.

"Where's Thraxa?" Sevro looks around.

"Here," she says, rushing up.

"Still got that baby nuke?" he asks, his face enraged.

"Yes, sir."

"Give it."

She unholsters the nuke launcher from the back of her armor and hands it to him. Without even lowering his helmet, he jumps thirty meters upward to clear the ridgeline. He hovers a half second in the air and fires. The small missile shrieks out of the tube. He lets gravity claim him and falls back to the beach as we rush to shelter against the ridgeline. He saunters over without a smile. There's a flash of blinding light. The earth shudders. A blast wave of sand and debris roars over our heads and huge waves crash against the island. In the distance, the black distortion surrounding the Ash Lord's island flickers and disappears, revealing the horizon.

I climb back out to see the devastation the half-megaton missile has caused to the island's coastline. Smoke and dust particles clog the sky. A horrible wound has been carved into the Ash Lord's island. The mushroom cloud blossoms. And above it, deeper inland where the white fortress of the Ash Lord towers upon the high peaks, sunlight catches on iron men.

Finally, the Golds have come to war.

I unfurl my razor and look to my Howlers. "For the Republic."

54

DARROW

Wrath of the Republic

I SOAR WITH THE HOWLERS into the wake of the nuclear blast, skinned in mechanized armor, smeared with char and blood, aimed like a driven spear toward the tower of the Ash Lord. The kill-squad of armored Golds races to meet us. They are nearly twenty in number. Each will be a sworn Peerless of Legio XIII Dracones—dragoons. His elite bodyguards and exterminators. It was men wearing the sea dragon badge who liquidated Reds on Mars by the millions and dropped the nuclear ordnance that destroyed New Thebes, and who dumped my men captured on the battlefield out the back of transport ships three kilometers up.

They must all die.

Fire and mini-missiles streak between the war parties. Shields flash and armor buckles as life is ripped from men. Thraxa fires an EMP missile. It detonates amongst the Golds. None drop from the sky. They have the new EMP shielding too.

A Howler's body is blown to bits in front of me. Two dragoons die as Sevro's particle cannon slices through their ranks. Using Thraxa's starShell to shield me in my thinner personal armor, I fly in her shadow and raise my razor ahead of me like a charging knight, the blade straight and true.

And then, just shy of the speed of sound, the two war parties of machine and men meet in the sky. They clang together like squadrons of fallen angels. A horror of metal. A scream of guns and fire and shimmering swords and engines. Milia spears a Gold through his head with her razor, then is cut in two by a passing sword. Her body divides and spins down without a sound. I block the same man's blade aimed at Thraxa's head as he rips past us. The force numbs my arm to the socket, but I hold on to the blade, plunging into their ranks. I launch off Thraxa's flank and gore the chest of a Gold as we slam together. I twist myself at the last second so his blade nicks off my helmet. Without the starShell's protection, I feel the wheeze of my bones as they nearly snap against the force of our bodies colliding. My vision wavers and we tumble.

We slam down on an outcropping of rock beneath, metal limbs tangled together. My helm is inches from his jaguar helm. He pushes his pulseFist toward my head. I let go my razor and use a kravat arm hold, pinning his arm to the side as I bring my own pulseFist to his belly and fire on full auto. His body melts in half and superheated stone kicks up from the mountain cleft to skitter against my visor. I push his smoldering corpse off and struggle to my feet as his legs flop off the ledge to the white rocks below. But before I can rise again into the air, I'm shot in the back. My skin sizzles as my pulseShield caves in and my armor melts into my lower back. I bellow in anger and jump off the ledge, swerving madly in the air to avoid my pursuer. I glance back just as Sevro smashes the Golden knight down into the mountainside with his starShell. Using the mech's incredible power, he peels off the man's arms and stomps his armored head flat. Another Gold rips past, strafing him with his pulseFist. Sevro lurches one of his starShell's mechanized hands up and grabs the Gold's foot. He jerks the leg so hard in the other direction that the opposing forces tear off the man's leg at the hip. He spins off and collides into the mountainside at two hundred kilometers an hour.

"Get inside the tower! There has to be a door on the landing pad,"

Sevro shouts. He fires up at the dogfight above him. "Without a starShell you'll die out here. Get the Ash Lord."

But it is my Howlers who are dying.

Our effort to pierce the Gold formation has failed. The battle has broken down into aerial dogfights and men killing each other on the face of the mountainside and against the walls of the tower. Our starShells gave us the edge, but the Golds are more maneuverable in their pulseArmor, and have the numbers. They're overwhelming the powerful mechs like jackals taking down lions.

I see Thraxa's mech fending off six Golds in an aerial cage. Men broken by her power hammer litter the mountainside below. She smashes another out of the air, but she's speared from behind. Another hacks off her mech's left hand. And a third stabs at her stomach repeatedly before Tongueless smashes into them. Below, in a ravine, Pebble stands fighting over Clown's broken mech.

"Rally to the roof!" I call over the coms, signal going through now that the darkzone interference has gone. Sevro echoes the call.

The remaining Howlers fight their way to the roof to join Sevro and me as we fly up the mountain toward the high tower. At the top, the landing pad nearly sixty meters across is being used by a Gray sniper team and Obsidian reinforcements. They retreat as we land, seeking shelter behind the long wings of the Ash Lord's personal shuttle.

Sevro and I land on the edge together and fight back a squad of Obsidians and Grays. I rocket into them at full speed, breaking the rib cage of a Gray against the concrete. Rolling up, I deflect the huge axe of an Obsidian and shoot him in the head. His helmet takes the blast, but I stun him enough to hew through his legs with my razor. I'm hit from the side by a Gold pulseFist before I can finish him. My shield absorbs it. I shoot up on my gravBoots, then straight down in front of him to exchange a series of razor slashes that ends with his arm off at the shoulder. Someone shoots him from the side. Sevro kicks a Gray off the roof with the boot of his mech. An Obsidian launches toward him and stabs a pulseSpear into his cockpit. He moves his head at the last moment, then pulls the Obsidian off. Blood showers his mech as he crushes the Obsidian's head with a squeeze of his mechanized hand. Green plasma rounds pound the legs of his mech, melting them inoperable. A squad of hunched Grays fires at him from across the landing pad with huge anti-armor plasma rifles. I fire at them, cutting a hole of steaming meat through their ranks. Too late. An EMP rocket slams into the chest of Sevro's mech. Blue electricity sizzles out, frying his circuitry. He manually ejects, shooting straight up, over the heads of Alexandar and Tongueless, who fight like mad together against the tide.

I lose Sevro in the fray.

The enemy presses in, firing at us from the air above, chewing into our ranks. I'm slammed sideways by a concussion munition. As I try to gain my balance, an Obsidian a head taller than me hits me in the chest with a pulseHammer. My pulseShield shorts out. My armor caves inward. I feel several ribs crack and I tumble back. He knocks me to the ground before I can lift my head. Stomps on my hand as I try to stab him with my razor. His axe lifts high into the air, the moment slowing. Thraxa lies pinned to the ground, a razor in her thigh. Alexandar tries desperately to reach me. I roar in fear as the pulseAxe comes down. It smashes through my helmet. The energy blade glows with a pale fire, its edge centimeters from my face, held back by squealing metal. The heat radiates into my eyeballs, filling them with aching pressure. The Obsidian wrenches the axe sideways. My helmet rips from its sockets. He cries his war chant and kneels on my chest, a crooked knife in his hand. He grabs my hair with an armored hand and saws on the front of my forehead to claim my scalp.

Bazzoooohhh. Bazzoooohhh.

A trumpet's clarion call rides in with the wind. The Obsidian looks up to see a flight of armored knights falling from the sky, a violent figure in purple Minotaur armor at their head. The Minotaur lands before the Obsidian and hacks him in half with a running two-handed upward blow.

Apollonius has come.

His knights fall upon the Ash Guard, carving them with razors and smashing them off the face of the landing pad till not one is left alive. Apollonius sings as he kills the Golds and lurchers who try to make a last stand at the doorway down into the fortress.

"I sung of Chaos and Eternal Night
Taught by the heav'nly Muse to venture down
The dark descent, and up to reascend!"

He picks up a Gray with one hand and smashes the man's skull into the hull of the Ash Lord's ship until there's nothing to hold on to. Fresh from the kill, he wheels on me, his Minotaur helm blood-soaked and battered, and for a moment I think he will strike me down. But his helm retracts, and from his sweaty face and tangled hair, he stares at me with wild, loving eyes. He helps me to my feet.

"What wrath we summon together!" he roars. "Reaper and Minotaur, legends unholy. We broke them on the beach!"

How in the hell did he do that?

He was outnumbered four to one.

One of his men helps me to my feet. I've lost my helmet, but my face is so covered in blood from the attempted scalping that even my own mother wouldn't recognize me. Apollonius skewers the heart of a wounded Gold and turns to his bodyguards. "Vorkian, Gaul, rejoin the hunt. Slaughter them to the last man."

His men jump from the tower back toward the battle, which rages inland of their beachhead below. Apollonius comes toward me and extends his arms, taking me into a hug. Bewildered, I stand there as he pulls back. "A divine spectacle, Darrow." He looks at my men with a smile. "A more glorious band of devils there is none. What a path you cut, like fallen seraphs amongst mortal men."

Sevro limps toward me. His left arm bends the wrong way at the elbow and I can see charred flesh through fissures in his armor. I scan the remains of my Howlers and realize with a sinking feeling that Pebble and Clown are nowhere in sight. Thraxa sits propped against a retaining wall as Tongueless administers first aid. Alexandar alone is uninjured. His shell is a smoking wreck, but he stands free of it, almost elegant amidst the carnage despite the shell-shock in his eyes. "Alexandar."

"Yes, sir?"

"Call the *Nessus* and hold the roof." I turn to limp toward the security door leading down from the landing pad into the tower. "Sevro, Apollonius, with me."

55

LYSANDER

Requiem

I WAKE FROM A FITFUL SLEEP and expect to see Cassius standing there, filling the door, asking me if it's the night terrors again. But he is gone. I remember slowly, then all at once. There's a presence in the room. By the window an old Brown watches me. I'm too tired to be startled. His bark-colored eyes smile with deep respect from underneath cirrus-cloud eyebrows.

"Dominus Lune, I beg pardon for interrupting your sleep. But your presence is requested."

"By whom?"

"A friend."

Seraphina? He walks past my pallet, careful not to trod on the fabric, and sketches a strange symbol onto the stone wall. It rumbles very softly, dilating inward to reveal a hidden passage through which he seems to have entered. I hesitate, wondering if it could be some sort of trap. He wags his hand impatiently. "Come, come, *dominus*. She awaits."

I follow the Brown in silence through the tunnels. He leads on through the darkness till we reach another wall where he sketches another symbol and the wall retracts. The Brown leads me into a sitting room and closes the new aperture behind us. He gestures to several silk cushions on the floor by the hearth.

"Wait here, *dominus*. May I prepare refreshment?"

"Tea, if you have it," I say instinctively. Then I feel my hunger. "And food. Anything will do." He bows and limps away. "Excuse me, steward. What is your name?"

"Aruka," he says softly.

"Thank you, Aruka." I dip my head in Rim fashion.

He bows again and leaves me there.

This room reflects the pre-Color heritage of the Raa more than any other. It is traditional and austere but for the use of wood. Tatami flooring, woven from pale igusa grass, stretches to a bank of windows overlooking the frozen waste. Entire tree trunks, stained a warm honey color, support the stone ceiling. A length of cypress forms the tokonoma, a raised alcove where a small tree grows and a razor hangs in midair above a gravWell. I'm drawn to the room's lone eccentricity: a grand old piano made out of heartwood. It is a marvel. Of course, Ceres and some of the larger asteroid depots have pianos, but those are cheap plastic synth jobs. The wood to make this must have come from Ganymede or Callisto.

I run my hands over the piano's keys. I was wrong. The piano is old. Perhaps older than the Society. Two golden S-shaped markings are imprinted on the fallboard above the keys. My hands run over the polished fiddleback grain. I close my eyes and imagine I can feel the energy that grew this tree on my face, that I can hear birds in the sky again. After ten years, they sing like I heard them yesterday. A flicker of a memory, no longer than the flash of a lighting match, burgeons in the recesses of my mind. A feeling, a scent of something lost.

Am I just homesick? Or is it something more?

"Do you know how to play?" a woman asks.

I turn to see Romulus's mother, Gaia, shuffling into the room. Her back is crooked, shoulders slumped. In her youth, she would have been a slight thing. Her wrists are fragile as the stems of wineglasses, and her skin paper-pale and veined like bleu cheese. In fact, it seems all that keeps her from tipping forward and shattering on the floor is a thin wooden cane and the enormous arm of the grand Obsidian who escorts her. She clutches to him as if he were an old friend. He is aged, like her. A hunched gray golem with intense beetle-black eyes buried deep in the folds of an ancient face. His head is a boulder. His ears chipped and pointed at the tips. The lobes filled with gold disks the size of chicken eggs imprinted with the lightning dragon. A long uncut white beard hangs down the front of his gray scorosuit and is tucked into his belt.

"No," I answer. "I never learned."

"A child of Hyperion alien to music? What a crime. But you must have been a busy little thing. Your grandmother no doubt teaching you the alchemy of turning moons to glass instead. Or were those lessons the province of your godfather?"

The senile mask she wore before her family is gone. Curious.

"My godfather taught me to finish a fight," I say. "Two hours of strategic instruction every day."

"If only he had taken his own lessons. Then Darrow would be a memory instead of a ten-year plague."

"My godfather is still the only man to ever best the Reaper in battle," I say. "And I rather think it the habit of an indolent mind to indict a single man for a civilization's failure."

"True. Back and forth they go. But now a peace."

"So they say."

"What a thing it must be for you. Lorn for a grandfather. Octavia for a grandmother. Magnus, Aja, Moira, Atalantia . . . trapped between so many giants and having to watch the birth of two more."

"Two?"

"Darrow and Virginia. I rather think it the habit of a boy's mind to believe the man could exist without the woman." She smiles.

I feel a sudden surge of enjoyment at the riposte.

I like this woman. She reminds me of Atalantia.

"All others here call him the Slave King, yet you do not?"

"That brat is flesh and bone. Why feed the legend?" She wheezes as her Obsidian helps her sit on the flame-maple bench. "Thank you, Goroth." He turns from her to take a place at the window, and as he does I see a screaming skull has been tattooed to cover the back of his head in blue ink. "Don't let the old blackeye frighten you," Gaia says.

"He's as batty as I am." Goroth shakes his head in disagreement as he reaches the window. "Oh, quiet, you." She pats the bench beside her as she produces a thin white pipe from her robes, along with a match. "Sit here with me, Lysander. I will teach you." She strikes the match on the calluses of her heel and holds the flame to the pipe bowl.

Glancing uneasily at the Obsidian, I sit down in the cloud of smoke at her side.

She pats the piano. "My husband gave this to me as a gift when I was twenty-nine. Do you want to guess how old I am now?"

"You hardly look older than sixty," I say with a smile.

"Sixty!" She cackles. "What a rogue you are! That Bellona philanderer rubbed off on you, I see." She scrutinizes me. "I hope you didn't catch anything from him."

"He was like a brother to me."

"Well, that's not saying much in the Core."

"My home is Luna. Not the Core."

"Pfah. It's all the same to us."

Why am I here? In accepting the invitation, I've walked into some scheme. Is this a test of some sort? Just because I'm grieving doesn't mean the dance has stopped. If anything, the pace has increased as the coup solidifies and the dissenters are clipped one by one. While Cassius may be gone, I still have Pytha to protect. Seems a lofty goal at this point.

Gaia is unaware of my inner turmoil as she touches the keys and strokes out a simple melody. A strange sense of belonging courses through me and I forget about the dance.

"Must be grotesque for you, seeing age," she says. "I know how the deviants in the Core love their rejuvenation therapy. Pfah." She hacks something into a crusty handkerchief, examines the prize, then makes the kerchief disappear back into her thick kimono. "Your grandmother never looked older than sixty, but I remember her when we were both girls dancing at her father's galas. I was a plain little thing to her. She had such jewels. Such refinement. But was always so haughty. Pretending she didn't know who I was. A sizable stick up her *gahja* ass, that one. But now I have the last laugh!" She cackles again. "How old are you, child?"

"Twenty."

"Twenty? Twenty! I've ingrown hairs older than you."

I laugh despite myself. "You're not very discreet, are you?"

"Ha! I've earned indiscretion." Her cloudy eyes soften and she pulls on her pipe before pointing it at me like a finger. "I know you wear the mask of court. What did they call it again?"

"The dancing mask."

"Yes. That. You Lunes are famous for it. The composure. I once saw your great-grandaddy bitten in the face by a Venusian manticore at his birthday gala. Took a chunk out of his cheek and he didn't even flinch. Just bit the thing back, threw it to its handler, and ordered champagne. Terrifying man, Ovidius. Might be too hot-blooded for the mask myself, but I see through yours. Your friend died today. And so did my grandson, granddaughter, and grandniece." She reflects on them for a solemn moment and drags from her pipe.

"I will miss them. Even that noxious scorpion, Bellerephon. But I will not say I am sorry. That is life, neh? Play with blades you get pricked. Like my kin, your Bellona made his bed long ago. But you are different. Your weapon is in there . . ." She pokes my head. "If you are wise and lucky and live long as me, you will learn this pain is just a drop in the sea." She sets a hand on my heart, her eyes intense. "So feel all of it, boy, before time makes you forget."

"Could you play something for them?" I ask.

"For them?"

"The departed. Cassius and your kin. A requiem, perhaps?"

She laughs. "Yes. Yes. I like your gray matter." She turns to the piano and begins a song, slow, mournful, that sounds like the wind in my dreams. As her fingers drift over the keys, the song wakes something inside me besides grief—a shadow, a shadow of a shadow in the library of my mind, something I never knew forgotten. I feel a presence at my back, though there is no one there. I smell a perfume that is not in the air, and feel a heartbeat against my spine that ceased to beat so many years ago.

Gaia senses my unease. "Are you well, child?"

"Yes," I say distantly, only now realizing that I've set my hands on the keys, blocking her from playing. I should take my hands back, but instead press down on a key. The note sings through my body. The memory coalesces. Warms. The shadow dripping from it like dirty snow from a statue. I find another key. My eyes close. My hands move and more notes emerge through me, taking me to another place, another time, a spirit inside guiding me, a spirit that has long been caged and hidden so I did not even know it was once there. But now it flies. The cobwebs of my mind burn away.

My hands glide along the keys and a song pours out, a requiem for Cassius and all those others I have lost. I'm swept away by its music to a far-off study where a fire crackles and a small leopard paces around my legs. She is behind me. Her hair falling around my cheeks. Her earthy scent filling my nose. Her dazzling eyes and truculent mouth. All of it, all of her in that moment rushing back on the wings of the melody. When the last mournful note hangs in the air and my hands linger on the keys, I sit there breathless, tears streaking my face.

I look over at Gaia, confused.

"I thought you couldn't play," she says.

"I can't," I murmur. "Unless I forgot."

"How could you forget something like that? It was splendid, child."

"I don't know." For a breath, for the briefest flicker, I saw her. The face of my mother. The soft skin. The small nose and strident mouth. Those eyes that burned in a face time stole from me. Or was it something else that stole it away, a lock placed upon her memory that the music unfastened?

"My mother played," I say, remembering now.

"And she taught you."

"Yes. I . . . I don't know why I couldn't remember."

"Sometimes bottling pain is the only way to survive."

"No . . . I don't forget," I say, somehow knowing there's more beneath the shadows that I've yet to remember. A whole life buried in my own mind. "I never forget anything. My grandmother said it was my greatest gift. . . ."

"Sounds more like a curse to me." She watches sympathetically. "My mother died when I was young like you. Even though she would be a withered fossil now, I remember her as she was young. Young death is divine. It freezes the flower in time. A gift in a way, to remember her as that instead of watching age ravage and devour . . ." Her blue-veined hands pull absently at the loose folds of her neck. ". . . till she is a shadow of what she was."

"I don't think you're a shadow," I say. "I think you are rather marvelous."

"I don't need your pity," she snaps, startling me. Then she smiles and taps me with her pipe again. "You're not as good at being a rogue as the Bellona. Are you? You flatter an old fool, but I think it's another who has stolen your heart." Her eyes twinkle with mischief. "My granddaughter."

"You're mistaken."

"There are easier women to fall in love with. But you know that. Don't you?"

"Love? There are more important things than love."

"Like?"

"Duty. Family. She let my friend be butchered. His death is on her." I hang my head. "And it is on me. There is no love between us. Only a slight mutual curiosity—understandable and now fled."

"She kept you from being tortured," Gaia says. "When her mother discovered it was Cassius behind that mask, Seraphina begged her to spare your life and to let Bellona have an honorable end."

"Before she knew who I was," I say. "The only thing Lune and Raa share is responsibility for losing the Society. For allowing Darrow to divide us and spending precious resources and ships against one another."

I turn to her.

"What do you want?" There's a dull ache between my shoulder blades that now is working its way into my head. I'm weary of this. She's talking like we're old friends, pretending that we mean anything to one another. On another night I might have patience for it. "Why did you bring me here? It wasn't to commiserate or show me your piano. I know I'm going to die. Is that why you've stopped pretending you're senile? Because you know I won't last the night?"

"No. It is because I want your help."

"My help?" I laugh bitterly. "Why would I ever help you? I gave you the war you all seem to want. Isn't that enough?"

"Who said *I* wanted war?" She tries to get up from the bench. Goroth rushes to help her, his own knees crackling as he comes. She shoos him away and manages on her own with great difficulty. She extends a hand to me. "Come. I will show you."

I hesitate, then take her hand. I support her as she leads us back through the door through which Aruka disappeared earlier. It leads us into a humid artificial solarium that smells like flowers and pastries. Luminescent ivy crawls up the walls. The steward is there, pouring tea at a low table at which sits a lone, hunched woman with short dark blue hair in a prisoner uniform.

"Pytha?"

She bolts upward and bowls toward me with her spindly limbs, shocking me by wrapping her arms around me in an embrace. She holds tight, the top of her head under my chin. The latticework of her rib cage presses against mine.

"You're alive," she says into my chest. "You're fucking alive."

I did not expect an embrace from her. I would not have given one myself.

"Pytha . . . there's something I have to tell you. About Cassius . . ."

She pulls back, eyes red. "I know."

I swallow the stone in my throat. "Where have you been?"

We sit sipping tea at the table as Pytha recounts her trials. She was not accorded the same comfort Cassius and I were. She was tortured by Pandora on the first night we were captured and has trouble remembering what she revealed. Here on Io, she's been treated well, but she's still famished and devours a plate of thin sandwiches that Aruka serves. I nibble on one without tasting it, mulling over what she's told me. Gaia picks tobacco from her pipe with a short knife.

"You still haven't told me," I say. Gaia looks up, confused. "What you want from me . . . from us."

"As you said, you are going to die. Soon. Both of you. I believe Dido will execute you after Romulus's trial tomorrow. Perhaps before. It will be quiet. A blackblood scorpion in your room. A needle drone. A poisoned cup of tea." I set down my cup uneasily. "She will want the grandson of Lune to disappear. You complicate her plans, Lysander. She can stand no challenges to her authority. So disappear you shall, regardless of Seraphina's intervention."

"Damn, you're depressing as an empty stimpack," Pytha mutters, but she's not depressed enough to stop eating the sandwiches. "So what do we do? Just wait to die like Cassius?"

"No," Gaia says. "I suggest an alternative: survive."

It's not the answer I expected, but it fits. "And how do you propose we do that?" Pytha asks sharply. "Even if we get past the guards and steal a ship, we need to get past Sungrave's guns. Then we need to get to orbit before warhawks shred us with railguns. Then we need to outrace the orbital guard. Then the fleets themselves. Prolly won't even chase us. They'll just send a long-distance missile and it'll do the work. We run, we die a dozen ways." She loses interest in her meal and pushes it away. "We're trapped on this shithole moon."

"I understand you are angry," Gaia says. "But speak to me in that way again, lowborn, and your tongue will fertilize my tobacco garden." Gaia puffs away on her pipe as Pytha blanches. "And, yes, you are trapped . . . unless . . ."

"Unless what . . . *domina*?" Pytha asks nervously.

"Unless Dido's not in power," I guess. "Unless Romulus defeats her coup. Then he may let us go."

"Romulus, who let me be tortured by that Pandora . . ." Pytha spares a quick look at Gaia. ". . . woman? Didn't you say he wanted to cut your head off and send the *Archi* into Jupiter? Aren't you a little raw about that?"

"It's in the past. And it made sense, considering his predicament."

"Killing you made sense?"

"Technically."

She considers. "Well, I have thought of it a few times."

I mull over an idea, seeing Gaia's intention. "You want us to help you. You want us to free Romulus from the Dust Cells." Gaia nods at me through her pipe smoke.

"So we can get killed by those turbaned psychopaths? Are you spacemad?" Pytha crosses her arms. "Don't you have your own men . . . *domina*?"

"All my men have been arrested or displaced," Gaia says. She gestures to Aruka and Goroth. "We crones are all that's left. What mischief could we do, feeble as we are?" Goroth bares his black teeth, chilling me.

"Golds wanting us to do their dirty work. Typical," Pytha mutters. "I don't want to die for them, Lysander."

"This might be the only way we don't die today," I say with a smile. But inside, behind the dancing mask, my logic is cold and clinical.

"Don't tell me you're actually thinking about this!"

"Dido is preparing for war, Pytha. We're afterthoughts to her. She'll delete us or use us . . . use *me* as a bargaining chip somehow. I won't have that. Not at all." I turn to Gaia. "Would Diomedes help?"

"No. The vain boy is a slave to his honor. He's bound by his oath to the Olympic Knights, and they've accepted Dido's coup. Romulus's trial begins tomorrow. Diomedes will deliver him to that trial for justice to be served there."

"His own father?" Pytha asks.

"It is our way."

"You have a plan, I assume?" I ask Gaia.

"So you'll do it?" she says slyly.

"I did not say that. What is your plan?"

"My daughter, Vela, waits in the desert with legions loyal to Romulus. They will begin an assault on Sungrave to capture Dido. But she cannot attack if he is a hostage. I need you to go to the Dust Cells. Free him. I've arranged for hoverbikes in a garage. You will need them to cross the Waste and reach Vela.

"It's not just about my son," she says, baring all her cards. "I was friends with your grandfather, Lorn. He was a stuck-up old goat, but so am I." She could be lying. "He came to Europa because he tired of the ambition of the young and the pride of the old. I tire of empire, just like Old Stoneside did. War eats families. I told my husband that when he went to Augustus's war and raced to fall in the Lion's Rain. He did not listen. My son did. All he's done, all he's hidden, has been for the good of the Rim."

"Did Romulus know Darrow destroyed the docks?" I ask.

"No. *I* suspected, and I counseled my son not to seek war with him."

"Logical, at the time, considering your losses. But dishonorable."

"Stupid boy. Do you know how many proud humans I've seen die for honor? Melted onto the floors of landing craft? Crying on the battlefield for their mothers as they try to push their guts back into their bodies? Honor." She sips her tea. "Romulus knows the cost. A leader may not always be logical and honorable. At times, he must choose. I'm surprised, of all people, your grandmother did not teach you that. Or are you trying to be Lorn?"

I say nothing. She makes a small noise of amusement.

"My son, for all his power, is a humble man. He listened to me. Because of him, our civilization survived the destruction of the docks, and the starvation and economic collapse that followed. We built new ships out of the ruins of the very docks that fell on Ganymede. Now we have peace. I want to die knowing that it will last and that the Venusian strumpet won't pull us into her planet's endless war."

Gaia does this to protect her family and the Rim. She could care less about the Interior and their people. Seraphina suddenly seems so very noble compared with her grandmother. The young girl's eyes were incandescent when she spoke of bringing peace to the Core.

There's only one answer I can give Gaia that will let me walk out of here.

"I will do it," I say carefully. "I will free your son. Pytha, you can stay here. . . ."

"Last time I did that, you slagged things up good and I got thrown in a cell," she says. She pushes away her tea. "I come with."

I eye her frail arms.

"Then you must hurry." Gaia stands with Goroth's help. "Dido is in council with her Praetors now. But soon she'll learn I brought you both here."

We follow her back into the main room. "I'll need something. A letter. A recording so Romulus knows you sent me," I say.

"You'll have a guide," she says. "He knows Goroth."

"Then why not just send him?"

"Goroth is not what he once was." She looks at the Obsidian with grave affection. "And he does not know how to pilot the hoverbikes. I assume you do."

I nod. Appraising Goroth, I look back at Gaia. "I'll need a weapon."

"Yes . . . Aruka, my hasta." Aruka rushes to the tokonoma and, using tongs instead of his hands, brings back the razor from its gravity perch. "Show him this. I have not held her for many years. Her name is Shizuka. She is yours until I ask for her again. Take it, boy."

I take the hasta in my hands. It is cold and alien and outlandishly long. Its handle is pale brown leather and is as long as my forearm. Its blade clear as glass, like Seraphina's. My hand touches the small activation toggle near the top of the handle and the whip snaps rigid.

Gaia glances nervously to the door, no longer the collected woman who sat with me at the piano. It took all her energy to make that show of confidence, to sell herself, the gambit. Now her own nerves and exhaustion betray her.

"You must leave now. Goroth will lead you into the tunnels." She guides me to a wall where she traces her fingers over the stone. The wall rumbles backward, revealing a dark passage. "We know the secrets of this mountain better than that Venusian tramp." She hands me a transponder. "Remember, as soon as you have him and can hide, signal for the legions."

"I will."

The old Obsidian joins us there and looks sadly down at Gaia, torn by the parting. Tears glisten in his black eyes. "Oh, don't weep, you old brute," she says to the giant. "Tears do not become us." He bends down suddenly and kisses her upon the brow with his tattered lips. She's so startled she barely has time to be offended.

"Farewell, *domina*," he rumbles.

She shakes her head and shoves him weakly in the chest. "Go!"

Goroth tears himself away and presses into the darkness of the tunnel. "Thank you for the sandwiches," Pytha says to Gaia. "If they find out you helped us, won't they kill you?"

"Stupid girl, not all who live fear death." She backs away, the door closes between us, but I hear her last words weakly through the stone. "Save my son."

56

LYSANDER

War of Dragons

GOROTH, PYTHA, AND I WIND through the bowels of the ancient city in a darkness so complete memory guides the man instead of his large eyes. Up and down and in twisting turns we go. Passing whispers that leak through the stone. Machines that shudder in unseen alcoves and rooms. Thin blades of light slice through the darkness from peepholes. I glance through them, hoping to catch sight of Seraphina, but the deeper we plunge, the farther from the Golds we go. What I see through the walls are Yellows hunched over holoDisplays, studying diagrams and videos, White hierophants reading in cloisters, carver laboratories alive with experiments, barracks of Grays, and great cisterns and botanical gardens abuzz with bees and Reds plucking fruits from rows of subterranean bushes growing under artificial light.

The tunnels are old and have their own humors. Wind rolls through them, whispering eerily. And deep in the darkness, as it bends around turns and passes over apertures, the wind howls. I walk closely behind Goroth. Without him Pytha and I might wander until we starve to death.

At each turn Goroth glances back to make sure we still follow, and

I worry that he knows what I'm thinking. Knows what I plan. He continues to guide us until we reach a freezing stretch of tunnel where ice slicks the stone under our feet.

"Here," he says. We stop and I hear his finger on the wall. The stone grumbles in complaint and then light seeps in through the expanding aperture, revealing a storage room on the other side of the wall. Goroth goes through first. I put a hand on Pytha to stop her from following. My hand trembles on the hasta. What if I miss? I find the toggle with my thumb. My fingers shake.

"Some ill wind, *dominus*?" Goroth asks, turning back when I do not follow. Now he senses my intentions in the air. I say nothing. His eyes narrow as he sees my finger on the toggle. Without a word, he lunges at me. His speed uncanny to his age and size. I activate the razor. The long blade springs into the space that separates us. I lunge for his kneecap, hoping not to kill him. It impales the bone and tendons, sliding through them as if they were not even there. Goroth's momentum carries him through the blade. His huge hands reach for my throat. Pytha screams and slips on the ice. Her legs knock out mine from beneath me. I slam down just as Goroth sails over me and crashes into the wall. He rolls over, reaching for me. I scramble away down the tunnel, trying to gain my feet. He manages to grab only my left hand. I try to bring the razor around, but he jerks me down. I fall facedown and he almost throws his body atop mine. A narrow miss. Still on my belly, right arm and razor pinned under my body, I kick blindly backward at him, hitting his face and shoulders, leveraging my legs against him to prevent him from crawling up my facedown body to pin me there. With his strength and weight, he would nail me to the ground and shatter my skull into the stone. We flail there in the darkness, grunting, his immense strength slowly overwhelming my kravat-learned leverage. I can't twist my right arm with the razor out from under me.

"Pytha!" I shout. "Pytha! Kick him."

I glance back and see her in the dim light that bleeds from the storage room into the tunnel. She's gained her feet and rushes up behind Goroth's prone body to kick him in the back of his head. His grip doesn't slacken. He's reaching up my body, trying to take the transponder that will signal Vela. Pytha kicks him again with the heel of her foot and, using the distraction, I manage to wrench my body around so that I'm on my side and can free my arm. I stab down at him again with the razor, this time in the arm that holds me. The blade gores his shoulder. He doesn't let go. His huge hand closes around my left hand, squeezing till I hear a popping like green wood over a campfire. The bones crackle and splinter under my flesh. Pain races up my left arm. I grunt and swing the blade down at his arm in frantic desperation. His grip slackens. I scramble to my feet, his severed hand still clutched around my left. I wheel around to kill him, but he's rolled back away from me into the shadows of the tunnel past the storage room aperture.

One breath. Two. He does not reappear.

I rush to Pytha, razor pointed warily at the darkness, and shove her inside the storage room. "Lysander, what the blackhell was that?" My hand throbs with pain. In the light I can see the mangled fingers and the swelling underneath the skin. We weave through boxes, fleeing the tunnels till we find a door and go through it into a cold hallway. We're in the Dust Cells prison facility. Cameras blink on the ceiling from behind small glass globes. "They'll see you!" I go to my knees in front of one and throw the razor on the ground. She retreats to the doorway of the storage room. "Lysander . . ." An alarm begins to howl out of the camera. Doors slam somewhere in the distance. Boots hammer the ground.

"Pytha, get on your knees with me. They'll be here soon."

"Lysander, what are you doing?"

"Choosing a side."

An hour later, Dido watches me after I finish my story. Pytha stands nervously with me; we're surrounded by a handful of soldiers, along with Dido and Seraphina, both of whom look to have been woken from their sleep. My left hand is in agony, swollen like a waterskin and throbbing a deep black-purple. The shock wore off half an hour ago. My teeth don't chatter anymore, but I'm sweating bullets. I compartmentalize the pain along with the fear, putting it in the void and focusing on my breathing. The pain becomes manageable.

"He had this with him." The centurion of the platoon that captured us hands Dido a plastic container that holds Gaia's razor, taking care not to touch the blade with his own hand. "It is the matron's razor, is it not?"

My evidence.

"It is. Seraphina, what do you think?" Dido asks.

Seraphina scrutinizes me from the corner of the room. "I wouldn't trust a Lune farther than I can spit." She looks at her datapad as it glows. "But they found a hand in the tunnel and Obsidian blood. Field DNA inspection says it's Goroth's."

"And that monster wouldn't take a piss if Gaia didn't tell him to." Dido cradles the transponder that Gaia gave me. "So he is telling the truth. Your grandmother is not so senile as she appears."

"Should we send a platoon to her quarters, *domina*?" the centurion asks. Dido's finger glides along the activation button.

"No . . . no, that would look tawdry. More family squabble." Seraphina breathes a sigh of relief. Dido's eyes glitter over at me. "We're not Lunes, after all. She is my mother-in-law. No. Search for Goroth, centurion." His men swallow nervously behind him. Dido doesn't notice, but Seraphina seems to have a better gauge on the pulse of the men. "Even with one arm, I don't like the idea of a Stained in the walls. And not a word of this to anyone. Last thing I need is all our new allies shitting themselves for fear of being skinned in their sleep." The soldier waits expectantly. "Something else? Pray tell."

"I don't have clearance for the tunnels, *domina*. Or maps."

"Did you know they existed before today?" Seraphina asks.

"Only rumors. And I was born in Sungrave."

"I can go, Mother," Seraphina says. "I know most of the—"

"No, I won't risk you chasing a Stained in the dark. Who else knows the damn tunnels?"

"Some Dragonguard," Seraphina says. "But most of the centurions are loyal to Father."

"Goryhell. Isn't there a map in the servers or something?"

"There was," Seraphina says. "When Fabii's hacker battalions corrupted the mainframe, the tunnel maps were casualties of the data purge."

"You mean they're lost and we're strangers in our own gorydamn home?" Dido laughs to me. "See? Always at siege."

"Marius was mapping them with the Krypteia, but I don't know how far he got," Seraphina says.

"Of course he would."

"He won't help us, not without Father's permission."

"I know. I know." Dido rubs her fingers into her temples, thinking. "Sera, summon Kurath. I want a hundred Obsidian bloodstalkers and kuon hounds in the tunnels by morning. Let them hunt their own." The Grays breathe a sigh of relief.

"And Marius's maps?" Seraphina asks. "There's thousands of kilometers of tunnel."

"I'll deal with the maps and your brother." Dido dismisses the Grays. The centurion asks if he should take me to a cell. "Let him stay." The Grays leave and Dido fondles the transponder that I gave her while looking me over.

I stay silent, knowing the die is already cast. Seraphina closes the door behind the Grays and looks at the transponder. "Are you going to summon Vela?"

"Perhaps." Dido purses her lips. "It seems the only proper move in the game. I can recall the legions I sent to take care of Kardiff and Iola. Under that shield, Vela can last for years. We lure her into the Waste, we can destroy her legion in an hour. Solidify our control. Without Vela who will they rally around once Romulus sees reason?"

"You think he'll see reason if you kill Aunt Vela?" Seraphina asks. "You kill her, you lose him. That's not what I agreed to. We've done this without tearing our family apart. That is a victory to build our war on."

I watch Dido for her reaction, gauging.

"Yes . . ." Dido's thumb continues to trace over the activation button. "Yes, of course you're right. We shall reason with Vela." She tosses Seraphina the transponder. "Do something with that." She turns to me. "Now, young Lune. This is the second time you've helped me. Considering the death of the Bellona, I am curious to know why you chose to betray my mother-in-law. Was is that you could not simply bear to be an honorable little boy?"

"Cassius died for his honor," I say.

"No. He died because he murdered my brother, my daughter. Are you too cowardly to follow him?"

I look past her to Seraphina. "Death begets death begets death. It's something my grandfather once said. And it's why I did not free Romulus. Gold blood would spill, and there's precious little of it left. Lorn au Arcos once said it is the duty of every man to listen to his enemies. When you spoke I listened. Your war is just. Cassius did not believe that, but he is gone. And to honor the dead at the cost of the living is a vanity none of us can afford."

Seraphina has had some difficulty in looking at me since I entered the room, even when I recounted my story, but now I have her attention.

"I saw the Rising claim Luna. And I have watched for ten years as their supposed liberty gave way to anarchy. It is time order and justice return to the realm of man. That is why I helped you."

"Not because you wish the Slave King's head on a pike?" Dido asks.

"The worlds would be better without him in it," I say.

"If you wanted that, you would have tried already," Seraphina says. "You would have gone to your godfather in the Core. But instead you hid."

"Cassius saved my life. I owed him a debt." I do not say that I was afraid my godfather would blame me for the Fall of Luna and my part in it. "But with his death, that debt is gone."

"Noble platitudes," Dido says, eyes wary. "But Lunes have ever had silver tongues. I imagine you would have me free you?" I nod. "Many of my allies cry for your head. I would hate to disappoint them."

"I have committed no crimes."

"You are the residue of tyrants and genocides," Seraphina snaps. "You are a Lune."

"So you judge me by the faults of my ancestors? I thought better of you."

"Interesting." Dido examines me with a Venusian eye, wondering if I'm more valuable dead or alive. "But as it is, the decision is not mine."

I frown. "Then whose is it?"

"Tomorrow's trial will be a sham," Dido says. "I've spoken to Helios, who will conduct the trial. He agrees, there is no evidence my husband knew about the recording. His containment of Seraphina's return can be excused by saying he was trying to protect the peace and his daughter from harsh judgment. There was no treason. But the docks were destroyed on his watch. He will be impeached *only* for negligence in wartime for not investigating the Reaper's duplicity. But then he will be freed and we will be on our course to war. As Rome had two consuls, we will have two Sovereigns. Husband and wife. Equals. He will have no choice but to lead at the front with me. So the fate of your life, Lysander au Lune, *heir of empire,* is not for me to decide alone. Together my husband and I will decide if you live or if you die."

When Dido is through with me, Seraphina escorts me back to my cell. There is little conversation between us. But when she goes to close the door, I block it with my foot. "Did your mother send you to my cell?" I ask. "I want the truth."

She stares back belligerently. "Since when has truth mattered to a Lune?"

57

EPHRAIM

Fit for a Duke

O VER THE COM CHANNEL, Gorgo gives the address of a restaurant and tells me to meet him there tonight. I manage to keep the nervousness from my voice, but my hand trembles when I hang up the com. It's a one-way ticket I'm buying. My only hope is that when I call in the cavalry, they come fast and hard. Otherwise the Sovereign's pardon will be for one.

I know Volga will use it better than I could anyway.

Holiday tries to get me to go to a government facility to wait out the mean hours till the meeting, but I finally convince her that it's better for the Syndicate to see me street-side during the day before miraculously showing up at the restaurant. She says goodbye without a smile and departs not back into the terminal, but through a maintenance door that leads under the docking platform. Lyria pauses at the door and turns back to me with my Omnivore in hand. "You're probably going to need this," she says. Holiday unlocked the trigger lock before she left.

"Sure you don't?" I ask.

"No." She frowns. "I didn't make a deal like you. Don't think they let you keep weapons in Deepgrave."

"That's why you never do anything for free," I say glibly.

"I'll keep that in mind." She turns to go.

"Rabbit." She turns to look back at me, and for a moment I wonder if I see hatred pass through her eyes. Did she say all that about Trigg just to get me to agree? She did. She was the honey to Holiday's vinegar. There's no forgiveness in her. Just exhaustion and anger at me and the world.

"What?" she asks.

The fleeting notion of apologizing vanishes. "Bit of advice. Get as far away from them as you can, as fast as you can. Or they'll just chew you up and spit you out."

"If I wanted advice, you'd be the last person I'd ask." With that, she leaves.

I arrive via taxi at the restaurant, a glitzy joint on upper west Promenade, and have to wait for an hour before Gorgo arrives. Nervously pushing aside my drink, I follow him from the restaurant to a flier where several slick thorns in dusters search me for weapons and, as I said they would, look for tracking devices. They take my pistol. When they've decided I'm clean, they put a distortion hood over my head that's set to submerge my senses in an arid, desert world.

Digital tumbleweed rolls across the cracked ground in front of me. In the distance, hungry wolves howl as my body jostles in the back of the flier as she ascends into the flow of traffic. Time distorts inside the hood as well. I can't tell if it's been an hour or four when I feel the ship's landing thrusters kick in and the gentle bump as she sets down. They unload me as I see wolves approach across the false desert, hunting my digital presence. I'm pushed along till I'm guided onto a couch and at last the hood comes off, just before the wolves pounce.

I face an immense ant colony that stretches the length of a wall, all the way up to the ten-meter-high ceiling. Acid-yellow ants the size of my pinky toil behind the glass. They swarm in a mound of legs and teeth over some carcass above the surface of the colony and make a line to carry the food from the top desert level down into the belly of their labyrinth, past storage rooms, barns for aphids, egg hatcheries and nurseries filled with squirming larvae. In the center of the colony, an obese queen the size of a small cat with a swollen, purple abdomen excretes transparent eggs that are ferried away in the mouths of workers with black mandibles.

A nauseating cocktail of curiosity and revulsion grows in me. Gorgo lounges on a couch across from mine, his huge body out of place in the finely decorated room. He lights a burner. His datapad sits on the table, Omnivore next to it. "'Lo, Gorgo. What's with the ants?"

"Duke says they soothe him," he says, watching me through the smoke.

"Got another one of those?" I gesture to the burner.

He hesitates and then proffers me a pack of White Dwarfs. I reach across the glass table and take one. He tosses me a lighter. I light the burner and lean back to admire the place. It's a trophy room. A rare diamond stolen a year after the Fall sits on a glass desk by the window as a paperweight. A war helmet with the crescent moon of House Lune hangs six meters up on the wall. A hundred other priceless treasures litter the room. Not one is nailed down or secured beneath glass, as if to say *No man would dare take me.* The arrogance is magnificent and balanced by menace. On a table sits the Duke's bonesaw.

"Did he steal all this?" I ask. In admiring the room, I've come to the conclusion that there's no way I can get across the table to my gun or his datapad before Gorgo kills me. He could crush my skull without breaking a sweat. He also has that weird locomotion they seem to breed into black ops Obsidians. He was probably a berserker, or maybe even a Stained. I've never seen one in the flesh.

How easy would it be for him to peel my arms from their sockets? I've seen Rising Obsidians do it to captured Gray legionnaires and Golds. Would I scream like those poor bastards?

"Eveything here he stole with his own hand. There was a Duchess before him. He stole her crown too," Gorgo says.

"Surprised he doesn't have the children in here on a pedestal." I fish for a hint of their whereabouts. Would be a shame if I called Holiday and the cavalry and had nothing to show for it. Gorgo doesn't take the bait. "Back to the ants . . . they soothe him? Is the

Duke an entomologist as well?" Gorgo does not reply. He just sits there like a cultured yeti with those eerie eyes bugging out of his cadaverous face. "You don't like me very much, do you, Gorgo?"

"No."

"May I ask why?"

"You talk too much."

"So?"

"Talking wastes wind, slows cogitation. Unlike you, I don't need to wag my tongue to soothe my nerves."

"Communication is the soul of civilization. Otherwise we're like them, aren't we?" I nod to the ants. "Carrying, ferrying, digging, and toiling. If you express yourself only through your work, what are you but an ant?" I want to get a rise out of him. His quietness irks me. "You really should try it."

"I told him he should kill you. Like that Green."

"I take it back. Maybe stick to silence."

"I still think he should kill you."

Gorgo isn't the sort of man you want envisioning your mortality.

"But death is so permanent. You'd miss me." I puff a cloud of smoke between us. "Any particular reason you want to put me in the ground?" My lungs feel tight tonight.

Gorgo doesn't answer. I eye his black duster and black boots. "I've always wondered, the dusters . . . do they give them to you when you sign your employment contract or do you go out and buy your own from a criminal apparel store?"

"You're funny," he says.

"Thank you."

"How's that working for you, Gray? Being funny."

I look around. "Pretty good. How's being the Duke's dog work for you?"

He just smiles that eerie metal smile of his.

The man puts the fear of hell into me. You can read most men, but not this gilded golem. I have no idea what he wants. Feigning boredom, I stand and walk the length of the ant colony. On closer inspection, I realize there are two species of ants, the colonies separated by a sliding glass partition near the ceiling. Hundreds of each gather at the partition. They're little trundling war machines. Larger than the worker ants, with thick plates of shell armor, oversized heads, and comically large mandibles. The yellow ants crane their bodies upward like howling dogs and wave their mandibles in the air while the blue ants throb their stingers in and out. I look again above the yellow ant colony and peer at the carcass that feeds them. I step closer to the glass to see past the squirming bodies. *Oh hell.* It's a severed hand nearly picked clean of flesh. Too large for the children. An Obsidian's crescent metal Sigil can be seen fused to the bone of the metacarpals.

Dread rises from my balls into my belly. So the Duke collected on his debt. Belog? Wasn't that the Obsidian's name? I have a sudden urge to vomit. They're going to murder me. That's why they brought me to see the ants. They're going to kill me and feed me to the fucking ants.

I turn away in disgust. Gorgo's watching me with those quiet eyes that promise so much pain. He gathers his datapad and my gun, and stands when the Duke enters several minutes later. My heart plummets even further into my intestines, hitting each rib on its way down, when two Obsidian bodyguards follow the Pink into the room.

"Have you two been playing nicely?" the Duke asks.

"Relatively," I say with an earnest smile of relief. "Gorgo is a bit taciturn."

"It's his charm. I don't need you anymore tonight, Gorgo. Go play with your little toys," the Duke says. "I took the liberty of refreshing your stock."

Metal glints between Gorgo's lips.

"His gun." Gorgo hands over my Omnivore and leaves with a short bow. The Duke wears a black robe with a purple sheen and black slippers. "Ephraim, darling. So dreadful of me to keep you waiting. I hope Gorgo wasn't too much of a bore."

"Quite a vocabulary on that cold fish in there. Where did you find him?"

"Oh, we've been acquainted for some time. Let's just say that we melted that gold in his teeth down together. Come. Come. I hope you're hungry." He keeps my gun and sets it next to the knives on his side of the table. Close enough for me to reach. I could get it and take his datapad to signal Holiday, but the Obsidians would peel me apart.

I watch them on the far side of the room while the Duke's servants open the bottle of La Dame Chanceuse as we sit across from one another at a long table. The Duke eyes me playfully. "I must admit, I did not expect to hear from you so soon. I feared I might have been a touch too enthusiastic about killing your friends."

"What friends? They betrayed me. Fuck 'em."

"Coldblooded," the Duke says. "I do like reptiles. Almost as much as insects!" He nods toward the ants. "Still, I thought it would take at least several weeks for the ennui to set in. It seems you are like me after all."

"How's that?"

"Restless minds make restless men."

"It's a terrible fault of mine," I say with a small smile for his benefit. "I grow bored quick." The man isn't bothering with coyness now that we're in relative private. His eyes rove my lips as he slips an apricot into his mouth.

"Not too quick, I hope."

I let him see me eyeing the servants in the room, playing up my discomfort. "Lamont, bring the food and let us alone," he says. "I think we can pour our own wine tonight." The servants bring several silver trays of food out and set them on the table before disappearing from the trophy room. He doesn't mention the trophies, but he wants me to see them else we wouldn't be dining amongst them. The two Obsidians did not follow the servants from the room. As long as they're here, I won't be able to get his datapad. They linger at the far door. I can't very well assault him with those two monsters in the room. They'll rip off my arms and beat me to death with them as easy as they would kill a cricket. I look at them pointedly.

"Pretend they're statues," he says. "Heads are full of stone already."

"I'm not used to having witnesses," I admit.

"Yet you left so many when you stole the children. I thought you would detonate a charge in the shuttle once you left, as I recommended."

"If you wanted murder, you should have sent Gorgo."

"Do I detect squeamishness?"

"I prefer to think of it as precision." I glance at the guards. "Can't we be alone? I feel like they're going to eat me."

"I'm sorry. They are here for my protection. I never go anywhere without them. A flaw in my physical design. Weak bones." The lithe man sighs as if he shoulders the greatest of burdens. "They never tell you this, but the peril of power is the people that come with it. Servants, bodyguards, aides. So many eyes and ears and little reptile thoughts in their brains. All those years I wondered what the Golds would do if they knew what went on inside our skulls. I don't think they did, or they would have exterminated the lot of us. Now I sit where they sit and I know what my men think. It's an advantage."

"And what do they think?" I ask, sipping my wine to try and calm myself down. My heart's slamming in my chest. It hasn't stopped since I saw the Obsidian hand in the ant colony. I dry my palms on my pant legs.

"Oh, tedious things. That they could cave my skull in with a wine bottle or slit my throat as I sleep or throw me out a window. The little fantasies of murder are what keep servants sane. They tell themselves they allow me my power. And if ever I become too dreadful, they will do me in and maybe take over. But of course they never do. They procrastinate their vengeance because deep down, they are afraid not just of me, but like all people they fear their own fantasies. Easier to cherish them and keep them inside where they are in control. Possible."

He forks a serving of charred octopus swimming in a dark vinegar sauce onto my plate. The sweet scent combined with my nausea almost makes me gag.

"Do you think I'm afraid of you?" I ask.

"Isn't that the heart of desire? No one wants to fuck what they don't fear, because then there's no validation from it, no power derived."

"Interesting opinion."

"That is why Roses were created. The first Pinks were more beautiful than we are now, but there was nothing inside them. No content beneath the shine. They were toys. Once you used one, the lust evaporated. So the Golds made us into inscrutable enigmas to hold their attention, masters of art, sex, music, and emotion. Enigmas they could never fully understand, and that lack of understanding is the heart of fear."

"So that was a yes."

"That was a yes. You are afraid."

I refill his glass, my hand trembling only slightly. He notices and thinks it's from desire, not zoladone withdrawal and sack-shriveling fear. "I'm curious, Ephraim. Why did you come back so soon? You have all the money you could ever need."

"Can people like you and me ever have all we need?" I ask.

He smiles. "You're insatiable. I love it. The best thing about this new world . . ." He waves to his trophies. "There's always more to take. But you didn't answer my question." His eyes go cold and he ignores the wine I poured for him. "Come now. Answer it."

"I want more." I pander, praying he can't see through this two-bit bullshit. "More than contracts. More than filling a bank account. There's no satisfaction to it. I want more out of this life than just money."

"And what do you think we make here?"

"After the kidnapping, I see there's more than money at play. You make power."

"Yes. Yes. That is a good reason to return."

"That and to visit the kiddies," I say with a laugh that comes out too loud.

He smiles, but watches me, the comment arousing his suspicion. Dammit, Eph, stick to the script. I glance at the ant colony.

"What do you imagine my role would be here?" I ask, deflecting.

He drinks his wine and plays a finger on the edge of his glass. "Well, you would work under me, of course. The rest would depend upon your imagination." I look past him to the patio outside. The glass is smoked, but I see the obscured outline of his personal yacht. The keys dangle from a gold chain on his neck. There's my exit.

"And professionally?" I ask.

He smiles. "As you have no doubt noticed, the era of the freelancer, the prowler, is coming to an end. What an era it was. So much art, so many treasures ripe for the picking. It gave birth to you. To me. But now most of the treasures are consolidated and hoarded by a small enclave of individuals. We must turn our gaze outward before we cannibalize ourselves. Find new ways to steal. That is where you would come in." He pours himself more wine. "I will need an architect who can create new unconventional streams of income. And I think that man could be you."

It's going to go like this for hours, I realize. The dance is more than half the fun to a man like him. But that still won't take the Obsidians from the room. If I ask about the children again, it might cost me my hands. And I'm not a good enough liar to keep pace with this prim courtesan. So instead, I lean back and slide my leg under the table to the inside of his right calf. "Bored now," I say. "Let's change topics." He watches me, eyes sparkling. He wets his lips, small, warm breaths escaping them as I slide my foot up his leg to the inside of his thigh. I feel him harden, so I push my foot gently down, encouraging him. Then, with a sigh, I pull my foot back to its original position on the floor. "But I don't play with an audience."

"Hvardin, Jorlnak . . ." He snaps his fingers at the Obsidians and they leave the room through the double doors. The Duke smooths out his robe and moves his fingers along the controls of an audio system. The deep percussion of synth music thuds through the room like the heartbeat in my chest, but the lights stay bright. He leans back. "Come around the table." I walk around the table, my body numb with trepidation, my gut grumbling for zoladone. He's moved his chair back so there's room for me. He reaches for the tie to his robe, a bright, hungry look in his eyes as I stand over him, blood thundering in my ears. The ghost of a smile plays over his lips. His slender hand runs from my knee up to my hip. The music beats faster, and I realize it's synced to his heart rate. "Go to your knees." I stand there looking down at his soft face and see the predatory self-ishness there. It eats the beauty like a cancer. "On your knees," he says in irritation. My heart sticks a beat, like I stand on the edge of a cliff. Time to jump.

"Nah. I'm good."

"I said . . ."

I flatten my hand into a blade and lurch it forward into his nose with a locked elbow. My basic instructor would applaud the strike. The base of my palm pulverizes the bottom cartilage of his nose. Afraid of killing the Pink, I don't use all my strength. Still, the blow rocks him back in his chair, stunning him. He reaches up to his face. I snatch up my Omnivore and point it at the door. No Obsidians come through. Knowing he must have some sort of panic device, I grab both his hands and slam them down on the table. I frisk him and pull his datapad from his pocket. I wipe blood from his face on the pad for the DNA lock and rip the keys of his ship from the chain on his neck.

"Move your hands or scream, I shoot you in the head," I say under the music. His nose is shattered, flayed up like a pig's. I grab it between my fingers. "Are the children here?" I squeeze. He gasps and nods. The music is throbbing now with his heart. I dial the number Holiday gave me. Her face appears in the air above the pad.

"Ephraim, where the hell have you been?"

"I'm with the Duke," I say over the music.

"It's been hours since you were picked up!"

"How long?"

"Four. The children . . ."

"They're here. Come save my ass."

Four hours?

"Tracking your beacon," she says. She curses under her breath. "Eph, you're on the far side of the moon. You're in Endymion."

The dread that I feel whenever I hear the name wells up in me, formless and absolute, threatening to pull me down into the darkness. I hear their screams. The whir of the laser scalpel . . .

"Endymion . . ." I whisper. While I was in the hood, we must have gone suborbital. I thought I was still in Hyperion. How did time pass so fast? "Don't you have local assets?" I ask.

"Not to punch in there. And none that have been vetted. I'm with Team One in Hyperion. Team Two is closest to you. They're already in the air."

"How long?"

"Two hours."

"Two hours," I repeat quietly. The adrenaline killed my nausea when I struck the Duke. But it comes slithering back now, accompanied by horrifying flashes of what the Duke's men will do to me. I can't keep him for two hours without his men knowing. They find out I have him, they'll move the kids or kill them, then make me wish I'd never sucked down air. Then it's a long goodnight for Volga. I look around the room with its trophies and thudding music and I laugh. Slag it.

"What the hell is so funny?" she asks, annoyed.

"Life. Same as always." I sigh, knowing I'm going to die, and knowing I made my peace with it hours ago. But maybe I can get the little shits out and Volga will walk free. Maybe. "If you gotta leave the field, best to do it in style, Holi."

"Ephraim . . ."

"Tell those bastards to fly faster." I force a smile. "Be seeing you."

I close the connection. The Duke was listening and he's recovered his senses if not his looks. "Why . . ."

"Where are the children?" He spits blood at me. I wipe it off my face. "Stay." I train the Omnivore on him and fetch the bonesaw from its table. Its shape is an acute triangle. "Now, how does this work?" I toggle the switch. The teeth saw the air with a low hum. A cauterizing laser glows above the teeth.

"You rat . . ."

"Sorry, slick, can't hear you. Speak up!"

"Gorgo!" The music drowns out his voice. I slap him anyway and turn up the music with his datapad so his screams won't be heard outside the room. I come close to his ear and hold his right arm on the table. "You killed one of mine. You owe a debt, Duke."

He looks up at me. "Kill me, and she will skin you alive. I'm a Duke of the Syndicate!"

"Where are they?" He just stares back, madness clawing out from inside his eyes. "All right. Time to collect." I lower the bonesaw into his wrist. The saw shakes in my hand as the tiny teeth serrate flesh and bone. Blood hisses as the cauterizer burns closed the capillaries. He thrashes and drools, screaming like my friends did all those years ago.

Being on the other end of the saw doesn't make the screams any better. I clap a hand over his mouth.

"Shh. You weren't meant for this sort of pain," I say in his ear. "You feel too much. Your nerves are too raw. There's no shame in telling me. Where are the children?"

"In the vault," he whimpers.

"Where is the vault?"

"Two floors down . . . East . . . wing."

"What is the combination?"

He hesitates.

"You have only one hand left, Sir Duke," I say.

"It's biometric." His teeth chatter. "Voice and retinal." *Shit*. I was betting everything that he'd have them nearby as part of his collection, but I gauged him wrong.

He sees me doing the mental math. "You need me."

"You're right about that. Anyone guarding the vault?"

"No. That's why we have a vault."

I let him go and he cradles his arm to his chest, whimpering in pain. "There, there," I say. "Let me see."

Tentatively, he shows it to me, and as I bend to look at the damage done, he lurches up at me with something long and sharp emerging from under the skin of his left hand. I twitch my head at the last moment. Blade misses my throat but goes into my face, through my cheekbone, rattling along the upper right molars and sticking into the gums. He twists it. I grunt and stumble back as he tries to pull the wrist blade out and stab me again. I grab one of the spent wine bottles and swing it at him. The bottle hits him in the right cheekbone, collapsing the frail bone. He grunts and falls down to the ground, his body heaving from shock.

I pull his blade out of my gums, hissing when it grates along the teeth and then slips out through the cheek. A subdermal blade. I hurl it to the ground and drool blood out of my mouth. The Duke is crawling away from me, his face bloody, stump on his right arm weeping blood from the charred skin.

Stupid, Eph. Stupid.

I grab him by the back of his robe and hoist him up. He's feather-light. I shove the gun under his jaw. "You try anything again and I peel your head off at the root," I say through the blood. "You're going to take me to the kids. Then I'm going to leave with them and you can go back to your life. Do you understand?" He looks at me with wild eyes. I slap him in the face. "Do you understand, Duke?" He nods.

I drag the man to the door. I don't know how I convinced myself this would go more smoothly. Can't believe the extent of the plan was to "call in the cavalry." Rolling in my own self-loathing, I tear off a piece of my shirt, ball it up, and stick it into my mouth against the wound. My eyes tear up. *Be slick. Calm down.* But I can't stop the hammering of my heart. It feels like I'm going into cardiac arrest. *Gotta move.* With a finger trembling from adrenaline, I unlock and open the door. It hisses back.

The hall is empty. No sign of thorns. I stare down the barrel of my trembling Omnivore. Nothing moves after a minute. "Guess they went to get a drink," I say with a laugh. "Never trust a crow to do a Gray's work." I push the Duke forward, letting him lead a little through the halls. We pass a doorway where his bodyguards are watching a race and smoking. I grind the pistol into the back of the Duke's head in case he might call out to them, then we're past and to the lifts. My body is pulsing with adrenaline. I press the button and wait for the lift, my bloody fingers leaving a smudge. I'm about to wipe it off when voices come from around the corner. I drag the Duke hard away from the lift to the hallway adjacent and hide around the corner just as the men come to the lift bank.

"—they say she's coming tomorrow."

"Not just sending the Collector?"

"Thank Jove, no. I hate that pervert. Something wrong with him down to the bone. Word is she's coming up from Lost City in the flesh to pay the Duke a call. Something to do with the big prize he just scored."

"I heard it was missiles."

"Idiot. It's not missiles. It's a Howler."

"It's missiles. The Howlers have all disappeared."

"Not all of them. Arrested a few on Mars and Earth and out on Mercury. Don't you watch the news?"

"Why? You watch for me. What do you reckon she looks like? Big tits?"

"Obsidians don't have tits. They have pectorals."

"I heard she was a White—"

The lift arrives and they disappear inside. When the doors close, I drag the Duke back out. The blood is still smeared on the call button. I wipe it off as I call another. Sweat slithers down my armpits. The next lift arrives, no one inside. We enter and I press the button to carry us down. The doors take forever to close. My mouth aches with pain. The cloth is already saturated with blood. I spit it out and stick in another swab. The Duke stands quietly facing the doors.

"How do you think this ends?" he asks.

"Probably with me in a furnace," I admit.

"They will catch you. The things they will do . . ."

"If I'm caught, you won't be around to worry about me."

"She won't just torture you, Gray. She takes her time." His voice has caged the madness, but its fingers work at the bars. This job was supposed to end with me dead. If it comes down to it, I'll put the pistol in my mouth and eat iron. Better my way than theirs.

I position myself behind the Duke and the doors open. I push him out and down quiet halls. Blood drips from my chin onto the floor. We come to a set of double doors, through which, ostensibly, is the vault. "Remember, keep your head," I tell the Duke. He makes no reply. I lean past him to open the door and push him in.

Three men lounge outside the vault, smoking burners in the windowless room. Their guns are on the table. They turn from their Karachi cards to see us and they freeze. I shut the door behind me. "Not a move or I kill him," I say, just a little less surprised to see them than they are to see me. One twitches toward his weapon. He stops when he stares down the barrel of my Omni. They watch it like it's the head of a snake, eyes darting to me, their guns, the Duke. "Not a move," I say, inching forward. "Tell them to get on their bellies," I tell the Duke.

"Get on your . . ." With a sudden scream, the Duke rears his head back into my nose. I hear a wet pop and see stars. Then I'm pitched sideways as the Duke throws himself onto my arm, wresting the Omnivore sideways. "Kill him!" he's screaming. "Kill him, you fucking halfwits!"

I punch the Duke in the side of his head and wrench myself away from him so that he sprawls out in front of me. The Obsidian has picked up his railrifle and is raising it. I shoot wildly and miss. I stare down the barrel of the Obsidian's railrifle. I shoot again. The bullet lances forward at two kilometers a second, sparks off the tip of his rifle, and carries on to take off the top half of his head. The other men grab their guns. One crouches and fires a pulseRifle. The sound consumes the room. I fall to my belly as a stream of fists of rippling translucent energy spew over my head, raining debris down on me. I fire from my belly on full auto. The bullets eat into his knee and torso, chewing half his body into a flopping, oozing mass. The last man drops his gun, surrendering.

I stand, my eardrums throbbing. The smell of ozone thick in the room. Holes from the hot metal smoke in my suit's long tails. The last man, a Brown with tattoos consuming the left side of his face, holds up his hands. I shoot him in the chest. He flies back into the wall and drips down, his suit catching fire at the edges of the entry wound. The barrel of the Omnivore smokes, so hot I can feel it on my knuckles. Sounds come to me like I'm underwater. Numb, I haul the Duke from the ground and push him past the ruined bodies to the door as the Brown's burning suit fills the room with smoke. My Omni has one slug left. I strip open the magazine on the dead Obsidian's rifle and push the larger-caliber rounds into the hilt. I close the bottom and the autonomous forge heats the handle as it forms new slugs for the hungry gun.

"Open it!" I push the barrel to the back of the Duke's neck, singeing his flesh.

He presses a series of commands into the door with his good hand. I'm out of my own body, numbed even to the pain of my mouth, the barbarism of the scene and what the gun in my hand did bringing back the hell of the block battles. I don't know how far the sounds went. A scanner slides open on the huge doorframe. The Duke presses his eye to the little light. It flashes and a green positive code flickers on the door's display.

"A murder of crows is nary a flock," he says hoarsely. The light blinks yellow and requests he try again. He clears his throat desperately. "A murder of crows is nary a flock."

This time it takes: a second light blinks green on the display and deep inside the door the tumblers begin to rotate and metal bars roll back. With a satisfying thunk the massive door unlocks. I edge past the Duke and haul it open. I push him through.

The inside of the vault makes me stumble.

It's like the dragon hoards from one of Volga's little storybooks. Mountains of cash and jewels and priceless works of stolen art fill the cavernous metal chamber. A fifteen-million-credit diadem lies errant beside a stack of Titians and Renoirs and Phillipses. A chest of Gold razors lies open; signet rings are heaped together like a child's collection of pebbles from an ocean shore. Samurai masks and framed documents in illegible cursive and real ivory tusks and precious gems as big as duck eggs.

And amongst all this, in a cleared space on the floor, lies a cage with a single mattress inside and plates of chicken bones, a half-empty jug of water, a bucket of human waste, and the most valuable children in all the worlds.

58

EPHRAIM

Halfbreed and Hatchetface

I RUSH TO THE CHILDREN'S CAGE. A curtain of humid, urine-filled air hits me as I enter the unventilated room. Throwing the Duke down on the ground, I look through the cage to the boy and girl. The singing of my eardrums is fading. "Hello, little humans, you might remember me."

The girl spits at me. "Syndicate scum."

"That's no way to welcome your savior. Your mommy sent me to get you out."

"My mother . . ." the boy says.

"Did I stutter?" I realize then that I'm slurring my words. I spit out the rag. Bits of skin from the wound cling to it.

"If Mother sent you, where are the Lionguards?" the boy asks. "The Telemanuses?"

"In the Citadel, shining their armor and jackin' it. How should I know?"

"Are you a lurcher?"

"Hell no." I bend to unclip the lock and then twist it so that the teeth of the lock disengage. I'm about to open it when I catch the girl's eyes again. "I'm on your side, girly. If you little brats want to see your parents again, you do just as I say. Otherwise we'll all get peeled apart like onions for a stew." I watch them expectantly. "This is the part where you nod." They both nod. First the boy, then the girl. "Good."

I open the latch and step back, keeping my gun trained on the Duke. The girl bursts out but the boy follows more tentatively, eyeing the Duke and me curiously. He's more tender and scientific than the girl, it seems. More willing to cooperate. I'll talk to him. Then I feel something cold and metal against the back of my spine. I turn slightly and see the girl holding a solid razor to my back, which she must have fetched from the stack. I laugh at the size of it in her hands, but there's no humor in the pale girl's eyes. I'd call her bluff if I didn't know who her psychotic parents were. The kid is feral.

"Very smart, little lady. Kill your ticket out of here." I step away from the razor. She shuffles forward, the blade never leaving my spine. I look to the boy. "Will you tell her to stop slagging about? We're wasting time."

"Electra, he's right."

The girl twitches her blade to the side and cuts me shallowly on the arm.

"Dammit. I'm bleeding enough," I say.

"That's a down payment," she replies. She reaches into the box of razors, trying them till she finds another blade. She tosses it to the boy. He catches it nimbly and spins it in his small hands.

Little warlords, I remind myself.

"What's our point of egress?" the boy asks me like he's a real soldier.

"There's a ship on a private dock two floors up," I say, holding up the key. "There's also a main garage, but it'll be swarming with thorns."

"Place will already be swarming," the Duke says bitterly. "You're dead flesh walking."

"He's right," the girl mutters. "You made hell coming in here."

"Sound might not have traveled," I say hopefully.

"We heard it through the vault, Gray."

"What's your name?" the boy asks me.

"My name?" I laugh. "Ephraim."

He extends a small hand. The little halfbreed is mocking me, but his eyes are sincere. I laugh again and take the small hand. There are no sigils on it, but I'm surprised by the calluses I find there. "Pax," he says. "Are the Telemanuses alive? The rest of the staff?"

"Don't know." I grab the Duke and haul him to his feet. "Up. Highness, you're our human shield." I straighten his jacket and leave him between the little monsters with their razors at the mouth of the vault. The Duke cowers. He's already attacked me twice. I was surprised. I thought he'd wilt like a flower soon as I threatened him. "Watch him for a moment. Stick him if he gets out of line."

"Immobilizing strike or just a flesh wound?" the girl asks.

"Goryhell. Just watch him. Little psycho."

The boy grows quiet and serious as he sees the bodies outside the vault. Unfazed, the girl turns back impatiently as I cram the bag I brought full of gems and bearer bonds. It breaks my heart to see how little I can fit in the bag and how much loot I'll leave behind. I could spend days in here. Place would have melted Cyra's circuits. "What are you doing?" the girl says, scowling.

"Sorry, I have a problem." I zip shut the bag and throw it up on my shoulder. I contemplate taking a razor for a souvenir, but the things are damn terrifying, so I settle for an old iron ring with a three-headed dragon snarling out from its surface. I'm about to leave when I catch sight of a familiar splash of blue and yellow paint on a canvas out of the corner of my eye.

It can't be.

"Gray, we have to go!"

I ignore her and rifle through the stacked canvases, tossing several million credits' worth of paintings on the ground, and pull out a small-framed oil-on-canvas painting. I laugh incredulously at the picture of Dalí's dread monster: in bright, cracked colors soft watches drape over a tree branch and against the corner of a brown shelf. It is *La persistencia de la memoria*. I'm suddenly conscious of the blood on my fingers. "Gray!" the girl shouts. Wiping my hands, I carefully cut open the back of the frame and slide the canvas out, rolling it gently and slipping it into the bag. Feeling a bit lighter, I join the children.

"I once investigated this claim. They said it was lost in a fire!" I say with a laugh. "I knew they were lying."

"Stealing even now," the girl sneers. "You're disgusting."

"Quiet, hatchetface." I grab the Duke by the back of his collar and push him through the entry room toward the double doors. "Everyone stick close to me. If anyone comes close, you stab them right in the jewels. Understand?" They both nod. The boy is a model of concentration. He paled when he saw the bodies I left on the floor, but now he's lowered his head in anger. Same dead-set jaw as his father, but his hands shake as they hold the too-large razor. Pretend to be spawn of the Reaper all he likes, he's just a terrified boy.

"You ready, little monsters?" They nod. I look at the closed door leading out of the antechamber back into the hall and feel the dread of what lies beyond it seep into me. "Let's go."

We open the door. Half a dozen guns roar. The door shakes and wood shatters as bullets and energy chew into it. I slam closed the door and duck with the children, hauling the Duke down into my lap. "You blind idiots!" I shout out over the Duke's head. "I have your duke!" No one responds from the other side. "You, peek out there," I tell the girl.

Her eyes widen. "What?"

"You're the most expendable, look out there and tell me what you see."

"Slag you."

"Fine." I grab the Duke and shove him out, then jerk him back. "What did you see?"

"Fuck you."

"Will no one cooperate?!"

"I'll do it," Pax says. Before he can move, the girl shoves him back and darts her head to look through the holes in the door, then dips back to shelter.

"Four Obsidian braves, six Grays, three Browns. Six EFC-37 rifles, two GR-19 pistols, two Eaglefor PR-117s, a Vulcan 8k pulseFist. Couldn't make out the rest."

I stare at her. "So, no dolls for you, huh?"

"Was this your plan?" she asks. "How is this your plan?"

"Yap yap yap. You're the one who got kidnapped, dumbass." I rise to a crouch and push my gun against the Duke. "Tell them not to shoot."

"Don't shoot."

"Louder, obviously." He glares at me like he has a choice. I grab his balls through his robe and twist.

"Don't shoot. This is your duke! Don't shoot." I dare a quick peek out through the door. A row of thorns clog the hallway. They look at each other in confusion.

"Tell them to put their weapons on the ground."

"Put your weapons on the ground."

I look out again. "Well, look at that." They're obeying. "We're coming out," I say. I push the Duke up and rise myself, using him as a shield, keeping an arm around his throat and the gun to his head. We shuffle out the door. I have to kick it open. Their fusillade knocked it half off its hinges. The children follow.

"Well, this is a bit awkward," I say, facing the line of cutthroats. Some are in their dusters, others look just roused from bed by the commotion. Their guns litter the floor. "I need you to back away. Down the hall. Then put your sacks and clams to the floor. If anyone rises or looks at me in a way that displeases me, I'll relieve the Duke of his head. Crystal?"

The men look to the Duke.

"Do it," he hisses. "Obey him."

The thorns back away from their weapons and lie on the floor. There's four Obsidians amongst them. Those I watch most carefully. Gorgo isn't there. Not good. We move quickly through the ceded floor. Pax grabs a small plasma pistol from the ground. The girl turns up her nose at this in favor of her razor. They follow tight behind me as I lead them to the lift bank. Electra hits the button with her razor's hilt. Pax's pistol suddenly goes off. The sound explodes in my ear. Plaster rains from the ceiling.

"Halfbreed! What the hell was that for?" I snarl.

"One of them was reaching for something."

"Well, then shoot him, not the ceiling!"

The lift dings behind me. We back into it. The Duke laughs a little mad laugh to himself but says nothing of substance. The children are terrified, even the nasty girl. "Professional recommendation," I say, looking back at the boy, "use that pistol on her, then yourself, if it looks like we're slagged." He looks down at the pistol. The girl glares at me. "Just trying to help."

There's no one waiting for us on the Duke's level. Word must have traveled. But still I expected Gorgo. We move quickly through the abandoned halls and make it back to the Duke's suite. Our dinner still sits on the table. Electra grabs a handful of octopus tentacle and jams it into her mouth as we pass. We access the patio outside, crossing a small gravel park with swirling white angel trees to reach the Duke's sparkling CR-17 Hornet. There's no sign of any thorns. Something is off. I keep the Duke between me and the building, then I have an epiphany.

"They're in the ship," I say. "Don't . . ."

Pax activates the door controls and the door hisses upward, revealing a dark interior. No one comes from inside. I look back to the building, not seeing any pursuers. Then I catch the glint of metal. Three stories up, through a plate-glass window, I see Gorgo's pale face to the side of a long barrel. There's a small flash. The window shatters. In this moment I suddenly realize why Gorgo smiled when I called him "the Duke's man." Something that feels like a hot hammer hits me in the right side of my chest. Everything goes very quiet and focused. Confused, I rock back on my heels, barely moved, and sway with the Duke. Like we're slow dancing. I take a step backward, trying to pull the Duke into the ship. My heel catches and I fall backward with the Duke on top of me. I stare at the back of his head and part of the sky and breathe his hair. I try to push him off and get up, but he doesn't move. I try to crawl out from under him. The Duke is making a rattling sound with his mouth. I crawl free of him and twist myself to my belly to try to stand. I can't get up. My right arm is too weak to push.

"Help . . ." I say distantly, quietly, confused at why I can't rise. "Help . . ." I'm not even sure who I'm talking to. I feel hands under my arms. The boy's hauling at me to get me up. I almost tip over again.

"Leave him!" the girl cries.

"Come on!" the boy shouts in my ear. I push with my legs and use him to stumble toward the door, leaving the Duke behind to bleed out on the edge of the ramp. I feel better with each step. The girl stands there with her legs spread, both hands on the boy's stolen pistol, firing wildly up at the window. The panes around Gorgo vaporize. Another shot from Gorgo slithers under my left ear, taking the bottom of the lobe. It slams into the metal of the ship and ricochets till it embeds itself in the floor. I duck away from the door, now inside the ship's main hall. *Must fly away.* "We have to take off," I say. With the boy following, I stumble to the cockpit and then sit down in the captain's chair. I stare at the controls, acclimating. I push the key in and twist. Lights come on the console.

"Greetings, Your Ethereal Majesty," the vessel purrs. I press the engine ignition. The Hornet's twin ion engines thrum to life.

"Close the door!" the girl is shouting. "Close the gorydamn door!" I look for the ramp retraction button and can't find it, still dazed. The boy reaches past me from the co-pilot seat and presses it. I feel the ramp retract into the ship. He asks me something. I turn to look at him.

"Hm?"

"Can you fly?" he asks me.

"Of course I can fly." I reach for the elevation thruster controls and activate them. The Hornet levitates up off the landing pad. I push forward on the main engine throttle and we rocket away from the landing pad out into Endymion's cityscape.

"Goryhell," the girl says. The tower shrinks behind us. "That was manic."

"You prime, Electra?" Pax asks. She nods.

"Is the Duke dead?" I ask.

"Hell if I know," the girl replies.

"Where are you taking us?" the boy asks.

"Back to the Hyperion. It'll take us an hour's flight time in this. I can get your mommy's men to rendezvous halfway. Syndicate will have this thing tracked, but short of military ships, nothing can catch a Hornet. Long as we don't set down, we're safe and you're home to Mommy."

"We should hail the local Watchmen," the boy says.

"And roll the dice that they're not on the Syndicate payroll? I thought your parents were geniuses."

"They are."

I grunt. "Must not be genetic." They're both staring at me funny. "What?" I ask. "Got something on my face?"

"Are you prime?" the boy asks me.

"I'm shiny."

"Shiny?" he asks.

"Dog tongue," the girl says. "You don't look shiny. You look like you're going to die."

"A regular font of cheer, you are." A localized burning pain on my right pectoral begins to grow and grow until it's a horrendous agony. My entire chest is starting to cramp. Something wet and hot trickles down my flank and soaks into my underwear. I look down and see a small hole in my suit. I stick a finger in and feel a sharp pain on the torn skin. It comes away covered with blood. Cool shock ignites in my cells from my nipples down through my legs and toes, like I've been dunked in ice water. "Oh. I've been shot," I say. It must have gone through the Duke into me. It seems obvious now, but in the moment I couldn't figure what happened.

"Have you been shot before?" Pax asks warily.

"Not exactly. Congratulations, you just saw me get my cherry popped," I say through chattering teeth. It hurts worse by the minute. I look down at the wound. I thought I'd go into shock sooner. Fighting alongside the Sons, I saw Golds bleed out from scrap metal to the thigh. Others I've seen take bullets or pulseblasts to the face and keep ticking with half their jaws hanging off. A Red once kept fighting for an hour with his arm a shredded stump from a grenade. Died after, but still. Everyone is different. I'm a little proud of myself.

But the pride is quickly eaten up by fear.

The wound is bad and there's no exit hole on my back. My fingertips are going cold. My teeth rattle together and the pain becomes unimaginable. I look over at the children, who talk amongst themselves, as we fly over the manufacturing districts of Endymion—areas hard hit by the Battle of Luna and not as well loved by Quicksilver—and wonder if they know how bad the wound is. I shift over to the ship's holopad, which rests to the right of the flight control console, and tap in Holiday's number from memory. She answers the call almost immediately. I face her, the Sovereign, and several others.

"Ephraim . . ." she says in relief. "Did you . . ."

"Right here," I say. I expand the camera view to include the entire cockpit so they can see the children too.

"Pax!" the Sovereign says, her voice almost breaking. Tears fill the Gold's obnoxiously symmetrical eyes.

"I'm here, Mother."

"Did they hurt you?"

"No," he lies. "I'm safe." The Sovereign looks to someone off-camera. "Call Victra, tell her Electra is alive."

"She'll hit the Syndicate if she knows."

"I'm counting on it."

The Sovereign looks back to the camera. "Where are you, Ephraim? Send us your coordinates and my men will rendezvous."

"No," I say. "I'm not going to risk you shutting me in prison. Release Volga, and soon as she's safe and tidy I'll dump the kids on a rooftop, then your men can find them."

"That wasn't what we agreed upon."

"Tough bloody luck."

"You're bleeding everywhere . . ." Electra says. She looks past me. "He's going to crash the ship anyway."

"I'll trust a backalley Yellow's clinic before I'll trust a Gold's word," I sneer.

"We're going to the Citadel," Pax says from behind me.

"Maybe you didn't hear . . ." I turn and find the tip of a razor centimeters from my right eyeball. He stands in a fencer's position.

"Comply, citizen. Or I'll be forced to learn how to fly a ship."

59

LYRIA

Forgiveness

F ROM A BALCONY, I watch a squadron of ripWings rise from the
Palatine landing pads up into the night. Their engines plume
blue and shrink in the distance, leaving the Citadel wall behind and
crossing the trees toward Hyperion.

The children are safe. And so is Ephraim. My own relief in knowing the bastard lives comes as a surprise to me. I've never been the
forgiving type, but I feel pity for the man and his pain. I recognized
the fear in him when he saw the Obsidian the Sovereign's men captured. He's a man. Like my father, like my brothers, raised in a place
without love, trampled by the same clumsy Republic that brought us
from the mines. I can't hate him any more than I can hate myself.
Maybe that isn't forgiveness, but it's all I have to give.

Just because he has pain doesn't mean he should bring others into
it.

That's on him.

Holiday stands motionless beside me, watching the ships, a wistful
expression caged by the hard lines of her face. The Sovereign held her
back from the mission. Says it was because she hasn't slept in forty-
eight hours, but even I know it's because of Holiday's connection to

Ephraim. There's no forgiveness in the hard woman. I wonder if she was always this intense.

"What odds did you give him?" I ask.

At first I think she doesn't hear me and might be listening to the pilots and commandos on her internal com, then I realize she's just ignoring me.

"I don't gamble," she says after a moment.

"Course you don't."

"Ephraim won't die," she says.

"He blessed or something? Touched by the Vale?"

"No. Not blessed," she says distantly. "He used to work for the Sons, you know. Joined after my brother died." Her voice is slow and robotic. "Served as a recruiter before becoming a scar hunter. Back before House Lune fell, before the Battle of Ilium even. When the Society's agents owned this moon, he brought in people like you. Like me. He taught them how to fight. How to survive so they could take back just some of what'd been taken from 'em. After Luna fell to the Rising, he was given a mission in Endymion to find a Gold who was organizing raids. It was a trap. They interrogated his men in front of him. Skinned them alive and made him watch. By the time we got there, he was the only one left. The Gold was captured with the peeling knife in hand." She pauses, disliking the memory. "But . . . the Gold had information the Sovereign needed, information he exchanged for a full pardon. Ephraim watched the man who skinned his friends walk free." She looks at me. "Point is, Ephraim wants to die, but he can't. That's his curse."

"That's why you took the Obsidian," I say. "Because he couldn't watch another friend die?"

She shrugs. "I know where to hurt."

There's no regret in her eyes. She seems a person made all of flint and iron, one who came into the world full-born, without mother or father or past or future. Less a woman than shovel or an axe. If there is more than that to her, she would never show it to me. "What sort of person does that make you?" I ask.

She doesn't answer immediately.

She points east to the New Forum on the far side of the Citadel grounds. The domed building is pale in the night and rises out of the trees around it like a hill of snow, stark in contrast with the brutal lines of the pyramid forum the Society used. "Beautiful, isn't it?" I nod. She stares on at it. "You think clean hands built it?"

The Sovereign is in conference with Theodora and Daxo when we join them. I keep my distance from both Pink and Gold, my arm still itching from the torture. Above the table, a map shows the progress of the squadron toward the stolen shuttle. The Sovereign watches it coolly as she converses with Theodora, but I can sense the underlying tension in her. Her eyes are bloodshot and heavy bags have formed under them. Coffee cups and the remnants of a meal litter the table. How long can a Gold go without sleep?

". . . could not have done this alone," Daxo is saying to Theodora. He cuts short when he sees me enter the room with Holiday.

"Continue," the Sovereign says.

Daxo hesitates for a moment with me in the room. "The Syndicate is working with someone. I recommend we conceal this from the Senate until we know more. My spies will have names by the morning. Heads by the end of the week."

"Theodora?" the Sovereign asks.

"You know my thoughts," she says. "The longer we hold this from the Senate, the more it discredits the transparency you promised them. Senator Caraval is already inquiring about the unusual traffic over Hyperion."

"It's stupid to go before them until my son is safe here, by my side," the Sovereign says. "I won't have those men saying a mother can't govern when her child is in danger. They'll smear me and call a referendum to make me step down before the vote. With Caraval and the Coppers lost, we're going to lose six to seven. My veto is all that can stop this absurd peace process."

"Who would replace you?" Theodora asks.

"The Senate would vote. Majority rules until next election," Daxo answers.

"Until we know who did it, there will be suspicion that this is a ploy to delay the vote . . ." Theodora says.

"I already know who did it," the Sovereign replies. Theodora and Daxo exchange confused glances. "The Syndicate was hired. But by whom? Who has the most to gain?" She waits for an answer. None comes. "It was the Ash Lord. He can't beat our legions, so he's after our Senate. Darrow was right. This happened because I was weak, because I was tired. I never should have let the Vox chase him away."

She focuses back on the holo of her son's ship making its way back to Hyperion, her long fingers tapping her side.

"Lyria," she says, eyes boring into me. I don't bow my head this time, but stare back at her, knowing this is when the axe falls. Yet her tone surprises me. "You made a dire mistake, girl. One that should end your service to me, to anyone. But without you, we would not have found this Volga and . . ." She spares a glance to Holiday. ". . . Ephraim. Soon my boy will be back with me, because you were brave enough to own your mistakes. I must now own mine." How could she ever understand what her mistakes cost me? She's lost her son for a few days and she thinks she knows. She'll never know the mud. The flies.

"You lost your family," she says. "You trusted the Republic and we broke that trust." Then I'm struck dumb. She goes to a knee. Her eyes on the ground. "I do not deserve it, nor must you give it, but I ask, all the same: Will you forgive us? Will you forgive me for not doing better?"

Forgive her?

I don't understand the idea. Nor do her councilors. They gawp down at her, as off-footed as I am. Her golden braids are even with my eyes. There's loose strands. The faint, earthy smell of oil and the coffee from her breath. I hear the air enter her mouth and fill her lungs and whistle out her nose, see her shoulders rise and fall. The power is shed, her naked soul there in front of me. She's just a woman. Just a mother with more children than any other. Maybe she does know my pain. Before this, she was a freedom fighter. A soldier. It's easy to forget that. She's seen mud, and now I think she remembers it.

I can't hold on to the anger or the pettiness or the pain. I want only to help her, to protect families like mine. Letting go of that anger doesn't spit on the memories of Ava or Tiran or the children. It honors them. And for the first time I can remember, I feel hope.

With a trembling hand, I reach and touch her head.

She stands afterwards. "Thank you." I nod, unable to put what's inside me into words that don't sound stupid. "A storm is coming to the Republic," she says softly. "This was just the first breath. You still have a part to play in all of this."

"What could I ever hope to do?" I ask.

"You have a voice, don't you? When I go before the Senate, I will need you as a witness. Your testimony will save lives. It will bring the men behind this to justice. Will you help me, Lyria of Lagalos?"

"If you promise me that Liam will be looked after, and his eyesight given to him. I know there's a way. But I don't have the money."

She looks down in amusement. "Are you negotiating with me?"

"I won't help you if you don't help him."

"Very well. It's agreed."

I spit in my hand and stick it out to her. She looks down at it in surprise, then shakes my hand.

I'm guided by Holiday to the door. There, I turn back around. "I wonder . . . could I see Kavax?"

"No," the Sovereign says. "I don't think that would be a very good idea right now."

I nod and follow Holiday out of the room.

At the doorway to my room, I stop. "Could you tell Liam I'm all right?" I ask her. "He must have been worried."

"He was told you were on an errand for Kavax," she says. "He wasn't worried."

"All the same. Could I see him? I won't say a thing to him."

"I'm sorry, it was risk enough bringing you to speak with Ephraim. We can't have any more security risks." She watches my face fall without sympathy. Then a sigh escapes her thin lips. "What if I take him candy or a little cake or something and say it's from you? Would that cheer you up?"

"You'd do that?"

She shrugs. "What's his favorite flavor?"

"Chocolate."

"All right." I wait expectantly, looking up at her. "What? You want a hug? Get inside." She shoves her fingers against the opening mechanism. The door slides into the wall.

"Oh," I say, and step in. "Thank you for the—" The door shuts in my face. "Fucking Grays," I mutter. The room is not grand, but it's clean and has a full water bathroom. Exhausted, I turn on the water to the shower till steam rises. I wriggle out of my borrowed clothes, awkward with the shoulder sling, and stand under the stream of hot water thinking of how lucky I am to be alive. To not be on the run.

You'd be proud of me, Ava. Ma. I know that. And there's more I can do. Help the Sovereign till this is through, and maybe we can bring all those bastards down. But it wasn't the Syndicate who killed my family. Whatever happens here, those Red Hand butchers will go unpunished. How can that be fair? How can it be right?

I turn off the shower and stand near the exit vents so the hot air can evaporate the water from my stomach and breasts. When I open my eyes, I see a pair of white maid shoes on the wet white tile. My eyes track upward. The woman is a Brown in her mid-thirties with two great moles, a hooked nose, and a bird nest of hair. She holds a gun in her hand. At the end of it is a large hypodermic needle that she pulls out of my chest. I take a step toward her and lose my footing. I don't even feel the ground come up to greet me. The world fogs and spins. And the last I see is the woman patting my face.

"Hello, traitor. House Barca sends their regards."

60

DARROW

Ashes to Ashes

Apollonius, Sevro, and I cut our way through the fortress guards. It seems most of the manpower was sent to fight beyond the walls, likely to stop Apollonius's force from ever making landfall. Those who remain offer thin resistance to our combined violence. After shattering a trio of Gold bodyguards near the grav-Lifts, we divide to search more efficiently for the Ash Lord. Sevro and I stick together, while Apollonius sets off on his own.

The search does not take long.

"This has to be it," Sevro says outside a set of double doors gilded with gold.

"There will be Stained inside," I say. "We should wait for Apollonius."

"You need him to wipe your ass too?" Sevro asks. He kicks open the doors. "Time for your bill, Ass Lord."

The room is quiet.

Despite the decadent floral moldings and whitewashed walls, the room is cavernous and sparse but for a large four-post bed that looks out an open balcony window to the sea. A pulseShield ripples faintly outside the windowsill. Around the bed squat a legion of hulking, polymelian forms. At first I think they are knights, but as a column of light from the outer suite illuminates the gray metal, I realize that they are not men at all, but medical machines. Small displays glow with life readings.

An old Pink in a nightgown and two Brown servants holding fire pokers guard the foot of the bed, shielding its inhabitant from us. The Browns charge, screaming at the top of their lungs. We take them down, trying not to kill them with our metal-covered fists. The Pink at the bed is wailing. "No," she screams. "Stay away from him!"

I pull her from in front of the bed as Sevro approaches it warily. She slashes at me with her nails, breaking them against my armor. "Monsters!" Her spit sprays my face. "You monsters." Sevro punches her in the back of the head. I catch her as she drops to the floor.

A deathly stench fills the room. Sevro stands at the base of the bed, his hand pulling back the silk curtains. His face is pale. "Darrow . . ." He jerks the silk curtains off the frame so I can see.

On the bed, lying in a nest of blankets, are the remnants of a giant. When I met the Ash Lord as a lancer to Augustus, he stood over seven feet in height and weighed as much as a Telemanus. At that time he was edging past a hundred. But he was still stately and spry despite his girth. That vigor he retained throughout our many bouts in the early stages of the war. And though his face has spoken on Core broadcasts over the last years, I see now that it was a ruse, and why he hides here in his seaswept citadel.

Barely a third of the man remains.

What does is emaciated and skeletal. His arms have shrunken in on themselves, the muscle withered away. The skin, once dark as onyx, is now loose and scabrous with yellow flakes, oozing pus into white bandages. His once-bright eyes are sunken into his head, which is bald, the skin tight and dry like a thin layer of scale over his titanic skull. Wires and fluid lines connect to the machines that guard his bed, cycling his blood and removing his waste. It's as if he has been devoured from inside.

"I wondered who knocked," he murmurs. His eyes—stained with a rotten yellow infection—watch me without malice. A hologram floats beside his bedside, showing us the battle outside. "I thought it the Saud, finally come to reclaim their planet. But now I see it ends as it should, with wolves." The simple words brook no anger. The voice alone remembers the man. It is drum-deep, defiant and proud, even trapped as it is in his wasted body, like summer thunder captured in a tattered paper lantern.

For ten years we've been adversaries. Have danced across the worlds in a never-ending duel. Each move countered by the other, then recountered in one giant game on many boards—first the metal jungle of Luna, the plains and seas of Earth and Mars, then the Core orbits, till finally the sand belt of Mercury, where I took the planet and he broke my army. Now all those vast theaters and the millions of men shrink down to this moment, to this small room on this far-flung isle, and none of it makes any bloodydamn sense.

"Am I not as you expected?" he asks with a smile.

"Let's just cut his head off," Sevro says.

"Not yet."

"What are we waiting for? This piece of shit needs to meet the worms."

"Not yet!" I snap. Sevro paces around the bed in agitation.

"You are precisely what I expected," the Ash Lord says. "The destroyer of a civilization too often resembles its founders." He wets his mouth from a water feeding tube and follows that up with a grotesque clearing of his throat. "I must apologize, Darrow. For not seeing you sooner—when you were just a boy who broke his Institute. Had I opened my eyes and noticed you, what a world we would still have. But I see you now. Yes. And you are *immense*."

It's admiration in his voice. It's familiarity. How few people left breathing could understand this man? How many men know what it is like to give a command that kills millions? I swallow, my hatred for him quieted by the wretched thing he's become, and my fear at heading down the same broken road.

This is not how I pictured our final confrontation.

"What happened to you?" I ask. "How long have you been like this?"

The Ash Lord ignores the question and searches my face. "I see you kept our scar. And our eyes. Then what of the Red remains?"

"Enough."

"Ah," he says quietly. "I suppose that is what every man must tell himself in war." His voice rasps and he sucks again on the water tube. "That there will be an end, and when it is done, enough of himself will remain. Enough to be a father. A brother. A lover. But we know it isn't true. Don't we, Darrow? War eats the victors last."

His words make a heaviness settle on me. I wish I could say I was different than him. That I will survive this war. But I know day by day the boy inside is dying. The spirit that ran through the halls of Lykos, that curled with Eo in bed, he began to die the day he watched his father dangle from a noose and did not cry.

"It's a price I'm willing to pay to be done with you," I say.

"That is part of your Red genetic character. Your yearning, your *need* to sacrifice. Brave pioneer. Toil, dig, die for the good of humanity. To make Mars green. We designed you to be the perfect slave. And that's what you are, Darrow. A slave with many masters. Change your eyes. Take our scar. Break our reign. It won't change what you are at your core. A slave."

Bombs rumble outside. Sevro spits at the corner, nearing the end of his patience.

"Lorn once said you were his greatest friend," I say. "That you were once a man to be admired. Before Rhea. Before you crowned yourself with ash."

"Rhea was a rational transaction. Sixty million lives to keep order for eighteen billion." His shrunken lips curl. "What do you think Lorn would have done if he saw what you were? Do you really think he would have spared you?"

"No, I think he would have cut my heart out," I say. He could walk away from his Society, but he would never let it fall. I hear a sound at the door. Apollonius enters, alone. The Ash Lord's eyes darken with hate. But in seeing the state of his nemesis, Apollonius does not look as dismayed as he should.

"Ah, I see the Ash Lord has become most literal indeed."

Apollonius sits on the edge of the bed and pulls back the sheets to see the cadaverous legs of the old warlord. He makes a clucking sound with his tongue and prods the flaking skin at the thigh, peeling off a small strip of the scale and grinding it between the metal fingers of his gauntlets till a fine powder sprinkles the bed. "Did the bite hurt?"

"So it was you," the Ash Lord murmurs. "Atalantia did not believe me."

"Even from the deep, I have teeth," Apollonius says. "I served nobly. Without deceit or graft. But you betrayed me to steal from me. You turned my blood against me. That, my goodman, was a dire mistake."

I feel a reptilian fear slipping into me. I back away from Apollonius. Sevro points his pulseFist at him. "You knew he was like this and you did not tell me?" I say.

"You son of a bitch," Sevro hisses.

Apollonius smiles. "The warden did not just buy me tomatoes and whores."

"You're dead, shithead." But Sevro doesn't fire.

"I did not know it worked," Apollonius says innocently. "But I am delighted by the results."

The Ash Lord tries to spit at him, but the feeble saliva catches on his own chin. "Is revenge worth sounding the death knell of your race, spoiled cur?"

"My race?" Apollonius stands. "No, no, my lord, I am a race unto myself."

"How long ago?" I ask, grabbing Apollonius by the throat. "How long ago did you do this?"

"Three years," he says, not liking my hands on him. "Are we not allies any longer?" He steps back measuredly, touching his throat. At the news, Sevro looks light-headed.

Three years. Three years like this . . . He can't have led his men or fleets on Mercury from here. The time delay would make battle command impossible. But how then did they resist me for so long? Who commanded them? Who is responsible for their new tactics? Who was really behind the holos of him on his bridge when we spoke those half dozen times?

"Yes," the Ash Lord rasps, as if he can hear my thoughts. "Do you feel the dread yet, slave? Knowing you came all this way, fractured your Republic, your family! Made a pact with *this* devil to kill a sick old man at the end of his days?"

I fight the urge to scream. I feel like I'm falling. What a waste. What an unbelievable waste.

"Who was it?" I ask.

The Ash Lord looks at Apollonius. "Who else? The only daughter you have left me."

"Atalantia . . ." I whisper.

"My last Fury." He smiles with pride. "You destroyed her home. You murdered her sisters. Now you come to take her father. She was a frivolous girl. She would have lived in peace, Darrow, but you have brought her nothing but war." He mocks me.

"All of this for nothing," Sevro murmurs to himself. "We killed Wulfgar for nothing. We came all this way. Darrow . . ."

I don't know what to say.

"Where is Atalantia now?" Apollonius asks.

"Far from here," the Ash Lord says. "The peace talks were her idea. She expected you to dissolve the Senate. Take the reins. But you left. You should have gone to your fleet, Darrow."

There were too few ships in orbit. I assumed most were on the far side of the planet. But now I know what he means. "Impossible," I say. "They would have been detected."

He smiles. "Ten years ago, you came upon Luna from the fog of war. She will fall upon your fleet over Mercury. It is at half strength because of your . . . tantrum in your Senate. It will burn. And your fabled army on the surface will burn."

Something inside me knows that he is right, because it would be too fine a world for this to end with him, today. If Atalantia has led his forces, if they are en route to destroy the Republic forces, then the war is not ending. It is beginning again. Around and around it goes. I do not know if the Republic can last another blow. It is my fault. I never should have launched the Iron Rain; but for hubris, for so many reasons, I let the Rain fall, and it has not stopped since. I shattered my family, killed Wulfgar, came here all for nothing.

The Ash Lord watches me realize this with little satisfaction. There is no joy in his final moments. No cruel relish. Just a great exhaustion.

"Orion and Virginia have to know that Atalantia is coming," I say, numbly. "We have to go."

"Do you think I would tell you this if you could hope to influence it?"

"Darrow, we have to let them know . . ." Sevro says.

"You came all the way here," the Ash Lord continues. "Across the great ink, thinking you could kill me and return home to your family. But now there is nothing to return to. No Republic. No family . . ."

"No family . . ." I echo.

Sevro takes a step forward. "Say that again?"

"You left your children behind. Didn't you?"

Sevro lurches forward and grabs him by the neck. "What the hell are you talking about?"

The Ash Lord smiles at him, their faces inches apart. "You are like me, in the end. I spent my children for my war. And now, so have you."

Sevro's grip goes slack.

"Your daughter." He looks at me. "And your son. They have been taken."

No.

My fingers curl around the wood post of this rotted man's bed and I feel the shifting of something inside me. The whisper of formless dread that attends when I wake from a horrible nightmare and for a moment forget my human delusions and see the world for as cold a place as it really is. Dark, hollow wind channels through my heart and I know I have lost. I left my boy behind.

"You're lying," Sevro whispers.

We're each in our little worlds of dread, each sinking into the darkness, each unable to grasp, to believe that he is telling the truth. This is the spite of a dying man. That is all it can be. That is all I can accept.

"You're lying," Sevro says again. His face is milk pale.

But he's not. There is too much satisfaction in him.

"Was it you?" I whisper.

"If only. It was one of yours."

"Who?"

The Ash Lord watches me and then turns his large head to look away from me out to the bright sea, where his spirit has already fled. "Lorn was right," he says in a rough whisper. "The bill comes at the end."

"Who took my son?" I shout. "Who?"

With an animal scream, Sevro launches himself past me and slams his fist into the Ash Lord's face. Again and again till blood coats Sevro's hands to his wrists and the Ash Lord's lips are mangled. I pull at Sevro. He hits me right in the jaw. I hold on, sagging against him as he hyperventilates. He shoves me off, wheeling back to the Ash Lord with his razor drawn.

"We need him alive," I shout. "We need to know more."

There's a soft pop and I look back to the Ash Lord to see foam bubbling from his mouth. He spits a false tooth onto the sheets. Apollonius picks it up and brings it to his nose. "Poison."

"Who stole my child?" I say, gripping him. "Tell me."

He smiles, baring his rotting gums.

"He won't talk," Apollonius says.

Sevro grunts. "Doesn't mean he gets to go easy."

"I agree with the halfbreed," Apollonius says. He grabs something from atop one of the medical machines. A bottle of antibacterial spray the nurses must have used on the equipment. He takes one of the candles from beside the bed.

"No . . ." The Ash Lord's eyes are wide with fear, his words slurred from the poison.

"Apollonius . . ." I move toward him. Sevro shoves me back.

"Burn the bastard," he sneers.

But Apollonius looks to me. "Reaper?"

The sorrow in me is fathomless.

I killed Wulfgar.

I broke my family.

I lost my son.

For this rotted slaver.

"Burn him."

"No!" The Ash Lord tries to rise from his bed. "Stop!"

"Ashes to ashes . . ." Apollonius turns the canister so it points at the Ash Lord. "Dust to dust." He depresses the canister's release button. Antibacterial residue hisses out onto the Ash Lord, coating him in chemical sheen. Then Apollonius tosses the candle onto the bed. Blue fire explodes as the candle flame catches the alcohol.

The Ash Lord screams. Fire races over the dry husk of his skin. He flails against the inferno like a thrashing mantis, his skin contracting and boiling and swelling and blackening as the air of the room fills with acrid smoke. The plastic tubes connected to his gut and arms snap taut and jerk the medical machines toward the bed.

Apollonius stands back from the horror in delighted satisfaction. The inferno dances in his eyes, and casts maniacal shadows over his high cheekbones. Beside Sevro, I feel no satisfaction, only a gaping loneliness. All the friends and family tattered and torn by my war, my choices.

Anguish saws at me inside with crueler teeth than these flames.

And as the Ash Lord breathes his last, I turn from the murder, as lost as I was when I walked the scaffold seventeen years ago and felt the rope around my neck. All I wanted to be then was a father. And now my son is lost.

61

LYSANDER

The Moon Lord

T HE IDLE CHATTER THAT FILLS the Hall of Justice in the Ionian
Golds' capital city of Sungrave evaporates when Romulus au
Raa enters the room. He comes in dignified silence, clad in a gray
kimono of rough-spun wool. Flanking him are his loyal kin: mis-
shapen Marius, ancient Pandora, a host of die-hard Praetors and
white-haired veterans. What is missing and notably absent is the
younger generation. Those of my age or thereabouts. The brilliant
students of the post-Rising generation all cluster worshipfully around
Seraphina, her Dustwalkers, and several other notable captains of
Ganymede, Callisto, Europa, and a contingent from Saturn's and
Uranus's moons up in the stone stadium seats.

The Hall of Justice itself is a dark treasure. All its surfaces are faced
in a shiny black stone. The nave is triangular, the south, north, and
west aisles steeped stadium rows. The towering ceiling narrows until
it makes a pyramid, the peak of which is iron. In the winnowing east
chancel, twelve Olympic Knights sit cross-legged in a bowed line on
an elevated white marble podium looking out at the nave. Each wears
a long cape in harmony with their title. Diomedes's is storm gray.
Helios's is brilliant white. Behind them, a marble, gold-tipped pyra-

mid floats. The old Justice sits to the right of the pyramid in her living chair of elm. The young Chance from the duel sits to the left in her chair of bone; one remembers, one promises.

After a welcoming benediction and customary rights, Romulus and his men take their seats in the center of the nave on thin cushions. His has been set apart at the peak of the forty others. Helios au Lux, Arab Knight of the Olympics, stares out from the shadow of his cape like an imperious falcon, long-necked, bald but for a long white mustache, the ends of which are held together by two iron clasps. Diomedes sits at his right hand. A toadish woman with huge eyes sits to his left wearing the badge of the Rage Knight.

"Romulus," Helios begins, his voice a hammer and lacking the nuance for duplicity. "Sovereign of the Rim Dominon, Dominatus of House Raa, you have been brought before the Olympic Council for an impartial hearing on charges brought against you by your accuser, Dido au Raa."

Alone, Dido sits beneath the council, cloaked all in black. To accuse before the council is a perilous endeavor. If Dido's charges are deemed false, she will suffer the fate that would have befallen the man were he convicted. Draconic.

"Accuser, present your charges."

Dido stands without flourish. "First charge: gross negligence during wartime." The Olympics wait for her to continue the list, but she sits down.

Whispers are exchanged in the crowd. She brings no charge of treason, just as she said she would not. She played everyone like a zither. Once her husband is forced to step down or accept co-rule, she will solidify her position. I overhear the two men next to me voicing a different opinion.

"Base cowardice on her, not bringing treason charges," one says.

"Nepotism there. He knew. He had to know."

The room quiets as Helios confirms. "You seek no charge of treason?"

"I do not." She says nothing more and watches her husband evenly.

"Very well, the accuser may present her evidence or witnesses for the charge of gross negligence during wartime."

"This first evidence you may have heard by now." She throws the holo up into the air and plays Seraphina's evidence of the Reaper's deception to predictable silent response. Romulus sits implacable on the ground, watching the docks die in the air above him and bathe him in the brilliant light.

The next item of evidence is Romulus's own communication with Darrow, taken from the sealed communications records of the Battle of Ilium. Romulus's helmet cam feed appears in the air. He's in a hallway filled with smoke. Dying men writhe on the ground around him as he stands, armor spattered in blood, surrounded by mechanized Golds and Obsidians in the middle of a firefight. His two sons Diomedes and Aeneas provide cover for him as he makes a desperate call to Darrow. His face is frantic with fear.

"Darrow, listen carefully. The *Colossus* has altered trajectory and is headed for Ganymede. . . ."

"He's going for the docks. Can any ships intercept?" the Reaper asks.

"No. They're out of position. If Octavia can't win, she'll ruin us. Those docks are my people's future. You must take that bridge at all costs. . . ."

"I'll do my best," are the last words of the Reaper.

"Thank you, Darrow. And good luck. First Cohort, on me!" The connection to Darrow cuts out and we see from Romulus's headcam as he and his sons charge down the hallway. A blinding flash of light goes off. The hull to the right ruptures open, and Aeneas, Romulus's eldest, is speared through the side of his head by a fragment of metal and then sucked out to space. The clip ends.

On the floor, Romulus sits in solemn silence.

One final clip is loaded. It is a conversation between Romulus and Darrow after the Battle of Ilium concluded. Romulus was in the Hanging Palace of Ganymede. Darrow was on his ship. Their two faces float in the air.

"As promised, you have independence," Darrow says.

Romulus sits on the floor, his face haggard, the stump of his right arm wound with white bandages. "And you have your ships," he says very quietly, the spirit stripped from him. "But they will not be enough to defeat the Core. The Ash Lord will be waiting for you."

"I hope so. I have plans for his master."

Romulus pauses. "Do you sail on Mars?"

"Perhaps." The Red's eyes mock, his tone insinuates, while Romulus maintains an even air of military civility. The man had just lost a son, an arm, to say nothing of the destroyed docks. What a picture of a Gold.

"There's one thing I found curious about the battle," he says icily. "Of all the ships my men boarded, not one nuclear weapon over five megatons was found. Despite your claims. Despite your . . . evidence."

"My men found plenty enough. Come aboard if you doubt me. It's hardly curious that they would store them on the Colossus. *Roque would want to keep them under tight watch. We're only lucky that I managed to take . . ."* There's static interference. *". . . bridge when I did. Docks can be rebuilt. Lives cannot."* It sounds like a threat.

"Did they ever have them?"

"Would I risk the future of my people on a lie?" The Slave King smiles cruelly. *"Your moons are safe. You define your own future now, Romulus."* His eyes narrow to two thin slits. *"Do not look the gift horse in the mouth."*

"Indeed." Romulus's silence is heavy as he swallows his anger, his pride, and lets the Slave King mock him. "I would like your fleet to depart before end of day."

"It will take three days to search the debris for our survivors." He insults Romulus's request. *"We will leave then."*

"Very well. My ships will escort your fleet to the boundaries agreed upon. When your flagship crosses into the asteroid belt, you may never return. If one ship under your command crosses the boundary, it will be war between us."

"I remember the terms."

"See that you do. Give my regards to the Core. I'll certainly give yours to the Sons of Ares you leave behind." The connection with the Reaper cuts off, but the image of Romulus floats in the air. He shudders, the calm wilting away and giving a glimpse of the broken man beneath. The image sputters out.

Dido looks at her husband, sharing the pain of Aeneas's death all over again. "Noting the duplicity of the Slave King's actions, it stands as plain fact that more investigation was warranted. Not only into the veracity of the nuclear threat, which was supposedly levied against us by the Sovereign. But toward the veracity of the Slave King's actions throughout and preceding the Battle of Ilium. The inquiry which was commissioned by the council was quickly scuttled by my husband. I do not believe there is evidence he knew the dark truth of the Slave King's actions against our docks . . ." She says this to temper the fury of the Ganymedi Golds, who built the docks and saw them fall on their cities. ". . . but I am not beyond bounds by saying more effort should have gone into assessing the truth. Now I would like to call Seraphina au Raa to the floor."

Seraphina descends and stands between Dido and Romulus.

Dido addresses her daughter. "When you acquired the hologram evidence of the destruction of the docks and returned with it into Rim Space, were you arrested by sworn men of the Sovereign?"

"I was. As I should have been."

"Did you divulge to them the nature of the information you carried?"

"I did not."

"Did, at any point, Romulus admit to knowing the truth about the destruction of the docks?"

"He did not." Seraphina looks at her father. "His actions toward me and the secrecy under which they were enacted were done to protect me from capital punishment for breaking the Pax Solaris. It was a father's love. Not a man's schemes. He knew I entered the Gulf. I do not know if he was aware of the reasons why. But he knew he would have to bring me before the Moon Council."

"Do you believe he committed negligence during wartime?"

"It is not my duty to judge."

"Thank you, Aureate."

Seraphina salutes with her fist to her heart and returns to her place amongst her friends. Dido closes her argument. "My charges are limited because, while I believe my husband misstepped by not investigating further, I do not believe there is evidence to prove he was complicit in hiding information from the council. I do not believe anyone here could call him a traitor." One of the Ganymedi shouts their dissent. "Thus, I ask only for impeachment from his position as Sovereign."

She sits down.

Helios continues. "Romulus. Do you contest these charges?"

Romulus stands. "I do not."

"You wish to offer no mitigating evidence?"

"I do not. In the charge of negligence, I am guilty."

Heads nod in approval. This is an honorable response, one they expected, one that an Iron Gold would give. On Luna, this trial would have stretched out over the course of years, with endless appeals and warehouses of evidence and armies of Copper lawyers. By the time it was through, half those involved would be dead or have had their relatives kidnapped and tortured till they came to the correct judgment. My grandmother would have burned the government to the ground before releasing her clutch on power.

She could have learned a thing or two from this man.

On the dais, Diomedes looks like a man freed from the gallows. His father will be stripped of the Sovereigncy for negligence, but any prison time will be commuted on the grounds of the pending war. Romulus will likely even lead his family's forces under Dido's command. It's a marvel.

But then, in the chancel, behind the Olympic Knights, a fragile chime shatters all well-laid plans. The council turns to look back at the sound. Chance, hardly ten years of age, stands barefoot and quiet in front of her chair, holding a small iron bell. Her white eyes stare out at the terrifying host. Dido frowns, confused. Seraphina whispers to her friends. I feel the rush of impending doom. The memory howls with warning, because I remember my tutor Hieronymous droning on about ancient codices outlining the rules of an impeachment trial. Most forget that the Whites are not set behind the Olympics for show: they cannot decide a verdict, but they do have one unique, archaic power. It is where the phrase "unless chance strikes" originates.

Helios beckons the small girl forward. She comes to whisper in his ear. His face tightens. She returns to her seat and the knights discuss amongst themselves. Whatever is said turns Diomedes sheet white. I glance up at Seraphina and can sense her distress even from across the room. Diomedes is shaking his head at Helios, as are two of the younger knights. The Death Knight, an older woman, walks from the end of the dais to confer with Helios and vehemently stabs her finger in the air. The younger knights don't like what she's said, but after Helios seems to agree, their objections fade and they slowly nod their heads in compliance.

Helios calls order to the room.

"We have discussed amongst ourselves and have come to an agreement. While it is seldom invoked, the Fates are afforded the right to levy additional charges against the accused on behalf of the State. It brings us no pleasure to voice these charges, but we, the Olympic Council, are bound by duty to charge Romulus au Raa with one count of arch treason."

The room upturns. Peerless bound to their feet. Dido raves on the floor. "I do not seek that charge!"

"It does not matter," Helios says.

"This is my trial! My charges!"

"It is the purview of the Fates to request to add charges. You know this. Now sit down."

"Diomedes . . ."

"The council has spoken, Mother," Diomedes says. He looks like he's going to pass out. "You must desist."

Enraged, Dido sits, casting a horrified look at her husband: the punishment for treason is death.

While his men behind him are in a holy rage, Romulus alone seems unaffected and waits patiently for Helios to continue.

"While the Fates may demand additional charges, it is not in their power to present evidence. Thus it should be a simple matter, and one that should be stated for the record so that there are no lingering resentments that might eat at the foundation of our Dominion as we enter our most dire hour. Our Chance was wise and correct to invoke her right. Let us clear the air and move forward as one people." He looks at Romulus with a sigh. "My friend, it annoys me to insult you, but I am bound by my office."

"Of course."

"Two simple questions, two simple answers, and we move forward. Did you know that Darrow of Lykos destroyed the docks, and did you conspire to conceal this from us? Yes or no?"

Romulus wears a tranquil expression. The same I saw on his face as he dissected his razor when we first met. He stands slowly and steps off his small cushion and lets his lone arm fall down his side to tug on the cape so that it is smooth behind him. He lifts his head to the council, then to his wife, with eyes that seem to gaze far beyond the people in this room.

"Romulus . . ." his wife whispers, knowing the spirit of him. "Don't . . ."

"Yes," says the Moon Lord. "I knew and I did so conspire."

The silence of the room shatters a second time. An uproar from the stands, from Dido, from all but Romulus's men and the council itself. Diomedes sits stunned. Seraphina looks around like a lost little girl.

"He does not mean it!" Dido hisses to the council. "He does not mean it. Strike it from the record and convene a new trial for that charge."

Helios is just as astounded. "I cannot."

"He's perjuring himself," Dido says. "It is a lie. He had no evidence. Supposition doesn't count. We all saw the recording. It can be inferred but not proven. All we have evidence of is his negligence. Diomedes, tell him . . ."

"Mother," Diomedes says helplessly, "by his own admission . . ."

"Damn his admission, boy. He's your father. He's Romulus au gorydamned Raa!"

My heart breaks watching her spin helplessly about, as if she were a drowning woman the rest of us could not help. I'm as lost myself.

"Dido . . ." Romulus says from behind her. "Please." She turns to him still in denial, but slowly as she looks into his eyes, she knows that there is no going back and all at once a shiver goes through her that I can see from forty meters back, as her reality, her family, are irrevocably shattered and she knows it is her doing.

"Tell them you're lying," she whispers. "Tell them you had suspicions but didn't know."

"But I knew," Romulus says. "I knew because the holodrop you sent Seraphina to collect was offered to me first."

"What?"

He looks up at the council as if he's already parted from the world.

"It was offered to me. Several images were sent. I invited the brokers to the Rim, where they met around Enceladus. I relied upon my reputation of honor to lure them and the original copy there. I took out a warhawk and killed them all and burned their ship. Of course, as you have seen, there was a copy."

"You did this by yourself?" Helios asks, looking at Pandora.

"I am Romulus au Raa." He smiles sadly. "You might ask yourself why I did this. Why I tell you this now when it will cost me my own life. All my days I have lived as honorably as a man can. But I have carried this secret for too long. And, as my father would ask, what is honor without truth? Honor is not what you say. Honor is what you do."

A cold stone settles in my throat as I watch Seraphina's heart break. Tears leak down her cheeks.

"We live by a code. I broke that code, even if my reasons for doing so were just. Let it serve as a warning to you all. I lied because I knew if we saw what the Slave King did to the docks, we would have no choice but to declare the peace void and sail for war.

"I believe that war will destroy us. All of us, Rim and Core alike. All that the Colors have built together. All we have protected. The legacy of the Society will vanish. Not because our arms are weak. Not because our commanders are frail. But because we are fighting against a religion whose god still lives.

"At this moment, he is mortal. He strains under the burden of rule, and the seams of their alliances fray. But if we sail on Mars or Luna, the Colors will unite. They will become a tide and their now mortal general will become, once again, their god of war. And if he falls, another will rise, and another, and another. We are too few. We are too honorable. We will lose this war just as surely as I will now lose my life.

"I urge you to feel my death. To let it be the last casualty, and not the first of this war that claimed my father, my daughter, my son, and now me."

Seraphina bursts into tears. Dido hangs her head, her body limp. I feel the stirring of my own grief, a reflection of the grief I felt for Cassius's death. It is tragic to see a man's nature doom him, especially when it is a nature so fine as Romulus's.

Helios stands. His voice barely even a whisper. "Romulus au Raa, you are found guilty of the charges levied against you. Guards, seize the convicted and prepare him to return to the dust."

62

LYSANDER

Iron Gold

Amongst a host of Moon Lords on a frozen sulfur dune, Romulus says farewell to his children. Only Raa are in attendance. I do not know why I have been invited. Wearing a kryll and a scorosuit, I watch from the end of their ranks as he bends to press his forehead against young Paleron's. The child weeps for his father. The tears freeze on his cheeks. Romulus stands before Marius. The two men press their foreheads together stoically.

"Forgive your mother. Honor me and serve the Rim," Romulus says.

"As you wish, Father."

Marius watches icily as his father moves on to Diomedes. The warrior looks down at his father like a giant child, hoping beyond all hope for the man to perform some miracle and make this all a dream. "I am sorry, Father," he says, a huge sob stuck in his chest. His father lays a firm hand his shoulder. "I have failed you."

"No. I should never have involved you in this. But what luck I have to call a man like you my son. It is an honor you cannot understand. One day you will have children and if you have just one who is as dear as you are to me, you will understand how blessed my life has been. Stay true to your own heart, no matter the cost."

They say farewell and Romulus goes to Seraphina. Guilt and grief rack her. He puts his forehead to hers. "My burning one."

She recoils from him. "You don't have to die."

"If I live, I divide the Rim. You might forgive, but how could the Codovans? How could anyone on Ganymede who lost a son, a daughter? They've been denied justice because of my lie. I hope this cools their blood. But . . . if the Rim does go to war, it must go as one."

Seraphina says nothing. He touches her face. "The same spirit is in you that was in my brother. Do not let it consume you like it did him. You have nothing to prove. Glory for others is nothing." He touches her heart. "What matters is in here. Honor your conscience, honor your family." His eyes crinkle as he smiles behind the kryll. "One day you will understand why I've done this."

"I will never understand."

He tries to embrace her, but she pulls back from him and walks away from the family across the dune as Diomedes calls to her. Romulus watches her go. He does not move on to Dido, or his mother, who chose not to come watch her son die, but instead he walks to me.

"Lord Raa," I say, lowering my head.

"There are some who would say I should bow to you, heir of Silenius," he says.

"Most who'd say that are dead," I reply. "Besides, I am a guest in your home."

"Very true." He motions for me to follow him and we walk a few paces away from his family. The cold wind howls around us, flinging debris into the reflective goggles I wear. The kryll warms the air as it passes through the membrane into my mouth. Romulus looks back to his family. "They wonder why I have brought you here."

"They're not the only ones."

He examines me with his lone eye. "You look very much like your mother."

"You knew her?"

"Not well." He sees me look at Seraphina, who sits on the edge of a distant dune watching us.

"Why did you ask me to come here, my lord?"

"There is still a chance to stop this war, Lysander. Maybe not to stop it from beginning. I fear the blood has risen too high for that. Even my death will not stop it. But there is a chance to stop it from destroying us all. Our strength before the Rising did not come from our arms or our ships. It came from our unity. Long ago, Silenius au Lune, your blood, and Akari au Raa, my blood, stood together. One the scepter, one the sword. They gave birth to the Pax Solaris. They freed us from Earth's dominion. You face a choice that will touch lives far beyond your sight. Run as you have these last years, or become the echo of those great men." He leans forward, his voice husky and full of emotion. That lone eye seems suspended in his face, celestial and untethered from its mortal body. He sets his hand on my shoulder. "You saved my daughter. Can you now save the worlds?"

He does not wait for a response, which I am far too stunned to give. He walks back to his family to say farewell to his wife. I'm left overcome with the weight of his question. I already took the first step in ignoring Cassius's dying wish. The second with the betrayal of Gaia. Do I have the strength to take the rest? Can I bear the burden of my blood?

I watch Romulus say his final farewells. The great man looks at Dido with so much love I know I can't fathom it. I have never known love like theirs. Seraphina sits alone on the dune and I wonder how Romulus felt when he first saw Dido all those years ago on Venus. If he loved her so much, how could he be so brave as to *choose* to say farewell? Is it really true, pure honor? After having been ripped from my family, I'm at a loss, unable to understand how a man, a father, a husband, could value something more than love.

It awakens something deep inside me. A desire to be as noble as he is now. A need to honor his memory, though I barely knew the man.

"These ten years I've been looking for the man I married," Dido says to her husband. I strain to hear them over the wind. "Now I see him again. The young Moon Lord who burned a city for a girl of the pearl shore. Romulus the Bold. Dido of Numidae. What a pair they were. What an end they had."

"No," he whispers. "This is not the end. I loved you before I ever met you. I will love you until the sun dies. And when it does, I will love you in the darkness. Goodbye, wife."

Stepping close, he removes his kryll and, holding his breath against the toxic air, gently unfastens Dido's to pull her into one last kiss. Steam billows from their lips as they cling at one another. Then Romulus pulls away and tosses his kryll on the ground to step backward down the dune.

Seraphina watches from her perch on the dune. It does not seem right for her to be alone now. I find myself walking toward her up the frozen sulfur. She says nothing as I sit beside her to watch her father's last rite.

Under the watchful gaze of two Obsidian adjuncts to the White Justice, Romulus removes his boots. His cloak. His scorosuit beneath. His liner and his undergarments, till he is naked and pale there on the frozen sulfur. Across the waste he must walk for eighty steps to reach the resting place of Akari au Raa, the founder of his house. The Dragon Tomb is a giant black obelisk shaped like a winged beast at the top of a stubby crag of rock. Hunched frozen bodies litter the dune around the tomb and cling to the rock formation itself—Raa who in old age or punishment or shame came here to die and in death seek to reach their ancestor and erect a humble monument to their own strength. Only four have ever made it to the Dragon Tomb. Romulus seeks to join the honorable dead.

It is below negative one hundred degrees Celsius. Convulsing from the cold, he turns to face us, hiding nothing. His chest is scarred and pale. His stomach flat and muscled. His ribs stand out. His remaining arm is corded with stringy fibers. And as the wind ripples across the waste, his extremities begin to purple from the cold. His hair unbound behind his head whips till the moisture in it freezes.

He roars.

"I am a son of Io. A child of the Dust." Steam clouds his words as he spends his last breath. His fist thumps his chest with each proclamation, leaving a shadow of pink over the paling skin. "I am a dragon of Raa. An Iron Gold. Akari, bear witness!" He whispers something to himself.

Then he turns and walks down the dune toward death, his hand at his side, his shoulders proud and square, head held back in defiance of the cold and poisoned air. The frozen sulfur crystals crack under his feet, wounding the skin. By the tenth step, blood smears a glittering red trail behind him. By the twentieth, his body shudders against the wind.

"Twenty-nine," Seraphina whispers, counting her father's steps. Romulus clutches his chest with his one arm, desperate to keep his spirit of warmth from the gnawing moon. "Thirty-two." His spine stands out as he hunches. "Thirty-seven." His hair is frozen and no longer whips in the wind but clumps to the back of his neck like a dead animal.

"Forty-five." He drifts sideways, his path bending away from the monument. "Fifty." He falls to his knees. Paleron sobs at his mother's side. Dido watches without blinking. Frost crusts her eyelashes. Romulus wills himself up. Blood pours down his knees and freezes to his shins as he stumbles on, his will inexorable. One foot after the other. They are black and red now. Blood frozen onto the bottom of the dead flesh to make a shoe.

"Sixty." Seraphina's voice grows louder, wishing her father a triumph in the end. "Sixty-four." The man will not stop. His will is immense. All the pain of all the years has culminated into this single testament of will to prove to the moon that despite its horrors, it is under his power.

"Sixty-eight."

I find myself wishing strength.

"Seventy . . ." Romulus takes another impossible step up the side of the dune. Then his legs betray him. He falls hard to the ground ten steps from the monument, striking his head on the ice before sliding back, supine. His black hand paws at the ground. Steam seeps from his mouth. But with one arm, he cannot lift himself up. He heaves himself upward one last time. The effort is in vain. He does not stand again. Soon, he does not move. Ice crusts over his white body amongst the corpses of his humbled ancestors. Ten steps from the honored Golds who reached the monument lies the greatest man of a people.

"Pulvis et umbra sumus," Seraphina whispers, and I alone hear her. Below, the family weeps. The moon howls, the darkness quickens, and the Raa leave their father behind and, like the dust, fly away with the wind and fade into the ebbing twilight.

63

LYSANDER

Lux ex Tenebris

DIDO SITS SLUMPED IN a low chair by a window that looks out over the sulfur plain. The weather is clear. Her arms hang off the edge of the armrests. Her large, angry eyes look out into the waste but are trained on her past. She is an island of regret, bled of pride, of spirit, and swollen with the torpor of loss.

"What is it you want, Lune?" She asks this without turning around when Seraphina and I enter the room. The young woman escorted me in silence.

"I'm sorry for your loss," I say. She does not respond. I glance nervously at Seraphina, knowing my presence here is unwanted in this moment of grief. The girl looks back at me with cold, inhospitable eyes. "He was the noblest of men."

"What do you know of my husband?" she asks harshly.

"From what he said to me before he died, I learned enough."

"He was something out of time. A paragon. His life spent honoring the Conquerors. But he was greater by far than they could ever have been. Now . . . such a waste." She shakes her head. "Uncurl your tongue, boy, and leave me to my grief."

"I wish to join your war," I say flatly.

She watches a lone volcano vomit ash into the chrome horizon.

Seraphina scowls. "There's no place for a Lune in our army."

"I beg to differ."

"And what good would you do me, Lysander au Lune?" Dido asks. "Can you skim a dune like a Dustwalker or fly a warhawk in storm or operate a starShell in an Iron Rain as your friends die around you?" She snorts. "You have no scar. You know theory, games. You were raised in a palace, raised to be a king. And there is no more wretched a creature than a king without a kingdom."

"I am not a king."

"Then what are you?"

What am I? I have been asking this of myself for a decade or more.

Little has been certain since my grandmother fell. I looked out at the worlds in flux, in constant motion beneath my feet. Denying me a foundation. Filling me with uncertainty, fear. I did not know my own heart. But no matter the shifting of the worlds, I know the bedrock of my soul. I know the foundation upon which I stand and no longer fear my blood. Just because my grandmother was a tyrant does not mean I will be.

I see the faces of those I left behind on the *Vindabona*.

They need a protector. A shepherd.

I know who I am, or at least, who I want to become. And with that realization, I feel the culmination of the souls who have filled my life. I feel my father's calm, Aja's love, my grandmother's brilliance, Cassius's honor, and even the faint heartbeat of my mother; and I know that Romulus spoke wisdom I somehow already knew deep in the heart of me.

"I am no heir of empire or conqueror of men," I say slowly. "But I have the same birthright as you. The same inheritance. We were created because Earth broke itself. Because man disintegrated into tribal strife. Chaos is the nature of man; order, the dream of Gold. We were made to shepherd. To unite, despite our differences—that is what Romulus said to me in the end. And he is right."

Seraphina stares at me, a rebuke frozen on her lips.

"You called my grandmother a tyrant. She was. But I am not her. I am not Aja. I am not my godfather. I am an Iron Gold."

Slowly, Dido turns around.

"As you gather your armada to sail on the Rising, send me to the Core with a cohort of your best. I will find my godfather. I will tell him that the Rim is coming, that the sins of the past must be forgotten, and that you seek an alliance against the Reaper so that Gold may be united once again. If peace must be brought with a sword, let us hold it together."

The silence stretches between us. She stands imperiously over me. Then her eyes narrow. And slowly on Dido's dour, grieving face, her lips curl into a smile.

64

EPHRAIM

Locust Queen

I SLUMP OVER THE CONTROLS, guiding us over the gray cityscape at high altitude. Electra sits in the co-pilot chair with the razor pointed at me from the side. Of course the little warlords know first aid. Pax has cut open my shirt and sealed the hole in my chest with resFlesh from the ship's medkit, but I'm in shit shape. Need a doctor and blood packs or I'll die, and soon. I'd rather bleed out in this ship than die in a cell, but that's not much of a choice anymore. I eye my Omni in Electra's lap and wonder if I could throw the ship hard to port and get a jump on the little bastards.

"How far are we?" Pax says.

"Republic escorts are twenty out." I eye the roofs beneath us and the flow of pedestrian traffic in the airspace below and wonder if the Syndicate can still reach us here.

"You going to make it?" Electra asks me.

"Do I look like a Yellow?"

"Can you feel your hands?" she asks.

"No." She looks back at Pax. "Don't look at him, hatchetface. I'd rather fly unconscious than let a kid behind the grip of a . . ." I grimace at the pain. ". . . of a Hornet."

"I fly gravBikes all the time," the boy says.

"This ain't a gravBike, kid."

A cold sweat soaks my body. I wipe my face and wish that Volga were here now. I feel naked without her, just as I did the entire time I was with the Duke.

"What's that light?" Electra says, pointing to the communicator.

"Incoming message," Pax says. "Could be Mother."

He opens the channel and a noseless face distorted by a facial scrambler appears over the holopad between the pilot and co-pilot seats. The pixels swirl together, looking like a plague of marauding locusts forming a head with gaps for the mouth and eyes and the twirling black tips of a ghost crown.

"Ephraim ti Horn," the disembodied head of the Syndicate Queen rasps over the ship's speakers. Whatever blood is left in me chills.

The children are struck dumb, smart enough to know when to be afraid.

"Let me guess, you'd be the queen bitch, eh?" I say thinly.

"You will return the children."

"Course I will. In exchange, I'll take a private island on Venus with a legion of Pinks to bring me cocktails in little coconut shells. Not a bad life, eh?" I laugh at the locust face. "Let me guess: you're going to offer me *three* islands. Well, fuck that and fuck you. I'm not afraid of dying and certainly not afraid of you. Ephraim out."

I reach and shut off the communicator, but the hologram doesn't obey. The empty eyes stare at me from the mutinous pixels.

"I gave this ship to the Duke," the shadowy face rasps. *"I own it. I own you. Soon I will see you in the flesh—while you still have it. Till then, thief."* The ship suddenly banks hard to port, throwing Pax sideways behind me. He slams against the bulkhead. My body jerks against the pilot restraints.

"What's happening?" Pax asks, picking himself up. His forehead is bleeding.

"The ship's turning around . . ." I whisper.

"Back to the Syndicate . . ." Pax says.

"Well, turn it back!" Electra shouts.

"Good idea! I'll just do that," I snap. The steering has gone dead.

The secondary electrical controls are off. "It's being flown remotely. Coms are dead." My mouth's gone dry. I look frantically for some sort of override, but the control isn't physical. It's coded into the ship's computer. "The escorts won't reach us in time . . ." I say. They'll land us at some Syndicate facility and that will be the last the world ever knows of us. But it won't end there. No, they'll draw it out for years. And what will happen to Volga then?

"Slag this." I totter to my feet, almost falling down. Pax catches me. I sway there, trying to slow down the spinning. "Thanks."

"What are you going to do?" Electra asks.

"Something stupid." She reaches for her restraints. "Stay, hatchet-face." I grip Pax by his collar and shove him to the chair. "Both of you, strap in." I leave them exchanging confused glances as they strap themselves into the pilot and co-pilot chairs. I stumble back through the ship, using the wall to support me. "Where are you?" I shove open doors and lockers, finding fridges of champagne and caviar and dining sets. Come on! Blackness is creeping into the fringes of my vision. I fall down, catching myself on the cushion of an inset dining area. I fumble with the zoladone dispenser in my pocket. I drop it on the floor and pick it up. I pop three zoladone between my molars. An electric thrill vibrates through my veins, numbing the pain in my chest. I struggle to my feet, and in the back of the ship, near the dis-embarcation ramp, I find what I was looking for—a walnut-paneled locker full of weapons. Beneath a row of pulseRifles and elegant rail-guns rests a stack of thermal grenades in formafoam. Someone is laughing. It's me. I pull the grenades out, clutch them to my chest, and shimmy to the back of the ship, toward the engines. I cluster the grenades on the ground near a cooling unit and shudder out a breath.

"Here goes something." I set the timer on one of the grenades to thirty seconds and, with a laugh, drop it amongst the pile. I race back the way I came. Well, I try to race with rubber legs, pulling myself back toward the front of the ship, using my arms to hold myself up, counting silently to myself. I reach the front cockpit, seal the door behind me, and collapse into a passenger chair along the wall behind the pilots. Pax and Electra stare at me as I buckle tight the safety re-straints. Jove on high, let there be crash webbing in this seat.

"What did you do?" Pax asks.

"Told ya, something stupid. Four, three, assume the position!" Their eyes widen and they cover their heads with their hands.

A deafening roar comes from the back of the ship.

The door to the cockpit buckles inward. The ship pitches sideways and begins to spiral down as the gravity thrusters fail in stuttering gasps. Then they give out and we're plummeting down, the city and sky whipping past outside the cockpit windows. As we careen down into the wasted, skeleton city landscape of one of the Jackal's craters, I can't help but laugh bitterly.

I knew this was gonna be a one-way ticket. . . .

65

DARROW

The Rending

WALKING OUT OF THE ASH LORD'S fortress, I am an empty shell.

The Howlers wait on the landing pad at the top of the tower. The *Nessus* hovers to the left of the Ash Lord's shuttle and is readying her to depart. Colloway's battle-scarred ripWing is docked on her top-side. Far below, the tattered remnants of Apollonius's forces and those of the Ash Lord fight a desperate running battle on the south end of the island. Our injured and dead have been loaded up. I don't yet know the tally. The jubilation my friends expected to feel with the Ash Lord's death never comes. Not when they see our faces. And when they hear of Pax and Electra, and Atalantia's fleet, they turn as pale as Sevro. Rhonna is stunned.

"No," she whispers. "It's bullshit. Virginia would have protected him. I know it. He fed you a line."

"Society fleet ripWings are eight minutes out," Pebble says. "We'll have to burn like hell to escape. At current orbit, we can be back on Luna in four weeks."

I barely hear her. My mind is apart from them, from this place. If only I could go back in time and never come to this hope-forsaken planet. I just want to hold my boy again in my arms. I would protect him from the worlds. I would never leave him. Is he even alive? Would I feel it? The horror grips me again. The world swims and I feel the tears of anger itch behind my eyes. Sevro is locked in his own rage. He storms up the ramp, shouting for the Howlers to load up.

But my feet do not follow. They cannot.

"Darrow?" Pebble murmurs. "What are you doing?"

Sevro turns at the top of the ramp to look down at me.

"I'm not coming," I say, and as I say it, I feel the last of my soul empty itself from the vessel of my body. Sevro watches me with contempt. "I'm not going back to Luna."

"Boss," Colloway says. "What are you talking about? They have your kid. We have to go back."

Pebble comes back to touch my shoulder. Her hands are coated with dried blood, likely her husband's. "You're in shock. You need to get on the ship."

"Whatever happened, it's over," I say. "If he was taken, Mustang will get him back as well as I can. If he is dead . . . there is nothing to be done." Even to myself, my voice is like that of a condemned man. Pax. I see his eyes as he watches me rise from Wulfgar's body. The key is so heavy on its chain against my sternum it's all I can do to remain standing.

"Don't say that, Darrow," Pebble says.

"Mustang needs you," Thraxa says; her own love for my son runs deep, just as it does in her whole family. Where were they? Why didn't they protect him? "Your family needs you."

I think of my wife. She won't survive this with the Senate. They'll say she's unfit to rule. Compromised. She might already be deposed. The life I left behind is shattered, and my fist put the first cracks in it. Whoever took my child did it to wound me and my wife. Our sins passed down to that perfect, innocent boy.

Death begets death begets death.

How many sons did Lorn bury? Four?

I have made my choice and it kills me to know I chose not to be a father. Not to be a husband. I failed at both when I chose the Rising over my family. And now it teeters on the razor's edge. Orion might already be lost. Our fleet, cobbled together, the product of ten years, might already be debris.

The Red boy inside me would run home to his family.

But I cannot.

The Ash Lord was right. Nothing of the Red remains. I am trapped in my duty. Like Lorn. Like Magnus himself. Like Octavia. Sevro and I did not understand them when we were boys. But now that we are men, we become them.

"My army needs me," I say. "Atalantia might already have destroyed the fleet. That means our men on Mercury are trapped. Fathers, wives. Nine million of them marooned under the city shields. They'll be exterminated like the Sons in the Rim. Like the Reds in the mines. I took them there. I will not abandon them."

"So you abandon your child instead?" Sevro asks, finally coming back down the ramp to face me. The Howlers back out of the way. "And steal me from mine?"

"We don't even know if they are alive."

"Shut up." His sorrow finds a home in his fist. It trembles at his side. "Slag you. How many times have I followed you? How many times have I trusted you? You were wrong! You didn't listen. But I followed. Like a good little dog. And now my daughter . . ." His voice falters. "My baby . . ."

"I'm sorry, Sevro. I am."

"You're a father!"

"I'm not asking you to come with me."

"Oh, trust me, I won't be."

"Take the *Nessus*. Reach Victra and Mustang and bring our children back to us."

"How will you get off-planet?" Pebble asks.

I turn to look at the Ash Lord's shuttle. "If I can't turn the tide on Venus and Mercury, they'll be coming for Luna or Mars next. You have to prepare the defenses." Done with me, Sevro turns to walk up the ramp into the *Nessus*. "Sevro . . ." He doesn't turn around. "Sevro . . ." He disappears inside and his name lingers in the air.

Too little, too late.

I stand alone in the Ash Lord's shuttle. The grim walls press in on me. I sit in the pilot's chair and begin the preflight procedures. There's a sound behind me. I turn to see Alexandar coming up the open ramp, leading the Gold prisoners we took from Deepgrave. Colloway, Tongueless, Thraxa, and Rhonna follow him, their starShells left dented and smoldering on the landing pad. They toss down several bags of gear, lock the prisoners in the cargo hold, and settle into the passenger compartment. "Sevro says you'd need them," Thraxa says.

Colloway saunters up, a burner hanging between his lips. "You're in my seat."

I get up and find my way back toward the passenger compartment. A lone figure stands at the bottom of the ramp in bloodied armor. "Apollonius," I say.

"The clock's still ticking," he says, tapping his head.

Sevro and I in our despair forgot about the man entirely. I look down at my dented datapad and pull up the program. Ten minutes left before the munitions in his head go off. "Are you a man of your word?" he asks.

I look down at the man and see nothing I value. Just a murderer who saved my life. But all the evils that have befallen us today, all the mistakes I've made, have come from my pride and the duplicity I've sown.

"Today I am." I deactivate the bomb. "Venus is yours, if you can take her."

"And the hostages?" he asks. "The Carthii and Saud family members you promised me?"

"We need them more," I say, and hammer my hand on the door control. The ramp rolls up, and the last I see is Apollonius staring at me in rage.

My men say nothing as I rejoin them in the passenger hold. I settle into my chair as Colloway lifts off and we trail in the *Nessus*'s wake. Thunder rolls outside as the frigate fires at the Society ripWings that pursue us. Colloway says something about capital ships cutting off our escape as we breach orbit. Over the com, I hear Sevro snarling at the Society Praetors, showing them pictures of the Gold family hostages we had in the *Nessus's* brig. Just as planned. Even as I mourn for my own son, we use the sons and daughters of the Golds of Venus to escape. The dark irony is not lost on me. All that holds the guns of Venus from destroying us is the love of parents for their children. They do not fire, and I wonder if I had my enemy in my grasp, would I have done the same?

I say no farewell over the com to Sevro and Pebble and Clown, friends who have been with me for half my life. People think I believe my own myth, that I'm a singular whirlwind of nature. I know I am not. I was the concentrated force of the people around me, balanced, hardened, inspired by Ragnar, Fitchner, Lorn, Eo. Sevro.

Now I sit a world apart, in silence as my friends lie dead and the rest return to my son while I race away from him toward the war. Accompanied only by the tattered remains of the Howlers, an old prisoner, and a girl of barely twenty years.

I feel lost. But in the void, drifting away from my friends, I feel something else. Something I have not felt for some time. The Ash Lord claimed he did not take my son. But I know his designs. It was not a friend who took them. He and Atalantia played me for a fool. She thought I would abandon my army, my fleet, and rush home to save my son. But she does not know what she has awoken.

I pull the key Pax gave me from my neck and put it in my bag, setting aside the father, welcoming the Reaper, and letting the old rage take hold.

ACKNOWLEDGMENTS

I NITIALLY, I WAS HESITANT to return to the world of *Red Rising*. Not for fear of the labor, though labor there was. Not for fear of doing the story justice. But for another reason altogether.

A single, standalone book is a fling. A series such as this is a relationship between author and reader. You trusted me to give me your time, your imagination through the initial trilogy. And, by buying this book, you trusted me yet again.

So my greatest thanks is to you, the reader, for that trust. Know that I do not take it lightly, and will not abuse it as we spin further down the rabbit hole.

Thank you for your time, your emails, letters, and thoughts, all of which breathe new life into the veins of Darrow's world and made me ache to return to the windswept tunnels of Mars, and the freezing sulfur flats of Io, and the manic boulevards of Luna.

Without you lot, this world would be the pale imaginings of a disconsolate wage-man.

Now, for more aimed acknowledgments. Cue the war drums. Cue the trumpets.

A hearty, backslapping, most-prime thanks goes out to the team at

Del Rey. Charging once more into the Red Rising breech was a daring affair, but you lot made it as easy as walking in the front door.

Thank you to Hannah Bowman for the brainstorm lunches and for believing in me from the first haemanthus blossom. And to Mike Braff for his editorial wizardry and for cackling every time I say "Space Vikings!" A better friend and collaborator, there is none.

Thank you to Tricia Narwani for the Herculean labor of making me stay on pace and deciphering my convoluted family trees. David Moench, Emily Isayeff, Julie Leung—I could type away all I like, but without you three no one would ever find my words. Thank you for your tireless efforts promoting the book and helping *Red Rising* find a place in the hearts of readers. Thank you to Scott Shannon, Keith Clayton, and Gina Centrello for once again having faith in the series. Keith, I fully expect more breakdowns of the thematic nuances within the *Fast and Furious* franchise over eccentric IPAs.

Though I was a bit more secretive with the text this round through, the book would never have been composed were it not for the legion of friends at my back.

Josh Crook, thank you for the constant inspiration, stalwart friendship, and collaboration even when I'm pacing a hole in the carpet and fraying your nerve endings. Eric Olsen, for your contagious, ebullient spirit, boundless dreams, and for introducing me to the peerless Olsen Clan. Babar Peerzada, for torturing the stress out of me through burpees and deadlifts and breaking stories on rooftops. Tamara Price, for your love, empathy, and for trusting me enough to say the words to bind you and Jarrett together forever. Jarrett for the constant generosity and introducing me as "*New York Times* bestselling author Pierce Brown . . ." every damn time I meet a new person. The Phillips clan for tending my sanity on the phone. Max Carver for giving me company in my insanity. Madison Ainley for WWW forevermore. Jake and Ruth Bloom for their humble wisdom, inside scoop, and our unending gastronomic tour of LA.

And thank you Lily Robinson, who, more than any other, was with me for every page of this new journey—from the glens of Wales to the coast of South Pacific Islands. You abide my madness, nurture my heart, and fill my dreams.

Thank you as well to the authors who have helped me tackle the multiple-narrator beast—Scott Sigler, Justin Cronin, and Terry Brooks. And the authors whose colossal shoulders we all stand upon—Robert Heinlein, Frank Herbert, Dan Simmons, George R. R. Martin, Bernard Cornwell, J. K. Rowling.

And last, but certainly not least, thank you to my family. My sister, Blair, for her efforts on behalf of the Sons of Ares and her enduring loyalty. There will be more cons to come, my dear! And to my parents—who have always given me the loving bedrock upon which to write and dream and live my life. You are a constant source of inspiration, love, joy, and faith, and continue to teach me how to live my life. Congratulations on thirty-seven years of a love and marriage under the stars, and here's to thirty-seven more.

Farewell for now, dear reader. Jove willing, we will meet again soon.

ABOUT THE AUTHOR

PIERCE BROWN is the #1 *New York Times* bestselling author of *Red Rising, Golden Son, Morning Star,* and *Iron Gold.* His work has been published in thirty-three languages and in thirty-five territories. He lives in Los Angeles, where he is at work on his next novel.

piercebrownbooks.com
Twitter: @Pierce_Brown
Instagram: @PierceBrownOfficial

To inquire about booking Pierce Brown for a speaking engagement, please contact the Penguin Random House Speakers Bureau at speakers@penguinrandom house.com.

ABOUT THE TYPE

This book was set in Garamond, a typeface originally designed by the Parisian type cutter Claude Garamond (c. 1500–61). This version of Garamond was modeled on a 1592 specimen sheet from the Egenolff-Berner foundry, which was produced from types assumed to have been brought to Frankfurt by the punch cutter Jacques Sabon (c. 1520–80).

Claude Garamond's distinguished romans and italics first appeared in *Opera Ciceronis* in 1543–44. The Garamond types are clear, open, and elegant.